THE QUEEN'S RISE

THE QUEEN'S RISE

Copyright © 2021 by Bethany Atazadeh

All rights reserved. Printed in the United States of America. No part of this book may be used or reproduced in any manner whatsoever without written permission except in the case of brief quotations embodied in critical articles or reviews. This book is a work of fiction. Names, characters, organizations, places, events, and incidents either are the product of the author's imagination or are used fictitiously. Any resemblance to actual persons, living or dead, events, or locales is entirely coincidental.

This book includes three full novels from The Queen's Rise series: The Secret Gift, The Secret Shadow, and The Secret Curse by Bethany Atazadeh.

For information contact: *https://www.bethanyatazadeh.com*

Cover design by: Bethany Atazadeh
Cover Character Art by: Alrun Maget (@alrun.art on Instagram)
Koda & Jezebel Character Art by: Hillary Bardin (@reebardin on Instagram)
Map Design by: Andrés Aguirre (@aaguirreart on Instagram)
Formatting Template by: Derek Murphy

First Edition: April 2024
10 9 8 7 6 5 4 3 2 1

THE QUEEN'S RISE

BETHANY ATAZADEH

GRACE HOUSE PRESS

Copyright © 2021 by Bethany Atazadeh

CONTENTS:

THE SECRET GIFT	9
THE SECRET SHADOW	127
THE SECRET CURSE	269
KODA'S CURSE	473
20 YEAR'S LATER	490
SERIES PLAYLIST	504

THE SECRET GIFT

1

"LET'S HOPE YOU NEVER develop that barbaric Gift your mother had," my father grumbled after his second cup of mead. He was getting an early start tonight. "That woman thought she could use me to hide her shifting? In the end, I used her Gift to *my* advantage far more than she ever—" The rest was too muffled to hear, but it was no doubt the same litany of complaints I'd heard every night for as long as I could remember.

I shrunk inward, shoulders curving forward, chin dropping to my chest. Focusing on the dirty plate in my hand, I scrubbed hard enough that there should've been a hole.

He tossed his empty drink in my direction.

I didn't need to duck, but I still flinched. The wooden cup bounced harmlessly across the wood floor halfway across the small room, dribbling liquid onto the surface that was covered in stains.

"Jezebel. Another," he mumbled, closing his eyes and burrowing deeper into his Lacklore-hide chair. He draped his arms over the bear-like paws, with claws still sharp, and leaned back beneath the ox-like head where it was stuffed and set into the tall back of the chair.

Growing up, I used to whine that he could take care of himself. Without fail, he would point to his legs—those legs that started out like any other Jinni male, but transformed into the legs of a goat. Hoofs and all. A permanent *gift* from my mother.

"Yes, father." I lifted my chin and obeyed, bringing him a third full cup, setting it on the table beside him. My hand shook slightly, straining against the desire to slam it down or scream at him. I kept my face serene.

Sometimes I secretly wondered how my mother had stopped at the legs alone.

Our home was small. Only a few steps to get back to the sink, where I continued to slowly do the dishes. If I looked too idle, it'd only encourage him to focus his bitter diatribe on me.

I stared out the kitchen window, past the faded blue curtains, at the street below where my few friends gathered, waiting for me to join them. They were the ones who mattered. They respected me.

Asher waved when he saw me, but I couldn't wave back without giving myself away. Pressing my lips together in a pained smile, though he was too far below to see, I wished I was with them.

Other Jinn my age had mentors after their discipline years ended, including some of my friends. As their Gifts manifested between the ages of fifteen to twenty-two, someone with similar Gifts would take them on and train them in how to use them. How to be a lethal weapon or a benefactor or anything in-between.

I was only seventeen, so some would say I still had time.

Clenching my fists underneath the hot water, I wrung the rag between my hands. I deserved a mentor. But I couldn't tell anyone that.

My Gift was still fairly new. It'd manifested a few short months ago, after I'd finished my discipline years. One night, I'd lain awake, wishing for something more. Wishing I could hide from everyone. Wishing I could be small. Like the little green lizard that crawled along my ceiling.

I closed my eyes, breathing deeply, picturing it.

Suddenly, the covers began to suffocate me. I opened my eyes to find myself buried beneath them. As I struggled to claw my way free, I emerged from beneath the blankets to find the moonlight shining down on shimmering, green scales.

I'd become the lizard.

Panic made my tongue flick in and out wildly. *How did this happen?*

Dizzy, oddly hungry, and confused, I searched for the Jinn who'd changed me. *Is my mother here?*

Shifting was her Gift—this had to be her.

But no one appeared. Nothing else happened.

I curled up on my pillow, squeezing my eyes shut tight. *Please, oh please, turn back. Turn back.*

Out in the main room, a glass clinked as my father set it down, making my heartbeat double in speed. *Turn back! Now!* I screamed at myself mentally. I could *not* be seen like this!

I envisioned my body as it should be—pale skin, dark hair that skimmed my lower back, sky-blue eyes, and my nightgown—and imagined myself shifting.

Like my mother.

At first, I couldn't, because part of me refused to believe it was even possible.

But what if it was?

Once I opened up to the possibility—that I might have the same Gift as my mother—my skin began to tingle.

With all my energy focused inward, I felt the change this time. Limbs ached as they shifted from little claws back into hands. Muscles in my legs popped and stretched as they grew larger and longer, until my toes once again hung off the edge of the bed.

It didn't hurt exactly.

But it didn't feel *good* either… It was like stretching a muscle to a breaking point, but instead of snapping, the muscle became flexible like soft clay and loosened into its new form. Or, in this case, its original form.

Breathing rapidly, I ripped the covers off and flung myself across the small room, as far from the bed as possible. I patted my sides and arms, searching for any remaining green scales.

None.

It was as if it'd never happened.

A cold sweat broke out across my skin.

My hands were clammy.

It can't be.

I shook my head, trembling fingers touching my lips in horror. *Anything but this.*

Shape-shifting was one of those rare Gifts that was considered *too* strong. It couldn't be controlled by the royal family and because of this, they feared it. They weren't alone. *Everyone* feared a shifter.

Because who could stop a shifter from impersonating another Jinni? No one.

To my knowledge, a mentor for shifters didn't exist, but even if someone knew how, none would ever consider working with me. It was too risky.

Swallowing hard, my mind tried to skirt around my next thought, which was too terrifying to even consider, but I couldn't help myself. *There'd be no way to stop a shifter from posing as someone in power—maybe even the king or queen themselves.*

How would my friends or acquaintances react if they knew I had this Gift? *Not well.* An understatement to say the least. And that wasn't even considering how a stranger might respond.

I sank down the wall until I hit the floor. Wrapping my arms around my knees, I buried my face in them, unable to stop shaking my head.

What the Jinn feared, they removed.

Which meant that a Gift like mine would either be carefully guarded or—if that was deemed too difficult—severed completely.

Once I reached this thought, I couldn't escape it. It taunted me, echoing in my mind.

No one survives a Severance.

Over and over, the words repeated.

No one.

A single tear trickled down my cheek, soaked up by my nightgown. Grumbles came from the living room. My father's hoofs tromped across the wood floor, paused as a glass clinked, then shuffled back. The chair groaned as he fell back into it.

He'd likely push for a Severance.

Who wouldn't?

It didn't matter that I hadn't asked for this Gift, that I didn't want it. If anyone found out, nothing would ever be the same.

I did *not* sleep that night.

An entire week passed before I dared to attempt my Gift again. Before I dared to even *think* about it again.

There was no doubt about it. I'd developed my mother's shape-shifting Gift.

Thankfully, no one else was aware.

And I, for the most part, was too terrified to use it.

Still, I would never have a mentor because no one could know my true Gift. I'd learned that from my mother.

Just five years old when she'd left, I'd gripped her short skirts and wrapped myself around her tall legs, pulling on her sandal straps where they laced around her calves. "Please don't leave, mama."

"I have to, darling," she'd said, ruthlessly prying me off of her before retying the laces and strapping on her ornamental breastplate. "When you have Gifts like mine, that's all anyone can see. The royal family fears this Gift and wants to take control of my abilities, as your father did." She stood. "I'm not going to let them."

"But papa loves you," I'd cried.

"He loves my Gift," she'd snapped, bending down again to face me. "And I plan to break him of that." Her grip on my shoulders hurt as she shook me slightly. "Always remember this: don't share your Gifts with anyone, Jezebel. People will use them and use you. Better to keep them for yourself." She'd stood, brushing off her hands against her skirts as if brushing me off for the final time. "If I could go back in time, I'd keep mine a secret. Then we'd know how your father really felt."

Releasing the rag from its chokehold, I frowned at the bit of blood in the water. My nails had dug into my skin and left a mark. Could I shapeshift away a cut?

I narrowed my eyes in concentration, searching for the way. Hissing in frustration, I gave up, returning to scrubbing another plate and setting it out to airdry. If there was a way, I couldn't find it. A mentor could've told me if it was possible.

The soap and unreachable answers just made the cut sting more.

Yanking my hands out of the water, I wrapped a rag around the tiny wound and viciously pressed down. The pain distracted me, but only briefly.

If my mother had known that I'd develop the same Gift as her years later, would she have stayed?

Or, better yet, would she have taken me with her?

I still didn't know the answer, but I'd never forgotten her words. Part of me wanted to believe she was wrong. The burning question came back as it always did: if I showed my true self to someone, would it change how they saw me? Would they still love me?

My father certainly wouldn't. He hadn't been the same since she'd left.

"Your mother's Gift was as useless as her," he said now, as if he'd picked up on my train of thoughts, sloshing his drink as he lifted himself out of the chair. He set the cup down and made his way to the bed on the far side of the room, falling into it. He'd moved it out of his bedroom to eliminate unnecessary steps.

That was my cue to go to my own room for the night, though it wasn't even dark out. Better to let him sleep it off than to make noise and risk waking him.

I dried my hands quickly. As I was dimming the flickering ceiling lamp and pulling my door closed, he muttered, "She was ugly besides."

Despite myself, I paused and looked back at him.

His cold eyes were on me, clear for once. "You look just like her, Jezzie."

My hands twitched, wanting to touch my long, black hair and my pale face. Lips too small and thin. Brows too thick. Nose too long. I knew it all by heart.

Instead, I let the door to my room close softly, refusing to give him the satisfaction. Though he didn't realize it, I could easily change all of that. And someday, I would. Someday, I promised myself I'd get away from him. And I'd never let anyone call me that nickname again.

The minutes passed slowly as I paced my tiny room from one side of the small bed to the other, past the bare walls with peeling gray paint, my few possessions inside the dark dresser, and the small gold mirror that hung above it. It was one of my favorite possessions—one of my *only* possessions. A gift from my mother.

Sometimes I stopped in front of the mirror to stare at my reflection. To see if the hidden power underneath my skin shone through. It never did, of course. But I still imagined what it might look like.

Outside, the sun began to set. The glow on my skin from the last golden rays gradually faded to gray, and my confidence dimmed along with it. This was all anyone could see.

Only when my father's heavy snores pierced the air did I finally tiptoe toward my window and crack it open.

Our cramped living quarters were on the third floor of the acropolis surrounding the capital. Hundreds of Jinn lived in the little apartments above, below, and on both sides of our own. Even more Jinn walked the busy streets no matter what time of day, so this was always a fear-inducing moment.

It was far too high to jump. And the spells surrounding the acropolis prevented traveling—a simple Gift that allowed a Jinni to instantly cross an enormous distance in the span of a heartbeat. Barely even considered a Gift, except to the rare Jinn who didn't have it.

Since I wouldn't dare sneak past my father, that left me with only one option.

I shifted as quickly as possible into a green lizard the size of my palm, just like the one I'd accidentally become that very first time. Glancing at the door, I kept an eye on it over my shoulder until the round curve of my skin grew flat and the cream-color turned green and scaly, along with my clothes, which ceased to exist. This form would be permanent until I chose to shift again.

Using my helpful sticky footpads, I crawled up my bedroom wall, out the window, and down one of the tall columns of the acropolis. There was a hidden corner near the main entrance. In the dark space where no one could see, I shifted back to my own form—short white dress, sandals, gold arm bands, and all.

Forced to keep my Gift to myself, I didn't always know exactly *how* it worked the way it did. As far as I could tell, it was like molding clay, reshaping it into something new. I had to do it a little bit at a time, but as I got used to sculpting certain things, they came to me quicker. Such as returning to myself; that form always snapped back into place effortlessly.

All four of my friends lounged in the deep shadows of the acropolis, by one of the passageways through it. They all had the typical ebony hair of the Jinn, with pale, almost translucent skin that hinted at our blue veins beneath. That, however, was where the similarities ended between us.

"Bel," Asher called softly, his deep-red eyes flashing in excitement as I strode up to them. He had a self-assured grin with just a hint of teasing that always set others at ease. "We were starting to wonder if you were coming!"

I warmed to him and the nickname as always, to the whole different person I became with them, though even here I kept my shifting a secret.

"You know I have to wait for old donkey-legs to fall asleep," I retorted, but I let the corner of my mouth tip up a bit. Summer heat still radiated off the darkstones that paved the street, even now after the sun had set. "What're we doing tonight?"

Besides Asher, our group was made up of three other adolescent Jinn: tiny Phillipa, whose strongest Gift let her sense when fruit was ripe, obnoxious Simon, whose main Gift allowed him to put himself and others to sleep, but only for a couple minutes, and the ill-tempered Miriam who—like Asher—couldn't claim a single Gift. Not even the most common Gift of traveling.

While it took an especially talented Jinni to cross vast distances such as from one floating island to another, almost all Jinn could travel at least as far as they could see. Which made it a forgettable Gift to me—except when I was around them.

As far as my friends knew, traveling was my only Gift, and only average distances, nothing extraordinary. Which meant I fit in with them perfectly.

Other Jinn our age looked down on us. Our old friend, Reuben, from our discipline years refused to even be seen in our presence. He said it might make a mentor reconsider working with him.

Even our parents saw us poorly-Gifted ones as a disappointment.

Since we weren't strong enough to be considered for the Jinni Guard, and most of us couldn't acquire a basic mentor, we were left to ourselves. Until eventually, one by one, we'd be forced to take on some kind of menial labor.

"We can't talk here," Asher whispered, pulling me out of my dark thoughts. His usual cocky grin stretched across his face hinting at all kinds of secrets. As my spirits lifted with anticipation, I grinned back.

2

SECRETS WERE JINNI BREAD and butter. It must be an especially good secret to worry that someone might overhear. "Take us to the usual place," Asher commanded, holding out a hand in my direction.

Times like this, when his insecurities about being Gift-less made him sharp, I oddly liked him more. To find pleasure in the little power he did have over us in moments like these—well, I knew the feeling better than he realized.

So, I simply took his hand and traveled with him to the ruins at the edge of the main island. The others appeared beside us a moment later.

When we glanced back at the enormous capital city of Resh we'd left behind, it looked like a miniature toy town in the distance, with the acropolis stretching protectively all around it. The castle rose above everything else in the center, glowing white in the moonlight.

Here at the edge of the island, clouds drifted past, close enough to reach out and touch. Somewhere far below, too distant to see from our elevation, was the human world. And there to the right, floating in and out of clouds, was Urim, one of the smaller Jinni islands. It was close enough that many Jinn could travel the distance between these particular islands and visit other cities without bothering to use the bridges.

Not the five of us, of course... but some.

Asher pulled his hand away as soon as we landed. I tried not to let my disappointment show. He turned to the others who stood in a half-circle. Miriam was next to Simon, since he'd brought her. Her wrinkled forehead and crossed arms said she felt the same as Asher about their lack of abilities. Simon might've brought Phillipa too, I couldn't tell; though she could travel on her own, she preferred to stick with one of us and fade into the background of our little group.

After a quick glance around the ruins, I frowned. There was nothing unusual here. Just a few white pillars that used to hold up a roof, tall grass swaying in bright moonlight, and a steep drop off at the edge of the island. I whispered, "You have to tell us! I can't stand the suspense!"

Asher's pinched lips relaxed into a smile. Knowledge was another kind of power. Something we all craved. He waved for us to follow him into the trees. "Remember our discipline years, when they taught us what a *Daleth* was?"

"A portal to the human world," Miriam snapped, though her expertise didn't seem to make her feel better. She hated nature. "What of it?"

"I found one."

Simon immediately traveled in front of Asher, though he'd only been two steps away. He liked to show off the meager skills he did have. "You're making that up."

"You wish," Asher said with a grin, hitting Simon's decorative silver breastplate as he stepped around him.

"Those don't just pop up one day out of nowhere," Miriam said, swatting at bugs as she followed. "How would no one have found it before? I doubt it's really a portal at all. You're just trying to trick us."

"You'll see." Asher kept walking, grinning over his shoulder. "This one is nearly impossible to stumble onto. If I hadn't tried to pick a specific herb right between two trees, I'd have missed it myself. My hand vanished!"

The details made me start to believe him. My heartbeat sped up. We could use information like that as a way to curry favor with the royal family—maybe find a better profession at the castle than what we were destined for.

It could even produce an opportunity to meet the handsome Prince Shem. I glanced over at Miriam and Phillipa, wondering if they were thinking the same thing.

Better yet, being introduced to such powerful Jinn could help me get away from my father for good.

The royals were always looking for Daleths. For whatever reason, they liked to have control over them. Probably because an unguarded portal was asking for trouble when it came to adolescent Jinn like us.

At the smirk on Asher's face, I sighed.

He'd chosen the trouble.

Leading us away from the edge of the island, on a curving path through the grass and the trees, he couldn't stop talking. "I found it when I was looking for some star anise." His cheeks blushed slightly blue. Since his natural-born Gifts were non-existent, he was determined to learn Jinni enchantments instead.

Truthfully, the idea of another kind of power intrigued me as well. Though we all knew this about him, he still changed the subject quickly. "Besides the Jinni Guard, no one we know has ever visited the human world."

"Except for Master Yeshiva," Miriam reminded him. All of our thoughts turned to the teacher we'd had briefly during our discipline years, right around the time we'd all met. He'd been banished to the human world for breaking one of the three Unbreakable Laws: *Never use a Gift to deceive, never use a Gift to steal, and never use a Gift to harm another.* To this day, we still didn't know which one he'd broken.

"Well, we don't know anyone who's ever come *back*," Asher modified. "We're going to be the first! We'll see this human world with our own eyes, instead of hearing dull bedtime stories about it. Maybe we'll even have a little fun with the humans themselves."

He and Simon chuckled as each tried to hit the other's breastplate first, making the showy armor clang loudly when Simon succeeded.

I shuddered at the thought of interacting with humans. Miriam, Phillipa, and I exchanged tight-lipped glances.

Humans were said to be slimy to the touch and terribly unsanitary. Their intelligence level was about the same as one of our mutton grazers. You couldn't approach them in groups or you'd be more likely to be attacked than greeted.

We had a few humans living in the capital city of Resh, but it was rare, and usually only for a short time before someone with the Gift of memories made them forget. They were usually employed by Jinn who thought they had a special talent or ability they needed. I couldn't fathom it. What could a human do that a Jinni couldn't?

Though the dangers of the human world didn't appeal to me, I trailed along behind them anyway.

Asher drew up next to a seemingly empty space between two trees that gently arched toward each other. Other than that, there was nothing to indicate they were anything special. If Asher hadn't stumbled across it while looking for herbs, it would've likely never been found. Gesturing to the bark on one, where some scratches created a poorly carved circle, he said, "I marked it so we can find it whenever we want."

"But do we *really* want to go to the human world?" I spoke up, arching a brow at him.

"Everyone knows they're inferior," Miriam agreed, though coming from her it didn't mean much. "I hardly see the point."

Asher ignored her and stepped through the space between the trees.

He disappeared.

"The *point*—" Simon mocked her "—is to have a little fun. But if you're as scared as an actual human and want to stay behind, then we'll see you when we get back." With that, he followed Asher.

Unlike traveling, where the whole body vanished at once, the daleth seemed to almost eat his body, swallowing it in pieces.

Miriam shook her head at the empty space, while Phillipa glanced between us.

I rolled my eyes.

When Asher stuck his head back through unexpectedly, I squeaked.

He roared with laughter. Miriam shoved his head back through and followed, no doubt anxious to prove herself. Giving me a small shrug, Phillipa stepped through next.

Once again, I brought up the rear.

Throwing my head back, I took a deep breath, then pressed through the invisible portal to the human world. The tingle of magic on my skin as I passed through made me shiver.

In the dark, it surprised me how similar the human side appeared to home. Though the moon above was naturally smaller from this lower vantage point, the rest of the landscape wasn't terrible. Wildflowers grew along the edge of the woods. A town on the hill ahead shone like a cheerful lamp, lights flickering in windows and laughter flooding out all the way to where we stood in a small clearing.

Asher was already moving.

From the dark edges of the forest, we were still invisible to the humans, but there were at least a dozen of them in sight, hurrying in different directions throughout the town like little ants on a mission.

"Slow down," I called softly to Asher, rushing to take his elbow and pressure him into waiting for the rest of us. Though I'd never made my feelings for him known, I liked to think I held *some* sway over him. He did slow a bit, even if he refused to stop altogether. I tugged harder to get his attention. "What exactly are you hoping to accomplish here?"

With a glance back at the others, he leaned in to whisper in my ear, "I'd like to talk to one."

I shivered. *A human? Why?* Glancing up at his feverishly bright eyes, I could tell there'd be no arguing with him.

Still I tried. "We won't blend in." I waved toward Miriam, Phillipa, and myself with our short skirts and sandals that laced all the way up our bare calves, then at the village ahead. "Human women dress much more conservatively than the Jinn."

Phillipa and Miriam nodded sagely, attempting to hide their relief as they slowed to a stop.

"That's fair. You can wait here, if you'd like," Asher said over his shoulder. Freeing his arm from mine, he tugged his ceremonial armor off and chucked it beneath some nearby bushes, not pausing in his stride. Simon imitated him, following on his heels.

I stuffed down my disappointment yet again. He could be stubborn when he was focused on something.

"We should probably make a plan first," Miriam tried, when I glanced over at her in desperation.

Finally, Asher stopped pressing forward. Turning to face us, he waved his hands wide. "Why must you all make everything so difficult? We're just going to talk to them."

"But what about the Unbreakable Laws?" Phillipa asked in her high, reedy voice.

"You think I forgot about them?" Asher snapped, fists clenched at his sides. "We're not going to use our Gifts to steal from anyone, deceive anyone, or harm anyone, because none of us has *any real Gifts* in the first place."

The reminder dulled the pulsing excitement in the air for a moment. Technically, we all had more Gifts than him except for Miriam, but he was sensitive to that, so none of us mentioned it.

I pondered the advantages of the human world as I searched their faces. What if I didn't even worry about talking to a human at all, but instead found a safe place to explore my Gift outside of the tiny boundaries of my bedroom at night?

I flexed my fingers tentatively.

What if I could test my limits? See what else I could do? The others never needed to know.

The freedom that had always been out of my reach tempted me like a rare dessert.

"Fine," I pulled away from our uneven circle, turning toward the town. "We'll all talk to a human. Meet back here by midnight." My strides started out small, but quickly stretched wider and faster as a tiny thrill tickled up my spine.

"Wait, Bel," Asher hissed as he caught up to me. "I, uh… I kind of thought we'd all talk to a human together."

"We can't," I said, ignoring the other's nods as well as the spark of pleasure at Asher admitting he wanted me there—even if he did lump the others in too. "If we all show up in one place, it'll be far too suspicious."

Not to mention it'd ruin my half-formed plans.

"We must each go alone. Avoid any crowds, only talk to a human if they're on their own, and make sure you have an escape route if it goes poorly. Understand?"

"Who put you in charge?" Miriam muttered, but she didn't seem to expect an answer, and I didn't bother to give one.

It was exhilarating to lead for once.

3

AT THE EDGE OF town, our collective nerves made us huddle together behind a big stone wall, just outside a ring of lantern light. "Who's going first?" I asked, trying to sound nonchalant.

"My eyes are going to stand out too much," Asher complained, blinking his red eyes owlishly at the rest of us.

"You always do this." I crossed my arms, irritated that his worries made me question my own decisions. *Am I being foolish? Is this is a mistake?* "You convince us to do something and then back out last minute."

As expected, this made him dig in his heels. "I didn't say I wasn't going. I'll just have to make sure they don't see my eyes, that's all."

Training on humans was part of our Jinni discipline years. We all had a basic understanding of how to interact with them—whether the ones allowed into our world or the ones met through rare travel, such as joining the Jinni Guard. They occasionally ventured into the human world for their own secret purposes.

The thing about humans that always stuck out to me, though, was how incredibly *little* they knew about our culture. They had many wild tales based on the occasional rare sighting of a reckless Jinni or two. But the current royal family had made it a precedent over the last couple centuries to erase any memories of our more distinct differences. Such as our wide variety of eye colors.

My own eyes, though a paler blue than any normal human color, would be far less conspicuous.

"We all have a handicap we have to deal with," I reminded him, pointing to my bare, sandaled legs. Those would stand out just as much in this town as his eyes. More actually, since they'd be much harder to hide.

Without another word, I strode past him into the perimeter of the town.

Alone.

Keeping to the shadows, I didn't glance back until I'd walked past a dozen buildings and at least as many humans. At that point, as far as I could tell, everyone had gone their own way. I had until midnight for my experiment.

Anticipation made me walk faster, until I was practically running, dodging down one dark alley after the next, avoiding the humans.

The first non-human creature I stumbled upon in the dark shadows of a private alleyway was a dog. It ignored me, rummaging through some garbage. No other living soul was nearby to see.

Without another thought, I attempted shifting into the same form, leaning into the strange feeling of my body stretching to a breaking point before softening and settling into a new shape. This was a breed we didn't have in Jinn, but the composition of the creature was the same: four legs on the ground, lengthier spine, and my nose extending away from my face as my jaws grew sharp canines. Once I'd seen it, it wasn't too difficult to replicate. The whole transformation took only a few minutes.

Letting out a cheerful bark at the real dog, I silently laughed as it backed up with hackles raised. I took off, racing along the packed dirt between homes at full speed, enjoying the wind in my fur.

I dug in deeper, taking one alleyway after another. Back home, I'd only dared the smallest of creatures, ones that a Jinni wouldn't look twice at. I reveled in this new form.

The downside of this creature, however, was the sense of smell. Some of these alleyways were full of human filth that overpowered my new nose.

Tentatively, I played with my Gift. Forced to feel my way through something that I should have been taught, it took multiple tries before I discovered how to block the nasal passage. Perfect.

Halfway down one alleyway, I drew up short, panting. There was a small human boy at the other end. Young. No more than a few years old.

My heart thudded heavily in my chest, and not from the exertion.

The boy blinked at me, then grinned.

He sees a dog, not a Jinni.

Even if he did recognize me, what could he do? He looked as if he could barely even speak. Fear faded and confidence slowly replaced it. Some part of me wanted him to see me—to see my Gift. My power.

That compulsive part of me that I'd let loose for the first time in months whispered, *Do it. Show the human child. Who can he tell?*

It'd stretch my abilities. In fact, it'd probably use up most of my strength.

I exulted in the challenge.

Shaping my fur into skin as I reformed my endoskeleton within, I shifted. It took far longer than the dog, as I'd never tried to emulate another person before—human or Jinni. I left the fine details of the little boy's face for last, adding a smattering of freckles under newly brown eyes and overly-long straw colored hair.

His eyes had grown large as saucers by the time I finished the transformation, but he didn't make a sound.

I took a testing step toward him, into the small ring of lamplight by the door.

The little boy's lower lip began to tremble.

I attempted to copy him.

He stumbled back against the wall of the home and let out a wail that pierced the night.

The door of the house flung open, bathing me in light. "Naseem," the woman cried, sweeping me up in her arms where I stood stunned.

My whole body tensed.

A human was touching me.

I wanted to make the same noises the child had at the awful sensation.

The real Naseem had cut off his cries when the door opened and met my gaze with shocked eyes as his mother whirled back inside, completely unaware, and shut the door between us.

"My little escape artist," the woman clucked as she moved toward a stove, bouncing me on her hip in a way that made my head hurt. I tried amidst the jiggling to get a sense of the small human home. There were two other children playing a game on one of the beds, and a stove took up the nearest wall. "Want to help me clean up dinner?" she asked, turning her face toward mine.

I panicked. Not only was I in the clutches of a human, but she was about to discover the truth any moment because I couldn't answer—the human child had never spoken! Even if I'd had practice in shifting my own vocal cords to match someone else's, I had nothing to match!

"What's wrong, Naseem?" The woman's forehead wrinkled, and she stopped the horrible bouncing to focus all her attention on me.

Not knowing what else to do, I burrowed my face in her scratchy blouse and hid.

A hand patted my head, comforting. Through my fear, I noticed it wasn't slimy like the stories said at all; her skin was warm and dry, like my own, though a bit rougher. Nothing like the rumors had said. That knowledge didn't make the danger any less though.

"Don't worry, Naseem," she said, going back to that unbearable bouncing. "Your baba will be home soon."

What's a baba? I wondered, but I didn't dare lift my head and expose myself to more questions.

This had been a huge mistake.

I never should've agreed to come.

What if I don't make it home? The humans would discover me soon and cook me in a stew. Or trap me in a cage to entertain them. Already the woman's arms had begun to feel like steel bars. Or maybe they'd just end my life immediately.

When she set me on a bed, I didn't hesitate to crawl under the itchy blanket and close my eyes, refusing to open them until her footsteps shuffled back toward the stove.

Long minutes passed.

I agonized over how to escape, still struggling to form a plan or even a coherent thought, when the wooden door swung open and a human man stepped inside, holding the *real* Naseem. "Look who I found outside again," he said, chuckling.

No!

Panicking, I flung the blanket over my head and shifted into the smallest creature I could think of, tinier than anything I'd ever attempted before—a flea.

If I hadn't already been smaller than usual, I wouldn't have been able to shift fast enough. But by the time the woman stepped up to the bed and flung back the covers, I'd burrowed into the thin straw mattress and was already halfway to the other side.

"What kind of Jinni magic—" the wife grumbled to her husband.

I stopped listening.

Crawling out from the bottom of the mattress, where a thin piece of straw poked through, I dropped into the darkness beneath the bed. There, I shifted into the one shape besides my own that was most familiar and would take the least amount of energy: the green lizard.

All that mattered right now was escape.

Crawling painstakingly around the furniture along the edges of the room, I managed to remain unseen until I was a short distance from the door.

Little eyes caught on me from across the room. That troublemaker Naseem had spotted me. As I slunk along the wall underneath the wooden table, he raised one chubby finger, pointing wordlessly in my direction.

Before anyone could follow his gaze, I ducked behind the table leg and shifted back into the tiny flea, hopping frantically toward the door. I slipped through the crack at the base.

Outside in the dark, I wanted to sob, but my flea form wasn't capable.

All this shifting had left me beyond exhausted.

Starving.

I struggled to return to my own form.

After so many shifts in such a short span of time, it took far longer than normal.

This had never happened before.

As long minutes passed, I feared I'd be stuck in this half-shifted form, vulnerable and exposed.

Aching, stretching, and shuddering through the changes, I pushed myself harder until finally I could wipe a tear from my own cheek.

Sobs broke free.

I stumbled away from the home into an alley where I dropped to my knees, shaking from how close I'd come to being discovered.

Then, I forced myself to stop crying.

I wiped my eyes with the back of my hand.

Drew a slow breath in.

Then another.

Years with my father had taught me to keep my emotions in check until it was safe, though I'd never been tested like this before.

Dragging myself to my sandaled feet, I nearly broke down again at the thought of trying to cross the entire town without discovery. I just wanted to go home. To never see or think of a human again.

A wave of dizziness hit me.

Leaning against the back of the house in the dark, I listened carefully for any sounds of approach while I tried to catch my breath and refocus my thoughts.

So many changes in a row and at such speed had sapped my strength to the point that my muscles trembled. I needed food and rest. As soon as possible.

Traveling was out of the question. So was changing into the dog form or any other. I couldn't shift in this condition. I could hardly think past my hunger.

What an awful night.

I needed time to regain my strength. Time I didn't have.

I could only hope the others would return home without me… Because I didn't know what I would do if they came looking.

4

MY FOREHEAD TOUCHED the rough wood. It scraped against my skin, bringing me back to myself. *I can't lean against the wall of this house all night, waiting to be caught.*

Taking a deep breath, I pushed myself upright, wobbling slightly. *All I need is a partial shift.* Something simple. Manageable. Just enough to make me inconspicuous.

Rubbing my hands across my face, I groaned. *Yet another instance where a mentor would've taught me how to handle the exhaustion. And how to shift in spite of it.*

Jealousy always hit me in waves, but this time it sucked me under, drowning me, leaving me gasping for breath at the intensity. Clenching my fists, I had to hold back a scream of frustration. *I could've learned how to handle a situation like this. I wouldn't need to be afraid.*

Another wave hit, and another. I might've stood there seething all night, if not for a circle of lantern light and male voices approaching. Ducking around the corner of the home, I strode down one dark, silent street after the next, trying to think of a solution.

There was *one* thing I'd never tried before...

Sticking to the shadows, I slowed down, checking to make sure I was alone.

In a normal transition my clothes always shifted with me, which meant I'd never changed only my clothing. I'd never needed to.

Since this part of my Gift had always come naturally, I decided to try it.

Lengthening my short skirts until they reached my ankles, like the ones the human mother had worn, turned out to be as easy as touching the fabric and picturing it longer. It took almost no effort and sapped almost no strength.

When I tried to turn my pale blue eyes into brown, though, I sagged against the dirty wall of a nearby home.

Once I finally managed it, I relaxed slightly. Now I would blend in.

Slipping out into the quiet streets like this, I allowed myself to draw a full breath.

There was at least an hour until midnight. I needed rest, and if possible, something to eat.

Hoping to regain my strength as soon as possible, I walked slowly, taking it easy. An apple pie sat cooling in a window, and I stole it without pausing, not even feeling guilty since it was made by one of those vile humans. I ate it in crumbly bites with my fingers as I walked.

Still ravenous, I used the tiny bit of energy the food gave me to travel inside a nearby home, hoping the lack of light under the door meant they were asleep. Shuffling through their kitchen, I ate anything and everything I could get my hands on, no matter how unfamiliar it tasted. Then, curling up in a dark corner in the pantry, I closed my eyes, leaned my head back against the wall, and rested.

Shifting eventually started to feel within reach again as the minutes passed. It was almost like when a leg or arm fell asleep—numb and foreign to the rest of my body, but then as the Gift woke up, a tingling sensation as it made itself known again. Prickling. Shivers of awareness spread throughout my body as my strength returned.

Satisfied, I traveled back into the dark streets, noting the time—close to midnight—and continued on.

By the time the outer wall of the village came into sight, most of my anxiety had melted away

I laughed softly, feeling foolish.

I hadn't been in any real danger.

The humans would never even know I'd been there. By the time that little boy was old enough to explain, he'd think he'd imagined it. And now, I was practically home.

After I passed a few more houses, I'd stop in the shadows to change my dress and eyes back to normal.

Part of me wished I would've enjoyed my time here a bit more. Now that I'd recovered my strength, shifting felt easy again, like I could become anyone or anything.

"Hello, sweetheart," a male voice said.

The corner of my mouth twisted upward. It was as if someone had granted my wish. If I'd still been tired, I would've simply traveled away, but my playful mood was back in full force.

I stood in a circle of lamplight, and the man was somewhere behind me. Taking advantage of this, I quickly grew facial hair, forming an entire beard like the so-called "Baba" had worn earlier. It was detailed work, but excitement spurred me on, making me add other details like wrinkled skin and bags under my eyes. A few tucks and tweaks to my body and clothing, and by the time I turned to face the voice moments later, I was an old man wearing a slightly odd robe instead of a dress.

The leer on the drunken man's face froze.

It was an effort not to burst out laughing. Staying in character, I raised my now bushy gray brows in disgust before I turned around and kept walking. Only then did I allow a smirk to reach my face.

The only damper in my fun was that I still didn't know how to shift my voice.

Another wave of jealousy stole my breath.

Trying to ignore it, I closed my eyes. Could I mimic the sound of a male voice in general?

Grumbles came from behind me as the disgusting man shuffled off, and I tried to imitate him. I visualized my vocal chords as new strings on a lyre, playing with them, stretching them this way, then that, testing the way they sounded with a tuneless hum. It was almost like learning a new song. Certain changes raised my voice until it was high and childish, while others lowered it.

"Good seeing you," I called after the man in a deep baritone. He was all the way down the street by this point, disappearing around the corner, and lifted his hand in a rude gesture without looking back.

I grinned.

But the smile slowly fell off my face. Could I ever learn to imitate a specific voice, like the little boy from earlier? That would be the only way to truly replace someone. Maybe I could imitate someone like my father, whose voice I knew all too well, but that would take practice and experimenting to know for sure.

I'd discovered my Gift months ago, and yet, I still knew so little.

Scowling at yet another reminder that I was weak without a teacher, I started walking again and forced a faster shift than normal, pushing myself. I returned to my true form—short dress, sandals, and long, dark hair grazing my bare arms and back—without pausing in my stride.

A gasp came from the shadows on my left.

The usual instinct to flee surged through me.

I swung around.

No.

Asher stood in the dark alley between homes, where he waited for the others to return. He might've never even left this spot.

My fingers curled into helpless fists.

How much did he see?

"Haven't you been hiding a valuable little secret?" he whispered, slowly grinning. "Wait until the others find out about this."

"What're you talking about?" I scoffed, hiding my panic. "Are you feeling ill? I've been here nearly ten minutes, and you've been babbling about all the humans you saw." I reached out as if to feel his brow for a fever.

He frowned, pulling back and shaking his head. "Nice try. I saw all of it. First, you grew a beard for that dirty old man, and changed your voice. Then you made all of it disappear just now in an instant." Every word made my heart sink. "You're a shape-shifter!"

For a beat, we simply stared at each other.

What am I supposed to say?

I'd always liked Asher, but liking and trusting were very different things.

"It's okay," he said softly, as if he could sense my uncertainty. "If you don't want me to tell anyone, I won't. You can trust me, Bel."

It was the nickname that made my mask slip. I stepped closer and hissed, "You have to swear to keep it a secret."

Though he swallowed hard, he didn't step back. That alone gave me hope. "I promise."

Another long silence passed between us, heavy with unasked questions.

"So, why *is* it a secret?" he blurted, curiosity making him lean forward. "You have a Gift that's actually *worth* something. Sure, it's considered a bit dangerous by some, but that's only because it's so rare. You could be working with a mentor right now—"

"It just is," I bit out. He didn't understand. As much as I wished for a mentor, I knew the truth—none would take me. Shape-shifting wasn't a Gift that anyone cultivated, it was a Gift to be pruned out of Jinn altogether. Whether by dimming its strength, overpowering it, or removing it altogether. I shivered at the thought. *A Severance.* Very few Jinn ever survived a severance of their Gifts.

Pressing my lips together bitterly, I crossed my arms. If only my secret Gift could've been shifting memories instead of physical shapes.

Before Asher could press for more, Simon materialized a few paces down the road, right under a street lamp, not the slightest bit concerned about humans seeing his Gift.

I supposed after what Asher had seen me do, I couldn't really judge him.

"You should've been there!" Simon chortled, completely unaware of the tension between Asher and I as he jogged over and joined us in the dark alley. "I put a whole tavern to sleep! It was exhilarating! I can't believe my mentor won't let me try this back home. I could do so much more than they think!"

The mention of a mentor made Asher swing back to face me, and this time, I couldn't break free of his gaze. I could hardly breathe.

Please don't tell him, I wanted to say.

Instead, I ripped my gaze away and gave Simon a terse nod.

"Where is everyone?" Miriam's voice drifted toward us from down the street. "This isn't funny," she whined, growing louder as she let her fear make her forget the nearby humans. "If you all thought you could travel home and leave me here, I'm going to mix up a curse so strong you won't be able to sit for a year."

Simon leaned out, not noticing Asher's stare or the way I stood too still. "Oh, get over yourself, Miriam. You couldn't curse a pinky toe if you tried."

His jab made me shake my head, breaking the spell. "Don't be so sure of that," I said to Simon, standing up for the sensitive Miriam. "You're practically begging to be her first true curse."

Once I'd looked away from Asher, I couldn't seem to meet his eyes again.

What must he think of me now? Any hope that he might return my feelings someday was crushed.

Stepping out into the street, I forced my hands to hang lightly by my sides and took casual strides, though the light made me feel exposed. Made me want to run. "Let's go home," I said to all of them as I passed Miriam, who fell into step behind me.

If they noticed the slight hitch in my voice, they didn't say anything.

We didn't find Phillipa until we reached the short stone wall where we'd first entered the town. She leaned against a tree, waiting for us with arms crossed, shoulders slumped, and ignored all of us as we drew closer, though we weren't making any effort to be quiet.

"What happened to you?" Simon asked, nudging her shoulder less roughly than usual.

"Nothing," she muttered. "I don't want to talk about it."

A piece of her dress was ripped at the shoulder. Though she didn't have the best life at home, I could've sworn it hadn't been that way when we'd first arrived.

I waited until the others moved toward the portal before I took her arm and tucked it under mine, bending to her ear to ask softly, "Did a human hurt you?"

"Nothing serious," she murmured back, staring aimlessly ahead. "I traveled away before..." She didn't finish whatever she'd been planning to say.

Despicable humans. I gritted my teeth, and fury made my whole body tremble with the desire to hurt something. Someone. "We should make him pay."

Phillipa's voice shook. "I just want to go home."

I was sick of bullies. My father was the worst of them. But they were everywhere. People—whether Jinn or human—couldn't seem to help preying on others. It was in our nature. And while the Jinn could be cruel, humans were without a doubt the lowest scum.

"Are you coming?" Asher called from ahead, standing beside the tree trunk next to our passage home. His eyes were on me.

When I met them, he held my gaze until I broke it again.

Phillipa's problems faded in the face of my own.

A piece of white ribbon from Miriam's dress marked the portal on the human world side. It clung to a skinny branch and danced in the breeze. The daleth itself was invisible. The trees stood so close together that to pass through and return home, we had to each take turns, sucking in our breath and squeezing past the rough bark to make it to the other side.

Asher led the way, followed by Simon, then Miriam, just like before.

"Go ahead," I told Phillipa, wanting for some reason to go last. As her foot disappeared, I stared at the dark patch of foliage beyond. A soft wind made the leaves rustle all around me and an owl hooted somewhere off in the darkness. From here, the town we'd visited transformed into a twinkle of lights in the distance.

What was I going to do about Asher? He wasn't known for being trustworthy. But that didn't stop me from hoping.

While I stood frozen, worrying over it, his head popped back through the daleth. "I haven't said a word to the others," he said, as if he knew I needed to hear it. "We can talk more tomorrow, but don't worry. I won't tell anyone." Winking, he added, "Yet."

He disappeared before I could reply, and I could only hope he was joking.

5

MEET ME BY THE *daleth*, his note had said. He didn't sign it, but he didn't need to, because only Asher slipped notes under the door when my father was out.

Normally, I loved this. I kept a jar of his previous notes beneath my bed—even if all they ever said were things like, *Boaz got a new Gift that lets him put all kinds of senses on the skin. Fire. Insects. Worse. Just a warning, in case you come across him. Don't let him touch you.* Or, *See if you can get me some Tradandar at the market for my new spell.*

Today though, anxiety chased me around the small apartment no matter how fast I cooked and cleaned. I managed to finish my chores and slip out before my father ever came home.

By the time I reached the daleth in the last bits of golden light before the sun set, Asher had clearly been waiting a while. "I brought you honey cakes," he said as I strode up the hill toward him. "But I ate them all." Crumbs dusted his upper lip, stuck amidst the slight dark stubble growing there.

I turned away to look at the view and smiled a little despite myself. Shading my eyes, I waited for him to lead this conversation.

From this height, the whole capital city of Resh stretched out below, seemingly calm from a distance. The river Mem lazily split the city in two, winding off to the north. Up close, it was a roaring giant, but from here it was as thin as a string.

"I was just wondering," he said, when I didn't turn around or speak. "Are you going to tell me at some point... about your Gift? About why you kept it a secret?" He stepped in front of me, so that I couldn't help but look at him. His brows lifted suspiciously. "Do you have *other* Gifts I should know about?"

I laughed. Shaking my head at him, I moved to sit on the grassy hill. "What a question," I answered in the usual Jinni way of not answering at all, giving him half a smile. That would most likely make him think I did indeed have other Gifts.

I did not.

At least, none that had revealed themselves yet.

But just like the others, I wished I did. Didn't all Jinn? Our abilities were everything: power, wealth, stability...

It might still be possible, I supposed, to have a latent Gift, not yet discovered. It happened sometimes.

At the very least, Asher wasn't the only one attempting to learn spells and more permanent enchantments in his free time. Though, unlike him, I didn't advertise the fact.

Accepting my non-answer, he simply shrugged and sat beside me, switching to a different question. "What exactly can you shift into? Can you look like other Jinn?" There was a hint of fear beneath his bravado. A slight tremor in his voice that he tried to hide with a laugh. "Can you become *me*?"

Instead of the landscape below, I saw the freckled face of the little boy from the human world. I shivered, knowing the answer, even without a mentor. I could shift into anyone or anything, as long as I had enough time to figure it out and enough energy to make the shift.

Part of me wanted to trust Asher, to open up about everything. Would he try to control me like my parents had constantly tried to manipulate each other? Like everyone else I'd known? Or could he be trusted?

"I don't know," I lied, finally. "I'm not sure if I'm that skilled."

"Why don't you work with a mentor and find out?" he asked, letting his arms hang over his knees as he played with a long strand of grass.

Back to that question.

"I can't." My voice came out almost in a whisper.

He waited patiently.

I ran a hand through the long grass between us. Sighing, I pulled my arms in to hug my bare legs. "People will want to exploit you," I quoted my mother the day she'd left us. "It's better when you don't give them something to use." Out of the corner of my eye, I tried to gauge his reaction.

He swung around to stare at me and scoffed. "That's ridiculous. Why do you think we all spend time together? It's not like any of us have a valuable Gift—" He caught himself, glancing at me. "None that we were aware of, at least. We *are* your friends, aren't we?"

I nodded. He had a point.

Hesitating, I considered telling him more. One huge secret was already out,

THE SECRET GIFT

what would another hurt? It might be a relief.

I made myself turn to him and be far more honest than usual. "You're right. We weren't spending time with each other for our abilities. But, maybe you did still want *something* from me?" I leaned in closer, letting my eyes drift to his lips and then slowly back up to his red eyes, making myself as clear as I could without spelling it out.

He laughed. "So what if I did? Or do?" he added, with a wink. I didn't dare move, staying slightly too close, feeling his breath on my face as he continued. "That doesn't mean I'm 'exploiting' you. Unless, of course, you aren't interested?"

I swallowed, heartbeat speeding up. He'd put me on the spot.

I should pull back. That'd be easier.

"That's not it…" I said instead. I planned to add more, but couldn't find any other words.

It seemed to be enough.

He leaned in, closing the remaining space between us. His lips brushed mine softly. "I don't want to take advantage of you," he said huskily against my mouth. "If anything, I want *you* to take advantage of *me*."

I felt his grin more than saw it, but was too caught up in the kiss to answer.

He took the hint and stopped talking.

This wasn't my first kiss, but it was the first that meant something. My whole body felt shimmery and light, as if I could turn into a butterfly just by sensation alone.

Was this what my mother meant when she said people used you? If it was, then she was wrong. It was worth the risk.

I kissed him back, tucking the thought away for later.

Pulling away unexpectedly, Asher whispered, "Show me what you can do?"

Eyes half-closed, it took me a moment to orient myself. I drew a breath to divert him again, then paused. The temptation to reveal my Gift to someone after hiding for so long tugged at me. Maybe just once? After all, he'd already seen it.

"Not here," I found myself saying. I wasn't about to let another Jinni accidentally discover my Gift again. Standing, I headed for the daleth, anxiety and excitement warring within me as I hurried toward it.

A glance over my shoulder assured me Asher followed, practically on my heels, and I slipped through the portal into the human world for the second time in as many days.

Again, it struck me how the other side was deceptively the same as ours. Green grass, tall trees, blue skies, and a gentle breeze, although the sun peeking through the clouds was smaller from this vantage point. During the day, we might never have discovered the town, without the lights drawing us toward it.

This time, we instinctively moved through the trees in the opposite direction, putting distance between us and the humans. Keeping secrets was in our blood.

"What do you want me to be?" I asked over my shoulder as we went, inexplicably shy.

"You mean who?"

"I haven't tried shifting into another Jinn," I admitted, studying my toes as we walked. "But I can be any animal you can think of—at least, I haven't found any limits yet."

"If you can shift into animals, then you can shift into people too," he declared, as if everyone knew that.

I hadn't.

"How do you know so much?" I asked suspiciously.

He shrugged. "I don't just read books about spells and enchantments. There are all kinds of fascinating topics you can read about. If you don't want a mentor, the least you could do is pick up a book about Gifts like yours."

Of course I want a mentor, I retorted inwardly. But I only murmured, "I didn't know they existed."

Waving his hands excitedly, Asher nodded. "There are at least three different types of shifters. I've read all about them. If you could only become *one* animal, that'd mean that most likely, you're limited to that specific form and your Jinni form, and that's it. But if you already know you can shift into *any* creature, then the other forms you could take are basically endless. You could become a Jinni or a human—literally anyone!"

Anyone? My eyes widened at the possibilities.

I shook my head, taking a slight step back. "No," I whispered. "I could never try that." That would be outright asking for someone to discover my Gift. It'd also give them immediate cause for a Severance. Impersonation wasn't taken lightly in Jinn.

Still... Asher's revelations left me feeling light-headed with newfound power. No wonder shape-shifters were feared. I could go anywhere, be anyone.

A small smile crept over my face. *I could pretend to be the queen. Or one of the fancy ladies who will most likely end up marrying the prince.* Shaking my head, I laughed away the idea. *I wouldn't mind being anyone else, if it would take me away from my father.*

My smile faded.

No. It's not realistic. Changing the outward appearance was only one small aspect of a person. Pretending to be someone else would come with a million other details, such as voice and memories—not to mention dealing with the real person. Because who would willingly let someone impersonate them? No, no one could get away with that.

Asher had trailed off at my expression. "Fine," he said with a sigh. "I admit it. I don't know anything else. The book only had a couple paragraphs on shape-shifting before it moved on to another Gift. But you *do* know how unusual this is, don't you? I haven't met a shape-shifter—especially not one with your range of skills—in... well, ever."

"My mother was the strongest kind of shifter too," I whispered. Neither my father or I had ever told anyone that since before she disappeared. It was her secret. When asked about his legs, my father would always say he'd offended a powerful Jinni who'd cursed him and leave it at that.

Asher stopped in a small clearing, whirling to face me. "Was *she* the one that changed him?"

The worry on his face made me lie without thinking. "No, of course not. She wouldn't break the Unbreakable Laws like that."

He mimed wiping his brow in relief and smiled, then straightened suddenly. "If you both have the same Gift, did she teach you anything before she left?"

I shook my head. The disappointment when I thought of her stole my voice for a minute. "I've had to teach myself," I repeated, souring more each time he made me say so.

Biting his lip, he swung around to sit on a fallen log at the edge of the circle. "Show me your favorite shift?" He carefully made it a question.

I swallowed hard and nodded.

6

THE LIZARD.

I stepped onto the log beside him, towering over him for a moment, which made him lean back at first, then forward in surprise as, a handful of seconds later, he peered down at my small, green, four-legged shape. I flicked my tongue out at him to signal it was complete.

"Wow," he said on a breath. "I'd have never..." He shook his head, searching for words. "Can you go smaller?"

I dipped my leathery chin in a nod, and shrunk down to the flea I'd tried the previous night. Because it was familiar now, the change was not nearly as difficult. In fact, I could still change two or even three times more before I'd begin to tire. If my flea form could've smiled, I would have.

As it was, Asher had dropped his face until he was level with the trunk, trying to find me.

I gave a little hop.

"Ha!" His response almost blew me away. Literally. "Can you grow larger as well?"

I took my time, answering by shifting, forming first a large body, then thick, muscled bear-like legs with elongated claws, and the ox-like head of a Lacklore.

This was a creature I'd never attempted before. Not only because it would've been impossible to hide my Gift if I'd attempted it in the city, but I'd also never seen a Lacklore alive in person. I'd only ever seen a stuffed one in a museum, and the partial pelt on my father's chair.

THE SECRET GIFT

As a result, this shift was far more difficult and time-consuming, as I tried to visualize the living version. I wished I'd brought a meal with me—after a change this drastic I was going to be famished.

When I completed the change and blinked my huge black eyes at Asher, he could barely blink back.

I studied the long length of the claws and the way they left deep gouges in the soft grass and dirt. Lifting those sharp claws, I wiggled them in a wave.

Asher leapt back. Blushing when he caught himself, he forced a hoarse laugh. "I don't know what to say. It's—You're—I just… I can't believe you've kept this a secret. Shift back so you can talk to me! Do you realize all the things you could do with this Gift?"

I took longer than I really needed to return to my Jinni form, partly to conserve my strength, but also to give me time to think about what he meant.

One thing I hadn't shown him yet, which I'd barely even begun to experiment with, was tiny, incremental changes to my own features. As I shifted back to my usual form, I enhanced my dark lashes and the rosy tint of my lips and cheeks, deepening the blue in my eyes from a pale shallow pool to a deep, clear lake. As my sharpened teeth returned to their usual rounded state, I made them straighter too. When I smiled at Asher, I paid close attention to see if he'd notice any of the minor changes.

He stood squinting at me with a small crease between his brows. "Why is it that I feel as if I'm seeing you differently? It's like I never truly saw you before…"

This time I did laugh. A light happiness settled over me. Instead of pointing out what I'd done, I just smiled at him.

I might keep the changes going forward. Maybe even make a few other adjustments. They were easy enough. So minor, in fact, that it took about as much effort as walking a step. And once I set them in place, they were as permanent as all my other changes, staying exactly this way until I made another change.

It occurred to me for the first time that perhaps I could slow down aging. That I might live longer than most Jinn, maybe even… forever?

My eyes widened.

Forever was an incredibly long time. Long enough to escape my father for good. To leave bad memories behind. I could become something—or someone—new?

Turning my back on Asher for a moment to savor this new revelation without letting him see, I walked to the middle of the clearing before I turned back to him.

"I guess I'm starting to realize what I could do…" I finally answered his earlier question. "Probably more than I ever imagined." Gesturing to my short day dress that ended above my knees, I touched the pale cream fabric to focus my ability, and it extended into an evening gown that brushed the soft, grassy floor.

This, I had learned out of necessity the night before. But now I took it a step further. Still clutching the soft fabric, I imagined it as a different color. The cream rippled and changed in a wave of color to a deep teal as if it'd been doused in a dye.

"Does it have to be touching you?" Asher asked with wide, curious eyes as he stepped closer to get a better look. "Or does it remain changed even when you... take it off?" A blue blush rose in his pale cheeks, though he held my gaze.

"Are you trying to get me out of my dress?" I meant to sound flirtatious and confident, but the words came out breathy and girlish.

Before he could answer and make the situation more awkward, I dropped to the ground to sit, pulling the dress back to view my sandals, which were laced all the way from my ankle to my knee.

The wrap style was way too thick and out of fashion. With a touch to the tan laces to orient myself, I attempted to thin them into the elegance of the current style, changing them to a shimmery teal as well, to match my lavish gown.

Though it worked, I bit my lip as I unlaced one of them slowly. Part of me wished Asher wasn't here. I didn't like to experiment when others were around.

Now that he'd given me the idea, though, I had to know.

Untying the last lace, I slipped the sandal off.

Asher crouched down across from me.

I met his eyes briefly before I set it ceremoniously between us... and let go.

It reverted immediately to its true form.

Thick, old, tan laces.

Clenching my fists, I struggled to breathe calmly and not show Asher how frustrated I was.

I hated failure.

"Bel," he said when I didn't look up.

I kept my gaze firmly on the sandal, pretending to study it as if I could somehow change the outcome, though I knew for a fact I couldn't.

"Bel," he tried again, moving to sit beside me. "This is a good thing."

I scowled at him. "How?"

"Now you know one of your limits." He spread his hands as if it were obvious. "You have to know these things to learn what you *can* do. Any mentor would tell you that."

I wrapped my arms around my legs and bit back the urge to say, *I wouldn't know.*

He reached out and tugged on the teal fabric of my gown, which hadn't changed. "As long as it's touching you, it sticks, right?" He didn't wait for an answer. "Does the change need to be on something living? Change *my* sandals. See if they revert back when you let go."

Despite the pit of doubt in my stomach, my spirits rose a little at his confidence in me. Maybe it wasn't *so* bad that he was here. Eyeing his sandals, which were out of date as mine, I smirked. With only a tiny bit of effort, I turned them into furry snow boots instead.

The look on his face made me giggle.

"Hey!" he yelled, but then we realized at the same time that when I'd let go, they'd remained changed. He shook his head, but his tone was calmer as he grumbled, "I expect you to change those back."

"Take them off," I suggested instead, both curious and growing tired. I needed to reserve at least enough strength to return my dress back to normal before I went home.

I leaned forward as he tugged one of the boots off and set it in the same place I'd put my sandal. When it stood on its own, it once again reverted to its original form. Asher didn't waste any time yanking the other snow boot off to get his sandals back, strapping them on again hesitantly, almost as if he expected them to have a mind of their own.

With a sigh, I laid back on the grass and stared up at the faraway human-world version of the clouds.

Asher flopped down beside me, eyes soft, lips curled in a contented smile. "It's an incredible Gift," he whispered, though no one else was around. "Beautiful. Jinn are foolish to be afraid of it."

I blushed. Though I managed to keep it from visibly reaching my cheeks, I couldn't quite stop myself from lowering my eyes to our hands between us.

He reached out, tangling his long fingers with mine, playing with them.

It was somehow more intimate than the kiss.

Another step across the invisible line between friends and something more.

But unlike the daleth, I didn't know if either of us were making it on purpose, or if it was inevitable. Something I'd wanted for so long that I wasn't sure what to do when it actually happened.

I closed my eyes and allowed a small smile.

"I know what we could try!" Asher's hand tightened on mine unexpectedly, startling me. I looked over at him.

He'd propped himself up on his elbow, and his sharp gaze pinned me in place.

I couldn't explain why his expression made me hold my breath. My heart began to race. As I sat up to listen, I subtly pulled my hand back into my lap. "As long as it's nothing huge. I don't have much energy left."

He just studied me.

"I'm waiting," I said, curling inward, away from him, as the silence stretched.

Not letting me rush him, he merely leaned closer. "Since you've obviously been keeping this to yourself, I assume you haven't had a chance to try shifting someone else..."

I blew out an anxious breath, relieved. "I already told you, I haven't shifted into anyone else." *At least,* I amended silently to myself as I remembered the little human boy from the other night, *not another Jinni. Not anyone I actually* know *personally.* And I didn't want to.

"No, no." He grinned, either not noticing or ignoring my discomfort. "Not *into* someone else, actually *shifting* someone else. Simple shifters can become one creature, right? More complex shifters can become multiple creatures or persons. But the rarest form of shifting—" he faltered over the next words, but I still heard them: *the most dangerous form.* He chose to skip over it. "The rarest is a Jinni who can not only shift their own form, but also *someone else's.*"

Though it wasn't really a question, I still shook my head, frowning. I didn't like where this was going.

He sat up and took my hand again, squeezing it with a gentle pressure. "Bel, what if you could?" When I immediately started to shake my head again, he squeezed harder, until it actually hurt. "Just think about it," he insisted. "Can you imagine all the things we could do?"

We? The choice of words didn't escape me.

"I can," he continued. "The possibilities are practically limitless! What could it hurt to try?"

"Maybe tomorrow." I put him off. His interest in my Gift had been sweet at first, but for some reason it was starting to make me uncomfortable. Why was he so fascinated by it? Was I becoming another one of his enchanted items—another obsession? I shrugged off the uneasiness. This was Asher. We'd grown up together. I was probably reading too much into it.

Still, I needed time to think. After another heavy silence, weighed down with all his requests, I stood and said, "I should get home before I'm missed."

7

ASHER WASN'T ONE TO forget or let something go. He pestered me about going to the human world again the next afternoon, and the next, and the next. "I'll tell the others we're busy," he said when I protested that they'd try to come. "They know you like me." He winked, and I blushed before I could stop it. "I'll tell them I feel the same way, and we need some time alone."

Since my father worked late, I eventually gave in on the fourth day. "If I try this, do you swear you'll leave me alone afterward? Stop pestering me to try new things constantly?"

"Of course," Asher agreed immediately, settling back into the wobbly chair with a grin.

I snorted. We both knew that was an empty promise.

He started rambling about the details of how I might attempt this particular shift, but I was too distracted to listen. Under the guise of needing more tea, I stood and moved to the stove, heating up more water, keeping my back to him.

The idea of changing Asher's form instead of my own was daunting. What if I wasn't capable?

On the other hand, what if I *could* learn, but only with a mentor to teach me all the things that would otherwise be impossible to figure out on my own?

I dragged myself out of the dark thoughts long enough to say goodnight to Asher as he left. He gave me a distracted kiss on the cheek and said, "Don't change your mind now, Bel, okay? I'll see you at the daleth tomorrow."

As I closed the door behind him, I couldn't ignore it anymore. My biggest fear, that I'd pushed to the back of my mind ever since he'd asked me to try, forced its way to the surface. *What if I can change him, but then I can't change him back?*

Still, it was Asher's choice. *He can imagine the danger just as well as I can.*

We met early the next afternoon and made our way through the daleth to the human side, to the clearing where we'd stood a few days prior.

Unlike last time, though, we were both quiet. Tense. No kissing or holding hands today, not with something this huge looming over us. Asher's usual pale skin seemed stark white against his standard day armor and tunic, and his throat bobbed nervously.

"You can change your mind," I offered. The first words we'd spoken since meeting.

He only shook his head. As if words were too much, and he might lose his nerve.

With a deep breath, I closed my eyes. I'd worried over how to do this for the last four days.

I'd decided to attempt a change that was similar to his current size.

A wolf.

Whether or not I needed to touch him was unclear. Pretending to be deep in thought, I imagined him shifting.

Nothing happened.

I hid my failure, though, feigning a new start, as I stepped up to him and took his hand.

Something about the contact told me instantly it would work this time.

He opened his mouth, probably to ask what was taking so long, but I'd already begun. Choking on whatever he'd been about to say, his eyes widened as his fingers transformed into a huge gray paw in my palm. His nose began to lengthen. Instinct made him lift a hand to his face, but instead of a hand he scratched his new gray muzzle with his other paw.

I tugged him down to the ground, keeping my hand on his hairy foreleg. This allowed him to stand on all fours while I finished the change down to the tail, making his clothes shift into nothing before they could rip, though I kept his red eyes the same.

In the span of a few short minutes, he'd metamorphosed into a powerful gray wolf.

Finished with the change, I let go.

As I'd expected, the change in him was as permanent as it always was in me; a living body would always hold a new form.

Part of me wanted to ask how he felt. Of course, that would be a waste of breath.

"Are you okay?" I whispered instead, as if anything louder might startle his animal nature.

Was he still himself, the way I was in animal form?

He dipped his big head in an exaggerated nod. A wolf-like grin appeared on his new face, tongue hanging out, sharp white fangs glinting in the light, ears up and relaxed as his red eyes danced.

With a soft growl that was almost a purr, he danced back, spun in a circle, and then without warning, took off.

"Wait!" I yelled, terrified that I'd been wrong. I'd thought for sure he was still Asher beneath the new façade, but now I wasn't nearly as certain.

Already, I'd lost sight of him.

Branches tore and sticks crunched beneath his feet, growing softer as he put distance between us faster than I'd have thought possible.

I brought my hands to my mouth.

What have I done?

Long minutes passed.

I paced from one end of the clearing to the other.

He didn't return.

I slowly moved toward the log where we'd sat so happily only a few days prior. My legs grew numb and unresponsive. I sank onto the rough bark.

This was it.

I'd be found out for sure now.

Mind racing, I frantically tried to think of what I could say to his parents. Maybe I could tell the Jinni Guard about the daleth. Say he'd gone through it but never came back.

They didn't need to know the details. That would be enough. *Would it though?*

Time dragged by.

Asher still didn't come back.

Shaking, I tried to stand, but I couldn't find the willpower to leave yet.

I shut my eyes, trying to hold back tears.

This was all my fault.

I should've told him *no*.

So engrossed was I in my despair that I didn't hear the soft, padding footsteps until they stopped in front of me and a warm furry head dropped onto my lap, poking a wet nose against my bare arm.

I screamed and fell backward off the log.

Asher—for, of course, the big gray wolf with impossible red eyes was Asher—yipped almost gleefully, jumping over the log and running a circle around me. His tongue lolled in a wolfish grin, as if my struggle to catch my breath was entertaining.

"How *dare* you run off like that?" I yelled at him, forgetting myself for a moment as the fading adrenaline made my muscles weak. I'd almost left him behind in the human world. My panic turned into guilt. "I'm changing you back right now!"

With a whine, he tucked his tail between his legs and backed away from me. Clearly pleading for more time.

Standing with precise movements to cover my embarrassment over being startled so easily, I brushed the twigs and dirt off my skirt and legs before I deigned to answer him, trying to hide how breathless I still felt. "Fine." I inhaled deeply and added, "But if you're not back within the next ten minutes, I swear on all of Jinn and the human world on top of it that I'll leave you in that form forever."

He bounded away without another sound, long legs launching him across the clearing and out of sight once more.

This time I buried my rising apprehension beneath slow, measured breaths and began counting. I told myself I was only pacing out of boredom. My lungs felt tight, though, and I couldn't seem to take in a full breath. This was too much responsibility. Like the first day he'd found out, I wished fervently that he'd never discovered my Gift and everything could go back to the way it used to be.

When he finally vaulted back over the log and into the clearing, panting hard, it was an effort to keep my spine straight and my face clear of emotion. I wouldn't reveal myself so easily again.

"Come." I motioned when he stepped out of reach.

What if I can't change him back?

The old fears tried to raise their voices, but I clenched my hands into fists and ignored them. At this point, he deserved whatever end result he received.

Another quieter part of me somehow knew, though, and was not afraid at all. *If I could do it once, it will work again.*

Bending, I touched his furry shoulder and began the process of changing him once more, bringing back his original form—height, clothes, annoyingly persuasive voice, and all.

A gasp came from the forest behind me.

I spun to face the intruder.

Searching for a human, I was prepared to scare them into submission, but instead I froze at the familiar face.

Simon.

8

***NO!* I SCREAMED INTERNALLY.** *Why is he here?*

I couldn't speak.

We stared at each other across the short distance. He kept glancing at Asher, who stood behind me, and then back to me.

He'd seen everything.

I opened my mouth to call him over.

His eyes flew wide in alarm, and he flashed away before I could say a word.

"Simon!" I yelled, not sure if he'd just traveled out of sight or if he was truly gone. "Simon, come back! I won't hurt you!"

"It's true, Simon!" Asher yelled too, as we each swiveled around, trying to spot him if he reappeared somewhere nearby. "She has to touch you to do anything. You're safe!"

As far as we know, I thought harshly. *But I'd make an exception for idiot, if I knew how.*

There was no response.

He must've truly left then.

My heart sank. *Did he go back through the daleth? Is he telling everyone? Did he really see everything?* Ice filled my veins. Even if he'd only caught the last few seconds, it was enough.

For the second time in less than an hour, I feared the worst: I'd return home to find my father had disowned me, my friends would all fear me, and the Jinni Guard would press me into forced service with the threat of being watched closely for my too-strong Gift. Or, more likely, they'd just go straight to a Severance.

"This is all your fault!" I whirled on Asher. "You told him we were here!"

It was only a guess, but he couldn't hide the guilt that crossed his face. "I've been meeting him here every afternoon because you refused to come," he protested. "I'm sorry, I forgot to tell him not to come today! I tried to warn you that I smelled him as you changed me back, but it was too late." Despite everything falling apart around me, he had the audacity to grin. "That change was so incredible! I never would've imagined!"

Crossing my arms, I strode away, furious with myself for continuing to trust this stupid boy who'd taken advantage of me.

Asher caught up to me, apparently realizing he wasn't quite forgiven. "Bel, I truly am sorry. You have to believe me. Normally he and I meet on the other side of the daleth anyway; I never would've expected him to come to the human side without me. Still, it's my fault. We should've gone farther in to be safe. I wish I could go back in time and stop it. If I had a Gift as powerful as yours, I would. I'll—"

I stopped at the edge of the tree line, throwing my head back, eyes squeezed shut. "Stop." The ferocity had drained from me, turning to a quiet despair instead. My life was over. "I know you didn't mean to. What's done is done."

For once, Asher listened. We stood silently for a long moment. Birds chattered to each other above us, and the wind tried to play with my hair. I barely noticed.

Eventually, I began walking again, slower this time. Simon had likely told a dozen Jinn by now.

We reached the bit of ribbon that marked the portal. It fluttered in the wind, like a white flag of surrender, growing closer with each step. Part of me was tempted to stay in the human world. It was dingy and savage, but at least no one could abuse me or my Gifts here.

Not for the first time, I wondered if that's exactly what my mother had done when she'd left years ago.

Without warning, Simon appeared through the portal a dozen paces ahead. On his heels were Miriam and Phillipa. All three of them stared at me as if I'd grown horns on my head.

My hand lifted of its own volition to check. I stopped it halfway to my head when they flinched, dropping it back to my side.

He'd told them.

The weight of discovery that'd sat on my chest for months had finally lifted, but instead of relief, despair flooded in, filling my lungs until I couldn't seem to breathe.

All four of my friends knew my secret.

They stood tense, almost crouched, ready to spring away from me.

As if I were a Lacklore. Or a human.

Instead of trying to explain my Gift to them or calm them down, I sucked in a painful breath. And then burst into tears.

Hurriedly, I turned my back on them, covering my face.

I couldn't stop once I'd started. Each thought washing over me just made me cry harder.

They hate me now.

I swiped roughly at my cheeks, as tears continued to flow over them.

I'll never be the same in their eyes.

I choked on a sob.

This is just a small taste of what it'll be like to go home.

It crushed me.

Even a Severance couldn't be worse than this.

Asher came to my side, trying to put his arm around my shoulders, but I shrugged him off.

I blamed him for this. If not for him and his pressuring, I could've gone on the way I was for many more years, if not forever.

He sighed, but it didn't sound regretful. More like he found my reaction overly dramatic.

I didn't take my hands from my face, unwilling to let any of them see my lack of control.

When his shadow faded away, though, I wanted to call him back. I used the edge of my sleeve to wipe my cheeks.

Soft whispers floated toward me from him and the others, but I couldn't make anything out.

Shamelessly, I transformed the inner workings of my ears to be as sharp as an owl, allowing me to listen in without turning around or coming near them. It took longer than a full shift, as I had to figure out how to match the changes to the rest of my body, but focusing on the details helped calm me a little.

"—like I said, she doesn't want to tell anyone."

"Obviously." Simon scoffed, although with my attuned hearing I noticed his voice shook a little. "But Miriam and Phillipa have a right to know. And so do I." His voice grew loud enough that I would've heard it even with regular hearing, no doubt his intent. "She *should've* told us."

As I listened, a tiny spark of hope rose. Did that mean he hadn't told anyone else? Just the girls?

I changed my hearing back to normal as I dried the lingering tears and turned to face them. "Have you forgotten what my father is like?" I'd meant to put some force behind the words, but they were as dry and brittle as an old, fallen leaf. "You can't tell anyone." And though it hurt me to beg, I added softly, "Please."

Grudgingly, Simon crossed his arms and shrugged. "I haven't told on you yet, have I?"

That was the confirmation I'd so desperately needed. Despite myself, my shoulders sagged in relief. Still, I gestured silently toward Miriam and Phillipa. They remained close to the daleth—to their escape route—though they'd ceased to look scared of me. More curious really.

Simon scowled. "Like I said, they have the right to know. We all should know who we're spending our time with."

Pursing my lips, I shook my head, hating how much this was out of my hands. "We'll agree to choose conflict, then," I ended the disagreement the way Jinn were often forced to.

Phillipa, always the peacemaker, stepped between us, drawing our attention away from each other. "Simon says you turned Asher into a beast? Can you do all manner of shape-shifting?"

I told them only what Asher already knew, and no more. Whenever I tried to hold back, he would fill in the blanks in excitement, either not catching my darting glances or disregarding them.

"Lovely." Miriam's eyes narrowed on my face. "So, if I understand correctly, you're one of the most powerful Jinn to ever exist and have been laughing at us poor, incompetent fools behind our backs all this time."

"No!" I was quick to argue, though part of me perked up at the backhanded compliment. *Most powerful? Am I? Is that why Asher won't leave my side?* Out loud I only said, "I would never laugh at you. You are *all* my friends."

Though Miriam only crossed her arms, mimicking Simon's discomfort, Phillipa smiled and moved toward me, taking my hand before facing the others. "It'd be good to have a powerful friend," she said to me, though her tone said it was really to the others. "I, for one, am very pleased."

I squeezed her hand gratefully. The tears threatened again, and I had to blink to hold them back. Until now, I hadn't realized how much their friendship meant to me. But did I truly still have it? Miriam and Simon both still stood apart and aloof.

Asher spoke up, "As Simon saw, Bel can change us as well as herself. I don't think any of you realize how valuable this is." He turned to me. "Even you, Bel. You're still treating it like a curse, instead of the Gift it is."

Standing there with half of my friends judging me, I only scowled at him and muttered under my breath, "If you had it, you wouldn't be so quick to say that."

Even as I said it, I knew that was a lie.

He would've embraced it to the fullest. I had the one thing he'd always wanted desperately: *real power.*

"Think about it," he said over me, excitedly waving us closer.

We reluctantly obeyed.

"As we all can imagine, an animal is a fun shift. Useful too, such as for hiding from say, someone with a bad temper, for example…" He didn't look in my direction, but he left a long pause as if waiting for me to jump in and agree.

I refused to respond.

"But the changes don't have to be so drastic," he continued without missing a beat. "You could also shape-shift one of us to be taller or more handsome." He paused again for dramatic effect, letting them envision the little changes everyone wanted. I didn't need to imagine. Did he know I'd already tried this?

Glancing around at each of us, Asher's gaze landed on me with a grin. "You could shape-shift into one of the Jinni Guards." Phillipa gasped, and Miriam shook her head. "Or even a *royal*." Simon crossed his arms, tensing even more, if that was possible. But Asher still wasn't done. "Better yet—you could change *the royals themselves*."

My jaw dropped.

Until Asher, I'd never allowed myself to consider what I could do to someone else, much less something as specific as that.

Transforming into someone else wasn't truly that useful though. Since I'd never met Prince Shem in person—very few in my social standing ever had—I doubted very much I could actually duplicate his exact features—or anyone else in the royal family—based on a mere image from a coin or piece of paper.

Still… I reconsidered the idea. I had in fact already transformed into someone else—into a human, no less—our first night here in the human world. That had been terrifying in the moment—but I could see how useful it might be.

Their eyes were on me, waiting for my reaction. But Asher had revealed enough of my secrets for one day. I needed to think things over on my own before anything else was shared.

"My father will be expecting me," I used the worn-out excuse gratefully. "We can talk more later, if we must. I have to go."

"Come on, Bel," Asher pressed, stepping up to me, lowering his voice to a whisper. "Just promise me you'll think about it?"

I nodded, and when he ushered all of us back through the daleth, he said in a firm tone, "We'll meet here again tomorrow evening."

I wondered if I really had a choice anymore.

9

I APPROACHED THE DALETH with heavy footsteps. Not only was I late, but for the thousandth time I contemplated not going at all. If only Asher hadn't seen me. If only the others hadn't found out. If only I didn't have this Gift in the first place.

My mother had been right. *People only want to use you.* And foolish girl that I was, I'd given them something to use. I should've pretended with Asher that I couldn't change him. But I'd given in to curiosity. I'd wanted to know for myself.

Now, if I didn't show, there was a chance—however big or small I wasn't sure—that one of my friends would reveal my secrets to the Jinni Guard.

Or tell my father.

I didn't know which was worse.

Closing my eyes against the worry, I forced myself to step through the portal into the human world.

Bird song greeted me, cheerful and carefree. Completely discordant with my current mood. Other than the wind blowing through the trees, I didn't sense anyone. The others must be in the little clearing already.

A small part of me hoped that somehow they'd all stayed home. As I thought this, however, laughter reached me through the trees. Muffled voices.

Though I did my best to approach silently, their conversation died off when they spotted me. Already our friendship had changed, maybe forever.

"We're all just a little nervous," Asher said at my expression, swinging his arm over my shoulder. I appreciated him trying to pretend the tension wasn't my fault. It barely broke through my concentration. I was too busy watching the others' reactions to me, looking for any warning signs. When I didn't say anything, he continued, "We decided to go back to the human town and try being humans for a day."

As his words hit me, I pulled back, confused. "What? Why?"

Grinning, Asher shook his head. "I'll tell all of you when we get there. For right now, we just need Bel to shift all our features to look like humans. Not a lot—just enough to fit in."

I expected one of the others to put up a fight, especially Miriam, who always argued against Asher's ridiculous schemes. Instead, she stepped forward, surprising me with an unexpected request. "I was thinking…" She hesitated, then spoke in a rush, "Can you make us look like anything at all?"

Biting my lip, I slowly nodded. "I think so…"

Miriam's thin face lit up. Her hand flitted past her nose and eyes self-consciously. Leaning toward me, she whispered her requests in my ear. "My nose is so sharp and pointed." I could barely hear her, she spoke so softly, "Can you make it rounder? And can you make my eyes a less dull shade of blue? They look like human eyes. And they're too small."

"Human eyes are what we are going for right now though," I whispered back. *Why am I going along with this?* "All our eyes need to be human shades if we want to blend in."

Reluctantly, she nodded. Glancing over her shoulder at the others, she paused, then asked, "Can you enhance them when we come back home, then? Will they stay that way after you change them?"

My spine stiffened at the assumption that I'd simply agree.

Miriam's normally flat, insolent expression was bright and hopeful for once as she gazed up at me.

Some of my tension faded. I could understand wishing to be different. After all, hadn't I just yesterday added enhancements to my own features? Sighing, I nodded.

With those requests out of the way, she let me remake her short dress in the longer human fashion without comment, and when she turned back to the others, she was a different person—not only on the outside, but inside too. Her smile lit up her entire face. Even if I hadn't changed her nose per her request, she'd have been stunning, though of course, she'd never believe me if I said so.

"I don't want you to change anything except my clothes," Simon snapped as he stepped forward next, not moved in the slightest by Miriam's unusual excitement.

I crossed my arms.

"Simon, be reasonable." Asher stepped between us before my glare could turn into anything more. "You have to at least change your eyes." He waved to Simon's iridescent green, common in Jinn, but an otherworldly shade for a human.

"We're trying to blend in, remember?"

"Fine." Simon braced himself, lip curled in disgust.

His dislike of being touched by me was the biggest issue; every time I started shifting him, he jerked back, and the change stopped. "Hold still!"

Though he continued to squirm, I tried to make quick work of his eyes and clothes, lengthening the tunic but not bothering to do much more, wanting to be done with him as much as he wanted to be done with me.

Asher went next.

He sauntered up to me with a half smile and quirk of his brow.

My face stayed flat and expressionless.

"Bel," he murmured, leaning closer, blocking the others with his back.

I glared up at him.

Whatever he'd planned to say, he swallowed it and stayed silent.

I did the same changes for him that I'd done for Simon, giving them both brown eyes and simple clothes. Though Asher squeezed my fingers afterward and gave me a smile meant to be comforting, that sensation of butterflies was missing.

We each removed some of our more decorative outerwear—arm bands, belts, hair pieces, and armor—and tucked them beneath some bushes next to the daleth tree. This allowed me to save my energy. Though I didn't reveal it to the others, I noticed that these more minor changes had barely made a dent in my strength.

Phillipa pulled me aside, waiting for the others to stop paying attention—which happened quickly as they admired each other's new features—before she timidly asked, "Could you make me taller? And maybe stronger?" Unlike Miriam, I knew immediately she wasn't asking for these changes out of vanity. The last visit to the human world had left its mark.

"Of course," I agreed immediately. Shifting her soft, yellow eyes into the same human shade of brown as the boys was quick work. With some difficulty, I also played with the round, innocent shape of her face to make it narrower. Without a visual to base it on, it was like creating a complicated painting from scratch for the first time as an amateur artist. It took a couple tries, before I surreptitiously tried basing it on the way Simon was glowering at me. That helped it look more natural.

Giving her additional height forced me to exert myself in a different way. Taller was simple in theory, but the stretching took more energy.

Adding muscle definition, especially to her arms, which I left bare in her new gown, proved to be the most simple of the changes she'd requested.

When I finished, she flexed them in awe, standing taller for the first time in weeks. Maybe months. I hadn't realized how much she'd slouched before.

For the first time since this whole experience began, I was happy to use my Gift for someone else.

THE SECRET GIFT

This time when we entered the town on a busy main road, the sun was nearing the horizon and there were humans everywhere.

Everywhere.

Without meaning to, we all froze at the outskirts like deer caught in a hunter's gaze.

The humans didn't even notice us.

Going about their evening, they moved at different speeds or not at all, dawdling in small groups to gossip. Some left town via the main road, while others were just arriving. The humans filled the air with yelling as they tried to sell their wares, while banging and hammering sounded from down the street, and children squealed as they raced past us in a group with a leathery ball made out of an animal intestine.

Such a primitive culture.

"Get out of the way!" a deep voice yelled, making all of us jump and then scramble to the side of the road as a driver prodded his horse and cart forward, nearly running us over.

"Where to?" I asked Asher, since this was after all, his idea.

He blinked his now dull-brown eyes, unsure.

Pointing to a sign partway down the road, he said, "I think that's a human tavern? Why don't we try one of their drinks?"

"We don't have any money," Miriam reminded him, but without her usual malice. She was smiling at the humans who passed by us, and beaming when some of them smiled back.

"I'll handle that," Simon said, disappearing from the middle of our group without warning.

"Fool!" Asher hissed under his breath, as all of us scanned the crowd in a hurry, worried that a human had seen.

We couldn't risk starting rumors of Jinn in this town. We weren't supposed to be here.

While the reaction of the Jinni Guard back home would be terrifying all by itself, the humans were actually far more dangerous to us than most Jinn realized. For one thing, they had superior numbers to the five of us—four now.

When Simon reappeared in the exact same place, we were ready this time. Standing in a protective circle, we acted as nonchalant as possible and studied the passersby carefully, searching for any hint that someone had noticed.

No heads turned.

No one screamed or fainted.

An *oof* sounded behind me, and I nearly leapt out of my skin.

Turning around with the others, we found Simon doubled over, clutching his stomach.

"What was that for?" he groaned to Asher.

"Next time you're stupid enough to travel in broad daylight *in front of humans* for no good reason, you're done," Asher's voice was low and furious, enunciating every word. "Is that clear?"

"Done?" Simon tried to joke, wincing as he stood back up. "With what?"

"All of it," Asher said in a flat tone, not smiling back. "Us. Coming here. You make a move like that again, and you're out."

"Fine." Simon scowled. He held out a little cloth bag and shook it, making whatever was inside clink together. "Sounds like you don't want the money I got us then."

Phillipa and I glanced at each other. She stepped forward a bit more, blocking the small bag with her body from any curious eyes around us, and whispered, "Simon, what did you do?"

"Don't worry about it," he waved a hand at her, smiling again as if he thought she was impressed. "The human I took this from was fast asleep."

Stole. The human he'd *stolen* from. What Simon had done technically broke the Unbreakable Laws. Even if it was a minor infraction, being that he'd used his Gifts on a human rather than a fellow Jinn.

Asher didn't praise him, but he didn't chastise him again either. Instead, he just turned on his heel, leading the way toward the tavern he'd pointed out earlier. The others followed.

I trailed along behind them, staring at their backs.

It didn't make sense.

Why didn't the others fear Simon and his Gift, when he used it with reckless abandon? Especially then? I'd only ever acted with extreme caution, yet they still feared me.

Though I was here with them now, it wasn't the same as before. As we entered the dimly lit tavern, none of them seemed to care if I followed or not.

We sat at the closest open table, furtively glancing around. The room was mostly empty. Meaning it had about a dozen humans too many.

Near the back, a young woman wearing a white, stained apron wove through the tables toward us.

I leaned forward and hissed, "Who's going to talk to the human?"

"Not me," Miriam said immediately. Both Phillipa and Simon were quick to agree.

"I vote you," Asher said to me. "You can use your Gift to calm her or something."

"It's shape-shifting, not *hypnotism*," I snapped, but I didn't have time to say anything else.

The woman came to a stop at our small table, and we all took in her freckles, red hair, and how her dress came up to her chin.

Simon's eyes had grown wide, whether in fascination or fear, I couldn't tell. Head tilted slightly, Miriam studied the woman's freckles, touching her own cheeks. Phillipa kept her hands pressed in her lap, sitting still enough to be a statue, while Asher merely turned to me, expectant.

"Welcome to the New Kings Inn," the serving woman intoned, wiping her dirty hands on her apron. "What'll you have?"

10

PANICKING, I POINTED TO the only table nearby with customers and blurted out. "We'll have the same thing they're having."

The redhead swiveled to look at their food: three drinks and three big plates filled with meat and bread. Turning back to me, brows raised, she asked, "Will that be for you alone or for the whole table?"

"All of us," I said quickly, wanting her gone as soon as possible. I took the little purse from Simon's hand and emptied the coin onto the sticky wooden surface. "Will this be enough?"

She blinked at me, raised brows coming together. "That's more than enough, honey. I only need six of those."

"Sorry," I laughed a little breathlessly, waving a hand as if embarrassed. "I wasn't paying attention."

She studied me as I counted out six coins and handed them over. With a shrug, she moved away to help another table of customers that had just sat down, saying over her shoulder, "I'll tell the cook."

I awkwardly began returning the rest of the coins to the bag.

"There's three of them, and five of us," Asher whispered as soon as she'd taken a few steps. "If she only brings three plates, that's not enough food for all of us."

"If you wanted something different, you should've ordered it yourself," I snapped, embarrassed. "Besides, why would she only bring three plates?" I lowered my voice. "Humans might be inferior, but they're not *that* stupid." I didn't think so, anyway.

Tossing the coin bag across the table to Simon, I added, "You'd better return what's left to the one you stole it from."

None of us mentioned that returning some but not all of the money was still breaking one of the Unbreakable Laws. It irked me to be part of it, but I couldn't say anything further. It was too late. I'd already participated in the violation simply by being present.

Simon rolled his eyes, but agreed. Underneath his cocky demeanor, he was clearly as spooked as the rest of us, jiggling his leg nervously as he took in the dark room.

More humans walked in, laughing loudly and heading in our direction.

Simon flinched as they pulled out chairs at the table next to us. We all did. Even me, if I was being honest.

If this goes wrong, I'll shift into a mouse. They're bound to be rampant in a place like this. If I had to, I'd leave all four of them behind. Crossing my arms, I studied each of them in turn. *They'd leave me behind without a second thought. I'm nothing to them anymore. They blame those with powerful Gifts, but when it comes down to it,* they *are the ones keeping themselves separate.* Bitterly, I dropped my gaze to the wooden table, focusing on the crumbs and the whorls in the dark wood.

Phillipa usually didn't speak in large crowds, but she surprised all of us by leaning across the table, saying to Asher, "I think it's time you tell us why we're here."

His throat bobbed as he swallowed. Glancing around the room, he leaned in too, waiting for all of us to do the same, before he whispered, "I want to steal one and bring them home."

One.

"One what?" I forgot to be quiet in my horror. I already knew the answer, but I hoped that somehow I'd heard wrong.

It took the others a few seconds longer to understand what he meant: *a human.*

Powerful Jinn sometimes enchanted humans with certain talents and brought them back to Jinn to work for them. No doubt Asher thought possessing a human would give him the same suggestion of power.

"Absolutely not." I moved my chair back to get up and leave.

Asher grabbed my wrist from across the table, and Simon put a hand on the back of my chair, helping him keep me there. "Don't make a scene, Bel," Asher muttered, squeezing hard until I allowed Simon to drag my chair back in.

Yanking my hand away, I rubbed my wrist, which stung. Surprise brought tears to my eyes. I blinked them away before they could fall.

For the first time since I'd met Asher, I hated his lust for power.

"She's right though." Miriam kept her voice low, wrapping her arms around herself and avoiding my gaze. "There's no way we could kidnap a human without leaving some trace. Do you think everyone back home is just going to accept that *you* of all Jinn have a human worker, without asking questions? The Jinni Guard would find out within the day, and you'd get the rest of us in trouble with you."

"The Jinni Guard brings back human workers all the time," Simon argued, seeming intrigued by the idea. Not surprising, since he usually agreed with Asher. He still gripped the back of my chair tightly, though I hadn't moved.

"We're not the Guard," Phillipa bravely whispered.

Asher's face grew blue as his blood rose. "You like to remind us of that, don't you? That we're not 'good enough' to do all the things that the Guard can do—"

Fury boiling over, I leaned across the table so far that Asher was forced to look at me and interrupted in a harsh whisper, "If you even *consider* making me an accomplice in this, I swear on all of Jinn that I'll turn you into a frog for these humans' table."

The serving woman set down a plate of frog legs on the table next to us right then, adding weight to my threat.

Asher scowled and sat back, crossing his arms.

He wasn't outright choosing conflict, but he clearly wasn't in agreement either.

If not for my newfound—or rather, newly known—Gift, he might not have listened to me at all. The fact that he had to, that I'd threatened him if he didn't, wouldn't be received well by any Jinn, least of all him.

The others glanced between us, paler than normal, and didn't say a word.

If someone had asked me in that moment why I liked Asher, I wouldn't have been able to think of a single reason. Right now, I felt like I didn't know him at all. And I didn't want to.

More customers came in, and the serving woman forgot about us for a while as she took more and more orders. It seemed the dinner rush had begun.

We sat in tense silence.

Asher fumed.

Half of me seethed as well, while the other half wanted to earn his forgiveness. I tried not to panic at the way everything was deteriorating. That it was falling apart *here* of all places. This was the worst place to not be able to trust a fellow Jinni.

When our food arrived, I couldn't even taste it. As we had waited for our meal, the entire tavern had filled to maximum capacity. The volume had risen along with the numbers, making it difficult to hear my own thoughts. We were surrounded by humans. It was like going into the lair of one of the ugliest, most dangerous Lacklores wearing only a thin Lacklore hide and hoping they didn't notice and eat us.

Asher still hadn't responded.

Something between us had shifted, and it felt permanent.

"This drink isn't bad," Simon said after we'd spent a minute or two of poking at our food, pretending everything was fine. "If you can get past that bitter taste."

"Let's just get out of here." My skin crawled with the sense of a hundred eyes on us.

Phillipa was quick to agree. "I don't know if I can last much longer," she murmured. "This many humans is too much for me."

"It doesn't bother me," Asher said, not even trying to keep his voice down. Eyes on me, he ignored the others and stood.

As he gazed around the room, staring at one human after another, he began to draw attention. His eyes settled on a pretty human girl waiting on tables at the far side of the room. I hated the tightness in my chest as he stared at her. "She'll do," he murmured.

I could picture the next moments vividly.

He'd lay a hand on the poor girl, and one or more of the dozens of human men surrounding us would instantly get involved. With his arrogance, he'd pick a fight he couldn't possibly win, and we'd be forced to either abandon him or fight with only our fists and feet like the humans. Most likely one of us—probably Simon—would use a Gift, revealing us to the whole town, breaking all kinds of rules, and then the entire Jinni Guard would come down on us.

The scene played out in horrific detail in my mind. I didn't need the Gift of foresight to know what came next.

Fists clenched, I debated standing up to him. He needed to be stopped. But if I spoke again, I could almost guarantee it'd make things worse.

Asher pushed his chair back and began to walk away. Miriam caught him with a tentative hand on his arm. She spoke just loud enough for our table to hear, "This town isn't going anywhere. If you're truly determined to pull off something like this, at least take the time to make a plan and do it right, so you don't get caught. Or, if you don't care about that, then at least give us a chance to leave first so we don't go down with you."

She paused, waiting for a response, but he just stood there, stubborn.

"Fine," she snapped after a few more strained seconds passed. "We're leaving." She glanced around at the rest of us for confirmation. Bobbing our heads in unison, we stood with her as she added, "Are you coming with us or not?"

His glare caused a few nearby humans to give our table a wide berth as they walked past, but finally he conceded with a short nod.

We left the half-eaten food and dregs of the drinks behind, scurrying out of the tavern on each others' heels.

Outside, I sucked in a deep breath of fresh air. *That was too close.* We waited in the back alley behind the tavern while Simon returned the remaining coins to their original owner.

Though he came back in a suspiciously short amount of time, none of us said a word. We made our way through the streets, which were much quieter now, toward the edge of town. The sky was deep black. The first stars began to twinkle. We'd lasted longer inside that awful tavern than I'd thought we would. Still, I would put up a fight before ever coming here again. I'd had enough of Asher's foolish ideas.

Glancing over at him, it was clear he still held a grudge against me as well. He wouldn't meet my eyes, and his fists were clenched.

Picking up our hair pieces, arm bands, belts, and armor, we crossed back through the daleth, reentering Jinn before any of us remembered we needed to change out of our human forms.

Asher demanded I change him and Simon back first. They traveled away immediately, not waiting for the rest of us.

Miriam stopped me after I'd changed her dress back to normal. "Could you—" she faltered with Phillipa right there listening, and tried again. "Could you let me keep a bit of it? Like the new nose?" she reminded me. "And maybe make my eyes a little more, you know, Jinni? Nothing obvious, of course, just a little bit brighter?"

As a friend, I couldn't find a reason to say no. It seemed cruel to refuse her when it was within my grasp. So I did as she asked.

When she stepped back, Phillipa took her place, meeting my eyes. "I know keeping this height and these muscles is asking too much," she began softly. "Someone would notice. But, perhaps I could keep the smallest amount today, and maybe add a little more every so often, over time?"

Once again, how could I say no? I understood why she wished for this completely. Her father and mine were so similar. I did as she asked, attempting to return the outer appearances back to what they'd used to be, while still retaining a bit more strength in the muscles beneath. They would serve her well.

"I'm so tired," I told them as I finished, eyes drooping, body sagging. Though the small, detailed changes only took a fraction of my ability, the emotional exhaustion threatened to overwhelm me. I couldn't face them right now. I needed to be alone.

"I'll take Miriam home," Phillipa offered, since Miriam hated being forced to walk. "You get some rest."

Nodding, I traveled straight home, dragging myself up the stairs of the acropolis, sneaking inside, past my sleeping father, and falling into bed exhausted before I remembered to shift myself back. *Careless.* I groaned. *No more mistakes.*

I hauled myself up and over to the small gold mirror on the wall. The girl staring back at me had deep bags under her strange, brown eyes, along with a lost, hopeless expression. I tried not to look too closely.

Though I didn't need the mirror to shift my eyes back to blue, watching them change colors grounded me. Seeing my ability in action made me feel more powerful and in control.

Something I desperately needed right now.

Touching the gilded edges of the mirror, I whispered to my reflection, "*You are the most powerful of them all. They don't control you. No one can.*"

I wanted to believe it.

Snores came from the outer room, and I pulled back from the mirror. My father's presence reminded me how small and out of control I truly was, but for once I was too tired to care. Pulling the blankets over me as I dropped back onto my bed, I fell asleep instantly.

✳ ✳ ✳

The next day, I ignored Asher's note to meet them at the daleth.

I was done going to the human world. Done doing favors for them. Done being used.

"Jezzie, where's the food?" my father yelled, pulling me out of my dark thoughts.

Asher knew better than to stop by when my father was around. So, for a while, he stayed away. I didn't know which of them was worse at this point.

But he must've been watching the acropolis closely. Because the following morning, just a few short minutes after my father left for work, there was a knock on the door.

11

"I JUST NEED A small favor," he said, before I'd even opened the door fully. The morning sun cast him in a glowing light that made him look far more innocent than he was.

No, *where have you been?* Or, *are you okay?* after I didn't show yesterday. More proof of how he really felt. I was just a useful tool to him. I couldn't lie to myself anymore when the truth was staring back at me.

Hot frustration seeped into my blood, making me spin away from him and stalk across the small room to the kitchen window.

Behind me, the door clicked shut. "I wouldn't ask if I wasn't desperate," Asher continued, as determined as always. "It's, well, I have this idea... It might be stupid."

Most of your ideas are, I thought traitorously. But I didn't say it out loud, because some part of me still hoped...

Hoped he wouldn't be stupid.

Hoped there was still some small chance we'd...

I didn't even know how to finish that thought. My clear—albeit boring—future had shifted all on its own into a bleak, dark cloud. It was impossible to see.

Did Asher and I still have a chance? Had we ever?

When I glanced at him over my shoulder, his head was bowed and he scratched the back of his neck, staring at the fading paint on the wall.

Sighing, I pulled a wobbly chair out from the little table and sat. "What is it?"

Instead of sitting, he started to pace. To the kitchen window, back to the door, and then the window again. "It's nothing, really... After you changed our clothes that day, I kept thinking about all the other things you could change. Or—" he corrected himself "—more specifically, what you could change them *into*."

Icy dread washed over my skin, leaving it pebbled with goosebumps.

Halfway through pacing back toward the window, he yanked a chair out from the table and dropped into it, leaning toward me. "For example: *coin*."

Already shaking my head, I was relieved to have an easy answer. "Metal isn't alive. It can't stay transformed on its own, remember? You were there when I discovered how my Gift works with lifeless objects. You already know this."

One side of his mouth tilted up. "It doesn't have to last though, don't you see?" He grinned wider as my lips parted in understanding. "It only has to fool someone for a minute! Then, you just slip the money into a coin purse to hide it as it returns to whatever it was, before you hand it over." He named the price. It was so outrageous.

"That's stealing," I said in a flat tone.

He ignored the words and gave me that smirk that he knew full well had always worked for him in the past. "Come on, Bel! It just has to be an item that sounds similar when you shake a bag full of them. Maybe tin... Or rocks... Or even shekels!"

Shekels had such little value that they were often tossed in the street for orphans or beggars to pick up, since you'd need dozens of them to buy something as simple as a loaf of bread.

While I had to admit, if only to myself, that the idea intrigued me, it was too risky. Even if I didn't care that it was wrong, it would alert the Jinni Guard to a Gift being misused, and that trail would lead them straight to me. "There's no way. We'd get caught." *Or rather, I would get caught.*

"Well, that's the best part," Asher was quick to say. "With your Gift, you can pretend to be anyone you want. After you use the fake coin and purchase the item, you can simply return to yourself. They'll never know. So, it has to be you, see?" He leaned back in the rickety wooden chair.

The certainty that I would listen to him and obey reminded me of my father.

"No," I bit out. He'd made me part of his schemes against my will too many times. Pressuring me to use my Gift on him. Telling my secrets to our friends without my permission. Including me and my abilities in his plans to steal a human. I'd broken the Unbreakable Laws simply by being around him as he did whatever he wanted. All of those instances were frustrating, yet they were nothing compared to what he was asking now. "This isn't a game. This is my life. I'm not doing it."

"Listen, I didn't want to say this, but... if you want me to keep your Gift a secret, then I need you to do this. For me. Please, Bel?" he added, putting a hand on my arm, as if that would somehow soften the threat.

My freedom leeched away from me as quickly as the blood drained from my face.

Quicker even, since it'd been gone the moment Asher walked into the room. He wasn't giving me a choice.

It hit me that I hadn't had a choice since the moment he'd found out.

If he had his way, I'd *never* have one again.

The sharp stab of betrayal was almost physical. It left me breathless. Unable to speak.

This was *Asher*.

I'd *trusted* him.

Years of practice hiding my emotions from my father helped me keep my face calm even while breaking inside.

I took a mental step back, behind my old, familiar wall of secrets, building it back up in my mind.

I'd been a fool to think he cared for me.

He patted my arm, still under the guise of letting me decide.

He knew he'd won.

When I could trust my voice enough to speak, I muttered, "What's this 'item' you need so desperately?"

Asher grinned and leaned forward. "You're going to love it."

He was wrong. I *hated* it. Hated that he'd still managed to hook me into his schemes like he always did. My stomach twisted and churned, fighting it. There had to be something I could do…

"It's a lamp," he was saying, holding his palms a short distance apart. "About yea high, with a solid gold base and a green, glass-blown top. Lamech just put it on sale yesterday."

"And what's so special about it?" I crossed my arms.

"It's spelled for travel."

Enchanted items and other tokens often enhanced Jinni Gifts. "I'm guessing it's meant to take Jinn further than they could naturally travel on their own?"

"Yes," he admitted. "But, think about it, Bel. Enchanted objects will also give you a Gift you *don't have*!"

Ah. It all made sense now. He'd always been jealous that the rest of us—well, excluding Miriam—could travel when he couldn't. It was such a common Gift that almost every Jinni had it, to some degree. Walking to a place like the daleth could take him an hour, while it took me only a split second.

I was tempted to poke at him and his sensitivity. But I knew from experience that would only make him dig in his heels more.

"Come on, Bel," he said again, leaning forward to take my hand, a gesture that would've given me butterflies in the past. Rubbing his thumb against my skin,

THE SECRET GIFT

he added softly, "It's really not a big deal."

I sat there, speechless. He wanted me to use my Gift in public, lie to a vendor who we both knew was going through difficult times, and steal from him. To essentially announce my presence *and* my fear-inducing Gift to the Jinni Guard themselves.

It was a *very* big deal.

No, I thought. *Absolutely not.*

But I didn't say the words out loud. I couldn't. Not with his threat hanging over me. There was no way I could agree to do this... and there was no way I could say no.

Patting the table, Asher stood, taking my silence as acceptance. "I'd better go before your father gets back, or you'll have to turn me into one of your lizard creatures to escape."

I didn't laugh with him.

At the door, he paused with his fingers on the handle. "Oh, can you do it as soon as possible, though?"

For a split second, I thought he meant the last thing he'd said: *turn me into one of your lizard creatures.* I blinked in confusion.

But I'd misunderstood. He was obviously talking about the lamp.

I shook my head slightly to get the image of Asher as a lizard out of my head.

He didn't notice, stepping over the threshold as he continued, "I don't want someone else to snatch the lamp out from under me just because we were slow." *Ah, yes. We.* Now he was insulting me on top of everything else, by pretending he somehow shared the risk I'd be taking. *If* I did this. I clenched my hands into fists. There had to be a way out. If I could just find one...

Pulling the door closed behind him, he paused, turning to face me once more, and added, "I can meet you this afternoon after you pick it up. Either here, or out by the daleth?"

I still hadn't spoken, seated in the same frozen position at the table. Had my feelings on this really not been clear? Did he care that little about what I wanted? I stared at him.

He just raised his brows expectantly. To him, there was no other option. He tapped a finger on the doorknob. How had I never noticed the calculation behind his small smiles.

"Was anything between us ever real?" I whispered across the looming space between us. "Or was it all a lie?"

"Don't be ridiculous." Asher laughed. "Nothing's changed. You're making this into something much larger than it is."

"Then why the threats?"

He rubbed his forehead with a sigh. "You're so dramatic." Something in my chest pinched. I hated being mocked, and he knew it. "It's not a threat. It's a fair trade."

I just shook my head wordlessly. He could spin anything. There was no reasoning with him.

"You know I'm right," he said when he glanced up at my expression. "You *have* to use your Gift. I'm *helping* you use it, one way or the other. With a mentor, or—" he smirked a little, pointing to himself "—better yet, with me."

1 2

WHEN HE'D SAID HE would turn me in, he meant it. His red eyes sparked mischievously, and my hope was extinguished. Snuffed out completely. As if a whole ocean had flooded over me and washed away any chance of flames catching ever again. Whether Asher called this a favor or a threat, it didn't matter. If he didn't tell on me this time, I had no doubt he would later. Whenever it suited him.

I needed some leverage over him in return, or this would never end.

An idea tickled the back of my mind.

"So…" he dragged out the word when I still didn't say anything. "Should I meet you here in a couple hours?"

"No," I snapped automatically, trying not to think too hard on the idea until he left. "Never come here again."

I hoped he'd hear the disgust in my tone, but if he did, he chose to ignore it. "All right, daleth it is," he said as he stepped into the hall, nearly running into the elderly Hanna, who owned this section of the acropolis, as she shuffled past us.

"Watch your step," she grumbled, eyeing us both before she continued on down the hall.

Behind her back, he mouthed, *Old Hag*. A lot of residents called her that since there were few Jinni as old as her. Rolling his eyes as she turned the corner, he added out loud to me, "See you in a few hours." He had the audacity to wink at me before he closed the door.

The apartment walls that had always felt like my prison seemed like nothing now compared to my own skin.

Once again, I walked through the chain of events that had brought me here, struggling to find the moment I could've escaped this destination.

I couldn't find one.

My feet moved with a mind of their own.

Without allowing myself to consider the possible consequences, I followed my instincts as a partial plan began to form. A plan that would make him pay. My jaw set in grim determination. He would regret asking me to do this.

Stopping in front of the mirror in my bedroom, I touched the gold edges, running my fingers along the curves.

When I lifted my gaze to my reflection, the girl gazing back at me had tears in her eyes. I hadn't even felt them. Raising a trembling hand to my cheek, I tried to steady my breathing and blink them away. *This is how it has to be. This is how he decided it would be.*

Of course he wanted to use my Gift for himself. I should've expected it. It was who he'd always been—the hunger for influence and power was a part of him just as much as his red eyes and cocky smile.

Another long inhale. Exhale.

Until the girl looking back at me in the mirror lifted her chin in an arrogance that could match Asher's own, and the shine of tears had disappeared.

He wanted to see who was the most powerful of all?

Fine.

He was about to get his wish.

But it wasn't going to be who he thought.

I shifted slowly. Carefully.

I became male, changing my clothes to fit my new form.

Taller. Shaggy dark hair. Deepening my voice until it matched the rest of my changes. A voice I knew so well that, after a half hour of experimentation and frustration, I managed to form what I thought was a close resemblance.

I finished with those red eyes.

They blinked back at me calmly in my little mirror.

I turned away, before I could change my mind.

Picking up my coin purse, which was currently empty, I left the acropolis. Once on the street, I traveled directly to a quiet alley right outside the emporium, taking every precaution possible to make sure no one would see me and connect the dots. Better to be overly cautious than to *ever* be caught again.

I strode through the back alleys, bending down over and over again whenever something shiny glinted in the light, until I'd collected a handful of shekels, listening to them clink together in my purse.

Once I had enough, I practiced.

A dozen times, and then a dozen times more.

Reaching into the purse, I shifted the small shekels into hefty gold coins the second I touched them, pulling them out to display them in my palm before quickly returning them to the bag.

Of course, the moment I let go, the metal returned to its original form.

My timing would have to be perfect.

"Asher!" the storekeeper called to me as I entered his store and the bell rang out. Lamech knew both of us in passing, which meant my impression of Asher needed to be as accurate as possible.

I imitated his cocky stride, flinging my shoulders back and grinning, ignoring the way my heart pounded. This next part would be the true test: I had to speak. Clearing my throat, I said, "I'm here for the lamp."

Lamech's brows rose, but his weak yellow eyes were pleased. "I didn't expect you to come back so soon. You understand, the price hasn't changed?"

Clearly, he didn't think Asher had the money.

He was more right than he knew.

A nagging feeling that this was going to make things worse instead of better tickled my neck, but I wasn't about to stop now. Taking out my coin purse, I smoothly changed the coins as I pulled them out. A spirit of showmanship struck me. I flaunted each coin, dropping it back into the coin purse one at a time, counting each one—careful to let go only once they were out of sight.

The *clink, clink, clink* made the storekeeper's eyes grow wide. He shook his head, clicking his tongue. "Where in all of Jinn did you find so much coin in such a short time? That's at least three months wages. I didn't take you for a hoarder?"

Swallowing hard, I managed to keep my grin in place and diverted him with a question, as all Jinn learned to do from a young age when we wanted to keep a secret. "Do you always ask your customers such personal questions?"

He held his hands up with a chuckle. "It's none of my business, of course. My apologies. You must have run across some good luck."

I tightened the string without answering and tossed the little purse onto the counter in front of him.

This was yet another opportunity to fail. If he double checked the coins now, he'd discover the truth.

Keeping my body relaxed and my smile in place, I waited.

Brows still raised, Lamech turned to the shelf behind his counter, where the more valuable items were stored.

Though there were multiple lamps, he didn't ask which one, just gently took down a small glass-blown lamp—with a gold base and a deep-green glass top, exactly like Asher had described.

Clearly, Asher hadn't hid his interest the last time he'd been here.

"You're very lucky," Lamech told me as he placed the lamp on the counter. It was the size of my palm. "More than a few others have eyed this today. I was considering raising the price."

I put two fingers on the little coin bag and thrust it across the counter toward him. "Good thing you didn't," I replied in a flat tone.

Fortunately for me, that's exactly what Asher would've done, so Lamech only huffed as he pulled out a paper to write a proof of purchase.

I took the lamp and the receipt, thanking him, and walked out.

It worked.

A slow smile stretched across my face. I couldn't quite believe I'd just done that.

The bell jingled as the door shut behind me, and I paused.

If I traveled from Lamech's shop, that would be a dead giveaway I wasn't Asher. Something I wanted to avoid at all costs. Not to mention, traveling itself would leave a trail far too easy to follow. A trail that would lead directly to me.

So, I threw my shoulders back and began walking instead.

All the way to the other side of the shopping emporium, I walked. And then on toward the river Mem, until there wasn't another soul in sight.

Only then, did I feel safe to travel.

I didn't want to go straight home though.

Inspiration struck me. I traveled to the daleth—partly because no one outside of our group knew it existed and partly because of where it led—and entered the human world.

A genuine smile curved my lips for the first time since Asher's visit. Straight ahead, the human town sat innocently on the hilltop. There, the humans went on with their day, oblivious to the Jinni in their midst.

I knew exactly where to hide the lamp.

Though I couldn't travel many places in the human town without being spotted, there was one dark, little cranny I'd become familiar with. A quiet place that, if I stopped by for a brief visit, or to hide something small, no one would ever see.

I lay down on the grass to be in the necessary position, and traveled.

Opening my eyes, I blinked up at the wooden frame of the bed and the straw mattress above me. Little Naseem's bed in the human house.

To my right was a wall, and to my left, bare feet under a dress moved about the room, unaware of my presence.

I only needed a moment.

Silently, I set the lamp down, all the way in the back corner, where it might easily go undiscovered for years.

The metal base bumped into the wooden wall with a tiny clink. I breathed in and out, trying to slow my racing heart.

The woman continued moving about the small kitchen, humming to herself. She hadn't heard.

Still, before I left I should make absolutely sure. As I lay there, the reality of what I'd done back in Lamech's shop began to hit me.

THE SECRET GIFT

My breathing refused to slow.

If anything, it grew more rapid.

I sucked in air as quietly as possible, staying under the bed longer than was really necessary.

After two long, off-key songs, when the human clearly hadn't noticed anything, I drew one last breath and traveled back to the daleth.

I'm going to do this right, I reminded myself. *No more getting caught.*

Re-entering Jinn, I made three more stops in the woods. That should hide my trail thoroughly. Even the most talented tracker would have trouble tracing me from Lamech's shop all the way home.

Swallowing hard, I traveled twice more anyway, across the river as an added precaution—to the opposite side, as far as my ability would take me, and then back—before I finally traveled to the acropolis entrance.

I climbed the stairs to our little apartment still in Asher's form, hoping I wouldn't run into Old Hanna. If she or any neighbors were watching, Asher was the only one they would have seen going in or out of our apartment today. If anyone were to ask, I—Jezebel—had never left.

Just outside the door, I stopped to listen, making sure my father wasn't home yet. No sounds from inside. Reassured that I was alone, I entered quickly and ran to my room, where I immediately shifted back into my own form as quickly as possible.

All the things that could go wrong flooded my mind. If I'd made even one mistake...

No more getting caught, I repeated vehemently. *No. More.*

From now on, every decision—and every shift I made—would only be allowed after careful analysis of the danger. Of the chances of getting caught.

I stood, staring into my little mirror on the wall. Though everything about my appearance had returned to normal, I didn't recognize myself in the reflection. Blinking my ice-cold blue eyes, I lifted a hand to my face, empty of expression. Something about the girl in front of me had changed. Permanently.

The hardness in her eyes scared me.

I couldn't look too long.

Guilt overcame my initial satisfaction as I hurried to finish my chores before my father came home.

This time, I'd broken the Unbreakable Laws all by myself. There was no one else to blame. And though I'd never admit it to anyone, least of all Asher, I'd kind of enjoyed it.

Asher would hate me for what I'd done to him and his reputation.

A small part of me still wished there'd been another way.

But the important thing was that it would force him to take the hint and leave me alone.

At least, that's what I kept telling myself.

He *had* to.

Belatedly, his other possible reactions flitted through my mind. Reactions that I hadn't allowed myself consider before...

No. It's too late now. It'd had to be done.

There was no taking it back.

I couldn't let him—or anyone else—exert this pressure over me anymore. I refused.

No more getting caught, I repeated my refrain, and added to it: *Whatever it takes.*

13

WHEN A FIST POUNDED on the door a few hours later, I somehow expected it. Only two Jinni I knew behaved like that.

And my father had no reason to knock.

Asher burst in as soon as I turned the lock. "What have you done?" he screamed. His red eyes burned like a hot fire, and his face was flushed.

Though I tried not to react, when he slammed the door behind him, I instinctively stepped back.

When my father got like this, I hid. As long as I was out of sight, he left me alone.

Asher wasn't going to let me out of his sight.

He grabbed my wrist, twisting painfully. "You used my face!" he shouted. "You knew they'd come after me as soon as they found out—if I had been home, I'd have been caught! You have to fix this!"

Swallowing hard, I tried to pull my arm away, but he only gripped tighter. "I thought you'd get the message," I tried to snap back at him, but my voice shook. "You can't control me."

"No," Asher growled, yanking me forward and grabbing my other arm, putting pressure on them until I stopped struggling. "Unless you want everyone to know your precious secret, you will *fix* this. Now!"

Panic caused my skin to flush hot and then icy cold.

An image flashed through my mind, unbidden, of Asher as a little lizard.

Powerless... Tiny...

I acted without thinking.

My arms were already pressed so tightly against him. It only took a small, excruciating twist of my wrist to touch his hand.

When my fingers touched his skin, his eyes widened in understanding.

"No—" he gasped, trying to let go and back away, but now I grabbed *him* and held on, shifting him as fast as my ability would allow.

In seconds, he shrunk down to just a few fingers tall.

Turned green and leathery.

And grew a tail.

I'd never know how he'd wanted me to fix it his way, but this was mine.

In his new lizard form, he scurried across the floor, trying to escape, but I caught him between my hands, trapping him.

When I picked up his tiny body, he struggled frantically, scratching my hands deep enough to draw blood. I ran to the kitchen. Dumping a glass jar of flour into the sink, I tossed him into the now empty jar and slammed the lid on top.

The lid didn't have any air holes.

Biting my lip, I tried to think. There was a matching glass lid on the sugar jar. Taking it off, I put my hand on it and attempted to use my Gift. Unlike my clothing, which was essentially a part of me, this object felt completely foreign.

Pressing it into my body, I tried harder, managing to shift the glass just enough that a tiny hole formed beneath my finger. The moment I let go, it disappeared.

This Gift was *useless*!

Shifting the spare lid again, this time I tried putting a knife in the hole before I let go. Then, once the glass had closed back in around the knife, I yanked until the knife came out. Once again, the hole closed up.

No matter what I tried, the jar resisted my Gift.

The one time I really need it!

Asher had stopped struggling. His lizard form sagged inside the glass jar as he slowly began to run out of air.

"Hold on," I murmured, touching the glass near his face.

He didn't respond.

Panicking, I snatched a nearby dish towel. I couldn't let him die. Grabbing the knife once more, I cut two slices of fabric from the towel. One, I bunched up and propped under the lid, until it held it open just enough to allow air in, but not wide enough for him to get out. The second, I used as a makeshift rope, tying it over the lid and around the jar to hold the lid firmly in place.

It *should* allow enough air in. I hoped.

As the fresh air seeped in, Asher's tiny green body twitched.

I breathed a sigh of relief.

Replacing the sugar jar back in the cupboard, I flushed the tell-tale flour down the sink and took the jar that now contained Asher to my room.

Setting him on my tiny dresser, I dropped onto the bed and let my head fall into my hands.

The full magnitude of what I'd done hit me.

I'd gone too far.

Sitting up to face Asher again, I found my own reflection staring back at me instead, in the little mirror over the dresser.

I stood unconsciously, stepping closer.

With a wordless scream, I flung my hand out at the mirror, knocking it off the wall with a clumsy swipe. It hit the floor with the sound of splintered glass. I crushed my fists against my eyes, curling in on myself, joining the mirror on the floor.

My breathing was ragged.

Remorse hit me instantly.

That mirror was one of the only things I had left of my mother.

Gently, I lifted the edge, turning it over to see the damage.

The gold frame was loose, and the glass had formed an enormous crack. It fractured out like a spider web with little splinters of glass all around it. Broken beyond repair.

It would never again be what it was.

I hadn't *fixed* my situation with Asher at all. If anything, I'd made it unfixable.

No matter what angle I approached it from, there was no coming back from this.

I drew a finger across the sharp glass edges, letting them bite my skin until a tiny drop of blood bloomed on the tip of my finger.

If Asher was returned to his own form, he'd either blackmail me for life or turn me in to the Jinni Guard. They'd no doubt throw me in the castle dungeon to await a Severance.

If he remained a lizard, however, I had no doubt they'd come looking for him. They'd discover what I'd done, and I'd *still* face the dungeon, and the subsequent Severance.

This was exactly why the Unbreakable Laws had been created.

Somehow, I'd broken all of them in just a few hours. I'd deceived. Stolen. And now harmed.

When I moved to sit on the bed once more, cradling the small, broken mirror in my hand, Asher's stare pierced me. Somehow it conveyed fury and disgust, even in his lizard form.

I stood just long enough to set the ruined mirror in front of the jar, leaning it against the glass and blocking Asher from view.

Turning off the light, I crawled into bed and closed my eyes. I'd figure out what to do with him—and myself—in the morning.

Long after my father stumbled home late that night, I still lay wide awake. My mind held onto the problem relentlessly, trying to untie it, like an impossible knot.

Very few ideas came to me.

Those that did were too dark to consider.

I didn't know what to do or who to ask. I couldn't trust anyone.

By morning, I'd barely slept.

I didn't get out of bed.

The front door slammed shut, signaling my father leaving for work. But I could only manage to briefly check that Asher was still breathing, before I curled up in bed once more.

My thin curtain allowed a square of sunlight on the opposite wall. I stared at it all morning as it crept across my room.

Afternoon passed even more slowly.

A knock on the front door made me frown. Was I supposed to be somewhere? I quickly ran a brush through my hair and straightened the clothes I hadn't bothered to change out of yesterday. With a swift glance in the fractured mirror that made me cringe, I strode into the main room and opened the door.

I froze. *No. It's too soon. How do they know what I did?*

A Jinni Guard with icy blue eyes and full body armor—designed for actual battle, not just as a fashion statement like Asher's and Simon's—stood on the other side. "Is the head of the household available?"

I managed to shake my head and cleared my throat. "I can pass on a message if you'd like?"

He ignored my answer. "Are you one of the companions of Asher, son of Methuselah, son of Obed?"

I didn't know what to say, so I just nodded. *Is he here for me? Or for Asher?* I pictured him finding the glass jar and piecing it together... Either way, this couldn't end well.

The members of the Jinni Guard were by far the most Gifted in all of Jinn. Rumor had it that some of them had the rare Gift of conviction: the ability to spot the difference between a lie and the truth. Every word I uttered had to be chosen carefully. "Is he... okay?"

"He has been reported missing and is wanted for some possible unlawful behavior. We are speaking with friends and family to ascertain his whereabouts."

Nodding slowly, I put a hand to my heart. Body language wasn't usually as decipherable by a Gift as words. I couldn't say, *I hope you find him*, or, *I'll keep an eye out for him*, because both of those would be lies. "Let me know when you find him?" I asked instead, squinting my eyes as if anxious—which wasn't hard since it was exactly how I felt.

THE SECRET GIFT

The guard gave a sharp bow, eyes never leaving my face. "My name is Eliezer, son of Japeth, son of Hezekiah. If you come across any new information, come to the castle and ask for me immediately. I'll be sure to follow up if I have further questions."

Not at all what I'd asked.

As he turned away and strode down the hall, conversation apparently over, I slid the door shut with a soft click. I couldn't determine if he was onto me or simply following protocol.

My stomach growled loudly.

Now that he'd pulled me out of my stupor, I realized I was starving.

All we had in the apartment was some stale bread and cheese. Scraping the mold off, I ate all of it. My father didn't always eat at home, but if he wanted to tonight... I decided to go pick up some fresh bread and supplies. Just in case.

The short trip to the emporium gave me something to do. More importantly, it gave me a chance to clear my head and get some distance from Asher, whose presence I could feel everywhere in our little apartment.

When I came back, I had yet to come up with a plan, but I could at least talk to Asher and explain myself, even if he couldn't talk back. He might be in a better mindset today. There might still be a way out of this.

I finished putting the food away right as someone knocked on the door again. The guard was back already? Was that a bad sign or a good one?

Wiping my suddenly sweaty hands on my dress, I cleared my throat and swung the door open. I took a startled step back at the glowering boy in front of me. "Simon?" My heart did an erratic dance. "What are you doing here?"

He pushed past, eyes searching the small room and its few hiding places. "Is Asher here?" he asked, turning to face me. His eyes narrowed, and he kept his distance. Wary. "He was supposed to meet me, but he didn't show. Last I heard, he was with you."

I widened my eyes, hoping the surprise seemed authentic, and shrugged. "I haven't seen him. What's going on?" Simon didn't have any truth-seeking Gifts, so I didn't hesitate to lie to him.

It turned out that was a mistake.

"A member of the guard was just at my place," he said in a low, dangerous tone. "Eliezer, son of Japeth, son of... I forget. It doesn't matter. He told me that he came here first. Said he talked to *you*."

"I swear, I don't know where Asher is." I spread my hands wide. "He's clearly not here. You can see for yourself."

I hoped he wouldn't take me up on it, even as I knew I couldn't be so lucky.

"I'll do that," Simon snapped, stalking around the room, leaving a mess in his wake, looking under my father's bed and even going so far as to open a small cupboard beside it that Asher couldn't possibly fit into. At least, not in the size that Simon was looking for...

He stormed over to the kitchen, opening all of the cupboards there as well, letting the doors swing wildly behind him.

Then, he strode toward my room.

Even before he pushed open the door, I knew what I had to do.

This time, I didn't hesitate.

By the time his eyes landed on the jar behind the mirror, where Asher was scratching at the glass walls in warning, my hand was on Simon's back, and he was shrinking.

Becoming a lizard too.

Darker green this time, so I could tell them apart.

He didn't have a chance to scream. Not even to say a single word.

Pouncing on his tiny lizard form before he could run, I moved the mirror out of my way, leaning it against the wall instead, and dropped Simon in beside Asher in the little glass jar.

Just like Asher had, he clawed the sides, desperately trying to escape, while his friend looked on in resignation.

"I'm sorry," I whispered, struggling not to cry—not just for them, but also for myself and my own stupidity getting into this mess. "I swear to you, this isn't what I wanted."

I sank onto the bed, my gaze swinging between them and my reflection in the broken mirror, where the girl inside looked ready to cry again.

"You have to believe me, I hate every part of this. I wish there was something else I could do..." I wrapped my arms protectively around myself, shaking my head at the way they looked at me. I could almost hear them: *You could turn us back.*

"No," I replied, as if they'd actually spoken. Standing to reach for the mirror, I placed it face down on the dresser, where I could no longer see my reflection. "I can't."

I turned away from the jar and its occupants, heading for the kitchen to avoid their judgment as well. Over my shoulder, before I closed the door, I added, "I can't let you turn me in." My voice cracked. "And I can't trust you not to. There's no other way."

14

THE NEXT DAY, I woke with a grim determination for what I had to do. It had always been an impossible choice. My friends, or my freedom. My innocence, or my future. But really, hadn't it already been made? At this point, my only choice was to finish carrying it out.

I was ready.

With careful efforts, I hung my fragmented mirror back on the wall once more, staring at myself in the largest piece as I created dark circles under my eyes, rumpling my clothes and hair as well for extra emphasis. I even tested my Gift to see if I could form tears on command. It would take more practice, but I thought eventually I could figure it out.

Phillipa knocked on my door first, around mid-afternoon, calling my name softly to let me know it was her. I leaned my forehead against the wall next to the door, taking a deep breath to bolster my resolve. I'd desperately hoped Miriam would be the one to come. It would've made this easier. Though not by much.

Still, I followed the plan I'd come up with the night before. "We can't talk here," I whispered as soon as I cracked open the door, pretending to look over my shoulder as if my father was asleep in the room behind me. In truth, it was empty. "Meet me at the daleth—on the human side—in a half-hour. Tell Miriam to come too."

Facing two of them would be more difficult than one. I'd eaten a huge meal and slept late into the morning in an attempt to prepare. I knew my extra training lately had strengthened my Gift, but by how much, I couldn't say. There was only one way to find out.

When the girls came through the daleth, I stood trembling on the human side with my bag on my shoulder. I pressed my hands together against my body to hide the shaking. Beneath them, my stomach churned, threatening to bring up everything I'd eaten earlier. *It has to be done,* I repeated to myself, as I had all day. *They know too much. It'd only be a matter of time before they figured out what happened.*

Inside my bag was a second, empty glass jar.

"I think Asher may have come to the human world to hide," I told them my pre-rehearsed story, urging those tears to appear. It didn't quite work. I still needed to see myself in a mirror to manipulate the tear ducts effectively.

From their worried reactions, my very real anxiety was enough.

"Why would he do that?" Phillipa asked. She drew her hands to her mouth, starting to shake her head. "Are you saying… The Jinni Guard was looking for him—are you saying he actually did something wrong? Did he break one of the Unbreakable Laws? He wouldn't be so foolish…"

"Oh, yes, he would," Miriam snapped, crossing her arms in a huff. "That sounds exactly like something he would do. So, why are we here?"

I cleared my throat, wavering. *No more getting caught,* I reminded myself. *Whatever it takes.*

I *had* to do this.

Miriam started to frown at me.

"I'll explain everything," I said. "But first, we should try to find him. Let's spread out. Meet back here by the portal in a quarter hour."

Phillipa was quick to agree. Anything for Asher. And while Miriam protested and put on a good show of disagreeing, she was already turning to begin the search.

Bitterness twisted inside me. Would they have done the same for me? After the last few days, I didn't think so. Had any of us ever truly been friends at all or had we all just been using each other?

I brushed aside the guilt nagging at me for what I was about to do.

We each went in a separate direction.

As soon as the trees hid me from sight, I looped back around to follow Miriam, traveling short distances to catch up to her, moving as silently as possible.

She never saw me coming.

Scooping up the little pink and orange lizard, I opened the jar and gently set her inside, whispering apologies, though I knew they didn't mean much.

I used the remaining time to capture crickets, adding them to the jar with Miriam, who scrambled away from the bugs, though she had to know they were meant to be food.

At the quarter hour, I traveled back to the daleth.

Phillipa was already there waiting.

"Anything?" I asked, pretending to search the horizon as an excuse to avoid meeting her eyes.

"No." Out of the corner of my eye, she crossed her arms, hugging herself. "What's going on, Bel? You seem like you know something. What did Asher do? Please, just tell me."

I sighed. There was no getting around what I had to do… I still faltered.

Phillipa hadn't done anything wrong, but she was still going to pay the price. She deserved to know the truth.

I decided to tell her a modified version. "Asher made me use my Gift to change shekels into much larger coin," I said slowly. "He used the false money to purchase an enchanted lamp, but after he left, the shekels returned to their original form." I spread my hands apart, wanting her to understand my side. "He knew my Gift only works when connected to living things. He *knew* it was wrong."

Phillipa was already nodding in agreement.

"Now he's in serious trouble." I finished vaguely. "You said that you had a visit from the Jinni Guard as well?"

"Yes!" She gasped. "That's what that was about? I thought it was because of the daleth…"

I just shook my head.

I needed to get this over with.

Stalling was only making it more painful.

Reaching out, I hugged her.

It was completely out of character for me, but after a moment of shock, she lifted her arms and embraced me back, comforting *me*.

"I'm so sorry," I said, squeezing my eyes shut against real tears this time. "I wish there was another way."

"What do you m—" Phillipa started to pull back, but she was already shifting beneath my hands, too startled to even fight back.

I chose yellow for her lizard form, to match her warm eyes, which now haunted me with that last look.

Slipping her into the jar, I paused at the way Miriam lay lifelessly at the bottom. Was the air not adequate? Was she suffocating? Panic gripped me. Holding Phillipa in one hand, I nudged Miriam's little body with my finger.

Her layered eyes blinked open. She lunged at my hand.

Tiny little teeth clamped down hard on my finger.

With a shriek, I flung her back inside the jar, tossing Phillipa in after her, and yanked the lid over them.

The bite had startled me more than anything. Despite her attempts to break skin, there was no blood, just a little sensitivity.

The assault made it easier for me to shove the jar back into my bag and pull the cover flap over it. With the jar out of sight, I returned to Jinn through the daleth, and, once confident that no one else was nearby, I traveled home.

Setting the second jar on top of my dresser beside the first, I dropped wearily onto my bed and stared at the four of them.

While Simon scratched at the walls of the jar—communicating with the girls maybe? I had no idea—Asher lay still. In the same place he'd been since I'd left earlier this afternoon. It worried me. He needed food and water.

I started with the first, since I'd brought home the crickets in the other jar.

To Miriam, I pointed a stern finger and said, "Try a stunt like that again, and I'll turn you into a fly for them to eat. Is that clear?"

Her tiny tongue flicked at me furiously. After a long second, she dipped her head once in what I took to be a nod.

To be safe, I didn't actually remove the lid, but instead untied the fabric holding it on, until I could lift it just enough to scoop up two crickets and pull them out.

Turning to the jar with Simon and Asher, I dropped the crickets in as quickly as possible.

Both of them turned their noses up at the offer.

"You'd better eat," I said, eyeing Asher especially. "I'll be back with water."

My father's favorite drinks came in big glass bottles, and the small, curved lids would make perfect water dishes. I pulled two out of the trash, filling them both to the brim, and added one to each jar.

Once that was done, I sat on the bed again, and we all stared at each other while the crickets hopped around, blissfully unaware.

"Eat," I said again, when none of them moved. "I'm not letting you out, so you might as well get used to it." The bugs would never taste quite right, even in their shifted forms, but their bodies would know what to do with them—would *need* them soon.

They ignored me.

All afternoon, we waited, though of course, they didn't know what I was waiting for.

Finally, the knock came.

Picking up my poor, cracked mirror one last time, I hoped my tears were ready. I strode to the door and opened it.

The same Jinni Guard, Eliezer, stood on the other side. At the end of the hall, Hanna peered out from her own apartment, but the guard stared at her until she pulled back inside and closed her door.

Just like the last time he'd come, he began by asking if my father was home.

Shaking my head, I summoned up the tears, letting them fill my eyes until they threatened to spill over. It was easier than before. Maybe because they were real. "No, but... I have to tell you something." I turned away, leaving the door open for the guard to follow, and started to pace. "I didn't want to say anything before, because I don't want my friends to get in trouble…"

When I trailed off, Eliezer stepped into the room, impatient. "Speak the truth. The guard will reward you for your honesty."

I stopped my pacing in the kitchen to dab at my eyes with a towel. Turning to him, I pulled my lips into my mouth, then blurted out. "I think they went to the human world."

His carefully blank expression altered, showing shock before he managed to hide it. "And what makes you think this is the case?"

Choosing my exact words with care, I said, "Asher found a daleth that no one knew about… He showed the rest of us. He wanted us to go through and visit the human world. Asher went through first, and the others followed." I then named each of my friends specifically and waited for him to write their names down. This was exactly what needed to happen. Now for the last half-truth. "I didn't want to go."

As soon as I said this, I pretended to sob harder, dropping into a chair at the table and putting my head in my hands. "I should've told you, I'm sorry."

"So, you're saying that they went through the daleth to the human world without you, and they never came back," Eliezer finished for me, wanting to end the story quickly and get away from my tears, just as I'd hoped he would.

He shook his head at my friends' foolishness, making notes for himself on the small pad of paper. "He must have been warned after he stole that lamp," he muttered.

To me, he added louder, "Where is this portal located? Do you think these friends of yours know about his theft?"

"I don't know." I sniffed. "Maybe." I gave him my best description of how to find the daleth, slowing the tears, but not cutting them off completely quite yet. I didn't honestly know if I could.

"Thank you," he said, standing and tucking his notes in a pocket beneath his armor. "I'll be in touch. Most likely the royal family will request your assistance in leading them to the exact location of the daleth."

I nodded, though he was already striding toward the door to leave. "I'm at their service, of course," I whispered, as the door shut on his heels.

Sagging back against the chair, I swiped at the new tears that continued to flow until they subsided. I inhaled deeply, filling my lungs until they burned before blowing out all the air.

This nightmare was almost over.

15

WHEN THE KING AND queen of Jinn summoned me to the castle that same day, I was so relieved that my father was still at work and wouldn't find out, that I forgot to be nervous until I reached the woven white gates. Very few Jinn besides the Guard and those in the upper circles ever had the opportunity to visit the castle.

The guard who met me at the gate led me through the giant front door and inside a receiving room the size of ten apartments put together. A flicker of excitement made me pick up my step as we walked down one of the red-carpeted halls that led deeper inside the castle. Glancing at each new piece of art as we marched down one hall after the next, I lost track of the different portraits, statues, decorative displays of armor, flower arrangements, and lounge furniture we passed.

This was luxury and power.

I bet the royal family never has to worry about someone using them. If anyone tried, they'd regret it.

When we strode into a smaller, but equally grand receiving room, the chandeliers and elaborate décor was overshadowed by the presence of Queen Samaria seated in the center. I recognized her immediately—both her, her husband, and her son all had their own coins in circulation with their faces stamped on them.

My friends and I had always considered Prince Shem incredibly handsome—or at least, his likeness on the coin was. For all we knew, he could be

THE SECRET GIFT

hideous in person. *We.* The accidental word made me cringe. There was no *we* anymore. No one I could tell, if I met the prince, whether he was handsome or not.

Clamping my jaw shut to avoid gawking, I bowed low. "Your Majesty," I murmured, meeting the queen's eyes. Her pearly white irises were rimmed in deep blue. Her pale Jinni skin was more translucent than most, and she was smaller and more frail than I'd expected.

King Jubal strode into the room from the opposite door, equally recognizable, even if he hadn't been wearing the enchanted crown that enhanced all his natural Gifts. His presence exuded control—of everyone and everything around him. It was the exact opposite of my life.

I'd never cared much for the politics of the royal family before today. Who would rule after the next fifty-year period bored me. The only thing that piqued my curiosity was the young Jinni prince who was so near my own age.

Until now, when sudden jealousy of their lives—of their power—gripped me. It was unexpected. I wasn't entirely sure where it came from, but I couldn't completely shake it.

The king bent to kiss his wife on the cheek and exchanged a smile with her before he noticed me standing there with the guard. "This is the girl who found the daleth, then?" he asked, shuffling through some papers on his desk. His hair was cut short, and he had a neat black beard to match. His energy level was the exact opposite of his wife.

"Yes, your Highness," I answered, wanting to come across strong and believable. "I can take you to it whenever you need." Hopefully right now. The sooner they sealed it off, the better.

"Unfortunately, I don't have a lot of time," the king muttered to his papers, looking up at us finally, eyes glancing over me, then focusing on the guard. "I've far too much on my plate dealing with last month's Khaanevaade attack. I need to focus on making the islands impossible to access." Turning to me, he said, "I've asked my son to take over this particular daleth."

Queen Samaria nodded with a pleased smile, leaning back in her seat. "It will be good practice for him. An opportunity to prepare for becoming king someday."

My heart beat a little faster. Was I about to meet the prince of Jinn? Though I'd considered that it could happen today, I hadn't actually believed it. Phillipa and Miriam would absolutely die if they found out. Once again, the thought of my friends distracted me— specifically where they were right now.

The king was still talking, though with his focus on his desk, I couldn't tell if he was speaking to me or the guard. "From my understanding, the daleth is in a remote location. Only a few of our own were lost to it, before it was reported."

"That's correct, your Highness," the guard replied.

Nodding to himself, the king stroked his beard for a moment. "I'd say it shouldn't require more than a half-dozen guards on rotation to keep others from going through." Turning to his wife, he added, "It's those poor children I'm concerned about. The parents will have to be notified. Shem will need to set a strict schedule to make sure the daleth is guarded at all times. We don't want the parents to go in after their children and lose them as well."

"Shem can handle it," Queen Samaria said soothingly as she joined him at the desk, placing a hand on his arm. She smiled and added, "You know he's been itching for a chance to get away from the castle."

"Yes, well. This might be more than he bargained for," the king grumbled. "It all depends on if they can find a recent trail from someone traveling. Each hour that passes makes it more unlikely. And by my count, they've already been gone for at least three or four."

Longer, I thought to myself, but didn't say anything.

"You may go," King Jubal said without looking at us. "The guard will give you your reward for reporting the daleth." As he said this, the guard pressed a small coin purse into my hand, turning me by the elbow at the same time.

"Wait." I pulled away, clearing my throat. I couldn't go home without knowing if the portal was closed or not. "Could I please speak with the prince? I'm worried that he'll have trouble finding the daleth."

King Jubal barely glanced at me, then sighed and nodded in agreement, already turning his back as he waved us out. Under his breath, he muttered to the queen, "If Shem would just choose a wife, we wouldn't have to deal with constant pursuit…"

Whatever she mumbled back to him was lost to me, as the Jinni Guard bowed, leading me from the room. My cheeks blushed furiously hot.

That was *not* why I wanted to speak to the prince.

At least, not the only reason.

I needed to be certain they'd seal the daleth immediately. An open portal was dangerous, after all—a human could just as easily stumble on it from their side and enter Jinn. Not to mention young Jinn like us could find it, like Asher had, and cause enormous amounts of trouble. Only a set number of daleths in strategic locations were usually left open.

"Wait here," the guard said, leaving me in another room decorated with a silver theme, not bothering to bow or say anything else before shutting the door behind him.

Twisting my fingers together, I tried to reassure myself. All of our traveling trails were far too old to be discovered. There'd be no trace of us at this point. If they thought to quickly find some young Jinn making trouble in the human town and return them to their parents by nightfall, they'd be sorely disappointed.

I remembered the coin purse in my hand that the king had given me and opened it. It held enough coin to buy two enchanted lamps, nearly three! *Or enough to leave here and start a brand new life somewhere else.* I tucked the little purse into my pocket to consider later, when I wasn't quite so overwhelmed.

While I waited, I explored the details of the room, which, although smaller, was as lovely as the previous one. The windows stretched from the floor to the ceiling, which was twice my height, and all five of them were framed with silver curtains. The furniture was soft enough to sink into, making me groan with pleasure as I sat down and leaned into it. I could happily stay here forever.

The thought put a dampener on my mood. It made me resent the two little jars back home, as well as my father, who was due for another one of his episodes any day now.

Could I find a way to stay here?

I sighed at the wishful thinking and closed my eyes.

A gentle hand on my shoulder startled me awake.

I lurched upright and almost knocked heads with the young Jinni who'd roused me.

Blushing fiercely, I apologized and lowered my gaze as I stood, barely allowing myself a glimpse of him. His black hair grew long enough to hang in his eyes slightly with wild waves that somehow fit him, a strong jaw, pale blue eyes, and a lopsided grin like we shared a secret. The young Jinni prince was every bit as handsome as the likenesses I'd seen, but much less formal. He wore a simple woven crown of white-gold on his head. And he had a dimple in one cheek when he smiled.

Bowing low, I said again, "My apologies, Prince Shem."

He laughed lightly. "I hesitated to wake you. Perhaps we should start off our daleth hunt with a nap?"

At first, I thought he was mocking me, but his smile was genuine and open.

When I stood there, lips parted and staring at him, not knowing how to respond, he just smiled wider. "I'm only teasing. What's your name?"

"Bel," I said, then corrected myself. "Jezebel, actually."

He bowed, which was completely unnecessary for the prince of all of Jinn to do, and had me blushing all over again. "A pleasure to meet you, Jezebel." Lifting his elbow out to me, he added, "Would you accompany me on a countryside walk to this daleth of yours? I'd love to take a closer look at it."

My mouth twitched in a small smile, and I took his arm.

✳ ✳ ✳

What I did not expect, however, was for the prince to lead me *through* the daleth to the human side once we arrived.

"Spread out," he told the four Jinni Guard members who attended us—one of whom was Eliezer. They'd followed us through, wearing their full armor, while the prince wore just a breastplate—a silver and gem studded breastplate, more decorative than useful. "See if you can track down any evidence of Gifts being used or a trail that might show us where they've run off to."

I waited until the guards obeyed his orders before I cleared my throat and asked, "Do you think they'll find anything?" My arm still rested in his, and I couldn't tell if my racing heartbeat was from that or the small chance that these Jinn might somehow be able to sense that I'd been here too. If they could, my entire story would be ruined.

He turned those incredibly pale blue eyes on me, the color of the sky on a cloudless day. Quirking one side of his mouth up at my question, he humored me. "They've been trained to use their Gifts to sift through the human town, as well as the surrounding area, without raising any suspicions or drawing any attention to themselves. The humans won't even notice their presence. They'll search for any unusual activity."

"Like Simon traveling in broad daylight?" I muttered. At the prince's glance, I added, "That's exactly something he would do." For good measure, I scrunched up my forehead in concern, staring out toward the town, which was visible over the hill. "I hope they find something."

"Don't worry," Prince Shem patted my hand, probably trying to be comforting. "I won't let them leave a human unturned. We'll continue the search, both here, as well as in Jinn, until all possibilities have been exhausted. Though I doubt it will take that long. Their parents will be notified within the hour, but my hope is that we'll deliver their children back to them by the end of the day."

I tried to smile through my frustration, pulling away. Gritting my teeth, I shaded my eyes from the sun, hiding the emotions that must be flickering across my face. *I just pulled away from* the prince. *What's wrong with me?*

"I've never been in the human world before," I said, trying to pretend nothing was wrong. Since the guards were gone, I lied through my teeth. "Is it dangerous?"

"Not at all," the prince said, voice lifting in excitement as he gave me one of his charming, dimpled smiles. He held out his hand again. "How about I show you some of the sights in the human world, since we're already here?"

His father was right, I thought. *He's itching to explore.* For the briefest moment, I forgot my anxiety. Hand hovering over his, I hesitated. "What kind of sights?"

"Nothing as beautiful as back home, obviously." He waved his free hand, still holding the other out to me. "But there are creatures you've never heard of before, mountains that rise almost to Jinn, and if that isn't enough to entice you, I could always take you to see the ocean."

I gasped. "We wouldn't go *in* the ocean, would we?"

"Maybe just a toe?" he teased, but I could see that he wasn't serious. "My parents would kill me. The truce with the Mere has been in place since my grandmother's reign. Don't worry, I'm not about to jeopardize that." He wiggled the fingers of his outstretched hand playfully. "Just do me a favor and promise not to tell the guards where we've gone."

This prince wasn't half as high and mighty as Asher and the others could be. I grinned and took his hand. "You have my word."

16

OCEAN WAVES CRASHED AGAINST the white sand beneath our feet, stretching, reaching, coming so close that the icy water tickled our toes. I squealed as it licked across my sandaled feet, leaping back.

Prince Shem laughed so hard he had to bend over and lean on his knees to catch his breath.

Part of me was still in awe of the enormous body of water, while the other part began to blush in embarrassment. I hated seeming foolish.

The prince waved a hand at my expression, trying to stop laughing, only half successful. "Please, don't be offended," he said between gasps, wiping a hand across his face, not quite able to wipe away his smile. "It's just been such a long time since I've enjoyed a reaction like yours. It makes the ocean feel new to me once more."

Skeptical, I raised a brow at him, daring to speak more freely. It was only the two of us after all. "You're laughing at my pain?"

"Hardly pain!" he said in mock horror. Holding a hand to his heart, as if in pledge, he added, "You must trust me, I would never allow you pain."

My smiled faded.

I glanced away, focusing on the next wave as it crept along the sand toward us, though not reaching quite as far this time.

Trust.

The one thing I couldn't give.

Especially not to a prince.

A throat clearing behind me reminded me of his presence, and when he spoke, he was closer than I'd realized, "I sense that's a delicate subject."

Turning to face him, I attempted a carefree smile. "Nothing that serious. Just an unfortunate reminder of my friends."

He misinterpreted that as I'd expected he would, and didn't push. He didn't leave either. Just nodded in acceptance.

A comfortable silence settled over us.

Prince Shem knelt to pick up rocks, attempting to skip them across the water, though more often than not, a wave rose up and ate the rock within one skip.

"I envy you, you know," he said, seemingly out of nowhere.

My head whipped up from where I'd been studying shells lying on the beach. He wasn't looking at me.

Instead, he gazed toward the horizon, speaking more to himself than to me, "What must it be like not to be trapped in a castle?"

Trapped.

Did he feel bound by something he could never be free of? Constantly controlled by what he *had* to do based on the people around him? I was far more familiar with the feeling than he knew. Trapped in a home I couldn't escape. By the Gift I hadn't asked for, but couldn't be rid of. Burdened by what I'd done because of it.

"I can't imagine your particular cage..." I finally murmured in response. "But believe me when I say, I have a cage of my own."

* * *

"We should head back," Prince Shem said, what might have been a few minutes later or a few hours. I'd completely lost track of time.

Despite the cold wind making me shiver, I wished we could stay. He'd given me a small window of peace in the midst of misery. Now his words brought me back to reality.

"Thank you, your Highness," I said, just loud enough to be heard over the crashing waves, still in awe of them. "I'll never forget today." I meant it.

He held out a hand to travel the two of us back to the others. "Please, call me Shem. After all, we're friends now."

I took his hand, and nodded. As if I'd do anything else. Friends with the *prince* of Jinn. I half-believed I'd wake up and find that I'd been dreaming.

Shem didn't travel immediately, instead holding my cold, wind-chapped fingers in his own, which were warm and strong.

"We really should go back," he said, not moving, and not letting go. "The guards are used to my wandering, but if I wait too long, we run the risk of them telling my father."

The way he still held my hand made me daring. "If it makes you feel better, I don't want to go back either."

That lopsided grin appeared immediately. "You know, it does, actually."

Another wave of boldness swept over me, like the cresting waves in front of us. "I know *my* reasons for wanting to stay, but what are *yours*, your Highness?"

"Shem," he corrected me immediately.

I hesitated, noticing how his pale eyes squinted when he smiled.

"Shem," I repeated, but hated the way my voice was soft. Pulling my hand away, I took a step back. "You must have a lot of admirers back at the castle," I said in a harder tone, before I could think better of it. "Someone with your charm, good looks, and title must get whatever—and whoever—he wants."

He blinked, taken aback, then unexpectedly burst out laughing. "Once again, you've caught me by surprise," he said with a shake of his head. With a sidelong look, his grin returned. "So you think I'm good looking?"

"And charming," I agreed, refusing to be embarrassed again. "And you know it."

Instead of laughing again at my honesty or trying to argue, he grew serious, coming to stand in front of me, closer than he had before, though he didn't touch me this time. Gazing into my eyes, he murmured, "I get the feeling that's not enough. To earn your trust."

I couldn't hold his gaze. Sudden shyness swept through me. Since it was a statement, I didn't answer. I just wished it wasn't true. "I'm sorry," I found myself saying instead.

He ducked his head a bit, just enough to convince me to look at him again. "Don't be. That's the way it should be."

This time, when I took the hand he offered, he traveled both of us back to the daleth and the human town where we'd begun the day.

Two of the Jinni Guard members sprang up, flashing across the clearing to where the prince and I stood, immediately beginning to berate him. "Your Highness! Your father has charged us with your care, and we had no knowledge of your whereabouts. You cannot continue this reckless behavior. It's been hours! We were beginning to fear the worst. If something were to happen to you, it would be our heads—"

They continued to scold the prince until the other guard members appeared. They must've also been out searching for the prince, because they heatedly joined in.

Shem nodded along, saying, "Absolutely," and "Of course," and "My apologies," wherever they left an opening. As if he'd heard it all before. Many times. Almost as if they went through this frequently.

Perhaps the guard's truly meant what they said, but after the initial impassioned speech, even they seemed more resigned to the situation than truly upset.

Though Shem kept a serious expression, his eyes twinkled when he met

THE SECRET GIFT

mine, and he dared to wink at me behind their backs.

I hid a smile, not wanting to draw their ire too. I didn't have a royal title to protect me.

Once done with their admonition, the guard's gave a stiff report of their findings. The day's search had ended as I'd expected it would from the start: in failure.

It was still an enormous relief. I hadn't had a backup plan.

Muscles relaxed that I hadn't even realized were tense, and a headache began to form. As we moved toward the daleth to return to Jinn, my feet dragged from sudden exhaustion. This day was almost over. They'd close the portal now.

I should be grateful, but as we each stepped through the daleth, re-entering Jinn, I found myself lingering. I'd never see the prince again after today.

Why did I pull away from him? I swallowed hard, wanting to kick myself for being so stupid. A friend in the palace would've been rare and valuable, and I'd ruined it.

"One moment," the prince said to the nearest guard, before turning to me and interrupting my dark thoughts. "You're welcome to come back and check on our progress again tomorrow." And in a softer voice that the guards couldn't hear, he added, "We could go on another adventure." He wiggled his eyebrows comically.

My hopes rose at the invitation, then plummeted as I registered his words. "You're coming back tomorrow?"

As soon as the words left my mouth, I wished I could take them back. *I should've said yes. Yes, I'll go on another adventure with you. As many as you'd like.*

"We are," he said, taking a step backward toward the guards, then another, turning away from me to join them. Over his shoulder, he added, "I'm sure this is just a hiccup, and we'll have better results in the morning. Tomorrow will no doubt be our last day."

One more day.

I could handle that.

Especially if it meant another day with Prince Shem.

"I'll be here first thing," I promised with a smile he didn't see. This time the guards took on the responsibility and effort of traveling, despite the fact that Prince Shem was likely just as strong in that Gift as they were, if not stronger. Before I'd finished speaking, they were gone.

On impulse, I decided to walk home instead of traveling. It gave me time to think.

Whatever happened tomorrow, no matter how anxious the open portal made me, I'd be a fool to pass up the chance to spend time with the prince. His attention alone could bring me into better circumstances. An actual friendship—if he really meant that—could bring me into an entirely new world.

As always, this made me think of escaping my father. The sooner, the better.

Next time Prince Shem offered an adventure, even if it was as mundane as going to the shopping emporium or the acropolis, I'd take it. I'd keep my eyes open for any opportunities that could come from this.

And I'd keep the reward money for myself.

When I got home, I hid the small coin purse in the back of my dresser drawer, avoiding looking at the two little jars on top of it and their inhabitants.

Unlike the first few days they'd been here, I didn't want to talk to them. I didn't want to try to justify myself again, or explain what'd happened today. It'd only ruin my excitement.

When my father came home late, I was already in bed, pretending to be asleep.

He didn't try to be quiet, but I didn't care.

Tomorrow, I had another date with the prince.

17

THE NEXT DAY, I traveled to the portal the instant my father left for work, as the sun was still rising. The parents of Asher, Simon, Phillipa, and Miriam were already waiting outside the daleth when I arrived, speaking with the guard stationed there. They greeted me, but were distracted by the prince and the rest of his guards arriving.

"Jezebel," Prince Shem said, giving me a brief nod before turning to the parents. "Good morning. As we reassured you yesterday, there's no need to worry. We have this under control. The Guard has handled similar instances in the past, and I've no doubt we'll return your loved ones to you soon."

I noticed he didn't say *by the end of the day* this time.

"Please, if you have work or other duties, feel free to attend to those. You'll be sent word the moment they're found."

Phillipa's father vanished as soon as the prince finished speaking, followed quickly by Miriam's and Simon's parents. Asher's mother spoke with the prince a bit longer, but after he continued to soothe her, she left as well, leaving only me behind.

"Let's make today count," the prince said to his guards, as he waved them through the daleth.

I bit my lip, thinking he'd forgotten I was there, until he glanced over his shoulder with a mischievous grin. "Aren't you coming?"

✶ ✶ ✶

Of course, the prince couldn't keep his promise to the parents, because my friends were nowhere near the human world, and any remaining trail from our original travels had gone cold, making them impossible to find.

Still, they continued the search.

Day after day, I got to wake up and spend long hours with the prince.

We traveled all across the human world over the next three weeks. As long as I showed up before him and his guards every morning, and stayed until after the worried parents left, he always invited me to join him. Whether it meant anything to him or not, *that* was a generous opportunity I wouldn't pass up!

My goal quickly became winning him over—as a friend at the very least. A friend in the highest of possible places. One who brought a smile to my face and opportunities to my door, instead of trouble and heartache. That was enough for now.

He laughed when I encountered my first camel—which spit in my face—caught me before I accidentally stepped on my first poisonous snake, and as we soaked up my first human sunset from a mountaintop together, his eyes were on *me* instead of the colorful sky more than once.

Is he like this with everyone? Or is it just me?

I sincerely hoped I was special, but I couldn't quite allow myself to believe it.

I sighed.

Back at the castle, he likely knew dozens of Jinni girls far richer than I, who'd had their sights set on him for far longer. What were the chances he'd be interested in someone like me?

I was a fool to even hope.

Shem—as I was beginning to think of him privately, instead of *Prince Shem*—did confide in me, though. As the days passed, he told me stories of growing up in the castle with its many secrets. How he'd eventually convinced the Jinni Guard to go along with his schemes and even let him disappear from time to time. Such as now.

"My father tries to understand," he said one day as we stood before a waterfall so tall it rivaled the castle back home. The rush of water thundered, even from this far away, and he had to raise his voice to speak over it. "He really does. But the problem is, it's been centuries since he was young. My mother too. They barely remember."

I laughed at the way he contorted his face in exaggerated pain. "Every parent is that way." My own father was only a century and a half—he and my mother had had me when they were young—but he could rival the king when it came to understanding his offspring.

"I don't think he *wants* to remember," Shem complained, yanking his tall boots off and tugging the bottom of his pants up around his knees.

THE SECRET GIFT

"What're you doing?" I interrupted.

He waved at the calmer pool of water in front of us, where the roaring water quieted. "It's hot," he said as if it was obvious. "I'm putting my feet in." He plunked down on a rock large enough for both of us plus a dozen more, patting the smooth surface next to him in invitation.

As a rule now, I always joined him in his escapades. So I unlaced my sandals carefully, glad that I'd worn another short summer dress, and slipped my toes into the cool water next to him. I moaned at how good it felt. Shem was right, the air was so hot it was suffocating. Cooling off instantly lightened my mood.

"Anyway," he continued, once I was settled. "My father has already seen the world a hundred times over. He doesn't understand that it's all new to me. It's just better if he doesn't know where I spend my days." He kicked his feet, splashing me a little, then leaned back until he was lying on the warm rock beneath us like a bed. It felt oddly intimate. Made me want to reach down and brush the stray hair from his eyes.

Shem was unaware of my distraction as he added, "Sometimes, I almost wonder if he *does* know when I disappear, but he's allowing it because he knows I'd go stir-crazy otherwise."

"*My* father thinks I'm working for the castle," I admitted out of nowhere. He'd been sharing secrets, so maybe it was time to share one of mine. "But unlike your father, I'm *certain* he doesn't know better. If he did…" I trailed off.

Shem waited, but I didn't continue. I'd only mentioned my father to him briefly. Just enough to answer questions. Probably enough to reveal the cracks in our façade as well, but Shem was too polite to say anything directly. After some time, he let it pass without comment, and we just sat quietly, enjoying the view.

Now that I'd brought up my father, I couldn't get him off my mind.

Back when we'd first started the search, I'd realized I'd be gone frequently and would need to give my father some sort of excuse for my absence.

That night, I'd fed and watered my little lizard friends, tucking them underneath my bed out of sight. Then, I'd waited.

When the doorknob finally turned, signaling my father's arrival home, I was past the point of trembling or twisting my hands anxiously, and in a state of numb exhaustion instead.

"What do you want?" he'd grunted, slamming the door behind him, and moving to the kitchen.

I'd trailed behind, clearing my throat. Better to keep it simple. "The Jinni Guard took me on for a short-term assignment. A few days—or weeks if I'm lucky. I won't be home much, but it's a paid position…" It wasn't a total lie. I'd thought of the coins hidden in my drawer.

"Fine," my father had interrupted. "Maybe you'll be worth something after all. Make sure you bring home every shekel."

It'd been harder than usual to keep my face calm. My father reminded me of

Asher, which reminded me of what he'd done, and in turn, of what *I'd* had to do.

My mother had been right: People used you. Better to keep them at a distance where they couldn't do any damage.

* * *

"You're nothing like the Jinn at court," Shem said the next day, laughing at my stories of the crowded acropolis.

My face must've fallen, because he was quick to add, "No, no—I *like* that about you."

His words hit me unexpectedly. They gave me the same giddy feeling that I had with Asher. Except this time the boy looking back at me might actually mean them... I wanted desperately to believe he did.

"Trust me, it's a good thing," Shem continued, unaware that my heart was sprinting ahead of him, full of dangerous hopes. "Everyone in the court is completely vapid. Conversation always turns to the crown, and if I'd ever consider sharing it with someone."

"Hmm," I dragged out the word playfully, stepping closer to him, pretending sudden interest. If I were being honest with myself, it was more like revealing feelings that had been growing all along. "And would you?"

When he rolled his eyes, I winked at him the way he was always winking at me and laughed. "You can't blame them for wondering. After all, have you looked in a mirror lately?"

It was easy to laugh with him, even if I was blushing because I meant it.

And I knew I was being hopeful, but as the weeks passed, part of me thought that when all of this daleth business was over, there might be a chance he'd still want to see me.

The only dark spot in my day was when I had to gather fresh food to feed my friends and refill their water before I left each morning. I tried not to think about them if I didn't have to. Showing up at the daleth as early as possible and staying as late as they allowed each day, I made the most of this short season. Shem made me feel safe for the first time in... as long as I could remember.

I knew they couldn't keep the search going forever, but I didn't want them to close the portal anymore. I didn't want this to end.

Still, my luck had to run out eventually.

"Tomorrow is likely to be our last day," Shem was saying now as we strolled through a rainforest, stopping to admire a colorful bird with a beak the same size as its body. We'd traveled three times to reach this unique location, stretching Shem's traveling ability—though in truth it wasn't much stronger than my own.

His voice was low, eyes downcast, as he added, "This isn't the first time we've been unsuccessful in finding missing Jinn, but that doesn't make it any easier."

He offered me a helping hand to step over a fallen log. When he picked a lush, pink and orange flower and held it out to me, my cheeks weren't flushed from the heat this time.

I tried to also seem disheartened at the news, instead of relieved. When I thought about not seeing Shem anymore after tomorrow, I didn't have to pretend to be disappointed. Searching for the right words, I cleared my throat and said, "I wish they'd never gone through the daleth. And I hate that we're giving up…" *Because I won't get to spend time with you anymore.*

Shem stopped to face me, waiting until I looked him in the eye to speak, "I need to apologize to you. For raising your hopes in what ended up being an impossible situation. I truly thought we would find them, and I feel personally responsible for the failure."

"It's not your fault," I murmured. If he only knew just how true that was.

We turned to continue walking in silence until I asked, "Will you tell the parents in the morning?"

"No." Shem turned away and shook his head, blowing out a frustrated breath. "We'll bring them to the castle and tell them after the daleth is closed. And after we've had a chance to plan a formal shivah to mourn their children's passing and honor their memory. I probably shouldn't have told you either, truthfully. But I thought you should know."

"I appreciate that," I said softly, smiling at him. "I'd always prefer to know." My words held layers of meaning.

"Oh, yes?" Though his eyes were still sad, he gave me a small smile. "And does that apply to everything? I suppose I should also let you know that you look very lovely today."

"Thank you." I smiled back. I'd shifted my face in small increments over the last few weeks to slowly add more color to my cheeks and lips, darken my lashes, and make my blue eyes sparkle with a hint of silver. The slight changes could easily be mistaken for makeup, and over time I hoped those who knew me would forget I'd ever looked any different.

The thought reminded me of my friends, still in lizard form, back at the acropolis. Still in their jars, but moved to a better hiding place beneath the bed.

I knew what I needed to do with them now.

Tomorrow was my last chance to do it, and I'd been putting it off over the last few weeks. There'd never been a good time. The prince had posted a constant guard by the daleth, day and night. And I'd enjoyed spending my days with him so much that I hadn't wanted to waste a second of our time sneaking away. But now it was necessary.

Before that portal was closed, I needed to bring my friends back over to the human side one final time… and leave them there.

I shivered, wrapping my arms around myself.

It has to be done.

Grimly, I pressed my lips together and lifted my chin.

Shem read my change in expression and misunderstood. "I really shouldn't have told you about tomorrow. You don't have to come if seeing them seal the daleth will be too difficult for you."

I turned away, lifting my hand to my eyes as if to brush away a tear, because I couldn't fully hide how I felt. A mixture of anxiety and anticipation. *The only thing that will be difficult is not getting caught.* After weeks of worrying they might somehow find evidence of what I'd done, the biggest clue was about to finally vanish. "It won't be too difficult," I managed to say, eyes downcast. *It will be a relief.*

But once again the reminder that it'd be my last day with Shem caused me a pang of disappointment. I'd have to make the most of our time tomorrow. "There's still a small chance they could be found," I said, clearing my throat as I turned back to face him. "I'd like to be there, if that's all right? I'll stay out of the way."

He smiled down at me, standing close enough to reveal the startling flecks of silver in his pale blue eyes. "I'd enjoy that very much."

18

MY FATHER SAT AT the kitchen table when I got home. As I slowly swung the door shut, he slammed his drink onto the wood, sloshing liquid over the edges. Next to his fist, was the broken mirror from my room.

Ice flooded my veins. *Did he see the jars? Does he know what I'd done?* Just as quickly as the thought came, I rejected it. *They're just lizards. He couldn't possibly know they used to be Jinn. He has no reason to suspect.*

Still, he clearly wanted a fight.

I tried to walk calmly past him.

"Sit," he growled.

I pulled out the chair across from him and sat.

He shoved the broken mirror across the table at me. "You think you can destroy my property? You'll be paying for that."

"That's mine." I wanted stand up to him, but my voice was weak. "Mother gave it to me—"

"I know who it belonged to," he snapped, snatching up the mirror and hurling it at the wall. This time, it shattered into a thousand pieces, littering the floor, completely destroyed. It left a jagged hole in the wall above it. "Clean that up."

Without a word, I stood to get the broom, stepping around the shards of glass, and began to sweep them up.

But he wasn't done. "Have you been paid yet?"

He didn't wait for an answer.

"No. You haven't," he snarled. "Because you're a filthy little liar. I spoke with a member of the Jinni Guard today. You're not working for them, and you never were."

I slowed, heart beating erratically.

Standing so violently that his chair fell back and crashed onto the floor, he stormed into the main room, moving toward his favorite chair. "Fetch me a drink!" he yelled, as he dropped into it. "That's all you're good for. It's time you get a real job and support your father in his old age, after all the years I've supported you."

Gripping the broom, seconds ticked by as I considered throwing it at him and telling him to get his own drink. Instead, my hands slowly leaned the handle against the wall, and my feet stepped carefully over to the glass toward the cups to obey.

"I expect you to come home with real coin by the end of the week—" he yelled, cutting off abruptly. Snatching up a dirty glass from the night before, he waved it wildly in my direction. "What's this? You were supposed to clean up!" It hit the wall with a heavy thunk, spraying dark liquid across the carpet and his bed, making a brand new mess to clean up.

Shaking, I didn't move or respond. I couldn't.

If I did, I might snap and do something I'd regret.

"Jezebel," my father raised his voice from the main room, getting to his feet threateningly. "Where's my drink?"

A knock on the door saved me from answering.

Lurching to his hooved feet, my father tromped over to yank it open, growling as he did, "What?"

On the other side, stood Old Hanna, the owner of our section of the acropolis. Of *our* apartment.

He immediately grew more subdued.

She only came up to my father's chest, and her once black hair had turned completely gray, with a heavy dose of wrinkles on her face to match. But as the owner, she controlled my father. With one word, she could kick him out.

"I received some complaints from your neighbors." Even her voice sounded ancient, with a trembling quality to it.

"So sorry, Hanna," my father said immediately, transforming into an embarrassed tenant. He *never* apologized. "Jezebel here accidentally dropped a plate and broke it. She's just cleaning it up now."

Hanna didn't reply right away, allowing her gaze to roam across our small place, lingering on my face. If she noticed the glass wasn't from a plate, she didn't say a word. After a pause long enough to make my father sweat, she gave a short nod.

"See that you keep it down," she warned, shuffling away without waiting for a response.

My father reached for the door.

Ducking beneath his arm, I rushed after the old hag—Hanna—without thinking. "I'll walk you home."

My father's eyes burned hot on my back. Though I listened for the sound of the door clicking shut, I didn't hear it.

I didn't dare look back.

When we turned the first corner, I realized I wasn't breathing and sucked in great gulps of air, trying not to panic.

Glancing over at Hanna, I found her staring back at me with a gleam in her eye. "I may be old, child, but I can get home just as easily as I could at your age."

"I—" I stumbled over an excuse. "I just thought it was a good night for a walk…"

"Of course, you did," she reassured, as if it was perfectly normal, but her sharp eyes examined my face, searching. As we reached her apartment at the far end of the hall, whatever she saw made her put a hand on my arm. "You must be hungry. Come in for a bite."

With nowhere else to go, I obeyed.

The owner's suite was much larger than ours, furnished with cozier chairs and a clean floor that wasn't covered in stains. Hanna was already in the kitchen. "Quickly now," she called back to me.

Swallowing hard, I entered her kitchen, once again noting the cheery atmosphere, with curtains that weren't faded and towels that didn't have moth-eaten holes in them. Without a word, Hanna held an apple out to me.

I accepted it.

Staring down at the little red fruit, my stomach revolted. I couldn't go home tonight. If I was honest with myself, I didn't ever want to go back. Clutching the apple tightly, I realized I had to. The reward money was hidden in my drawer. And my friends were still in the jars under the bed… I couldn't *not* go back. The thought made me sick. "I'm sorry," I whispered, shaking my head. "I don't think I can eat."

Hanna tilted her head, then took the apple back. Moving to her stove, she dipped it into a cauldron.

At my frown, she cackled. "It's just my nightly sleeping potion, deary. The sweetness of the apple helps counter the bitter taste. I thought you might have use for it. Perhaps you might give it to your father when you return home. That's what I used to do for my own father when I needed a bit of… *peace*." She emphasized that last word, making it sound strange. Like she meant something else altogether. *Space? Freedom? Relief?* Possibly all the above. After all the years she'd lived down the hall from us, she might've seen more than I'd thought.

With a knowing look, she shook the shiny apple dry, setting it on top of the others in her basket, where it rested with an extra sparkle. "You could just use it for yourself to get some sleep and give him one of the others, if you'd prefer." Lifting the little basket, she handed it to me. "Up to you."

When I didn't take it, she sighed, lowering it. "You can either avoid him or face him, but your problem isn't going to disappear on its own."

"I don't know what you're talking about," I mumbled.

She ignored me, thrusting the basket into my hands. "I recommend the second option. Avoidance never lasts. We all have to stand up for ourselves eventually."

With that blunt advice, she took my arm, walking me back to the door. "Good night, child," she said before she shut it. "And good luck."

For a long while, I stood transfixed in the hallway. I could try to wait for my father to fall asleep on his own, and then sneak back in. He might even be asleep already.

Hope carried my feet back down the long hall, around the corner, until I stood outside my front door.

At first, there wasn't a sound.

Then, a heavy thunk of a drink being slammed onto a table.

He's waiting up for me.

19

ANY OTHER NIGHT, I would've gone to stay with one of my friends. Regret stung my conscience when I remembered that wasn't an option anymore. Even if I'd had somewhere to go, I couldn't leave them behind. They were sealing the daleth tomorrow. My window of opportunity was closing. I had to get those two little jars, as well as the reward money I'd hidden in the drawer, before I could leave for good. I'd go somewhere far from here. Use my Gift to disappear.

For any of that to happen though, I had to first go through this door in front of me.

Inspiration struck. My father was afraid of Hanna. If she offered him the apple, he'd take it. With a quick glance around to make sure I was alone in the hall, I shifted.

Wringing my hands, I glanced around to make sure I was still alone as I stopped to quickly consider all the possibilities.

As long as Hanna was telling the truth about the sleeping potion—*and* as long as my father took it—that would give me enough time to get inside, pack my things, and get out.

But if, for some reason, things didn't go according to plan, I could take my leave and try to come back in the morning after he left for work.

No. I closed my eyes and rubbed at the ache beginning to form along the back of my neck. *That just extends the risk into the morning.* Leaving me with no money, and nowhere to go. I might miss meeting Shem if I was late, and then not be allowed to enter the human world at all.

I had to act now.

After one final scan of the hall, I made a hurried decision and cleared my throat. Humming softly to myself, I experimented with changes in my vocal chords until my voice deepened and warbled like Hanna's. I knocked.

Stomping hoofbeats signaled my father coming to the door. When he opened it, I tried not to flinch at his frown. "Hanna? Back so soon?" He leaned out to peer down the hall in both directions. "Is Jezebel still with you? Is she causing trouble?"

"I sent Jezebel out on an errand," I lied, choosing my words carefully. The voice wasn't quite right, but hopefully it was close enough. I added a bit of a rasp. "I apologize for the intrusion, but Jezebel reminded me it's been a while since I did an inspection. She asked me to take a look at the window in her room in particular. Something about a draft."

"Did she," he asked in a barely contained growl, crossing his arms. As long as he was angry at his daughter instead of his property-owner, that's all that mattered.

"I brought a gift as a consolation for the late hour." Holding up the basket of apples, I gestured toward the kitchen. "May I?"

He blinked, caught by surprise, and I took advantage of it, entering without permission and setting the basket down on the kitchen table.

Irritation flared in his eyes. He slowly closed the door, where he still stood. "You want to do the inspection *now*? In the middle of the night?"

"It'll only take a moment," I said, hoping my imitation of Hanna's voice would hold up.

As his eyes drifted to the basket of apples, I gave up trying to find a convincing reason for him to eat one that didn't sound strange. Instead, I just plucked the shiny one off the top and offered it to him. "Apple?"

He took it, but didn't bring it to his mouth.

Tottering toward my room before he could ask more questions, I said over my shoulder. "This is your daughter's room?"

He stepped in my path, looming over me, with a suspicious glint in his eye. "Perhaps you can come back in the morning."

I stepped around him, pretending that my heart wasn't pounding so loud that I could hear it in my ears. "I'll just be a moment. Have an apple while you wait." *Just take a bite,* I urged him silently, thankful that my back was to him so he couldn't see the panic starting to rise in my eyes.

But his hand caught the doorknob before mine could. "I'll take care of the draft Jezebel mentioned," he said with a false smile and a firm tone that I knew from experience meant he wouldn't budge. "I'm sure it's a simple fix."

The apple dangled uselessly by his side, bruising a bit from his grip.

Though I was tempted to step back, I stood my ground.

THE SECRET GIFT

You can either avoid him or face him, but your problem isn't going to disappear on its own, Hanna's words came back to me as I stared up at him.

I can't do it...

As the silence stretched, I almost walked back out as Hanna. But I was *so* close. I just needed one more minute to pack my bag. If I didn't deal with this now, I'd lose my chance to change things for the better.

He won't tell anyone, I told myself. *He had a thousand chances to turn my mother in, and never said a word. He's too ashamed of our secrets.*

I didn't know what I'd do if I was wrong.

No. I'm not *wrong.* He'd been afraid of my mother, and once I revealed myself, he'd be afraid of me. Obviously, he'd disinherit me immediately. Make me pack my things and go. But that's what I was planning to do anyway.

I couldn't think of any other option.

Though it was the last thing I wanted, I'd tried everything else. It was time to face him.

He was frowning at me.

I made my decision.

I'd face him if I had to, but first I'd give myself one last chance to sneak around him.

Instead of pushing past him as Hanna—or as myself—instead I shifted into my favorite form.

The little lizard.

I made the change so fast that I dropped to the ground on silent clawed feet, and his eyes didn't immediately follow.

Scurrying through the gap underneath my bedroom door before he spotted me, I shifted again the moment I was on the other side.

If I was lucky, he'd think Hanna had somehow found a loophole in the acropolis enchantment that allowed her to travel.

A wave of dizziness came over me from the reckless speed.

I shook it off and lurched toward the bed, tiptoeing so my father wouldn't discover where I'd disappeared to.

I wanted to go back to Hanna and hug her.

Someday, if I ever had a daughter, I'd name her after the old hag as a thank you.

I should've stood up to my father a long time ago.

Yanking my small bag out from underneath the bed, with the jars containing my friends already inside, it only took a few seconds to dump the contents of my top drawer in as well. The little coin purse that I'd hidden in the back of the drawer clinked softly as it fell.

I froze.

The door swung inward and slammed against the wall so hard that the plaster cracked.

My father loomed in the doorway, taking in my transformation with widening eyes. His face grew paler than our dirty, white walls. "I should've known," he whispered.

I pulled the bag over my shoulder and raised my chin, glaring at him.

Astonishment kept him paralyzed. Maybe a little bit of fear as well. *Thanks to mother,* I thought. *And those legs.* But that might not last long.

I needed to get past him.

Unfortunately, my last trick wouldn't work while carrying my bag. And I couldn't leave it behind.

Time to face him, I told myself, squeezing the strap on the bag to hide the way my hands trembled.

His own hands clamped down on the apple so hard that it crunched as he broke the skin.

He tossed it in the corner and took a step toward me.

The shock hadn't lasted as long as I'd hoped. Fear washed over me like a sickening wave, making it hard to think straight.

"You're just as vile as your mother." He sneered, taking another slow step, arms lifting to block any attempts to run. "You've had her curse all this time."

He was moving in on me like a dangerous animal.

I staggered backward without thinking and nearly tripped over the bag on the floor where I'd accidentally dropped it.

He followed.

"I should turn you in," he said, as he took one slow step toward me after another.

No, I wanted to cry. *You wouldn't.* But I didn't really know what he'd do anymore.

I moved around the bed, slowly backing into the corner, heart racing.

Panic blurred all rational thought. *I should've gone out the window before he'd blocked it*—but then I'd have had to leave my bag behind. *I shouldn't have backed up and given him the power*—but my feet had moved of their own volition.

He stopped suddenly, pointing down at his hooves, "Change these back, and I'll consider letting you go."

I'll consider... Ha! I knew better than to believe that.

His words sunk in. *Change these back.*

He wanted me to shift him.

I could shift *him.* Not just his legs... *him. I* had the power in this situation. If he pushed me, I could turn him into anything I wanted. And he *knew* that.

Another step, and he was close enough that his foul breath washed over me. He swayed slightly, but his eyes never left my face.

"No," I whispered.

It might as well have been a shout.

"Then it's time I do what I should've done years ago." He lunged.

I froze.

I couldn't help it.

Instead of stopping him like I had with Asher, I panicked, and my body stiffened for just a moment too long—it was all the time he needed to seize my wrists.

Ice cold terror flooded my body. *He knows I need my hands to shift him.*

Too late, I reacted, throwing my whole body into the struggle, kicking and bucking, trying to get some contact with his skin. Even just one finger could be enough.

He was too big.

And he knew what I was trying to do.

"The Guard will reward me handsomely for exposing an undisclosed shapeshifter," he got out, breathing hard, as he dragged me out of my room by my arms. "They might let you live," he chuckled darkly. "Might even let you keep your Gift. But I doubt it." He knew as well as I did that a Severance of a Gift was as good as death. Jinn who lost their Gifts lost their will to live.

My struggle grew weaker. I'd been wrong in thinking he wouldn't turn me in.

Trust had betrayed me once again. But there was still time—this wasn't over yet.

I reacted instinctively.

One moment, I'd been pulling away in fear; the next, I cut off the emotion and saw what I had to do with perfect clarity.

I shifted my fingers into sharp claws that matched those on the Lacklore hide chair behind us and suddenly stopped struggling. Using his own momentum, I was yanked toward him, not able to aim, just hoping to get close enough to cut. Curved and wicked, the claws sliced across his stomach without warning.

He shrieked in pain, blood dripping from the three long gashes that'd cut through his clothing and into the skin beneath, and let go.

With my hands freed, I shifted my fingers back and wrapped them around his wrist.

One moment, his large hands, dripping blood, were trying to jerk away from me.

The next, his entire body could fit in one of those hands. He landed on the floor with a tiny thunk. Dizzily, he tried to run.

I caught him by one of his tiny clawed feet.

Standing there, holding him, I tried to catch my breath. It came out in ragged gasps.

I hadn't wanted to do this. It didn't matter though. Once again, I was left with no choice.

Even if I'd wanted to bring him back, I couldn't. He'd said it himself. He'd turn me in to the Jinni Guard immediately.

Holding up his tiny form, I whispered down at him, "You should've taken the apple."

* * *

Though I brought my bag along the next morning, with the glass jar that held all my lizard friends hidden inside, Shem would not leave my side long enough for me to do anything with it.

This was the *last* day that the portal would be open. Ever since I'd shared its existence with the royal family, it'd been guarded. And every time I'd been allowed to cross over to the human side, I'd been with the prince the entire time. I wouldn't have changed that for anything, but now—there wasn't time for this kind of interference!

"I don't want you to face this alone," Shem said softly at the start of the day.

I tried not to flinch at the reminder of just how alone I truly was and smiled my thanks. The tension in my shoulder blades and neck grew painful enough to cause a splitting headache.

As the day passed, we ate fruit and cheese from the castle and waited for the guards to return from their final search. Today, we didn't stray far from the daleth, keeping it and the hilltop town within eyesight as we picnicked.

When Shem asked why I'd brought my bag, I said, "It's for good luck, I guess..." I slipped my hand inside without opening the flap, pulling out one of my gold armbands that I'd included for this exact reason. "Just some of their things in case we find them today."

That was enough to keep him from asking more. But not enough to distract him from his mission. Shem fastened himself to my side, determined to be there when I broke down.

I considered faking it, then brushed the idea aside. By the end of the day though, I could hardly think, much less answer Shem's persistent questions.

Fortunately, he interpreted that as anxiety over my lost friends.

Still, when Eliezer gave his evening report to Shem, I asked them for one more hour. "Please," I begged, pressing a hand to my face where I'd managed to summon a sheen of tears. "A little bit longer. Just in case?"

Shem was quick to agree.

I waited until he'd sent the guards out again before I pretended to panic, whirling to face him. "Have they checked the human towns thoroughly? Because Asher was bragging about trying to take a human captive, but..." I paused to shrug delicately. "The truth is, he's Giftless. Do you think there's a chance the humans took *him* hostage instead?"

"It's doubtful," Shem said, pursing his lips, though his eyes strayed to the town. "They've done quite a few searches in that vicinity already without disturbing the human life in the area. I hate to disappoint you…"

"I understand." I put a hand on his arm, lowering my gaze. "Would you consider asking Eliezer to check just once more, for my sake? Please?"

Again, the prince was as moldable as if I'd shape-shifted him myself. "Of course. That's the least I can do. I'll catch up with Eliezer and ask. Be back in a moment."

The instant he left, I strode a dozen paces to make tracking me more difficult, and traveled as well, multiple times, to the farthest place I could think of: the rainforest we'd explored the day before.

Kneeling next to a moss-covered fallen tree, I opened my bag and pulled out the jar, lifting the lid and pouring out the lizards inside onto the wide log.

"You're free," I whispered, feeling as lost as they looked.

Asher and Simon blended into the moss easily, and with a simple touch, I shifted the vibrant pinks, oranges, and yellows of Miriam's and Phillipa's scales to green as well.

"This will help you hide from any predators," I said softly, though no one else was listening. I didn't need to understand them to know what they were thinking. "You can never return to your true forms. I'm sorry, but you've forced my hand in this."

My grief was real for once, and I had to look away at the foliage around us as I struggled with guilt. "I wish I could trust you. But you'd only continue to use my Gifts or turn me in. Maybe both. I hope someday you'll understand that you did this to yourselves."

Phillipa and Miriam's tongues flicked out furiously. "Yes, including you," I snapped. "Don't you remember? You made me use my Gift to change your appearance. More than once. What would you have done if I'd said no?" I crossed my arms, looking away. "We all know how this would've ended."

Why couldn't they have just accepted me? Treated me like anyone else? It wasn't fair. I hadn't wanted any of this. They'd forced my hand. And I hated them for it.

"This is *your* fault," I repeated for emphasis, wanting it to be clear. "All of yours. *Not* mine."

If I could go back, I don't know what I'd have done differently. It was their choices that had led us here.

I shook my head and finally, reluctantly, turned to the fifth lizard.

The one I'd added last night.

My father.

20

I'D CARRIED HIM WITH the others throughout the day up until this moment.

I stared down at him now where he crouched, stiff and frozen, apart from them, tongue flicking wildly, probably trying to scream at me.

He didn't blend into the foliage like my former friends; I stared down at him, considering.

"I should've known it would end this way," I whispered to him. "After all, my mother left me all the signs. She knew what you deserved."

He reared up on his back legs, perhaps trying to appear larger and more intimidating. It only emphasized how small and weak he truly was. How weak he'd always been, really.

I should've stood up to him a long time ago.

He'd tried to make me small my whole life, when the truth was, I'd had this power over him all along. I was more powerful than anyone I knew. And I would *never* give that up again.

"Let's see how you like it," I murmured, bending until I was at his eye level. "When you're not the strongest anymore. When you have to trust someone else will treat you right."

He only bared his tiny teeth at me.

Trust. I'd trusted others not to use me, but that'd been a mistake. I wouldn't make it again. In fact, I'd go out of my way to avoid it.

In the end, I left his coloring a vibrant red.

Though I'd barely been gone five minutes, I returned to find Shem pacing. His hair stood at odd ends, as if he'd run his hands through it multiple times. Had something happened? He couldn't be this concerned over my absence alone...

"Where were you?" he called, running toward me, scanning my body as he approached. "I was frantic!"

"You were worried for me?" I processed the words. "Truly?"

"Of course!" he said, shaking his head as if it should be obvious. "I thought we'd lost you as well." *Ah, he didn't want another missing Jinni on his record.* Disappointment stung unexpectedly. When had I started to care this much?

Shem reached out and lightly touched my arm, drawing my attention back to him. "I was terrified. I don't know what I would've done." He pulled back, but held my gaze, looking unusually vulnerable. "We've spent... quite a bit of time together. I've grown rather fond of your company."

I struggled not to read into it or hope for too much. *Fond of my company.* It could mean a *lot*...Or it could mean very little.

Instead of answering, I reached into my bag, pulling out a large pink flower that faded into a soft orange center. Biting my lip, I held it up to show him. "I just wanted a little keepsake from our time here," I said, dipping my head to hide my eyes and any impossible feelings that might show through. I snuck a glance at him through my lashes because I couldn't help myself. "I should've told you, but I worried you'd think it was silly."

He touched the soft petal of the flower, smiling easily as he blew out a breath of relief. "I don't think that's silly at all."

"Good," I said, trying to fight the butterflies in my stomach into submission. I reached into my bag again to pull out a second flower, unable to look at him this time as I held it out. "Because I picked one for you too." I couldn't hide the blush on my cheeks.

His fingers brushed mine as he accepted it. "I should've known you'd have a purpose for leaving," he said. Startled, I glanced up to find him twirling the large flower in his hand, studying it. "You always know what you want."

What if I want you? came my traitorous thought. "Knowing what I want and actually getting it are two different things," I answered cryptically, aiming for a lighthearted tone that wouldn't betray my gloomier thoughts.

He considered me, raising one brow with a hint of a smile. "I'd guess that you probably get most things you want as well."

I didn't know how to answer that.

Thankfully, the Jinni Guard began to return one by one, pretending not to see the way their prince stared at the lowly Jinni girl. I tried to pretend too. It might not mean anything. *But what if it did?*

Once we were all there, we returned to Jinn through the daleth, and the Guard began the slow process of sealing it shut.

Permanently.

The others would never be able to get home. Never be able to take advantage of me again, or tell anyone my secrets.

A small pang of guilt reminded me there was also no taking this back. No changing my mind.

Once the portal was sealed, that was it.

"I'm so sorry we didn't find your friends," Shem said, putting an arm around my shoulder—not to lead me anywhere this time, but simply for comfort.

I blinked back real tears, though I probably could've let them fall. Clearing my throat, I said softly, "*I'm* sorry they ever found that awful daleth in the first place."

I meant it. Even though they'd done this to themselves—even though I wouldn't change anything I'd done—I would still miss them. Most of all, I'd miss the way things used to be. Without them and with my father gone as well, I was truly alone.

Taking my first deep breath in weeks, I wondered why I didn't feel better. No one was hounding me anymore. If I had anything to say about it, no one would control me ever again.

It was unexpectedly lonely.

Leaning into Shem slightly, I imagined that he also held me a little tighter. Then, I sighed. Pulling away, I forced myself to let go of him. I shouldn't let my imagination run wild.

Better to be alone and accept it, than to hope for love from the wrong person again.

When Shem also sighed softly, I tried to ignore the sound. *It doesn't mean anything,* I told my treacherous heart. And then, when that didn't work, I envisioned dropping my heart in a glass jar just like the ones I'd used for the lizards and sealing it in with a lid.

Down the hill, the Jinni Guards standing in front of the daleth stepped back a bit.

The space between the trees began to glow white, growing brighter until I had to squint.

As the guards continued to chant too quietly for us to hear from where we stood, the glow outlined the invisible portal, making its full size and scope clear.

Eyes stinging, I was about to look away when the glow snapped together and vanished.

All at once, the trees on each side seemed lifeless and dull. We waited anxiously as the first guard stepped through the unremarkable space between the trees, followed by the others. They tested every speck of the former portal to be certain it was gone.

No one disappeared.

All four members of the Jinni Guard stepped back as one from the now insignificant spot, signaling that they were finished sealing the portal. They turned to walk up the hill toward us.

This would be the last time I'd see Shem.

On a whim, I blurted out, "Is there any chance you have other portals you need help sealing? Or… searching for…?" I trailed off, realizing I hadn't actually done either of those things. Technically, my presence had been completely unnecessary after day one.

"Now that you mention it, I believe there might be." His wink gave me little flutters of excitement in my belly. "Perhaps I can call on you and your father soon with a new assignment?"

I stiffened.

"What is it?" he asked, stepping closer and daring to reach out and tilt my chin up, until I met his eyes. "What's wrong?"

Once more, I called up tears, letting them hover right on the edge of overflowing. I'd gotten quite practiced at this particular skill. All I had to do was think of all the things that'd gone wrong. "My father's gone. He left me and made it clear he wasn't coming back."

Shem frowned in confusion. "It's almost unheard of for a Jinni father to abandon his children. Did he give a reason? Or a clarification on when he'd return? Or… any explanation at all?"

"No…" I searched for the right words. I didn't want to lie to him if I didn't have to. "If you were to ask around or send your guards to inquire for you, I promise you it wouldn't take much searching to discover that's exactly the kind of father I have."

A vision of a bright red lizard on a mossy log flashed across my eyes, but I blinked it away.

"No need," Shem said softly. "I believe you." After a quiet moment passed, he added in a lighter tone. "My guards vetted your family weeks ago anyway."

Startled, I laughed.

He spread his hands wide and shrugged. "It's a requirement before I'm allowed to spend time alone with someone, as I'm sure you can understand."

"Of course. I'd expect nothing less." I was extremely thankful that I hadn't lied. At least, not about that.

"What will you do now?" he asked when I didn't say anything further.

I had the reward money to cover expenses for at least a few more months. That should give me time to find a smaller, more affordable place to live.

I didn't say that though.

Giving him a sad smile, I just shrugged. "I'm on my own. I may not have my home for much longer, so I'm not certain. But as long as I'm still there, I'm at your service."

"Leave us," Shem said in response, waving at the guards who'd just reached us, not breaking my gaze.

The guards didn't *actually* leave, but they did travel a good fifty paces away to keep watch over their prince from a distance instead, giving him the privacy he'd requested.

To me, the prince said more gently, "I can't imagine why your father would leave. But I hate to think of you alone." He lifted my hand, pressing his other hand over it. An intimate gesture. *Wasn't it?* I didn't know him well enough to be sure. "Come back with me to the castle for the day," he continued. "We can introduce you to some people, and I can ask around to see if there are any open positions…"

It was more than I'd dared to hope for. Of course, every girl in Jinn wanted to spend time with the prince, including me—but now, I wanted to spend time with Shem. With my friend. Even if that was all we were, even if I wanted more. His friendship was all I had left. "Are you certain?"

"Very." He grinned.

Summoning the guards to return, he told them, "Bring Jezebel with us."

"Your Highness?" Eliezer said, glancing at me with a slight frown.

"Let's go," Shem replied. "We have a shivah to plan in memory of the lost children of Jinn."

Ignoring the pang of guilt and the rudeness of the guards, I took Shem's hand with my chin held high. He wanted me with him. It might only be for the day, but I'd savor every minute.

The guards didn't question him further, and within seconds, they traveled us back to the castle gates.

Just like the acropolis, enchantments surrounded the structure, preventing traveling across the castle walls. That left only a select few carefully guarded entrances.

In the company of the prince, we swept through immediately, passing everyone waiting in line.

A thrill of second-hand power swept through me. The taste of what it must it be like to be in the royal family made me crave more. Just like the last time I'd been here, I imagined them as the puppet masters with everyone else doing their bidding. *No one* pulled their strings.

The gleaming white stones of the castle walls rose above us, with light blue turrets that looked like pointy hats, and lavender flowers stretched out in all directions around the castle, like a purple ocean.

Last time I'd been here, I'd been brought in through what I now realized was just a side entrance. This time we used an enormous set of double doors and entered a huge receiving room full of Jinn.

They all turned to stare. Not just at the prince, but at me as well. Above us, the ceiling rose a stunning four levels high, allowing a glimpse of balconies on the second, third, and fourth floors, which were also sprinkled with onlookers.

Craning my neck back, my jaw dropped at the giant shimmering chandelier that, if it fell, could've easily crushed multiple Jinn. Someone tittered. My teeth came together with an audible click. A furious blush rose so fast, I couldn't manage to keep it back completely, which only made my cheeks burn hotter.

I might not belong here, but they didn't need to know that. I kept my gaze level after that, no matter how many things sparkled in the corner of my eyes.

Whispers followed Shem wherever he went. Though I'd been here once before, this visit mattered far more. What happened next could influence the rest of my life. Gossips eyed me and my proximity to Shem, murmuring in each other's ears.

Pulling my shoulders back, I stood taller, lifting my chin. They wanted to talk about me? Fine. That just meant I was worth mentioning. Maybe *I* would learn to pull some strings.

I tried to keep my face empty of emotion and hide my shallow breathing.

It was impossible not to feel self-conscious though. I wore a simple white day dress, cut short above the knees to highlight the sandal straps that wrapped around my calves. Everyone else wore their finest evening wear. The women wore luxurious floor-length gowns that sparkled with jewels and other decorative pieces, complimented by the shining, ornamental armor worn by the men.

Intimidating didn't even begin to describe the feeling.

Though some of the Jinn moved toward us as if to engage in conversation, Shem led us away, down one red-carpeted hallway, and then another, flanked by the guards, even within the castle walls.

"These are my rooms," he said to me, as we came to a stop before an ornate wooden door, carved with detailed depictions of dragons. *His rooms?* I didn't know how to react or what to focus on. The fact that he had multiple rooms? Or that they were *his*? If it'd been any other Jinni, I'd have assumed ill intentions, but this was Shem. He'd never given me any indication that he thought like that before.

At my frown, he quickly added, "I should clarify, this is the entrance to my council room. I meet here with my personal council." *Ah.* Relief flooded me.

"They aren't all in the castle at the moment," he continued. "But every member of the royal family has their own personal council. My father, of course, runs the kingdom with his. And my mother prefers to focus on the inner workings of the castle, like her mother before her."

"I believe I might have heard of the royal councils," I managed, when he seemed to expect a response. I didn't know what else to say.

What did this have to do with me? Why would he introduce me to them? *He wouldn't.*

21

SHEM'S HAND DRIFTED TO the doorknob, but didn't turn it, reinforcing my growing certainty that he was trying to dismiss me. He licked his lips, as if trying to find the right words. "I expect at least half a dozen council members will be present. They're most likely already waiting on the other side…"

He was trying to find a graceful way to say goodbye. When he'd offered to find a position for me in the castle, he'd no doubt meant that someone else would figure it out.

"I understand completely," I said, backing away. "I'll wait in the servant's hall." If he remembered to ask if there was room for me, I'd be grateful. If he didn't, I could try to make a connection on my own. Either way, I'd hold my head high until I left the castle.

"Wait—" Shem pressed a hand to my arm. "Please, stay. Just give me a moment to explain."

He murmured to his guards to resume their normal rotations. Three of them vanished, presumably to another part of the castle, since the outer walls were enchanted against travel. The fourth moved a few paces away to stand by the door, facing the hallway. The carpet muffled his footsteps. Suddenly the space felt empty and overly silent.

Turning back to me, Shem looked at the door instead of my face, touching his decorative armor, then scratching his hair, and running a hand across his face. "I'm not explaining myself very well. I'm not… used to being so honest with someone."

My brows shot up.

"Not that—I'm not saying that I'm not honest…"

Seeing his nerves, when he was always the confident one, somehow calmed my own. I pressed my lips together to hold back a smile.

"It's just that, if you'd grown up here in court, you'd know that no one ever says what they're really thinking. It's too vulnerable."

I nodded. It wasn't just that way in court. All of Jinn was like that.

"It was a refreshing change of pace while we were away," I filled in the rest for him, helping him with what I knew he was trying to say. "But now that we're back, it needs to end. I truly do understand."

"No!" he exclaimed. "The opposite, in fact. It's more than refreshing. It's… indispensable."

I got the sense he'd wanted to say something else, but I didn't know what.

For all his talk about being honest and forthright, he didn't elaborate. If anything, he seemed to reel himself back in, becoming more formal again, placing his hand on the door as if to ground himself. "What I'm trying to say is, most royal children in the past used their council to plan elaborate celebrations and other frivolous things. But I've strived to make mine mean *more* than that. To make a difference. Whether that be searching for missing Jinn, closing a wayward daleth, discussing how to better prepare for attacks from the Khaanevaade, or…"

"Or planning a shivah," I whispered. Perhaps he was still being vulnerable after all.

"Or planning a shivah," he agreed, looking relieved that I understood.

Glancing at the lone guard just a few paces away, I lowered my voice, "I'm sorry, but… what does that have to do with me?"

Surprise lit his eyes. "Is it not obvious? I was hoping you'd want to join."

My brows rose. I tried to find words and stuttered, "You—It was definitely not—I mean…" I paused, chewing my lip, and tried again. "What are the requirements for entry?"

"An invitation from the prince." The corner of his mouth tilted up. "Which you have."

Clearing my throat, I nodded brusquely. "All right, then."

"That's a yes?" he asked, starting to turn the doorknob.

A smile slipped out between the two of us. "It is."

Shem swung the door open, pausing to speak with the guard again briefly, gesturing for me to enter first.

The council room was not what I'd expected. Instead of long-faced elders sitting in uncomfortable chairs, most of the Jinn were young—within their first century for sure. The large room wasn't ugly or bare, but instead filled with luxury, including a second floor balcony and a cozy fire burning in the hearth. There *was* a long mahogany table where a few Jinn sat, but the seats were high-backed lounge chairs covered in cushy, blue velvet. Three of the four walls were covered in bookshelves, and the fourth held a window that took up most of the wall.

A handful of Jinn sat by the fire, and two more peered down at us from the balcony.

There were more women in the room than men, but *all* of the eyes pinned on my face were shrewd and calculating. I could practically hear their thoughts: *Who is she to invade our space?* I was clearly an intruder and would be treated as such.

No one greeted me right away, acknowledging the prince instead with nods and a few hellos as he stepped inside.

"Is the daleth closed?" a female asked, absently brushing her long black hair over her shoulder as she stood, pushing back her chair. With a glance at me, she waved to the tall candles spaced across the table. Flames sprang up from the wicks.

Here's what I offer, she might as well have said out loud. *What do you bring to the table?*

Though the blatant use of Gifts was an obvious challenge, I didn't take the bait.

Shem pulled out a chair for me to sit, then took the one beside me. "They sealed the portal less than an hour ago," he confirmed, folding his hands in front of him, growing serious. "The lost ones were never found, and we'll be planning a service to honor their memory."

"And your guest?" another female Jinn at the far end of the table purred, leaning back in her seat as if she didn't have a care in the world. Her sharp eyes studied me momentarily, before dismissing me.

"Yes, thank you, Milcah," Shem said, shoving his chair back to stand and raising his voice. "Everyone? This is Jezebel. She was a close friend of our lost Jinn and will be helping plan the details of their shivah. Please welcome her to the council."

Sharp eyes around the room pinned me to my chair.

I didn't know what to say, but they were clearly waiting for me to begin. "How do you… normally proceed with planning a shivah at the castle?"

"We try to think of the family first," Shem said gently, giving me an encouraging nod. "You know them best, so we will follow your advice."

Scooting to the edge of my chair, I leaned onto the table and tried to project confidence that I didn't feel. "Well…" I pictured my friend's parents, one at a time, trying to envision how they'd respond, and spoke slowly, "Phillipa's mother will most likely be inconsolable, but she'll still want to share a few words, so we should arrange for someone to speak on her behalf."

No one said a word, and I paused, uncertain, until Shem said, "Go on."

"Asher's father won't want to attend, which will upset his mother, so perhaps…" I inclined my head toward Shem, recognizing the audacity of what I was about to say, "Perhaps the royal family could offer a small financial incentive? To make it more worth his time?"

Though I caught a few raised brows out of the corner of my eye, I kept my gaze on Shem, who nodded and said, "More than fair. We make it a priority to take care of the grieving family. Consider it done."

A small but powerful win.

Inwardly, I cheered at the little victory. On the outside, I focused on being firm and decisive, expanding on the ground I'd gained.

I was a *council member* now. It was more than I'd ever dreamed possible.

I might be a little insect beneath their notice at the moment, but not for long. I'd *make* them accept me.

"With the extended family and friends, it might be nice to gather written condolences for the parents to read later." I grew more confident with each word. "That way, if they're not up to talking to anyone, they can still have something to hold onto and hear on their own terms."

"We should make notes and assign these tasks to individuals," Shem said, gesturing across the table to Milcah.

She grudgingly sat forward, picking up a blank sheet of parchment, and began to write my suggestions down.

"You're forgetting food," she grumbled.

A male Jinni sitting close enough to brush shoulders with her quickly agreed. "We'll need quite a bit of food for those who want to sit shivah past the first day."

"I know," I said a bit too sharply. Softening my tone, I added, "That was my next request. Enough food to last seven days." The parents would likely choose to sit shivah for the full week, meaning they wouldn't wash their clothes, bathe, work, or travel more than a short distance until the mourning period was over.

As I continued, a few other Jinn chimed in. I didn't worry about names or what they thought of me. All that mattered right now was impressing Shem enough that he would ask me to stay on long term.

That, and giving my friends a true shivah to honor their memory.

I grew quiet for a minute, letting the other council members edge me out of the conversation. I couldn't change what I'd done—I didn't *want* to, because it was the only way I could be free—but I could mourn my friends and give them the farewell they deserved. I'd make this shivah the best it could be. For them.

Once everyone had exhausted their ideas, Shem assigned different duties to everyone, then clapped his hands on the table and stood. "Let's adjourn for the evening. Everyone, please get started as soon as possible. We'll meet again in the morning to finalize plans."

I stood with the others, lingering next to the table as they filtered out of the room, one by one. Awkwardly, I cleared my throat to get Shem's attention, as he finished speaking with two council members who pretended not to see me as they swept out of the room.

Quietly, so the last few Jinn still in the room couldn't hear, I murmured, "I just wanted to thank you before I went home. And... I'll see you in the morning?"

"Well," Shem dragged out the word. "If it's not too forward of me, I took the liberty of asking Gabriel to prepare a room for you." He gestured toward the door, where he'd stood outside speaking with the guard when we'd first come in. "It's located in the residents wing of the castle," he added with a lopsided grin. "In case you decide to stay."

I forgot about the remaining council members, bringing my hands to my mouth. I hadn't dared hope for so much. "Truly?"

"Of course," he replied, smiling down at me. I might've been imagining it, but he almost seemed to be blushing slightly.

"I don't deserve your kindness," I said softly, bowing my head.

Asher, Phillipa, Miriam, and Simon's faces flashed through my mind, one after the other. I could picture them shaking their heads at me.

Agreeing.

But this was my future—which had been essentially non-existent—opening up before me. This one opportunity held a thousand possibilities.

One of whom, stood right before me.

Still smiling.

"You *do* deserve it," he urged when I didn't say anything further.

I didn't want to hesitate anymore or let the past hold me back. I needed to do whatever it took to make this situation permanent. To never, ever suffer the manipulation of others again. If that meant accepting a place in the castle with Shem, I would take it, gladly. If it meant covering up what I'd done—what I'd been *forced* to do—I'd do it. And most importantly, if it meant I had to do it again... I knew now, I would.

Slowly, holding my breath, I dared to reach out and take his hand. "I really don't," I answered him honestly. He'd never know how to true that was. Bowing low, I pressed my lips to his knuckles, and gave him a rare, true smile as I added, "But I humbly accept."

THE
SECRET
SHADOW

1

"THIS WILL BE YOUR room." Prince Shem unlocked a solid wood door and handed me the gold metal key. With a glance I could only describe as thinly-veiled annoyance at the two guards on his heels, he added to me, "I'll show you where you can put your things." He stepped inside, waving for me to follow.

Before I could step forward, both guards moved between us. "Your highness—" one of them began, with a sharp glance in my direction.

Without a word, Shem took my hand and gave it a tug, forcing his guards to allow me past.

He put an arm around my bare shoulder, making my skin tingle. His ornamental armor pressed against my side, cold and solid. "I'm not expecting an attack in Jezebel's empty room," he remarked dryly. "But I promise I'll call for you if the furniture rises up against me."

Both guard's eyes locked on me, narrowing. Their prince might not see me as a threat, but they certainly did. I couldn't tell what bothered them more—that I was a common Jinn from the acropolis or that I was allowed to be alone with the prince without being vetted.

Shem winked at me, ignoring them. When the door swung closed, he added softly, "It seems you're a bit of a legend already."

I scoffed.

THE SECRET SHADOW

"It's true," he insisted. "They may have noticed that I took you on many of my latest adventures to the human world…" He gave me that co-conspirator grin I'd grown fond of. Those warm blue eyes carried a disarming friendliness that was impossible to ignore. Paired with his sharp jawline and disheveled black hair—and of course, being the prince of Jinn—he was naturally irresistible. But his genuine interest in his people—in *me*—was what truly drew me in. Blushing, I said, "A few little adventures hardly makes me a legend."

"On the contrary." He laughed, rubbing the back of his neck. "I apologize in advance, but the Guard seems to have marked you as someone to watch."

My brows rose. I tried not to react further, but my heart rate picked up. "Wonderful," I muttered.

"Take it as a compliment." Shem winked and added, "Legend."

Some of my tension faded at the nickname. I laughed and changed the subject, "I believe I was promised a tour?"

"Ah yes—" His grin disappeared briefly as he put on a mock serious expression. Bowing, he waved an arm, "—Welcome to your room."

Turning to take in the space, I tried not to gape at it like a common Jinni from the acropolis. If my younger self had visited the castle, I'd have sworn this space was the king's own room. My entire acropolis apartment could've fit inside.

"Bed, wardrobe, desk, attached bathing room, window… all the standard features," Shem teased, but they didn't feel standard to me at all.

Above us, a chandelier almost as tall as me hung from the high ceiling. Both the desk and the wardrobe he'd mentioned had delicate designs carved into the dark wood hinting at how expensive they must be. And the bed was a huge four-poster with a canopy over it and a white fur rug beneath.

As I moved toward the window, my jaw dropped at the view of the lavender garden stretching out in the distance.

I felt like an imposter.

Shem and I had met less than two months ago, by accident. Or rather, by unintentional design. After betrayal forced me to turn on my only friends, Shem was tasked with finding them, and we'd been drawn together during the search. But while he spent hours working with his Guard to find the lost Jinni children, they'd been under my bed in lizard form the whole time. Until the last second, when I'd slipped them into the human world right before the portal was closed—and left them behind.

I didn't deserve to be here.

Shem shifted behind me, making the wood floor creak, but he didn't speak and I didn't turn around. The grief came at the most inopportune times.

Another minute passed before he cleared his throat. "If you don't like it, please don't be afraid to speak up. We have many other rooms—"

"Oh no." I turned to reassure him. "It's not that at all. I'm just… overwhelmed by your kindness."

"It's nothing." He grinned and added, "Legend."

At the ridiculous nickname, the tension in my shoulders eased. I laughed softly. "Thank you."

I didn't know what else to say, but the corners of his eyes wrinkled as he smiled back, and I knew he understood.

A few days ago, Shem had sent a formal invitation to join his council and come live at the castle. When he'd first heard my father was gone and I had nowhere to go, he'd offered it immediately, but I hadn't truly believed him until that day. Lots of people made promises, but Shem actually kept them.

I'd packed my bag that same night.

Partly because living in the castle was a dream come true, but mostly because I didn't have anywhere else to go. Not after what I'd done to my friends—and my father.

As I'd left my apartment for the last time, I'd tucked that empty jar—the one I'd used to trap them—beneath the clothes in my bag. I wanted it with me. Not as a memory, since I'd never forget what I'd done, but more to remind myself never to let something like that happen again.

Setting that same bag down on the bed, I stepped subtly away from it. Though I returned my gaze to the garden, I barely noticed the Jinn strolling along the walking paths.

I never wanted to hurt anyone with my Gift again.

If I wanted to avoid repeating my past, no one else could ever learn my secret.

Not even Shem.

My eyes locked on his reflection in the window as he leaned against the wardrobe, running a hand through his hair and rubbing the back of his neck. "If it's not the room, is there something else bothering you?"

I swallowed hard, forcing a smile. "Nothing that can be fixed, I'm afraid." Taking a deep breath, I tried to say something close to the truth. "I just wish I didn't need your generosity as badly as I do."

"It's not your fault your father abandoned you," he was quick to say with a rare frown.

But it was.

Clearing my throat, I ignored his comment, gesturing around us instead. "The room is incredible. Thank you." The trembling in my voice wasn't from the view.

He smiled and accepted the subject change. "I haven't shown you the best part yet."

Shaking off my dark thoughts, I gave him a curious glance.

"Are you aware of the protection spell over personal rooms in the castle that prevents traveling?"

THE SECRET SHADOW

Most Jinn could travel long distances in the span of a breath. It was considered one of the lesser Gifts—unless a poor Jinni didn't have it.

Unfortunately, it also meant that there was no such thing as a locked door to a Jinni who could travel right through it. That's why most Jinn used the protection spell for privacy. It acted as a lock, preventing unwanted travel into personal spaces.

I nodded. "The acropolis uses the same spell."

"Well, the royal family created a second spell that forms a loophole of sorts."

Intrigued, I raised a brow. "Oh? I've never heard of it."

"You wouldn't have." He came to join me at the window. "It's reserved for those the royal family trusts. And well-guarded for obvious reasons. There wouldn't be much point to the spell preventing travel if *everyone* in the castle knew how to get around it."

He glanced my way with a smile and caught me studying him. I blushed as his words sank in: *Reserved for those the royal family trusts.*

I ducked my head. *Does he trust me?* I wanted to ask, but I wasn't nearly as forward as he thought I was. I chewed on my lip instead.

"Come. Let me show you." Shem waved a hand at the wardrobe. Patting the dark maple wood, he leaned casually against it. "This particular spell creates a 'room' within a room. You simply need something large and enclosed, like your wardrobe here."

I stopped close enough to feel the heat from his arm next to mine. He smelled like a pine forest with the barest hint of cinnamon. It tickled my nose. I leaned a bit closer, pretending to inspect the detailed carvings, and my long black hair brushed his arm. He didn't seem to notice. This close I could see a hint of dark stubble.

I startled when he spoke, "Unlike your room, this smaller space doesn't have a spell preventing travel."

"The loophole," I whispered, coming back to the conversation. My lips parted. *Impressive.*

Shem's eyes flicked to my lips and then back to the wardrobe.

For weeks now, there'd been this tension between us. Brief touches, stolen looks. Half the time I wondered if I imagined it, but the other half—moments like this—I wondered if there was something between us.

Was the wardrobe a declaration? A way to reveal how much he cared without saying it out loud?

I took it in with new eyes.

It stood on four little legs that lifted it off the floor, making it slightly taller than Shem. Through the intricate carvings, the inside was visible.

It was empty now. But once I unpacked, it'd barely be half-full. I only owned a handful of dresses and a few pairs of sandals. Nothing like the grandiose outfits I'd already seen in the castle so far. Everyone else on Shem's council likely had ten times as much.

"You'll receive a stipend for more clothes," Shem said, as if he could read my mind.

My cheeks filled with heat. I wrapped my arms around myself, wishing I could burn this simple day dress.

"I'm sure you don't need it," he rushed to add. "It's just that council members are often required to attend extravagant events, so the royal family feels it's only right to compensate everyone for that."

The royal family. Did he distance himself on purpose? The uncertainty of it all, constantly going back and forth on what things meant, made my mind spin.

"Thank you." I acknowledged the offer, trying to hide my shame. I gestured to the wardrobe—the more personal gift. "It's incredible."

He shrugged off the praise. "It's useful. The enchantment against travel is intended to keep unwanted guests out. This way, you're able to keep the privacy benefits, but you don't lose your freedom to travel *unobserved*." He emphasized the last word. I didn't need him to elaborate to know he was referring to the castle gossip.

"I love it." Daring to place a hand on his arm, I smiled up at him. "How does it work?"

"Step inside," he directed, opening the thin door for me. I did, turning in the small space to face him. "Now, close the door behind you to seal the room." He pressed it closed as he spoke, and the wardrobe door clicked softly shut.

Through the gaps in the decorative wood, I stared into his pale blue eyes.

A heartbeat passed.

Instead of traveling to test out my new freedom, I gently pushed the door back open and stared at him, gathering the courage to ask, "Why would you do something like this for me?"

I wasn't sure what I hoped he'd say.

But I couldn't help wishing he'd stop the usual Jinni hinting and be straightforward for once.

I wanted to believe there was more to our relationship than simply a prince and his new council member.

Shem waved a hand and smiled. "It's really not that special. Everyone on the council has a loophole spell."

My little bubble of hope popped.

Deflating, I hid my disappointment behind a forced calm.

"Consider it a thank you," he continued, moving to the side so I could step out of the wardrobe. "It's one of the many privileges of being one of my advisors." His cheeks dimpled as he grinned, and I forced myself to smile back.

This wasn't a romantic gesture after all.

While I hadn't met all of them yet, Shem had almost three dozen council

THE SECRET SHADOW

members.

It stung.

Turning away, I touched the carvings on the wardrobe door and gently closed it, avoiding Shem's gaze. I wanted to kick myself for getting my hopes up.

"Let's continue your tour, shall we?" He smiled, seemingly unaware of my inner turmoil.

I pressed my lips together in an imitation smile.

The two members of the Jinni Guard trailed after us as we walked. "The rest of my council, as well as my mother's and father's councils, all reside in the south wing as well," he began, gesturing down the long hallway.

Doors led to individual apartments, just like the acropolis. Except here in the castle, the hall had lush blue carpet, solid limestone walls in a crisp shade of white, and expensive décor carefully placed in small alcoves. There were dozens of vases, paintings, and even a full suit of ornamental armor that likely belonged to a former king.

We passed an open seating area with comfortable lounge chairs and heavy drapes beside floor-to-ceiling windows. Shem continued past with a familiar nod to those seated inside, but he didn't stop.

As we reached the heart of the castle, he gestured to the hallways on either side of us. "The royal family lives on the east side. And most of the long-term servants live on the west."

I tilted my head back to stare at the stained glass window four stories above us in awe. Sunlight filtered through, lighting the large, round room with dozens of bright, flickering colors.

"The north wing holds the largest rooms, including the dining hall, which I'll show you later." Shem's voice came from further away, and I hurried to catch up before he noticed me dawdling. "There's a smaller throne room, meeting rooms for all of the councils, and over here—" I spun to look where he was pointing, at a heavy-looking set of double doors twice as tall as him, "—is the grand throne room."

As we continued on, Shem glanced over. "It can be a bit overpowering at first."

I cleared my throat. "It is. But I'll get used to it." I'd make sure of that—I'd spend my nights exploring in lizard form until I knew these halls better than anyone.

A few Jinn headed toward us from the opposite direction. All eyes fixated on my bare, sandalled legs. Here in the castle, the dress code was clearly more formal.

The first woman wore a sleek, backless gown, made of a dusky blue that grew darker as it neared the hem, looking exactly like the sky at twilight. Lights twinkled along the bottom half of the dress like stars. Beside her, the other woman's vibrant red dress had feathered sleeves that reminded me of a cardinal.

Between them strode a man in ornamental armor. Unlike the sharp silver armor of the Jinni Guard, worn from head to toe, this shining surface was a soft, gold metal that would never hold up in a real battle. It was also studded with diamonds. Definitely not intended for combat, then. It was flashier than anything I'd ever seen Shem wear.

Even before I'd come to the castle, I'd heard of the fashions here, but seeing it in person was an entirely different experience.

They bowed to the prince, ignoring me entirely.

I raised my chin, gazing past them and pretending not to notice.

"The council meets in the east wing," Shem said, picking up the tour where he'd left off. "The royal family's quarters are also in the east wing, so the Guard will require you to pass through a checkpoint each time you enter."

"Is that where we're headed now?" I sounded shy. Childish. Gritting my teeth, I pulled my shoulders back, determined to fake confidence if I couldn't find it on my own.

"It is." Shem placed a hand on my arm, guiding me toward the stairs.

He let his hand fall, but it'd drawn my attention to my simple attire once again. I had on a single gold armband and my short white day dress with otherwise completely bare arms and legs. Did the stipend Shem had mentioned include jewelry as well? My own small collection was cheap in comparison. I'd be lucky if I could afford any of the latest fashions here.

As we entered the east wing, the thick carpet changed to a deep red to signify the royal family. We walked in silence, until finally Shem cleared his throat. "I should probably share before we arrive, that there's been a bit of contention in my council over my decision to bring you on."

I stiffened.

"Nothing to be concerned about, of course."

Swallowing, I nodded, but I didn't believe him for a second. "What're their concerns?"

He hesitated. Gesturing for his guards to wait, we walked a bit further, before stopping out of hearing. "I'll be as honest with you as you've been with me," he murmured. "There's talk that you won't know the customs and that you won't respect the way the council works. Some think it's disrespectful to the institution and the monarchy. And a small number feel that your upbringing…" He faltered again.

"My upbringing?" I repeated, frowning. "You mean, growing up in the acropolis?" Our little apartment was just one of thousands within the thick acropolis wall that surrounded the city. Though it was on the outskirts, that didn't make us less civilized than anywhere else in Resh. "Surely not everyone on the council grow up in the castle?"

I expected him to say no, but he slowly nodded.

"Oh…" I shrunk back. I'd worried before about fitting in, but now I felt certain I wouldn't.

"Most of my personal council is around our age," he continued. I tried to follow his train of thought, unsure how that was relevant. "What I'm trying to say is, they aren't set in their ways. They may have formed an opinion now, but once they meet you, they'll see you're more than capable."

Am I though?

I didn't know how to respond to that, because I was half-convinced they were right. Instead, I changed the subject again. "Is the entire castle spelled so you have to walk everywhere? Or do you travel sometimes?"

Shem chuckled, waving for the guards to rejoin us as we began walking again. "Fair question. We often stroll for a bit of exercise, but traveling is perfectly acceptable in the main halls. It's only the personal and private rooms that are spelled to prevent traveling in and out. Oh, and the throne rooms and the dining hall."

Chewing on my lower lip, I hummed my understanding.

"Here we are," Shem said before I could ask anything else. "You'll likely remember some council members from when you were here before." He gestured toward a set of double doors in a hall with a guard posted outside.

"Gabriel," Shem called as we drew closer. "You remember Jezebel?"

"Of course," he said, bowing stiffly.

We'd met before? His face wasn't memorable. *It doesn't matter. He's just a guard. They're not important.*

Gabriel's dark eyes narrowed almost imperceptibly. He looked down his nose at me, raising a single brow, then turned to Shem, dismissing me. "Most of the council is in attendance, your highness," he said as he pulled the door open for us.

"Very good." Shem gave him a nod as we passed.

The door nearly clipped my heels as it closed behind us, and I jumped, whirling around. Gabriel's back was turned, but I could've sworn he'd done that on purpose.

The door clicked softly shut.

Shem stopped in the small entryway unexpectedly. I almost bumped into him.

"Did they teach you how to guard your mind during your discipline years?" he asked without explanation, standing closer than Jinn usually did.

His nearness distracted me for a second. I nodded, faintly remembering the teaching. I'd been good at it, but we'd only spent a few days on the training before moving on. "A bit. Why?"

He cleared his throat, leaning close enough to whisper, "Guard member's Gifts aren't usually disclosed unless necessary, but you should know Gabriel has a minor ability to read minds."

I sucked in a breath, tensing.

What was I thinking in the hall? I tried to remember, my thoughts scattering frantically. Had I thought of my shape-shifting Gift? My breathing sped up. I put all my energy into slowing it back down. I didn't think so? I couldn't remember!

Hair rose on my arms as another thought occurred to me, and true panic kicked in. "Can he read minds through the door?" I glanced back at the dark, stained wood.

"No," Shem reassured me, and I blew out the breath I'd been holding. "Most, if not all mind-readers need a visual for their Gift to work. And like I said, Gabriel's Gift isn't terribly strong."

"But he's on the Guard," I whispered back. Which meant it was strong enough. It was *mind-reading* after all. The Gift I'd feared most when trying to decide if I should come here.

"He usually doesn't hear anything, unless a thought is being broadcast."

Like mine probably had been.

They came to me then.

Just a guard. Not important.

I sighed. Had I already made an enemy before the morning ended? I'd find out soon enough.

"Ready?" Shem waited for me to nod, before leading me out into the council room.

I'd been here once before. I'd had a temporary seat on the council as we planned a mourning event to honor my missing friends. The room was familiar, with its long wall of books, dark blue velvet furniture, long mahogany tables, windows that stretched from floor to ceiling, and an upper level with a balcony and more bookshelves.

This time, however, at least two dozen Jinni faces stared back—they'd been waiting for us.

2

GABRIEL'S WORDS CAME BACK to me: most of the council *in attendance.* Shem had planned an event? As I trailed him to the center of the room, I wished he'd given me a bit more information. What was expected of me?

"Come, sit with us," a nearby woman said when I hesitated. She had sleek waist-length hair that matched her black dress and gold accents that complemented her yellow-gold eyes. I vaguely remembered meeting her before.

Warily, I took the seat. The sharp points of her dress poked me in the shoulders as she shifted to make room. She didn't seem to notice. Smiling, she whispered in a slightly condescending tone, "I wouldn't expect you to remember us, but my name is Jerusha. This is Milcah."

Turning to glance at the woman on my opposite side, equally young and pretty, she gave me a closed-lip smile before returning her attention to Shem.

I tried not to stare at her decadent dress. It was also black, with a delicate trail of white flowers along one side from head to toe and a plunging neckline. Was everyone wearing black? I glanced around the room, confirming they all were. Was there a dress code I wasn't aware of? I frowned as I turned back to Shem. His armor gleamed silver and his crisp shirt and pants were white. Not a trace of black on him. I rubbed my forehead, trying to make sense of it. It was almost as if they were dressed for mourning.

Shem finished speaking with a nearby Jinni and stepped to the front of the room, clearing his throat. "Thank you, everyone, for taking time to be here today. Most of you remember Jezebel, I hope?"

The Jinn around the room smiled at me pleasantly enough. Maybe Shem was worried for nothing.

He nodded to Jerusha and Milcah on each side of me. "Thank you both for taking the initiative to welcome Jezebel to the council. I will place her with your circle first, and potentially long-term if it's a good fit."

I raised a brow at the unfamiliar term, hoping it was a good thing.

"I'll keep my speech brief, as I'm sure you're all excited to get to know our newest council member. Feel free to mingle. The noon meal will be delivered shortly."

His easygoing leadership clearly trickled down to his council, as they immediately began talking and the volume in the room rose. Before I could think of something to say to the women next to me, Shem joined us.

"I probably should've asked you ladies first," he began, pulling up a tall blue-velvet chair to sit with us. "I do apologize. I got caught up in the moment."

They glanced at each other so briefly I almost missed it. Jerusha waved him off. "Nonsense."

Milcah nodded in agreement. Both of them leaned forward, smiling, drawn to the prince like dragons to their prey, and Milcah said to him, "We're honored, in fact, that our circle would be your first choice."

They probably didn't realize I had no idea what they were talking about. I cleared my throat. "Circle?"

Milcah was making eye contact with someone across the room, gesturing for them to join us. Jerusha didn't seem to hear me either, smiling at Shem instead. "No doubt she'll be a good fit, once she... adjusts to our customs."

"The circles are smaller work groups within the council," Shem explained when they didn't, focusing on me. "I pair Jinn together on smaller projects so the council can work on multiple issues simultaneously. Occasionally we come together for bigger concerns, but often you'll work more closely with a specific few on the council: your circle."

I tried not to flush from embarrassment at how obvious that was once he said it. "How many others are in our particular circle?"

"Just a few," Jerusha said vaguely. To Shem she added, "We'll introduce her, don't worry about a thing."

Hesitating for a second, he smiled and thanked her. "I'll be nearby if you need me," he murmured to me before standing to face another Jinni waiting at his shoulder.

"Tell us about the acropolis," Jerusha jumped back into conversation before he'd finished turning, grinning at me. "What's it like living by the river? Did you

THE SECRET SHADOW

have discipline years? Or did you skip those and stay at home to work?"

I blinked at her words, which were mildly insulting. It didn't *seem* intentional...

"Yes, do tell," Milcah added, ignoring the nearby Jinn who'd approached us.

The flood of questions overwhelmed me almost as much as the dozens of eyes. Should I introduce myself to the others? Or answer Jerusha? It seemed like Shem valued resourcefulness, so maybe Jerusha and Milcah expected me to take the initiative with meeting everyone.

"Ladies," a Jinni tsked as I wavered in indecision. She slipped through the crowd, lowering herself elegantly into the chair where Shem had sat. "Don't be ridiculous. You're acting as if you've never been outside the castle to see the acropolis with your own eyes. And all Jinn attend their discipline years. Even the lowest Jinni deserves to learn with their peers."

Once again I didn't know if I should be insulted or thankful for the rescue.

When she smiled at me, it *seemed* genuine.

"Not at all, Dorcas," Jerusha replied, and her brows drew together as she turned to me. "I do apologize if my questions were intrusive. I simply wanted to get to know you better and hear about common life outside the castle."

Her apology appeared authentic as well, despite the snub. It was as if they couldn't help themselves. Or maybe they were good at hiding their true feelings...

"The acropolis apartments are certainly modest, compared to the castle," I admitted, lifting my chin. I met their gazes through sheer force of will. Whether it was well-intentioned or not, their scrutiny was uncomfortable. "We still have many of the same luxuries, as well as a beautiful view of the River Mem. Incomparable, really." I wasn't as skilled in subtle jabs, and the poke at the castle views landed awkwardly, leaving a beat of silence in its wake.

"I'm sure you miss it." Dorcas patted my arm, managing to sound superior even when offering comfort.

Jerusha reached forward to touch my bare knee. "You won't miss that wardrobe though," she teased. "I'm sure you're dying to get out of those old things and wear something more fashionable."

Heat flashed through my whole body.

I wrapped my arms around my waist as I mumbled, "Yes, of course."

"Give the girl a rest," Milcah inserted herself with a mothering look in my direction. "She's intimidated enough by her drastic change in circumstances without you pressing her for information. Aron, what is your circle working on?"

At first, I was grateful for the reprieve. But as they discussed terms I'd never heard before, my body tensed, forming the beginnings of a headache. I was in the center of the group without a clue what we were discussing. If they asked me to weigh in on a subject, I'd look like a fool. Fortunately, no one did. It was as if they'd forgotten I was there altogether.

The noon meal arrived, and the group dissipated, leaving me alone with Jerusha and Milcah again when Shem rejoined us.

"I trust everyone is making you feel welcome?" he asked, glancing at the ladies. I swore something like a warning flashed in his gaze as he addressed them. Something almost protective. My stomach fluttered.

Their eyes landed on me.

"Absolutely," I replied with a small smile. I still couldn't tell if their offensive comments were calculated or accidental. What Shem had said before we'd entered came to mind, about the council not being thrilled about my joining them, but I still hoped that wasn't the case for everyone.

Shem's shoulders relaxed. As we all moved to the dining table to eat, I tried not to frown. He was doing everything he could to make a place for me, but in the end, it was up to me. It was normal to have a little awkwardness when meeting new people, but I'd make friends soon enough. Maybe even someone I could trust. At least, I hoped so.

* * *

AFTER A WEEK, however, I was quickly losing hope.

Every interaction with council members led to embarrassment. I laid awake at night pulling apart each conversation, but I couldn't put my finger on the reason for it. No one acted unpleasant toward me on purpose. It was more that I seemed to naturally make a fool of myself. Sometimes, I didn't need their help at all. They'd laugh and someone would tell me, "Not to worry. You'll adjust to the castle eventually."

Today, after an hour of conversation, I needed a moment of peace. I'd hidden behind some bookshelves on the balcony.

Below, a low woman's voice drifted up to me. "The poor girl. It's not her fault she's so simple. Growing up in the acropolis doesn't afford someone the luxury of good taste. Or *intelligence*."

Her listeners laughed.

"I truly don't understand why the prince spends so much time with her."

"No," a second voice agreed. "And I can't say I like it either."

"Neither do I. Perhaps there's something more there than meets the eye, but I cannot fathom what it might be…"

As I listened, I flushed hot and then cold.

Footsteps sounded on the stairs.

They were heading toward me.

I needed to leave before I burst into tears.

If I could've traveled away, I would have, but the council rooms had the usual spells that prevented it.

THE SECRET SHADOW

Which meant my only way out was to walk right past them.

Keeping my expression cool and composed—or as close to it as I could under the circumstances—I swept out from the bookcases and brushed past them without a word, chin high.

It was Jerusha and Milcah.

"Oh my," Jerusha stage-whispered. "Do you think she heard?"

Ignoring the muffled laughs that followed, I strode down the stairs toward the door, past the blurry shapes of the Jinn on the first floor.

"Jezebel?" Shem's voice floated toward me as I twisted the door handle. I ignored him too.

I couldn't let him see me like this.

My feet hit the thick carpet of the hallway, and I traveled.

Reappearing outside my room, I shoved through the door, slamming it behind me, and burst into tears.

I didn't belong here.

I knew it. They knew it. The only one who didn't was Prince Shem. But if he hadn't figured it out yet, he would soon.

A soft knock sounded on the door seconds later.

I barely heard it at first, through my sobs.

Another knock.

This time, I caught myself, silencing my cries so they couldn't be heard through the door, though the tears didn't stop flowing.

"Jezebel?" It was Shem's voice. "I don't mean to intrude, but you looked upset."

I hesitated.

Swiping at the tears with my sleeve, I tried to force a calm I didn't feel before I swung open the door.

"May I come in?" he asked, mostly as a formality, since I'd already stepped back to let him enter.

The door clicked softly shut behind him and we stood in silence. I tried to think of something to say, staring at his polished silver boots that matched his decorative armor.

"What happened?" his voice was a little unsure, something I hadn't heard from him before.

I raised my gaze to his. The concern in his eyes made me give in. With a sigh, I chose my words carefully. "I think you were right about the council not wanting me here."

He stood, agitated. "Who's making you feel unwanted?" Beginning to pace, he ran a hand through his unruly hair and turned back to me. "Give me their names. I'll make certain they don't mistreat you again."

Instead, I pressed my lips together. If I told him about Jerusha and Milcah, he'd remove me from their circle, but would any other circle be better? Especially if they thought I was complaining about them to Shem? Unlikely. At least in this circle I knew who I couldn't trust. "It's not important," I murmured, lowering my gaze.

"Jezebel." Shem's tone was fierce. He knelt beside the bed until I met his gaze. "If someone is causing you pain, you *must* tell me."

I pressed my lips together, attempting a small smile. "I promise I'm stronger than you think. I'm probably a little homesick, that's all."

Shem gave me a look that said he didn't believe me for a second. Rubbing a hand across his face, he blew out a breath and leaned against the window ledge. He stared out at the gardens below.

After a moment, I joined him, touching his fingers lightly. "They just need more time to get used to me. I'll sway them, don't worry."

The tension in his shoulders eased slightly. He sighed, curling his fingers around mine and squeezing once before letting go. "I know you will."

We stared out the window without speaking. Below, at least a dozen Jinn strolled along different garden paths or lounged on wooden benches. I could only make out a few recognizable faces from this distance.

I lifted my gaze past them to where the enormous River Mem flowed through the middle of the city. It passed through the acropolis, which circled the city, entering on one side and exiting on the other.

Even from this distance, the fierce waters raged and churned, reflecting my inner turmoil. I kept my face smooth, not wanting Shem to see. While I pretended confidence with him, I'd learned not to trust others once before, and I shouldn't have hoped it'd be different here. I wouldn't expect to make any friends on Shem's council. If anything, I'd already made some enemies.

"It's my fault you were unprepared." Shem broke the silence finally, shaking his head. "I should've warned you."

"Of what?"

"Life in court involves a lot of... maneuvering. It's something I've always lived with. I'm afraid I've grown so used to it, that it didn't occur to me I should give you some training."

"All right," I said slowly, frowning. "Train me."

Whatever that meant.

He smiled a little. "There's that charmingly stubborn streak of yours." He gestured for us to sit.

I sagged onto the bed as he pulled up the desk chair to sit across from me. "It's all about learning how to twist their words before they can twist yours. After time you'll begin to phrase things more carefully as well, which will remove their own opportunities for insult. You are just as intelligent as they are—more so. Your lack of pretense shouldn't be mocked. It's a noble quality more Jinn should have—it's what drew me to you in the first place."

THE SECRET SHADOW

I tried not to scoff. That felt like a lie to make me feel better.

"Truly." He must've seen through me. He leaned closer, more sincere than I'd ever seen him. "You've just never required the skill of manipulation before."

After a pause, he added more softly, "That's something I very much admire about you."

* * *

TWO MONTHS LATER, Shem's declaring how he felt had turned out to be a rare occurrence. But I *had* begun to find my feet in the council's slanted conversations.

Sometimes.

As I strolled through the gardens, enjoying the sweet smells and the shade along one path, I refused to admit I was avoiding my circle today. I simply needed some fresh air.

Whether that was true or not, it didn't matter.

From the opposite direction, a small group of council members approached, glancing at each other.

"Jezebel," Milcah greeted me from the front of the group. "You must be taking a glory walk as well."

Someone snickered at my confused expression. "She doesn't know what that means, dear."

Milcah sighed, patting my arm as if I was a child of eight and she was an elderly old woman, though we were both an equal eighteen-years-old. "It's a castle term, I do apologize, everyone else would know it." They weren't being very subtle today. "It essentially means taking full advantage of a beautiful sunny day because you can afford to—that would explain why you'd never heard of it before."

Soft chuckles came from the others as I flushed.

Before I could answer, a member of the Jinni Guard flashed onto the path before us. "I come from the castle with a message from the prince for his council." Though I was closest to him, he handed the note to Milcah instead. He didn't give me a second glance before traveling away.

Without a word, Milcah read the message, then passed it to the Jinni behind her. She traveled.

"What does it say?" I asked, as the next man read it and imitated Milcah, handing it over and disappearing as well.

Irritated, I refused to repeat myself. I waited for my turn, but when the last council member finished the note, he simply let go and vanished, leaving me alone.

The paper fluttered to the ground, then took off down the path, carried by a sudden gust of wind.

I was forced to chase it.

Grunting, I snatched it up, pulling the hair out of my eyes as I tried to catch my breath and read the note:

There's been a discovery. Council meeting at your earliest convenience.
—Shem.

Short and straightforward, they could've easily conveyed what it said before they'd left.

The real message from all of them was clear: I was *not* one of them.

Though their scorn was usually more veiled than this, their intent was obvious. And the Jinni Guard went out of their way to confirm the sentiment, as if despite the simple upbringing many of them had, they were somehow also above me.

I did *not* belong.

The worst part was, I felt the same way.

3

"I NEED TO SEE the prince." I strode down the hallway, stopping before the double doors that led to the council chambers. As expected, no one had waited to make sure I was coming.

Thick red carpet muffled my voice and the clink of polished silver armor as Gabriel, one of the Jinni Guards, shifted his crystal spear to block the entrance.

Neither his armor or weapons were nearly as intimidating as his expression, however. Impassive, yet unapproachable, it hid the Gifts that lay beneath the surface, but I hadn't forgotten what Shem said: *a mind-reader.*

Most castle residents spent years learning to shield their minds, while I'd only truly begun practicing two months ago. I was still in many ways an untried beginner.

I envisioned a wall around my thoughts as a mental defense, like I'd been taught back in my discipline years. It took effort to carefully lay brick after brick until the imagined wall grew thick and strong. Was it enough? I worried he could somehow hear my heartbeat quickening.

He lowered his gaze to mine. Silence stretched between us, making my eye twitch.

It took everything I had not to look away.

If there was another way to see Shem today, I wouldn't be here.

But he was on the other side of that door.

Despite the fact that Gabriel knew me well, he still kept his crystal spear barred across the gilded gold door, unmoving. "Business?"

"Council meeting." The same thing I always said. I could share details, but like most Jinn, I preferred my privacy.

The prince's council was smaller than both the king's and the queen's. Somewhere between two and three dozen Jinn. But he used his for more meaningful ventures than planning frivolous parties like his mother or getting caught up in politics like his father. Since I'd joined his council a little over two months ago, we'd searched for missing Jinn, closed wayward portals, discussed the growing attacks from the Khaanevaade, and dealt with spells, enchantments, and other equally important things.

Since Gabriel wasn't part of Shem's council, however, none of these things were any of his business.

"Take a seat, and I'll be with you shortly," he replied finally.

It's going to be one of those days, is it?

"I'm in a bit of a hurry," I said with false cheer, speaking slowly as if talking to a child. "Maybe you could practice your castle defenses on someone else today?" I didn't need anyone to tell me that he was yet again attempting to read my mind, stalling in case I slipped and gave him an opening.

"Apologies," he said, though he barely hid the glint of enjoyment in his eyes. "Occasional delays are just a precaution for the prince's sake."

And if it's for the prince, how can I argue? I pressed my hands against my skirts so he wouldn't notice when they trembled.

I'm strong enough to keep him out. Or at least, that's what I told myself, trying not to think what might happen if I dropped my guard and let him see something from my past.

No doubt that's exactly what he hoped for, and the reason he made me wait so long and so often.

Despite living in the castle for months now, visiting the prince's council rooms almost daily, Gabriel and the others in the Jinni Guard still didn't like or trust me.

Maybe they never would.

Though there were comfortable chairs conveniently placed along the wall for instances like this, I didn't sit like Gabriel requested—that would only fuel his misguided power-trip.

But I did take a step back, crossing my arms and drawing in deep breaths for patience. This wasn't the first time Gabriel or the other guards tried to put me in my place, and it probably wouldn't be the last.

That didn't make it any easier to ignore his eyes on me, though.

Ever since I'd arrived, I'd been on their bad side. None of my offenses were intentional. But in some ways, Shem's council was right, I was an outsider. I didn't understand the customs of the castle. I was bound to break some rules.

"Do you take issue with all of Prince Shem's council members? Or just me?" I muttered under my breath, trying to hide the growing sense that maybe he *should* keep me out.

He acted as if he hadn't heard.

In fact, he wasn't even acknowledging my presence anymore, staring blankly at the opposite wall.

The arrogance of the Guard, I was used to. But the poorly veiled contempt always reminded me I might never find a place here. How many years would pass before they'd consider me one of them?

Briefly, I imagined striding down the red carpet that led back to the heart of the castle, then on to my room. It was tempting. Shem would probably never learn that I'd been here in the first place. But I didn't want to hide any more than I already had been.

I also didn't want to complain to Shem. He'd done so much for me already. The problem wasn't just Gabriel anyway; all the Guard members had taken on his opinion of me. If it wasn't him denying me entrance, it'd be another.

I was gripping the sleeves of my dark green, floor-length gown unconsciously. With effort, I relaxed my fingers. I turned away from Gabriel, pretending to study the artwork hanging on the wall across from us instead.

Smoothing out the crumpled fabric, I let my arms hang loosely so I wouldn't be tempted to wring the poor dress any further. I'd shifted the fabric to give it a slight shimmer of gold beneath the first layer, with thicker threads of gold woven through the bodice and sheer sleeves.

It was nothing like the simple short dresses and sandals I was used to. Yet it still didn't measure up to the stylish dresses some of the other council members wore—gowns made of seemingly liquid gold, fabric that rippled like fire, a skirt full of flowers that bloomed on their own, feathers of all shapes and sizes, mermaid scales… really anything that glowed, swirled, or seemed impossible. Spells always enhanced them somehow.

I could only do simple shifts to my clothing before my abilities lost their effect, but truthfully that was for the best. Anything more extravagant and someone might question how I could afford it with the modest clothing budget Shem had provided.

This dress was purchased from that budget, which meant that technically it was from him. I pressed my fingers into the sheer fabric along my sleeves trying to draw strength from that.

He wanted me here, even if no one else did.

That was the reason I didn't give up or complain, despite over two months of this treatment.

"Gabriel," a female voice said behind me in a warm tone that suggested a smile. I recognized her voice instantly. *Jerusha.* As one of Shem's council members since the day he'd begun working with a council, she and the prince had grown up together in the castle. She'd let me know on my first day here that she and the prince had been friends for years. *Chased after him for years, more like it.*

I turned to face her, momentarily stunned, as usual, by her dress. The top piece was an ebony corset. Decorative gold chains delicately held it up, wrapping around her neck and shoulders. But my gaze was drawn to the skirt, where the black flowed like lava into molten red, orange, and even small flickers of yellow fire as it billowed out and *moved* around her legs.

Her eyes slowly trailed down my own dim, green dress, hanging flat and lifeless. A slit along one side revealed my favorite pair of sandals, wrapping around my feet and calves, but they were plain leather. No embellishments or decorations.

A flush of shame rose to my cheeks. Under her gaze, my clothes seemed childish. She'd never wear something so simple. But no one on the council shared their clothing spells with me, and I had too much pride to ask. It'd only fuel their gossip about how little I knew about castle life.

Gabriel lifted his spear, allowing her to pass.

My whole body clenched.

Jerusha's mouth twisted up at the corner. She didn't bother to vouch for me or reprimand Gabriel, though he was clearly making me wait longer than necessary. Turning the door knob, she chuckled softly as she entered. "Perhaps we'll see you inside."

The door closed with a heavy thud.

I shrugged as if I couldn't be bothered to care, struggling to keep my hands loose and relaxed. Forcing my chin up, I leveled a bored look at Gabriel.

I could've sworn his lips twisted up slightly in a smirk.

He and Jerusha both seemed to take pleasure in undermining me—everyone in the castle did. Always imperceptibly. Like this, in a way that couldn't be called out without sounding foolish.

If I put in a complaint about Gabriel, he'd only protest that he was doing his job. He'd swear he gave me the same treatment as anyone else: a routine check for threats. Worse, he might take my unwillingness to be detained as an opportunity to question my loyalty to the crown.

On the other hand, if I accused Jerusha of allowing the slight, she'd place a hand over her heart, as she said to Shem in a condescending tone, "I do apologize, your majesty. I didn't realize the girl needed a babysitter."

They knew what they were doing.

I stood awkwardly in the quiet hall, ashamed, waiting for Gabriel to stop denying me entrance to the council.

THE SECRET SHADOW

This could last a few more minutes, or, if he was feeling spiteful, a few more hours.

I'd had enough.

I refused to spend any more time standing humiliated in the hall.

My voice broke the silence, startling both of us with the forcefulness. "This seems to be either a deliberate slight or a disturbing loss of memory." I almost broke off there, but forced myself to continue, pretending confidence I didn't feel. "Since I can't *imagine* a member of the Guard being intentionally disrespectful to a royal council member, I have to assume it's the latter." I gave an exaggerated sigh, shaking my head at Gabriel. "Perhaps the prince should be informed. I was under the impression the Guard needed to be sharp-witted." I started to turn away. "I suppose I'll have to let him know that not everyone in the Guard is up to the royal family's standards."

I strode down the hall.

"Wait," Gabriel called after a few steps.

I turned, arms crossed.

Grudgingly, after a long pause, he pulled back his spear. He didn't apologize, refusing to even meet my eyes as he allowed me to pass.

I gave him as much space as possible, holding back a shiver as I slipped through the large door.

Smoothing my face as I entered the large council room, I made sure not to show any sign of my embarrassment from the hallway.

A couple Jinn glanced up from where they were browsing the dark mahogany bookshelves or seated in the surrounding blue velvet furniture. A large fire roared in the hearth that stood as tall as some of the Jinn nearby.

Dust motes danced in the light shining in through the wall of windows. It gave the whole room a magical feel.

On the balcony above, a murmur of conversation drifted down, but otherwise the room was fairly empty. There were a handful of council members with Prince Shem, gathered around one of the large tables.

Milcah was the only one who saw me coming. She wore a gown that made her look like midnight incarnate—a deep blue with diamonds flickering all across it like stars in the night sky. The diamonds trailed along the low neckline heavily to draw attention there, as well as lined a cape that looked like a shooting star flowing behind her.

She stood as I entered, drawing nearer to the prince where he hunched over something at the long table. Whatever she murmured was too soft for me to hear, but it distracted him from my approaching footsteps. Her silky black hair cascaded down her shoulder and arm to land on the table, creating a thick curtain that blocked my view of whatever they were working on.

Frustration mixed with shame, but I kept those feelings hidden as I crossed the council chambers to join them.

Clearly I was late for some new finding.

Despite being paired with this circle for months now, none of them cared if I attended this meeting or not.

Face burning, I didn't say a word about the exclusion. Whenever I did, Milcah would cheerily say something like, "Oh this? We didn't call an official meeting darling, we just *happened* to all be here. No need to get all worked up over a chance conversation." Or in this case, since Shem *had* called a meeting, she'd probably ask why I'd dawdled. I pictured her turning my delay into a question of my commitment to the council.

I'd rather not be forced to swallow another story like that today, so I kept my mouth shut and joined them.

Dorcas glanced up next. She stood beside the table instead of sitting, likely because she didn't want to crush the vivid red flowers that circled her white skirts. They grew along layers designed to look like hills, leading up to the massive red mushroom cap that circled her tiny waist and emphasized her hips. Sparks of light dusted the skirts and bodice, giving everything an otherworldly glow. Her dull blue eyes darted between me and the prince, as if she was torn between acknowledging me and pretending not to have noticed my arrival, but she didn't have a chance to decide.

"Jezebel," Jerusha's cheerful voice rang out in the library as if she hadn't just seen me in the hall. She was louder than necessary, making Laban startle and drop his pen.

He turned toward me with a wide grin, taking off his reading glasses. I could never decide if his attentive gaze and abundance of questions were due to interest or ulterior motives. Since he spent time with the Jerusha and Milcah, I tended to assume the latter.

His decorative armor gleamed silver with gold embellishments, just as much the height of fashion as the women. The stomach muscles on the armor were chiseled to look extremely defined, which made me want to roll my eyes. Laban rarely even walked anywhere if he could travel, much less took the time to build his physique.

When I finally allowed myself to sneak a glance at Shem, his eyes were already on me.

"Someone found a *Kathenoth* and delivered it to the castle," Jerusha said before Shem could greet me. "It's a thrilling find—oh, I don't suppose you know what a Kathenoth is, do you, dear?" Unlike Milcah's tactic of edging me out of conversations and opportunities, Jerusha had a different strategy. Whenever possible, she found a way to make me seem simple. Useless.

I sent her a scathing look behind Shem's back, but I didn't expect any less.

"Everyone in Jinn knows about Kathenoths," I replied with a sweet smile, as if I hadn't even noticed her attempt.

THE SECRET SHADOW

A Kathenoth was simply a fanciful term for a journal that you *meant* for someone to read.

As Jerusha passed the small book to me, I hid my distaste and took it. It felt heavier than it really was, like the secrets it held weighed it down.

Every paranoid Jinni with enemies—which described almost everyone in the castle—kept at least one Kathenoth. Usually they were strategically placed somewhere they could easily be found if their owner vanished.

Pretending to study the book, I swallowed.

It wasn't a perfect fail-safe. There was still a chance no one would happen upon it, or at least, not in time to reverse the damage done.

I offered it to Laban, who was closest to me, wanting to be rid of it.

"I've already had a turn," he said. The others refused it as well. Shem reached out to take the little book, and I held back a sigh of relief.

He set it on the table and slowly flipping through the pages. We looked on, waiting quietly. I kept my eyes on his hands, ignoring the others, until a servant stepped up. Passing the book to Jerusha, he stood to speak with them.

A Kathenoth offered protection from the *Shakach* spell—often referred to simply as the forbidden forgetting spell. Shakach was a hard word to translate, but it meant something between ignorance and withering. And that was exactly what it did: it erased a Jinni from existence, even in their own mind. It made them—and everyone else—forget who they were, filling in the holes left behind until they weren't even noticeable anymore.

Jerusha stroked the pages of the little journal where it lay open on the table, drawing my attention to the delicate handwriting, before she snapped it shut.

I shivered.

Without a Kathenoth, you might never be found.

It occurred to me that the others were uncharacteristically quiet as well, and I risked a glance around the table. Perhaps they were equally unsettled.

If a Jinni wrote down evidence of their existence—as well as what to do with their belongings if the discovery happened after memories grew too fragmented and distant to repair—those they left behind had a very small chance of breaking the spell.

That was the key to a Kathenoth: having someone who would find it.

As the servant spoke with Shem, I snuck a glance at his profile.

I wasn't sure I did.

Though I'd never tell Jerusha or the others, I hadn't bothered to make a Kathenoth of my own because I was afraid. If I left bread crumbs behind, there might not be anyone to follow them. The only person who'd care if I disappeared was Shem. And only three short months of memories needed to be erased before he'd forget me easily.

What if no one had found this little book? The embellishments on the cover were beautiful, but nothing guaranteed it would be noticed. What if it'd gone undetected for years, until it was too late, and the memories were impossible to bring back?

Shem turned back to us.

Jerusha's lips were turned up in a cat-like smile.

Now that I'd had time to think of an insult, I wished I could've recommended she make ten Kathenoths since she seemed so concerned about being forgettable.

I might've come up with the response sooner, if the discovery hadn't left me flustered.

Even when I'd abandoned my friends in lizard form in the jungle, I hadn't dared to do a Shakach spell on them.

Not only did it break our strict code of ethics, including the Three Unbreakable Laws, but it also came with consequences. The dangers of a spell like that weren't worth it. It could backfire and obliterate the memories of the spell-doer just as easily as the intended victim. Yet there were Jinn who disregarded the potential repercussions.

Stepping closer, I peered down at the little book.

It terrified me to imagine being erased from memory so completely that I'd never be missed.

Or rather, I'd never even be *remembered.*

I determined then and there to start a journal tonight. I'd leave it in the middle of my bed where it'd be impossible to miss.

"Interesting," I lied. "My Kathenoth is a similar color."

"Oh, darling," Jerusha tsked, interrupting my thoughts. She held a dramatic hand over her black leather corset and the gold chains that held it in place as she shook her head. "Don't tell me you only have *one* Kathenoth?"

4

I FLUSHED, FRUSTRATED THAT she'd somehow managed to turn that back around on me.

Jerusha would be merciless if she discovered I didn't have even one Kathenoth hidden for someone to find.

Keeping my gaze on the little journal to avoid looking at Shem and giving myself away, I wondered yet again if he'd feel the hole of my absence deeply enough to come looking for me, despite the lack of memories. Ever since arriving at the castle, my feelings for him had grown, but I still didn't know how he felt. I wavered between believing his feelings were there, beneath the surface, and at the same time, convincing myself that I'd imagined everything.

"Perhaps fresh eyes will help." Shem saved me from having to answer the taunt. "We've hardly made any progress on discovering the owner of this Kathenoth. Why don't you see what you can make of it?" He smiled and waved me forward.

His decorative armor was understated compared to the design of Laban's chiseled abdominal muscles, though it still included shoulder wings and a brace along each forearm. The metal gleamed in the light and had the royal family's insignia embossed across the breastplate.

His kindness encouraged me, even though after months at the castle, I now knew he offered this same consideration to everyone he met, not just me. It was a quality I both liked and disliked about him. Right now, his smile included the others equally, and I felt a twinge of jealousy.

Still, I stepped close enough that the sheer sleeve of my gown brushed his forearm. Catching Milcah's frown from the corner of my eye, I smiled up at him.

Laban's slight smirk told me he was equally aware of the tensions around this table.

The only one who seemed oblivious was Shem, leaning around me to point at the open page where the handwriting was nearly illegible. "Listen to what it says here…" His warm fingers brushed over mine, distracting me slightly as he turned the page and began to read, "'I didn't intend to go to the anointing. But in the end, I made an appearance…' Do you realize what this means?"

He grinned at me, brows raised.

The anointing.

An anointing only took place before a Crowning Ceremony, which only happened twice in a century.

Every 50 years, on the last day of summer, the reigning sovereign of Jinn would remove the enchanted crown that enhanced their natural Gifts, strengthening them and affording them absolute control. The removal severed the enchantment.

If the ruler stood uncontested, they'd be crowned anew, but if an heir to the throne stepped forward, the ruler would concede the throne—and the crown—to their heir.

Though the last two centuries had passed with King Jubal wearing the crown, he'd made it known that he was preparing to pass it on to Shem this coming year.

Shem's Crowning Ceremony was still almost a year away, but the anointing—one of the first steps that would lead to Shem's succession—had just taken place last month.

The night before the anointing, I'd been sneaking through the halls in lizard form, still familiarizing myself with the castle, when I'd caught Shem deep in conversation with his parents. Queen Samaria had been lecturing him, "It's time you grow more serious about preparing to rule. You're setting the example for all of Jinn."

King Jubal had chimed in, in a much harsher tone, "These little explorations were fine when you were younger, but it's time to give them up."

And Shem had.

Not only had he stopped inviting me to go on adventures with him outside the castle, but he'd also called an official council meeting the next day, speaking more solemnly than I'd ever seen him, "My father trusts that I will be the leader Jinn needs. As such, I plan to dedicate more time to the tasks he gives me. We

THE SECRET SHADOW

will take on more duties as a council as well."

My brow had furrowed, but no one else in the room seemed surprised.

As the anointing came and went, I'd seen Shem less and less.

My depressing thoughts distracted me from Shem's question long enough for Milcah to beat me to the answer. "Your anointing was last month," she stated the obvious, making me want to roll my eyes. "And there hasn't been another in over a century. Which means that unless this journal is over a hundred years old—" she stroked the open page, which still looked brand new, giving the prince a sultry smile— "This Kathenoth was abandoned recently."

As she leaned back to lounge against the blue velvet chair, she ran graceful fingers through her dark hair and smiled at me innocently.

Laban scowled. "That makes this entire situation much more urgent," he said, leaning over the table. "If it's that fresh, there's still a very real threat until the one who cast the spell is found. What if one of us is next? Or the royal family?"

Someone willing to use the Shakach spell once wouldn't be afraid to use it again.

That sobered the rest of us, even the prince.

"It's impossible to know for sure whether or not the royal family is in danger," Shem said after a beat of silence. "Ultimately, there are many precautions in place to defend ourselves from such attacks, but I will entrust this Kathenoth to your circle and have full faith you'll find the owner shortly."

There were layers of pressure within that statement. I wanted to find the owner for Shem's sake, but also for my own, to prove to the council that I was worthy.

I sank into an open chair. The others frowned and I realized it'd belonged to Shem. "So sorry," I murmured, moving to stand, but he waved me back into it.

"No apology necessary, I need a moment anyway," Shem said, brushing off my embarrassment. He strode across the room toward the windows where he began to pace.

Turning back to the table, four sets of eyes gazed at me with varying levels of irritation. It was hard to say if it was at the situation or at my claiming the prince's attention. Maybe they simply didn't think I was capable of solving the Kathenoth. But to avoid direct conflict, which was rarely done in the castle, I turned my gaze to the open journal on the table and began to read.

One page at a time, I poured over each detail, trying to get a sense of the owner. The one who'd been erased.

The library grew dark as the sun set. Candles were lit to make up for the difference. I barely noticed the hush fall over the room as most of the council left for dinner.

"What do you make of it?" Shem leaned over my shoulder unexpectedly. His eyes, so light blue they were almost white like his mothers, met mine. In rare moments like this, when it was just the two of us again, it felt the way it had when we'd first met. I could almost feel a tangible thread connecting us, telling me I must mean something to him, because he'd come to mean so much to me.

"What do *you* make of it?" I asked to hide my surprise—I hadn't heard him return. I'd gotten so caught up in the writing that I'd even managed to tune out the soft murmur of conversation from the others.

In response, Shem sat in Milcah's open chair, which she'd abandoned at some point in the last hour or so to speak with Laban by the fire. Her eyes bore into me, but I ignored her.

"It's obviously a woman," he began. "And it seems to insinuate that there are multiple threats to her life." He flipped back a couple pages, still near the end of the book, where the writing stopped and the remaining pages were blank. He pointed to a blank space where a name should've been but the spell had erased it. "This would suggest she had good reason to be concerned."

I cleared my throat, and he paused, nodding for me to go ahead. "I noticed that," I began softly, hoping no one else would join us, in case I was wrong. "It's just... It's almost..." I searched for the right word. "Forced? As if the author is trying to mislead anyone who reads it?"

Shem's brows rose, disappearing under his unruly dark hair. Frowning down at the page again, he tilted his head and scooted closer, spinning the little journal to face him. "What makes you say that?"

Though Dorcas had long since left for dinner, Jerusha came to stand over us with crossed arms, trailed soon after by Milcah and Laban. I could almost feel them sifting through what they'd overheard to find a weakness.

I shut them out and tried to focus.

Milcah leaned in, wedging herself into the small space between Shem and I, under the pretense of studying the journal closer.

Reluctantly, I leaned back.

It was either that or press my face into her generous chest.

Another council member named Risha, with a fiery orange dress the same color as her eyes, drew closer to our little group. Though she wasn't part of this particular assignment, Shem's excitement had clearly caught her attention. Whatever I said next was guaranteed to spread throughout the rest of the council and be twisted as it fit their needs—especially if I accidentally misspoke.

"It's in the little details." I cleared my throat again, lifting my chin and straightening my spine. "The beginning doesn't line up with the end... At first, the owner of the Kathenoth is smitten by a young man. She doesn't name him, but you can tell from the context that they spend a lot of time together. She also cites quite a few comments from family members against him... I think—" My mouth was dry enough that I had to swallow before I could keep speaking. If I was wrong, the others would love to rip me to shreds and declare me unfit for the council. They'd been looking for excuses to do so since I'd arrived.

THE SECRET SHADOW

Though I trailed off, Shem's frown deepened, as he reviewed the text in this new light. When I still didn't continue, he glanced up impatiently. "Please speak your truth, Jezebel. We have all made guesses in our time that required the inspection of others. No one will judge you for attempting to decipher what happened here. Your guess is as good as anyone else's."

Inhaling deeply, I hid my relief. They certainly couldn't judge me now, after *that* speech. At least, not openly.

"Here, she says she wants to leave Resh with this unnamed man for one of the smaller islands. He's mentioned on nearly every page. Then, suddenly..." I flipped a couple pages, finding the one that had caught my attention. "Here. The tone shifts. It sounds as if an entirely different person wrote the following pages, which doesn't make any sense." Jinn with Kathenoths didn't share.

"It makes me wonder..." I cleared my throat. "I think she made a decision to portray a different story on purpose."

"Why would she do that?" Shem asked and murmurs of agreement came from the others.

Ignoring their skeptical looks, I made my tone firm. "I believe the owner of this Kathenoth cast the Shakach spell over herself."

Slowly Shem exhaled, dragging a hand down his face, shaking his head.

My heart sank.

I'd gone too far. Clearly I'd imagined it. Though he'd barred the others from judging me, he was obviously forming a poor opinion of me himself.

"How did we not see it?" he whispered.

My breath hitched. "What?"

"It's impossible to miss, once you point it out," Shem said in awe, letting his gaze drift up to meet mine. An incredulous smile slowly stretched across his face. "It's such a risky move that it hadn't even occurred to me. Especially since it'd require additional protection spells to allow her to keep her own memories, while everyone else forgot."

I bit my lip.

When he said it like that, it sounded even more implausible. I began to question myself along with the others.

But Shem continued to nod and murmur to himself, as he flipped through the pages. "Yes. I believe that may be exactly what she did."

"You're not truly considering this story she wove out of nothing?" Jerusha protested.

Now that my heart rate was returning to normal, I let my lips curve into a smile.

Shem's response was polite on the surface, but his tone held an edge. "Where you see nothing, Jerusha, there is in actuality an extensive trail of breadcrumbs that Jezebel has found." He smiled at her to soften his words, but they cut off her objections just the same. While the prince was often free with his compliments—

a fact that normally bothered me—I basked in Jerusha's annoyance now.

He wasn't done. "Jezebel, you seem to have an unparalleled ability to dig up the truth in texts where others see nothing."

My smile didn't slip, but a small part of me grew still.

My understanding came from my own secrets.

Suddenly, I wished I'd let someone else solve the Kathenoth, rather than put myself under the spotlight.

The eyes on me were like hot coals raking across my face.

Prince Shem stood unexpectedly with a relaxed stretch, smiling at everyone. "I believe that's our cue to retire for the evening. We'll still study the Kathenoth privately until we can break the spell and verify this story with a name, and I'll have the Guard review it as well, but I think we can all agree that there's no threat here. I believe the owner simply doesn't want to be found."

As we all turned to leave, Shem brushed my arm lightly, signaling for me to stay behind. Though Jerusha, Milcah, and the other council members who'd joined us all likely noticed, they respected the prince enough to continue exiting.

As the door clicked shut, Shem turned to the fire, putting a little distance between us. Things like this confused me. Was he shy? Or maybe he wished to avoid any feelings he might have? Perhaps there were no feelings to evade in the first place. The clues he gave me could lead equally to both possibilities.

"I don't know how you do it," he said over his shoulder with a smile.

I shrugged, even though he wasn't looking, and joined him at the fire. Compliments from Shem would never get old. At least I could blame the heat of the fire for my rosy cheeks.

"You look for complicated solutions," I replied in a soft voice. "Usually our wants and desires are far more simple: Survival. Protection. Love."

The last word came out a bit breathy.

I averted my eyes to the Kathenoth that he still held. "In this case, the owner seems driven by fear. She made foolish decisions, and was forced to protect herself."

I could see it so clearly, because the owner might as well have been me.

Closing my eyes for a moment to hide the feelings that surged up, I tried—unsuccessfully—to push away what'd happened a few short months ago.

Unbidden, the memory of holding a small glass jar made my fingertips tingle, as if I were experiencing it now. As if it was just yesterday that Asher had threatened to reveal my secrets. In the heat of the moment, I'd used my shape-shifting Gift to turn him into a lizard on instinct. Forced into the awful choice to protect myself or lose everything, that choice had led to the same fate for the rest of my friends. A rash chain of events had followed. I still wondered if I could've stopped it somehow.

Blinking, I pasted a smile on my face as I met Shem's gaze.

THE SECRET SHADOW

"Is everything well?" Instead of his usual scholarly gaze focused on some internal thought, his piercing eyes were now pinned on my face, seeing more than I'd meant for him to.

I was tempted to tell him.

My desire to be honest with Shem grew each day that I spent in his presence. Biting my lip, I hesitated. I couldn't share such a terrible secret until I knew if I were truly special to him, or if he simply made everyone feel that way.

If I revealed that I was both a shape-shifter and the reason for my friends' disappearances, he might never see me the same again.

I was terrified to take that risk.

Rejection would be the least of my problems, though. I'd also be forced to leave my new home in the castle. Depending on the severity of my offense, I'd end up in the dungeons, in servitude, or on the run. But worst of all, they'd undoubtedly sever my Gift and leave me to slowly deteriorate until the Severance caused me to give up on living.

I took a deep breath and released it. "Nothing important." I gave him a small smile. It was the best I could do.

"If something is bothering you, I hope you'll share with me," Shem tried again, not moving. The firelight flickered in his eyes, turning them into a pale blue fire of their own.

I considered it. *What if I told him the truth? What would he do?* There were too many unknowns. I'd paused too long to simply brush off his concerns though. "I'm just… thinking of my father."

A partial truth.

After all, when everything had happened, I *had* included my father. I'd abandoned him along with the rest of my friends in the human world. It was harder to regret that particular choice, after everything he'd done.

Shem didn't know that though. I'd led him to believe my father had abandoned me.

"I… wonder if he's thought of me at all in the last few months," I managed to say. Silently, I added to myself, *And if he's still alive…*

That seemed to satisfy Shem.

He placed a warm hand on my arm for a brief second before removing it. "Come," he said with a soft smile. "Let's go to dinner. The others will talk if we don't leave soon."

That was a perfect opportunity for me to ask, *Is there any truth to what they're saying?*

But he'd already turned to leave, taking hold of the door and swinging it open for me.

For the thousandth time, the moment had passed before I could catch it.

5

"LET'S TAKE A QUICK detour." Shem said, as he stepped into the hall and held up the Kathenoth. "I need to put this away." He stretched a hand out to me, indicating that he wanted to travel directly.

I accepted with a smile. "Where're we going?"

"Have you ever been to the vault for enchanted objects?" His fingers curled around mine. We both ignored the pointed look from Gabriel.

My excitement rose as I shook my head. I didn't even know where it was, and I'd explored most of the castle at this point.

"It's deep within the east wing, above the king and queen's private chambers," he said with a grin. That explained why I'd never seen it or heard of it. This side of the castle was heavily guarded and off-limits to most residents.

My sole visit to the east wing beyond Shem's council rooms had been in fly form, late at night. After dodging multiple guards, flying so hard my little heart nearly gave out, I'd decided it wasn't worth the risk to go back.

"If we hurry, we'll have time for a quick tour," he said now, with a squeeze of my fingers right before he traveled, taking me with him.

One second we stood in the bright light of the red carpeted hallway, and the next, we were in a similar hallway, but darker—there weren't any windows here. If Shem hadn't said it was above the royal chambers, I'd have guessed it to be the

THE SECRET SHADOW

lowest level of the castle, instead of the highest. The air was hushed. As if no one came to this floor.

At one end of the hall stood a member of the Guard. Turning my head slowly, so as not to seem suspicious, I looked in the opposite direction.

Another guard.

Her eyes narrowed on my face, but with the prince there, she didn't say anything.

Shem nodded back, acknowledging her briefly, but he was focused on the dark blue door in front of us. The decorative black iron swirled over it creating a design that looked like dozens of thin snakes, woven together in intricate patterns from floor to ceiling. A soft vibration came from the metal. It seemed to expand and shift ever so slightly, almost as if the snakes were alive.

The vault door.

Shem touched the door handle. Without warning, two of the iron snakes uncoiled their heads and struck the prince's hand, wrapping tightly around his wrist, holding him firmly in place.

I hissed in surprise, but Shem didn't flinch.

If I had to guess, I'd say the iron was also spelled against travel. Quite an effective lock.

He waited patiently.

After a long pause, the iron unwound, slithering back into place with metallic scrapes.

The lock clicked open softly.

"It's enchanted to allow my family in, but all others need a key," Shem explained, as the door creaked open. He entered, still holding my hand.

I trailed behind him, blinking as my eyes adjusted to the dark room. There was only one window at the back wall. It created a square of sunlight on the dark wood floor, but otherwise only dim light reached the shelves along the walls. Various tables filled the room, covered in objects, seemingly without rhyme or reason.

Shem lit a candle by the door. It caused a chain reaction spell until all the candles around the room were lit.

My eyes were immediately drawn to the opposite side of the room where an entire wall seemed to glitter.

Light bounced off of countless jewels—rings, earrings, necklaces, and even multiple crowns sat on carved wooden heads designed to display them. In the corner, a dress made of gems sparkled so brightly it made my eyes water. Rubies, emeralds, topaz, sapphire, diamonds, amethysts, onyx, and so many more, were all sewn into the lace. It must weigh more than any woman wearing it ever could, which most likely meant it was enchanted to carry itself.

"This is where we store all Kathenoths." Shem strode toward another shelf, running a hand along all the different bindings before placing the newest

Kathenoth beside the others. I'd barely noticed the bookcase because it was so ordinary. But the shelves were full of journals in all shapes and sizes. Some seemed new, while others looked brittle and ancient, like they'd fall apart if anyone tried to read them now.

Turning away from the books with a shiver, I stepped further into the vault, trailing a hand along a nearby table. It had beautiful carvings all around the mahogany edges and a red velvet cloth on top. There were different display cases for every item.

"Each table holds enchanted objects that somewhat belong in the same category," Shem explained as he joined me.

A key, which didn't seem significant in any way, sat above a handwritten description with a looping cursive. *Enchanted to unlock any door in the world.*

My brows rose. That could be useful.

I slowly circled the table.

A knife... *enchanted to always hit the intended target.*

If someone had that, they'd never lose a fight.

Lifting my gaze, I spun in a slow circle taking in all the other tables with what must be hundreds of objects displayed. Most appeared simple at first glance, but each one came with an inscription for its usage: a lamp, a mirror, a spindle...

There was a magical quality to the air, almost a heaviness. As if the history in these objects was making itself known.

"Feel free to look around." Shem waved a hand at all the tables. "This is the royal family collection. It's been built up over the centuries."

As I passed a mirror, I expected it to show my reflection, but it remained dark, nearly black. Uncomfortable, I didn't stop to read whatever enchantment made it that way, moving away from the enchanted objects instead. "Does anyone use them?"

Shem shrugged. "I'm sure they've all been used at some point. I've studied many of the objects in this room myself, but I still don't know half of them." He lifted the key I'd noticed before, then set it back in its stand gently, before drawing his finger over the spindle beside it. "Some of these were created by the crown for a specific purpose. Others were confiscated—sometimes before they could be used, but usually after."

I drew a shallow breath, feeling like I should whisper. "There's so many."

"Isn't it incredible?"

I nodded, hand hovering over the same table, too awed to risk actually touching anything. "Very."

"Well," he said, gesturing to the shelf of Kathenoths. "Now that that's taken care of, time for dinner."

* * *

THE SECRET SHADOW

NORMALLY WHEN DINING with the prince in the evenings, I found myself competing for his attention with at least half a dozen council members. We rarely spoke. I could only hope it was because he didn't want to play favorites.

Today, however, we entered the dining hall together. I threw my shoulders back and lifted my chin, daring anyone to question it.

At the far end, a long table stood slightly raised for the royal family. It had a dozen extra seats for whichever honored guests they invited to join them. At their backs was an enormous window overlooking the entrance to the main gardens.

The nearest three tables were reserved for the three royal councils. Many more tables filled the large room for other castle residents and guests.

Shem often sat with his council instead of on the raised dais with his parents, especially when they weren't yet present or when he arrived late.

As we reached the council table, he pulled out a chair for me and took the one right beside it.

Over half of his council was still here. Some seemed nearly finished, but they immediately slowed upon Shem's arrival. My best guess was that they'd already dragged out their meal as much as possible. Others looked like they were just beginning. They'd probably circulated throughout the room making conversation, waiting for the prince to show.

Before I could think of something witty to say, Milcah immediately engaged Shem in conversation from across the table. "We were discussing some particularly juicy gossip about her Majesty's newest council member," she murmured, loud enough for us to hear, but not so loud that the unfamiliar woman seated at the queen's council table next to ours would overhear.

"Oh?" Shem replied politely, ever the gentleman. Queen Samaria frequently added to her council and had twice as many members as both the prince and King Jubal's councils put together. Her council table wasn't nearly large enough, so the members tended to rotate between their table, the dais when invited, and whatever open seating the main tables had available.

Since it was common for those on a council to travel for the crown—and in the queen's case to also remove council members on a regular basis—it was difficult to put an exact number on how many she had. But the queen was rumored to have hundreds in her employ.

"What're they saying?" I chimed in, determined not to be ignored.

Though Milcah's mouth curled slightly in distaste, she couldn't avoid a direct question. Still, when she answered, she focused on Shem, as if he were the one who'd asked. "Supposedly she has a strong Gift. Maybe even dangerous."

Servants slipped up to our table unobtrusively, placing the first course before the prince and I, filling our drinks. Because it was Shem, one of them also stayed close by along the wall.

Laban reached for his drink, swirling the dark liquid and gazing thoughtfully out at the gardens. "Perhaps a water-based Gift? Or fire?"

Those Gifts tended to cause the most accidents before the owner got them under control. The king was rumored to have the Gift of fire, though like all Jinn, he tended to keep his Gifts to himself.

Did they have a conversation like this about me when I first joined the council? I held back a shiver. I could only hope they'd been as far off base in their guesses then as they likely were now.

"I think we would've heard of the damage if it were something so obvious as that," Jerusha scoffed, smiling with her teeth bared.

Quirking a brow at Shem, who'd quietly picked up his silverware and begun to cut into the meat on his plate, I asked, "What do you think it might be?"

He set down the heavy silver knife, chewing thoughtfully. The nearby council members all tried to pretend they weren't hanging on his every word as they waited. "I do have to agree with Jerusha. A physical Gift would be fairly noticeable. It's likely more of an internal ability. Something they can use without others being aware of it."

"Such as?" *He means a Gift like mine. Is he going to say shape-shifting?*

A sensation unexpectedly swept over me, almost like being inside a bubble, where the voices around me dimmed and a cool wave washed over my skin.

A small part of me wanted him to say it, if only to know what his reaction to the idea might be. Would he abhor it? Or find it fascinating? Or something in-between?

"I don't know…" It seemed like he cut off for some reason. Then the bubble burst and everything rushed back into clear focus. I sucked in a steadying breath, taking a drink to hide my reaction.

Shem tapped his fingers against the table, considering. The candlelight in the center flickered across his face, highlighting the sharp angles of his cheekbones and jaw. "Perhaps another mind-reader?" He shook his head again at all the possibilities, though he didn't seem concerned—his mental defenses were likely ten times stronger than my own. More likely he was curious.

My shoulders relaxed.

Just last month, a young Jinni from a few islands over, a distant relative of the royal family, had inadvertently revealed a newly formed mind-reading Gift. She'd immediately been pressed into joining the Jinni Guard, with its many checks and balances.

If a Jinni from a powerful family refused an invitation to join the Jinni Guard, it could lead to being banned from Resh, our capital city, for good. All in the name of protecting the royal family, of course. Many Jinn were, in fact, banned from visiting this island due to possessing dangerous Gifts of some kind.

But I'd gathered through hints and whispers that others from less-influential families weren't always offered those options, and often ended up in the dungeons instead. For those who had no family ties to protect them at all, their Gift might be severed completely. It was rare and cruel, but it happened.

A Jinni seldom survived a Severance.

I shivered. Picking up my fork to mask the involuntary movement, I focused on my meal and tried not to think about my utter lack of connections, family or otherwise.

For the rest of the evening, I ignored the conversation swirling around me, not wanting to draw attention. Shem's eyes caught on mine briefly in silent question. I just smiled at him and took another bite.

He'd grown quieter as well, allowing the others to drive the discussion, providing short, simple answers when addressed directly. A few more times, he glanced my way. Both of us knew better than to have an intimate conversation here. But when a server came to refill our drinks, Shem faced him as if to ask a question, murmuring to me instead, "Is everything all right?"

Out of the corner of my eye, Milcah leaned forward a bit, so when I smiled softly and nodded, I pretended my response was to the server as well.

The thin Jinni kept a straight face as she lifted the water carafe and the towel that caught condensation. She was more than used to such things, moving on to refill the other council members drinks without skipping a beat.

Shem met my gaze and licked his lips, seeming to consider.

Before he could say anything, a hand landed on his shoulder. "Your highness."

"Josiah," Shem said, blowing out a breath, turning to face him. I noticed the younger guard was attempting to grow a straggly beard. The prince's face reflected oddly in Josiah's thick armor breastplate. "Is there an urgent matter?" A polite way of asking why he'd so rudely interrupted us during dinner.

I pretended not to listen while peeking over my shoulder at them. Josiah had pulled back his hand and stood at attention.

"Actually yes, your highness—" Josiah's frown landed on me briefly, before darting around the table, "—it is urgent. The castle has been placed on high alert."

Without being obvious, I used my drink as an excuse to turn, surveying the room as I took a sip. Where one guard usually stood near each table, now there were three. They weren't eating or even joining in the conversations. If anything, they eyed the familiar dinner guests with narrowed eyes.

My skin prickled.

Instinct told me something was wrong.

"I've been asked to bring you to the royal chambers immediately," Josiah continued.

The king and queen's rooms.

The heavy carpet gave a soft whoosh as Shem pushed back his chair and stood, folding his napkin and depositing it neatly beside his plate.

"Alone," Josiah added, as his eyes swung to mine once more.

I hadn't realized I'd stood.

I flushed.

Lowering myself back into the chair with grace, I pretended not to notice his disdain or the council members murmuring about my audacity.

"My apologies," Prince Shem said to the table, but his eyes stayed glued to mine. He wrinkled his nose in annoyance. "I'm sure it's nothing. I'll be back promptly." To the rest of the table, he added with a wave of his hand. "Please don't wait on ceremony, continue with your meal."

Nodding with the others, I stared at his back and watched his leather boots until they disappeared between tables, heading for the large doors at the dining hall entrance, where they would travel the remaining distance to the east side of the castle.

I softly let out the breath I'd been holding.

"Is there something we should know about?" Jerusha's loud voice drew everyone's attention back to me.

When I gave her a blank look, she waved in Shem's direction. "You seemed to believe you belonged in a high security meeting?"

Oh, *that*.

I flushed again and cleared my throat, taking a sip of water in a desperate attempt to buy time to think. "I'm afraid the guard misunderstood," I said lightly, careful not to blame Jerusha, or she'd dig in her heels. "I was about to go to the lavatory. The timing was coincidental." To prove it, I pushed back from the table and stood again. "The Guard is always trying to cause a spectacle. Thankfully, our *council* is above such things."

Before she could question me further, I slipped away from the table, keeping a casual pace until I reached one of the doors and exited the room. Once out of sight and away from the enchantments in the dining room that prevented travel, I immediately flashed away to a familiar, dark alcove near Shem's council rooms.

Something told me this crisis, whatever it was, would affect me. I needed to get closer so I could overhear.

Hidden away in the shadowy corner, I peeked out briefly to make sure I was alone, before shifting.

Small, smaller, and smaller still.

Tiny insect feet replaced my limbs.

Membrane-thin wings stretched out from my back.

My two eyes altered to become a few thousand on each side.

I was a fly on the wall.

Pushing off, I flapped my new wings with all my strength, racing toward the royal quarters.

As I passed the tightly closed door to their rooms, I shot down the hall and back, mind racing. *How do I get in?* I knew from experience and court gossip that

THE SECRET SHADOW

the royal chambers didn't have many weaknesses. The outside windows were spelled even when open, so it wasn't possible to get in from outside. As far as the interior, the chambers had multiple doors, but they were all currently closed.

At the end of the hall, a meeting room frequently used by the king and queen was propped open. It wasn't connected to the rooms they used now... except, possibly, by some lavatory pipes between the bathing rooms...

I veered sharply toward it.

I can't believe I'm about to do this. Though I'd entertained the idea a few times before, I'd always dismissed it. I'd never been this desperate.

Inside the meeting room, I headed straight for the lavatory, where the yawning dark hole led to a series of pipes that eventually drained out of the castle.

Since I'd refused to stoop this low in the past, I could only hope it connected to the lavatory in the royal chambers as well.

Interesting.

The smells that would've disgusted me in human form seemed strangely normal. *This shape has some benefits.* Flying through the nearly pitch-black pipes, I hit an intersection that led straight ahead, as well as upward, and down. I followed my instincts.

Up.

Light appeared above.

I hurtled out of the disgusting pipes and into a fancy, tiled bathing room. I headed toward the connecting chambers—what I hoped were the *royal* chambers.

Voices grew louder as I flitted inside and landed on the back of the first chair I could find. Slowly, I crawled with sticky insect legs along the fabric until I could peer over the edge.

Across the room, near the door, at least ten guards stood surrounding the king and queen. Two more guards stood at the entrance with Prince Shem. Captain Uriel joined them.

I rarely saw the captain of the Guard.

If he was there, it must be serious.

Prince Shem clearly had a similar thought. Frowning, he asked, "What's going on?"

"Sit with your mother," the king answered instead, waving him and Queen Samaria in my general direction. The queen lowered herself onto a warm green sofa nearby, small and fragile against the enormous furniture. Though her dress seemed to be a delicate silver silk at first glance, it was iridescent, reflecting a rainbow of colors beneath, whenever she moved.

Shaking his head, Shem gestured back toward the door. "I was in the middle of dinner. Couldn't this wait?"

"I'm afraid not, son." The king rubbed a hand across his wrinkled brow, turning to pace. The decorative chains on his heavy boots clinked with each step. "You need to be briefed by the guard. We must make some decisions immediately."

Frowning, Shem crossed the carpet to sit beside his mother. "Well then, by all means, begin."

Uriel cleared his throat. *Is he nervous?* I could understand a younger guard fidgeting under the pressure of speaking to the royal family, but not Uriel. My own anxiety level rose in anticipation.

"There's a threat in the castle, your highnesses," the captain began slowly, gripping the crystal spear at his side so tight his knuckles whitened. "We've discovered a shape-shifter."

My tiny insect heart nearly gave out.

They found me!

I took off flying before I even had a direction.

A wall rose up before me, and I had to veer right, spiraling wildly as I lost my balance in the air, barely slowing in time for a rough landing on the carpeted floor.

The queen had jumped up from the sofa. "We must evacuate immediately!"

Oh, don't worry, I'm already gone! I thought in a panic.

But my wings trembled so hard I couldn't fly.

The room spun.

Calm down, I berated myself. *They can't possibly know it's me.* That thought sped up my racing heart to dangerous levels. *Do they?*

This was so unfair. Just when I'd been falling for the prince, I had to lose him too. Now I'd have to run before they caught me.

Perhaps they were already searching my rooms.

I should try to learn as much as I can about their plans to catch me before I sneak out. Logical thinking didn't help my nerves at all.

The queen swayed slightly. Prince Shem stood to put an arm around her. "What do you mean a shape-shifter? Is it truly in the castle? How did it get past the guards at the first and second gate? Or the entrance? Are you certain?"

It? I rolled my many eyes at his ignorance, but his last question caught my attention. *Yes, are you certain?* I fluttered my wings, hopeful. *Maybe they don't know for sure.*

Even as I thought this, I sagged in defeat. It didn't matter if they knew for sure or not. Now that they were on the alert, it was only a matter of time. *I still have to go.* I focused on calming down enough to fly out the way I'd come in.

The king stopped pacing, coming to put a hand on his son's shoulder. "Unfortunately, my son, we have proof."

The queen sank onto the green cushions, shuddering, as if she couldn't hold herself up any longer.

My bug eyes would've widened if they could have. *Did I slip? When?*

"A serving woman by the name of Hila approached the head of staff in his office less than an hour ago, inquiring after new guests and employees in the castle."

But... I didn't do that.

If I could've shaken my head, I would have.

The shifter wasn't me.

For one thing, I didn't like to shift into another Jinni, whether known or unknown. Not after what'd happened with Asher. More importantly, it was far too risky.

Creeping along the floor on all six legs, I tried to get closer.

"I fail to see how that would raise an alarm?" Shem was saying to both his father and the guards.

"Hila hasn't been employed by the castle in over a decade," Uriel said in a flat tone. "Not since she died."

My chest grew tight.

"Ah," the prince said, absently lowering himself to sit beside his mother, dragging out the word as he slumped back against the sofa. "I see."

So did I. *It's hard to argue with that evidence.*

For once, the Jinni Guard was right.

There was another shape-shifter in the castle.

6

THE QUEEN PALED AT the revelation. "Why didn't the head of staff apprehend this shifter right then and there?"

That would've certainly made my life easier. The many eyes of my fly form were giving me a severe headache. My wings finally felt steady enough to fly, but now I couldn't leave without gathering more information.

I flew up to the mantle for a better view, landing behind a small statue set of the royal family, peering out from behind a miniature, marble Shem.

"He assumed that this shifter was more dangerous than it appeared," the king took over the explanation for the guard, whose shoulders slumped slightly in relief. "And rightly so."

There they go calling the shifter an "it" again. I itched to get away from this anxious hatred of my kind, but hearing the details was more important than my comfort right now.

The king strode to sit beside the queen as well, taking her hand. "Fortunately for us, the head of staff was clever. He made excuses to the shifter about needing a different ledger to get the information she needed, and if she would wait in his office, he would fetch it."

When the king waved toward the guards, I flinched automatically. *They don't know I'm here,* I reminded myself.

"The head of staff instantly summoned Captain Uriel," the king continued. "And half the Guard closed in on the room." He stood again to pace, gesturing for Uriel to continue the story.

I crept out from behind the little statue of the prince, forgetting myself, wanting to lecture them. *If this other shifter wanted to hurt you, you'd never have had a chance.* Scoffing, I added to myself, *You don't think like a shifter or you'd have searched this room much more carefully.* They could get wise at any moment though. I pulled back out of sight once more.

Uriel stepped forward. "The shifter must've known she'd been discovered. When we entered the head of staff's office, she attacked the first guard in lion form, forcing her way out of the room and tearing down the hall. By the time we'd rounded the corner, the shifter was gone."

Impressive. Whoever she is, she's fast. I'd picked up speed over the last few months, but if that'd been me, they would've caught me mid-shift for sure.

"Most likely this shifter went to the first window they could find," Shem's voice lifted, almost hopeful, as he turned to his father. "Surely they wanted to vacate the premises straightaway."

Agreed. People underestimated Prince Shem because his head was so often in the clouds, but he was more perceptive than most realized.

"Not possible." Uriel shook his head, bringing his hands behind his back, standing stiffly. "When the head of staff alerted us to the danger, we immediately enacted the castle defense enchantments."

My tiny lungs couldn't seem to suck in enough air. I hadn't heard of any defenses that prevented someone from fleeing. That didn't bode well for me at all.

"They fell into place before we reached the office, less than an hour ago," he continued.

Was *that* what I'd experienced earlier when I'd felt that sensation like a bubble bursting around me? It'd been so subtle I hadn't recognized the hint of magic sweeping over me, but looking back it was perfectly clear.

"All inhabitants are currently locked inside the castle walls until the spell is lifted," Uriel finished. "Which also means we're trapped here. With the shifter."

My tiny stomach—or were there multiple stomachs?—curdled in a split second. Could a fly throw up? I was about to find out...

I'm trapped.

I couldn't leave even if I wanted to. Everything in me wanted to test the spell by flying through the nearest window here and now.

Don't do anything foolish.

If I set off the enchantment and alerted the Jinni Guard to my presence, there'd be no escape.

"Shouldn't we lift it to allow the Guard to get you and mother to safety?" Shem asked, frowning.

Queen Samaria lifted a shaking hand to her forehead. "I quite agree."

"The enchantment won't be lifted. Not until the shifter is caught." King Jubal cut a hand through the air with finality. "It's too risky. If we allow the shifter the chance to escape, we'd give them free reign of the kingdom. They could attack at any time. We would be in even more danger if we let it loose, than we are now."

All the little hairs along my tiny body lifted as his words sunk in. *They're not going to stop until they find a shifter.* Any *shifter. Whether it's the one who caused this uproar or not.*

This other shifter clearly knew more about their Gift than I did. They probably knew exactly what the Guard would do in a situation like this and would be prepared. Which meant they weren't likely to get caught.

That led to an even worse realization.

They're not going to catch the intruder… They're going to catch me.

7

"I HATE THIS," SHEM said.

Silently, I agreed with him.

"Don't fear, your majesties," Captain Uriel reassured the royal family. "Even now we already have measures in place that will help us catch the shifter." He gestured vaguely. I tensed. What measures? How could I avoid capture if I didn't recognize the trap?

Off the top of my head, there was only one Gift I could think of that might discover a shape-shifter: mind-reading. Was Captain Uriel a mind-reader? Or one of his guards?

Creeping back, I let the little statue of the prince block my tiny body from view. I checked my mental walls, and then built them even higher.

Unless a Gift was exceptional, even a powerful mind-reader usually needed to focus on a subject to hear their thoughts, but that was the extent of my knowledge—I didn't know if "focus" meant an intentional stare or if a passing glance at a seemingly-innocent fly in the room would spell my doom. When it came to the Guard members, chosen for the strength of their abilities, it wasn't worth the risk.

"What do you think the shifter is after?" Shem asked, ignoring Uriel's attempt to placate them. "How do you know they're even a threat?"

King Jubal scoffed. "*All* shifters are a threat. They could replace any one of us in a heartbeat—and if they were smart, no one would be the wiser. No other Gift is more dangerous to us. Use your head, boy."

Shem flushed, but his mother put a soothing hand on his arm and added, "We wouldn't expect you to have considered all the angles, dear. You've never faced a shifter before. But your father and I had an unfortunate encounter, many years ago. The danger is quite real."

My heart stuttered.

My mother had been a shifter—could they be talking about her? After all, she'd been in their Guard. I'd always wondered why she'd left so suddenly...

Shem paled. "You think they'd replace *you*." It wasn't a question.

A heavy pause filled the room.

"They could take anyone's place, really," Captain Uriel dared to re-enter the tense conversation. "We developed a rough plan the last time we were in this situation... There's a spell that can leave an invisible mark on a Jinni—one that a shifter couldn't possibly replicate, as they cannot see it."

"Ah yes," Queen Samaria's face lifted, and she sucked in a hopeful breath. "The mark. It doesn't fade for weeks. We'll need to begin interrogations at once."

"Interrogations?" Shem frowned at his parents.

His father stared into the thick carpet, lost in thought.

Captain Uriel glanced at the king, who remained silent, before he cleared his throat and said, "We will determine with one hundred percent certainty that a Jinni is who they claim to be, before giving them the mark. If we make our way through the castle this way, in theory, we could complete the interrogations by the second day. Or the third at the very latest."

"Perhaps we could call it an 'interview' instead?" Shem suggested, running a hand through his hair and wincing. "They're not going to like it."

"They don't have to like it," King Jubal declared in a sharp tone that made me flinch. I hadn't thought he was listening. "They'll do what their king and queen demand."

"We have full confidence we'll catch the shifter," Captain Uriel inserted before Shem could protest further, turning to the queen with a smile. "Most likely within the day."

She smiled back, shoulders relaxing.

My wings vibrated with renewed panic.

My chances at a full life here with Prince Shem were absolutely and without a doubt over.

Without connections or family in power like the other council members, if I was caught I'd spend the rest of my life in the dungeons below. That wouldn't last long though, since they'd probably punish me with a Severance as well. If my Gift was severed, my remaining days would be few.

THE SECRET SHADOW

Slowly, staying out of sight as much as possible, I used the sticky pads on my tiny feet to crawl down the wall to the thick, patterned carpet, heading as quickly as I could in such a tiny form toward the bathing room: my escape.

It was time to find a way out of the castle.

At some silent signal, the guards began to spread out across the room.

I tucked myself behind the leg of a chair. Burrowing into the carpet, I waited for the nearest guard to pass by. As he headed for the lavatory, the queen followed in his wake, waiting for him to pronounce it safe.

She closed the door on his heels as soon as he did so. My heart sank.

My only exit was barred.

I managed to stay ahead of the guard searching my section of the room. When he paused to respond to the king, I quickly flew behind him. Whether or not they could sense me, I didn't want to stay and find out.

I need to get out of here. Now. Every second I stuck around, I was asking to be caught.

Flinging out my wings, I took a risk.

I flew straight up to the ceiling—the least likely place they'd look. Once there, I flew horizontal along the surface, so hard my little heart almost exploded.

Upside down, I landed. All my eyes were trained on the Jinn below me. After a second to catch my breath, I pushed off, aiming for the entrance.

Dropping onto the tiny ledge above the double doors, I pressed against the wood. From this height, I shouldn't be noticed.

For good measure, though, I flipped onto my back, feet in the air. *Play dead.*

While I impatiently waited for the guards to finish their search and open the door below, I tried to calm my beating heart. If I listened for helpful information, maybe they'd give me a clue on how to survive this.

"The royal chambers are safe, your majesties," the youngest Jinni guard finally said with a bow. "We've searched every room thoroughly, both before and after your arrival. We recommend you remain here while we begin our search throughout the rest of the castle."

"Apologies." Shem stood from where he'd waited on the sofa. He wasn't apologetic at all. "I'm afraid I can't do that. I can't in good conscience leave my council members unaware and unprotected."

King Jubal held out a hand, barring Shem from moving toward the door. "You must tell no one."

Fists clenched at his sides, Shem sidestepped the king. "I have to warn them."

With a flick of the king's hand, four members of the Guard fell into position in front of the double doors, spears crossed.

"Father," Shem snapped, turning around. From my vantage point, I could only see the top of his head.

King Jubal crossed his arms. "We cannot lose the element of surprise," his voice overrode whatever Shem had been about to say, unyielding.

"What surprise?" Shem scoffed. "The shifter ran from our guards. They most likely tried to escape shortly after and have already discovered the enchantments that hold them prisoner in these walls."

Did that mean the enchantments didn't include a trap when tested? I wouldn't risk trying it yet, but that was a tiny ray of light.

"There's no *element of surprise*," Shem continued, advancing toward his father slowly, stopping in front of him. "They *know* we're looking for them."

His father said nothing, expressionless, as if he wouldn't back down now, even if it did appear foolish.

Shem visibly took a deep breath, ignoring the guards. Focusing on his father, he murmured, "Let me warn my council. They deserve to know." Another pause, and he added, "The court will piece together that there's a threat once the interviews begin anyway."

Grunting, King Jubal relented and nodded to the guards. "Just wait long enough to get the mark before you go."

"How long will that take?" Shem glanced between his father and Uriel.

The captain cleared his throat. "It's a complicated spell. Hopefully within the next hour we'll have gathered everything we need."

"A lot can happen in an hour. I need to warn them. You can give me the mark when I get back." Shem stepped up to the four guards blocking the door, waiting impatiently for them to step aside and open it.

"Son—" the king cut off, darting a look at Queen Samaria as if asking her to intervene.

She merely shrugged. "He's with his guards. And the shifter isn't going to attack them in a crowded dining hall full of powerful Jinn. Let him do what he needs to do. He'll be back shortly."

Shem strode through the door before she'd finished speaking, flanked by two guards rushing to keep up. As soon as they stepped past the enchantments that prevented travel, they vanished.

My racing heart picked up speed again. This was my chance to escape the room as well.

All eyes were on the door below.

I couldn't fly through the exit without risking being seen.

The guards were closing the doors behind the prince. In a few seconds, I'd be locked in once more. This was my only chance.

This is insane.

I *should* stay put. Wait here in the *one room* in the entire castle that they'd pronounced shifter-free, where I could be confident that I wouldn't be caught. Where I could wait it out.

If nothing else, I certainly *shouldn't* put myself directly in the guards' line

THE SECRET SHADOW

of sight.

The king turned to speak with Uriel, and the queen's eyes latched onto them as well. Below, two of the four guards at the door had already taken up position with their backs to it, and the remaining two weren't looking up. If I remained above eye level, I might make it through unseen.

It was now or never.

The crack between the door and the frame was narrowing.

With only a few fingers of space left, I leapt off the ledge and flew through the door, nearly clipping my wings as the heavy wood thudded closed behind me.

Shem was already gone, of course. The hall was empty.

On instinct, I tried to travel too. The most common Gift in Jinn was traveling from one distant place to another, and I had just as much range as the prince, if not a little bit more. I swore silently as nothing happened—I'd learned very early on that I couldn't travel while in animal form, but I used the Gift so often it became muscle memory and I sometimes forgot.

Shem and his guards would've already arrived at the dining hall entrance.

If I didn't follow suit shortly, he might come looking for me. He wanted to warn his entire council after all.

My absence would be highly suspicious behavior at the absolute worst time.

It was too late to pretend I'd never left the dining hall, but I could still get back before he finished warning the others.

I pushed my tiny wings to their limits. Heading down the empty hall, I searched for a safe place to shift back into my true form.

A Jinni with dark eyebrows and graying hair passed by below me, heading in the opposite direction. I nearly grazed the high ceiling in my attempts to hide from him. He never looked up.

At the sight of an open tea room down the hall, I changed direction.

I circled the room, still near the ceiling tiles, trying to capture every angle through my bug eyes.

It appeared empty.

I dropped onto the table in the center, landing on a teapot—it was cold.

No one was here.

It still felt too exposed.

Pushing through my exhaustion, I forced my wings to carry me to a hidden space behind a lounge chair.

I shifted.

After straining so hard in my fly form, returning to my true self took the last of my energy. The transition was sharp. It felt like yanking off a piece of clothing so roughly that it ripped out bits of hair and scraped against tender skin.

My weakness wouldn't be noticeable to anyone else, but I could hardly stand.

I leaned against the back of the chair. For a long minute, I simply breathed in and out, eyes closed, and tried not to faint. I needed food and rest as soon as possible to regain my strength.

One problem at a time.

Right now, my secrets still remained my own. If I wanted it to stay that way, I needed to calmly return to finish my meal and act as if nothing had changed.

Bones aching, I stood and forced myself to travel to the dining hall entrance. Exhaustion made me stagger as I materialized.

Prince Shem's voice floated toward me from within. "All council members please report for an emergency meeting."

Still breathing hard, I gulped a few deep breaths to steady myself before I wove back through the tables toward him. His back was to me, as he spoke to our table, "I'll explain more once we're all together. Please spread the word and make sure everyone is gathered in my chambers within a quarter hour."

Though their faces held questions, none of the council members challenged his request, nodding before they strode out into the hallway and disappeared. Milcah's gaze caught mine briefly as the hall door was closing, before she vanished as well.

Smoothing out my face, I shoved my terror deep down, until I could almost pretend it didn't exist. I casually approached the table, touching Shem's arm lightly.

He flinched. It was almost imperceptible. When he turned to face me, he was calm, but there was more under the surface than he was letting on. "Jezebel," he said on a breath, seeming to relax slightly. "I was worried you'd gone off alone."

Pretending confusion took every bit of my willpower. "Why shouldn't I be alone?"

I tried to memorize his face without being obvious. That way I could take a piece of him with me when I left. The thought made me want to cry. I crossed my arms and bit the inside of my cheek to hide the rush of emotions.

He stared back, not moving, as if he wanted to tell me right then and there, despite the rest of the dining crowd listening in.

His guards stood on each side, and one of them shifted on his feet, breaking the spell between us. "This isn't a good place to share." He ran a frustrated hand through his hair, glancing at the guards again. "I've called an urgent council meeting. Please go join the others, and I'll explain everything shortly."

I obeyed, traveling to the hall outside his council chambers, arriving at the same time as a few others.

There were two guards outside his rooms now, instead of one. I slipped in on the heels of another circle, not giving either guard a chance to protest.

Once I snuck inside, I sank into a chair against the wall, partially hidden in the corner. I ignored the gossip buzzing around the room and closed my eyes to prevent anyone from trying to speak to me.

THE SECRET SHADOW

When Shem arrived, he strode in with a grim look. He didn't stand on ceremony, beginning his announcement right away, "The castle—and perhaps the royal family in particular—is very likely under attack."

He continued on ruthlessly over the gasps across the room. "I have it on good authority that we have a shape-shifter in our midst."

Now he did pause, allowing that to sink in.

Utter silence met his announcement, as we eyed those around us.

"I must ask that you keep this information to yourselves, as we are trying to avoid a widespread panic in the castle while we search for the shifter."

He briefly explained the enchantment over the castle locking all of us in with this shifter, but he didn't say anything I didn't already know.

"I trust each of you know how to handle yourselves in this situation," Shem continued. "But I would also recommend that you begin a habit of traveling in groups, as well as bringing up your history with each other whenever you meet, as a precaution."

To check if you're speaking to a shape-shifter, he meant.

I swallowed hard. That would be effective.

It might also give me the slightest edge over this other shifter. They might have some knowledge of the castle, but if their shifting into an old staff member was any indication, their information was at least a decade old, if not more.

I, on the other hand, knew most of these council members personally. And they knew me, whether they wanted to admit it or not.

Shem rubbed his brow, as if a headache plagued him. "I'm afraid I'm duty-bound not to share further details at this time. Please return to your regular activities. Once I'm able to say more, you'll be the first to know."

The dismissal was clear. Council members slowly trickled out of the room in pairs or larger groups, as Shem had suggested, until only the prince was left.

And me.

I hadn't meant to stay behind, but my legs wobbled slightly beneath my dress, not ready to carry me anywhere just yet. "I'm sorry," I whispered when his gaze found me in the corner. "I need a moment."

He misunderstood. "I should be the one to apologize," he said, striding to sit on the sofa across from me, leaning on his knees so that only a small space separated us. "It's my fault you're in this situation. If I hadn't asked you to stay at the castle, you wouldn't be in any danger."

"There's always danger in Jinn," I said with a soft laugh, waving off his worries.

"That may be so." He remained serious, reaching a hand toward mine. "But I still fear for your safety."

Swallowing the lump that brought to my throat, I looked away from his earnest eyes and down at his hand where it covered my own. Though I wanted to respond in kind, I froze. "I don't suppose there's a way I could avoid this awful business altogether?" I finally managed to say, trying to keep my voice light.

He squeezed my fingers. "I'm afraid not."

I'd assumed as much. I shouldn't push him to tell me anything else, no matter how desperately I wanted to know what the Guard was planning.

He wants me to ask questions, I told myself. *Otherwise he would've asked me to leave.*

I met his eyes and placed my other hand over his, not daring even to blink as I whispered, "Please… if there's anything else, you'd tell me, wouldn't you?"

"Yes…" he whispered back, uneasy, but not looking away, almost as if trapped by my gaze.

"Please?"

He gave in unexpectedly. "They're going to question every single resident in the castle."

The interviews.

Some sort of one-on-one examination.

It went unsaid that the Jinni Guard would be using *all* their resources during these polite interrogations, including every available spell and Gift.

I bit my lip.

Ducking my head, I sucked in a breath.

For a split second, I considered telling him the truth. If he heard it from my lips, would he believe me? *Shem, I have to tell you,* I'm *a shifter… But not the one you're looking for, I swear.*

I shook my head, rubbing my forehead with my free hand.

Put it like that, and I don't even believe myself.

"What's wrong?" Shem responded by moving from the sofa to a chair right next to mine, ducking down a bit, trying to catch my gaze.

As I lifted my eyes, a movement caught my attention in the balcony above. Milcah stood in the shadows. She'd never left. My heart rate doubled at the realization I'd almost spilled my secrets in front of her.

When she saw I'd spotted her, she stepped forward to lean casually on the balcony railing, eavesdropping without shame.

I was at a loss for words.

I pulled my hand from Shem's without thinking. It fluttered around like a bird without a perch, lighting on my hair, my earrings, my lap, and up again.

I couldn't tell him. Clearly.

Even if Milcah wasn't here, I knew better than to trust anyone with my secrets.

Shem's frown grew deeper the longer I was silent. "Jezebel, whatever it is, you can tell me."

I fiddled with my hair, tucking stray pieces back beneath my decorative headband. "You know the Guard makes me uncomfortable," I said slowly,

THE SECRET SHADOW

searching for something I could tell him *and* Milcah at the same time, since she showed no signs of leaving.

Shem sat back in his chair and sighed. "I do. Your first few weeks here were an adjustment period to life in the castle... The Guard should've been more understanding of that. But what does that have to do with the shifter and the interviews?"

"I just..." I hesitated, then decided to simply tell the truth. Or part of it. "I'm not the shifter they're looking for, Shem. I'd rather not deal with them at all, if I didn't have to."

"They'll be completely professional," he assured me, brows drawing together in sympathy. "I wish I could allow you to keep your distance, truly. But you have nothing to worry about. They're only doing their job."

He's not going to bend.

Casting around for the next best solution, I leaned forward to take his hand again, despite Milcah's presence—or maybe I was daring *because* she was watching.

I swallowed hard before I could meet his eyes and speak, "Would you consider another favor then?"

Nodding, he held my gaze, absently stroking my hand.

"Can you tell them to interview me last?" I rushed to explain, "That way I'll never have need to speak with them."

"Oh? How so?"

I twisted my mouth into a semblance of a smile, hoping it seemed genuine. "I'm sure they'll find this dangerous shifter long before it's my turn for an interview."

The excuse sounded weak.

If he had any reason to suspect me now, he'd likely have me go first instead. Asking for this had been a mistake.

Yet, after a short pause, he nodded again in agreement. "I'll see what I can do."

My eyes widened. Normally he didn't like to give individual council members any special treatment. *Does that mean...* My traitorous heart soaked up the moment despite my fears. *Maybe he does feel something for me. Why else would he agree so quickly?*

"May I also request the same favor, your highness?" Milcah's voice floated over to us as she gracefully descended the stairs from the balcony. "I did not mean to overhear," she lied blatantly with wide eyes. "But I would ask that you might extend the same favor to myself and the rest of the council. Perhaps even in order of seniority?"

I glowered at her. That would move me from the last interview right back to the somewhere near the top of the list, and she knew it.

Politics in Jinn dictated that Shem always consider his council's wishes, so he murmured in agreement, trapped by the request as much as I was.

After Milcah thanked him, she stood over us for a few moments as the awkwardness grew.

"Well," Shem said, standing. "I suppose I should go make the request to the Guard."

We followed him out into the hall and the door clicked softly closed behind us.

"Wait!" I grabbed his hand once more to catch him before he traveled away. Milcah paused as well, but I gave her my shoulder and a brief, impatient glance over it to make it clear that this didn't include her.

With a barely contained huff, she turned on her heel and traveled away.

Once she was gone, I turned back to Shem and bit my lip hopefully, knowing I was about to ask a lot. His fingers were warm in mine. "Don't tell the Guard that I was the one who asked? I don't want to give them another reason to dislike me."

Once again, he surprised me by agreeing immediately. "Of course. Don't worry over the Guard, Jezebel. You're safe here." Cupping a hand over my cheek, he smiled. "I'm sure they'll find the shifter within the next few hours. In the meantime, stay in your room and lock the door, just to be safe."

"I will," I agreed on a breath of relief. But it was short lived. I'd only bought myself a short delay. The Guard was still coming.

Shem gave my fingers a gentle squeeze, then let go.

He vanished.

I traveled as well, heading to my room as he'd asked.

While I didn't fear the shifter the way the others did, that didn't mean I wanted to get caught roaming the halls. That might seem suspicious.

Unlocking the door, I entered my room with a sigh. I'd remain here for now.

I didn't really have a choice, since I couldn't escape the castle, and I couldn't avoid the interview. My time was running out.

Unless... what if I found the other shifter and turned them in, before the Guard ever got close to me?

It was half a plan, but at least it was something.

I'd find a way to catch this other shifter myself.

8

THE SMALL CLOCK ON my desk ticked softly, counting down the hours until the Guard would discover my secret, sever my abilities, and send me to the dungeons for the rest of my short, Gift-less life. Not a single acceptable strategy for catching the shifter had come to me.

The empty glass jar on the desk beside the clock reminded me of the awful choices I'd made in the past when pressed into a corner.

I didn't want to hurt anyone this time.

Especially not Shem.

Crossing my arms, I paced between the window and the door, feeling a pressure building up behind my eyes.

If I couldn't find a third solution, he'd suffer either way: he'd either discover my secret or find that I'd disappeared without a goodbye.

It'd been at least a couple hours since dinner and the emergency council meeting. The Guard could arrive any minute. Being exposed as a shifter was simply not an option.

Time to test this enchantment.

It was designed to keep Jinn in, but maybe it would allow an animal to pass through… Only one way to find out.

Biting my lip, I unlatched the window, pulling it inward to open. It was better for everyone, including Shem, that the truth remained hidden.

Shifting into my favorite form, I became a little green lizard. It came to me easily now. I crawled up the wall to the window. My scaley sides expanded in a deep breath.

Smack.

I hit an invisible wall.

It knocked me backward.

Dizzy, I shifted even smaller, into a tiny flea. I crept toward the open window, more tentative this time.

The enchantment threw me back again.

Oof.

That hurt.

I couldn't leave, even in animal form.

Unfortunately, I'd half-expected it.

That crossed my last remaining option off my list.

Though it was extra work to shift back into my own form, I did so anyway, because I desperately needed to cry.

I flung myself across the middle of my bed and let the tears flow.

Gradually the ticking clock reminded me that nothing had changed. I was still on a deadline.

Tracing the decorative carvings on the bed post, I tried to focus on finding another way out of this.

My stomach growled.

It always begged me to eat after expending so much energy shifting.

I rang a little bell that would sound in the kitchens.

While I waited impatiently for someone on staff to answer my summons, I shifted one of my fingers into a talon and began carving into the thick bed post, between a design of two dragons that wrapped around it. If I dug deep enough, I could create a thin but prominent shelf to place my first Kathenoth. Shem could find it and hopefully think someone had put a spell on me. Or maybe, if I was sure I could escape, I might write the truth...

My eyes caught on the glass jar on my desk. If I had a Kathenoth, would it include that story?

I flipped onto my back so I wouldn't see the jar anymore.

I'd have to write a Kathenoth for it to be found, and I didn't have the words. Not even one.

Dragging my dark thoughts away from their hopeless spiral, I forced my attention to the shifter problem.

I imagined somehow trapping the intruder myself, bringing them before the king and queen as a hero, and watching them lift the castle enchantments without ever discovering my secrets. In that scenario, I could stay here, free and happy,

THE SECRET SHADOW

with Shem.

I chewed on my bottom lip.

How will I even track them down, much less detain them, if they don't want to be found?

I wouldn't recognize the other shape-shifter unless they used their abilities right in front of me.

I need to make them use it.

This was where I'd been stumped for hours.

Meanwhile, every available member in the *entire* Jinni Guard—one thousand of the crown's most trusted and elite servants in the entire kingdom, at least half of whom lived here in the castle—were interviewing the occupants of the castle right now, at what I could only assume was a breakneck speed.

Shem had promised to do what he could, but at any moment they'd knock on my door. Perhaps they'd force me to use all my Gifts? Or maybe, the interview would be simpler than that. All they needed to ruin me was a truth spell.

Then, I would betray myself.

My stomach was hollow. I couldn't tell if it was from fear or hunger pains.

No one from the kitchens had answered. It'd been over an hour. Maybe the king and queen had given them a curfew. Either way, it looked like I wouldn't get anything to eat tonight.

Ignoring the pinching in my stomach, I climbed off the bed and paced to the window. Below, the luscious royal gardens sprawled out as far as the eye could see, with intricate paths between the different flora and fauna, and an enormous fountain in the middle. Normally, at least a few dozen Jinn strolled the footpaths at any time of day—even any time of night.

Now, though, it was empty.

Thanks to the barrier placed over the castle by the still unknown enchantment, it would remain that way until the shifter was caught.

Two days, the captain had said. *Three at most.*

Had any castle residences been caught outside the perimeter of the spell? They would've been left to puzzle out what happened on their own.

News of the enchantment would spread fast inside the castle though. They might not know *why* the castle was locked down, but it wasn't the first time the royal family had been under attack, and it wouldn't be the last. Most castle residents would take the temporary imprisonment in stride. I wondered if they'd feel the same way about these so-called "interviews."

Shem wanted us to remain in our rooms until it was our turn to speak with the Guard, but I'd lose my mind being locked up like this.

Every bone in my body wanted to do *something*.

I shook my head. Most likely there were guards in the hall.

Leaving would look suspicious.

My eyes drifted to the unassuming wardrobe in the corner, and my lips twisted up.

Thank goodness for Shem and his loophole spell.

I crossed the room and placed a hand on the delicate, dark wood. It begged me to use it. I could sneak into the kitchens and feed myself. At the thought, my stomach growled again. I pressed a hand to my belly.

Inhaling deeply, I sighed.

There might still be staff in the kitchens, preparing for breakfast tomorrow.

"Soon," I whispered to myself. I'd wait until the middle of the night. "Just a few more hours."

As I paced, my eyes continued to flit back to the wardrobe.

The loophole spell worked two ways, after all.

Someone could also visit, *if* they wanted to.

A small part of me that I refused to acknowledge hoped that Shem might use it to come to me.

Another, more realistic part knew he had dozens of princely duties with this shifter situation keeping him busy—especially now that his father was preparing him to be king. Facing constant threats such as this would become his job soon enough. Even if that wasn't the case, he wasn't obligated to check on me. There were a thousand reasons I shouldn't expect him. But I couldn't stop myself from hoping.

As the midnight bells rang, a shadow crossed beneath my doorway in the dimly lit hall.

I held my breath.

The shape continued on without stopping.

It was probably a guard on rotation.

I finally acknowledged the sharp pang of disappointment.

Shem wasn't coming.

The Guard hasn't come either, I reminded myself. *They would've started here first, if not for Shem requesting them not to. That has to mean something...*

Milcah might've requested the same favor, but he'd seemed more invested when he'd promised it to me. *Hadn't he?* My mind would drive me in circles if I let it.

Were the servants still in the kitchen? I should wait another hour... I paced away from the wardrobe and back to the window. At this rate, I'd create a groove in the floor.

On a normal night, I'd have traveled to the kitchens right after dinner. It was easy enough to find a staff member who didn't know I'd already eaten and request a meal tray be delivered to my room.

Whenever I practiced shifting, I did this out of necessity. I'd learned the hard way that if I strained my Gift too far without feeding it and getting rest, my body would betray me. Once, I'd collapsed in front of Shem. He'd worried for days.

THE SECRET SHADOW

An invisible hand grabbed my insides and twisted painfully as my stomach gurgled.

I needed to eat more than the half-dinner I'd had hours earlier.

Taking a deep breath in and out, I closed my eyes.

Just a little longer.

My feet moved on their own, returning me to the wardrobe. Again, I dragged myself away.

Only a shifter would show up demanding food right now. The kitchens will be empty soon.

If another hour could be considered soon.

My body stiffened. I stopped so abruptly that I nearly tripped over my own feet.

Whirling around, I stared at the wardrobe.

I know exactly how to find the shifter.

A little laugh escaped. I instantly felt lighter. The answer was so obvious I couldn't believe it hadn't occurred to me sooner.

While the Jinni Guard wasted time on their precious interviews, all I needed to do was sneak into the kitchens and wait. The intruder had shifted as much as I had, maybe more. If they'd stayed hidden since their encounter, they wouldn't have had anything to eat since this afternoon.

Unless they had a stash somewhere, they were probably exhausted and growing desperate. There was only one place they could go.

I'll find them in the kitchen.

9

A KNOCK SOUNDED ON my door.

Shem came after all!

I dashed across the room to let him in, throwing on my robe so it'd look like I'd been sleeping. When I swung the door open, it wasn't the prince.

It was Gabriel.

A second Jinni Guard that I didn't recognize stood behind him.

"Can I help you?" I asked in an icy tone. Only my ability to shift my features kept the flush of fear from reaching my cheeks. Slowing my breathing was much harder, but I concentrated my efforts on not giving away how frightened I was.

Gabriel spoke in a monotone as if repeating something he'd said a few dozen times already. "By order of the king, the Jinni Guard is appointed to speak with all castle inhabitants." He stepped forward, waving for the other guard to follow. "We are to conduct an interview focused on Gift—"

"Wait!" I put my hand on the door and pushed back, glaring. "You can't force your way into my room without asking!"

"Castle safety overrides privacy in this instance," Gabriel replied, meeting my gaze with a dark smile, as if he knew I was supposed to have more time, but was choosing to ignore it.

My heart pumped like I was facing a Lacklore instead of one of my least favorite castle acquaintances.

If I took this interview, I would fail.

Keeping my hand pressed firmly against the door, I lowered my voice, hoping it wouldn't shake. "Prince Shem didn't speak with you? He gave me—and the rest of his council—special status for the interviews. We're to go last, as we have too much work to do right now for us to waste our time on this."

"I'm afraid I don't know what you're referring to," he replied.

I didn't believe him for a second. His narrowed eyes hadn't blinked. "You're one of the newer residents in the castle," he added, as if that explained his decision.

My newness shouldn't affect whether I was the shifter or not in the slightest. It simply made him more suspicious.

I let out a sigh, clutching my robe together at the neck. "You've roused me from bed without even checking the order of the interviews? I was *clearly* moved to the bottom of the list. I think the prince would find it highly disrespectful to hear you're disregarding his request."

Had Shem actually made the change? I had no idea.

I took a chance and began to swing the door shut as if the matter were already resolved.

Gabriel's hand slammed over mine, fixing the door in place. "Now that we're here, it'll be easier if we just move forward with the interview."

I snorted. "Easier for you, maybe." I tried to hold the door in place while sliding out from under his grasp, but his grip was firm. He put more pressure on the door. The muscles in my arm began to tremble.

I glared at him. "Why don't you do your job and go find the real lawbreaker? I have better things to do, and you're wasting your time with me."

He surprised me by pulling back so fast that I almost fell through the open door after him. "I suppose we should interview someone else," he said to his fellow Guard.

Turning on his heel with a slightly vacant look, he left without another word.

The other guard frowned, glancing between us, then shrugged. She murmured to Gabriel as they moved away, "I *told* you about the special status…"

I stood there blinking a second or two longer before I shook myself out of the stupor and swung the door closed.

Leaning against it, I frowned. *That was odd.*

They'd moved on to the next room.

I peeked out, listening through a crack as they knocked.

The room beside mine had been vacant since I'd come to stay at the castle. Since this residence hall was set aside for council members, I knew the occupant, whoever they were, must be on one of the royal family councils.

No one responded. The second guard spoke, "This occupant is listed as employed on another island for six months."

Gabriel grumbled, "We'll have to check the logs."

They moved on to the next hall, leaving mine empty.

All across the castle, other guards were conducting the same interviews. It was hard to guess how much time I had before they'd come back.

I let the door click softly closed.

Leaning back against the wood, I chewed on my nail, until it matched the others I'd gnawed on earlier.

While I might not be bothered again until morning, there was an equal chance that I might only have an hour or two before Gabriel returned.

It'd be foolish to question my good fortune when I should be taking advantage of it.

All that mattered right now was that they didn't come back until the other shifter had been caught—until *I* caught them.

Striding toward the wardrobe, I was already inside before it occurred to me: I still didn't have a real plan.

Guessing the shifter's location was really only the very beginning of a plan.

While it'd be easy enough to hide in the kitchen pantry until the shifter showed, the *capture* part still had me stumped.

It wouldn't do any good to find them if I lost them immediately.

I stepped out to pace the length of my room.

Every few rounds, I paused by the door to listen.

Glancing at the jar on my desk, my fingers trembled slightly. I didn't do well under stress.

This other shifter clearly knew how to use their abilities. They'd embraced their Gift, probably had years more experience than I did. Maybe they'd even had a mentor and real training.

A run in with someone like that could easily backfire, if I wasn't careful. It paled in comparison to being interviewed by the Guard though.

At least with the shifter, I had a chance.

If only because I had the element of surprise.

Earlier, I'd considered becoming a tiny poisonous phidar. I'd crawl up the oblivious shifters clothing until I found exposed skin, and sink my fangs in.

They'd never see it coming.

In that form, though, just one bite and the shifter wouldn't wake without the help of a castle healer. Possibly not even then.

Not to mention there was a very real possibility of being stepped on before I had a chance to bite anyone.

It was too risky.

Animal forms in general were limiting.

Maybe I could pretend to be a clueless servant—or even the king or queen? But if the shifter attacked me in those forms, I'd be more vulnerable…

THE SECRET SHADOW

I blew out the little candle by the bed and the room fell into darkness. I didn't need light to pace. At least I could pretend to be asleep while I schemed.

The hall was quiet. Only a hint of moonlight streamed in through my bedroom window.

Time was running out.

Desperation made me consider the Lacklore. A hulking beast with the head of an ox and the body of a bear, with bone-slicing claws the length of my fingers, dangerous horns, and sharp, wicked teeth.

But what would I do in that form? Cut the shifter into ribbons and deliver the pieces to the royal family?

There wasn't time for this debate. If I wasted any more time, the shifter might visit the kitchen and leave before I ever had a chance to confront them.

I needed to already be in place when the shifter arrived.

If fortune worked in my favor, they'd be starving. Exhausted. Weak. Maybe they'd make a mistake.

Stepping back into the wardrobe, I pressed the dresses out of the way and closed the door behind me, traveling to the kitchen pantry before I could talk myself out of it.

I'd improvise if I had to.

If I couldn't think of a way to capture the other shifter, then at least I could get a glimpse of them and maybe follow them to wherever they were hiding.

Once in the kitchens, I immediately shifted into Farah, one of the serving girls who usually worked during the day. She shouldn't be anywhere near the kitchen at this time of night.

More importantly, if I accidentally stumbled into someone besides the shifter, no one would report seeing *my* face here.

With that larger shift complete, I followed it with a smaller shift of my innerear until it was shaped like an owls', making my hearing so acute that it could catch the smallest whisper of sound. I did this whenever I snuck into the kitchen, so I was used to it and only needed a minute to complete the change.

I crouched in the dark pantry, waiting.

The smaller shift gave me an idea.

I could transform a tiny part of myself into something poisonous and catch them unaware.

A small part of me whispered that learning minor shifts took a lot of practice. Time I didn't have right now.

Not helpful.

What mattered most wasn't using my Gift perfectly, but my ability to deceive. To make the shifter believe I was harmless and unimportant. Hadn't I been doing that my entire life?

I can do this.

Turning my teeth into the venomous fangs of the phidar wouldn't work. In a larger mouth, they were almost guaranteed to have too much venom.

I squeezed my eyes shut, trying to picture the book of creatures I'd studied in the library.

There was a cone snail. Tiny, but deadly, they had a single stinger. Shifting my finger into a stinger would probably end up fatal, since the true size of their stinger was closer to an eyelash.

I heard a rustling.

Leaning forward onto my knees, I peered out. If that was the shifter already, I needed an answer to click into place in the next few seconds. My mind was blank.

When I cracked the pantry door open, it took a second for my eyes to adjust, but there was no one there.

After another pause, the rustling came again.

This time I could see what made the sound—it was just a towel fluttering in the breeze from an open window.

I sat back, blowing out a breath.

The hungry pit in my stomach ate away at me.

I scarfed down some old bread from one of the pantry shelves, trying to make it go away. But the ache didn't fade. It wasn't the hollow hunger that followed shifting. It was fear.

Stealth was my strong suit—if it came to a fight, I wasn't nearly as sure I could win, which meant poison was the answer. It was just a matter of finding a toxin that wouldn't kill the shifter instantly. I needed them alive if I was going to save my reputation and place in the castle.

Closing my eyes, I envisioned the book of creatures again. There was a blue-ringed octopi. My hopes rose. That was a better size. Then the text I'd read came back to me: the toxicity level could kill up to 26 Jinn.

What had been the creature on the next page...

My eyes flew open.

The poisonous dart frog.

Perfect.

It carried a similar paralyzing toxin that could be transmitted through the skin, but in a much smaller quantity. The recipient would never see it coming.

Best of all, I'd actually seen a dart frog once in the human rainforests with Shem. This firsthand knowledge should help me transform correctly.

Satisfied, I shifted the skin across the fingers of my right hand until they each turned vibrant blue with black spots, filled with the poisonous dart frog's toxins.

Then I pressed my sensitive ear to the pantry door to wait.

Ten minutes passed.

Then fifteen, twenty.

THE SECRET SHADOW

Thirty.

More.

My sense of time began to disintegrate.

It had to be nearing two in the morning.

My eyes burned, begging me to close them, but I forced my body to stay alert.

I wouldn't leave until I was one hundred percent certain that the shifter wasn't coming.

But what if they already came and went?

Shoulders sagging, I scooted back until I sat on a sack of potatoes, dropping my head into my hands.

If I was forced to wait until tomorrow, it might be too late.

There was no guarantee the shifter would even return here.

This was a stupid plan.

Every second I spent not trying to escape, I might as well be locking myself in a cell in the dungeons below.

The Guard would come for me soon.

I'd fail the interview.

My leg tingled as my foot fell asleep beneath me. I wiggled around on the sack of potatoes, trying to find a more comfortable position. My right arm ached from the tension of holding my poisonous fingers away from the rest of my body. I rested it on a shelf. Without a mentor to teach me the inner workings of my Gift, I'd never learned if I could poison myself—and I wasn't going to risk finding out now.

Through the crack in the pantry door, the pitch black kitchens showed the first hints of dawn, only an hour or so away now. The kitchen staff would be here soon—including my look-alike, Farah. Shortly after that, the rest of the castle would rise, and I'd have wasted my entire night on this foolishness.

Exhaustion tugged at my eyelids. It'd make me even more likely to crack when interviewed by the Guard tomorrow.

I gritted my teeth, squeezing my burning eyes shut to stop the salty tears.

Time to give up.

I'd go back to my rooms and fight sleep as I tried to come up with a new plan.

Rubbing my backside as I stood, I stretched to ease the stiffness, then froze at a sound.

What was that?

I held my breath. It'd been the tiniest sigh of a door opening on the other side of the room.

Light footsteps sounded now on the stone floor.

They padded closer.

If it was a staff member, I'd be in trouble.

But what if it was the shifter?

It was too early to start breakfast—I gripped the door handle.

This was the chance I'd been hoping for.

I had to make it count.

With one last deep breath, I picked up a random container, labeled "salt," taking care not to let my right hand touch any other part of my body.

I stepped out.

10

LETTING THE PANTRY DOOR close with a bang behind me, I was intentionally noisy, as if I hadn't been hiding there all along. This was part of the act, along with the apron I'd put on over my head when I'd first arrived.

Don't leave, I begged the shifter, even as I pretended not to notice their presence right away. Setting the container down on a random counter, keeping my shifted hand hidden behind it, I finally allowed my eyes to lift.

My heart sank.

It was just Naomi, one of the morning cooks.

I held back a groan.

Pretending to fold napkins, I snuck another glance at her from across the room.

She wasn't wearing her apron yet and her gray hair was uncovered, hanging down her back. Unusual to see when the cooks always kept their hair bound up during the day. But then, she was here before her shift started, likely too anxious over the latest castle drama to sleep. I couldn't blame her.

Now I'd have to pretend to be Farah, make some excuse to leave, and when the real Farah arrived, they'd realize it was another shifter sighting. That would add more fuel to the fire, and the Guard would work twice as fast to complete the interviews. It'd be all my fault when they got to me by midday.

Naomi moved slowly around the kitchen, ignoring me, opening cupboards in search of something.

I hesitated. Maybe I still had time to slip away.

Before I could decide, she turned in my direction, and her gaze briefly touched mine.

"Morning, Naomi," I said, when she didn't speak. My voice came out rough with its first use since the evening before and I cleared my throat.

"Morning," the older woman replied, but didn't stop her search.

Something struck me as odd.

I couldn't quite put my finger on it.

Was it the way she scrounged through the cupboards as if she'd never seen the contents inside before?

Or maybe it was the sudden lack of concern for her long hair draping over kitchen counters where food was prepared—something Naomi would never have allowed if she'd seen anyone else do so...

As she continued to ignore my presence, my confidence grew. Naomi would've taken one glance at me, a lowly Jinni girl from the acropolis, and put me to work.

This wasn't Naomi.

It was the shifter.

"Can I help you find something?" I asked in a cheerful voice, with a respectful dip of my head. That's how servants always greeted me when I stopped by the kitchens.

I hadn't realized how stiff the shifter was until her posture relaxed. When she smiled back at me, I was struck with a strange sense of deja-vu. "I'm looking for some fruit."

"Here," I said as calmly as I could, while my heart beat so hard it could knock my apron off. Careful to hide my hand covered in tree frog spots, I picked up the fruit bowl and carried it to her, clenching my toes in an effort to stay steady.

I held it out.

She slipped a bunch of bananas from the bowl, then pocketed an apple, and another, and a third.

I moved the bowl slightly to one side as she reached out again.

Our hands met.

I knew the poison was fast-acting, but I still gasped at the way her face paled.

She took a step back.

Then another.

Frowning, she stared down at her hand, then up at me, as her breathing grew ragged.

The toxin was taking effect.

"What kind of poison is this?" she murmured to herself.

THE SECRET SHADOW

She was so compelling, I almost answered.

Eyes closing, she sank to the floor, pulling in on herself and shutting me out.

I stood awkwardly over her, waiting.

Once she stopped moving, I'd run to fetch the Jinni Guard. Or maybe a healer first... She wasn't looking so good. Was she going to make it that long?

"Ah... yes," she whispered suddenly, between deep breaths.

Was it my imagination, or was her breathing returning to normal? It didn't make sense. That wasn't how the poison worked.

I gasped. *Her coloring!*

In the dim light of the kitchen, with her head buried in her knees and arms, I hadn't noticed—her skin was now a vibrant blue and black, just like my hand.

Like the poisonous dart frog.

If she'd shifted, did that mean she was immune to the poison?

I tensed, ready to travel instantly if need be.

But I held off, hoping I was wrong.

Maybe the poison was slower than I expected... I didn't want to lose this one chance if I could help it.

On a deep breath, she drew herself to her feet, back to me. Her gray hair shimmered, turning black, and her skin returned to normal.

What was she shifting into now?

A tremor ran through my body. Whatever her plan was, this couldn't be good.

Run! My instincts screamed, but I was too frightened to react.

Especially when the shifter spoke in a calm voice, "Well done, darling, I'm impressed."

I went numb.

Impressed?

"Next time, consider a sleeping potion or enchantment instead." She turned to face me with a smile that was oddly affectionate. "Far more effective against another shape-shifter."

The words unstuck my feet.

I stumbled back, eyes glued to her face. It couldn't be...

She'd transformed into her true form: long, black hair, jade-green eyes, and a confidence in her stance that couldn't be feigned.

I knew it was her true form, because I knew *her.*

I took another step back.

She followed me, step for step.

My breath came in panicked gasps. I didn't have to pretend to be terrified.

"Sariah?" I said under my breath, too soft for her to hear. My back hit the counter where I'd gotten the fruit. Somewhere in the back of my mind, I registered the clatter of the bowl hitting the floor as I dropped it. The remaining apples and pears rolled around our feet. Neither of us glanced down.

She gave me the same steady, unyielding gaze as when I'd been a child.
The shifter is my mother.

11

I CAN STILL TURN *her in.*

That was my first thought. Followed immediately by, *Could I live with myself if I betrayed my mother?*

Standing there, breathing raggedly, I thought I knew the answer.

After the choices I'd made the last few months, if it was between me or her, I'd do whatever it took to survive. Especially since she'd done the same to me. She'd abandoned me to grow up alone with my father all those years ago.

But my feet didn't move. My arms dangled limp by my sides.

Giving myself a mental shake, I reached back and drew a butcher's knife from the wooden block on the counter. I held it out between us. "Don't move."

The corner of her mouth tilted up in a smile, but she didn't protest.

Time to call for a nearby guard.

I was going to turn in my own mother.

When I opened my mouth to yell… I couldn't do it.

I couldn't pretend she was a stranger and still turn her in.

Not when she was the only family I had left. Not when she'd finally come back, after all these years.

Her smile softened as she waited patiently.

I lowered the knife.

"Come now, Jezebel," she said. "Let's drop the pretense, shall we?"

My lips parted.

How does she knows it's me?

My poisonous fingers gave away my Gift, but how did she see through my disguise? Or... did she even know it was a disguise? It occurred to me that she hadn't seen me grow up. That she didn't truly know what her own daughter looked like anymore.

Gripping the knife, a new fear flashed through my mind: what if my mother revealed my Gift to the Jinni Guard?

She knew it was me. And she'd seen me shift.

This was the woman who'd left me with my father without remorse, disappearing for years. I'd never gotten an apology or even an explanation. It wasn't hard to imagine her exposing my Gift, if it'd allow her to escape.

After wavering, I decided not to trust her further and remained in my false form. At least this way, if she betrayed me and named "Jezebel" as the shifter, she'd be pointing to a kitchen serving girl.

That would lessen her credibility.

It was best to assume this was her plan. If I expected the worst, I couldn't be surprised by it.

Still holding the knife, I made my voice cold, "What're you doing here?"

The early dawn light illuminated her face just enough that I caught a flash of something—disappointment? "I suppose that's fair. I shouldn't expect you to trust me after all these years. But I've seen your face, darling. After my attempt to get your information from the clerk failed, I braved the dining hall, and I would've recognized you anywhere. You don't need to wear this other girl's body for my sake."

I swallowed hard.

So much for my plans to confuse her.

She crossed her arms, waiting.

Fine.

Careful to check the windows and doors first, I shifted into my true form.

I forced my arms to stay loose at my sides, pulling my shoulders back and lifting my chin. "Do you truly recognize me?" I meant to sound sharp. Instead, I came across weak and unsure. I cringed inwardly.

"Of course," my mother widened her eyes. "I'd know your face anywhere." As I was about to soften, she ruined it by adding, "I also casually asked someone to point you out to be absolutely certain. I've been watching from a distance, waiting for the opportunity to talk to you."

"Why?" I stepped sideways as I spoke, subtly putting myself between her and the door. "Why have you been watching—more importantly, why are you here at all?"

THE SECRET SHADOW

"I came here looking for you," she replied, answering without giving me any new information.

I frowned and repeated, "*Why?*"

Once again, she didn't answer directly, in typical Jinni fashion. "Rumors said you'd come to live here at the castle. I wanted to look at the books to confirm. How was I to know the servant I pretended to be was gone? It seemed like a simple way to gain access to the books—if they didn't lock them up, it would've been a lot easier." She laughed then, a soft, bell-like sound that teased my mind with buried memories.

"You've caused a lot of trouble for me, you know." I decided to be direct. There wasn't time to play games right now, with my fate in her fickle hands.

"How so?" she raised her brows innocently.

I didn't buy that for a second. "You revealed your Gift in front of the entire Jinni Guard—"

She scoffed lightly. "Not the *entire* Guard—"

"—and now they're looking for a shifter in the castle," I spoke over her. "You've jeopardized my position here."

"I swear to you, that wasn't my intention," she replied, but she didn't seem overly concerned.

It was my turn to scoff.

"Jezebel, I truly didn't mean to cause you pain." Her brows pinched together. I couldn't tell if it was annoyance or sincerity. "I should've researched more carefully before I infiltrated the castle staff."

"Too late now," I mumbled, feeling oddly childish.

All the things I'd wanted to say to her when I was a little girl came flooding into my mind.

Why did you leave? Why didn't you take me with you? Why did you never come back?

But none of them were worth saying out loud because I knew the answers already.

The answers had become clear years ago.

Because she didn't care.

My voice came out flat, "I'll ask one last time: why are you here?"

Spreading her hands wide, gesturing to the room where we stood, she tsked at me as if it were obvious. "For your 18th birthday, of course."

A small pang in my chest tried to make its way to my face.

I refused to show it.

With a sigh, as if bored, I shook my head. "My birthday was weeks ago."

She tilted her head and then sighed as well, glancing around the room and twisting her hands instead of meeting my eyes. "All right. It was more than that."

Was she finally going to be honest with me? I tried not to hold my breath.

"I have someone back home who watched over you from a distance. To be my eyes and ears while I was away. They checked in on you now and then to make sure you were well. They kept me updated."

I blinked a few times, letting this revelation sink in. Did that mean she *did* care? But if so, why couldn't she have sent this person to take me in when my father became unbearable? Or bring me to her? It didn't make sense.

When I didn't respond, she continued, "They sent word that the old apartment was occupied by a new family. And that you and your father were nowhere to be seen. I had to come back, to make sure you were well."

Once again, I shook my head. Unable to help myself, I crossed my arms and tried to subtly put pressure on my chest to stop the pain there. "I've been in the castle for weeks now—over two months."

I didn't address the part about my father, banking on the fact that she'd never cared about him before, and she likely wouldn't start now.

Her gaze took in my closed-off expression, crossed arms, and stiff back, before drifting to the floor, as if the answer lay somewhere at my feet. "Coming back was an enormous risk," she said more softly, sounding unsure of herself for the first time. "I had to put plans into place, prepare multiple escape routes..." she trailed off.

That triggered a memory. A vision of her in armor—real armor, not the decorative kind that so many Jinn wore as a fashion statement. Not just a simple breastplate or arm plates, but full head to toe armor. If I closed my eyes, I could see the spot on the table where she used to set her helmet at the end of the day.

"You used to be in the Guard," I whispered, remembering again what the queen had said about an "unfortunate encounter" with a shifter. I narrowed my eyes to study her more closely.

She dipped her head in acknowledgment.

What did she do to make them so terrified?

Maybe one of my questions was still worth asking. I tried to sound nonchalant, but my voice came out soft, almost shaking. "Why did you leave me?"

As soon as the words left my lips, I wished I could take them back. I didn't know if I wanted the answer. She'd left because she didn't love me enough to stay. It was that simple. Hearing her say it out loud would only make the pain fresh.

I drew a breath to say never mind, but she spoke first, "It's a long story. Let's just say the Jinni Guard might know exactly which shifter they're looking for."

When she said that, she didn't look scared in the slightest.

The knife slipped through my fingers. It clattered onto the stone floor. "You were expecting to be discovered."

"Not that quickly," she replied in a wry tone. "I should've researched more carefully before choosing that particular Jinni form. Faulty information, but I still could've checked my sources."

THE SECRET SHADOW

If she'd anticipated being exposed, then she also had to know how the Jinni Guard would react. What she'd said earlier finally registered: *multiple escape routes*.

She had an exit strategy.

A muscle twitched in my jaw. She was going to leave me behind once more, after sentencing me to the worst fate in all of Jinn.

If she could betray me a second time, then I could do the same.

I allowed my irritation to show and turned away, using it as an excuse to scan the kitchen. Most of the counters were wiped clean and bare, but there were a few cast iron pans on a drying rack.

"Your birthday gift to me was to cause the entire Jinni Guard to search for a shifter?" I swallowed, throat tight. I tried to match her casual tone, not completely succeeding. "I wish you hadn't left behind a trail that leads directly to me."

"I didn't intend to do that," she protested.

When I refused to look at her, she reached out, clutching my arm. "Jezebel, I swear to you, I didn't know." She sighed. "I should've guessed. But before tonight, I had no idea I'd passed on this Gift."

I finally met her gaze, searching.

Her eyes were shadowed in the dark, seeming dark grey instead of the green I knew they were, but there was enough early dawn light to see her tentative smile.

She let go of my arm, but didn't step back. "I won't waste your time. Especially when we both know this isn't the safest place for us right now." Clearing her throat, she clasped her hands in front of her, and this time her voice cracked. "I came to ask if you'd leave with me."

"Leave?" I squeaked, taken aback. I coughed, and tried again, but it still came out higher-pitched than I meant it to, "With you?"

"Yes. I'd like you to come with me to the human world. I've made a home there, and I believe you'd be happy," she continued. "I realize I haven't been here for you the past few years."

"Twelve," I corrected in a flat tone. "Twelve years."

She shrugged, as if that didn't matter. "You had your father. I was on the run in the human world. I promise I'll explain everything when we have the time, but it was for the best. Trust me."

I scoffed. Moving toward the pan, I crossed my arms and allowed myself to sulk visibly. Let her think that was why I was moving away. Hopefully, she would follow and fall right into my trap.

She did.

As I turned, I found her much closer than I'd anticipated. With the drying rack directly behind me, I let my hand drift back to wrap around the handle of the pan. It'd only take one step plus a solid swing. She'd be out cold.

I'd call for the Guard and explain that I'd caught her shifting. They'd take her away. It'd be over, just like that.

Swallowing again, I sucked in a deep breath around the tight muscles in my throat.

"I *am* sorry," my mother whispered, when I didn't say anything else.

I waited, expecting more.

Nothing.

My hand gripped the pan.

I tensed, preparing to swing. *It's nothing she wouldn't do to you.* My muscles trembled, but my body wouldn't move.

I couldn't do it.

As much as I wanted to, I couldn't hurt my own mother, even if she'd hurt me like this before. Even if she *was* the shifter they were looking for. Even if she deserved it.

My eyes watered.

When my mother brushed away the first tear that trickled down my cheek, they only fell harder. She reached behind me to take my hand and slowly pried my fingers off the pan, one by one. Then, gently, she pulled me into her arms and hugged me.

Despite myself, I sank into the warmth that I'd missed so much all these years.

I sobbed.

"Shhh." She rubbed my back, setting the pan down with a soft thunk on the counter. "I know. I've been in your shoes. If I'd known you'd developed this Gift, I'd have found a way to come back sooner and help you." She pulled back a bit so she could see my face, tipping my chin up and frowning at me. "My source never saw a single sign." She studied me closer. "You hid it so well, I'd never have guessed if I hadn't seen it myself?"

She phrased it like a question, like she wanted to know why I hadn't revealed it to anyone.

I shook her arms off and stepped back. "Tell me," I said, unable to hold back some of the bitterness. "Did it go well for you when you revealed your own Gift?" Knowing the answer, having grown up with her complaints about my father and everyone else using her, I spoke before she could, "No. So why would I expose myself?"

"Fair point." She surprised me by smiling again. "You remind me so much of myself at your age."

I wrapped my arms tighter around myself. If the counter hadn't been directly behind me, I'd have taken a step back. "You might want a reunion right now, but I don't have the time. I'm too busy trying to avoid being framed for what *you* did." I ripped my gaze away and glared out the window, not wanting her to see more tears.

Her presence hadn't really changed anything. The Jinni Guard still had to

THE SECRET SHADOW

catch a shifter.

It was either her or me.

If anything, I had more problems now because I didn't trust her. She might give them *my* name. That meant it was in my best interest not to turn her in—at least until I knew if she'd keep my secrets. Which meant I was back to square one: no way to escape and about to be caught.

"What if you didn't have to worry about the Guard anymore?" my mother interrupted my dismal thoughts.

Glancing over my shoulder, I frowned. "I don't see a way around them…"

"Like I said," she spoke slowly. "I came to ask if you'd like to leave with me. You're not safe here. It was only a matter of time before something gave you away—if they weren't looking for you now, they'd be looking for you next month or next year, because at some point, you'll leave a trail. Trust me."

There were those two words again. *Trust me.*

I didn't.

But I *did* want answers.

The kitchen walls were turning golden with the first hints of sunrise. Someone could enter at any moment.

"Why should I?" I demanded. "You broke my trust when you left. You can't honestly believe I'd go with you, even if we could lift the enchantment spell locking us inside the castle."

"Don't worry about that, darling." My mother waved away my worries. "It's nothing I can't handle. If you come with me, I'll teach you multiple ways to get around enchantments, as well as dozens of other things a mentor should've shown you."

It was as if she knew my weakness.

When I'd first discovered my Gift, I'd wanted a mentor more than anything. Everyone else's Gifts had flourished under careful supervision and training, while mine grew stagnant. I'd been isolated. I still wondered sometimes what might've happened if I'd had more guidance—if Asher would've been able to force my hand and if my friends would still be gone.

A mentor would change everything for me.

While I didn't want to leave Shem behind, I was surprisingly tempted.

As I wavered, she cocked her head to the side, turning as if something had caught her attention.

The heavy kitchen door groaned.

Around the corner, still out of sight, someone shuffled into the kitchen.

We both froze.

A loud thunk sounded as they put a wooden door block in place, and then their footsteps whispered across the floor, heading in our direction.

My mother reacted first, leaning forward to whisper in my ear, "I understand this is all a bit sudden. Sleep on it. I'll find you later."

Before I could reply, she vanished.

A split second passed before I shook myself out of my stupor and traveled too, flashing back into the wardrobe in my room.

Four dark wooden walls surrounded me with the dresses still pressed against one side. The fabric rustled as I sank into a crouch. *What just happened?*

With my hands over my face, I drew a few deep breaths, struggling to find a sense of control after my entire foundation had been shaken.

Stepping out of the wardrobe, I fell face first onto the bed, exhausted. My body sank gratefully into the soft mattress.

I should try to think of a new plan, but all I could think of was catching a few hours of sleep before facing my imminent doom.

12

A FIST BANGING ON my door woke me. Sun streamed in with full force, making it clear I'd slept away most of the morning.

Is it already time for the noon meal? I blinked away the fuzzy remnants of sleep, dragging myself out of bed. Yesterday's dress was wrinkled from sleeping in it. As I turned to the door I paused. *I never called for anyone to bring a meal...*

It was the Guard, coming for my interview. It had to be.

A reply caught in my throat. If I wasn't here, they couldn't accuse me of missing an interview…

Without giving myself a chance to second guess, I rushed to the wardrobe and stepped inside. I shut the door softly, then traveled.

They couldn't interview me if they couldn't find me.

Reappearing one hall over from the council chambers, I sagged against the wall, breathing hard, as if I'd run around the entire castle instead of across my little room.

Close call.

I was safe for now.

Unfortunately, unless I found a more permanent way out of the interviews, it wouldn't last.

I threw my shoulders back and forced myself to breathe deeply as the rising panic threatened to take over.

Long moments passed.

It was only noon.

I didn't have a plan or even the first hint of one, but I couldn't stand here all day.

Glancing down, I groaned.

I was still wearing yesterday's dress.

The council already judged my every move. If I was seen in the same outfit two days in a row, they'd not only mock me for my attire, they'd start asking more dangerous questions. Either way, it wasn't worth drawing their attention.

Glancing around, I slipped into one of the little alcoves that lined the hallways, holding décor. I'd hoped to hide my shifting behind one of many full-blown suits of armor, often displayed from historical Jinni battles, or at the very least behind a vase filled with ever-blooming flowers. This one held only a painting featuring an ancient royal I didn't recognize. It'd have to do.

Pressing back against the wall, after checking the empty hall once more to make sure I wouldn't have an audience, I shifted my gown.

I couldn't do much beyond simple color changes and shape, but I tried to make it count. The forest green color turned a dark red. Where the fabric split to tastefully reveal one leg, I couldn't force it together, but I was able to lengthen the straps of my sandals where they circled my calves. I then turned them from tan to black, until they swirled delicately around my thigh, becoming a pattern of sorts before disappearing beneath the red fabric. The only other change I could think of was to raise the sweetheart neckline until it stretched to my neck, wrapping it around and leaving my back bare.

No one would believe it was the same dress.

Satisfied, I stepped out of the alcove. In the past I'd been tempted to create more striking shifts—I could've easily formed butterfly wings or peacock feathers that would've shocked the court with their realism—because they would've *been real*—but ultimately, I'd decided it wasn't worth the risk. If someone ever tried to search my wardrobe, I couldn't explain the absence of such a memorable gown.

Striding around the corner toward the council door, the guard there was unusually quick to grant me admission. I barely noticed, too desperate to find Shem and ask him to extend my immunity. He was my only hope.

When I entered, I jerked to a halt.

The entire council was gathered.

Colorful gazes around the room all turned to me, pinning me in place. I'd never seen this room so full. Almost three dozen council members filled the chairs, spilling past them to stand around the edges of the room and the balcony above. Shem must've called an emergency meeting and every single council member was in attendance.

THE SECRET SHADOW

Except me.

Shem paused in speaking to turn, and relief flooded his features as he let out a breath. "Jezebel. Thank goodness, you're all right. I was told no one could find you, but you must've got my message."

The knock on the door. Embarrassed, I managed to nod and duck my head, murmuring apologies as I pushed through the crowd without looking at anyone. *It hadn't been the Guard, it'd been Shem's messenger.* I found an open space to stand along one side.

As the heat of humiliation faded, though, I scowled at the Jinn around me. Whoever'd told him they couldn't find me hadn't even tried; before his messenger, no one else had knocked on my door.

"As I was saying," Shem resumed his speech, meeting the eyes of Jinn around the room as he spoke. "The Guard will continue to do interviews throughout the day. They should be able to complete them by this evening at the latest. We can expect them to begin working with council members near the end of the day."

No.

I shivered. I had roughly half a day left of freedom.

The thunder of my pulse in my ears made it hard to hear what Shem said next. I took slow breaths, focusing on drawing the air in and then out at the same pace. To say I was running out of time would be like saying the room was crowded—so obvious that it was suffocating.

"I called this meeting to ask that we conduct the council interviews here, in the back rooms," Shem was saying as I forced myself to pay attention. "To help it go as quickly and smoothly as possible."

I hadn't thought it possible to tense further, but the muscles in my back and shoulders spasmed painfully.

There'd be no escape here in the council chambers. No wardrobe to run to.

No privacy either.

I could envision the whole spectacle as if it were happening now—everyone would watch as I stepped into the back room with a guard. Jaws would drop as they dragged me back out again a few short minutes later. They'd declare that I was the hidden shifter and haul me to the dungeons to await my fate.

"Your highness," someone spoke up.

Chairs creaked around the room as dozens of Jinn shifted in their seats to look at the speaker. It was an elderly Jinni with streaks of silver in his hair and thinly veiled irritation. "May I ask what these interviews will consist of?"

"Of course." Shem moved to lean against a tall table, as if he needed the support. He stared at his hands for a moment. Inhaling, he straightened to look at all of us. "They're using a spell that pulls the truth from you. I allowed them to test it on me—" his mouth twisted upward slightly on one side. "With restrictions. Just a few pre-determined questions." He fiddled with the rings on his fingers, eyes falling to them, then stilled. "I tried to resist." Glancing up, his eyes met mine briefly. He smiled and said in a lighter tone, "I was curious."

A chuckle spread across the room.

I couldn't help but smile back, picturing it.

It was so like him. Always curious.

"It was..." his voice grew so soft that those in the back leaned forward. "I would call it uncomfortable. Heavy... I couldn't resist for more than a few seconds."

Swallowing hard, I tried to hide my anxiety, but it wasn't necessary. Nervous murmurs filled the air.

"None of you have anything to worry about," Shem spoke over the rising volume in a reassuring tone. "You merely need to speak the truth."

This was worse than I'd thought.

As I listened to Shem share more about the enchantment, I stiffened my resolve: I had to avoid this interview at all costs.

My mind ran through my limited choices for the thousandth time. There were really only two: besides getting caught—which was *not* an option—I could either flee or lead the Guard to another shifter.

My mother had offered a chance to escape with her, whatever that meant.

I might have to take her up on it.

As far as I knew, there weren't any other shifters in the castle. Even if I was wrong, they'd never reveal themselves now. With a day and a half or less, finding another shifter to turn in besides my mother was impossible.

I paused, chewing on the inside of my lip.

An idea slowly formed.

While my mother and I might be the only true shifters in the castle, the Guard didn't know that.

It was far-fetched, dangerous, and maybe not even possible, but it might work.

I can frame someone.

13

"IF YOU'D LIKE TO volunteer," Shem was saying, and my attention snapped back to him. *Volunteer for the interview?* I barely caught myself from scoffing out loud. *Never.* "You can approach any member of the Guard, and they'll direct you."

This caused a stir across the room. Or rather the absence of one, as every Jinni in the room grew still and an unnatural quiet settled over us.

Obviously volunteering would look good to the royal family. But it wouldn't happen. Every single person here had secrets. It didn't matter if they were related to shape-shifting or not—a truth spell was incredibly vulnerable. No one wanted to submit to the Guard.

Shem deflated slightly at the reaction. "If you'd rather wait for your turn, I completely understand. However, I must ask that you please do not roam the halls in the meantime, as it will make the guards work more difficult. If you're comfortable waiting here until the end of the day, we'll have food brought up for meals. But if you'd rather return to your rooms, just let the guard at the door know where we can find you before you leave."

With that, he ended the meeting abruptly.

Conversation slowly picked up in murmurs. A few council members approached Shem.

I stayed where I was.

There might still be time to frame someone, if I worked fast. Hopefully I had at least a few more hours. I needed to test every angle, make sure nothing would go wrong, and find an unsuspecting Jinni.

Though some council members remained seated, the chairs around me emptied rapidly. I slipped into a small blue velvet chair in the corner until the noon meal was delivered.

While some tried to discuss unrelated things, the main subject as everyone gathered to eat was the interviews. I tried to tune it out, keeping to myself.

On my right, a quiet woman named Eden leaned forward, hands pressed over her brow. Whenever I saw her, she was alone. If I framed her, would anyone speak up?

As if in answer, another council member approached the table, taking the seat beside her and rubbing her back. He murmured that they'd catch this awful shape-shifter soon.

I sighed, turning away from the sight.

I'd forgotten about her husband. He'd likely fight the accusation, making it harder to stick.

Finishing my meal, I couldn't listen to them calmly discuss the interviews any longer. I left the table to casually walk around the room, searching for the right person to frame.

My gaze landed on a Jinni by the bookshelves named Noam. He hadn't moved since the meeting, besides an urgent tapping of his foot.

I imagined shifting into his form. I could stroll out in front of a Guard member—Gabriel maybe—and then shift again. I could choose an animal that was difficult to catch—something with wings perhaps. Once out of sight, I'd return to my own form and then hide in my room while they hunted.

Noam wouldn't see them coming. They'd find him immediately and interrogations would begin. Would they question him much, if they'd seen him shift with their own eyes? If he had an alibi or could prove his innocence, it might only be a temporary solution.

But perhaps, considering the way he was tapping that foot, he had his own secrets that could distract the Guard for a while.

I sucked in a breath, trying to ignore the twinge of guilt at framing someone I barely knew who hadn't done anything to me.

It felt like what I'd done to Asher all over again. In some ways, at the core, it was exactly the same, because it boiled down to one thing: survival. It was either him or me.

As always, if I had to save myself, I'd do it. *Whatever it takes.*

Turning to the window, I pretended to stare out at the stunning landscape, stretching out in the distance, so no one would notice what I was really looking at: Noam's reflection where he sat behind me.

There was still one enormous flaw in my plan though. Both Noam and I had to leave this room for it to work. In his case, he needed to leave because staying here would give him an obvious alibi. Meanwhile, I had to somehow get out of this room without anyone noticing that I'd ever left to keep my own alibi intact.

I stayed there for a long time, keeping Noam in the corner of my eye. But he didn't leave, or even move, except to make up a plate of leftover food from the noon meal and return to his seat.

I couldn't slip away either without drawing suspicion. Not when the only way out was past the Guard. They'd make careful note that I'd left.

All around the room, tension built as the hours passed.

Dinner arrived. It was a light fare, since not many felt like eating.

I was running out of time.

"Ah, Jezebel," Jerusha's voice snaked up my spine, making me tense. "So good of you to join us earlier."

Turning to face her, I found Milcah, Dorcas, and a few other council members I'd worked with on occasion, Salman and Kareem, in her wake. I'd never worked closely with them. But I knew from experience that Kareem was a flirt, while Salman went out of his way to avoid me because, in Milcah's words, "He prefers not to speak to new council members until they've gotten a few years—or decades—of experience."

They stopped in front of me now, like a pack of wolves circling their prey.

Jerusha absently pet the thick white fur collar along the neck of her dress, which only added to my mental image. "Yes, I'm sure Prince Shem appreciated you attending the mandatory meeting."

My face flushed.

I tried to remember Shem's training back when I'd first arrived here. *Don't give them any ground. Don't reveal the effect of their words. That will only turn them into sharks with blood in the water.*

My cheeks burned under their intimidating gazes.

Too late.

I should frame one of them, not poor Noam. Unlike him, if Jerusha or Milcah had to undergo an interrogation from the guard, I wouldn't feel guilty at all.

Straightening my spine, I pretended a cheerfulness I didn't feel. "Yes, I understand someone sent for me? I'm sure I'll receive that message about this meeting eventually."

I doubted they'd ever sent one. If not for Shem's messenger, I wouldn't have known of it at all.

It wasn't my best comeback, but I was frazzled at the moment.

Always, if possible, turn their words back on them, Shem's voice came to me. As usual, I struggled to do so. *They* hadn't been late to the meeting.

Milcah's eyes narrowed slightly, calculating. "Were you not in your rooms for the messenger to reach you?" The question seemed innocent, but they were leading me somewhere... What if they actually *had* sent someone?

"I was sleeping," I replied lamely. "They should have knocked louder." I needed to get out of this conversation as soon as possible.

Turn their words back on them.

If they were insinuating that I might be the shifter, I could do the same. "If the shifter was pretending to be a council member, they'd be the *first* to arrive at a meeting, to avoid suspicion." I paused for a second before I drew my brows together. "What time did you say you got here?"

Milcah's answering chuckle was forced. "Fair point, dear."

I *hated* being called that.

Framing either her or Jerusha would be almost gratifying. I crossed my arms, considering. While Jerusha liked to condescend, Milcah had gone out of her way to actually damage my relationship with Shem.

I made my decision.

Smiling at her, I didn't bother to reply.

There was something about holding a secret power over her, knowing what I was about to do, that took away her edge and made her seem small.

As if she could feel the change, she frowned. Gesturing to the others, she said, "This whole unpleasantness is exhausting. I'm going to go lie down in my room for an hour or two. I'm sure it's not my turn for a little while yet anyway."

She headed toward the door, while the others broke off to join nearby groups.

My hopes rose. Milcah had just solved half of my problems for me without even realizing it. Alone in her rooms, she'd be easy to frame.

All that was left now was finding a way to sneak out of here unnoticed.

I blew out a breath.

With only one exit, barred by the Guard, that would be a challenge.

"Were they bothering you?" Shem's voice behind me made me jump.

When I turned to face him, my smile was genuine. "Nothing I can't handle, thanks to your tutoring," I teased, keeping my tone lighthearted to hide how unsettled I was.

His shook his head as if he didn't believe it for a second. "You don't deserve this constant ribbing. I'm growing tired of the culture in the castle that shuns outsiders instead of welcoming. We should be more open to change."

The fact that he'd noticed should've lifted the weight, but I was starting to wonder if I'd ever find my footing here.

He rubbed the back of his neck unconsciously, as he gazed around the room, both of us aware of multiple council members subtly watching our exchange. "I wish we could escape this madness together," he said with a sigh. "I don't think I realized how much I'd missed our adventures."

I didn't know what to say. "Me too," I whispered.

He was the calm in the storm swirling around me. For one brief moment, I could take a full breath.

"How are you handling the stress of the last few days?" he asked and the next wave of anxiety came crashing down.

The Guard was coming, I was a threat, and my solution was still full of holes.

"It's been… challenging," I said, choosing a word that didn't really reveal anything. "But I wouldn't want you to worry over me. You have enough going on."

He let out a soft laugh. "Enough going on could qualify as a grave understatement. But that doesn't mean I don't have time to care."

About me.

It was unspoken, but the implication hovered over us.

"Thank you," I murmured, leaning forward. "I've been concerned about you as well."

Not for the reasons he might think, of course, since I knew he was in no danger from a shape-shifter.

"Well, no need to fear much longer," he replied, relaxing back on his heels, putting his hands in his pockets. "It's only a matter of hours before the shifter is caught and brought to justice. I have complete faith in the Guard."

I dropped his gaze immediately, unable to hide the sheer panic that caused. I hoped he would misread my reaction as shyness.

His feet moved into view, and his warm hand came up to cover mine, as he tilted my chin up with the other. Waiting until I met his gaze, he repeated, "On my life, Jezebel, you're safe here."

Tears formed against my will.

Blinking quickly, I tried to hold them back. One slipped through. He caught it on my cheek, wiping it gently away.

"Thank you," I whispered finally, because I had to say *something*. He had no idea how false that was, but that wasn't his fault.

I swallowed the rest of the tears building in my throat, trying to find a peace I didn't feel.

Turning my fingers over in his hand where he still held mine, I touched his skin lightly. "It means a great deal to me to hear you say that."

He gently squeezed my hand in response, not letting go. "You look like you need to get away from this chaos for a little bit."

I held on like he was an anchor in the midst of a storm, attempting a small smile. "You see right through me. But I don't want to unnecessarily draw anyone's suspicions in a time like this…" I waved in the direction Jerusha and Milcah had gone, knowing he'd understand exactly what I meant.

He gave a short laugh, shaking his head. "Understandably so."

Gazing at him, I felt safe. Enough so to softly add, "I just wish I could go back to my room and lie down for a bit…"

His eyes grew a little vacant, and I thought he was about to pull away, when he surprised me by nodding. "I might have a solution."

I stilled.

With a hand on my arm, Shem turned us slightly so his back was to the room and lowered his voice. "Use the staircase. Make it seem like you're going up to the balcony or the library to read a book. No one will think twice about it."

I squinted, trying to understand what he was saying.

Even softer, he added, "As long as both doors are shut, and no one sees, you can travel."

I stared at the unassuming door to the stairs, eyes widening.

He nodded. "The staircase is my version of your wardrobe."

I quickly slammed my jaw shut, hiding my surprise from anyone watching by pretending to fix my hair. I'd never have guessed that.

"You're revealing your private traveling room?" I whispered. "To me?"

As far as I was aware, no other council member knew of this. Jinn protected their privacy, and the royal family even more so.

"I'm happy to," he replied, though his eyes still seemed slightly empty. He blinked and the feeling was gone. Maybe I'd imagined it. "Especially if it keeps you from traveling the halls. I worry for your safety when you're alone."

I waved a hand. "I promise I'll be fine."

"It's not just the shifter." Clearly he'd noticed my skepticism this time. I needed to hide it better. "The Guard has also been marking those who've undergone the interview so that they can see at a glance who's been through it."

Marking.

"How?" I whispered. The back of my neck tingled in premonition. "What does it look like?" Something told me this was another step on my path toward the dungeons.

"I don't know. Only my father and the Guard know. But apparently I have it."

I pulled back to look at him more closely. His pale eyes lacked their usual energy and his dark hair hung even more disheveled than normal, but otherwise he seemed the same. "I don't see anything."

"Exactly." He raised a brow. "So you have nothing to fear. The shifter has no idea how close we are to catching them."

A shiver raced through me. I had to clench my jaw to avoid my teeth chattering. *Oh, I have some idea.*

"Now go," he said with a smile, seeming a little more like his old cheerful self. "I'll make sure the Guard and this nosy council of mine never know you left."

Swallowing hard, I stepped closer to Shem and placed a hand on his arm, raising on my tiptoes to kiss his cheek, which was more than I'd ever dared to do. "Thank you," I whispered, meaning it more than he knew.

THE SECRET SHADOW

Now I had both an alibi *and* an escape from this room all in one. Shem had just given me the opportunity to frame Milcah.

14

HEART POUNDING AS I left the prince behind, I moved toward the staircase.

Conversation buzzed around me as I wove through the main floor, overhearing gossip about who the shifter might be. I didn't stop to talk or meet anyone's gaze.

Most council members remained on the main floor, but I still had to take the stairs up and then back down twice before the staircase was finally empty.

I waited for the doors at both ends to shut.

Immediately, I traveled.

Landing in my room, I entered through the wardrobe as usual, breathing an enormous sigh of relief.

But even here, the pressure on my chest didn't let up.

My comfortable room was beginning to feel like a prison cell.

Maybe my mother had the right idea. As each passing hour dragged on, I grew more tempted to leave with her.

If my plan didn't work perfectly, I might still have to.

This constant dread was giving me a headache.

I pressed my hands to my temples, rubbing circles in an attempt to ease the steady throbbing.

THE SECRET SHADOW

Ever since my mother had arrived, a hopelessness had slowly started to swallow me up. I couldn't breathe. I couldn't think. I couldn't seem to catch a break.

But if the Guard began interviewing the council soon, they might clear Milcah of suspicion before I had the chance to frame her.

Adrenaline surged.

I was out of time.

Stepping up to the full-length mirror that hung on my wall, I ran through the hazy plan one last time to solidify the details.

Milcah should be alone in her room by now. For the next hour or so, she shouldn't have an alibi.

On the other hand, as far as the Guard was aware, I was still in the council chambers. Since Shem had declared everyone must ask permission to leave, my own defense would be ironclad.

Once I shifted into Milcah's form, I simply needed to walk out my door and find the nearest guard.

Then, as Milcah, I'd shift again, right in front of their eyes—maybe into a Lacklore though, instead of a bird? That way, if the guard tried to use their crystal spear, I could knock them down with a massive paw...

I nodded to myself, and my reflection nodded back.

While the guard was unconscious or on the run from the dreaded shifter, I'd find a hidden alcove to return to my own form, travel to the council room through Shem's secret loophole in the staircase, and simply wait for the official announcement that the shifter was caught.

Milcah could be named the shifter within the hour.

The plan will work, I tried to reassure myself.

Using the mirror, I stepped close enough to see every detail and began to shift.

Eyes first. Then face, hair, body, and finally, an attempt at her swooping forest-inspired dress that she'd worn to the meeting earlier. I couldn't quite get the greenery right—it'd looked like actual branches encircling her long legs, with revealing but subtle glimpses of skin. Hopefully, no one would think to question any minor differences.

At the bottom mirror, movement caught my eye.

A thin strip of wood peeled away from the rest.

I stopped breathing.

Between one blink and the next, a tiny insect-like creature became a slender Jinni woman, forcing me to back up or be squished.

My mother.

How long had she been here?

She moved to sit on my desk, studying my new form, frowning. "Is this a spontaneous shift or are you planning something?"

I blinked, trying to orient myself. No "hello" or "how are you handling the pressure?" I pressed my lips together, unsure I wanted to share my plans. Instead, I gestured toward her. "What kind of creature was that?"

"The humans call it a 'Walking Stick'," she said with a grin, hopping off the desk and moving toward the window, glancing outside before continuing to wander the room. "They're not the most creative."

"Who? The Walking Stick?" I frowned.

She laughed as she traced the carvings on my bed post, swinging around one before peering into the attached bathing room. "No, the humans. The Walking Stick itself is actually quite creative when it comes to hiding in plain sight."

"Is that something you do often?" I asked boldly. Why bother beating around the bush, when she clearly didn't?

"All the time," she replied, grinning as she faced me finally. "Now, tell me." She waved at my disguise. "What is all this about?"

I hesitated. Might as well tell her. "Milcah is going to be our shifter. You and I will be safe once they think it's her."

For some reason, I expected a bit of approval or at least a hint that she was impressed.

Instead, she twisted her lips to one side, head tilting, then shook her head. "This plan seems underdeveloped."

I scoffed. "How much *development* does it really need? Pretending to be someone else is fairly straightforward for the two of us."

She ignored my sarcasm. "The Guard is alert and quick on their feet. And they have Gifts you don't even know exist. What if they're able to capture you? It wouldn't matter if they knew who you were or not—you'd still end up in the dungeons."

Rubbing my eyes, I sighed. "Then I'll wait to shift into an animal form until I'm out of reach." When she opened her mouth to argue again, I added, "And I'll shift multiple times. By the time they think to look for a different animal or person, I'll be long gone."

One brow rose skeptically. "It's still reckless. All it would take is one deviation from the plan—one little detail going wrong—and the trail would lead directly back to you."

I crossed my arms, and a long pause stretched between us.

She's right.

I blew out a breath. "It's the only plan I have!" I never yelled like that. Stepping back, I dropped onto my bed, lowering my head into my hands. It was too much. She'd just torn my last remaining hope into shreds.

"You also have to consider, how long would this solution even last?" My mother continued mercilessly. "Once they find out whoever *this* is—" she waved a hand at Milcah's body—"she'll most likely find a way to prove her innocence

THE SECRET SHADOW

in a few short weeks or even days. Then what? If they ask who framed her, who will she consider first?"

I swallowed hard.

Even if she *didn't* suspect me, my name would likely still be the first one on Milcah's lips.

"And what if they don't lower the enchantments around the castle while they interrogate her? You wouldn't even get the opportunity to run. And you would *have* to run eventually, because this is only a temporary solution."

I clenched my jaw and looked away. I wanted her to be wrong. Desperately.

But the truth was, she had a point.

If Milcah showed her face as I tried to frame her, it'd be over. If they *caught* me while framing her, it was over. If anyone suspected there was more going on than met the eye? Over.

"I told you I had a way to leave, darling," my mother said when I didn't answer. "You don't need to put yourself through all this emotional distress."

I flushed. "I don't *want* to leave." As soon as the words left my mouth, I blinked in surprise. I couldn't remember the last time I'd been so candid with anyone. Not even myself. But at this point, I didn't have anything left to lose. In a whisper, I added, "I don't have a choice anymore."

My mother tilted her head, studying me. "You always have a choice," she said with a slight frown. "You're one of the most powerful Jinn in the world. You simply need to decide what you want and then make it happen."

"I want to *stay*." I said immediately.

She shrugged. "So stay."

A knock sounded on the door before I could answer.

I leapt off the bed, panicking at the sight of the hands fluttering up to my mouth.

They weren't *my* hands.

I was still in Milcah's form.

Could I frame her now? Coming out of *my* room? Not likely.

Quickly, I shifted back to my own form.

It wasted precious seconds.

As I did, I wondered darkly if maybe I should just give myself up.

At this point, probably nothing could save me.

"I didn't think the Guard would come back again so soon," I whispered in despair, unable to make my feet move toward the door.

My mother laughed lightly and waved me forward. "It's not the Guard."

I still didn't move. "How could you possibly know that?"

She grinned as she moved toward the wardrobe to hide in the corner, out of sight. "Because I ordered a noon meal delivered."

My jaw dropped. "You let them *see you*?"

Again, she chuckled, shaking her head. "Of course not. I let them see *you*."

Lips parting, I stared at her. She could successfully impersonate me after only our brief meeting in the kitchen earlier? It took me ages to convincingly shift into another Jinni—even Milcah's form was difficult for me, despite enduring her company for months now. Was this something I could learn under her tutelage? A longing stole over me as I was torn between wanting to stay and wishing I could take her up on her offer to leave this place and mentor me.

My mother made a shooing motion with her hands, distracting me from the internal debate. "Hurry up. I'm starving."

Swallowing hard, I forced myself to open the door. Sure enough, it was someone from the kitchen. Instead of letting the serving girl carry the tray in, I reached out to take it, thanking her and shutting the door as fast as I could without seeming suspicious.

My mother took the food before I could set it down, snatching up a piece of toast.

"How'd you know the kitchen would bring a tray?" I asked, frowning as my stomach rumbled softly. Normally this is what I would do, and I hadn't eaten much today. I wandered toward the window, away from the delicious smells, but they followed me. "How have you waited this long to eat but you're still able to shift? Did you have food stored somewhere?"

She laughed, holding up her hands in surrender at the volley of questions. She dusted off the breadcrumbs and picked up the fork, taking a bite of eggs before answering. "I have some insight into the castle patterns from back when I lived in the barracks with the rest of the Guard," she began.

That sparked a whole new set of questions in my mind, but she continued, "I don't have any remaining food stores, but I can usually shift at least a dozen times, if not more before things get desperate. Why do you ask? Is it different for you?"

Very different, I wanted to say. *I can only shift a handful of times at most before my Gift gives out.* I shrugged. "A little." Apparently my Gifting wasn't as strong as hers. At least, not yet. If that was the case, was there any limit to what she could do?

"Let's come back to the more important topic," she said, before I could ask anything else. "You want to stay."

My heart squeezed painfully in my chest.

I could only nod.

"Well then. What's your plan?"

I clenched my teeth. Wasn't it obvious? Crossing my arms, I turned to stare out at the gardens. "I had one, but thanks to you I don't anymore."

"You mean you don't have a *working* plan." Silverware scraped the plate as she tried to get every last bite.

My stomach clenched painfully. I wished she'd saved some for me. It'd look odd to request a second meal tray from the kitchens, which meant now I had to wait until tomorrow to eat.

Taking a deep breath, my mother dabbed her lips with the napkin. She pulled the desk chair out, then dragged it a little further into the corner, dropping into it with a contented sigh. "You have to put yourself in the *mind* of another Jinn, as well as their body. Think outside of what you would do, and ask what you would do as someone else."

"I wouldn't know where to start."

"Try. Picture yourself in the royal family's shoes—what would make you innocent in their eyes?"

I sighed. Just like when I was younger, she was relentless. It was a waste of time to argue. "They'd probably have to see another Jinni shift while I was in the same room, at the same time, in *this* form. Since they believe there's only one shape-shifter in the castle, that would prove my innocence." I shook my head, moving to sit on the bed. "It'll never happen. I'd need to touch someone else to shift them, and there's no way to do that without being seen. They'd figure it out."

"Mmm," she hummed, tilting her head, considering. "I'll admit it'd be difficult…"

"It'd be impossible," I said flatly, falling back on the mattress. I stared up at the silk canopy above.

Silence filled the room until curiosity made me prop myself up on my arms to look at her. She gazed at some spot over my shoulder, unseeing. After another long moment, she shook her head. "Perhaps you're right. What's another way you could claim to be innocent?"

"I could figure out this invisible mark they're putting on people and find a way to get it for myself," I said impulsively, thinking of Gabriel and how that would finally wipe the superior look off his face.

"It has potential." She smiled a little, the way she had when I'd tried to poison her. "I'm impressed." As my chest swelled a little at her praise, she added, "Unfortunately, it won't work. I'm fairly certain they're keeping track of who's marked."

I deflated. They'd be fools not to track the mark, and I knew she was right.

We were silent again.

Somehow, that was worse than her pushing me to search for solutions. It told me she didn't see an alternative either.

Though she'd never admit defeat, we both knew the Guard was slowly closing the trap with me inside it.

"Come with me instead," she spoke softly, confirming my guess. "We'll leave this place together."

"We can't," I reminded her with a half-hearted laugh. "The enchantment prevents everyone from leaving, have you not tested it? Unless you know something I don't?"

"Don't worry about that." Her face lit up, as if excited by the challenge.

I shook my head. She'd always been more optimistic than me. More willing to take risks. "I tried leaving in animal form already. It doesn't work. We can't leave, and we can't lift the enchantment."

Her laugh sounded like low bells. "Are you sure about that?"

Before I could answer, she began to shift. But not into a creature like I had... instead the queen of Jinn formed in front of my eyes, taking my mother's place.

My lips parted despite myself. "You'd dare to impersonate Queen Samaria?" I whispered.

"Guards!" she said in such a convincing tone that I jumped slightly. "We must lift the enchantment immediately, by order of the crown! The shifter was just spotted outside the castle, and they're escaping!"

I gaped at her. *Why didn't I think of that?* As she shifted back to her true form, I snapped my mouth shut. *Because I wouldn't have the nerve.*

My mother returned to her own form, picking up the cloth napkin as she sat down again, dabbing her lips as if this were normal dinner conversation instead of a life-changing option.

Possibly my *only* option at this point.

I couldn't deny that leaving was tempting.

After spending two months on the council, I didn't feel like I belonged here anymore than the day I'd arrived. Less, if that was possible.

Sighing, I crossed my arms. Shem's face appeared in my mind again along with a twinge of pain. If there was even the slightest chance, however improbable it seemed, I'd much rather stay. He was my one friend in the world. And I was lying to myself if I didn't wish he was more than that.

"Maybe we can discuss—" I began, when the wardrobe next to my mother made shuffling noises.

Someone had just traveled inside.

The door swung open.

15

SHEM'S GRINNING FACE APPEARED inside it. "I was able to get away after all, and I thought you might want company—are you talking to yourself?" he asked, stepping out and swinging around to glance at the corner where my mother sat.

I sucked in a breath.

But, of course, the corner was empty.

The speed of her shifting never failed to surprise me.

"I'm… practicing something I wanted to say to you," I said the first thing that came to mind. It was hard not to glance around the room and search for my mother.

"Oh?" He put his hands on his hips and faced me. "All right then, I'm ready."

"Ah," I fumbled for something to say, regretting my choice of words. "I need a bit more time to get my thoughts together."

"Take your time." He moved to lean against the wardrobe with a small smile.

Was I blushing? Normally I could stop that, but around him I got so flustered that I didn't notice in time.

He waited patiently.

I had to actually come up with something.

The silence lengthened, and under pressure I couldn't think. Swallowing, I opened my mouth, hoping something reasonable would come out, "Are you taking time to reassure all the ladies—" I winced at how jealous that sounded, "—council members, that is, individually?" I hoped he wouldn't notice.

Shem didn't smile for once. His serious gaze made my heart drop. "I haven't had a chance," he said quietly, stepping closer. "But I also don't have any desire to. I only wanted to see you."

I searched his eyes for meaning. He'd never been this forthright before. "Me?"

He swallowed and took one of my hands in his own. Was he nervous? "I find myself thinking about you often lately. Especially now, when everything seems so uncertain."

"Me?" I repeated again, feeling flustered. "Why?"

Blinking, he began to withdraw his hand. Was that hurt flickering in his eyes?

"I'm happy to hear that," I rushed to say, grasping his hand between my own. "Because…" I struggled to be as straightforward as him. "I've been thinking of you too."

"Have you?" The corners of his eyes creased as he smiled gently and squeezed my fingers. "I know you've been anxious about everything." He waved a hand in the air, gesturing to the castle as a whole. "The interviews are invasive, I'll admit, but they're quick and painless. This will all be over before you know it."

"I suppose it will be my turn soon," I whispered.

"It probably should be…" I glanced up at the smirk in his voice. "But I made sure your name was near the bottom of the list in the last fifty or so."

I bit my lip, unable my relief. "The others would hate it if they knew." Milcah and Jerusha in particular.

He grinned back. "They'd be livid."

A laugh slipped out as I pictured their reaction, but then my smile fell. This morning, he'd said the interviews should be over by the end of the day. The last bits of golden sunlight touched his face now, highlighting the evening shadow along Shem's jaw. It was almost the end of the day. It'd been a kind gesture, but it likely didn't buy me much more time. The Guard could still arrive any minute.

I stared at our hands. Neither of us had let go. I savored the small connection.

Lowering my voice, I murmured, "Does Gabriel know? Because he's stopped here multiple times already." Impulsively I added, "I don't want to suggest something that might cause more anxiety for the royal family, but… it almost makes me think he's hiding something. Why else would he be so persistent? Have the Guard members undergone interviews or are they considered above reproach?"

Slowly Shem pulled his hands from mine with a frown.

I shrugged, spreading my hands wide. "It's truly none of my business." Maybe I'd pushed too far. "I just thought you should know."

"I haven't noticed anything out of the ordinary…" he trailed off, lips pressing together, glancing at the door.

I put my hand on his arm, feeling his pulse under my fingers. I waited until he met my gaze. "Just… maybe see if he has an alibi?" I asked softly, trying to sound uncertain. "Better to know if there's something to know…"

He nodded then, with a vacant look in his eyes. Shifting his stance, he refocused on me. "I'm sure you're right. I'll look into it."

Surprised that he gave in so easily, I hesitated, trying to think of something else to say while my mother was eavesdropping somewhere in the room. Now that he'd finally come here to see me, I hated that all I could think about was how I wanted him to leave.

"Thank you," I ended up saying lamely. "I appreciate it."

He slipped his fingers beneath mine once more, lacing them together. It felt natural. "Is there anything else I can do to make this time less difficult?"

I chewed on my lip. There was, in fact, something I wanted. I'd hoped for months now that it might happen naturally, but it never had. Now, for all I knew, this might be my last chance. *So what if my mother sees?*

I threw caution to the wind. Stepping toward him quickly before I could lose my nerve, I tilted my face up, lifted onto my toes, and kissed him.

His lips were warm.

Eyes closed, I sank into him for a second, before realizing he hadn't moved.

Pulling back slightly, I looked at his full lips, reluctant to meet his eyes. Suddenly I was terrified that I'd made a mistake.

When he sucked in a breath, he confirmed it.

I'd gone too far.

Humiliation washed over me as I jerked away, unable to look at him.

Immediately his arms caught me, folding me back in. He gently lowered his face to mine. "Jezebel," he whispered.

And then he kissed me back.

Warmth chased the fears away and for a long moment I forgot everything else.

My shoulders relaxed as tension left my body, leaving me loose, almost giddy.

He brushed a hand over my cheek as he pulled back, tucking me into him and resting his chin on my head. Both of us breathed deeply, not saying anything. We didn't need to. The unexpected stillness was sweet.

"I should get back to the council or they'll wonder where I am," he said softly, as if this moment somehow required whispering. "But I'll come check on you as soon as I'm able to get away."

I only nodded. My voice would tremble if I tried to use it now.

He climbed back into the wardrobe, and closed the door. Through the tiny openings in the wooden carvings he was there one second and gone the next.

I let loose a heavy breath.

The wardrobe was empty. He was gone. It was what I'd wanted a few short minutes ago, except I didn't anymore.

I touched my lips. They were curved in an unconscious smile.

Shaking myself, I blinked to refocus and opened both wardrobe doors wide. This way no one could travel into it again until the doors were closed.

That would prevent any more surprises, no matter how sweet.

"Mother?" I whispered, turning to the corner where she'd last been.

Searching for the tiny stick creature, I found her peeling away from the foot of the wardrobe where she'd blended in.

She grew to her full size in a few short breaths.

"Ah," she said softly once she could speak. "*Now* I understand why you're so insistent to stay." She strode over to the window, eyes on the gardens, or maybe on something only she could see. "I had something similar myself once."

"With father?" I asked.

She scoffed. "Not exactly. Your father... well, he helped me in many ways, but no. No, there was another here, in the Guard as well..."

She didn't finish the story, and I didn't know if I wanted to hear the details. They wouldn't change anything. In the end, she'd left, and that was all that mattered.

Turning away from the window, she faced me and sighed. "I might not have had to run if I'd had *that* particular Gift. Why haven't you used it yet? Are you saving it as a last resort?"

What? That didn't make any sense. She *did* have my shape-shifting Gift... This conversation felt like trying to untie an impossible knot.

I shook my head. "Are you saying you can't travel?" That was my only other Gift. That didn't make sense. *How does traveling help me in this situation?*

She only laughed. "You don't have to pretend with me, darling. I'm not going to turn you in. If I was, I would've done it already, don't you think?"

My head ached like it might split open. "Can you say it plainly? I'm not following."

"You really don't see it?" My mother frowned, gesturing toward the open wardrobe where Shem had last been. "You manipulated him so easily. Gifts like that usually take time to master and become so natural."

Manipulated?

"I would *never* manipulate Shem!" I yelled. Pulling back sharply, I glanced at the door, hoping no one was in the hall to overhear.

Grinding my fists against my eyes, I found them wet with tears I hadn't even noticed were falling. I drew in a ragged breath.

THE SECRET SHADOW

Technically, I *had* convinced Shem to do some things for me. But that was because he cared for me.

Wasn't it?

Little splinters bit into my fragile heart as my confidence wavered. I reached for the bed post beside me, needing to steady myself.

Had I used a Gift on him without realizing it?

I tried to remember our conversations. He'd agreed to help me avoid the interviews when the search first began. Had that been regular persuasion or something more? Milcah had been there! Surely she would've noticed a Gift like that being used and exposed it...

But then there was earlier today. He'd clearly wanted everyone to be available for interviews, and yet when I'd wished for an escape, he'd provided one.

A very private escape, no less...

No. I refused to believe it.

"Someone else maybe," I said in a firm, low voice, glaring at my mother. "But not Shem."

Someone else.

The words hit me as a face came to mind, unbidden. I wanted to deny it even as the reality sank in.

Gabriel.

I'd manipulated Gabriel.

There was no one in the castle who liked me *less*, besides him. Unlike Shem, he had no reason to listen to me. Yet he'd been determined to do the interview one moment and abandoned it a second later. After I'd told him to...

It was suspicious behavior all on its own, but when added to all the rest, the evidence loomed large.

A tiny part of me allowed myself to consider it.

It would explain so much.

A chill snaked down my spine as I accepted the truth.

I have another Gift.

Trembling fingers lifted to my mouth. My hands were cold.

My mother studied my face, softening. "You truly didn't know, did you? You were so caught up in the chaos going on the last few days that you didn't recognize your own salvation was right under your nose."

I shook my head, tears in my eyes. The shock of it made me numb. "I knew it was possible for Jinn to get latent Gifts," I whispered. It was rare, but it could happen as late as age twenty-one. I was only eighteen. "I just thought that dormant Gifts all happened at the same time. After the shape-shifting, I thought that must be it for me..."

Gently, my mother took my hand. "Looks like you were wrong."

When I didn't respond, she reached out and tipped my chin up until I met her eyes. "Jezebel, this is an unparalleled Gift. It's not something to fear, but to value."

She was wrong. It was another formidable Gift, yes, but that only made it another reason for Jinn to fear and renounce me.

"It must be powerful, for it to come to you so naturally," my mother added softly, letting go of my chin.

I cringed.

"Why does that upset you?"

A knock sounded on the door, startling both of us.

In an instant, my original problems came rushing back, reminding me that this new Gift wasn't my only concern. "That has to be the Guard," I said on a gasp. "It's time for my interview. What do I do?"

"Jezebel!" My mother took hold of my shoulders and shook me. "Think! This is the solution you've been looking for."

She meant manipulate the Guard.

That's treason.

Automatically I shook my head. "If they found out I used a Gift like this, especially to avoid a royal order, I'd be sentenced to death."

"Who's going to find out?" she pushed.

Knocking sounded again, louder this time. "Open up in the name of the king!"

"One minute!" I called out frantically. "I'm—I'm not decent!" My voice cracked, and I could only hope they'd listen.

"This is a much easier option than your plans to frame someone," my mother whispered now as she backed up to the wardrobe, stepping inside. "Convince them you're innocent and you'll get what you always wanted: the ability to stay here."

I'd have to be insane to consider what she suggested. It went against the first Unbreakable Law of Jinn: never use a Gift to deceive.

Could I truly use a Gift like this to my advantage, when it meant disobeying the royal family—including Shem?

Maybe.

If I could even figure out how to use the Gift in time.

Closing one of the wardrobe doors, my mother paused with her hand on the other, to look at me. "Unless you'd like to come with me? The offer still stands."

16

I WAS TEMPTED.

Evening light trickled in through the window as the sun set, casting everything in my room in gold. My lips still tingled from when Shem had kissed me. Inside the wardrobe, my mother waited, hand outstretched slightly.

I didn't want to lose any of this.

But I had to make a choice.

Turning my mother's words over in my head, a rising sense of hope filled me. Maybe she was right. This unexpected Gift was the impossible option I'd been searching for. It could allow me to stay after all.

"Your minute is almost up!" a gruff voice yelled from the other side of the door. It sounded familiar.

"If the interview goes poorly, I'll come with you," I whispered to my mother, taking a step back. "Hopefully, you can find me after."

She nodded, hearing what I left unspoken. If I wasn't here, she'd look for me in the dungeons.

With a soft click, she pulled the wardrobe closed. A second later, she vanished.

I started shaking.

Could my new Gift help me around the truth spell? What if I failed?

Convince them you're innocent.

Rushing to my attached bathing room, I hurried to splash water on my face.

My eyes were red and my skin blotchy. Staring into the mirror, I carefully shifted my features until I'd removed all evidence of my tears. It ate up precious seconds, taking far longer than it would've taken my mother. I was starving by the time I finished such detailed work, but it would do.

I wished I'd had a chance to practice this new Gift—to use it intentionally at least once before I had to use it to save my own life.

A heavy hand banged on the door again. "By order of the King and Queen of Jinn, if this door does not open soon I'm commanded to—"

"Yes?" I swung it open before the guard could finish.

It was Gabriel.

Of course it was.

A female Guard named Kinah stood beside him.

Anyone else would've been better—

No, I stopped my train of thought and smiled. *He will be perfect.* I'd have no qualms about testing out this Gift on him. No guilt to distract me.

I took a step back and wordlessly waved them in.

Gabriel strode inside, eyes sweeping the room, while Kinah went straight to my little desk with a small case and set it down beside my glass jar.

The hair on the back of my neck rose at the sight of it.

Unclasping the lock, she opened the lid to reveal ingredients for what I suspected was the infamous truth spell. She poured a cup of water and began to mix in different ingredients, making the liquid change from clear to a muddy brown with a hint of blue.

I stood by the open door, unable to swallow.

This may have been a huge mistake.

Glancing at my wardrobe, I almost made a run for it.

What if I can't make the Gift work on demand?

There was no room for error, and I had no idea how or where to start.

Gabriel paused in his search of the room to glance back at me, and I finally remembered to close the door.

It was like closing myself into my own tomb.

Forcing a swallow, I cleared my throat and moved closer to Gabriel. *Do I need proximity? What if it doesn't work on both of them at once, and I tip the other off?*

Questions surged as I stood there blinking.

Gabriel frowned and crossed his arms, making his armor clink together. "Have a seat on the bed."

I did as he asked, struggling to figure out my new Gift before it was too late. Something that Kinah wouldn't find suspicious if it didn't affect her in the same way...

"There's no need to hurry," I tried, attempting a trembling smile.

Gabriel's stern features didn't change in the slightest. He merely looked down his nose at me. I bit back the urge to shift Gabriel into a little bug and see how self-important he was then.

"Ready," Kinah said behind him.

He turned to take the cup from her.

Icy panic gripped me.

Before I realized it, I was standing, tensed to run.

"Remain seated," Gabriel snapped, fingers tightening around his crystal spear.

I'd never make it to the wardrobe.

Unconsciously, I placed my hand over where he gripped his weapon. "It's okay," I said urgently, trying to convince him for real now—Gift or no Gift. "I'm not a threat."

Behind him, Kinah glanced up from where she'd been putting away the remains of the enchantment ingredients. Her eyes met mine, then darted to Gabriel. Apparently, she didn't find anything to be concerned about, because she turned back to the box.

I dared another glance at Gabriel.

He hadn't moved.

Beneath my fingers, though, his hand had relaxed on the weapon.

Had it worked?

When I raised my gaze to his, I recognized the slightly vacant look.

It seemed like it.

If that were the case, then it seemed like I needed to touch him for the manipulation to take effect, at least for now. I disliked how limiting that made the Gift. Hopefully it might develop into something stronger in the future...

I didn't have time to consider it further.

"Drink," Gabriel said, holding out the cup to me.

I couldn't.

But I couldn't say no either.

"Of course," I said, as calmly as possible, reaching for the cup.

Kinah would join him any second now. I needed to move quickly.

Here was the true test.

I held Gabriel's gaze as I wrapped my hand around the cup, making sure to also touch his fingers. Quickly, without breaking eye contact, I whispered the same word back to him, "Drink."

I spoke so softly I worried he wouldn't hear me, or that Kinah *would*.

He lifted the cup obediently.

Once again Kinah paused in her work, turning to check on us.

I caught Gabriel's wrist before he reached his lips, preventing him from tilting his head back and giving us away. He stared at me, and I held his gaze, terrified that breaking it might decrease my control over him.

She couldn't see our silent exchange, but in the corner of my vision she frowned slightly. Then she shrugged and turned back to the case.

As soon as her gaze left us, I let go.

He drank.

I took the cup back from him, keeping my hand firmly around his wrist.

Eyes still locked with his, I spoke louder now, for Kinah to hear. "It's done." And then in case that wasn't specific enough, I added for good measure, specifically to Gabriel, "I drank all of it."

Watching both of them carefully for any sign they weren't convinced, I slowly let go and waited.

Gabriel crossed his arms and nodded, seeming to return to his usual arrogant self. "Have a seat and get comfortable. We have some questions for you."

Easing myself back onto the bed, I tried to appear relaxed and confident. As long as neither of them became aware of what I'd done, the worst of the interview was behind me—I hoped.

Gabriel turned to drag the desk chair across the floor, making me wince at the sound. He slammed it down to sit in front of me.

Kinah closed the lid of her case with a light snap and came to stand behind him.

They were close, but not close enough for me to touch. Which meant I'd have to finish the rest of this interview without my manipulation.

Hopefully I'd done enough.

"You should begin to feel the effects of the truth spell soon," Gabriel began in a flat tone, as if he'd said this a hundred times before. "You may feel a bit light-headed. And you'll find that fighting against the desire to tell the truth will make you physically ill."

That's when I knew for sure.

It'd worked.

Gabriel hated me as much as I loathed him. Ever since I'd come to the castle I'd stumbled through the court etiquette, offending him and the rest of the Guard constantly. I was no one, yet I'd been elevated to a status above his own, and he'd never forgotten the slight.

Gabriel would never willingly go along with my ruse. Which meant he truly believed I'd drank the cup dry.

I'd made him believe it.

Convince them, my mother's words came back to me, and hope freed my tense muscles, allowing my shoulders to sag and my clenched hands to loosen. I couldn't help smiling slightly. She'd known what I could do. "I'm ready whenever you are."

"We've already begun," Gabriel snapped, crossing his arms. He tilted slightly to one side before he caught himself, blinking.

The light-headedness. I held back another smile.

Frowning, he rubbed his brow slightly and said, "Tell us your full name."

"Jezebel, daughter of Sariah, daughter of Aziza," I whispered, feeling exposed, though this particular truth wasn't what they'd come here for. Had my mother returned to the room? Was she here now, watching? More importantly, did anyone still know her from the past that might recognize my family name?

It didn't seem so. Gabriel continued without pause, although he did seem to be blinking more than usual. "Now, tell us your name is Queen Samaria."

I opened my mouth obediently, barely catching myself. Instead of speaking, I made a show of clutching my stomach, hunching over as if in pain. "I… can't," I said finally, peeking up at them beneath my lashes, hoping this was a typical reaction. If they'd lied about how the spell worked, I'd know soon.

"Don't push yourself," Gabriel said, though he'd certainly waited long enough, letting me experience the supposed pain. He pulled out a small booklet, tearing out a piece of paper and handing it to Kinah.

She moved to my desk to write, although she was forced to stand since Gabriel had taken the only chair.

"Let's move on," he continued. "Tell us your Gifts, starting with the least important and moving to the most important. Don't leave any out."

I tried not to gape at the invasiveness of the question. *This* was how they chose to go about finding the shifter? Not, "Do you have a shifting ability?" or "Are you Gifted with changing shape?" but instead they were gathering a full list of every single castle inhabitant's Gifts?

Gifts were incredibly personal.

Some Jinn preferred not to share theirs with anyone, and that had always been our right. No one should be forced to reveal something so private.

And yet, here we were.

They'd have record of every Gift in the castle by the time this was over.

It made my blood boil.

Kinah had dipped her pen in the ink pot and now held it hovered over the paper, waiting.

Seated across from me, Gabriel kept his features still, hiding most emotion, but I could've sworn a small smirk touched his lips. "Resisting the urge to tell us will only prolong the interview, and as a result, your discomfort," he said after a long moment passed. "The king and queen require this information, but it will not be shared with the general public."

As if that made it acceptable.

At least, since he'd made that declaration without difficulty after taking the potion, I knew he was speaking the truth.

Eyes narrowing, I hoped it was normal for those under the truth spell to be furious, because I couldn't hide my disgust. "Traveling," I spat.

Nodding, he turned to Kinah and waved for her to write it down.

The sound of pen scratching against paper was the only sound in the room. Once done, the silence stretched louder than ever.

"Continue," Gabriel said, eyes pinned on me.

How long did my newly discovered Gift last? Did it convince him permanently or would he start to have doubts?

"That's it," I replied, crossing my arms and lifting my chin. Though I pretended calm, my whole body tensed. If I needed to, maybe I could lean forward to touch him again for my Gift to work. Would Kinah notice? I'd have to be quick…

He squinted at me. "That's all?"

Does he not believe me?

I bit my tongue, barely managing to keep my face void of emotion. Subtly, I leaned forward, ready to spring.

"Can you repeat that?"

I ground my teeth together. He wasn't questioning out of disbelief—he was trying to humble me.

"My *only* Gift is traveling," I growled. Even though it wasn't true, my pride smarted.

He let out a short contemptuous laugh. "Does the prince know? I would've thought—" he paused, wincing as if whatever he'd been about to say was causing him physical pain. After drawing a deep breath, he said instead, "—I always thought council members were supposed to be skilled."

I flushed hot from head to toe, shaking. Not from fear anymore, but pure, scorching fury.

I should use my Gift to make him strip naked and stroll through the castle halls. Or better yet, maybe I should reconsider framing someone, and frame *him*.

Another chuckle slipped out as he shook his head. Standing, he brought the chair back to the desk, where Kinah blew on the ink to dry it before handing him the paper. He added it to the little book, which he then tucked into a pocket beneath his armored breastplate. I took solace in the way he seemed paler than usual and swayed as if dizzy.

Once again his voice returned to the monotone of repetition, "Thank you for your cooperation. The crown will let you know when circumstances change and the threat is neutralized."

It's over? I succeeded?

If traveling really *had* been my only Gift, I'd have been terribly offended that I'd been forced to reveal that, so I tried not to let my excitement show as I stood too.

I can't believe it worked.

THE SECRET SHADOW

Kinah pulled a royal signet from her pocket, meant to seal a letter. It was dry.

Without warning, she placed it on my forehead, pressing, as if there were truly ink there.

I tried not to frown.

She removed the seal, inspecting her work.

My hand itched to touch my brow. I couldn't feel a thing.

At my expression, she held up the signet briefly. "It's enchanted. The Guard will see you're marked and it will prevent multiple, unnecessary interviews."

The mark.

I blew out a breath of relief.

If I'd known it was that easy, I might've tried to steal the signet and simply mark myself instead.

I nodded understanding, moving to open the door for them.

All that mattered was that they'd believed me.

As Gabriel exited and Kinah followed, I couldn't resist saying, "I'm so glad the interview went well, and that I was proven *innocent*."

I emphasized the last word. Gabriel's lips turned down in annoyance as he reached in to take the door handle and yanked it shut.

Blowing out a heavy breath, I sagged back against the wall, exhausted.

That could've gone horribly wrong.

I smiled, turning away from the door. My eyes caught on the wardrobe.

On the eyes within.

Pale blue and familiar.

Staring out at me.

I would know those eyes anywhere.

Shem.

17

"HOW LONG HAVE YOU been there?" My voice shook.

More importantly, how much had he seen?

He swung the wardrobe door open slowly on silent hinges. The dresses swished softly as he brushed past them and stepped out.

For a long minute, he didn't speak. I'd never seen him stare at me so coldly before. "You used a Gift on the Guard."

I opened my mouth, but nothing came out. To deny it would only make it worse.

"You forced him to drink the elixir instead of you," he whispered.

I winced.

Now I knew how much he'd seen.

Forced was a much harsher word than convince.

But I couldn't deny it.

"Did you use this Gift of manipulation on me as well?" he asked, dragging his eyes from the door back to mine. The hurt and betrayal in them brought tears to my eyes.

This is what I'd feared most. Why I'd never gotten the nerve to tell him my secrets. I deserved his hatred.

"Not intentionally…" I closed my eyes so I couldn't see the horror on his face. "I am so sorry. I didn't know that I was doing it. I—it was only an hour ago that I learned of its existence, I swear to you."

When he didn't immediately reply, I risked a glance at him.

He stood rigid with his hands clenched at his sides. "So," he finally replied. "You knew of it when the interview began."

My stomach dropped.

"Meaning, you knowingly used a Gift against the Jinni Guard in an interview—"

"Not against them!" I protested. "I just wanted to protect myself."

"Does that mean you are the shape-shifter as well?" he spoke over me.

I couldn't speak.

He looked stricken.

For a long moment, neither of us spoke, until finally, he whispered, "I suppose I must take that as a yes."

"Not—" my voice sounded strangled. I cleared my throat and tried again. "Not the one they're looking for."

Rearing back, Shem paled further. "There are others?"

I winced. "As far as I know, just one other. You have to believe me."

"I don't have to do anything," he said in a dark tone, stepping back without ever taking his eyes off me.

"Shem," I pleaded with him. But when I took a step toward him, he took two more back, moving too fast toward the wardrobe.

"Please," I stopped, holding my hands out in surrender, whispering through the tears. "You can trust me. You *know* me."

He put one foot in the wardrobe, hesitating. Lifting his eyes to my face, he whispered, "Do I?"

That struck me like a blow.

"I've been here for months now. I've never—" my voice shook so hard that I couldn't speak. Swallowing I tried again. "I've *never* used any of my Gifts against you."

He stood as still as a statue. One foot was still in the wardrobe, and his scowl was pinned to a spot on the floor.

"I don't know how to prove myself," I said through the tears sliding down my cheeks. My voice was thick with them. "Except to promise you on my life that I would never hurt you."

"And yet you already did." The wardrobe door cracked shut between us, punctuating his words. It hit so hard that it bounced back open, revealing an empty wardrobe, besides the few dresses that hung inside.

Sobbing, I crumpled to the floor.

I couldn't chase him. He'd only fear me more and likely call the Guard. Maybe he was calling them now.

I didn't move.

If he did turn me in, I deserved it. It was my fault he'd found out this way. No, more than that, it was my fault he didn't trust me, because without realizing it, I'd used my new Gift on him more than once.

Looking back at the last few days, I brought a shaking hand to my lips.

Possibly many times.

Burying my face in my knees, I let the tears come.

He called it manipulation, the same word my mother had used that I'd despised. And he was right.

If he hated me, it was only fair.

I tried to pull myself together, to hide my anguish, in case my mother came back. But I couldn't stop the flood of tears. I'd never admitted to myself how much I'd come to care for Shem. And now I'd ruined everything.

He'd never forgive me.

Swiping at the wetness on my cheeks, I yanked myself to my feet. I could *make* him forgive me...

I shook my head, ashamed that I would even consider it. Sinking onto the bed, I fell back on it, staring up at the canopy.

Was there any other way to salvage this?

I desperately wanted to avoid repeating past mistakes.

I wanted to be the good, noble, innocent Jinni girl that Shem had thought I was.

What would *that* girl do?

It was tempting to chase after Shem and figure it out later, but some part of me knew that would end in disaster. If I was to win his trust back, I needed to somehow come clean. It was a paradox. Because it was too late—wasn't it?

Maybe there was another way to prove that I could be trusted.

I bit my lip, considering.

I could tell his parents.

My heart dropped just thinking about it, and there was a good chance it wouldn't work...

But how else could I show Shem that I was on his side?

Jumping off the bed, I took a few precious seconds in the bathing room to dry my face and pull myself together, before I stepped into the wardrobe to travel.

I took a deep breath and fresh tears came to my eyes. Shem's unique scent of cinnamon and pine still hung in the air. My hand brushed against something, and for a second I could've sworn it was a hand, but the wardrobe was empty. My mind was creating a phantom touch, wishing he was still there.

My fingers shook, despite my resolve, as I took the knob and pulled the door closed behind me.

This could either go really well or horribly wrong.

So far, every single one of my plans had been the latter.

THE SECRET SHADOW

But there was only one way to find out.

18

I TRAVELED TO THE royal chambers. Or rather, to the entrance on the east side of the castle. Before I could stride down the long hallways to the royal family, I had to get past this checkpoint first.

Six guards stood watch.

Which meant six crystal spears were pointed at my face.

I attempted to appear calm as I swallowed, hard.

An icy wave flashed across my skin, and my ears felt like they might pop. The sensation of being in a bubble flooded my whole body, then swept away as I forced myself to focus.

I was going to turn myself in.

This is for Shem.

I pointed wordlessly to the mark on my forehead, mouth so dry that I had to swallow twice more before I could speak. "I've been cleared."

The guards exchanged glances. They didn't lower their weapons immediately, but one stepped forward to touch my brow. It tingled under the touch, responding. Some of the tension in the air faded at whatever they saw. "Business?"

That part of me that always whispered to use my Gifts reared its head again, but I shoved it down. It was time to be honest. This is what I should've done all along. This is what Shem would want me to do. It might very well be my downfall, but at least he'd see that I'd tried.

Gathering my nerve, I took a deep breath. "I have urgent news for the king and queen."

"It's not a good time," the lead guard said. "Give us the message, and we'll see they receive it."

I shook my head. "No," I croaked, clearing my throat. Pressing my shoulders back to project a confidence I didn't feel, I said, "It's about the shape-shifter. They need to hear it from me."

He broke his stern façade to glance at the other guards. If I lied, he'd be responsible. But if my claim was true, turning me away could anger the royal family. Most of them knew I was on the prince's council, which I hoped would work in my favor.

Finally, he nodded. "Come with me."

He nodded to the female Jinni beside him, who took over pointing a weapon in my face. They led me down the hall to a large meeting room between the king and queen's chambers. He knocked, then entered, shutting the door behind him.

Standing in the hushed hallway, surrounded by the other guards, I focused on my breathing which had grown shallow, and rehearsed what I would say.

Once again, I could've sworn I smelled the sweet fragrance of cinnamon and wood. A breeze blew across the back of my neck like a breath. My skin prickled. When I glanced around, no one else was there.

One of the guards frowned at me.

I stopped fidgeting.

The door opened after another long minute. "They'll see you," the first guard said, with narrowed eyes.

Smiling sweetly, I enjoyed the small victory. Halfway through the door, he shoved me forward, making me trip slightly, and both guards followed me in.

It wasn't the grand entrance I'd hoped for.

King Jubal and Queen Samaria sat on the soft green sofa straight ahead. The queen held her teacup paused halfway to her lips. Impatiently, the king gestured for me to come forward. "We accepted your request for our son's sake," he said briskly, by way of a greeting. "But be quick about it. Why are you here?"

Why was I here?

"I—" The guards shut the door behind me with a loud thunk and all my flowery practiced words flew out of my head. He wanted me to be quick. And Shem would want me to be honest. Best to get to the heart of it, then. Swallowing hard, I said, "I've come to tell you the truth."

Frowning, Samaria lowered her teacup, setting it down on the small table beside her.

I pressed on, hoping I'd somehow say the right thing. "I made a discovery, only an hour or so ago, that I have a new Gift."

It wasn't unusual for someone my age to continue developing Gifts.

They both nodded understanding, watching me warily. "Is this relevant to the crown?" the king asked when I didn't immediately continue.

"It is," I managed to say, clasping my hands in front of me where I'd been wringing them. *Stay calm. Make them trust you.* "As you know, I could keep this Gift to myself, but out of loyalty to the crown—and to your son—" I added, wishing Shem could hear and know how much I meant it, "—I feel it's important for you to know."

My fingers refused to stay still. Bringing my hands behind my back where they wouldn't be seen, I tried to stand tall and project confidence. "Before I share with you what the Gift is, I want to make it clear that I believe it can be of enormous value to you."

Their flat expressions didn't change.

I was tempted to draw a bit closer. Close enough to take their hands and use my new Gift on them, to help persuade them to my cause.

Just a tiny push.

No. I took a deep breath and blew it out. *That wouldn't be true honor. Shem would only think worse of me.*

The king's foot tapped irritably.

"I think this new Gift could make me a powerful ally for you. I can help you track down the shifter you've been looking for."

"How so?" the queen asked.

At the same time, the king leaned forward suspiciously. "What is your new Gift? Tell us immediately."

Though it was risky to disobey, I said instead, "I must beg you not to tell anyone else. It would break my heart to be feared for no reason, when I would never harm anyone." For good measure, I bowed my head. Using my Gift, I formed a tear and let it trickle down my cheek.

They sat stoically, unconvinced.

I dropped to my knees, abandoning self-respect to truly beg now. The tears that followed were real. "Please," I said in a voice barely above a whisper. "Let me work for you and use my Gifts on behalf of the crown. I want nothing more than to help. I'll do anything."

When I dared to glance up, the king and queen were exchanging a look I couldn't read.

"Get up," the queen said finally, with some compassion. She waved for me to sit across from them. "You can trust us to react calmly. Tell us now, what is this new Gift that's causing such fear?"

As I lowered myself onto the soft sofa, I turned to look over my shoulder at the guards standing by the door. "Please don't make me tell you in front of them." I dropped my gaze to my hands. "It would spread through the castle in less than an hour. And," I added, "Once it's made known, it won't be nearly as helpful to the crown."

The king raised a single brow, intrigued now. He waved a hand at the guards. "Go back outside. We'll call if we need you." Clearly, he didn't find me much of a threat, despite how I'd described my ability.

Waiting until the guards slowly turned and left, closing the door behind them, I sucked in another breath.

I still couldn't find the courage.

"You can restrain me, if that will prove my loyalty," I said, holding my hands out in front of me, hoping they wouldn't notice I'd said this only after the guards left.

"It won't be necessary, child," the king said gruffly. "Now. Out with it. Don't make us wait any longer."

I cleared my throat and nodded. My mind spun wildly as I tried to decide where to start. Perhaps before I shared my newest Gift, I needed to share the one that had caused me so much heartache from the start. "It's... multiple Gifts, really. But the most important thing you should know is that, while I am *not* the shape-shifter who is threatening this castle... I do have a slight shape-shifting ability."

I tried to minimize my strength in the Gift, but still winced as I said it.

The words could never be taken back now.

The queen stiffened, gripping her skirts as her eyes grew wide, though to her credit she did attempt to remain calm as she'd promised.

The king, on the other hand, did not, roaring, "What?"

I tried to curl inward and seem as small as possible. "Please, hear me out." I brought my hands together in supplication. "I think—I might be able to help you find the other shape-shifter, or at least, serve as one in the Guard?"

"We would not allow a known shape-shifter to be in the Guard," the queen said, putting a horrified hand to her chest.

But the king paused.

Staring at me for a long moment, he tipped his head, seeming to consider it.

The only sound in the room was the tick of the clock on the mantel.

At the risk of digging an even deeper hole—it couldn't get much worse now—I spoke up, "I can become both animal, human, and Jinni..." That seemed to make them tense, and I tried to backtrack. "Truthfully only animals come naturally to me, but in animal form I could make a valuable spy—"

"We cannot," Samaria hissed to her husband, interrupting me. "Not after what happened last time."

His voice was a low rumble as he finally spoke, "If, as she said, my dear, her secret is *not* known..." He ran a hand over his carefully trimmed beard. "There is some truth to her claims. It *could* be very useful to have someone with her skills working for us."

"I'll do whatever you ask of me," I promised, lifting my gaze to his. "If I ever fail you, you may have my Gifts severed."

Of course, they didn't actually need my permission for a Severance. If I ever crossed them, or if they simply decided not to trust me, that's exactly what I'd be sentenced to.

Still, it might help my case to offer.

A Severance was the most severe penalty in Jinn. Far worse than even death. To have your Gifts severed meant a miserable existence with a slow, agonizing decline until eventually one couldn't stand the pain anymore.

Instead of answering, the king paused, lifting his eyes to the wall behind me.

Shem's voice came from the same place, "You're attempting to manipulate my parents with your lies as well?"

Eyes wide, I spun to face him. *Where did he come from?* "No, of course not!"

He stood only a few steps away. There was no furniture nearby to hide behind. And I hadn't heard the door open... *Has he been here all along?* For a split second, I wondered if he had a secret Gift of his own?

"You didn't give me a chance to explain," I said softly, almost forgetting his parents were listening.

Shem's gaze lifted over my head, to his father's. He strode around the sofa, giving me a wide berth, coming to stand beside his parents. In a hard tone, he told them, "You really shouldn't have sent the guard into the hall."

King Jubal sighed. "Don't be overly dramatic. You know we each have protections in place for shifters." His hand strayed unconsciously to the large ruby nestled among a dozen other jewels in the center of his ornamental armor.

Enchanted in some way, most likely. How he thought it protected him from shifters, however, I couldn't say, since it hadn't seemed to respond to me in the slightest.

I kept my mouth shut.

"We already know about her Gift," the queen said, placing a soothing hand over Shem's on her arm. "She told us everything."

Well, not everything, I thought, wondering if I should speak up about that now or later. I hadn't had a chance to finish sharing my other dangerous Gift. Odds were good they'd like it even less than they liked shape-shifting, but perhaps they'd also see it as useful.

Before they could argue further, I pressed my hands together and repeated, "I would *never* hurt you or your family. I'm loyal to the crown. I've already told your parents that I'm here to serve, whether they want to expose my Gift, or..." I paused, hoping for the second option. "If they want to use my Gift in secret. Either way, I'm a humble servant."

Though still seated on the sofa, I bowed my upper body and kept my head down, terrified to look at Shem's face. Tears filled my eyes as I pictured the fear and distrust from earlier. Or had it been disgust?

If he still felt that way, even after my risking everything to tell the truth, I couldn't bear it.

I waited for him to speak now and twist his parent's view of me, to tell them of my *other* equally threatening Gift. But he was silent.

"I would never hurt any of you," I whispered to the floor, when the quiet stretched longer than I could bear.

If my eyes hadn't been trained on my feet, I wouldn't have noticed it.

A tiny creature on the ground.

Slowly, it peeled away from the wooden leg of the sofa. It waved a tiny twig-like arm up at me.

A walking stick.

Mother.

19

NO! I WANTED TO scream as she began to shape-shift.

But I couldn't without giving myself away.

Instead, I gaped from my chair as she exploded into the room, filling it in a few short breaths, shifting until her body reached all the way to the high ceiling.

In the form of a dragon.

She winked one oval, predatory eye. As her neck hit the plaster above, making it rain down on us, her razor sharp claws knocked down the blockade beside the door making it drop into place, locking us in. She fell onto all fours with a crash, claws making deep gouges in the floor.

I was still seated on the couch, too stunned to move.

Each time I thought my mother might finally care about me, she proved me wrong. She *knew* how badly I wanted to stay, and yet she seemed determined to ruin it. I didn't even know why I was surprised anymore.

Her red scales shimmered over huge, muscled thighs. Her long tail swung toward my face.

I ducked.

I'd never encountered a dragon in real life, so I'd never had the opportunity to try this shift—or even to think of it—but clearly my mother had.

Shem and his parents leapt back from their sofa, scrambling to retreat as she

THE SECRET SHADOW

turned to roar at them.

Their mouths were open in silent screams—or maybe not silent, and I just couldn't hear over my mother's roar and the blood rushing into my ears.

The queen trembled, seeming unable to react or use whatever Gifts she might have. Perhaps her Gifts were useless against a beast. But King Jubal reacted immediately. He spread his hands in front of him, creating a wall of fire. It roared to life in a heartbeat. This was the kind of Gift most Jinn feared.

Unfortunately, it did next to nothing against a dragon.

A growl ripped from my mother's throat as she side-swiped a heavy table with her tail, sending it crashing against the door and stepped right through the king's wall of fire.

Shem stood stunned into inaction.

I launched out of my chair finally, moving toward him on instinct. "Don't you dare hurt him!" I screamed, adding silently, *If you do, I'll* never *forgive you!*

Queen Samaria screamed and turned to run, trying to drag Shem with her, while the king yelled for the guards. Why weren't they answering?

Thudding noises against the main door registered faintly in the back of my mind. They were certainly trying.

King Jubal yanked a ceremonial sword from where it hung on the wall and stood in front of his wife, with only the dull blade and his decorative armor, prepared to fight the beast.

My mother lowered her head, eyes pinning them in place, stalking them.

Unhinging her jaw, she bared her teeth.

Heavy breaths in and out stoked the fire blooming in her chest, visible through her scales. Smoke began to pour from her open mouth.

She wouldn't.

"Stop!" I screamed again.

She didn't listen.

I dodged in front of the royal family, daring to put myself between them and her. "Don't hurt them!" I pleaded with her, silently begging her not to take this away from me too.

She was about to set my last chance to stay in the castle on fire.

Maybe that was why she was doing this.

She thrust me aside, talons scraping my skin and tearing my clothes, as her yellow eyes never left the royals. Rearing back, her head hit the high ceiling. Another roar made the furniture shake.

Tears sprung to my eyes—she was going to incinerate them!

I leapt forward.

Shifting faster than I'd thought possible, I copied her dragon form—the muscles, scales, fangs, and most importantly, the fire.

The dragon form was surprisingly similar to my favorite lizard form. I made my scales deep green like I always did. That way Shem would know it was me—

I hoped.

Using my powerful wings, I shoved her back, forcing her to give ground and shielding the royals with my body.

Once again, she unhinged her jaw and smoke poured out, warning me of what was coming.

Flames blasted me back.

I screamed.

In my dragon form, it came out as a screeching roar.

It shouldn't have even stung. But I'd never seen a dragon's scales before this moment, and I hadn't imitated them as well as I'd thought.

My left wing and shoulder had taken the brunt of the burn.

Limping, I held my wing at an odd angle and swung around, using my huge tail to knock her off her feet.

My heavy body slammed into Shem by accident.

I winced as he fell back a few steps.

I hadn't meant to do that.

A roar behind me was my only warning before her body crashed into mine.

It was a surprisingly light hit.

My feet clawed deep slices in the floor as I slid back, but I barely felt the impact. Instead, I felt the king's body bouncing off mine. He was flung back against the wall, where he sagged as he slumped down. Out cold.

Shem and his mother grabbed him by the arms, dragging him out of the way.

I stamped my feet and growled fiercely at the other dragon.

Was it my mother?

I wasn't sure anymore. I couldn't fathom why she'd do this.

Head lowering, haunches tensing to leap, I bared my teeth at her and snarled.

Either way, I was done holding back.

"Guards!" Shem yelled over the rumbles in our throats. The other dragon and I began to circle each other, each huffing breaths to stoke our fires.

He didn't bother to yell after that. It was useless, and he knew it. The guards were on the other side of a heavily enchanted door meant to protect the most important Jinn in the floating islands. Those spells wouldn't be broken quickly.

He and his mother hurried to barricade themselves and the king in the bathing room. As the door swung shut, I caught a glimpse of the king lying prone on the tiles behind them, not moving. The white tiles had a long streak of dark red.

Heavy pounding filled the air as the guards continued to attack the enchanted wood. It splintered and cracked. But thanks to the magic meant to protect the royal family, it held strong.

Muffled voices argued. Probably quarreling over whether they could use a Gift to burst through without harming a royal by accident.

THE SECRET SHADOW

The dragon attacked while I was distracted.

Throwing her whole weight against me, she tackled me to the ground, bending my injured wing at a sharp angle.

I gave a strangled roar.

She came at me once more before I could find my footing, throwing me back, almost as if she were trying to push me away from the royals.

I swung wildly with my claws and attempted to breathe fire.

Only a huff of hot air came out.

Another sharp scratch against my—unfortunately very penetrable—scales, and I fell back.

Crashing through the door frame, I created a much larger hole in the wall as I stumbled into the adjoining room.

It was a bedroom, and it was much smaller. Despite the tall ceilings, we barely fit, but she forced her way in after me anyway, teeth bared.

I braced for another attack.

With a roar, she flung herself upward instead, away from me, bursting through the ceiling above.

I gaped at the hole she'd created. The damage lay all around me, but her tail disappeared through the opening and heavy footsteps sounded above.

None of this made sense.

The footsteps grew lighter.

Was she back in her Jinni form? Or was she another creature now?

Meanwhile, crystal spears slammed against the door in the next room. Enchanted with power, meant to take down anything, they were thwarted by their own spells protecting the door from intruders, but they were slowly breaking through.

It shouldn't be long now.

I heard a soft click in the other room. Was Shem peeking out through the crack? Was he headed this way? My mother hadn't gone far, and Shem could easily get himself killed if I didn't figure out how to face her.

I gathered my haunches beneath me.

Launching myself upward, I landed in the dark, unknown room above.

It was filled with shelves and tables, covered in objects of all shapes and sizes.

It took me a moment to recognize the space.

The last time I'd been here, Shem had brought me through that ornate, blue door fortified with iron locks and spells: we were in the vault for enchanted objects.

My mother's entrance had toppled one of the larger tables, and it now lay with the mahogany wood cracked in half, ruining the delicate designs carved all around the edges.

And it *was* my mother.

She crouched over the mess in her true form.

I'd thought it couldn't really be her, or that somehow she'd been forced to act the way she did, but she appeared relaxed, as if she'd already forgotten the battle below.

Fury rippled through my whole body.

The fire that I'd struggled to find finally ignited in my belly with a dull roar. *How could she do this to me?*

I stayed in my dragon form, not trusting her in the slightest, and not at all sure what she was doing. Lowering my long neck to her eye level, I let a rumbling growl rip through me.

She ignored me.

I blinked.

Had she not *just* attacked me mere moments ago? Had I imagined the whole thing? I tried to make this scene mesh with the one from downstairs, and my head started to throb. *What's going on?*

She was sorting through the objects on the floor, keeping most of them. Her pockets were bulging as if she'd already gathered quite a bit. Glancing around, she murmured, "I need a satchel."

The pounding below didn't seem to touch her concentration as she found a nearby bag that apparently suited her needs.

"You're looming, Jezebel," she said when I wafted smoke in her direction.

I desperately wanted to ask *what in the name of Jinn* she was doing, but of course, I couldn't speak in this form.

Hesitating, I slowly shifted back to myself. As I did, a bone-deep exhaustion stole over me. I couldn't match her frequent shifts without time and food to regain my energy. If she attacked me again, I didn't know if I could shift fast enough to fight back.

But she didn't *seem* hostile.

I frowned, sagging against the side of the broken table. My wounded arm dangled uselessly at my side. Shock had kept the pain at bay, but sharp stabs grew stronger by the second, making me cradle the limb gently. The room spun. I sucked in a deep breath, and tried to focus. "Have you lost your mind?"

Below a heavy table scraped across the floor. The banging on the door renewed but with the crackle of wood splintered after each hit now, as if it was finally beginning to break. Was the enchantment on the lock broken?

I tensed, turning to the hole in the floor.

We had maybe another minute if we were lucky, and if the guards chose to approach with caution.

"We don't have much time," she murmured, still sorting through the objects on the shelves around the room. "I have to make it count."

A small knife, a handheld mirror, and an ink pot, all went into the large linen

THE SECRET SHADOW

bag.

Finally, she glanced up. "I thought if you were intent on staying here that we should make it look good, darling."

Dozens of Kathenoths were stacked neatly on shelves along one wall. She passed over those.

My mouth hung slightly open. "Are you trying to justify what you did? By saying you somehow did it for me?" I shook my head. That seemed far-fetched, even for her. "They're going to be here any minute. I'm sure I *will* stay here now—in the dungeons, thanks to you."

On another table, she sorted through a variety of household objects, as if she hadn't even heard me. Adding a few to her bag, she paused on a spindle. It belonged to a spinning wheel, though only the top piece was here in the room. She ran a finger up the length of it, contemplatively, though she avoided the sharp tip. Just when I thought she wasn't going to answer, she murmured, "You want them to trust you, don't you?"

"They *do* trust me," I snapped, cradling my injured arm where the burn was beginning to make me shiver as the pain set in. "I was doing fine on my own." An inner voice questioned, *Was I really?*

"It doesn't hurt to have them in your debt," my mother tsked, gesturing to my arm as she moved through the room toward the window. "Sorry about that. It was necessary for the ruse to be believable."

Frowning, I tried to clear my thoughts. It was beginning to feel like my skin was still on fire. But what she was saying... almost made sense. I shook my head. Maybe I was losing it too.

I followed her deeper into the room toward the sole window, glancing over my shoulder anxiously. "This 'ruse' isn't going to last much longer. As soon as they figure out what—and who—you are, they'll throw us *both* in the dungeons."

She smiled as if I'd described a tea party. Reaching over, she tapped my chin lightly. "You're such a worrier," she teased. "You get that from your father." Tucking a stray piece of hair behind my ear, she added more seriously. "Your beauty and brains are all from me, though. Use them wisely, darling. And embrace that Gift. It'll do more for you than anyone here ever will."

Pulling the window open, she paused to add over her shoulder, "Unless you've changed your mind and would like to come with me to the human world after all? It's quite fun. *We* are the royals in their minds, and no one tells us what to do."

Mutely, I shook my head, frowning. "Even if I wanted to, we can't leave...?" I hadn't meant for it to come out as a question, but it did. The enchantment spell would stop her from using the window to escape—wouldn't it?

"I took care of that little problem right before you arrived to see the king and queen." She laughed. "Didn't you feel the spell lift?"

My mouth fell open. I *had* felt the bubble pop, yet once again I hadn't recognized it. I'd attributed the reaction to my panic over what I'd been about to do. Looking back it was once again blatantly obvious.

My mother's short dress barely touched her thighs, exposing her long sandalled legs, as she lifted one foot up to the window and pulled herself onto the thin ledge. She hefted the bag over her shoulder and braced a hand against the frame, grinning at me. "Somewhere downstairs, there's a guard who'll wake up soon wondering why King Jubal commanded him to end the enchantment then knocked him out immediately after."

I met her smirk with a blank stare.

Even after the last few days with her, I still couldn't predict what she'd do. She moved faster than anyone I'd ever known.

Though we'd moved away from the hole in the floor, the crash of splintering wood and raised voices grew louder. They'd finally broken into the royal chambers.

She held out a hand. "Last chance, Jezebel."

My mouth opened and closed.

"I could teach you so many things," she whispered, hand still outstretched.

I bit my lip. Part of me wanted to go with her. To leave this place behind and start fresh…

It tempted me more than I'd expected it to.

Did I go back and face the royal family—now that they knew of my Gift and might imprison me for life, or equally awful, now that Shem might cast me out and never speak to me again? Or should I flee with my mother?

We'd spend the rest of our lives on the run, feared by everyone, unwanted.

Not to mention, she was a stranger to me.

It wasn't the life I'd dreamed of.

Staying here could be…

My muscles tensed, as if my body had already decided.

I had to stay.

Loud voices filled the room below. A door opened and closed. Probably the bathing room.

Queen Samaria's sobs reached us as she yelled at the guards, "Help the king!"

As soon as the king was deemed safe, they'd come for us.

For me.

They were probably on their way already.

Though I almost expected it to change my mind, it didn't. I couldn't imagine leaving.

"I can't," I whispered.

Despite everything, Shem was the one place where I'd truly belonged. He'd become my home. I couldn't leave him behind.

THE SECRET SHADOW

With a nod, my mother stepped down from the window and took my hand, giving it a squeeze. "I can't guarantee I'll come back in the next century," she said calmly. "But I'll try to visit once things have died down a bit."

She pulled the sharp spindle out of her pocket, turning my hand over.

I opened my fingers instinctively to accept it, but she didn't set it down.

When I glanced up, she was staring at me. "Do you remember how we met in the kitchen?"

I nodded warily. "When I tried to poison you?"

She surprised me by cracking a smile. "Exactly. What you should've used was a sleeping spell. It doesn't give a shifter time to fight it—"

Before I could react, she pricked my finger with the spindle.

Sleeping spell? My eyes widened.

A tiny spot of blood pooled on the tip.

I stared at it.

It was a tiny injury compared to the burns covering my arm, yet I sensed it was about to get much worse.

"Don't worry," she murmured, pulling me into her arms for a one-sided hug. "It'll wear off within a few hours. Or days... I'm not entirely sure."

I couldn't fight back or even speak as my mother gently lowered me to the floor, as if she was simply putting me to bed the way she had when I was a little girl.

Disbelief stole my breath.

Or maybe it was whatever spell the spindle held. I could feel it entering my bloodstream at a rapid speed.

And then, I couldn't feel anything.

I never should've trusted her.

"I'm sorry this visit caused you so much trouble," my mother's voice whispered in my ear, but I found that I couldn't turn to look at her. Or lift my chin. Or move at all.

My breath came in great gulps now, eyes widening. Panic gripped me as even those small actions grew nearly impossible.

"We made it look good," were my mother's last words as she leaned over me, winking, before she stepped back toward the window.

Breathing hard, I felt a tear slip from one eye.

I never should've let my guard down.

I'd never forgive her.

The worst part was, I didn't know what hurt more, my future with Shem being ripped out of my grasp for the thousandth time, or my mother proving once again that she didn't care about me.

She never had.

With a glance over her shoulder, she shifted.

Voices grew louder behind me.

I couldn't turn to look, but I felt every shake of boots pounding on the floor.

My mother became a phoenix with red and gold feathers, perching on the window sill. In her beak, she gripped the bag. With a burst of wings flapping, she launched into the air.

From the floor, I couldn't see where she went.

Guards filled my vision, blocking the window. Maybe they chased her or threw a spear. I'd never know. My vision faded, growing black around the edges.

Someone grabbed me harshly by the wrist, restraining me, yelling to others.

The last thing I felt before I lost consciousness was a sharp tug as someone dragged me across the floor.

20

WHEN I CAME TO, Shem's face hovered above mine, dark brows pinched together. He hadn't been this close to me since we'd kissed. For a second I forgot everything that'd happened in between and just stared into his eyes. They reminded me of a cloudless summer sky. Warm. And open.

"You're okay," he breathed. "Can you speak?"

I tried, but I couldn't.

When I attempted to shake my head, I couldn't do that either. The looseness I'd felt a moment ago evaporated. My mind reacted violently, but any physical reaction was invisible.

"Blink if you're all right," Shem whispered.

Immediately, I blinked.

He let out a heavy breath, leaning back against the sofa, closing his eyes in relief. A second later, he stood, saying as he moved out of sight, "Let me get you something to drink."

I lay prone on a soft surface. Eyes shifting to one side, I found green cushions the same color as the green sofa where the king and queen had lounged earlier. Was I still in the royal chambers? How long had I been asleep?

My mother's wild outburst of shifting, thieving, and enchanting all came back to me in a rush.

Straining, I urged my body to sit up.

I could almost wiggle my toes.

Whatever the enchanted spindle had done, my mother had at least told the truth—it *was* wearing off, even if it was agonizingly slow.

My eyes flitted around the room, taking it in from this strange angle, searching for the king.

He'd been injured, badly.

If he didn't survive, I feared that I might not make it through the day either.

When I spied him on the opposite sofa, my breath caught.

He was still. Pale.

I feared the worst until I noticed his chest moving in steady breaths.

An elderly Jinni hovered over him, tentatively pressing bony fingers around the king's shoulder, which looked swollen.

"Just do it," the king growled, eyes still closed, startling both me and the other Jinni. If I'd had control over my body, I would've flinched, but then relaxed.

The king was fine.

With a sharp yank, the healer popped King Jubal's arm back in the socket, causing the king to hiss in pain and then yell, "Enough. Leave me!"

Jumping to obey, the healer backed up, leaving my line of sight.

When Shem's face appeared over mine again, he held a glass of water and his gaze was pinned to my shoulder. "That looks painful."

I frowned. It didn't *feel* painful? Which was odd, because I remembered the burns and the way they'd set my body on fire.

Now there was only a slight tingling in my limbs.

Maybe that was the one upside of this enchanted sleep—it'd removed *all* sensation from my body, including the pain, providing temporary relief.

"When the healer returns from fetching ice for your father, we'll have him see to her," Queen Samaria's voice came from somewhere above my head.

My eyes widened.

She was offering me their personal healer?

Maybe my mother's meddling had had better results than I'd expected. I wanted to shake my head and smile at the same time. I couldn't decide if I was thankful or annoyed. Or both.

Shem smiled slightly, and I realized it was in response to my own expression. The feeling was returning to my face.

He ignored the chaos surrounding his father—as healers and guards came and went, reporting on their findings in hushed voices—and just sat with me.

At some point, as sensation continued to return, I realized he was holding my hand. He gazed at our fingers, head bowed, deep in thought.

I squeezed his fingers weakly.

"Are you in pain?" he asked instantly, studying me.

Clearing my throat, I attempted to speak again. "A little." I grimaced. My voice was ragged. Managing a wobbly smile, I forced myself to continue, "I'm so sorry. Truly."

"I know," he said, pulling my uninjured hand closer, taking care not to move abruptly.

"She's awake?" the king's gruff voice reached us.

This time, when I tried to turn my head to look, my neck slowly obeyed.

His sharp eyes dug into mine. "Where's the shifter?" he demanded.

"Gone, your highness," I croaked.

Another voice spoke up. "She watched the shifter fly off, your highness. Didn't even try to stop her."

I'd know that voice anywhere, especially after the interview that'd happened a few short hours ago.

Gabriel.

Another guard, whose voice I didn't recognize, chimed in, "To be fair, she'd clearly been immobilized by the spell. She was in no position to stop it."

Thank you, I wanted to say, but I held my tongue.

Shem leaned forward, but he wasn't looking at me. His gaze was pinned on his father. "We watched her—" his hesitation was so slight that anyone else besides his father, mother, and I would never guess he'd almost said "shift" before he caught himself—"step between us and the shifter."

Gesturing to my wounds, he added, "She *saved your life*."

I glanced down to see what he was pointing at. It made my stomach riot. I had to look away. The skin was exposed to the air by the burned remains of my dress, bubbling unnaturally, blistering red and even charred almost black in some places. I gagged softly. The pain increased tenfold once I'd seen it and now I was fully aware of the awful heat rippling across my skin.

"I know that," the king snapped, but behind him I caught multiple guards exchanging glances. They had *not* been aware. Their eyes drew to my injuries.

My mother had set this up for me.

Making me the victim had been a calculated move.

Despite the throbbing along my chest and arms growing with each passing second, I found myself grateful for the hurt.

Each time I thought I knew her plans, I was wrong. She thought a hundred steps ahead, while I only thought of what came next. Though she may never be an official mentor to me, I could still learn a thing or two from her.

If I wanted to benefit from this moment, I needed to begin thinking like her.

Removing all suspicion was the best place to start.

Everyone's eyes were on me.

As the pain intensified, I shivered. Moving as if to sit up, I fell back on the couch and let the throbbing bring tears to my eyes. It wasn't hard. In fact, it was growing increasingly hard to think past the pain.

"Stay still," Shem said, tightening his fingers around mine. "The healer is bringing ice that should help with your burns."

I nodded, clearing my throat, and let more tears fall as I said to the king, "I'm so sorry, your majesty." Turning my head back to Shem, I added, almost in a whisper, "I couldn't stop it."

Shem rubbed a thumb absently against my palm, and his face relaxed. It wasn't until I noticed the slightly vacant look in his eyes that I realized I'd accidentally used my new Gift on him. Again.

It wasn't on purpose. I cringed inwardly. *And it's the* truth. *So it doesn't count.*

King Jubal grumbled, but didn't question me further.

"It's the fact that you tried to stop the shifter that impresses me," Shem said softly, brushing a hand over my cheek, careful not to graze the burns with his sleeve.

"You were all perfectly safe," Captain Uriel said in a soothing tone. "Your enchanted armor would've protected you, if this young lady had not gotten in the way."

When Shem turned to face him, his tone was like ice. "Those enchantments were useless. Look at my father." King Jubal, along with all the guards around us, glanced down at his ceremonial armor, where the ruby rested beside multiple scrapes and dents. "While you were all wasting time in the hallway, Jezebel fought the shape-shifter. She is the *only* reason we are all largely unharmed. Your disrespect is disgraceful."

The captain mumbled apologies to me, looking chastened. "I only meant the danger wasn't as awful as it may have felt."

When Shem merely glared at him, he cleared his throat and made his excuses to leave. As he bowed to the royals, he included me as well.

Gabriel stood posted by the door, within my view from the sofa, and he looked down his nose at me, skeptical. He'd *just* completed my interview, which meant he knew all my Gifts—or thought he did. I could almost hear him wondering how someone with only a traveling Gift had stood up to a shape-shifter.

If I made it through this day without ending up in the dungeon, I'd make an effort to find him alone soon and *convince* him to leave the matter alone. Using my new Gift for that would be my one exception.

Fortunately, Gabriel remained silent for now. He wouldn't argue publicly with the prince, especially not after the way his captain had been reprimanded.

The remaining guards silently waited for a command.

Queen Samaria finally moved into my line of sight as she sank onto the sofa beside the king.

Both of them eyed me.

I tensed.

Please don't reveal my secrets, I tried to silently beg. The king's stern expression didn't change, and the queen was unreadable.

I'd never had a chance to tell them about the second Gift. But their awareness of my shape-shifting was enough. More than enough, if they decided I wasn't worth the risk.

Shem, on the other hand, knew *everything*.

He still sat close enough to hold my hand, pressing his palm into mine to offer silent strength.

As the king considered me, I forgot to breathe.

Finally, he turned to the guard. "The prince speaks the truth. This young Jinni was attacked first when the shifter struck. She fought back. It is to her credit that she stood between the awful creature and the royal family, and she is to be commended for her bravery."

He didn't mention my Gifts at all.

Queen Samaria, who'd been speaking with a servant, paused, then nodded. She didn't say anything either.

When I turned to Shem, he gave me a subtle nod.

Fresh tears filled my eyes. When Shem brought my hand to his lips and kissed it, I couldn't stop them from streaming down my cheeks. He and the others called for the healer to hurry with the ice packs, which they gently placed over the burns, working to salvage enough of the skin for the healer's Gift to restore it.

Despite the agony, I was able to take a deep breath for the first time since the shifter's presence had been announced in the castle.

I might still have a place here after all.

21

A FEW DAYS LATER, I paused at the grand entrance to the dining hall.

My wounds were fully mended, thanks to the healer's Gift.

Chandeliers sparkled, flashing bits of light across the high ceiling, which was painted with different scenes of Jinni history.

Every table was full. In the din of conversation, no one noticed me hovering outside in the hall. Members of the Guard were posted by the exits, and throughout the room, but no more than usual during an event like this.

In some ways, it was as if nothing had changed.

Yet despite the cheerful scene, everything was different.

All anyone wanted to talk about was the shifter, or how I'd fought against it, or my mother's dramatic exit. I didn't have to fight for a place at a table or in conversation anymore; people made room. They truly wanted to know me. And if, for some reason, someone didn't… A tiny smile touched my lips. If I truly wanted to, I could *make* them like me. Technically, I could force them do anything at all.

My new Gift tickled my mind at times like these, reminding me that I would never again have to suffer gossip or rude comments, if I didn't want to.

It was overwhelming.

And incredibly, wonderfully satisfying.

THE SECRET SHADOW

I'd never use it on Shem, of course, but he wouldn't care if I occasionally used it for our benefit, would he?

On the far side of the enormous room, the royal family all sat at their private table, surrounded by three separate tables for each of their councils. Each one was filled to capacity. Even from across the room, I spotted Milcah, Jerusha, Dorcas, Laban, and at least two dozen of Shem's other council members.

Every single council member I'd met in my time at the castle was in attendance, as well as some I hadn't, who'd traveled back specifically for this occasion.

I brushed a hand down the floor length gown that the queen herself had commissioned for me. I was still in awe. The gold shimmered in the light, gleaming like a newly minted coin. Along one arm and leg, the fabric turned sheer with stunning golden spirals embroidered into the clear fabric, which ran all the way to my hip as well as across my collarbone like delicate gold lace.

Knowing the queen, she likely wanted the patterns in the lace to resemble the scars I'd had before my burns healed, as yet another reminder to everyone of what I'd done. As if anyone needed it.

When I stepped into the dining hall, a hush slowly took hold with each table I passed, until it crossed the entire vast space, causing all eyes to turn to me.

I kept my chin high, eyes forward.

Whispers tickled my ears.

The words weren't clear, but I didn't need to hear them to guess what they were saying: "How did *that* girl face a shifter?" and "What Gifts could she possibly have that allowed her to survive?"

Without meaning to, my gaze drifted slightly, to the members of the Jinni Guard on duty along the back walls. They each stood stiff and composed. But rumors had probably begun to circulate in their barracks as well. Because *they* had a record somewhere, written and stored by Gabriel, listing exactly what Gifts I had.

Or at least, so they thought.

And while they'd never question the royal family outright, it had to be obvious to them that something didn't add up.

I reached the council members and stood before the dais that raised the royal family's table. In the corner of my eye, both Milcah and Jerusha seemed to eye my dress. I hoped they were jealous. I didn't dare look, keeping my gaze focused on the royals.

After my shoulder had finished healing, Shem had revealed that the king and queen chose to keep my secret at his request. He came by my room frequently, if I wasn't meeting with one or both of his parents.

I'd never had a chance to tell the king and queen about my second Gift, though. When I'd asked Shem to give me time to find the right words, he'd agreed without blinking an eye. I didn't *think* I'd used my Gift when I asked, but I wasn't entirely sure.

And none of them—not even Shem—knew that the shifter was my mother. It would only hurt him to know.

It seemed King Jubal liked the idea of having a secret shifter working for him behind the scenes. He had a gleam in his eye as he set his fork down to acknowledge me.

I stopped before the dais and bowed deeply.

As I sank low, I allowed myself to peek over at Shem's council table beneath my lashes. Milcah was flushed, and Jerusha's fists were clenched in her lap. I smiled to myself, lifting my gaze back to the king as I stood.

"Jezebel," his voice boomed, carrying throughout the whole room. "As this dinner is in your honor, we invite you to join us at our table." With a flourish, he motioned toward an empty seat beside his son.

Beside me, Milcah inhaled sharply through her teeth.

My cheeks dimpled with the effort of holding in a grin. Solemnly, I nodded my thanks.

Coming around the table, the chair beside Shem was so tall it looked like a throne. Before I could touch it, a member of the Guard stepped forward and pulled it out for me.

I sank onto the soft velvet cushion, barely feeling it as I placed my hands on the white linen tablecloth.

Next to me, Shem gave me a wink, the way he used to, before I'd broken his trust.

A trust which seemed to truly be restored.

All around the room, everyone's eyes were on us. I hid a smile, tucking my napkin in my lap, enjoying the way Milcah fidgeted jealously with her own.

Clearing my throat, I accepted a plate of food from a servant and picked up my fork, but the king wasn't done with making proclamations. "Let's raise our glasses to Jezebel," he declared in a deep voice that carried over the still hushed room. "And rejoice that we are safe and the shifter is gone!"

A cheer erupted across the dining hall.

Though the Jinn were naturally reserved, we were too relieved to stand on ceremony tonight.

Drinks flowed, and courses came and went.

I barely had a chance to say two words to Shem, as different council members stopped by the table to speak with him and his parents.

I tried not to look at anyone in the Guard, but a prickling sensation on my neck made me feel like their eyes were on me.

According to Shem, they'd put new safeguards in place to protect everyone in the castle from future attacks. Privately though, the king and queen had assured me that I wouldn't be affected by these changes. That I could come and go as I

THE SECRET SHADOW

pleased without triggering any alerts.

I'd thanked them, glad that I didn't have to force them to trust me. Real trust was far more compelling. Although I wasn't above planting a false faith in me, if necessary. Sometimes I even contemplated telling them to forget what I'd revealed to them. I was still trying to find my footing in this new world where others *knew my Gifts*.

It was only Shem, the king, and the queen—and my mother. But what if one of them told someone else? With each passing day, I grew a little bolder. It couldn't hurt to use my Gift to enforce the secret, could it?

Yesterday, the healer had pronounced me officially restored, shaking Shem's hand as he'd left the royal chambers.

I'd tentatively caught Shem's hand before he followed and whispered, "Can I ask a favor?"

"Anything," he'd said instantly, smiling.

I'd glanced at the guards near the door and stood, drawing Shem toward the window where we wouldn't be overheard.

Tendrils of guilt had swirled around me as I'd used my new Gift on him intentionally for the first time. "It'd mean the world to me if you didn't discuss my... newest Gift with your parents. If they—"

I'd prepared a long explanation of how they didn't really need to know about my Gifts, besides shape-shifting, and how I didn't want anyone to accidentally overhear and discover, but he'd interrupted, "Of course. Your wish is my command."

I'd paused, studying his eyes for the vacant look that I was coming to recognize, but they'd twinkled slightly as he'd smiled, pressing his lips to my forehead. The warmth had made me flush. Those little attentions raised hopes that I was terrified to entertain, but too thrilled to fully ignore.

Now, beneath the banquet table—as the dessert course was served and Shem had a brief respite from conversation—he reached out to take my hand, curling his warm fingers over mine.

Leaning close, until his lips brushed my ear, he said softly, "I should've trusted you. You've always had my best interest at heart."

A twinge of guilt pinched me. He wouldn't trust me if he knew about my mother. Or about what'd happened to my friends when we first met. And I still wasn't sure whether or not I'd used my new Gift to keep him from telling his parents, or what he'd think if I used it to swear the king and queen to silence as well.

You've always had my best interest at heart.

I silently vowed to him that I would do exactly that going forward, including when I used my Gifts. Especially then. Nodding, I managed a small smile.

His chair squeaked against the floor as he shoved it back unexpectedly and stood.

"What're you doing?" I whispered, squeezing his fingers. I let go before anyone noticed that he'd held my hand.

"You'll see," he said with a grin and another wink.

Nearby tables grew quiet, but it wasn't until he used his silverware to clink against the glass that the stillness spread to the rest of the room.

He cleared his throat, drawing out the suspense.

What's going on?

Raising his voice so that the entire room could hear clearly, he addressed everyone, but kept his gaze on me. "Today we gather to honor someone who's grown to mean a great deal to me."

A buzzing lit in the back of my head, a tingling sensation that something big was coming. I didn't know what to expect. In all my time here, he'd never made an unrehearsed speech like this before.

"You've proven yourself to the royal family in a way that few ever will." His pale eyes were almost gray in the candlelight, flickering with an emotion I couldn't name. "More importantly, this latest crisis has revealed to me how much I've come to care for you."

Out of the corner of my eye, Jerusha's hand flew to her mouth. I snuck a glance at their table to find her sagging back in her chair. Milcah was as still as death.

My eyes flitted back to Shem.

I didn't know where this was going, but I sensed there was more.

For a long moment, he was quiet, staring into my eyes. I began to wonder if I should reply—then I caught the glisten of unshed tears. He was composing himself.

Reaching out, he took my hand gently.

I froze.

We'd never held hands publicly before. Was he making a declaration?

Squeezing my fingers lightly, he led me around the table to stand in front of it, before letting go.

He lowered himself to one knee.

All at once, I knew where this was going.

My hands flew to my cheeks, and I almost shook my head.

I hadn't dared to believe this could actually happen.

My heart beat unevenly.

"Jezebel," he said softly, not caring if anyone else could hear. "You really are a legend."

In the corner of my vision, his parents leaned closer.

Everyone was leaning in.

He rubbed a thumb across my hand. "Will you do me the honor of becoming my wife?"

THE SECRET SHADOW

My lips parted.

Is this real? I rapidly inventoried the last few days...

Was it was possible I'd somehow used my Gift to make this happen?

No.

I hadn't said a word that might lead him to this conclusion.

This is all him.

I blinked back happy tears as his face began to blur and nodded. "Yes. Yes, of course!"

He leapt to his feet, pulling me into his arms. The room broke out in cheering and applause. I laughed with him, allowing myself to feel truly happy for once.

This was real.

I hadn't forced this—not really.

A few secrets could hardly be considered an issue. Every Jinni had them.

Shem distracted me from my thoughts with a finger on my cheek, leaning in, until his lips were a breath away from mine.

"May I?" he whispered.

My whole body flushed.

He wanted to kiss me here, now, in front of everyone. There was no more pretending to be calm. I was smiling so wide my cheeks hurt as I closed the distance.

At first, he kissed me softly.

I threw my arms around his neck and leaned in.

He lifted me, deepening the kiss with a laugh, and as he lowered my feet back to the floor to the sound of thunderous applause, a new revelation hit me.

I'm marrying into the royal family...

I pulled back, staring into his handsome face, as the implications swept over me like shock waves.

The girl who didn't belong anywhere now had a permanent place at the heart of the kingdom.

I could hardly dare to think the words, but they snuck in anyway, making me grin back at Shem.

Someday, I'll be queen.

THE
SECRET
CURSE

1

I WORE A DELICATE white-gold crown that signified my engagement to Prince Shem. This morning, I'd specifically chosen a white dress, and not just because it matched the crown. Embroidered gold leaves lined the neckline and hem. Shem's fingers wove through mine, another not-so-subtle reminder of my status to the crowd around us.

I might as well have been invisible.

Smoothing my face, I refused to let them see how much it bothered me.

Shem nodded politely to another group of Jinn. They flashed him smiles that sparkled as brightly as the jewels in their ears, hair, and clothing, managing to make small talk without hardly a word to me before moving on.

We stood at the edge of the Tel Sheba Conservatory, which was an indoor garden named after the same floating island it'd been built on.

"It's an honor having you here with us," Judge Baruk, the city judge of Tel Sheba, said to Shem. He took Shem's elbow as he spoke, swiveling almost imperceptibly, until I stood on the outside of their little circle.

When Shem tried to turn back to me, the judge added, "Perhaps, if you have a moment, we could speak privately?"

"Anything you'd like to discuss with me, you can share in front of Jezebel," Shem said in a gracious, but firm tone, drawing me back into the circle and

THE SECRET CURSE

looping my hand over his elbow.

I blew out a soft breath of relief at finally being acknowledged.

His crown looked like white fire in his black hair, somehow giving him an air of authority I couldn't replicate, no matter how hard I tried.

The judge bowed slightly, still not making eye contact with me. "It's nothing. Truly. I won't bother you with it now, when it's almost time for your speech. Come, let's make our way to the front."

Under my fingers, Shem's muscles tensed in response, but he was too aware of Jinni politics to call attention to the slight, as I'd learned over time.

It was like this on every one of the floating Jinni islands we'd visited so far on our engagement tour, which had been scheduled to span the last three months leading up to our wedding.

The wedding that was meant to happen today.

I lifted my arms, wishing I hadn't chosen this particular dress, which clung to my skin. It was far too heavy for the humid space. The sun baked us through the glass ceiling and windows, though no one else seemed affected. Sweat dripped down my back. Even the air was damp.

We'd been here almost an hour, and while the line of attendees at the entrance was finally dwindling, we had at least another hour of mingling with the hundreds of Jinn present, as well as Shem's speech.

If only I could travel briefly outside for a breath of fresh air. But the conservatory walls were spelled with a boundary against travel, making it impossible to pass through them using the Gift, like most other buildings in Jinn. The only escape was the tall doors at the opposite end of the rectangular room—too far away to slip out unnoticed.

"This conservatory was just completed a few days ago when they filled the spring with water," Judge Baruk said to Shem as we walked, pausing by the stream that trickled down the center of the gathering, It ended in a quiet pool full of water lilies. Pointing it out gave him an excuse to fully turn his back on me.

Under different circumstances, I might've admired the space.

Today, I could've sworn the tropical plants sucked all the cool air out of the room—or maybe that was the company.

"It's breathtaking, wouldn't you agree, Jezebel?" Shem replied, which forced the judge to turn and reluctantly acknowledge me.

I gave the judge a pinched smile. "Very beautiful," I agreed, and couldn't resist adding, "It'd make a lovely venue for a wedding."

Though we didn't currently need one.

"Oh, it's not nearly large enough for that," he replied smoothly, then tapped his chin. "Though it'd help a small wedding party seem larger, I suppose."

My cheeks burned. He clearly wasn't referring to the prince's lack of guests.

"Unfortunately, that wouldn't work for us," Shem said, drawing me closer. "Jezebel draws quite a crowd."

"Apologies, I didn't intend offense," the judge lied to our faces as he bowed his head.

These little victories were sweet. Shem could put the judges in their place in a way that I couldn't.

The win was short lived though.

"I feel terrible that your wedding had to be delayed," the judge said in a distinctly *un*apologetic tone that made me wish he was still ignoring me. "I'm sure you worry it might never happen."

All the time.

"I appreciate the condolences," was all I could say as my throat closed.

Ever since Shem had proposed, the king, queen, and their councils—really the entire country—seemed to be against us. Jinn loved their secrets and traditions, and my very existence threatened both. After all, who was I? Just an unknown Jinni girl who'd come from a poor home with no influence to speak of. While they'd happily recognized me for saving the royal family during a dangerous moment, it was quite another thing to say I was good enough for their prince. Especially when so many more eligible Jinni daughters had vied for the position.

They did *not* want me to become queen.

"Judge Baruk," Shem scolded with a smile, though his tone was icy. "You know as well as anyone that it'd be poor taste to hold a wedding while the Khaanevaade attacks continue to increase."

"I didn't mean to suggest—"

Shem continued as if Judge Baruk hadn't said a word. "We don't want to celebrate while our people are wounded. But as soon as we gain their surrender, the wedding will be rescheduled."

I pressed my lips together in a strained smile as Judge Baruk murmured more insincere apologies and I pretended to accept.

Shem squeezed my fingers where I held onto his arm, and with effort, I smiled at him more warmly.

It wasn't his fault the wedding was delayed.

He'd always obeyed his parents, and this instance wasn't any different. Being a prince came before being a husband. I'd never needed him to explain that to me.

And I wouldn't complain either.

The only one who wanted this wedding to take place—besides me—was Shem. I wouldn't risk alienating him. That might be exactly what King Jubal and Queen Samaria were hoping for.

Instead, I'd become as obedient as the prince.

Even when it chafed.

That's why we were here on our thirty-fourth stop in the courtship tour,

THE SECRET CURSE

despite the painful date.

It was also why I ignored Judge Baruk's insults with a false smile, like I did with every other city judge ruling over the different Jinni islands.

The tension in my shoulders crept up my neck, forming a headache. Light poured in through tall windows on all sides, making me fight the urge to squint.

"Come." Judge Baruk startled me out of my musings. "It's time to begin the formalities." He turned toward the low stage at the front of the room. It'd caught my attention when we'd first arrived because of a beautiful arch taking up the entire front half of the platform. The arch rose halfway to the tall ceiling, perfectly centered on the stage, covered in thick vines with sparkling white flowers.

Staring at the judge as he led us to the stage, I studied his thinning gray hair and his ceremonial robes, trying to picture him treating Queen Samaria this way. Somehow, I couldn't quite imagine it.

As we followed, he slowed again unexpectedly, forcing me to let go of Shem or run into the judge's back. "We timed the grand opening around your visit," he said, taking Shem's arm and continuing without breaking stride. "So that we could dedicate it to the crown today."

The prince's political training took over, and he fell in step with the judge, giving me a rueful glance over his shoulder.

I trailed after them, face burning.

Taking a deep breath, I held onto my calm expression by a thread. My goal on this tour was to demonstrate I'd make a good future queen, despite the people's goal of proving the opposite.

I rubbed my brow subtly, trying to ease the throbbing behind my eyes.

At least Shem found it as frustrating as I did.

A hush fell over the room as Judge Baruk led Shem up the two steps to the low stage. They stepped through the flowering arch, stopping in front of an iron railing.

I faltered.

The space was only wide enough for two people to stand—making it impossible for me to join them.

I'd already climbed the steps, which left me standing awkwardly to the side of the arch with Shem's four assigned Jinni Guard members, one of whom was Captain Uriel himself, as they kept a watchful eye on the crowd.

We were obscured by the thick foliage woven through the arch, only partially in view of this ridiculous conservatory.

As every Jinni face turned toward us, they didn't see the prince with their future princess on his arm, but instead were met with the prince alone with their judge.

Behind them, I went unnoticed.

No doubt exactly what Judge Baruk intended.

After a short foreword—which I couldn't hear past the buzzing in my ears—

he turned to let the prince speak.

Shem immediately beckoned me forward, forcing Judge Baruk to step back, and introduced me.

I held back tears and faked a smile at the blurry crowd as I stepped up to the railing.

The damage was done.

Back when Shem had proposed, I'd thought I'd finally belong somewhere.

I gripped the railing, knuckles whitening. Each time I met unsmiling Jinni faces in the crowds, that hope faded.

"Jezebel will make a fine queen one day," Shem was saying.

I managed to smile, as he thanked them for "so kindly welcoming" me.

Dozens of narrowed eyes pinned on my face made me want to use my Gift to shift into something as small as they made me feel. Something that could scuttle away and hide, and not have to deal with these constant politics anymore.

Pulling my shoulders back instead, I lifted my chin higher and carefully loosened my grip on the railing.

"The royal family wants to send reassurance over the recent Khaanevaade threat," Shem began his practiced speech. "While there are some unforeseen developments we've been forced to handle, we are not concerned."

Having heard this next part dozens of times by now, I was still impressed at the passion in his voice, as if he was saying it for the first time.

"Though the Khaanevaade people have never intimidated the Jinn in the past, over the last several months they've somehow gained access to restricted Jinni magic that allows them to open *daleths* between the human world and our own."

A typical Jinni understatement.

These Vaade burst through the portals and assaulted everyone within range, then disappeared back into hiding, closing the portals behind them. Worse—though the royal family wouldn't admit it publicly—they seemed to be untraceable, making it impossible to find them. It forced us to defend our islands reactively.

"There's no rhyme or reason to their attacks. At least, none that we can see," Shem continued, letting his gaze touch on individual Jinn around the room. He didn't let any of his frustration over this show, though I knew it bothered him to no end.

Personally, I thought they might be searching for something, or maybe someone. But I'd kept my opinion to myself, not wanting to seem foolish if I was wrong.

"No one knows when or where the next attack will be." Shem's hands clenched at his sides briefly. He caught himself, relaxing his body. "The disruption naturally has many of you feeling anxious."

THE SECRET CURSE

A better term would be dazed. Like a helpless mouse in a field staring up at a hawk, not knowing what to do. The Jinn were used to being the predators, not the prey.

Despite the dangers, their reactions were muted. Either they'd heard this news already, which was likely, or they were practiced at keeping their emotions hidden. Probably both.

Before this engagement tour began, all I'd known about the Vaade were the brief mentions during council meetings that made them sound insignificant. To hear those at the castle talk, one would think they were simply humans with startling eyes who disliked Jinn more than the average human.

During these tour speeches, however, Shem painted a very different picture. "If you have the misfortune of a Vaade crossing your path, you *must* let the Jinni Guard handle them. You'll recognize one instantly if you see it, by their eyes, which have an uncanny resemblance to a dragon's."

As he spoke, he tugged at the ceremonial breastplate he always wore, hands drifting to check the leather buckles and gold braces along his forearms. I'd noticed weeks ago that his tour armor appeared far more functional than the usual trendy pieces he wore in the castle.

The fidgeting was so unlike him. That was what had led me to finally start taking the Vaade seriously.

"They're stronger and faster than any Jinn," he continued. "Challenging us in a way no other race in history ever has, not even the Mere in the oceans below. As one of the only creatures in existence that can threaten the Jinn, it makes them extremely dangerous."

As always, I scoffed inwardly, though my face remained composed. These Vaade didn't frighten me.

"Their senses are enhanced like dragons—besides their distinctly dragon-like eyes, their powerful hearing, and an unparalled sense of smell, their skin is also thick like scales, almost impossible to pierce. And they can leap such great distances that they almost seem to fly."

King Jubal called this part of the speech fearmongering, but Shem felt the people should be prepared. I had to agree.

Behind closed doors before our tour began, Shem had revealed the Vaade race may have originally been created by a powerful Jinni—and that this history had resulted in a centuries-old power struggle between our people.

Wanting to be the strongest creatures—to not have a higher power hovering over them like a threat—was frankly something I could understand better than I wanted to admit.

Once Shem finished his warning, he thanked everyone for supporting our engagement, reminding them that we'd choose a new wedding date the moment the Vaade threat was extinguished.

He made it sound like victory was imminent.

I tried not to get my hopes up.

As soon as Shem's speech ended, conversation picked back up, and Judge Baruk hurried to meet us at base of the stairs, forgetting to maneuver around me in his concern. "We'd heard of these attacks, but I'd assumed the Jinn were being taken by surprise, correct? And you're merely exaggerating the danger for the public?"

Shem hesitated, lowering his voice. "Unfortunately, no. The Vaade raids are moving from the smaller islands to the more heavily populated. Until we can pinpoint where they'll be next, we need every island prepared." He leaned toward the judge, speaking softly so no one nearby would overhear. "Our Gifts don't always seem to affect them."

Judge Baruk's eyes widened. "Have they attacked any islands as large as Tel Sheba?"

When Shem nodded, he murmured a hasty, "Please excuse me," and disappeared within the crowd.

Almost immediately, a nearby group of Jinn called to Shem, drawing him into conversation. We moved from one group to the next, following the paths between the flowers. Colorful Jinni eyes watched my every move, but none of them drew me into conversation beyond a greeting or a passing comment on the weather.

Eyeing the opposite side of the room like a finish line, I held back a groan.

Despite the heat, a sudden shiver traveled down my spine.

If I'd actually been involved in the conversation, I might've missed it…

A crackle of magic filled the air.

2

A SWIRLING CIRCLE OF white light the size of my palm appeared beside the stream flowing down the center of the conservatory. It looked like a hundred bolts of lightning, flashing back and forth, fighting each other, but the light grew steadily stronger—and larger—by the second.

It reminded me of when I'd seen Shem's men close a daleth once.

Except, it almost seemed as if…

A portal was opening.

The sheer brilliance burned my eyes the way sunlight did when a curtain was yanked back in a dark room. I ripped my gaze to the side.

Shem had cut off mid-sentence, shielding his own eyes with his hand.

Backing away from the spot, the nearest Jinn started to recognize it for what it was—a daleth forming.

They fled.

Traveling from one side of the room to the other, they burst through the exit, shoving each other out of the way.

It caused mass panic.

Chaos descended over the room as they crashed into each other, piling up in front of the exit.

Captain Uriel and his three guards—Noam, Tirzah, and Boaz—surrounded

Shem and I, aiming their crystal spears at the daleth as it grew rapidly.

"Your Highness," the captain yelled over the din. "This same manifestation occurred on the island of Zipporah, and the Khaanevaade—"

"I know what it is." Shem cut him off.

My heart was racing.

We all knew what it was.

Shem wrapped an arm around me, tugging me closer.

"We must get you out of the building immediately." Captain Uriel's voice rose over the crowd. He used his body to shield the prince. The other three guards held a protective configuration around us. "It's not safe to stay any longer."

My jaw dropped at the sheer panic in the captain's eyes. I'd never in my entire life witnessed a member of the Jinni Guard afraid of anything.

I tensed. They wanted us to travel? The only way out of the conservatory were the doors on the far side of the room, blocked by dozens of overly-dressed Jinn fighting their way through.

"To the exit." The captain gestured for the other guards to join hands with us. "Now!"

"No!" Shem stopped them. "I'm tired of this game the Vaade are playing. Every attack ends before we have a chance to fight back. This time there are four of you. You can take the Vaade by surprise."

Captain Uriel finally tore his gaze from the nearly man-sized portal to give the prince a harsh look. "Your parents would have my head if anything happened to you. My first responsibility is your safety."

"Jezebel and I will hide." Shem gestured to the flowering arch on the stage where we'd stood not long ago. "We'll be perfectly safe."

When the captain began to protest, Shem interrupted, with iron in his voice. "Go now, all of you. That's an order."

"You first." Captain Uriel stood stubborn and unmoving.

With his arm still around me, Shem traveled both of us across the room to the stage, landing directly under the arch. The décor of flowers and leaves was thick but not wide enough to conceal two people on the same side. "Hide here," Shem murmured, pointing to one side of the arch. "Stay out of sight." Meeting my gaze, he added with a careful choice of words, "Whatever it takes."

Use your Gifts if you have to, I heard the unspoken request.

My brows rose. It would only take one single Jinni witnessing my Gift and exposing it to lead to a severance. If he thought it was worth the risk, he was more worried than he was letting on.

As soon as I nodded, he darted across the stage to the other side, hiding behind the opposite column.

Peeking out, we had a perfect view of the entire scene. Captain Uriel gave us a curt nod before turning to face the daleth with the other guards.

THE SECRET CURSE

Across the room, Judge Baruk's face was turning violet screaming for an orderly evacuation.

No one listened.

When a figure leapt through the portal in a blur, I forgot the chokepoint at the door completely. He launched over the guards' heads, landing in an empty space a dozen paces away.

Shouting orders, Captain Uriel led the attack. But before the Vaade had even fully landed, he leapt again, flying through the air toward the exit.

He was going after the fleeing citizens.

All four guards gave chase.

Though Captain Uriel threw fire at the Vaade with his Gift, it fell on empty space. Noam tried to throw a wall of air at him next, but the Vaade moved too fast. The strange man was a blur of motion. He slammed into a screaming Jinni, knocking her to the ground. Before I could blink, he'd done the same to three more Jinn.

Boaz and Tirzah joined in the fray. All four guards were completely oblivious to the flash that came from the open portal behind them.

Shem and I gasped as another Vaade stepped through.

He was enormous.

While his friend distracted the guards, he stopped to scan the room, unknowingly giving us a chance to size him up as well.

His bronze skin was a few shades lighter than his brown hair that hung in rope-like tangles past his shoulders. His bare arms displayed rippling muscles as he tensed, searching for something.

I ducked further back behind the arch, peering through the leaves.

Unfortunately, I couldn't see him now either.

My view of the room was restricted to one side.

The other Vaade stepped into my line of vision, chasing a small Jinni woman.

She traveled, but he was too fast.

He caught her foot as she vanished, taking him along with her.

The two of them reappeared beside the wall—the enchantment had blocked her from leaving.

The Vaade man fell to the ground clutching his head. He shook it a little, almost as if disoriented by the travel?

It didn't last long though.

He pulled himself up, widening his stance to fight, and grabbed her wrists.

As she tensed, I could've sworn she tried to travel again, but this time, neither of them moved.

Her face paled.

She screamed as he threw her against the wall. The glass shattered. She scrambled to her feet on the dirt and grass outside, covered in bleeding scratches.

Before he could follow, she disappeared.

Multiple Jinn at the back of the crowd recognized this as a new escape route. Seconds later, a dozen more jagged holes broke the glass walls.

The first Vaade was already turning back to the crowd. Jinn didn't like physical combat, preferring to use Gifts against any attackers, but they might need both to face him.

I tore my gaze away as the second Vaade quietly prowled along a garden path into my line of sight.

With a gasp, I ducked back again. *Had he seen me?*

Shem held a finger to his lips.

I nodded.

But as the seconds passed, screams across the room drew me until I couldn't help risking another look.

The second Vaade faced the first now, allowing me a soft breath of relief.

He tilted his head up, sniffing the air—what was he searching for? He slowly turned until I could see his profile.

For the first time since their arrival, he was close enough to see defining details. He wore some type of leather hide vest and pants. Buckles in a dozen places held knives and other weapons I didn't recognize. There were no sleeves on those large arms. Anxiously I compared his and the other Vaade's muscles to the Jinn—without Gifts, it didn't seem like a fair fight.

Though a few hundred Jinn had fled the building already, a small number of citizens had turned to stand their ground and fight. They formed a line behind Shem's guards, prepared to reveal their personal Gifts if they had to.

Tirzah was currently engaging the first Vaade, leading him away from the remaining citizens, while the other three guards flanked him, trying to cut him off from the people as well.

The muscled man lunged for her unexpectedly.

She dodged—barely evading him—by floating high off the ground toward the glass ceiling.

But that didn't deter him at all.

The big Vaade launched himself into the air, capable of nearly the same heights as she, grasping for her ankles.

I squeaked.

Clapping a hand over my mouth, I yanked back behind the arch again as the second Vaade man swung around.

I held my breath.

Through the little leaves I caught a glimpse of his legs.

They bent, then disappeared as he launched himself into the air.

He landed near the stage, closer to us than ever.

A tiny motion caught my eye from Shem. He held his palm up, gesturing for

THE SECRET CURSE

me to stay hidden.

I nodded, peering through the leaves of the arch as the closest Vaade sniffed the air again. He followed some unknown path that fortunately took him in the opposite direction.

Risking another glance at the fighting while his back was turned, I found Captain Uriel leading the guards and citizens in creating some semblance of a perimeter, closing in on the Vaade with caution.

The beast of a man knocked Noam's weapon aside, tossing it across the conservatory. It landed uselessly in a rosebush.

Tirzah leapt forward, capturing the Vaade's brawny arm and traveling, taking him with her.

Just like before, this seemed to overwhelm him, forcing him to slow down.

But when she attempted to travel a second time, the Vaade stayed rooted in place.

Only Tirzah disappeared.

In a flash, she reappeared, trying again.

The Vaade didn't budge.

Though Captain Uriel and the others tensed to fight, they couldn't do much without risking Tirzah as well. A few more citizens took the opportunity to slip out the exit.

With a wicked grin, the Vaade flung Tirzah into Noam. The crash of armor echoed loudly through the nearly empty room. The two guards fell to the ground, unconscious.

Why did the traveling stop working?

Captain Uriel and Boaz raised their weapons higher, calling for the citizens to step back and use caution. They didn't advance. Were they using other Gifts that we couldn't see? If so, it didn't seem to affect the Vaade in the slightest as he prowled forward. How could they fight an enemy who seemed oddly resistant to their Gifts?

A soft thud sounded on the hollow stage.

I yanked back out of sight, heart beating frantically.

I'd forgotten the other Vaade.

He was only a few steps away.

Clutching the little vial that hung on a necklace beneath my dress, I steeled myself.

Though Shem had asked me not to join the fight, I might not have a choice…

I was prepared though.

Just a few months ago, my mother had used an enchantment to paralyze me. I'd spent weeks searching for something similar, finally stumbling across a mixture of foxglove and bloodroot that made a potent black paste. To use it, I simply needed to scoop out a bit of paste and place it over a cut. The moment it entered the bloodstream, it took effect.

I gripped the little vial around my neck tighter, pulling out the stopper.

By using the paralytic, I could protect myself without exposing my Gifts.

Soft footsteps crossed the stage.

A few more, and he'd be here.

If I subdued the Vaade, the Jinn would revere me. They'd *have* to.

With a low growl, the brute stopped directly in the center of the arch.

Directly in front of *me*.

Gasping, I flinched, glancing across the space at Shem on instinct.

Except, Shem wasn't there.

My racing heart skipped a beat. Had Shem traveled somewhere else within the room and left me here alone?

Shock left me slow to react as the Vaade took a silent step toward me.

When I glanced at his face, I sucked in a breath.

His eyes...

My lips parted. Honestly, I hadn't believed Shem's stories, but I couldn't deny what I saw.

His black pupils were long and thin, pointed at both top and bottom, and the iris was the color of a deep amber like the gold that dragons were always said to hoard. Within the amber were deep orange and yellow flecks, like a burning sunset.

I should've run, but I could only stare back at him, too stunned to move.

Stopping close enough to loom over me, he tilted his head slightly, not taking his eyes from mine as he sniffed the air with a frown.

I still held the open bottle with trembling fingers. But how could I get the paralytic to enter his bloodstream? There wasn't a cut on him.

When he blinked, it shook me from my stupor.

Use the paralytic.

I began to shift my fingers into claws sharp enough to slice his skin.

To distract him, I shifted my eyes at the same time—to match his.

Just one quick slash across his chest, then wipe the paralytic on after.

But the way he watched my every move made my heart sink.

With his speed, I'd only get one chance to surprise him. Once I cut him, he'd knock me out before I ever reached into the vial.

The animalistic shape of my eyes did make him pause, though.

His own eyes narrowed.

Instead of attacking, he spoke, in a deep voice that raised the hair on my arms. "Where's the prince?"

Though I wanted to glance over his shoulder and search for Shem too, I managed to shrug, despite my racing heart. "How should I know where he is?"

Now he *did* growl.

He might have done more than that, if not for the approaching guards.

THE SECRET CURSE

Attempting to trap the first Vaade as he ran toward the open daleth, they flung out a wall of energy in our direction.

It knocked us back against the thick glass and into the smaller shrubs along the wall, which scraped my arms and face.

From the ground, I stared at the Vaade as he launched himself into the air. He landed heavily on top of the arch. A cracking sound came from the wood as it swayed dangerously under his weight.

"There's two of them." Captain Uriel's panicked voice came from somewhere on the other side of the arch as the Vaade leapt off the arch in their direction.

I scrambled to my knees, shifting my hand back to normal before the captain or any of the guards could see. Crawling forward, I peered around the arch.

The Vaade had landed in front of the portal.

I stood, taking a step toward him, though there was nothing I could do.

With one last furious glance in my direction, he stepped through and vanished.

The other Vaade led Boaz and Captain Uriel on a wild chase around the room, landing in one smooth motion in front of the daleth. He disappeared through it as well.

The two guards traveled to the portal seconds later.

But it'd already flashed closed.

The Vaade were gone.

Sudden deafening silence filled the broken conservatory.

"Find the trail." Captain Uriel's command made me flinch.

"I can't sense it," Boaz replied.

Tirzah roused on the other side of the room where a few citizens stood over her and Noam to protect them. She turned to wake Noam next.

Soon all the guards were yelling back and forth as they actively searched the space for any remaining threat.

So much for my half-formed plans.

I had to admit I was relieved, since the chances it would've worked had been extremely low.

Corking the little vial around my neck with a sigh, I replaced it beneath the collar of my dress.

As I let go, a warm hand touched my back.

I startled.

There was no one behind me.

Heat radiated from the empty space.

Reaching out, a cold, familiar armor hit my fingers, and I let out a relieved breath.

I should've guessed.

My hands ran along unseen leather armbands with a mind of their own toward invisible shoulders. As I splayed my fingers across a strong chest, Prince Shem appeared beneath them.

His own hand, now visible, came up to cover mine.

3

A GIFT OF INVISIBILITY was even more rare than shape-shifting.

And equally powerful.

A twinge of apprehension passed through me. Was this how he'd felt when he'd learned of my Gifts? It was uncomfortable.

Shem tucked a finger under my chin, raising it until I finally met his eyes.

There was a slight line between his brows—was it worry? Did he not trust me? Or was he wondering how I might react? A dozen more questions came to mind, but there were still other Jinni ears nearby that might overhear. I kept silent.

We stood like that, eyes locked, not saying a word, until Tirzah approached, breathing hard.

I broke first, dropping my gaze to the ground.

"We must leave immediately, Your Highness," she said, clutching her weapon against her chest, eyes darting around as she spoke. Touching her head, she winced.

"What about the citizens?" Shem asked, though there were hardly any remaining.

"We'll send support once you're safe," Captain Uriel replied as he joined us. "I never should've agreed to stay in the first place. Protocol states we return to the capital immediately." There was no room for argument in his tone.

Reluctantly, Shem agreed, though he insisted that he and I stay together.

We traveled to the now-empty exit, crossed the boundary of the enchantment in a hurry, and immediately traveled again.

At first, the island landscape was fairly open with minimal trees and smaller towns, allowing us to cross long distances as far as we could see. Each time we landed in soft grass, whether on a hilltop or in a valley, it put more space between us and our attackers. We flashed across Tel Sheba in a half-dozen leaps. A smaller island floated beside it, so close that even a human could've almost jumped across, and we were able to travel onto it without looking for a bridge.

"Your Highness." Captain Uriel held up a hand for us to pause. "I'm afraid we're going in a direction I haven't come before."

"I've studied all the islands, Captain," Shem reassured him, slowly scanning the landscape. "This is Tel Yevah. It only has one town, but three bridges. Follow me."

Though Shem could've gone straight to the bridge, the unfamiliar island kept the rest of us limited to what was in sight and slowed everyone's travel.

As we appeared and reappeared in the distance, leading the way, Shem and I whispered in the brief moments it took the guards to follow.

"You weren't supposed to engage," Shem murmured in my ear with an anxious frown. "Remember? *Whatever it takes*." He'd wanted me to shift—or, more specifically, to use my ability to hide.

Captain Uriel flashed into sight behind us with Tirzah and Boaz, who carried a limping Noam.

When I glanced down, my fingers were trembling—now that the danger was past, my body finally reacted. The Vaade had been more of a threat than I'd realized.

We traveled again, landing first.

"I was trying to distract him so he wouldn't keep looking for you," I lied, clenching my fists so Shem wouldn't notice the shaking. Telling him that I'd wanted to be a hero was too embarrassing.

The guards reappeared, and we traveled again.

A little town emerged with a smaller version of the acropolis we had back home, white pillars rising to the sky with a majestic statue of one of the past Jinni kings standing prominently in the town square.

We traveled past the town, landing on a small hill on the other side.

"I was going to stop him," Shem replied at the next opportunity. "I was right there, but I couldn't knock him out without risking your safety. You should've run."

Captain Uriel caught his last words, giving us a look, and when the six of us traveled again, we stayed silent.

THE SECRET CURSE

A quarter-hour of this passed in a blur, hopping from one island to the next, though most of the time we were forced to search for a bridge.

At one point, we paused again to rest. The guards discussed the fastest path home.

"Tel Haifa would take us in for the night," Tirzah suggested.

But Captain Uriel shook his head immediately. "Returning to Resh is our ultimate priority."

I stood in the group but felt like an intruder.

I knew next to nothing about Jinni geography—my discipline years had spent very little time on it.

Noam shaded his eyes, glancing out at the soft white clouds floating by the edge of the island we'd stopped on, as if he could somehow see the vast connections in the distance. "Bir Harim is close. From there, we can stick to the larger islands, which could help us avoid the Vaade's notice, if that's your concern?"

Though Captain Uriel's brow wrinkled at the mention of the Vaade, he nodded, coming to a quick decision. "The strongest travelers should take over and carry the others. We'll take turns if need be."

"I'll stay with Jezebel," Shem replied. "There's no real chance of another attack at this point."

The captain shook his head, leaning forward to grab Shem's armor and giving it a slight shake. "I risked your safety once already today. Don't ask me to do it again." He turned to Boaz. "You'll take the prince."

When Shem pressed his lips together, looking ready to argue, the captain added quietly, "You need to save your strength. Just because another attack isn't likely doesn't mean it's impossible."

"I'll go with Tirzah," I spoke up, trying to make it easier on Shem. Even I knew the captain wasn't going to budge on this one, and I'd only been in the castle for a few months. Protecting the royal family came before all else, and Shem was the only heir. Captain Uriel had risked his entire career following the prince's command earlier.

Shem ran a hand through his hair. "Fine." He turned to me. "As long as you're comfortable with this."

I tucked my hands beneath my arms and nodded.

Tirzah politely held out a hand and we continued on, though her presence wasn't nearly as comforting as the prince's.

None of us spoke.

Each time we reached the edge of an island, we'd stop at the guard station beside the bridge. One look at the captain's insignia—and face—and the guards posted there waved us on.

Not long after this, we were forced to slow again, both because our line of sight became impaired by more trees and cities, but also to conserve energy.

We didn't normally travel at this speed.

The guards were stretched to their limits.

After another argument, Captain Uriel allowed Shem to transport the others as well, to relieve the exhausted guards. Boaz stayed with Shem, while Tirzah and the captain quietly decided to take turns traveling with Noam, who still had a slight limp, leaving me to travel by myself—I could've taken three or maybe even four at once, but no one asked.

After keeping my true Gifts and full strength to myself for so long, I didn't offer.

Though I should've been looking over my shoulder, watching our surroundings like the rest of them, my eyes kept drifting to Shem instead. How many times had he used his Gift around me, without my ever knowing it?

My eyes widened as I remembered odd moments—the way he'd appeared, seemingly out of nowhere, when I'd gone to reveal my Gifts to his parents, despite the closed doors and the guards outside them. Gasping quietly, I remembered the way I could've sworn I'd felt his presence in my wardrobe as I'd traveled to the royal suites that same day.

I ignored the sunny skies and the thundering waterfall just behind the city ahead, as I thought back over the entire time I'd known him. For once, I understood how such a powerful Gift could make someone afraid.

At this pace, we needed only one more break for everyone to rest before we reached the capital city of Resh. The royal family's spring and summer castle stretched proud and tall in the distance beside the enormous River Mem.

By the time we crossed the border at the bridge and set foot in the city itself, we were all so thoroughly exhausted that we walked the final stretch to the castle. Originally, I'd wanted to find a quiet moment with Shem once we arrived. Now, all I wanted was a hot bath and my own bed. I could learn more about his Gift tomorrow.

At the gate, Captain Uriel gave hurried orders to those on guard, and we were unceremoniously dumped in a secure room covered in heavy protection spells deep in the heart of the castle. There were no windows. A small, round table only large enough for a handful of people filled the center.

I looked longingly at the door. Straightening my shoulders, I tried to unobtrusively shake the cobwebs from my head and focus. This could be my opportunity to finally show my value to the royal family. I had, afterall, gotten a good glimpse of the Vaade—and spoken to him! No one else had done that. Pride put a small smile on my face, and I was determined to stay as long as necessary, despite my exhaustion.

The guards who'd been on tour with us took up position along the walls. Shem pulled out a chair for me and we sat, but we didn't speak by silent agreement. Even the guards gossiped sometimes, and every other word from me

THE SECRET CURSE

lately seemed like it was misconstrued. Better to keep quiet and wait until we were alone.

Along the opposite wall, a large map caught my eye. No—I frowned and looked closer—it was actually two maps.

The left one held dozens of floating islands, names written beneath each island as well as each of their major cities, and the number of bridges—or lack thereof—between the islands.

But it was the little red pins placed at seemingly random locations across the islands that drew my attention. Because on the second map, there were an equal number of red pins, almost as if corresponding to the first map, though not always in the same position.

This second map held cities I'd never heard of. At first, I thought it was a much closer look at a specific island, since the map didn't document any airspace. But a massive mountain range stretched across the upper half of the map denoting steep cliffs along one side in particular.

We didn't have many mountains in Jinn, and certainly nothing that expansive.

It wasn't until my eyes caught on a small drawing of a horde of dragons that my mouth dropped open in understanding.

It was the human world.

The corresponding pins suddenly made sense.

They were daleths.

Shem would certainly love to use the one by the cliffs where that dragon was pictured. He'd always wanted to see them up close. Squinting, I made a mental note of where the pin was so I could tell Shem about it later. It was hard to tell without knowing the scale of the map—it could be anywhere from a few hours to a day's travel from those cliffs—but it was close.

I was busy trying to find the corresponding pin on the Jinni map, when the king and queen swept in with their own set of guards.

Shem and I both stood.

"What's going on?" the king asked the closest guard, Noam. "I was in the middle of a meeting."

"My apologies, your majesty." Noam bowed low. "There's been another attack."

Queen Samaria put a hand to her chest, and Shem moved to comfort her.

I followed unconsciously, then caught myself, stepping back to stand awkwardly near the wall.

"We chose to bring all of you to one of the secret rooms until we could guarantee your safety," Noam was saying. "I'll let Captain Uriel explain the details of what happened."

Stepping back, he gestured toward the table. Tirzah pulled out the closest chairs for the king and queen with a slight bow.

The king and queen took the offered seats, and Shem joined them.

Captain Uriel took the fourth and final seat in front of me before I could move and began to brief the king and queen on the incident, starting with the daleth.

Standing in the dim light, I leaned forward a bit, waiting for someone to notice, but no one did.

I tried to ignore the way they were treating me as neither friend nor foe, but simply as someone of no importance at all.

While I might expect this behavior from the king and queen, who seemed to think of me only when it suited their needs, I'd expected more from Shem. He scowled at the table, lost in thought.

I cleared my throat.

When he glanced up, he blinked at me, brows rising, and turned to the guards still standing. "Could someone please bring another chair for Jezebel?"

Noam nodded and left.

With a glance at the prince, Captain Uriel waited for his nod, then continued speaking.

I pressed my shoulders back and stood taller than I felt. Shem had defended me all day—even now he was trying. It probably didn't occur to him to offer up his own seat, but maybe that was to be expected. He was the prince after all.

"We felt it best to leave immediately." Captain Uriel finished explaining our time-consuming escape.

I noticed that he didn't add another red pin to the map. Since the Vaade had closed the daleth behind them, that must mean the red pins only marked open portals. Though I should've been paying attention to the conversation, that preoccupied me briefly. There were far more open daleths than the citizens were aware of.

"Why not wait to discover the city's plans for adding extra protection?" the king snapped. "We'll have to send someone out. It'll be hours before we get word. For all we know, there could be another attack." King Jubal's fickle temper irked me. It was probably *his* orders Captain Uriel had obeyed to prioritize the prince's safety, but he'd either forgotten or put it out of his mind on purpose.

"There won't be another attack," Shem replied, saving the captain from an impossible position. He flattened his palms on the table in a move that seemed calm but also practiced as he met his father's gaze. "They were looking for me."

Queen Samaria sucked in a breath, hands trembling slightly before she tucked them in her lap and out of sight. "How do you know?"

"I heard it from the Vaade himself," Shem said grimly, lips pressed together in a flat line. A heavy pause said more. The queen nodded at whatever was unsaid.

I frowned.

He'd overheard the Vaade say this when he was invisible, but he wasn't

THE SECRET CURSE

saying so, which meant the other guards were unaware of his hidden Gift. The king and queen probably assumed I didn't know either—and likely didn't want me to.

I shrank back farther into the shadows. My back hit the wall, stopping my unconscious retreat. No one noticed the soft thump.

Noam returned quietly, holding a small chair.

There was no room for it at the table.

He placed it against the wall without a word, turning to stand with the other guards, unwilling to interrupt.

I chewed my lip as I considered dragging the chair up to the table somehow, but the king was in the middle of a rant.

"We need to discern how these anomalies are taking place. I've said it before, and I'll say it again: we have to be more prepared the next time a daleth forms unexpectedly. How do the Khaanevaade sense them forming? We must find out as soon as possible, or they'll continue taking advantage of it."

I frowned, distracted from the chair. His portrayal of the Vaade didn't make any sense. There was no way that portal had created itself. The Vaade man had clearly been standing ready to use it, which meant he—or someone else in his tribe—had opened it on the other side. Intentionally.

Swallowing, I tried to find an opening to insert my suspicions into the conversation. This was more important than a chair.

"That's the fourth time this month," the king was saying, as he pounded a fist on the table. "This cannot continue!"

"I understand, Your Majesty," Captain Uriel replied, but the king didn't give him a chance to say more.

"We need to train all Guard members in the details of closing a daleth." The king stood to pace.

The moment for me to speak up seemed to have passed. Clenching my hands together, I squeezed my fingers anxiously. Should I tell them my misgivings? Maybe I was wrong...

"The engagement tour is postponed until further notice," the king continued, gesturing in Shem's direction, but ignoring me. Perhaps he didn't realize I was still here. I'd blended into the shadows against the wall. A gloom settled over me at the thought of delaying yet another aspect of our future together. It played on my worst fears that the wedding might never happen.

"You'll be safe on the main island," Queen Samaria told her son, patting his hand with a small smile, though her eyes were creased with worry.

"I don't think that's the case, though," I blurted out.

All eyes turned to me.

"I think—" I hesitated before stepping forward, suddenly doubting myself. "Well, I'm not certain, but it's possible that the Khaanevaade are forming these portals themselves...?" Under the intimidating stares of the royal family, the statement turned into a question.

"Impossible." The king scoffed, waving a hand at the idea as if swatting a fly. "The Vaade are not nearly advanced enough to accomplish something so complex. They're mere beasts masquerading as men."

He acted as if he wasn't even worried.

But I *knew* that wasn't the case. The Vaade had abilities we didn't understand. Even simple traveling affected them differently.

For three months now, I'd kept quiet around the king and queen, allowing them to view me as unimportant—encouraging it even, if it'd make them see me as less powerful. As the only other Jinn in the realm who knew of my shapeshifting ability, besides their son, my entire goal had been to seem like less of a threat. But now I could see it'd backfired. I opened my mouth to speak—

"You must be exhausted after this ordeal, dear," Queen Samaria cut in, coming around the table to place a hand on my shoulder. She squeezed my arm gently and smiled. "It seems we're all perfectly safe within the castle, so why don't you go get some rest? I'm sure you need some time to recover from this awful turn of events."

I sucked in a breath, too stunned to hide my reaction. But she'd already moved to return to her seat.

I'd been dismissed.

Every muscle in my body tensed. If Queen Samaria had glanced back, she'd have found fury radiating from every inch of me.

I *hated* being ignored.

Glancing at Shem, I expected him to counter their command and ask me if I wanted to stay. Instead, head in hands, brow furrowed, he stared down at the table lost in thought.

Logic overpowered my rage.

With my future wedding dangling by a thread, I couldn't risk cutting it with an outburst. King Jubal or Queen Samaria could use a single word of defiance against me. In a room with this many witnesses, one claim of aggression against the royal family paired with a revelation that I was a shapeshifter, and my entire life would be ruined.

"I'll bid you all goodnight then," I murmured, cheeks burning in humiliation as I strode to the door.

Shem glanced up at my words, brows knitted together, but still he didn't contradict his mother, only nodding distractedly. "Get some rest. We'll speak soon."

Bowing, because I didn't know what else to do, I allowed a guard I didn't recognize to take me by the elbow as we stepped into the hall. Once outside of the enchantment that protected the room, he instantly traveled with me to the hall in front of my own chamber door.

THE SECRET CURSE

With a brief nod as the barest sign of respect, he vanished.

I attempted to sense the trail back to the room we'd been in, wanting to rebel against the queen's wishes and return to the discussion.

They wouldn't be able to silence me so easily once Shem and I married, would they?

Once I was a future queen, they'd *have* to listen.

My eyes widened as I discovered the trail from the guard's travel was somehow hidden completely. Not even the slightest trace was left behind.

A Gift perhaps? Or maybe an enchantment over the room we'd met in?

It didn't matter.

Either way, I'd been belittled and insulted.

It left a bitter taste in my mouth.

"Hmm. You're back early," a feminine voice hummed.

In the alcove at the end of the hall, a dark shape rose from one of the lounge chairs in the communal space, stepping into the light of the hallway. It was Milcah.

I wanted to kick myself for not noticing her presence. Not only did she know I was supposed to be on my engagement tour, but she'd seen the guard drop me off without a single word. Any Jinn could read embarrassing things into this situation, but Milcah could manage to spread an especially humiliating story if she chose to.

"There was a Vaade attack," I said without further explanation, hoping to distract her from my solo return.

"Oh my." She fluttered a hand to her chest, highlighting the low-cut dress. "What are the king and queen planning to do about it?"

"You'll find out in the next council meeting, I'm sure," I told her, turning toward my door.

"Ah, I see," she said softly, making me tense. "You don't know."

Hand on the doorknob, I searched for a response that would fool her. My mind was blank.

The long pause was enough to confirm the truth.

"You know, Jezebel," Milcah said as she strolled over to me. "If you want to take control of your life, you have to take it." Her tone was mocking. She'd made it her personal mission to paint me as weak. Probably half the rumors circulating the castle came from her.

Gritting my teeth, I twisted the knob, opening my door. As I entered my room, I gave her a cool look. "Shem knows my value. I don't have to force myself on him the way *some* people do." Before she could come up with some other response to further rub salt in my wounds, I added, "It's been a long day with the attack and all. I'm afraid I'll have to say goodnight."

I let the door slam shut in her face.

With the curtains closed, my room was dark and had a stale smell that meant no one had bothered to clean it for me while I'd been gone. It was empty. I tried to imagine it filled with a welcoming party or even a small group of friends, but I couldn't picture a single face.

Unstrapping my sandals, I flung them at the wall where they made an unsatisfying clack before falling to the ground. I sat on the bed, wishing that it—or anything in this room—felt like coming home. Like I belonged here.

Instead, I turned, only to come face to face with my beautiful white lace wedding dress.

It hung on the side of my wardrobe, waiting for the wedding that was meant to happen today.

When Shem had first suggested we postpone, he'd said, "It'll be brief. Only another month or two. We'll use the time to schedule more courtship tours, to let everyone get to know and love you."

"Of course," I'd agreed, hiding the fact that I hated it. One month had turned into two, and then three.

As of now, our original wedding day had officially passed without any sign of setting a new date.

The one time I'd mentioned it to Shem after the first month had passed, he'd wrapped his arms around me in comfort. "I know," he'd said. "But we have to put our people above everything else, even our wedding. That's the price of joining the royal family." Pulling back, he'd gazed into my eyes. "I hope it won't be too much for you?"

I'd shaken my head. "Not at all." And that was the last time we'd discussed it.

Pinching my eyes shut, I avoided the nagging feeling that no one would mind if the wedding never happened.

Just like no one missed me back at that table.

I ground my teeth together.

I should've made them listen, or at least tried harder to explain my theories.

There was nothing to stop the Vaade from forming a portal here in Resh.

The very first attacks had happened on the far islands, while today's had been much closer to home—to the prince. I had no doubt they'd figure out how to hit their target eventually.

Once they did, they'd come after Shem, as they so clearly wanted to.

My body itched to leap up from the bed and return to that meeting room. I reminded myself that even if my presence was allowed, I didn't know where it was.

It doesn't matter, I repeated yet again.

Not the location, or whether they'd accept me, or even if I was right about the Vaade planning to attack here in Resh—maybe even in the castle.

My opinion wasn't necessary or wanted.

THE SECRET CURSE

I was merely an accessory for the prince to pull out during times of peace. Not someone with a seat at the table. Not someone with any real power.

I clenched my fists until the nails broke my skin and drew boiling, furious blood.

A year ago, I'd been no one. I'd accepted a life without power, without much at all really.

But how could I go back to that now that I'd had a taste? I was *someone* here. Or at least, I'd thought so, when I'd accepted a seat on the prince's council, and especially once Prince Shem proposed. That should *mean* something. I rubbed my eyes and groaned.

The rest of the night was spent stewing, waiting for Shem to come find me, only growing more upset and confused when he did no such thing.

4

I WOKE DETERMINED NOT to wait for Shem another second. Dressing carefully, I chose an off-shoulder red dress that made me feel powerful, even if all evidence spoke to the contrary. The top layer of the dress was a deep red fabric and nearly transparent, exposing the soft white material underneath. Crystals decorated the red layer where it cinched in to form a tight waist, before fading into a pure white toward the bottom where it swirled prettily around my legs as I walked.

Holding my head high, I strode through the halls toward the garden.

When Shem found me strolling there some time later, he gallantly held out an arm as if nothing were wrong.

Pretending not to see it, I brushed past him with a curt, "Good morning. Did the king and queen agree on a good solution for the Khaanevaade problem?"

"We think so," Shem replied easily, falling into step beside me, waving at some of the ladies approaching us from the other end of the path. "I know you're frustrated with my parents after they delayed the wedding. I can try not to discuss them or the Vaade attacks, if that would help you feel better?"

"Good," I said in a flat tone. "That will solve everything."

"Do I sense that you're upset with me?" he murmured, after the small group had passed us and moved out of earshot.

THE SECRET CURSE

I snorted. Jinni men thought they were so intelligent, but they missed the most obvious things. He'd think I was being childish if I complained about his mother, but after spending months in the castle I'd learned how to bring a problem up indirectly. "I feel certain that the Khaanevaade could attack here in Resh as easily as any other island, and yet, when I made my opinions known, I was dismissed from the conversation completely."

Shem lifted his hands in a helpless gesture, making a sympathetic face that only irked me further. "I know my parents can be abrupt and set in their ways. It's difficult for them to hear outside counsel—"

"From me, you mean," I cut him off. "It's difficult for them to respect and listen to *me*. They had no problem listening to the guards. Ever since our engagement, they've made it clear they don't trust me—they don't think I'm good enough for you."

"Well..." Shem faltered. "They don't know you as well as I do. And what they do know..." he trailed off, reminding me of my confession just a few short months ago.

I'd planned to tell the king and queen *all* my Gifts, but we'd been interrupted part way through. They didn't know I could persuade them to do almost anything—even now I tensed at the thought of telling them, grateful I hadn't gotten the chance. They *did* however know about my shape-shifting abilities.

So far, they hadn't asked me to use them on their behalf. I'd assumed it was because of our engagement—that they no longer felt right about making their future daughter-in-law spy for them. But Shem seemed to be subtly hinting that it was something else: trust.

"They need... time," he was saying. "It's a lot to ask someone to trust another's Gift, but especially to ask it of the king and queen. Surely you can understand that?"

"I can," I said in a soft voice, turning to begin walking again so I didn't have to look at him. "That's why I'd hoped you might stand up for me." And though I didn't want to think ill of him, I couldn't help wondering if his guilt was the reason he hadn't come to see me last night.

"I apologize," he said from behind, taking long strides to catch up. "I was thinking about other things, but that's no excuse. I should've joined forces with you and convinced my father to listen. Truly." He put a hand on my arm, urging me to slow down and listen.

"What other things?" I demanded, more heated than I usually let myself speak to him, spinning to face him. "What's more important than worrying about where they might attack next? They're looking for you. Who's to say they won't come here?"

"I don't disagree with you." He held up his hands, palms out. "But I was contemplating how we might've reopened their portal and followed their trail." His hands fell back to his sides when I didn't interrupt. He ran a hand through his dark hair. "If we wait for them to come to us, we're at a disadvantage. The only way we have a real chance of stopping the Vaade is if we go on the offensive. But we can't."

"Why not?"

"Because we still don't know where they're located. They're nomadic. And the only sites we've found so far were already abandoned."

We started walking again, more slowly this time, as I processed his words. Our wedding depended on stopping the Vaade, and he was saying that was impossible.

My heart sank.

I couldn't speak past the lump in my throat.

Only when I could manage to sound calm, did I reply, "I still think you should be more prepared for another attack here."

"We discussed where the Vaade might attack last night as well," he assured me. "In fact, that was the reason we finished so late, or I would've stopped by to check on you. I've been worrying over how you fared since the assault."

Pressing my lips together, I stared at him.

His brows nearly met in the middle as he stared back.

Softening, I took his arm when he offered it this time, slowing to walk beside him beneath a trellis covered in red roses. "I've been well enough."

Sneaking a glance at him, I plucked one of the pretty roses in full bloom. The vivid red was the same color as the top of my dress. As I sniffed it, I dared to add, "Well enough to wonder about your sudden disappearance during the attack…"

He sucked in a breath. "Yes. I—Thank you for reminding me. We should discuss it." Clearing his throat, he fiddled nervously with my fingers where they lay on his arm. "I hope… I'm afraid I must ask if you'll keep the details to yourself?"

"I swear on all of Jinn, I wouldn't tell a soul."

We began walking again, and when the path forked, we turned away from the castle toward the apple orchard. For a long moment, I thought he wasn't going to trust me.

"There aren't many details," he said finally. "But I'll show you what there is to know." Tugging me toward the orchard with a smile, Shem waited until we were hidden by the trees before he pulled me off the path. With one last glance around to check that no one was looking, he vanished in front of me, still holding my hand.

It felt like my mind was playing tricks—he could've just traveled away. It could be that my fingers only continued feeling him because they wanted to.

But then, he squeezed gently.

I grinned.

THE SECRET CURSE

"Incredible," I whispered.

He let go of my hand, and a moment later his soft voice came from behind me with a smile in it. "You think so?"

I whirled around to face him, laughing. *Invisibility. What a Gift!* It was as powerful as my own, maybe even more so in some circumstances...

"This is why I'm not worried anyone will catch me." His laughing voice came from further away now.

Before I could say anything else, a roar came from the other direction.

Something—or someone—crashed into me.

The massive weight knocked me down, crushing me.

I couldn't breathe.

Dirt covered one side of my face, my shoulder ached where it'd taken the brunt of the fall, and my heart thumped wildly.

Coughing, I turned to the face hovering over me. It came into focus.

My heartbeat kicked up.

A Khaanevaade.

"Where is your prince?" a deep voice growled. "He was just with you!"

"He's not here," I said loudly, hoping Shem would hear me and stay invisible. His Gift would allow him to take this Vaade by surprise. He would fight for me... *wouldn't he?* My body trembled, giving away my fear to the big man pinning me to the ground. My arms were trapped.

The Vaade spat a curse. "Jinn and their traveling!"

I chanced another look at him, only to find his terrifying, dragon eyes studying me like a predator when hunting prey. I flinched. Shutting my eyes, I waited for him to strike. Those eyes burned themselves into my memory—like a sunset, but with a black, oval sun in the center.

When I risked another glance, he grinned wickedly, dropping his head lower until his tangled dark hair framed our faces, forcing me to truly look at him. It was impossible not to notice the strange white paint drawn across those fiery orange eyes, like two fingers scraped from forehead to cheek. The white streaks continued in strange designs across his chest where he pressed against me. "I remember you."

Trying to see past the paint, I took in his strong nose, full lips, and the way his thick strands of dark brown hair tickled my bare arms.

It was the same Vaade from the engagement tour.

I sucked in a deep breath, remembering how he hadn't hurt me then. Maybe he'd liked my courage. Despite the way my heart thundered in my chest, I cleared my throat and pretended to be unaffected. "Are you sure we've met?" I asked calmly, as if we were at a tea party instead of pressed up against each other. I dragged my eyes down his body to where the paint disappeared, noting an enormous tooth dangling from a string of hide around his neck, before returning his gaze. "I don't recognize you."

As soon as I said the words, I regretted them. I shouldn't have antagonized him.

He grunted, eyes narrowing.

Shem only had seconds to attack if he was going to rescue me before—

Unexpectedly, the Vaade smirked. "You wouldn't be so calm if you were alone." He lifted his head, sniffing the air. "Is your prince around here? Are you hoping he'll come rescue you?"

Though I didn't like the way the Vaade sounded so excited for the prospect, I certainly hoped so. Or, if Shem had left, I hoped it was to rally the Guard and return immediately.

The way the Vaade stared to one side, nostrils flaring, made me nervous.

If Shem *was* drawing close to attack, then I needed to distract the brute.

Pretending a bravado I didn't feel, I gave the empty orchard a mocking glance. "Do *you* see him?"

His hands curled tighter around my arms, as he focused on me, murmuring, "You were close to him before as well." The way his voice rumbled from his chest into my own was unsettling. "You wore a crown."

Paling, I searched for an explanation. "Lots of Jinn wear crowns." That was a poor lie, but I said it with a straight face and a partial shrug, as much as I could while pinned to the ground.

The Vaade's lips slowly curled into a smile, and with a sinking feeling, I knew I hadn't fooled him in the slightest. "No. They don't."

"How would you know?" I challenged him, stalling. "I doubt you spend a lot of time in Jinni circles."

Instead of answering, he sniffed the air again, eyes scanning the same trees to one side. My heart raced faster. Shem was trying to get close.

Though I didn't want to compare him to the Vaade, the thick arms pinning me down were twice the size of Shem's and likely making him hesitate. Knowing his preference for strategy, he'd be waiting for the right moment. But if he didn't hurry up, there might not *be* a right moment. Trying and failing to take a full breath under the weight of the big man, I sucked in shallow breaths instead, with rising speed.

If Shem didn't act soon, I would.

"I was hoping to finally catch the prince," the Vaade murmured without taking his eyes off the empty space. "But we've run out of time, so you'll have to do."

Eyes widening, I was about to shift into something—anything—with claws, no longer caring if another Jinni saw my secret Gift anymore, when his weight suddenly lifted.

I could breathe again.

The Vaade had disappeared completely.

THE SECRET CURSE

Whipping my head around, I leapt to my feet, trying to watch every part of the orchard at once.

Was that Shem? Had he traveled with the Vaade?

There!

A few dozen paces away, the Vaade reappeared, stumbling into a tree. Just like in the first attack, they hadn't gotten far before he seemed to drop out of traveling like an anchor. "You!" he roared, pointing at me. "What did you do to me?"

I tensed to travel.

With a leap, he crossed the distance between us faster than I expected, crushing me in his grip and hauling me over his shoulder.

My head whipped back painfully.

I had only a split second to search for Shem as the Vaade flung us through the open portal.

There.

His horrified face appeared in the same place the Vaade had materialized.

After that, it all happened in a single heartbeat.

My whole world shimmered and shifted around me.

The cheerful orchard with its carefully groomed walking paths turned into a dark forest full of thick undergrowth that swallowed us up.

Thin pine trees shot up all around us, so tall that I couldn't even see the top through the branches covered in needles.

Even the sun was smaller.

We were in the human world.

From behind me, a new voice called, "Close the daleth!"

5

I WAS SURROUNDED.

Khaanevaade loomed over me on all sides with blank, unreadable faces. At least a dozen men and women, all streaked with white paint, wearing animal furs that blended in with the forest around us.

Light hardly dared to peek through the trees, turning them into dark silhouettes in the dusky green gloom. Leaves and twigs crunched beneath me as I struggled against the Vaade's hard body. A violent tearing sounded as my skirts ripped.

He eased back suddenly.

I lurched forward, but his strong hands held their grip on my arm, tightening when I resisted.

Taking in the fearsome group surrounding me, I tried to think past the panic clawing at my mind. If I shifted now, I'd have to make it count. There were so many of them. And where was Shem? Had he traveled after us? Had there been enough time?

Even as I searched the surrounding forest for a glimpse of his face, some part of me knew he hadn't followed. He was the sole heir to Jinn. He'd never put himself in that type of danger, not even for me. His father had drilled it into him at a young age.

THE SECRET CURSE

Still, I dared a glance at my captor, hoping to see him sniff the air for Shem again.

Instead, he lifted me to my feet roughly.

"This is not the prince," one of the other Vaade snapped at him. "Your father said to get the *prince*."

My kidnapper snorted and didn't bother to explain himself, holding me tight. "Make sure they can't reopen the daleth before we go."

My free hand lifted halfway to the little vial around my neck, still hidden underneath my dress. This was my chance to use the paralytic.

Almost a dozen eyes followed the movement.

I changed direction and pulled a twig out of my hair.

There were too many of them.

The vial only held enough for two or three at most.

My mind raced through the other possibilities.

I could shapeshift into a little creature and run, or a large creature and fight, or use my manipulation to make them let me go—though that would only work on one or two.

If all else failed, I could simply travel away, couldn't I?

From what I remembered of the last attack on Tel Sheba, the Vaade man had grown disoriented when the Jinni dragged him along. If I traveled enough times, he'd let go, wouldn't he?

Unless he somehow anchored himself again, like he had before...

Around us, the Vaade moved on silent feet where the daleth had been.

When I tried to peer over the shoulder of the big Vaade holding me, he put pressure on my arm to hold me back. With a frustrated glance, I turned away to find a dozen more dragon eyes pinned on me. It gave me the distinct impression of how a wolf might study a helpless sheep.

Though I wasn't completely defenseless, the sheer number of them made me tremble.

I could fight, poison, or outrun one or two Vaade, but over a dozen?

I wasn't sure.

With the Vaade's big hand wrapped around my arm, I was afraid to start something that I might not be able to finish.

As if he could hear my heartbeat pick up, his fingers tightened to a bruising strength, and I could almost sense him growing roots. He expected me to fight back. Maybe he even *wanted* me to attack.

"That hurts!" I hissed at him under my breath.

"Then stop acting like you're about to run," he replied easily, but his fingers loosened a bit.

A small chuckle ran through the Vaade, making me blush.

"Who says I'm planning to run?" My voice quavered slightly. I cursed the way the adrenaline made my fears rise to the surface.

Though I hadn't expected him to answer, his deep, calm voice said, "Your heartbeat sped up and your whole body tensed."

He had an entirely unfair advantage.

If I traveled now, I might accidentally drag him with me. Once I revealed my ability, I'd lose the element of surprise, so I needed to time this carefully.

"You're misreading the situation," I lied. "I'd be foolish to run when I have nowhere to go."

"You speak the truth," he said with a slight grin, as if we shared a friendly exchange.

Something about his words caused another ripple of laughter among the other Vaade, though.

"Then, we're in agreement. You might as well let me walk on my own."

He chuckled as if that was part of the jest. "Not a chance."

Huffing in frustration, I didn't bother to answer. He couldn't hold my arm forever.

Reminding myself to act fearful, like the foolish little Jinni he took me for, I bowed my head and stayed still.

The panic wasn't fully an act.

He seemed pacified, though, turning to study the Vaade behind him. Careful not to move my arm, I leaned my head forward and managed to catch a glimpse of what they were doing. They'd drawn shapes in the dirt and were now sprinkling ashes across the space where the daleth had been.

"It's sealed," one of the Vaade told my captor. "No one will follow us."

My heart sank.

That meant Shem couldn't reopen them like he'd hoped. If the daleths were sealed, he'd have no way to find my trail.

"Back to camp," the big Vaade said.

Without another word, he began to drag me through the heavily wooded area. There was no sign of a path.

I tensed. My heart leapt into my throat, racing fast enough to make the Vaade tighten his grip.

We don't know where they're located. Shem's words came back to me.

If the Vaade brought me back to their camp, no one would be able to find me.

With every passing second in this vulnerable position, my fear grew. None of the Vaade spoke as they traipsed through the woods, but they held their weapons ready. They'd fight if I tried anything.

I wasn't pretending to be afraid anymore.

I was alone and painfully aware.

Stay calm and focus on gathering information. I'm sure Shem's rallying the Guard right now. Maybe one of the Jinni Guard members would have a Gift for tracking lost Jinn? It was a stretch, but I clung to the idea.

He'll find me, I promised myself. *And if he doesn't...* Swallowing hard, I made myself finish the thought. *If he can't for some reason, I can save myself.*

When the right moment presented itself, that's exactly what I'd do.

I shivered. *Hopefully.*

I'd never attempted to fight so many at once... I could only hope the Vaade would leave me alone at some point.

Distracted by my thoughts, I tripped over the ripped piece of my dress where it dangled crookedly. The fabric tore again. A strip of dirty white fabric fluttered to the ground.

The gruff Vaade yanked me upright, keeping me from slamming face first into the ground.

I pressed my lips together, unwilling to thank him. All he'd done was remind me of his disproportionate strength.

When the time came to fight back, I wouldn't underestimate the Vaade the way the royal family had.

No, I'd wait to use my Gifts until the opportune moment, when they least expected it.

Despite my strategy, my skin tingled feverishly as we wound deeper into the woods until I was thoroughly lost. Every tree looked the same: thick trunks so tall they blocked out most of the sun, with pine needles covering all the branches.

It was suffocating.

I nearly risked shifting into a leopard and making a run for it, just to make the panic stop.

The Vaade's fingers curled tighter around my upper arm when my heart rate increased.

I tried to slow my breathing.

Don't give yourself away yet. There's only one chance to surprise them.

I allowed him to shove me on through the endless trees.

An hour passed. Maybe more.

If there weren't a dozen Vaade following us, I might've tried to cut my dress and drop scraps to leave a trail.

Each time I glanced back over my shoulder, however, a dozen dragon-like eyes in varying shades of fire stared back at me from dark faces streaked with white paint.

Many of these Vaade had the same thick tangled hair as my captor, with little gold circlets decorating some of the rope-like strands. They wore animal hides and furs with splashes of color in a necklace here, feathers there, or sometimes red paint streaked across a chest or face. Despite the cool shade, there were a *lot* of bare chests and arms.

Though my heart continued pumping rapidly, the chaos in my mind was clearing with the quiet walk.

They were taking me to their *camp*.

The one location that Shem said our people had been unable to find.

And they were taking me directly to it.

What if I let them?

If I pretended to be weak and defenseless a bit longer, they'd lead me right to it, finally revealing their home. I could escape with the knowledge of where to attack.

It could change the entire war.

Not to mention, I'd finally get to set another wedding date.

I made my decision.

He'd kidnapped the wrong Jinni.

When the time was right, I'd make them pay.

Despite my decision to stay of my own free will, the instinct to flee refused to fade completely, making me jumpy.

A wiry older man strode forward, pushing through the group. When I saw his bare, muscled thighs and chest, I realized his only covering was a small flap of animal hide over his groin and backside.

My face flooded with color. I whipped around to face forward.

It didn't do me any good.

Seconds later, he fell in step with my captor and I at the lead, giving me an eyeful of his chiseled arms and chest that almost rivaled my captor's own, despite the gray in his hair. "You can't bring it back to the camp," he hissed. "Koda, your father will be furious."

If I hadn't been forcibly connected to the Vaade, I wouldn't have noticed the brief hesitation. His face didn't change. His feet didn't slow. But one stride faltered slightly. This "Koda" jutted his chin out. "I don't care."

With a glance at me, the other Vaade shoved himself in front of Koda until he couldn't continue without running the man over. As he swung around, a long bow and a quiver full of arrows on his back became visible.

For a split second, it looked like Koda might keep walking right through the other man. He stopped so close that they breathed the same breath, both scowling. "Ahriman. Move."

Ahriman only stared back at him. His face was hard and unreadable. Like Koda, he had heavy brows and a strong nose, but unlike Koda, his lips were thin and pressed together.

Shoving me roughly behind him, without loosening his grip on my wrist, Koda hissed something else in Ahriman's ear. The exchange was brief and too soft for me to hear. I wanted to make this Koda regret turning his back on me—a foolish mistake—but I also didn't want to give away my strength quite yet, while I was still outnumbered, so I waited impatiently.

When he finally stepped back, my brows shot up at his next words. "We'll use a blindfold." It wasn't spoken to me. He didn't even look at me.

"No, thank you," I replied anyway, but they all acted like they didn't hear.

I considered using my newest Gift of manipulation. Since I'd yet to learn how to use it without both eye contact and somehow touching my subject, I'd be forced to twist at an awkward angle to look at Koda. *If* he let me. While the other dozen Vaade stood on and watched.

I chewed on my lip. It might ruin the element of surprise if I couldn't manage to control him or if the others stopped me.

Act naturally, I told myself, turning to attempt it without anyone else catching on. Koda clamped a hand on my shoulder, stopping me.

I drew in a deep breath and sighed, pinching my eyes closed, and spoke without my Gift. "I'd rather not have a blindfold."

"It'd *rather not*," another Vaade mocked, and they laughed as a female Vaade stepped forward.

I tensed.

She wore a long deerskin tunic with a wide neck that bared her graceful shoulders. Pulling a wicked looking knife from her belt, she bent to cut a strip of the thin hide from the bottom of the dress.

I frowned as the strip formed.

She stood.

My hands trembled.

It was torture to keep still. I reminded myself of my new plan: *find their camp. Wait until they let their guard down. Then escape with a clear path and valuable information.*

Glancing at me so briefly I almost missed it, Koda held out a hand to the Vaade woman. "Give it to me."

I matched the Vaade woman's scowl as she stepped forward to hand it over.

Koda turned to face me, blindfold in hand.

Shaking, I imagined shifting my fingers into claws and slashing it into pieces—or wrapping my hand around his wrist and whispering, *You want to let me go.*

With a frustrated breath, I lifted my chin and glared at the Vaade.

While the blindfold wasn't ideal, it didn't affect my plan. Once they brought me to their camp, I'd flee. There'd been over a dozen daleths on that map back in the castle—if I could remember where even one of them was, I could travel there and return to Jinn. I'd alert the Guard immediately and they could follow my trail back to the Vaade camp. We'd finally have the upper hand, thanks to me.

While Koda wrapped it over my eyes, I stayed still, hands clenched at my sides until he finished.

"We should take its clothes," someone sneered. "A naked Jinni is a humble Jinni."

I tried to hide the way I clutched the skirts of my dirty red dress. It'd felt so empowering this morning, but now it felt like my last defense against them.

Absolutely not.

I might be forced to fight after all.

"The Jinni needs a lesson in humility," someone else snapped. When a few of the other Vaade yelled in agreement, I instinctively stepped away from the sound.

And right into Koda's hard, bare chest.

"No," Koda said simply. This time when he pressed me behind him, I didn't mind nearly as much. "We'll blindfold her and no more." Koda didn't raise his voice, but he clearly expected obedience.

I hope he's their leader. It'd seemed like it at first, but when he'd submitted to Ahriman, I'd assumed it must be him instead. Now, though, they *all* complained about my presence loudly as if each had a say.

I shivered, unable to help myself.

They argued as if there were no consequences. In Jinn, *no one* argued with the king and queen. If they did, they'd be silenced immediately.

"At least make sure it can't see anything," a male voice said, and the bitter grumbling sounded like Ahriman.

Koda listened to him and pulled on the cloth, tugging a piece of my hair caught up in it.

I winced. "How far do I have to walk like this?" I dared to ask, trying to appear unfazed.

No one responded.

Without my sight, I felt off-balance. The Vaade were so quiet that if Koda's hand wasn't around my wrist, I'd have thought they'd left.

We began moving again.

Almost immediately, I tripped.

When Koda moved his hand from my wrist to my arm, I flinched.

It could be worse, though.

Most of these violent Vaade wouldn't think twice about killing me, but my captor at least seemed to be sane... More than the others, anyway.

Maybe he could even be reasoned with.

"I can work with you, if you'll let me," I tried in a quiet but firm tone. "We could come up with some terms for peace that I could bring back to the royal family?"

"We don't want peace," he growled in my ear, tugging on my arm to keep walking.

I stumbled a bit, mostly because it was unexpected. Once I righted myself, his grip on my arm kept me surprisingly steady. "What *do* you want, then?" I said back without thinking, and accidentally let some of my frustration seep into my tone.

Instead of infuriating him, it made him chuckle. "Many things."

I drew in a deep breath, trying to keep my temper, and replied in an even tone, "Such as?"

"Power," he replied simply.

Frowning made the blindfold shift, and it began to itch. I reached up a hand to rub the spot, but someone on my other side yanked my arm down roughly. I yelped.

There were sounds of a scuffle.

For a brief second, my captor let me go.

I stood still.

A thump sounded, followed by a grunt of pain.

Someone fell to the ground near my feet and I jumped back instinctively. As I did, I tripped over an unseen root. A warm hand caught my waist, keeping me upright, then wrapped around my wrist once more.

What just happened?

My body tensed, not knowing who held me now, until he spoke, "Come." After a slight pause, he added, "And don't touch the blindfold."

I recognized his voice. Relaxing, I let Koda lead me through the woods, finding myself leaning closer to him now.

Behind us, the other Vaade followed silently.

My mind raced as we walked.

If I'd interpreted it correctly, that was twice now he'd kept me safe. I would stay close to him. Not that I'd be with the Vaade much longer. Only long enough to find their camp and have something to report back home.

Koda surprised me by continuing our conversation, though his voice faded as he turned away, almost as if he were talking more to the others than to me. "We want power over the Jinn—not to abuse it, but to be stronger and better so that your kind never take advantage of ours again. And we're prepared to take it."

A few grunts of agreement came from behind us. "More than prepared," one of the men added, and a few others laughed.

That caught my attention. "Take it?" I repeated softly, not liking the sound of that.

"Yes," he replied with another one-word answer, and this time it was clear I wouldn't get any farther.

Unease crawled over my skin.

Was learning the location of their camp really the advantage Shem hoped it'd be, or was an attack from Jinn exactly what they wanted?

6

AFTER WALKING AT LEAST an hour across uneven ground, my ears picked up voices in the distance, growing louder as we approached. We must be nearing their camp. As we stopped weaving around unknown obstacles—trees, I assumed—our path smoothed out as well. A clearing? Or had we left the forest behind altogether?

I tried to control my nervous reaction, to keep my heart from picking up speed. It was almost time.

Koda's grip tightened anyway.

My feet ached and my arm was already sore, so I opened my mouth to complain, but before I could, his deep voice whispered in my ear, "Don't speak. You'll regret it."

Pursing my lips to hold back the torrent of questions, I scowled in his general direction.

He probably didn't even notice.

What did he mean? Who would make me regret it? Him? Or was he warning me about someone else?

Only his actions back in the woods convinced me to listen.

For now.

As soon as I confirmed this was their camp, however, I planned to run.

THE SECRET CURSE

"Dragon." Koda's tone was deferential.

Not a *real* dragon? An involuntary shiver touched my skin. I caught myself and shook my head. It must be a strange title for the Vaade leader... Despite the obvious logic, my fingers itched to rip off the blindfold to confirm.

"The prince continues to evade us," Koda was saying. "But we stole something equally valuable to them."

Some*thing*? I had to bite my tongue to keep from snapping, *I'm not a thing!*

"They only have one son!" a voice even deeper than Koda's rasped. He even sounded like a dragon. I shivered again. "Any other Jinni is worthless! Get rid of it."

Eyes widening behind my blindfold, I could only assume he meant to kill me. The way he spoke sounded like he was used to being obeyed too.

Against Koda's advice, I called out, "I'm not worthless! I can influence the royal family!"

There was a long pause.

A growl so animalistic it made the hair raise on my arms came from the same direction as this "dragon's" voice.

As I flinched back, the blindfold shifted the tiniest bit, allowing me a glimpse of two moccasin-covered feet coming to stand in front of me.

When he answered, that deep voice held a tremble of barely contained fury. "What does it mean?"

It.

He wasn't even addressing me. He was talking to Koda.

"She's important to the prince," Koda replied, fingers squeezing my arm to convey his frustration.

"His betrothed," I corrected.

His fingers dug into my soft skin harder, and I gasped.

Another stretch of silence passed.

"Take it to one of the longhouses."

"I'm not sharing space with *that*," someone yelled, and what sounded like a few dozen other voices echoed the sentiment, startling me. For some reason, I'd imagined the Vaade fighters as a smaller group. How many Vaade were here?

The leader allowed the dissent, just like Koda had. Even more shocking, he *listened*. Raising his voice, he called, "Where would you have me put our prisoner, then?"

"A deep ravine!" someone snarled.

"Below ground," said another.

It took all my willpower not to recoil.

Koda's calm voice spoke up, and while it was probably meant to be a question, it seemed more like a statement. "The smokehouse."

Chatter quieted.

"Acceptable," the Dragon said, voice fading as if he was already turning away. "It will need to be spelled. Take it to the longhouse until the smokehouse is prepared."

Without further debate, I was dragged forward through a hissing crowd. Holding my head high, I ignored the urge to cower away from sounds, to hide behind Koda's big, bare shoulder. I wouldn't let them see the pure terror snaking through my body.

Unfortunately, my uncontrollable trembling told Koda the truth.

My plans were falling apart. This was the Vaade camp, but with each new Vaade voice I heard around me, fleeing seemed even more impossible. How could I take on so many?

Bright sunlight beaming through the blindfold cut off abruptly, turning my world pitch-black.

I shuffled forward.

"Stop there or you'll hit a wall," Koda's voice rumbled beside me as he tugged my arm.

I sucked in a breath and stumbled slightly when the blindfold was ripped off.

At first, I thought we were in a dark cave. But as my eyes adjusted, the room took shape.

It was truly a long house, like the leader had said, with one big room stretched out, made of thick logs and some kind of sweet-smelling mortar.

We stood at the far end, tucked away in the back, next to a pile of animal skins resting on the dirt floor. Beyond us were sleeping bunks built into the walls that went on and on, though most were empty at this time of day. They hinted at a huge number of people living in this building alone.

One of the longhouses, the Dragon had said. There were more of these? Clearly the royal family underestimated the Vaade numbers.

In the center, a cooking fire was surrounded by dozens of tree stumps, which Vaade were using as seats. Men, women, and even children moved around the fire, shooting curious glances in our direction. Or, at least, the children were curious. Most of the adults were openly glaring.

Directly above the fire, a single opening in the ceiling allowed wisps of smoke to curl up and out while the Vaade around it cooked and ate. Sunlight lit up the cozy circle, but couldn't quite touch us this far back.

It was oddly communal.

Koda let go of my wrist.

I'd grown so used to the pressure that I felt almost weightless. *Free.* I could travel if I wanted to.

Though I tried to hide my reaction from him and the Vaade who'd entered behind him, he caught my expression. "The longhouse is spelled against traveling, and the smokehouse will be very soon as well. Something we learned from *your* people."

THE SECRET CURSE

Just like the castle. Hearing this and knowing it to be true were two different things, however. *What if he's only saying that to prevent my escape?* Now that we were here, I couldn't stand to wait anymore.

I attempted to travel outside the longhouse.

A barrier stopped me at the wall, flinging me back.

Oof.

I fell on the hard-packed dirt.

My chest ached. The enchantment had knocked the breath out of me. Coughing as my lungs spasmed, I blinked, trying to clear my head.

I hadn't tested a boundary spell since I was little. I'd forgotten how much they hurt. But my pride hurt more. Cheeks burning, I ignored Koda and the others looming over me.

Though he kept a straight face, the others chuckled.

"They never listen," one said.

Another agreed. "They always think they know better than us."

Mutters of "fool Jinni" and "the Dragon should never have allowed this" followed that statement, and some of the onlookers opened the door to leave.

I pulled myself to my feet, trying to ignore them and the pain in my backside that rose with my fury.

If they thought they wouldn't have tried too, they were lying to themselves.

Though I fully intended to feign indifference, my eyes still flew to the door as it closed, marking the loss of my only escape route.

"Two guards at all times," Koda was saying as he moved through the group. "Bull and Kele to start."

I panicked slightly as two of the Vaade swung around to face me with hands on their unsophisticated weapons—mostly knives in a variety of sizes, though all of them were large enough to slice off an arm. One of them also carried a bow and arrows. "You're not staying?"

Koda didn't look back at me. He barely even hesitated at the door, but it was long enough for the other Vaade to begin jeering, "Koda and the Jinni? Who would've thought—the Dragon's son has a soft spot for one of the lying snakes."

That confirmed my suspicion that he was the leader's son.

He didn't answer the taunts, or me, shoving through the door and slamming it behind him.

That left me with the two guards and a handful of other Vaade staring at me like a prized horse. "Did you see how it talked to Koda? How strange…" One of the women spoke to a friend loud enough for me to hear.

With a huff, I turned my back on them and dropped down to sit on the pile of furs. My vibrant red and white dress looked especially out of place against the dirt floor. Next to their simple deerskin tunics and colorful woven skirts, my crystal covered gown stood out, and not in a good way.

Though it was difficult to ignore dozens of eyes on me, I pretended not to notice, tentatively leaning back against the wall. Instead of being rough and scratchy, as I'd expected, it was rubbed smooth. I was surprisingly comfortable. Or, at least, I would've been, if I hadn't had an audience. I felt like a captured Lacklore put on display for entertainment.

I wished I hadn't waited to run. I should've pulled free back in the forest. All I would've needed was a moment of surprise, but I'd hesitated too long.

Closing my eyes, I drew my hand slowly over the soft pelt beneath me, over and over, calming myself with the motion. It worked briefly. Until my troublesome mind pointed out that I was petting a dead animal, specifically one that the Vaade had killed.

Heartbeat in my ears, I stilled through sheer willpower, pretending to fall asleep.

Stuck here without a plan, I finally faced the questions I'd been avoiding—why did they take me prisoner? What were they planning for me? And more importantly, how would Shem find me if they'd never been able to find the Vaade camp before?

I needed to get out of this longhouse and travel back to Jinn—or rather, to the nearest daleth.

Peeking out beneath my dark lashes, I confirmed that the dozens of eyes in the room were all still aimed in my direction.

If I shifted into a flea, odds were good they'd step on me before I could crawl out through a crack in the wall. Even if I shifted into a large animal to attack these two ridiculous guards, and somehow fought past all the others, I didn't know if there was a portal nearby. During the Vaade's last attack, they'd traveled a good distance from camp before opening a daleth.

If they were opening and closing the portals as needed, that likely meant we were a good distance from any nature-made daleth.

Keeping my eyes closed, I tried to envision the map of all the daleths in the human world—why hadn't I studied it closer? Though I had a rough sense of the landscape, I couldn't picture the names of any of the nearby human cities.

Maybe it'd only take a day or two to find a daleth, but it could just as easily take weeks. Especially if there was nothing marking the portal's presence.

I nearly groaned out loud. I hadn't thought of that before.

My earlier plans to travel straight home from the Vaade camp felt foolish now.

A traveling trail faded in a few days at most.

If it took longer than that to find a daleth, any trail I might leave behind would be long gone.

Even if I somehow marked the trail physically or remembered landmarks that could lead me back, that plan still depended on the assumption that the Vaade wouldn't pick up and move.

THE SECRET CURSE

The seemingly simple task I'd created for myself now seemed impossible.

My shoulders sagged.

Hot tears pricked my eyes unexpectedly.

I'm in over my head, I finally admitted.

If the only way to prove myself to the royal family was through dying here in the Vaade camp, I'd prefer to remain insignificant and live.

Blowing out a breath, I returned to my original plan: I'd cut my losses and look for the next chance to run.

The opportunity would present itself if I could be patient. Perhaps when they transferred me to this "smokehouse."

The number of Vaade increased as they gathered around the small cookfire at the other end of the room for the noon meal.

Everyone left to join them except my guards.

I sat up expectantly.

My mouth watered at the smells of bread and meat cooking, but no one offered me anything.

As the afternoon passed, the sunlight pouring in through the opening in the roof grew dimmer much sooner than I expected, hinting at either a storm approaching or some other enormous form blocking the sun. A mountain perhaps? That could help me find my bearings once I got away.

I will *escape,* I assured myself again as my stomach growled, trying to keep my spirits up.

Wrapping my arms tightly around myself, I glared at the onlookers who'd returned to ogle me. They discussed me with each other like a fancy pet.

"It's bad-tempered," a nearby Vaade woman whispered.

I rolled my eyes. "*She* can hear you."

The woman spat at my feet. "You are not to speak." Turning to the two Vaade that Koda had set to guard me, she snapped, "Punish it."

The one with his knife out at the ready leaned forward on the balls of his feet, as if tempted, but something held him back. "Not worth it." I probably had Koda's reaction back in the forest to thank for that.

With a huff, the Vaade woman turned on her bare heel, storming out of the longhouse. A few others followed. As the hours passed, and I ceased to do anything else of interest, the group of onlookers slowly dwindled again. After the evening meal, only the two guards were left.

This might be my best chance. Maybe even my *only* chance.

"What am I to do for personal needs?" I asked as delicately as I could, slowly standing, pretending not to notice the way they tensed. When their faces remained blank, I sighed, shifting on my feet as if my need was urgent. "Is there a bathing room, or somewhere I can go for privacy?"

This time, the blank faces had to be intentional. I clenched my fists. "I'd like to hope that your people don't usually soil the floor in their own home," I said, gesturing to the space around me, as I moved toward them. "So I'll be going outside to—"

They stepped in front of me, blocking my path.

"Go get Koda," I tried next. "Explain to him that even a Jinni has needs…"

They refused to respond.

Fine. I'd take my chances.

Narrowing my eyes at them, I moved my hands behind my back and began to shift. "If you insist on treating me like an animal," I said softly in a dangerous tone. "Then maybe I'll act like one."

Without warning, I finished the shift. Looming over them with the height of a bear and the claws to match, I lunged.

I landed on empty space.

Where the two Vaade guards had stood, now there was only hard packed dirt beneath me.

Roaring my fury, I spun around.

Something sharp plunged into my shoulder. With a yelp, I flung the attacker off.

He slammed into the wall behind me.

Before I could react, the other Vaade was on my back, pushing that knife in my shoulder deeper. Pain streaked through my body.

Swinging around, I raked my sharp claws across the Vaade, grabbing him by the shoulder and slamming him to the ground, unconscious. Instead of long, deep gouges along his body where my claws landed, there were only light scratches.

There was no time to process that.

The far door burst open, crashing into the wall, and Koda strode through it.

He was the only one who'd treated me even remotely decent. I didn't want to hurt him… but I would if I had to.

Snapping my sharp teeth in warning, I darted away from him toward the door at my back.

Once again, the Vaade strength and speed caught me off guard. He crossed the room in one big leap. A heavy weight crashed into me before I could squeeze through the exit, forcing me to retreat.

I eyed him for only a moment, then lumbered as fast as I could in bear form across the longhouse, aiming for the door on the opposite side.

He landed in front of it while I was still a dozen paces away.

Digging in my heels, I stopped in the middle of the room.

We stared at each other.

He was effectively blocking all the exits, unafraid of me. And why should he be? These Vaade were more powerful than I'd been willing to believe. Shem's claim that they were true rivals of the Jinn might actually be true.

THE SECRET CURSE

I couldn't win this way.

So, I did the one thing he wouldn't expect.

Backing up slowly, I stepped beneath the circle of light from the smoke hole in the ceiling.

I leapt into the air, shifting at the same time.

Koda's eyes widened.

With one powerful push off the ground, he soared through the air in my direction.

My bear form had taken me over halfway to the ceiling as I shrunk smaller and smaller, until I was a tiny fly—a form I'd shifted into often enough to know it would come quickly.

I flapped my clear, membranous wings the last few beats to the opening.

I still underestimated Koda.

His eyesight had to be incredible.

Though I made it through the opening, wings pumping, his huge hand shoved through after me, nearly snatching me out of the air.

His fingers closing in a fist below me caused an air current so strong I was flung forward, spinning end over end, flying wildly until I could right myself.

A second later, his hand disappeared back inside the longhouse.

He'd be outside and on me before I knew it.

The fly form wasn't good enough.

With no time to waste, I shifted into an eagle with a generous wingspan, pushing myself to make the change faster than I ever had before.

I flew straight toward the sun, where it was making its way across the sky. *How high can the Vaade jump?* I didn't know the answer, and I couldn't risk misjudging again, so I soared past the tall trees and then higher still, until the air grew thin.

Like I'd guessed from inside the longhouse, a mountain range trailed along one side of the Vaade camp.

Despite the throbbing pain, hope rose.

There.

In the distance, the mountains formed steep cliff walls—just like the map of the human world back at the castle.

Though I didn't see any dragons from this distance, it *had* to be the same one. After all, how many massive mountain ranges in the human world could have a sheer set of cliffs like that?

Circling, letting the air currents carry me along, I searched for a nearby human town.

Nothing.

Doubt dragged me down, but I pushed through it, turning back to the mountains. I'd paid careful attention to that daleth so I could describe its location to Shem. The one defining detail I remembered was the town close by. If it wasn't here, then it must be on the other side of the mountains.

Looked like I'd be crossing them.

I risked a glance back.

The Vaade camp was already far behind me. Koda would be a tiny speck, but in my eagle form I might still be able to spot him.

Other Vaade milled about their camp—a few hundred, maybe more, including women and children, which was far more than I'd expected from the voices I'd heard—but Koda was nowhere to be seen.

It didn't matter.

I knew where to go now. All I had to do was make it to the other side of the mountains.

I pushed myself on, aiming for the summit of the nearest cliffs.

As I flew, the shock and panic wore off, and my wing began to burn where the knife had struck.

Ignoring it, I glided on. But as time passed, it became harder to overlook.

I tried to move the wing less and less. That caused me to sink lower in the sky, dropping toward the forest.

The searing ache steadily grew, turning intense. I couldn't go much further. Floating in a slow circle, I would've frowned if this form was capable. I could hardly keep the wing extended, much less reach that peak in the distance.

Perhaps I should land briefly to rest and catch my breath.

The cliff heights I'd originally aimed for were still so far away.

Too far.

But the wound in my shoulder threatened to give out.

If I didn't land soon, my body might force me into a dangerous descent.

Since the Vaade camp was no longer visible behind me, I gave in to the urge.

Flapping the damaged wing as little as possible, I glided down into the woods and landed on an open branch near the top of a tree.

For a long minute, I just perched there, trembling.

My body hurt too much to shift.

So, I simply sat.

The shaking continued as I waited for my strength to return, but it didn't. After not eating all day and shifting so many times, I would've been exhausted anyway, but with this wound, I could hardly see straight.

I didn't know how much time was passing but I also didn't care.

The Vaade threat was over.

My concern now was this wound. If it was as bad as it felt, I didn't know if I could continue flying or if I should settle in for the night.

Finally, I twisted my neck to look at the damage. Fresh blood still leaked from the deep wound, dripping down to the forest floor. The sight made me dizzy. I nearly fell from the branch and had to flap my wings to catch my balance. The movement shot agonizing pain throughout my whole body all over again.

My wound was worse than I'd wanted to admit. If I didn't get back to Jinn soon, I might die out here.

I needed to find that daleth.

Racking my brain for a sense of where I was, based on those nearby cliffs, I tried to decide if I should shift so I could travel or remain in this form and attempt to fly again.

My energy was draining fast. Maybe I should shift while I was still capable.

But traveling would be restricted in the trees. With the density of the woods, I could only see a short distance, which meant it'd hardly be any faster than walking.

Flying was the obvious decision—but when I tested my wing, trying to lift it, black spots filled my vision.

I breathed shallowly through the pain.

No. Flying wasn't an option.

Something tickled the back of my neck, an animal instinct of sorts, making me look down just in time to see a Vaade form launch himself off the forest floor and up through the trees toward me.

Squawking, I flew without thinking, barely making it out of his grasp. A sharp yank on my tail feathers made me screech again.

Circling away, out of range, I let out another angry caw at the sight of two of my tail feathers in the Vaade's fist.

It was Koda.

7

THOUGH MY INJURED WING ached so badly my eyesight blurred, I strained toward the cliffs once more. I'd fly higher. Ride the air currents. Push past the all-consuming fire in my wing.

Somehow, I'd get to that daleth.

The sun was setting where it peeked between the mountains, casting the tops of the trees in a golden light.

"I only want to talk," Koda called after me, before I could fly out of earshot. "I have a deal to offer you."

When I ignored him, he yelled louder, "I tracked you here. I can find you again!"

I hesitated, letting myself sail on an air current for a moment, resting my throbbing wing.

"Even if I couldn't smell your blood, your magic is a trail, plain as day!"

My hopes sank.

It didn't matter if I flew for the portal or not. He'd capture and kill me before I ever had the chance to find it.

I'd never get home.

"Come speak with me," he yelled, though his voice was growing faint in the distance. "I mean you no harm."

THE SECRET CURSE

Lies! I wanted to shout back. But perhaps he might pretend a truce long enough for me to recover?

After another long beat, I finally circled back. *I'm listening,* I thought, as I hovered on an air current, wishing he could hear my response. Flapping my wings only when I absolutely had to, I stayed in the air. He'd have to take the hint because I didn't dare land. He could make all the promises he'd like, but that didn't mean I trusted them. Trusted *him*.

"I want to make a deal," he repeated, head flung back, waving an impatient arm for me to land.

My only response was to look away toward the cliffs. *Talk fast,* I thought now, struggling to stay airborne. I couldn't do this much longer, and there was no way I'd come any closer.

Were other Vaade hiding somewhere nearby? I couldn't see them anywhere, but that didn't mean much. I hadn't seen Koda coming either. Even if I landed far away from him, they could easily ambush me.

"I came alone," Koda called now, as if he'd guessed my fears. "Not all Vaade would be so lenient. Come. Hear me out."

I don't believe that for a second. I spun away on the wind again.

A few more seconds, and then I had to leave, whether he'd said his piece or not. *Hurry up,* I tried to urge him mentally.

As the air current disappeared and I was forced to flap my wings again, pain speared my shoulder so intensely I nearly blacked out, spiraling out of control, heading for the forest floor at breakneck speed. I pulled up with extreme effort, wanting to weep at the pain, but I could barely control my descent as I came hurtling through the trees.

I hit the ground in a bone crunching landing.

Koda crashed through the woods toward me, not bothering to hide his advance now.

He'd be on me in moments.

I screamed as I shifted faster than I'd ever done in my life, shuddering through the pain, forcing myself to take on the shape of the most dangerous creature I could think of: the Lacklore. Part bear, part ox, with talons as long and sharp as a dragon, and wicked teeth and horns to match.

It was less agile than the bear I'd chosen earlier, but far more deadly. I only hoped it might be enough.

That last push strained my energy to the point that I could barely stand. If I tried to shift into any other form besides my own right now, I'd fail. Even my own form would be difficult, draining the last of my energy reserves. I hid my unsteadiness by leaning subtly against a tree as Koda came into view.

He slowed, eyeing my new form. His nostrils flared as he openly sniffed the air, then he nodded to himself. "This is a fascinating Gift you have," he said without a trace of fear, stopping only a few paces away, as if the fact that I could skewer him with one swing didn't bother him at all.

If anything, he seemed intrigued.

I couldn't help but be impressed by his reaction—both to the Lacklore form and my Gift.

A Jinni would've run in the other direction.

Instead, he continued as if there was nothing unusual about it.

"My father wants the prince of Jinn to make a covenant with the Khaanevaade," he began without preamble. "We've spent years crafting this enchantment to mutually benefit our people."

An enchantment? I wanted to ask, but of course I couldn't. It was an intriguing idea, but it could be a bluff. More likely they wanted to kill Shem and end the royal family lineage. Jinn had long lifetimes, but rarely had more than one or two children, if that. Did the Vaade not know that new rulers were chosen once every fifty years? Shem wasn't guaranteed to rule—though, of course, he would. He was loved by the people. Still, if they somehow took his life, another would take his place.

Keeping one eye on Koda, I tried to also watch the forest, flicking my ears back, listening for any surprise visitors. This Lacklore body might've been a mistake. It was better suited to offense than defense, with terrifying fangs and razor-sharp claws. Hopefully the massive body would at least deter any unknown attackers—and Koda.

His sharp eyes took in my response, and he crossed his thick, muscled arms, leaning against a tree as well. "My father believes we can only deal with the prince. But we haven't been able to speak to him. Now that you're here, we might finally get his attention."

Get his attention—for negotiations? Swinging back to face him fully, I considered his words. *Or use me as bait in a trap?*

"I'm the only one who wants to help you," he continued reasoning, though I found that hard to believe. The question wasn't whether or not he had ulterior motives; it was what exactly were they? "The others would happily let you die out here in the forest," he added, making it sound inevitable.

A little voice whispered that maybe he was right. I hadn't even crossed the cliffs yet. Once I did, what if I couldn't find the daleth on the other side? What if I bled out while looking?

Noticing the direction of my gaze, he turned to glance over his shoulder, where the cliffs rose above the trees. "If you go that way, you'll die even sooner," he said with a shrug, crossing his arms as he turned back to me again. "The dragons live in those cliffs. They don't always listen to the Vaade anymore, especially during hatching season. I can't guarantee I'd be able to stop them from eating you."

Trembling overtook my legs. I leaned harder into the tree. *Dragons.* I didn't

THE SECRET CURSE

want to believe him, but my weary mind chose that exact moment to remember the map back in Jinn. *The drawing of dragons.* That little detail was exactly why I'd remembered the location of the daleth in the first place, when I'd wanted to show Shem.

I squeezed my eyes closed briefly.

"If you come with me"—Koda's voice drew closer—"we can discuss terms with your prince that will allow you to return home."

My eyes flew open. I glared at him until he slowed to a stop, hands up.

Though I hardly understood what he was offering, I was tempted to agree. The burning wound in my shoulder had yet to stop bleeding. Exhaustion threatened me.

Not taking his deal was becoming more of a risk than taking it.

As I deliberated tossing my desperate plans to the wind and accepting the dangerous offer, Koda slowly crouched, glittering eyes on me. "I can see you're spent," he said in a low voice that held a promise of something. "You couldn't beat me in a fight anyway."

I snarled at him.

When he leapt, I expected it this time.

Hurtling my huge body at him, we slammed into each other, but my extra weight took him down.

We hit the ground hard.

Just like the other Vaade, Koda's skin seemed nearly impenetrable—my talons left only shallow scratches along his shoulders and stomach, and he laughed in my face.

I roared my fury and pounded the ground next to his head.

Without warning, his thick arm pulled free and he hit my shoulder, right where the knife had gone in.

Mid-roar I shifted to a scream, snapping back into my Jinni form without thinking, a protective reflex to return to myself before I physically couldn't anymore.

He immediately rolled on top of me, looming much larger now that I'd shrunk to my normal size. Those huge, muscled arms trapped me in on both sides, and his body pressed tightly to mine, making me acutely aware of him. It pressed my wound into the hard ground, setting my entire shoulder on fire.

"Not. Fair." I gasped.

His face was so close that his warm breath brushed my face.

For a long second, I thought he'd kill me after all.

Then he grinned. "Fair doesn't win fights." Slowly, he peeled himself off me, clearly enjoying the way I grew flustered. He crouched next to me, leaning back on his heels, but made no move to capture my wrist or arm.

He probably knew it wasn't necessary.

Breathing hard, I held in a groan.

"Can I trust you to stay?" he murmured as my breathing slowed.

I nodded, wincing when I moved to sit up and it set my shoulder on fire once more. Instead of taking the hand he held out, I sank back to the ground and closed my eyes. I'd reached my limits.

"I knew it," he said on a laugh. "I *knew* you were pretending to be fine."

That annoyed me enough that I cracked open my eyes to glare at him, but I didn't waste any energy on speaking. The woods around us were starting to spin and grow dark at the edges. Or was that my vision playing tricks on me?

"Stay with me," Koda's voice murmured somewhere to my left, but I didn't hear anything more as I lost consciousness.

8

THE SMELL OF SOMETHING spicy and sweet cooking woke me. Opening my eyes was an effort.

Sure enough, to one side, a little more than an arm's reach away, was a cozy fire with a makeshift spit hanging over it, cooking a small, bird-shaped animal. Koda's glowing eyes met mine from the other side of the fire as he turned the meat.

It was dusk now. Stars had yet to come out, but it'd be fully dark soon.

The reflection of the embers gave him a predatory look and yet when I shifted to sit, I discovered a clean bandage wrapped around my shoulder, smelling of an unknown herb that seemed to be doing wonders for my pain.

I crossed my legs awkwardly beneath my long dress, copying Koda's relaxed posture across from me, ignoring the way the white fabric at the bottom of the dress was now a dirty brown.

Pulling the food away from the fire, he finally spoke. "You shouldn't push yourself so hard next time you try to escape."

I coughed. "Next time?"

His lips curved in a wolfish smile.

"Is that—" I tried to find a polite way to ask about the food, but when his grin grew wider, I frowned and got to the point. "Can I have some?"

Nodding, he stood and passed the steaming meat across the fire to me on a stick, returning to a crouch.

I took the stick gingerly. No silverware or plates out here in the forest, but after not eating since the previous morning, I was too hungry to care. Burning my fingers as I held the stick, I ripped meat from the bone with my teeth and gulped it down.

Koda watched me eat in silence, not saying a word when I ate the entire small bird—or was it another animal? I didn't know, and I didn't care. All that mattered to me right now was food and rest. I couldn't shift in my current condition and that left me more vulnerable than I wanted to admit.

When I handed him the stick with only the bones remaining, he tossed it in the fire without taking his eyes from mine. From his pack, he pulled out some yellow bread, pulling a hunk of it off and handing it to me.

"So, you'll come back to camp?" he asked finally, once I'd finished and was unashamedly licking my fingers.

It took me a minute to remember what he was referring to. Negotiations. Convincing Shem to listen, though the details were a little too vague for my comfort. I couldn't remember much else. Maybe he hadn't said. Either way, I didn't really have a choice, did I?

I pursed my lips. "I will if you get rid of the guards."

"Not possible," he replied without missing a beat.

I chewed on my lip, knowing he was right. They'd never allow it. "*You* guard me then."

For the first time since he'd tracked me down, he shifted uncomfortably. "That might raise questions."

"That you might actually *care* for a Jinni?" I asked sarcastically, remembering the way they'd mocked him back at the longhouse. "I doubt anyone will truly believe it."

The silence stretched as he considered. "If you're with me, you won't be able to stay comfortably out of sight."

I snorted at that. "You must not have seen all my visitors."

"We were preparing the smokehouse to hold you," he said, scowling. "They didn't like sharing their space either."

He unbent from where he crouched across the fire, straightening to his full height, towering over me. "I may have conversations where you're not allowed to listen. You will agree to let my sister guard you at these times."

It made sense. They'd never let a Jinni hear important plans. I couldn't think of an argument for this.

Though I kept my face smooth, my hopes rose. This arrangement might suit me perfectly. I could recover my strength while with Koda and test my Gift of manipulation on them when the opportunity presented itself. It might be too good to be true... But once I was in better condition, perhaps I could manipulate him into leading me directly to a daleth.

If he could be believed, this was a much safer way to get home.

Sighing, I nodded. "Deal."

"Good." He took two steps around the fire to where I sat, leaned down, and offered me his hand.

Hesitantly, I took it. His skin was warm from the fire, and though he could easily crush my fingers, he kept his grip gentle as we shook on it.

I swallowed at the gravity of our deal.

Shaking on it made his shoulders relax, as if he truly believed I'd keep my word. I nearly frowned. I couldn't put my finger on why his trust bothered me, but I wished he wouldn't.

"We should leave," he said, letting go. I almost missed his warmth. "It's a long walk back."

I waved a weary hand in dismissal. "Give me a little more time, and I can use my Gift to travel."

"Absolutely not," he said in a flat tone.

My eyes, which had fallen to the fire, swung up to meet his. "What? Why not? Walking would take the entire night."

"No traveling," he snapped, moving around the fire restlessly. He picked up his pack and went through the contents, almost as if for an excuse not to look at me.

I waited.

If he wanted me to press for answers, he'd be disappointed. I didn't care.

Studying him, I frowned slightly. Okay, fine. I wanted to know a little, but it was purely curiosity. "Why?"

Throwing the pack down roughly after a few more moments, he crouched in front of the fire with a scowl and met my gaze through the thick strands of tangled hair that hung in his face. "Traveling feels akin to riding a dragon hurtling directly down the side of a mountain at breakneck speed."

Raising my brows, I leaned back against a nearby tree. "Do you know what riding a dragon feels like from experience?"

He smirked as he looked up. "Yes."

That left me speechless.

As he returned to his pack, I tried to hold in a groan at the thought of walking. Back when Koda had attacked our engagement tour stop, I'd seen the Jinni travel with him, and it'd clearly left him disoriented. On top of that, it *did* require a certain level of trust. Clearly, I'd misread him. He didn't trust me any more than the other Vaade.

Still. Walking when I felt like this sounded not only miserable, but impossible.

"If we take much longer to return, your father will likely send others out looking for you—and for me," I dared to argue. "And then you won't have your heroic return." *They also might not let you keep your end of our deal,* I added silently.

Yanking the pack closed without pulling anything out of it, he crossed his arms and studied me. "If you're not up to walking, just say so."

"I'm *not* up to walking," I said immediately.

He nodded to himself, calmly setting the bag down. "Then we'll stay here until you are."

I drew in a deep breath and blew it out, confused. Apparently, I'd guessed wrong, and no one else would come looking for us. Or maybe they would, but he didn't care? "Why did you come alone?" I asked finally.

"Because I don't need help to track a lone Jinni and bring her back," he said with a smug expression that grated on my nerves.

"You would if I wanted you to," I muttered to myself, tipping my head back against the tree to look up at the first few stars peeking through the branches. When had it gotten so dark? I'd spent hardly any time in the human world at night, and had forgotten how dim the moonlight was here compared to back home.

"No," he said with that irritating confidence, reminding me the Vaade's hearing was better than most. "I wouldn't." Dropping down to lay by the fire, he closed his eyes, shutting me out.

The arrogance made me want to shift into something with claws and teach him a lesson.

Maybe I would.

My eyes burned, and I struggled to keep them open.

Maybe in the morning, after a good night's rest and more food. Then I'd show him who he was dealing with. He wouldn't be so quick to underestimate me then.

✳ ✳ ✳

Despite the hard ground, I didn't wake until something touched my arm. I lashed out blindly only to yelp at the sudden agonizing pain of moving my injured shoulder.

Blinking away tears, I found a blurry Koda crouching just out of reach, shaking his head at me.

"Typical Jinni," he said with a scowl. "Attacking the hand that feeds it."

At the possibility of more food, I bit my tongue and sat up, keeping my retort to myself. "Breakfast?"

"More like a late noon meal." He handed me some more of that yellow bread he'd kept in his pack, letting me have most of the loaf.

I'd slept through the morning?

THE SECRET CURSE

As I sat up, another sharp twinge in my shoulder made me flinch.

While I was still rubbing my watery eyes, Koda reached out to unwind the wrapping on my shoulder without asking.

I recoiled slightly before controlling my reaction.

He slowly tugged the bandage around and around. The pressure from his hands was surprisingly light. "Do you foresee the prince coming after you himself?"

Pausing mid-chew, I lowered the yellow bread, insulted that he'd even ask. I wanted to yell at him that Shem cared for me more than any Vaade was capable of understanding. But something held my tongue. Would Shem send help? I hoped so. Would he come for me himself? As much as I'd like to say yes, I couldn't imagine his parents or the council allowing it. "You're fishing for information?" I said instead. "Is that why you're helping me?"

"One of the reasons," he said simply.

Words escaped me. I searched for an underlying meaning—some sort of subtext beneath the simple words like every conversation in Jinn—but failed. "What's that supposed to mean?" I finally snapped.

He hesitated. "Some in our tribe don't feel as strongly about the Jinn as the elders and my father."

I tried to read between the lines. Was one of his reasons... to protect me?

"Some," I repeated. "You being one of them?"

He didn't answer.

"Would admitting it mean crossing a line of some sort?" I said, almost teasing, surprised to find the big, scary Vaade struggling with anything.

Instead of answering, he tugged the last of the bandage from my shoulder. When I glanced down at the exposed wound, I winced. It didn't hurt that badly—it was mostly numb thanks to whatever he'd given me—but seeing the mangled flesh caused a fresh burst of pain.

He took a wooden bowl and a sickly yellow plant from his pack, using a nearby rock to mash the herb until it turned into a thick yellowish paste. "Yellowroot," he said simply, before scooping it out with two fingers and gently spreading it over my wound.

Though he didn't press hard, I still gasped at the sharp pain, tensing. But it faded almost immediately as the paste soaked in and began to work.

He finally met my gaze, and a hint of a smirk crossed his lips. "You point out my pride while ignoring your own. I'll admit to whatever you'd like, if *you* admit that you could never outrun me in your condition."

I scoffed. "I could've gone on for days."

One brow twitched up and back down, so fast I might've missed it if his face weren't inches from mine. He couldn't hide his grin for long though. "Is that a challenge?"

For some reason, my face flushed, and my arm tingled where his fingers brushed the bare skin. "Maybe another time," I said finally, trying not to sound breathless. "When I'm not wounded."

That irritating smirk didn't change, but he didn't remind me that only moments ago I'd claimed that I could outrun him *even* when I was wounded.

"Tell you what," he said, using the edges of the stained bandage to wipe his hands before taking a large hunting knife to the edge of his long deerskin tunic. I frowned at the sound of the hide tearing. "We have a long walk ahead of us. Half a day at least, maybe longer if you're slow. And we also need to hunt."

I noticed he didn't ask if I could walk this time. Apparently, it wasn't optional anymore. Drawing a deep breath, I was surprised to find I felt up to it.

He twisted to continue cutting the long strip from the bottom of his tunic. "Let's just say if you choose to make our walk interesting and try to relocate, I'm not worried." *Relocate? As in travel?*

Now I raised a brow. "You're so sure of yourself?"

He grinned. "Absolutely."

Ice slid over my skin, though I kept my face expressionless. Could he really keep up with me if I traveled? Glancing around at the thick forest, my heart sank. With the density of the trees, I couldn't see more than maybe a few dozen paces—and without familiarity of the forest, I could only travel as far as I could see.

Having seen Koda's speed up close, and the way he could leap so far it looked like flying, reality slammed into me with unfortunate clarity.

He wasn't bluffing.

Not only could he keep up with me in these conditions, but he might even be faster.

If Koda heard my heartbeat speed up, he didn't give any indication.

When he took the fresh strip of soft deerhide that he'd cut from his tunic and began to wind it around my arm and shoulder, I swallowed hard.

For an enemy, he didn't seem so terrible.

"I'm not really in the mood to go exploring on my own right now," I said after watching him wrap my wound more carefully than I probably deserved. "I'll keep the invitation in mind for another time, though."

To keep myself from staring at him too closely, I stood as soon as he finished tying the hide tight.

"Though I have no doubt you can take care of yourself," the Vaade's deep, rumbling voice came from behind me in a murmur. "I'd suggest you stick close to me, just to be safe."

Safe from what? Animals? Or other Vaade out looking for me?

When glanced back at him, my eyes caught on the rippling muscles in his arms as he lifted his pack and straightened, and I forgot whatever I'd planned to say. Instead, I nodded at him like a fool, before turning away to hide my burning face.

THE SECRET CURSE

As his nearly silent footsteps took him away from the fire through the trees, I followed. A twig snapped under my foot. Then another.

Koda sighed and sheathed his knife. "Have you never gone hunting before, Jinni girl?"

I scowled. "My name is Jezebel."

He just looked away.

"And no. Why would I?"

Another long-suffering sigh and he moved forward without another word.

Though he acted nonchalant, if I stepped too far off the path he made through the trees, I always found his eyes on me.

Small twinges of pain pulsed rhythmically in my shoulder as we walked, making me move slowly. I tried to listen to the forest but couldn't hear whatever prey Koda was tracking, if any.

"You walk like a buffalo after eating mushrooms," he complained for the hundredth time. "You're scaring all the animals away."

I stifled a laugh. He was accidentally teaching me quite a few things about the animals in this forest.

As the afternoon passed, he taught me how to walk without disturbing all the twigs and leaves until I could manage a nearly soundless approach—at least for Jinni ears. Whenever my stomach growled, Koda pulled out dried meat or flat bread or berries, letting me eat to my heart's content without judgment.

If I ignored the way my shoulder ached and the fact that I'd had to pee behind a bush earlier, this was almost pleasant.

Koda had taken to circling a bit further out from my "stomping footsteps," so when he strode past on silent feet, I didn't flinch.

Without a word, he stilled and put a finger to his lips, staring at the foliage as he pulled a knife from his belt.

He threw it.

The leaves shook with a little tremor, then grew still.

Frowning, I crossed my arms. "Well done," I said dryly. "You killed a bush."

He chuckled.

Part of me wished he'd be more annoyed by my attitude so I could continue to hate him. It was all too easy to forget he was the enemy when his company was better than almost everyone back home.

Striding toward where the weapon fell, he stooped down, pulling what looked like a dead pheasant from the ground.

My brows rose.

I hadn't even seen it there.

"We should get it cooked for dinner," he said as he gathered nearby sticks for a fire.

My stomach growled.

How had it gotten so late? The entire day had passed, and I'd only thought about escaping a handful of times.

Even now, all I could think about was food.

Without waiting to be asked, I started gathering firewood too, watching him discreetly for a sense of what kind of sticks to gather.

"That should be good." His words pulled me out of my relaxed state of gathering to find he'd already built the beginnings of a flame and was plucking the feathers while he watched the fire grow.

He cooked the bird, and we ate without speaking.

"We should've gotten back to camp by now," he finally said, as the sun dipped below the mountains for the second time, painting everything around us a golden orange and pink. His words seemed overly loud after so much quiet. "We took longer than I expected."

"Is anyone out looking for us?" I wondered out loud.

No answer.

"Or maybe they don't really expect you to bring me back," I taunted, trying to get a reaction. Frustration seeped into my tone when he didn't even glance up. "Well, in that case, we wouldn't want to keep them waiting, would we?"

He turned his back on me.

I shook my head, crossing my arms. Just when I'd almost forgotten our places, he reminded me. I couldn't stand being ignored.

It occurred to me with growing satisfaction that, unlike the engagement tour, I didn't have to accept it this time. "I realize the Vaade are uncultured, but you should know it's rude to ignore someone when they ask a question."

He snorted. "I haven't decided yet if you deserve an answer."

That did it. My calm mask snapped. "If you can't decide whether we're friends or enemies, then let me make it simple for you. *I'm* not the one who kidnapped someone, wounded them, and is holding them hostage."

Those intense fire-colored eyes of his lifted slowly to meet mine. "You weren't the one we wanted." It seemed like he might say more, but then he pressed his lips together. Turning away from me again, he packed up his bag and hoisted it over his shoulder.

The message was clear. *We're done talking.*

I scowled at him. *Enemies it is.*

As the sky continued to darken, he kicked dirt on the fire. Apparently, we weren't staying here. How he thought we could keep going in the dark, I didn't know, but I wasn't about to ask. Maybe his Vaade senses compensated for the lack of light.

Leaving the now smoky pit behind with a creeping sense of anxiety, I trailed after him through the shadowy trees.

His words left a strange sting behind. Obviously the Vaade didn't want me. I'd already known that. He didn't need to explain for me to understand that the prince had value, and I did not. I was no one and nothing, just like I'd always been. Powerless once more.

Darkness slowly settled over us.

The stiff branches and pine needles irritated my skin as I started to brush up against the nearby trees by accident.

The Vaade's big, muscled body, strong nose, and dark hair all became one solid lump ahead of me. An outline that could be mistaken for a small tree or a bush when he was still.

Opening my mouth, I snapped it shut multiple times, before finally blurting out. "I can't see anything."

"That's your problem." His deep voice floated over to me lazily.

In spite of his sluggish tone, I was clearly slowing him down.

I let a layer of condescension fill my voice, as if talking to a child. "Any chance you've gotten over your ridiculous fear of traveling?"

A growl came from his silhouette ahead, and I allowed myself a small smirk in the darkness.

"My shoulder hurts," I whined next, though the ache was surprisingly minimal. If he didn't slow down, I was going to run face first into a tree. As if to prove my point, in my hurry to catch up to him, I tripped over a tree root.

Koda's voice startled me, closer than expected. "If you're waiting for me to carry you, you'll be waiting a long time."

"It's dark!" I snapped, taking a tentative step forward, then another. My hand caught the bark of a tree right before I would've walked into it.

"Is it?" he asked in a shocked tone. "I hadn't noticed."

Snorting, I stopped walking and crossed my arms.

"Do all Jinn throw childish tantrums? Or just you?" he taunted.

I ignored him, trying to focus.

Carefully, I shifted my eyesight to imitate an owl. Shifting only one body part was always tricky. It needed to still speak to the other body parts and fit seamlessly, despite being at complete odds with the rest of my body. Not to mention the energy it forced me to expend as I shifted. Though we'd eaten an enormous amount a few hours prior, my stomach gurgled softly.

I ignored that too.

Opening my eyes, I blinked a few times to adjust to the new vision. Everything was grayscale, but the trees were darker and Koda's outline a few steps ahead was now clearly visible. Though I couldn't read the details of his expression, I thought his brows seemed to rise when I turned and stared directly at him. Could he see the change even in the dark? That alone made the shift worth it.

Striding past him, I walked with confidence now, able to see the roots trying to trip me and stepping over them.

"You're going in the wrong direction."

Halting, I clenched my fists and turned. "Well, maybe if you'd walk faster, I wouldn't have to guess."

He lifted his arm and pointed to his right.

Refusing to give him the satisfaction of showing my embarrassment, I simply turned in the direction he pointed and began walking once more.

"Are you always this antagonistic?" he asked as he fell into step beside me.

I huffed a laugh in disbelief. "Me? Once again, I ask you: who's the prisoner here and who's the captor?"

He chuckled. Softly, but I still caught it.

Slowing, I allowed him to pass me and take the lead, but instead he kept even with me, walking side by side.

For a few minutes, silence reigned.

"Are the rumors true?" Koda's voice broke the hush unexpectedly.

"What rumors?" I took the bait without thinking.

Out of the corner of my eye, his dragon-like eyes were pinned on me. "They say you enchanted the prince."

"Who says that?" I snapped, whirling toward him. Were they using that particular word for dramatic flair, or was someone actually suspicious of my Gift?

He held his hands up, palms toward me. "I have sources."

"Sources?" I repeated, barely noticing that we'd stopped walking as my mind spun with the new information. I didn't know what to focus on first. "That would mean a Jinni willingly shared information with a Vaade. *False* information, by the way."

I started walking again, pushing a branch roughly out of my way as he followed, letting it fling back in his direction. A soft *oof* rewarded me. I started to relax as I finished my thought. "Since I know that's not possible, that means you made up this so-called rumor yourself."

He laughed audibly now. "While I'd love to take credit, I'm afraid I can't."

My mood soured. If he was telling the truth—a big *if*—then I couldn't honestly say I was surprised. Though no one would say something so disloyal to my face, I didn't doubt some were thinking it.

We didn't have time to walk all night. I needed to get back to the Vaade camp, glean as much helpful information as possible, and return to Shem before this insufferable Vaade managed to ruin all my plans for the future.

I'd had enough of this charade.

The sooner this was all over, the better.

While my familiarity with the forest was limiting my traveling to what I could see, there was one place in the human world I'd already seen well enough to travel there.

Reaching out without a word, I gripped Koda's big, muscled arm.

And traveled us back to their camp.

9

WE LANDED DIRECTLY IN front of the longhouse where they'd kept me the first time, since that's all I remembered clearly from my rushed escape.

This time, however, it was dark. Through the woods, I made out three more longhouses, visible only because of the soft glow off their fires inside. Smoke curled out through a hole in each round roof and into the starry night sky.

The line of buildings was slightly uneven as they curved around one side of a large bonfire, where a small number of Vaade huddled.

With a growl, Koda ripped his arm away from me and hurled himself out of reach. Though he caught himself, he nearly tripped as his balance was thrown off. "I told you, *no traveling*!"

I tried unsuccessfully to hide a smirk. "Your way was too slow."

Grudgingly, he returned to my side as nearby Vaade turned to look at us. Some of them stood from the fire and moved in our direction.

Averting my owl-like eyes, I shifted them quickly back to normal.

It was pure instinct.

After so many years of hiding my Gift, it didn't occur to me until I'd finished that it was a waste of energy. Multiple Vaade had seen me shift just the day before.

For the first time in my life, it wasn't a secret.

I shivered, feeling exposed.

Koda stepped closer to add under his breath, "Don't *ever* use your Gifts on me again."

I barely heard him, but his words caused some of the approaching Vaade to titter. He glared at them in return. Their remarkable hearing never ceased to surprise me.

"Where did it go?" one of the women asked Koda, eyeing the bandage on my shoulder.

Half my mind wondered what she was referring to, while the other half slowly registered she meant me.

My mouth soured.

Refusing to react and give her the satisfaction, I instead turned my focus to studying the camp. If I squinted, I could make out some smaller buildings along the far side. A small fire illuminated a structure large enough to house one or two people. Another partial building stood near the big bonfire with only a roof and one wall to shelter a huge pile of stacked wood. And on our side, there was another, even tinier shack. It wasn't nearly large enough to live in. I frowned, wondering what it was for.

When the girl turned her violet dragon-like eyes on me, I ducked behind his big body.

Koda ignored the girl, walking toward that smallest building.

I hesitated.

He'd promised I'd get home.

Though I didn't know if he could be trusted, I could hardly make a second escape this exact moment.

Rest. Eat and drink. Pay attention to anything that could help Shem. Despite my promises to Koda, I'd still run if I had to. But if his way was easier, I'd give it a chance. Shivering at the thought of the dragon cliffs, I tried to shake off the image of dying in the forest that he'd planted in my mind.

I could make it if I had to.

I just hoped I wouldn't have to.

Though it was a war camp, the sounds of children giggling floated on the air, making me wonder if they brought their whole tribe with them each time they moved—or if maybe this settlement was more permanent? The longhouses looked time consuming to build, but then again, what did I know about their construction? Perhaps they built them quickly and then moved on just as fast.

Tilting my head at all the noises coming from within the big building, I couldn't fathom why anyone would want to live in those, without any semblance of privacy. Then again, with their ridiculous sense of hearing, smell, and sight, maybe privacy didn't really exist for the Vaade.

I shrugged, tucking away the information to share with Shem when I returned. I didn't have to understand the Vaade; I only needed to keep my eyes

THE SECRET CURSE

open.

One of Koda's friends elbowed him in the ribs for "letting the weak little Jinni get so far away." Another chimed in, "Took you long enough."

I bit my lip, trying not to smile at the deepening frown on Koda's face and tried to look appropriately subdued. *Maybe I'd been more difficult to apprehend than he let on.*

Behind the longhouse, a small group of Vaade stepped out and strode past. The firelight flickered across their painted faces, arms, and chests.

Koda noticed them at the same time I did. "Where are the warriors going?"

Warriors?

I took a second glance. It looked like the war paint the group had worn when they'd captured me. The hairs on the back of my neck rose at the implication.

The same friend tilted his head meaningfully in my direction, answering Koda, "You know we can't tell you in front of one of them."

Koda blinked away whatever thought flitted across his face, too fast for me to catch it, taking hold of me again—I noticed he chose my uninjured arm, whether by choice or by accident, I couldn't say. He turned and tugged me toward the longhouse. "You'll *stay here* this time. I'll come back shortly."

"No!" I dug in my heels, not caring anymore how it looked. "You promised!"

Ahead of me, inside the longhouse, multiple pairs of dragon-like eyes glowed in the dark shadows. Possibly the same Vaade that I'd left behind last time. My heartbeat kicked up, and I gave Koda a pleading look that I fully expected him to ignore.

His eyes returned to the warriors, where they'd disappeared into the woods. Arguing with me would waste time that he seemed anxious not to lose. "Fine," he snapped, grabbing a torch from one of the Vaade nearby, though they muttered it was a bad idea. He pulled me forward so suddenly I nearly stumbled. "Let's go."

I tried to keep up with his long strides, thankful for the light of the torch. Though he didn't *seem* to be slowing down for me, we somehow couldn't catch up to the others.

Almost as if... were we trailing behind intentionally?

I would've assumed we'd lost them once the trees hid them from sight, but Koda sniffed the air, following his nose, and continued on. I waited until we were—hopefully—out of earshot of both the camp and the so-called warriors, before I whispered, "What does the paint mean?"

I was terrified I already knew the answer, but wanted desperately to be wrong.

"We wear it for significant events," he replied. "Different lines mean different things."

That told me nothing.

I rolled my eyes. "Yes, but what does *this* design mean?"

He didn't answer.

Irritation prickled my skin, but I refused to make myself look weak by asking again, so we walked on in silence.

Far ahead, a flickering light shone through the trees—glowing, like flames from torches, but also the cooler, ghostly glow of magic—answering my question without him needing to.

A daleth.

"You're still attacking the Jinni islands?" I hissed.

He didn't reply, but the orange torchlight flickered across his face, revealing an uncertain frown.

"Why aren't you with them?"

He growled—actually growled—and kept walking.

Oh right... That was my fault.

Tripping over yet another tree root and wishing I'd kept my night vision, I had to jog a little to keep up. "Your father doesn't trust you to lead the attacks anymore? You'd think he'd wait for you." I probably should've kept my mouth shut.

He whirled to face me, stopping so suddenly I slammed into his chest and nearly bounced off him, grabbing his soft deerskin tunic to keep my balance. My palms flattened across his chest, feeling the muscles tense underneath. While he still held the torch, his free hand had caught me at the small of my back and remained there, warm and steadying. He seemed as surprised as I was, neither of us moving.

Until I cleared my throat and pulled back.

Koda's face flickered with an unreadable emotion, but when he spoke, he was calmer. "I don't know if it's an attack. I don't know where they went tonight. I don't know why they went without me. I've been pursuing *you*, remember?"

My traitorous face blushed. I wasn't going to apologize for that, but I fought not to take another step back, lifting my chin defiantly instead.

"My father may still believe he can capture the prince," Koda said, offering more than I'd expected. "I, however, believe there's a hidden reason we've not been able to locate him so far. A certain Gift..."

I tried not to react.

He studied my face, staring down at me, unblinking.

I swallowed, and it was audible in the quiet forest. The pressure built. If I denied it, that'd only make him more suspicious, but I refused to betray Shem's trust either. So I said nothing at all.

Koda dipped his chin in the barest nod, as if my silence confirmed something. "That's what I thought," he said simply, turning to walk again, though at a slower pace as we drew closer to the daleth.

Now I wanted to kick him. His straightforward conversation had tricked me

THE SECRET CURSE

into letting my guard down, revealing more than I'd meant to. It wouldn't happen again.

I clamped my mouth shut and didn't try to talk anymore.

The portal came into view ahead, flashing with the same white light as the previous one, which I was starting to realize probably meant it was temporary—or somehow still in the process of forming? As if it was not yet stabilized like the nearly invisible daleth I'd seen in the past.

The Vaade warriors were nowhere to be seen.

"They all went through?" I whispered, briefly forgetting my vow to stop speaking to Koda. "And left the daleth unguarded?"

"Who would we guard it from on our side?" Koda countered.

Good point.

Still, was it my imagination, or did Koda approach with caution?

"Are we not supposed to be here?" I spoke louder this time, just to annoy him.

He didn't flinch—probably because our obvious torch light was already a dead giveaway we were here—swiveling to pin me with a look. "No," he said slowly, as if speaking to a child. "*You're* not supposed to be here."

Oh.

That made me glance around for any hidden Vaade as we stopped in front of the portal.

I shifted on my feet uneasily. There could be an attack happening on the other side right now.

Frustration creased Koda's face.

He wanted to go, but clearly wasn't going to bring me.

Attack or not, though, this was a portal to Jinn.

My first real chance to get home.

Despite my deal with Koda, there was no way I was going to pass this up.

Before he could stop me, I dove for the daleth.

As I crossed through, a rough hand wrapped around my wrist.

Koda followed through on my heels.

The air changed, growing thinner with the elevation. Glancing up, I confirmed my suspicions when the moon appeared twice as large.

We were in Jinn.

On what island, I had no idea. I didn't recognize the surroundings, though there wasn't much to see beyond the trees lit by Koda's torch. It looked exactly like the forest we'd just left, though perhaps the trees weren't quite as large or tall here.

Listening closely, all I could make out was the wind in the trees and the soft song of crickets.

No voices, no lights, no sign of a city or buildings of any kind. Even the warriors we'd been following were nowhere to be seen.

"So much for our agreement," Koda growled, gripping my wrist tighter.

"You clearly wanted to come," I reasoned with him, still studying our surroundings for some clue of why the portal was here. "And I'm still with you, aren't I?"

Koda didn't argue, and that alone told me how badly he wanted to be here.

A slight frown flitted across his face.

It smoothed out so quickly, I almost thought I'd imagined it.

"Is this normal for an attack?" I pressed, knowing full well it wasn't.

Koda's fire-colored eyes fixed on my face. "It's not an attack." He'd lowered his voice to a soft rumble.

Without warning, he turned the torch upside down and slammed it into the dirt. It killed the fire immediately, turning the woods around us into pure darkness.

"The negotiations have begun."

10

SHEM WAS NEGOTIATING FOR *me.*

A hopeful breath filled my lungs, and for a brief moment, I didn't even notice the throbbing in my shoulder. If Koda was right, maybe I'd make it home tonight after all. Unless negotiations went poorly, and the Vaade were merely using it as an excuse to capture the prince, in which case…

My breath hitched. Suddenly I hoped very much it *wasn't* Shem they were meeting. Would he risk being involved?

I turned to beg Koda to let me listen in on the negotiations, but he was already moving, tugging my wrist to pull me after him. "Not a single word once we see them, do you understand?" he murmured in my ear.

I nodded eagerly.

My foot crunched on a stick.

With a hiss, Koda scooped me up and slung me over his shoulder.

I bit back a gasp as the blood rushed to my face, gripping the back of his tunic in my fists. In any other circumstances, I'd kick and scream until he put me down. It was utterly humiliating.

Though he didn't change his grip on my thighs, all my senses narrowed on the warmth from his hands.

As we crested a ridge a long minute later, he lowered me to the ground.

My entire body was tense.

He wasn't even out of breath.

I tried to yank out of reach, but he kept a solid grip on my arm, ignoring my glare. *Koda, the anchor,* I thought irritably.

Calmly, he tipped his head toward the valley below, where the trees cleared and moonlight shone down to reveal the warriors.

Over two dozen of them in all, both men and women, stood on one side of the clearing, all holding torches, lighting up the empty space, waiting.

While Koda and I were hidden in the foliage, and the portal was on lower ground, blocked from view by the hill, the Vaade below us seemed oddly... exposed. Though they stood tall, the open space clearly made them uncomfortable. Their eyes darted in different directions, shoulders tense, and some of them shuffled their feet.

"What—" I began to question Koda, but he waved a hand and cut me off.

"Shh," he whispered directly in my ear. His hot breath tickled the sensitive shell, making me shiver. "My father will hear you."

I frowned, grabbing his tunic and tugging at him until he caved and bent down, allowing me to whisper back, "You can hear across this distance?"

Warmth gusted over my ear again, as he hissed, "Only if I have *silence.*"

I rolled my eyes. Fine. Why beg him to explain when, with a little effort, I could match his hearing? It took a few precious moments, but I carefully shifted to the hearing of a majestic eagle, known to hear their prey squealing underground from high in the air. Now, if things went south during these negotiations, I would know. Maybe I could even prove my value to Shem and his parents by joining the fray and thwarting the Vaade's plans.

Though it was frustrating to leave my vision normal, I chose not to risk the owl eyes a second time when the Jinn would be here soon and might see. It made the faces below hard to read in the dim torchlight.

The thought made my heart skip a beat.

What if that was the point of meeting so late? The Vaade had the advantage with their ability to see in the dark... If they doused their torches—

Koda's fingers tightened on my arm in response to my rapidly beating heart, probably worried I planned to run again.

But I hardly noticed.

I couldn't seem to catch my breath.

What if Shem showed up to this meeting and it was a trap?

A small retinue of Jinn flashed into existence in the clearing. From here, I registered their heavy armor first. It wasn't decorative the way it was usually worn in the castle. And instead of primitive torches like the Vaade, they'd enchanted their breastplates to have a white orb in the center, glowing white.

Most were members of the Jinni Guard.

THE SECRET CURSE

After scanning the group for another long second, as well as the Vaade reactions, I blew out a breath, both relieved and disappointed.

Shem wasn't with them.

Of course he wasn't.

King Jubal and Queen Samaria would never risk their only son on negotiations when his council could do the job.

Sure enough, the guards surrounded three equally armored Jinn from Shem's council in the middle. I would've recognized Milcah by her extravagant peacock feathers anywhere. Beside her on each side stood Jerusha and Laban.

"We're here on behalf of the royal family of Jinn," Milcah declared so loudly I probably would've heard it even without my advanced hearing.

I itched to step forward and reveal myself to them, to yell, "Take me home!" But I didn't want to ruin the negotiations by causing a fight to break out—Koda would drag me back through the daleth in a heartbeat and the Jinn were more outmatched by these Vaade below than they realized.

I forced myself to wait until they asked for me.

Though I tried not to get my hopes up, I couldn't quite help myself. *I'm going home!*

Up until now, the royal family had refused to meet with the Vaade, so Shem had likely had to fight for this meeting.

I wished there was a way to let them know I was here without alerting the warriors.

Maybe they'd attempt to bargain first, or maybe they'd decide to fight...

Either way, I'd be ready.

From the front line of the Vaade, an older man with long white hair and a wrinkled face took a few menacing steps toward them.

"The leader of the Vaade, the Dragon," Koda murmured in my ear, and after a slight hesitation, he added, "My father."

I bit my lip.

Something about him set me on edge.

Milcah lifted her chin at his approach, making those ridiculous feathers flare, but she didn't flinch.

The Jinni guards, on the other hand, quickly raised their weapons higher.

A tense silence filled the woods.

The whistling of the wind through the trees was the only sound that reached us. Not even the crickets were chirping now.

Beside me, Koda leaned forward, as if he was preparing to forget about hiding and leap into the clearing.

But the Dragon surprised me—and the council as well, judging by their startled expressions—by smiling and spreading his hands wide. "We welcome you to this meeting of good faith," he finally replied. "Despite your prince not bothering to show."

My eyes narrowed.

Was he mocking the council? Were they about to die? Though I couldn't think of anyone I liked less in the castle, without them I'd remain a hostage. I desperately hoped they'd ignore the slight.

Milcah's lips curved in a matching smile, and though I couldn't tell for sure from the distance, I could almost guarantee it didn't reach her eyes. "We should be the ones welcoming *you*, since you're on *our* land."

I nearly groaned, running a hand across my brow.

Koda snorted softly beside me.

His fingers had noticeably loosened on my arm. I was tempted to try pulling away again. Unconsciously, I tensed, which immediately made him tighten his grip.

I sighed softly. *Patience.*

Milcah continued before the Dragon could react, voice laced with thinly-veiled annoyance. "We understand you've taken a hostage. We would like to negotiate her return along with a truce to cease all future attacks."

Finally.

The first thing I'd do when I got home was take a long, hot bath, followed by a proper meal at a table with silverware and napkins. Nothing like the messy meals over a tiny fire with Koda. My mouth watered.

"You understand correctly," the Dragon replied, managing to sound like he was speaking to a child. It made me wish I could see Milcah's face more clearly. I allowed myself a tiny smile. "Tell your prince that in exchange for the female, I would like to use a Jinni enchantment to form a binding covenant between our people."

My ears caught on the word *covenant* and the fact that he'd said it was a *Jinni* enchantment. It seemed significant.

Even from here, I caught the way Milcah shifted to glance at the others, but she spoke calmly. "This is a term we are unfamiliar with. Before we bring this message to him, would you care to elaborate?"

Though her tone would've raised the hair on my neck, the Dragon merely laughed. "I wouldn't expect *you* to know it."

I shook my head, holding in a soft laugh of my own. Milcah had met her match!

Turning, the Dragon waved a young Vaade woman in the group forward.

Koda tensed.

"What?" I hissed. "What is it? Are they going to attack?"

"No," Koda snapped, forgetting to be quiet, though the murmurs below hid his voice. His orange and yellow eyes glowed with fury.

The Dragon placed his hands on the woman's shoulders, drawing her forward, toward the Jinn. From here, I couldn't see the details in her face, but she

THE SECRET CURSE

looked young and pretty, with long dark hair split into two thick braids and a colorful patterned shawl over her shoulders. She stared at the ground between the Vaade and the Jinn.

"Then what?" I asked louder when Koda didn't answer.

Lips pressed together in a silent snarl, he didn't take his eyes off the clearing, but finally he muttered, "That's my sister."

That didn't clear anything up for me.

"A covenant between our people would mean an end to the fighting between us," the Dragon declared, cutting off my questions. His word choice made me want to scoff. The only ones attacking were the Vaade. "We would not only agree to terms of peace, but if this covenant is put into place, both our people would be magically bound by it." His words struck me as funny as I remembered Koda's words the day I'd met him. *We don't want peace.*

"For this to be possible," the Dragon was saying, "the covenant will be completed in physical form through the unity of my daughter, Tehya, and your prince." He paused, and enunciated clearly as he clarified, "In marriage."

Cold shock flushed through my whole body.

The council members gaped at him.

His daughter's arms were crossed tight as she glared at the Jinn, and her sleeveless deerskin dress revealed tensed muscles almost as large as Koda's.

The Dragon raised a hand to grip his daughter's shoulder, holding it for a long moment until she dropped her gaze. Her chest rose and fell rapidly in heavy breaths.

Tell them, I mentally urged Milcah, the council, or even the Jinni guards—someone—to speak up. *She can't marry him because the prince is* already engaged.

But they didn't.

"This is your bargain?" Laban spoke up for the first time instead, studying the tall girl standing beside the Vaade leader. "Would you perhaps consider—"

"I will consider *nothing* else," the Dragon said with a note of finality.

Laban drew a long breath, looking to the women. When they nodded, he turned back. "We will bring your request to the royal family. Wait here."

He, Milcah, and Jerusha disappeared.

How far they had to travel to reach the prince, I didn't know, but a long minute passed, then another, and the Vaade stood tense and silent across from the Jinni Guard. Both groups glared at each other. Tehya yanked her multi-colored shawl back over her shoulders. The Dragon gave her a quelling look.

I barely noticed any of it.

My heart pounded so loudly in my ears, I doubted I would've heard them if they had spoken. Slowly, I registered the fact that Koda *was* speaking. It seemed almost under his breath.

"What?" I tried to snap, but it came out as a whisper. I couldn't focus on him. My eyes drifted back to the clearing, waiting for the council to return and say, *Absolutely not. The prince refuses your request.*

Shem *would* refuse.

But if he did, the Vaade would have no more reason to keep me alive...

I shivered, blinking rapidly, trying to clear my head.

"Breathe." Koda's voice finally reached me.

I sucked in a deep breath. Then another. My hands trembled. Wrapping my free arm around my ribs, I gripped the layers of my ragged dress hard to hide the weakness. But with Koda holding my other arm, he no doubt felt it.

I slowly became aware of the way his other fist clenched and unclenched, as if around someone's throat.

"It won't happen," he assured me without sparing a glance in my direction. Louder, he added, "My father is a fool."

The Dragon's head slowly swiveled to face us.

I paled.

Koda didn't flinch under his father's stern gaze, but he also didn't say anything further.

When Milcah, Jerusha, and Laban reappeared, the Dragon turned back to face them as if no time had passed. He waited patiently.

"We will need to see the hostage to verify her safety before we can give you our answer," Milcah said.

The Dragon didn't hesitate. "Not possible."

I whipped my gaze to Koda's. He knew we were here! He'd *seen* us.

Koda never took his eyes off the group below.

"Well then, perhaps we can meet again tomorrow, and you can bring her—"

"No."

Milcah paused, speechless for once, then tried again. "I'm afraid that—"

"You brought someone with the Gift of truth, did you not?" the Dragon interrupted in a bored tone.

My eyes widened. How did he know the Jinni Guard always used a Jinni with that Gift in negotiations? He seemed to have quite a bit more information on the Jinn than King Jubal realized.

"We happen to have someone here with that Gift," Milcah gritted out the words.

"Then you'll know I tell the truth when I say our hostage is alive and unharmed. And I will give you no opportunity to steal our bargaining piece." The Dragon crossed his arms, face unchanging as he added, "Either the prince accepts the covenant, or the Jinni girl dies."

Though it was hard to judge Milcah's expression from here, she seemed to pale. Subtly she glanced at Laban, who hid his responding nod by stepping

THE SECRET CURSE

forward to speak, placing his hands on Milcah and Jerusha's arms. "We'll confer with the prince."

They vanished again without another word.

It was time to make a move.

As soon as they returned, I'd travel directly behind Milcah and yell, "Run!" It'd have to be timed perfectly.

I drew a deep breath, tensing.

Koda responded immediately, shifting on his feet, almost as if planting himself.

He's worried I'm going to travel with him again. I held back a snort. As if I'd take him with me.

Taking slow, steady breaths, I did my best to seem calm as I prepared for the Jinn to return.

The second Milcah's face appeared, I tried to travel.

Nothing happened.

I felt the blood drain from my face.

Tugging on my arm, I strained my Gift to its limits, struggling to get away from Koda both physically and magically.

He wrapped his arms around me, holding me firmly in place.

I opened my mouth to scream.

Heavy fingers clamped down over my mouth and nose, muffling my shrieks. Multiple Vaade from the group glanced toward us, all quickly returning their gaze to the Jinn as soon as they saw me and Koda.

The Jinn, thanks to their pathetic, *normal* hearing, were too far away to hear a thing.

"Be still," Koda snarled in my ear. "My father would happily kill you in an instant along with all your friends. You'll only give him the opportunity."

I slowly lost the fight in me as I absorbed his words. But it was the way the Dragon tilted his head in our direction, while at the same time letting his hand casually land on the wicked long sword at his waist, that finally stopped me.

I sagged back against Koda.

He didn't remove his hand.

In a strange way, I was thankful he took away my choice, since part of me still wanted to risk it.

"The prince..." Jerusha was saying below, pausing to clear her throat, "has decided to consider your request. He asks for a fortnight to negotiate the details of this covenant with you and gain a better understanding of the full enchantment. If all is as it appears—and as long as your hostage remains unharmed—he will accept your offer. We'll meet again tomorrow to begin discussions."

Without another word, the entire Jinni party vanished.

I barely noticed the way Tehya cried out in frustration or Koda's hiss of breath beside me.

Instead, I replayed Jerusha's words over and over, piecing them together, searching for a hidden meaning. Shem had *decided to consider their request.*

Shem couldn't possibly want this.

He was equally trapped.

Wasn't he?

If he said no, he couldn't guarantee my safety. So he'd made my wellbeing a requirement for his participation. Logically it made sense, but... he'd still agreed.

I mentally curled inward, allowing Koda to pull me along by the elbow back toward the daleth, stumbling frequently, uncaring.

Focusing on my breathing, I tried to make it even out.

Hurt weighed down my bones, making me sluggish.

Shem didn't have a choice.

I imagined him struggling with this decision—how he'd pace the length of his council room, staring at the bookshelves, as if they held answers to yet another impossible dilemma. His options were to let me go—which he'd never do—or refuse, knowing the Vaade would go on attacking our people, after killing me. But maybe he'd seen a third option...

He asks for a fortnight to negotiate the details, Jerusha had said.

Two weeks was a long time. Negotiations could easily go sideways. I read between the lines, hope rising. Shem had said they must *gain a better understanding of the full enchantment.* I sucked in my first deep breath since the meeting took place. He was going to look beneath the surface of the enchantment for a loophole. *That's his plan.*

Drawing a deep breath, I nodded to myself. He'd find a reason to back out, but he'd *had* to say yes for now to keep me safe. His agreement was only a way to stall and search for a weakness while he came up with a plan. He always put his people first. He was doing this for them.

He didn't *want* to abandon me. He just couldn't help it.

Either way, though, he wasn't here. Even as his betrothed, I was powerless. Alone.

When I pulled my attention back to the present, the Dragon, Tehya, and his warriors, all holding torches high, were approaching fast.

Up close, rage contorted the girl's face, but even then, I could tell she was gorgeous. Glossy brown hair framed her perfect, heart-shaped face with honey-colored skin, full lips, and thick brows. Her cheeks were flushed dark red. Shem would probably think she was beautiful.

Her feelings clearly didn't matter. If the Dragon continued to lead the negotiations, then this covenant—this *marriage*—would happen.

I winced.

There were still Jerusha's final words to consider: *if all is as it appears—*

THE SECRET CURSE

meaning if Shem couldn't prove the Vaade had some ulterior motives for this truce—*he will accept your condition.*

"The filthy Jinn aren't worthy of marriage!" Tehya protested as we approached.

No answer.

"I want to marry Akeena!" she yelled next, though it continued to land on deaf ears.

The Dragon's voice interrupted my examination of her. "What is it doing here?"

My eyes snapped back to him and widened.

In our last encounter, I'd been unable to see him through the blindfold. Now I took in his long white hair and wrinkled face in the torchlight—the way his mouth turned down made him almost seem to have jowls. His fierce, dark eyes with flecks of fire reminded me of his son's. Unlike Koda, though, his eyes were deeper set, almost buried in the folds that came with age, but if possible, they were even more piercing. Though he wasn't taller than the other Vaade, he somehow loomed over us. His glare made me shiver.

"You were supposed to leave it in the smokehouse."

I tensed.

"No time," Koda lied. "And good thing, too, since you were able to use it against their truthsayer. If we hadn't been here, negotiations would've failed."

He was a quick thinker.

The Dragon's face didn't change. I couldn't tell if he was pleased with Koda or furious. Without a single glance in my direction or his daughter's, he waved everyone toward the glowing daleth a short distance ahead.

In my anguish, I hadn't been thinking logically. I should've shifted and fought Koda one-on-one while I had the chance.

Now, not only did Koda's firm grip somehow anchor me, but we were also surrounded by over two-dozen burly Vaade warriors. Beneath the white paint streaked across their faces, they were all scowling, itching for a fight. If I became a Lacklore, two dozen swords would run me through. If I became a tiny flea, they'd smell me out and crush me. No matter how many possibilities I considered, there wasn't a single scenario where I could win.

I glanced longingly over my shoulder for any Jinn who might've remained behind on Shem's orders, but the forest around us was empty.

Of course it was. I sighed. They hadn't known I was here.

When we reached the daleth, I reluctantly allowed Koda to lead me through.

11

"HOW DARE YOU GIVE me away like a prize horse?" Tehya's voice rang out through the otherwise quiet forest as she and her father stepped through the portal a minute later, followed by the remaining Vaade warriors.

Her father's only response was to turn to the last two coming through the daleth. "Close and seal it." With a dark look in Koda's direction, he added to them, "Wait until we're gone. I don't want it"—he gestured in my direction—"to see."

They nodded.

The Dragon then extinguished his torch and gestured for the others to do the same. He probably didn't want me to see the way back to camp either. As if I cared.

I could easily shift my vision back to spite him, if I was willing to waste the energy.

Licking my lips, I imagined shifting into an actual dragon and attacking him from behind. He was the reason all of this was happening.

As my muscles tensed, Koda's fingers tightened on my arm in response.

I tried to think, but I was distracted by the way the Dragon's daughter continued to berate her father so freely in front of his men. And also by the warm, muscled arm that brushed against mine as Koda led me through the forest.

When Tehya ran out of steam, the Dragon finally replied in a calm but firm

THE SECRET CURSE

tone, "We'll speak later." She took another breath, and he spoke over whatever she planned to say, adding sharply, "In private."

After that, she fell silent.

Gratefully, I let my gaze fall to my feet and tried to think.

I had two weeks.

Two weeks to find an excuse not to go through with the Vaade covenant.

Shem would be doing everything he could, but the answers were here. In the Vaade world.

Barely holding back a groan, I swallowed the sour lump in my throat.

I had to stay and learn more about this covenant—and how to stop it.

Nothing else mattered.

Not even escape.

A nagging thought came to me, and once it was there, it refused to be ignored: if I returned home now, was I still engaged to Shem? Did I even have a place in the castle if the covenant moved forward? If I didn't end these negotiations, there might be nothing to go back to.

Lifting my chin, decision made, I almost tripped at the sight of everyone waiting for us in their camp. The small group of Vaade returning merged with dozens more, until we were surrounded, despite the late hour.

I fought the growing feeling I'd just missed my last opportunity to get home.

There was no "home" until we stopped the covenant.

Pressing my lips together, I breathed slowly, inhaling through my nose, then a long exhale.

I would find answers.

If I was forced to stay here, I'd learn everything I could about these people—especially their weaknesses. The thought made my breath hitch. I hoped they *had* a weakness. For Shem's sake, and my own.

Because as much as I wanted Shem to come save me, the truth was King Jubal and Queen Samaria would never willingly send their son into danger, even if they did know where the Vaade camped.

Though Shem would do everything in his power to rescue me, I feared, after witnessing the Vaade up close, it might not be enough.

I had to save myself.

Bitter disappointment flooded through me. Nothing ever really changed.

The Dragon headed toward one of the longhouses, calling over his shoulder, "Lock it up, Koda."

Cold snaked down my skin as the surrounding Vaade eyes all swung to me. The group slowly began to break up. "I was hoping for more of a fight," one of them mumbled, and another thumped him on the back. "I'll give you a fight." That group moved toward the forest, while others followed the Dragon into the longhouse or headed for the bonfire in the center of the camp.

Tehya huffed, throwing up her arms, and turned on Koda unexpectedly.

"You have to talk to him."

Nodding, he lifted my arm toward her, as if it was a rope to hold onto. "Stay with her."

"I'm in no mood to babysit a Jinni." She glared at him. "Get someone else to watch her."

At least she hadn't called me an "it" like the rest of them.

Fist clenching as he lowered our arms, Koda watched her stalk off into the forest alone.

When Koda glanced at the fire, I thought for sure he was about to break our bargain. "Please," I whispered, not knowing how to plead my case but knowing I should.

He couldn't drag me along to talk to the Dragon. Even *I* knew how that would go. But he couldn't help his sister if he stayed with me either.

Tension built in his shoulders.

I clenched my fists, struggling not to say more.

With a growl, he spun on his heel toward the forest in the opposite direction of his sister, tugging at my hand for me to follow. "Come."

Pure gratefulness flooded my body like soothing cool water. I hadn't been sure he'd honor our agreement.

Blowing out a heavy breath, I hurried to keep up with him. We crossed through camp, passing all four longhouses and the bonfire to the side, heading for a smaller building nestled between two trees on the edge of the clearing. It was barely larger than my bed back at the castle. This must be the smokehouse they'd mentioned.

He pointed behind the building. "If you need to relieve yourself before you sleep, go now. This is your only opportunity until morning." Before I had a chance to get flustered, he added, "You have one minute, and then I'm coming to get you." The implications were clear—whether I was still peeing or trying to flee again, I wouldn't get far.

I only hesitated a moment before quickly hurrying into the dark to take care of business, tripping over roots as I went.

With heat reaching all the way to the tips of my ears, I returned. As someone raised in an extremely private culture, every aspect of the Vaade's world left me completely unbalanced.

When he opened the wooden door and gestured to the pitch-black space inside the smokehouse, I took one look at his brooding face and obediently entered.

It would be spelled against travel at this point, unfortunately, just like the longhouse. But escape was a secondary goal now—first I needed to gather all the information I could on this covenant.

Two weeks, I reminded myself yet again. *That's all.* I only needed to endure

THE SECRET CURSE

for two weeks and be ready for any opportunity that arose to gather information or escape.

That didn't stop me from imagining shifting into a little flea the moment Koda closed the door and slipping out into the night. Though I had no plans to follow through, I bit my lip. Could Koda smell my magic even if I shifted to that size? An image of him finding me in that form and using one of his big hands to crush me made me flinch.

Don't cause trouble. The Vaade had promised to keep me alive. I'd be a fool to test how much they meant it.

I took a few steps further into the smokehouse.

There were no windows.

The light from the bonfire was too far away to illuminate much without shifting my eyes again. I nearly ran into the opposite wall, which was only a few steps in.

The door banged shut behind me.

Yet again, my hopes plummeted. How was I supposed to gather information alone in a locked room?

A hot breath tickled my neck.

I jumped and spun around.

Koda's shadowy outline blocked the faint line of the fire shining through the cracks in the door. He loomed over me.

"What're you doing?" I blurted.

"Did you change your mind?" I couldn't see his expression, but his tone was bored. "I'd be happy to leave someone else to guard you."

"No...?" I didn't understand how that answered my question.

"Then my options are either to stand outside or inside, and I don't trust you out of my sight, even if it is a warm night."

He's sleeping in here. I processed his words, swallowing nervously. Somehow, though I'd slept across the fire from him once already, this little room felt far more intimate.

"Sit," he said when I didn't immediately move.

Eyes still adjusting, I moved toward a lump in one corner, hoping it was a chair. Feeling carefully, I found a small stool with a large pile of furs laid over it. Not wanting to upset Koda further, I sat.

A few cracks in the wooden walls allowed a bit of moonlight in. Not enough to make out much of anything, though.

A flame flickered to life between Koda's hands as he lit a candle. He placed it in a holder by the door that I hadn't seen.

I took in the small space again. There was no bed. No other furniture. In fact, the room was so small I didn't know if someone Koda's height could lie down without knocking their head or feet into the walls.

Soft candlelight danced over his scowling face. I couldn't tell if he was upset with his father's plans or with me—probably both.

When he turned to lean against the door, arms crossed, I looked away quickly, not wanting to upset him more.

On the other side of the tiny room, what I'd mistaken for a wall when we'd first entered was actually a second door. "What's behind that?" I asked without thinking.

"Not your concern," Koda muttered.

My shoulders tensed at his tone. It reminded me too much of my father growing up. I chose to stay quiet after that. I wasn't usually curious, but if it was another way out, it'd be good to know. I had limited time to figure out the details of this so-called covenant and then find a way to nullify it.

Carefully avoiding Koda's gaze, I bit my lip, considering. From the way he'd reacted to the negotiations back in Jinn, there was a good chance we wanted the same thing. I just didn't know how to broach the subject when he was like this.

"It's where the meat is kept," Koda said on a sigh out of nowhere.

I blinked. It took a long moment to realize he was answering my question from earlier, as if the last few minutes hadn't passed in silence.

When I didn't respond, he growled softly, grabbing the second door without leaving his post, swinging it open with a rough gesture. "The meat. Smoking. This is the smokehouse."

Sure enough, venison and other meat hung above a vent that poured out heat and smoke into the room, slowly cooking and preserving the meat. I blushed at how obvious it was in retrospect, especially as my nose finally registered the smell.

The smoke started to fill our room as well and Koda was quick to shut the door, though he didn't slam it this time. "This side is for storage. *And* detaining annoying Jinn."

I stared at him, lips parted. Was he making a joke?

"You wanted to know," he mumbled when I still didn't speak. He crossed his arms, returning to scowling at the wall.

I slowly released a breath, unsure what to say. "Thank you...?"

In response, he lowered to a crouch and sat against the door, getting comfortable.

I sighed at the idea of sleeping here, but doubted I had a choice. It couldn't be worse than a forest floor. Standing, I took a bunch of the furs from the stool and began to spread them out across the floor, layering them until they made a surprisingly comfortable bed.

Koda watched without a word, but when I started making a second line of furs for him, trying to get in his good graces, he snapped, "What are you doing?"

I froze, cringing back instinctively. Some things I'd learned growing up with

THE SECRET CURSE

my father would take a lifetime to unlearn. "I assumed we were spending the night. Do you prefer the hard floor?"

"I won't be sleeping." His tone was less annoyed now, more carefully flat.

I frowned. "You barely slept last night either." *Or at all?* I'd been unconscious so I couldn't be sure.

"I'll be fine."

I drew a breath to argue, then let it go. Why did I care? *I don't,* I told myself. *I just need him to trust me.* Keeping that focus in mind, I rebuilt my nerve and turned back to the furs, dragging the remaining ones off and building the second makeshift bed around him, while saying, "Fine. Don't sleep. But you can at least be comfortable."

When he narrowed his eyes at me, I pretended to be far more confident than I felt and tossed the last two furs in his direction. "It's not like I'll be able to get out, if you're blocking the door."

He still didn't respond.

Or move.

My logic was sound, and I frowned, not understanding, until it dawned on me. *He thinks I want to escape while he's sleeping.*

I crossed my arms, unreasonably irritated. It was a smart move on his part. After all, I *was* planning to escape eventually, when the time was right, and I'd learned everything I could. I could've shifted to attack him in his sleep. Or used the paste that still hung in a jar around my neck to paralyze him, roll him away from the door, and run. But the frustrating part was that hadn't been my intention at all.

I laid down with my back to him, pretending to get comfortable, determined not to say another word all night.

Candlelight wavered across the rough wood wall in front of me. The furs prickled a little, but were surprisingly thick and soft. I'd thought I'd need at least one as a blanket, but with the warmth of the smokehouse right next door, I found myself pleasantly warm.

If not for the soft breaths coming from behind me—and, I admitted to myself, the slight throbbing in my shoulder—I could've fallen asleep in a few moments. I didn't want to use my small store of energy on shifting my ears back to normal—I might need the extra-sensitive hearing again tomorrow—but between the lit candle and Koda's obnoxious breathing, sleep evaded me.

It had to be nearly midnight. Maybe later.

Exhaustion turned the soft lighting and gentle breaths into torture.

I gave in and shifted back to normal, throwing an arm over my eyes for good measure.

Drawing in a deep breath, I blew it out, and tried to ignore Koda's presence. It didn't work.

I could *feel* him an arm's length away, even if I didn't hear him anymore.

If I couldn't sleep and he refused to, I might as well try to gather some information.

Taking another fortifying gulp of air, I rolled over, sitting up. His fiery eyes pinned me to the wall, unreadable. For a long moment, we only stared at each other, before I got the courage to whisper, "You don't want this covenant to happen either."

It wasn't a question, really. But I still wanted to hear his answer.

His frown returned. Pulling up his knees, he rested his thick arms across them, staring aimlessly at the wall behind me. "Not with my sister," he said after a long pause, just when I was beginning to think the conversation had ended before it'd begun.

"What does that mean?" I asked without thinking.

Koda pressed his lips together.

"Who am I going to tell?" I asked, gesturing to the four walls around us. "I'm clearly not going anywhere."

"It was supposed to be a hostage situation," Koda snapped, almost before I'd finished speaking, as if he'd desperately needed to say this to someone. "Not a marriage. My father was going to force the prince to complete the covenant with us, swearing peace between our people, and shifting the balance of power to—" he cut off. "It doesn't matter. That's no longer how it will work."

No, I agreed mentally. King Jubal and Queen Samaria would've never allowed that. *But will they actually consider a marriage between our people?* I honestly didn't know if the negotiations were a front, or if the royal family was truly contemplating it...

It only served to remind me how much this covenant could *not* happen.

Maybe this barbarian might even be willing to help me stop it...

"I don't want Shem to marry your sister any more than you do," I said, nearly choking on bitterness toward the council. They hadn't even *tried* to argue that Shem was already engaged. "Believe me. If there is *anyone* who hates this plan more than you, it's me."

Some of the tension in the air around him seemed to melt away as he stared at me in the soft candlelight. I met his gaze, unsure what else I could say to prove it. Whatever he saw seemed to make him believe me, and he shook his head ruefully. "My sister would disagree with you." Rubbing a hand across his face, he sighed. "If you think Tehya wants to be bound to a Jinni, you'd be a fool."

"Shem's not so bad," I murmured, struggling to console him when I wanted to shout that she didn't deserve him.

I had so much more to lose.

If Shem married another, not only was I no longer engaged to a prince, with a future as queen, but I likely would lose my place on Shem's council. I doubted his new wife would want him spending time with a former betrothed. If I wasn't

THE SECRET CURSE

on the council, then I wouldn't have a place in the castle anymore, either.

I squeezed my eyes shut, trying to stop the tears before Koda saw them.

Glancing at him once I'd regained control, I could tell he thought I was mourning the loss of the prince. He respectfully kept his silence and averted his eyes.

But the truth was, I was mourning more than losing Shem, my place on the council, and my current home. If this Vaade revealed my shape-shifting Gift to anyone else, I could never return to Jinn at all. The Dragon could choose to reveal my secret during negotiations, or worse, he could be planning to kill me once the negotiations were over. Or, at least, to try. Quietly to myself, I admitted there was an even greater chance that there was nothing I could do about that.

After all, Koda had captured me.

I hadn't gone easy on him, no matter what I'd pretended. The Vaade were more powerful than I'd imagined, and I was no longer certain my Gifts gave me much of an edge.

One thing was certain, if this covenant wasn't stopped, I'd be back to who I was before I'd met Shem: a nobody with no future.

I gritted my teeth.

It was time to try using my newest Gift of manipulation again.

We were alone. No one besides Koda would notice if I reached out to touch him.

For the thousandth time I wished that part of my Gift wasn't necessary, but the ability was still new to me. I had yet to manipulate others without that extra support.

Koda sat just out of reach.

In other circumstances, I'd say he was too close, but for my purposes, he might as well be as far away as a Jinni island.

I needed to be subtle.

I cleared my throat, which made him meet my eyes, brows raised.

Though I'd learned to be delicate in many things, this wasn't one of them.

The silence between us grew thin. If I didn't speak soon, any action on my part would seem suspicious.

"What is this—" I reached for the large tooth that hung on a string of hide around his neck, intending to brush his skin and use my Gift as I held it.

Instead, he caught my hand mid-air.

12

HIS GRIP WAS FIRM, unyielding.

My mouth was suddenly dry.

I cleared my throat. "I was going to ask about the necklace," I whispered, oddly afraid to meet his gaze, even in the dim light of the lone candle. It felt like he could see through me. Forcing myself to look up, I pasted a smile on my face and added, "Are you scared of a little Jinni girl?"

His lips twitched. "Ask whatever you'd like."

When he let go, my sense returned, making me want to groan. I should've used his defensive reaction as an opportunity. I could've manipulated him while he held my hand.

I cleared my throat again, trying and failing to think of a clever way to try again when my focus had never really been on the necklace. He waited impatiently, so in the end, I asked the obvious: "What animal is it from?"

"Dragon."

Eyes widening, I gave the tooth a closer look. It was about the length of his palm. "I thought dragons were bigger than that?"

"It was a hatchling," he said calmly, not seeming offended, but also never taking his eyes off me. When he saw my furrowed brow at the idea of hurting a baby, he added dryly, "It tried to take a bite from my leg. Believe me, it could've gone much worse for the beast."

Taking a tooth from a dragon and evading certain death seemed pretty fearsome to me. I tried not to show my awe.

If possible, that made me even more nervous to touch him.

Two weeks, I repeated to myself, trying to see it as a positive though it was beginning to feel like a nightmare.

I should try again... It's not like I had anything better to do.

"Koda," I began, trying to prepare him for my movement this time, inching forward until I could reach his knee and set my hand down. It looked anything but casual. His eyes fell to my hand, making me want to pull it back. I forced myself to wait until he looked back up. Making sure his eyes locked with mine, I put all my energy into my Gift as I said, "Tell me about the covenant."

He didn't look away.

My shoulders relaxed as a small smile touched my lips.

Finally, things were going according to plan.

A long pause followed.

He must be fighting my Gift.

No matter, it would win.

It always did.

Koda's eyes drifted across my face, lingering on my lips, before falling back down to where my hand rested on his knee. He tilted his head thoughtfully. When his gaze returned to mine the strangeness finally registered: his eyes were clear. Bright, intelligent, and devoid of the typical indifference usually brought on by my manipulation.

In fact, he was smirking.

"Did you just try to use a Gift on me?"

I flinched and yanked my hand back. In hindsight, it was the worst possible reaction.

I should've feigned innocence. He couldn't prove anything.

Except, now I'd given myself away.

Though my mouth opened, I couldn't come up with a single explanation.

Koda's smirk turned into a full-blown grin, and he shook his head. "You Jinn and your secrets. This is what the Vaade have never understood. You try to control and drive a conversation instead of being willing to simply ask a question. This constant attempt to conceal things from everyone, including your own kind, is what will allow us to win in the end."

Crossing my arms, I scowled at him.

It only made him grin wider. "For example, here is a secret that your kind clearly kept from you: the Vaade are immune to Jinni Gifts."

My jaw dropped, and I breathed, "Impossible."

He only shrugged and gestured toward my hands, where they were tucked tight against my body. "The evidence is before you. Our minds are too strong to be twisted by your wickedness."

Snorting, I looked away. But I turned over his words. That wasn't exactly immunity, was it? There was a loophole in there somewhere... Their *minds* were too strong, he'd said...

It hit me.

"I *traveled* with you!" I sat up straighter, eyes widening as another memory came to me. "And during the other attack, one of the Guard members traveled with you too! Until you—" I cut off, remembering how he'd suddenly become rooted to the earth, like an anchor held him in place.

He shifted uncomfortably, avoiding my eyes. "That was a moment of weakness."

Their minds weren't always strong...

But something told me it was more than that.

He hadn't seen Shem either, and he'd certainly been trying his hardest. And what about when I'd shifted? The Vaade's immunity seemed more defensive than anything, almost like their thick skin made magic bounce off them, but did nothing to stop Gifts used on someone else.

Contemplating what this might mean, I jumped when he leaned toward me. When I met his gaze, he spoke slow and clear, "It won't happen again." *Traveling,* I reminded myself, trying to calm my frantic heart. *He's talking about traveling, not using my other Gifts.*

He waited for me to nod understanding before relaxing back against the door.

We were quiet for a minute.

When I risked a glance in his direction, curiosity shone in his colorful eyes. "Have you considered I might answer your question without your useless Gift?"

I lifted my chin, pinning him with my gaze, and said in a flat voice, "Fine. Tell me about the covenant."

Tilting his head thoughtfully, he paused, and for a long moment I was sure he'd been taunting me, but then he said, "Tell me about the Gift you tried to use on me, and I'll tell you about the covenant."

Absolutely not.

He was a Vaade, so he didn't know what he asked, but it still made me flush with anger.

I turned away from him and lay back down.

This conversation was over.

I thought he felt the same, but then I heard shuffling behind me. I peeked over my shoulder to find him laying the last two pelts across the floor and stretching out across them beside me. It was oddly intimate. Was that his way of saying he was trusting me?

He lifted his muscled arms and flexed, placing his hands under his head to

THE SECRET CURSE

stare up at the wood ceiling.

I was mesmerized.

Calmly, as if long minutes hadn't passed without talking, he continued to stare at the ceiling as he asked, "What do you have to lose?"

I blinked at him. What a ridiculous question.

Back home, I'd have *everything* to lose.

Breathing slowly, I took in his handsome face, only a few breaths away from mine, allowing myself a chance to stare for once. Who would have thought I'd be considering what a Vaade said?

But he was right...

Here, everything was already lost. Now there was only gain.

He rolled onto his side to face me, waiting less patiently now.

"I—" Heat flooded my face before I even began. Everything in me resisted telling him, after keeping it hidden for so long. "I don't completely understand the Gift myself yet. It's still new..." It felt traitorous to tell him even that, but I made myself continue, in the hopes that by sharing, he might choose to share with me as well. "...It seems to make people believe what I say and"—I had to clear my throat before I could finish—"want what I want."

He burst out laughing.

Startled, I froze, unsure what to do.

"That *would* be convenient," he said on a chuckle, relaxing onto his back again, shoulders shaking with mirth. "I can see why you'd try it."

Scowling at him, I rolled onto my back as well and crossed my arms. "It certainly would be useful right now," I agreed.

When he started laughing all over again, I glared at him. "Not everyone finds it so funny, you know. Back home, they'd sooner sever my abilities than trust me with them."

His laughter cut off, and I tried not to miss it. I didn't know why I'd told him that.

"And the Jinn think *we're* barbaric," he muttered, shaking his head.

"You're saying you wouldn't do the same thing, if you had the opportunity?" I challenged, meeting his piercing stare.

"Never."

He hadn't hesitated for a second.

I didn't want to believe him, but... I did. Skirting away from the personal, I came back to the point. "You promised you'd tell me about the covenant in return."

"Why do you want to know about it?" he asked in a soft tone.

"That wasn't the deal," I argued, sitting up again. "I don't have to tell you that."

"How could I forget," he said, and without moving a muscle, the cold distance returned between us. "You Jinn and your secrets." He snorted. "Why share something unless you absolutely *have* to?"

I was tempted to brush him off again and demand answers, but his earlier words came back to me. *What do I have to lose?*

"It's not really a secret." I leaned back against the wall, wincing when I accidentally bumped my sore shoulder. "I would've thought you'd already guessed—I want to stop it."

Koda didn't react.

Had I lost all the progress we'd made by saying that? I'd thought he wanted to stop it too…

He continued to stare at the ceiling.

I squinted at him. It seemed almost as if he'd forgotten I was there.

Finally, he blew out a breath. "I don't want Tehya forced to marry your prince."

"Then we're in agreement. Let's find a way to end it."

"There's only one other way." He slowly met my eyes with a fiery intensity, as if he knew what I'd say. "We take your prince as our hostage instead."

Never.

My sense of self-preservation kept me from speaking right away. I pretended to think. "Obviously that's not possible or you would've done it already. And the covenant isn't an option either. What else would you do?"

"There is no alternative," he muttered darkly.

"There has to be another way," I said, though I wasn't sure I believed it myself at the moment.

A pause hung over us as he sulked and I tried to think.

"Tell me more details about how the covenant works," I said finally, unsure if he would listen. "How does it benefit your people—or mine? And why does your father want it so badly he'd give up his own daughter for it?"

When he still didn't answer, I added, "You can trust me. In this, we're on the same side."

13

"**THE SAME SIDE?**" **KODA'S** stillness had lulled me into such a peaceful state, I startled when he leapt up to pace. In a space this size, he could only take a step and a half before turning, which gave the impression of bouncing off the walls. He seemed to come to the same conclusion, stopping to crouch in front of me instead. "I was raised to believe the Vaade and the Jinn are *never* on the same side."

His breath tickled my nose, an odd thing to notice. My own breath was faster than I'd like, but that was only because he'd scared me. *Wasn't it?*

Hesitating, I licked my lips, noticing that this drew his gaze. "I understand. The Jinn are taught that *no one* is on their side. And yet…" I cleared my throat. "We want the same things. Which means we *are* on the same side, whether we like it or not."

He leaned back abruptly.

I would've moved back too, but there was nowhere to go.

Koda settled against the opposite wall, studying me before giving in. "At first glance, the covenant is a marriage ceremony—but the Jinni enchantment built into the vows forms a magical truce."

"What kind of truce?"

"Neither side can harm the other. They become incapable of it."

When he didn't continue right away, I frowned. "A marriage is between two people. This truce would only affect Shem and your sister."

He shook his head. "Using blood, rings, and an ancient spell, the enchantment imbues the rings with the power to speak for the entire race."

I was sure he could hear my heart skip a beat. My mouth was dry. "If anyone can do this covenant, why wouldn't someone have tried to form this truce before?"

"Not everyone can." Koda stared up at the ceiling as he spoke. "Only a royal can imbue a ring with that power."

I tilted my head at that. "You mean, it'd have to be done by King Jubal or Queen Samaria."

Koda cleared his throat. "Or your prince."

That's why they'd tried to capture him.

"And once this covenant is complete, it prevents both sides from harming the other," I repeated.

Fidgeting with the dragon tooth around his neck, Koda didn't answer. His words when I'd first met him came back to me: *we don't want peace.* That must've changed.

"It sounds too good to be true." I scoffed. "How does the enchantment work?"

He paused longer than seemed necessary, making me wonder what this supposedly straightforward Vaade might be hiding.

"The most important requirement, according to the spell, are the 'sacrificial' rings," he said slowly. "That's what my father and your prince are currently negotiating right now. Both sides must imbue the rings with the power to speak for their people through their blood. We believe the rings will then draw out our abilities once the covenant begins—that's the sacrificial part."

"Draw out..." I repeated, not understanding.

"Like a weakening," he explained. "Both the Jinn and the Vaade will slowly lose all our unique strengths and abilities until we become like the humans."

My pulse picked up, though I kept my face neutral. "That doesn't sound good."

He smiled at me wryly, letting me know that I hadn't hidden my reaction from him at all. "It's only temporary. And a required part of the sacrifice—we must willingly give up a part of ourselves."

"That's... unusual." An understatement. It must be an old spell to have so much emotion written into it. Jinn these days avoided doing spells so based in passion. Or in most cases, any spell that needed a second person. It required too much trust. Who would risk it?

"It's meant to be a true marriage covenant based on love." Koda unwittingly answered my unspoken question. "But we've been led to believe that the magic also works with a real trust."

THE SECRET CURSE

I snorted at that. "Trust is for fools. Which is what someone would have to be to willingly submit to that."

"That's the whole point of the sacrifice," he snapped. "To have the benefits, they must risk everything."

I had to bite my lip to keep from smiling. He was a secret romantic, it seemed. "I still can't imagine it. I'd never *choose* to weaken myself for someone else."

"It's not permanent!" He threw up his hands, exasperated. "Unless the covenant is left incomplete, it's just a symbolic gesture."

"Of what?"

"Of *trust*," he said, shaking his head at me as if it was obvious. "Something you clearly know nothing about."

No, I thought darkly, *I know all about it and how impossible it truly is.*

"It doesn't matter anyway," he added, bringing my attention back to his smirking face. "No one's asking *you* to complete a covenant."

Once again, he'd managed to wound me.

I glared at him. "You Vaade can keep your covenant and your *trust*," I retorted, crossing my arms, hating how he made me react when normally I could keep a calm mask. Taking a careful breath in and out to control my temper, I added in a detached tone, "As far as I'm concerned, you all have a strange obsession with weakness."

Koda didn't seem offended or entertained by that. If anything, he grew more serious. "Yes. We do."

I blinked at him, not knowing what to say in the face of such honesty. After spending so many months in the castle, my mind was trained to search every phrase for subtext. But with this Vaade man, it felt like looking for the answer to a riddle I wasn't even sure was there. It was draining.

I rubbed my forehead. This whole day had been overwhelming. The thought of sharing anything further of myself with Koda frankly scared me. Turning my back on him, I lay down, mumbling like a coward, "We should get some sleep."

From the lack of sound behind me, I knew he stayed upright. But I wasn't his caretaker. If he wanted to be exhausted tomorrow, that was his problem.

My mind, however, refused to rest. Wrapping my arms around myself to keep from tossing and turning, I couldn't stop thinking about this covenant and all the details he'd shared. I tested them from different angles, trying to find a weakness or catch.

Instead, I kept coming back to the same question: *Would Shem really agree to this? Or is he stalling?*

From the sound of it, the magical truce would stop all Vaade attacks forever. If he thought of his people alone, he might say yes.

But he would also consider me and what this covenant would mean for us, wouldn't he?

I hated that I didn't know for sure.

Biting my lip until it hurt, I tried to distract myself from the salty tears filling my eyes, but they fell anyway, crossing my cheeks and slowly soaking the fur beneath my head. I hoped Koda couldn't somehow smell them.

It's not final, I reminded myself yet again. I still had two weeks to find a way out of the covenant for Shem. Tomorrow, I'd win Koda over with false kindness and convince him to tell me more about it. He'd obviously been holding something back. If I continued to remind him that we wanted the same thing, I could persuade him to help me. It was a flimsy plan, which didn't provide much comfort, but at least it was something.

At some point, Koda's soft breathing seemed to even out, and after listening to it for a while, so did mine, until I drifted to sleep.

* * *

"Wake up, Jinni girl." Koda's voice startled me out of a nightmare. Shem had been apologizing to me while holding Tehya's hand, calling her his *new wife*. It left a sour taste in my mouth and put me in a foul mood.

Rubbing my eyes, I winced at the headache forming. Forgetting my plans to be charming, I snapped, "I have a name, you know."

Unfazed, he swung open the door. "I'm sure you do."

Though the sun was peeking over the horizon, leaving the air misty and softly lit, the sudden change in lighting still hurt my eyes. I shaded a hand over them, squinting at Koda's outline.

"It's Jezebel," I reminded him in a more neutral tone. I attempted a smile as I stepped out of the smokehouse, but it probably looked like a grimace. "Where are we going?"

He nodded toward the longhouse and strode off, clearly expecting me to join him. Gut twisting at the thought of interacting with the other Vaade here, I sighed and followed. "Can you at least tell me more about the covenant if—"

My question was cut off when he whirled to grab me by the arms, glancing around to make sure we were still alone. "Do *not* mention the covenant."

When he didn't explain further, I frowned, trying to pull away, but stopped at the way it made my shoulder hurt. "Why not?"

His grip was firm, and he held my gaze. "My father would be... upset with me for sharing the details with you."

Having met his father, upset was probably putting it nicely.

I nodded. "Understood."

Finally, he let go, heading for the longhouse again. Thinking of the Dragon being nearby, I stayed on Koda's heels.

Over his shoulder, he said, "It might be best if you don't talk much around

THE SECRET CURSE

the others in general. At least until they get used to you. A lot of them have strong feelings about the Jinn."

I snorted. "I hadn't noticed."

That earned me a slight smile, which I only glimpsed because I'd caught up to him, standing beside him as he reached for the door to the longhouse.

"Wait!" I didn't realize I'd grabbed his arm to stop him until he glanced down at my hand. I pulled back, forcing myself to meet his piercing gaze. "Before we go in, will you keep my last Gift a secret?"

His forehead wrinkled. "Why?"

Taken aback, I could only blink at him at first. "Because of the consequences. If they knew what I could do…" Each reason made me stumble when it suddenly didn't seem valid here. In Jinn, my Gifts might be severed, but the Vaade didn't know how to do that. And if the Vaade were truly as immune to Gifts as Koda had led me to believe, they wouldn't care about my abilities anyway. "I just—I would feel more comfortable if they didn't know," I finished lamely.

Considering me, his frown deepened. "I don't want to keep secrets from my people."

My shoulders sagged. I nodded at his feet, understanding. Why would he keep an enemy's secret? I shouldn't expect anything less.

"If it doesn't come up, I won't bring it up."

Sucking in a breath, relief flooded through me. I opened my mouth to thank him, but he'd already opened the door and started through it.

This far side was quiet, full of empty bunks. A small group of Vaade sat talking and eating around the fire in the center of the longhouse, a few dozen paces away. Smoke drifted up through the hole in the ceiling that allowed light throughout the rest of the longhouse, though it was much darker on the ends where we were.

I'd only just closed the door, eyes still adjusting to the gloom, when Tehya stepped out of the shadows to one side, blocking our path. Close up, her deep-brown eyes made the dragon-like irises even more startling. She wore a chunky blue necklace over her pale deerskin dress. "What Gift?"

I gaped at her.

When I didn't answer, she turned to Koda, hands on her hips, long braids swinging over her shoulders as she turned. "She has more?"

I faced him too, silently pleading with him not to tell her.

He spread his hands wide and shrugged, as if to say, *It came up.* To Tehya, he said, "She travels, shape-shifts, and apparently can trick the weak-minded into doing what she wants."

"We already knew about the first two," Tehya said, waving them off as if they meant nothing.

My mouth hung open at the way she casually dismissed my abilities.

Without a second glance, she turned away again, moving toward the cookfire at the heart of the longhouse.

I glared at Koda. "Good to know you can keep a secret for a whole two seconds."

He shrugged again. "It's not my fault you chose to speak within earshot of a Vaade."

My skin crawled at having all my secrets exposed like this. It only annoyed me further that he was right. Forgetting about their ridiculous hearing was my mistake.

No wonder the Vaade didn't keep many secrets. How could they?

The smell of food wafted toward us, and my stomach growled.

Koda's mouth twitched. "Come." He waved toward the center of the longhouse, adding over his shoulder. "Breakfast."

Tehya was leaning over the group, gesturing toward us as she spoke, and eyes were turning in my direction.

Now, I *did* groan.

Not knowing what else to do, I dragged my feet after Koda toward them.

14

WE'D BARELY REACHED THE small cookfire and the wooden stumps around it where half a dozen Vaade were seated, when Koda put a hand on Tehya's shoulder and said, "Watch the Jinni girl until I get back."

She scowled. "He won't change his mind."

Did she mean the Dragon?

The fact that Koda didn't immediately argue said a lot. "Tehya," he murmured after a long pause, "I have to at least try to talk to him."

The others around the fire kept their eyes on their food, pretending they couldn't hear every word. "If you want my help, watch her."

Tehya gave him a short nod, turning away.

Startled, I opened my mouth to protest too.

Koda cut me off with a sharp look, as if to remind me of our deal. "Stay."

Glaring at his back, I wrapped my arms around myself, wrinkling my nose at both Koda abandoning me and also a little bit from the way I'd started to smell after living in the same clothes for so long.

Tehya studied my dirty red and white dress with a similar expression. "Come with me," she said on a sigh.

Following her through the bunks, we stopped halfway down the row, stepping between two of them, where Tehya dug through a wooden box until she found whatever she was looking for.

"Here." The cloth hit me in the stomach, and I caught it instinctively.

Standing again, Tehya pulled the blankets from the bunks on each side down, forming a privacy screen. "Change."

"What about a bath?" I countered, wishing I could scrub an entire layer of dirty skin off.

Tehya shrugged. "Only if you want to do it with company."

Glancing back over my shoulder at the other Vaade, I wordlessly shook my head. I'd ask again later and hope for different results.

Unraveling the bundle of clothes, I found a sleeveless deerskin dress with a pretty, blue pattern sewn around the neckline and waist. It was simple compared to my multi-layered, off-the-shoulder gown, but it was clean.

With a glance at Tehya, who simply stared back, I figured she wasn't going anywhere, so I stripped without complaint.

As soon as the stiff red and white fabric hit the ground, I breathed a sigh of relief. The soft deerskin dress felt like wearing a cloud after being so tightly wrapped for the last few days.

Tehya picked up the dress, leading me back to the fire, where the Vaade all blatantly stared at me. A delicious smell wafted through the air that had my mouth watering. They were eating something that looked like yellow-colored bread or cake.

As I watched, Tehya poured a similar yellow liquid over a large flat rock in the center of the fire. It sizzled, starting to cook instantly.

"What is it?" I asked, trying to sound indifferent so they wouldn't know I was drooling over the sweet smells.

"Corn cakes," Tehya replied without looking at me. She made a few more circles of the thick liquid until the rock was full, then sat, still not looking at me.

The tense atmosphere reminded me oddly of the Jinni castle. I scowled, not liking the comparison. Oddly enough, though, the hostility was almost relaxing in its familiarity.

A short log beside her was open. It didn't look like I was going to get an invitation anytime soon, and I didn't want to stand all day. I lowered myself onto it.

No one stopped me, but they didn't acknowledge me either.

My stomach growled. Loudly.

There was no way the Vaade's sharp ears hadn't heard, but they all continued quietly going about the meal without speaking. One woman worked on weaving an intricate basket, one piece of thick dried grass at a time. The man next to her shucked corn, while a third man was deftly skinning a small animal. I averted my eyes, before I lost my appetite.

"Can I?" I asked finally, sounding more sullen than I'd meant to. I gestured to the corn cakes that for all appearances seemed done cooking. The edges were

THE SECRET CURSE

turning a golden brown.

Raising a single brow at me, Tehya shrugged. "Help yourself."

I glanced around for a plate or any other serving tools, finding none, and under Tehya's cold stare, I licked my lips and reached forward to pick up one of the thick corn cakes with my fingers.

"Ah!" I howled, tossing the steaming bread from one hand to the other as it burned my skin. Blowing on it to cool it down, it was still too hot to hold, forcing me to set it on my new dress to avoid forming blisters.

Chuckles came from the Vaade around the cook fire as well as a few more around the room that I hadn't realized were there.

Tehya tried to hide her smirk, but not very hard. Nodding to my lap, she said, "Don't waste that."

I didn't know where Tehya's dress had been. But I was too hungry to argue with her and too humiliated to agree, so I chose to copy their silence, ignoring them completely.

Blowing on my fingers to cool them, I was wishing for ice, when she calmly reached out and picked up one of the hot cakes.

My mouth fell open.

Steam curled up in a thin smoky wisp above her hand, yet she didn't react. Letting it rest in her hand, she gave me a cheeky grin. If my fingers weren't burning, it might've tempted me to smile back. As it was, I leaned into my irritation instead. I hated being the focus of ridicule.

Bizarre Vaade skin.

I let my eyes skim over her, then lifted my chin and looked away, as if unimpressed.

Only yesterday I'd seen what should have been a fatal injury cause a mere scratch, so I shouldn't be surprised. The lack of plates or serving tools made sense now. Why worry about hot food if the heat didn't bother them?

My own little hot cake had cooled enough to eat, even if it burned my tongue a bit. I swallowed the last bite, but I was still starving. They were so small.

Uncertainty and hunger twisted my stomach, making me less reasonable than usual. It wasn't like me to use my Gifts recklessly, not to mention, in front of anyone else—but they already knew about them.

Koda's words from the night before floated back to me.

What do I have to lose?

I made a split-second decision and shifted.

My fingertips grew long and sharp, thick and pointed like claws.

Tehya's eyebrows rose, grudgingly impressed. A couple other Vaade nudged each other and studied me. But every face around the fire was curious. None of them held fear.

My shoulders lowered from where they'd unconsciously risen to my ears, and I let out the breath I'd been holding when I'd shifted.

They didn't care.

Using my new claws, I scooped up two more steaming hot cakes, not feeling the heat at all. I couldn't help a self-satisfied smile as they watched.

Tehya waited until I chewed the last bite before speaking up, "We should fight."

I choked, tensing.

"Not like that." She rolled her eyes as I coughed, trying to catch my breath. "For fun."

Fun? I blinked at her, not understanding.

"I've heard all about your shape-shifting and now your mind-tricks. I still think I'll win."

She let the challenge hang in the air.

A fight. For fun. I couldn't wrap my mind around the concept. "I'm injured…"

"It's not that bad," she scoffed, dismissing my shoulder wound in a handful of words.

I glanced over my shoulder, hoping Koda would rescue me from his crazy sister.

"Koda won't like it," one of the Vaade murmured, obviously thinking the same thing.

Tehya shrugged. "Don't care."

I couldn't help but compare her to the Jinn back home. Instead of fearing my Gift, she wanted to test it, to face me head on. Part of me was intrigued. "What kind of fight?"

Jumping to her feet, eyes lighting up, she gestured for me to follow. Instead of answering, she cheerfully called to the rest of the room. "To the clearing."

I hadn't actually agreed to the fight, but curiosity took over. When she took my arm at the door, I didn't protest. This was my opportunity to learn more about the Vaade—their strengths *and* their weaknesses. It could be valuable information to bring home.

Even if none of those things happened, it'd be easier for Shem to rescue me if I was *outside* the longhouse, wouldn't it?

Tehya surprised me by letting go of my arm. I supposed she wasn't worried about an escape when there were so many of them to give pursuit and only one of me.

Every other Vaade in the room trailed after us. The idea of fighting one of them was intimidating on its own, but having an audience nearly made me change my mind.

All of my instincts screamed to run.

Logic took over, reminding me I wouldn't get far in an area like this. I couldn't see past the surrounding trees. With their speed, they could probably run as fast as I could travel. I needed to play along with Tehya's challenge.

THE SECRET CURSE

As we passed through the camp, other Vaade seemed to recognize the direction we were headed, joining us until our small group held a few dozen. The majority chattered excitedly, although I heard a few grumbles about how Tehya "shouldn't allow the Jinni brat to wander around camp."

"We allow attacks in most forms," Tehya was saying, and I made myself pay attention. "But no going for the eyes or the throat."

Odd. A shiver of anticipation mixed with dread washed over me. "What if I hurt you?"

Tehya and a few others laughed. "Do your worst," she said. "You won't get past me."

Her reaction was so unexpected that I slowed.

Grabbing my elbow, she dragged me on. "Keep up," she said, but not angrily. It was almost as if the idea of a fight had raised her spirits.

"Do you do this often?"

"Sometimes."

We reached the clearing she'd mentioned, and I knew she'd been playing it off. It looked like it'd been used at least a hundred times before, like they came here often, maybe even daily.

Were the Vaade not as nomadic as the king and queen assumed? I filed away this new information, hoping it might mean something, even if I didn't know what right now.

The dirt was packed down, with a circle in the center created out of logs, with taller tree stumps cut and placed around it as seating around the little arena. Though the nerves made my skin tingle, the excitement was starting to take over.

I'd never had a chance to test my Gifts publicly before. Not only was everyone okay with it, but they wanted to *watch*. I didn't scare them at all. Part of me liked the reaction more than I would've expected.

But when Tehya stepped into the circle and waved for me to join her, I balked. "I've never fought anyone before."

She jutted out a hip and crossed her arms, frowning at me. "You're saying you just let Koda capture you?"

"That's different," I mumbled. And the truth was, I kind of had. I'd never needed to know fighting tactics before. If I ever made it back home, I'd make sure that changed. "How do we know who wins?"

"First person, or Jinni"—she added with a wicked smile—"to step outside the circle loses."

I frowned. "That doesn't seem like a test of our abilities?"

Hiding her thoughts behind an innocent mask, she spread her hands wide and said, "Why not enter and find out?" Almost as an aside, she added, "You can also yell 'defeat' if you find it's too much for you."

Some hecklers who'd joined us shouted insults, while others looked genuinely curious to see how this fight would go. One angry voice yelled, "Give up while you still can!" I recognized Ahriman by his seemingly permanent scowl.

My pride immediately rejected his suggestion. But this wasn't a simple fight either, and I didn't want to appear foolish. If I stepped into the ring in front of her, she'd use her Vaade strength to shove me out. This seemed like an unfair advantage. It was her strength against my wits.

But if I use my Gifts... There was something thrilling about the idea of using my Gifts so openly. It was just a fight. The worst that could happen would be if Tehya humiliated me, and that couldn't be much worse than what I'd endured here already.

I grinned.

15

STROLLING AROUND THE CIRCLE to the other side, I kept my eyes on Tehya. She smiled at me and allowed it.

Trying to catch her off balance, I leapt into the circle without warning, running toward the center, where I planned to hold my ground, shifting into a Lacklore as I ran.

Even after multiple encounters with the Vaade, I still managed to underestimate how fast they were.

With one leap, Tehya crossed the circle.

On all fours, claws partially formed, my body was still growing to the full Lacklore height, when she slammed into my side. A half-scream and half-roar ripped out of me as I forced the rest of my shift. Baring my teeth, I bit her arm and flung her toward the boundary lines.

She flew through the air in a graceful arc, landing on her feet like a cat, eyes flickering as she glanced down at the shallow puncture marks on her arm.

I hadn't held back.

Drawing in a frustrated breath, I realized breaking her skin would never be an effective way to win. I needed a different method.

At least she approached more warily now, though she circled me with the determination of a wolf hunting its prey.

She pounced and managed to wrestle me to the ground until I rolled, crushing her with my weight briefly before a well-aimed kick at my shoulder made me retreat with a yelp. We landed on opposite sides of the circle, panting.

I moved on instinct as she continued to attack without giving me a chance to recover. Snarling, I extended my claws, swiping wildly to fend her off. She dodged near and away, not giving me a chance to think.

She caught me by surprise, tossing me across the ring. I dragged my claws, barely catching myself before I slid out of the circle.

Cheers disrupted my focus. This was Tehya's element. Maybe I should let her win and get this over with.

"What's the matter?" she mocked when I remained on the other side of the circle instead of charging her like before. Looking me over, she tsked. "If you're the best Jinn has, we should skip the covenant and just invade."

Cheers sounded from the onlookers, along with a few more choice insults about the Jinn. For some reason, though, those didn't sound as light-hearted as Tehya's had.

Pride smarting, I shook my head and hauled myself to my feet, teeth bared. A memory of Koda fighting the first time I'd seen him came to me. I'd have to time it right…

She prowled toward me, which was her first mistake.

It gave me time to shift.

Pushing my body, I changed as fast as I had when Koda pursued me.

I returned to my true form.

A split second later, I traveled, landing behind her.

Wrapping my arms around her waist, I caught her off-guard, traveling again immediately.

It worked!

She wasn't mentally prepared, and I was able to take her with me, just like the guards had taken Koda. I could've traveled outside the circle, but then I'd lose too, and I wanted to *win*.

So I dropped her at the edge of the circle, as close as I dared, and gave her a push.

She wasn't nearly as confused as Koda had been, though. It was almost as if she'd prepared for this—she caught me by the arms, twisting and using my weight to pull herself back, nearly making me fall on top of her.

I traveled again in a panic.

It worked, but she held onto me so firmly that I couldn't shake her when we reappeared.

I traveled again, and again. A fifth time, a sixth. She was like a leech. It was almost as if she was letting me travel with her…

It was wearing me out, but if I stopped for too long, she'd defeat me, so I kept going, flashing from one side of the circle to the next. I tried landing closer and closer to the edge. If I could put her across the line, I could still win.

Suddenly she wasn't moveable anymore. She slipped from my arms as I traveled, ripped away from me like an anchor from a current.

I reappeared alone on the other side of the circle, whirling around, confused. What'd changed? Had *she* done that?

I didn't have a chance to think it through, as she sprang at me with a snarl.

I traveled out of the way.

She landed awkwardly as she wrapped her arms around thin air.

On the defensive now, I stood right next to the edge, hoping she'd jump too far, but she was too smart to fall for that. She stalked toward me with careful steps.

When she neared the center of the arena, I traveled behind her, attempting to use the full force of my Gift of manipulation as I commanded, "Stop!"

Instead, she flung me backward across the circle.

I landed on my injured arm and gasped.

The pain blinded me for a moment.

Dragging myself to my feet, I wiped the sweat out of my eyes with my good arm, trying not to cradle my injured arm too obviously even though it throbbed to the point I could hardly think straight.

Tehya didn't press her advantage, which a quiet voice in the back of my head whispered was odd.

She kept near the edge instead, stalking me.

I moved in the opposite direction, keeping my distance.

The Vaade around us were hooting and calling out encouragement to her, but she only circled cautiously.

I tuned them out.

I couldn't afford a distraction right now.

She *had* to have felt me trembling during those last few attacks. Why didn't she attack?

Keeping one eye on her, I took in our surroundings, searching for something I'd missed—was Koda here? Was she somehow injured too and hiding it? Nothing made sense, but as I listened to the Vaade around us jeer at me, one of them yelled, "Stop going easy on her!"

I frowned.

Glaring at me, as if somehow I was doing this wrong, Tehya swung her eyes toward the sky and back, trying to communicate something to me.

Whatever it was, she clearly didn't want to say it with the Vaade around us listening in.

I squinted at her. She wanted to fight in the sky? No... It was almost like... My eyes widened as it hit me. She wanted me to shift into a bird and fly away like I had the day before. That couldn't be right...

I tried to tamp down my reaction as we circled each other warily, looking for an opening. She made the gesture a second time. I hadn't imagined it, then.

All at once this strange fight made sense: she wanted me gone. If I wasn't here anymore, the Vaade would lose their negotiating power with the Jinn. Shem would refuse the marriage that *she* didn't want to happen in the first place.

She wanted me to escape.

Subtly, I shook my head at her, gazing around the circle of Vaade and then down at my injured arm to send her a silent message in return: *not like this.* Not surrounded by enemies, while hurt.

That wasn't a quick getaway, it was a death sentence.

Maybe she knew that and hoped I'd take the chance anyway? I couldn't say for sure, but in my irritation, I went on the offensive.

This time when I traveled, I landed in front of her, eye to eye, and whispered, "Back up."

Her sharp eyes dulled.

With the added eye contact, my Gift was taking effect!

She stepped out of the circle obediently.

The Vaade fell silent.

I should've been worried, but instead I grinned.

Someone clapped, and others joined in with cheers. Tehya's trance broke at the sound. She shook her head to clear the cobwebs.

Angry shouts broke through the conversation, as a handful of Vaade glared in my direction, while others stormed off as if they couldn't be in my presence another moment.

I waited for the punishment. It was my own fault for giving in to my frustration. No one liked their free will being taken.

It didn't come.

Shaking her head at me, Tehya gave me a reluctant nod and held out her hand to shake. "I should've been more prepared. I'll admit, I'm impressed."

A few more Vaade spat on the ground at her admission and stormed off as well. But most of them stayed, and there was more than one nod of agreement at Tehya's statement. I caught myself smiling. It was only because my plan to get them to trust me was working.

"Come," Tehya said, not bothering to hold my arm as we took the path back to camp. "Let's get something for that shoulder."

The throbbing intensified when she brought my attention to it. Between the injury, my exhaustion, and the number of Vaade still fairly close by, even if I'd wanted to run, I wouldn't have made it far. That didn't stop me from giving the sky one last longing glance before turning to follow her.

For all I knew, Shem might have a rescue planned. It could happen any minute now. Better to accept their food and medicine, and be fully rested when the time came.

She left me at the big outdoor bonfire, where I sank down among the other Vaade without a second thought because I'd pushed too hard again. I didn't even

THE SECRET CURSE

realize Tehya had left me alone with strange Vaade until she was halfway back from the longhouse.

When she crouched beside me, I tensed. As she reached for my arm, I unconsciously leaned away.

"If I had your magic, I'd tell you to sit still," she grumbled, pulling me back toward her. "Don't move, or it'll hurt more." She rubbed a salve that looked and smelled like the one Koda had used into my arm, but instead of wrapping it again, she left it exposed to the air. "It'll heal faster this way," she said without further explanation.

She left me unguarded for a second time as she returned the medicine to wherever it was kept.

Colorful eyes around the fire watched me closely. Unguarded wasn't the right word; I was far from alone.

Her mouth twisted almost like disappointment when she returned to find me in the same place. She must have a severely low opinion of the Jinn if she thought I'd run in my condition—not only did my arm ache, which meant there was no way I'd be able to fly right now, but after both the fight and the shifting, I was also starving.

Someone passed around some smoked meat and a type of thick bread, similar to what we'd eaten that morning. I took a second helping.

"Time to put you to work," Tehya said around a mouthful, pulling up a stack of long, thick reeds. "I'll teach you."

I wrinkled my nose. Grass baskets wouldn't hold any secrets on the covenant. Glancing around for Koda, I sighed. Unless he reappeared out of thin air, it didn't look like I had a choice.

We spent the afternoon making baskets—or in my case, attempting to.

"Like this," she said with a grunt, when I mixed up the fourth and fifth weave yet again. "Like a little deer running around its mother's legs, and then beneath, coming out the other side. Then the dragon eats it."

I snorted at the image.

She demonstrated with the strands, but I couldn't picture these deer she described, much less the dragon weave. Rolling my eyes, I muttered under my breath, "If you wanted a fancy basket, you should've asked someone else."

"Who says I want a fancy basket?" she retorted. I'd forgotten about her impossible Vaade hearing. "Maybe I just want to torture you."

"With basket-weaving?" I laughed at the ridiculous idea. "By all means then, torture on. We'll see how effective it is."

Instead of stiffening from my comments like Milcah would've, Tehya burst out laughing. "Prisoners of war sent to a basket-weaving class spill all their secrets!" She threw her head back as she cackled. "Can you imagine?"

I laughed too, caught off guard.

Tehya shook her head as we returned to the baskets, almost as if surprised by our easy camaraderie.

That made two of us.

The sun was low in the sky now, and Tehya had started looking over her shoulder constantly by the time Koda finally reappeared.

"Any luck?" she murmured to him, forgetting me completely.

He hadn't, however. Taking her arm, he led her a few paces away where I couldn't overhear, before whispering. The sun on the horizon turned them into silhouettes.

I considered shifting my hearing, but they were done before I had the chance.

Fists clenched and red-faced, Tehya stormed off toward the longhouse without so much as a goodbye.

Koda came to sit by me, also without a word.

Stiffening in his presence, I realized how much I'd let my guard down today. During my short time with the Vaade, Koda had usually been the one to give me a sense of safety, but not right now.

Every muscle along his large arms rippled as he reached for a log from the pile behind us and threw it in the fire with such force I wondered if he'd imagined it was a person. He gripped another log, squeezing it as if wringing someone's neck.

I focused on weaving the basket I'd started hours ago. Without Tehya to show me where I'd gone wrong, the whole thing was hopelessly tangled. I started to sigh, then caught myself.

Too late. I'd drawn his attention.

Koda straightened. His face grew blank as he visibly shut the door on whatever bothered him. He tossed the second log on the fire much more gently. "I trust you've behaved yourself, Jinni girl?"

"Jezebel," I reminded him casually, attempting a smile. If I could, I hoped to make him see me less as a hated Jinn and more as a person. That would increase my chances of getting information from him. "And yes…" I hesitated, wondering if I should skip telling him about the fight earlier.

"Why does your yes sound more like a no?"

If he'd asked with a scowl, I'd have protested, but his slight smirk was returning. The golden light danced across his face, giving him an otherworldly glow. With that strong nose, thick brows, and mesmerizing eyes, he could rival Shem's good looks. He was like the sun—warm, strong, full of life—I stopped myself before I had any other traitorous thoughts.

"It was Tehya's idea," I began, holding my hands up in the universal sign of helplessness. "She—"

"Wanted to fight," he finished with a sigh, shaking his head.

"How did you know?"

"Tehya's always wanted to fight a Jinni, but our father refuses to include her on the raids."

THE SECRET CURSE

I read between the lines. Koda had been on the last two, and I assumed probably the ones before that as well. Tehya and her brother had seemed close, to the point that I'd felt a twinge of jealousy, wishing I'd had a sibling who could care about me like that—but this hinted at a jealousy between them. Koda had something she didn't.

Keeping my voice neutral, I shrugged. "She got what she wanted."

"Who won?"

The fact that he didn't automatically assume it was his sister sent warm tingles through my body. "Who do you think?" I taunted, genuinely wanting to know who he'd bet on. But I couldn't help a small smile that gave me away.

His brows rose in appreciation, but he pursed his lips and tilted his head, teasing back, "So, Tehya then?"

"Tehya was the rightful winner," one of the Vaade on the other side of the fire slurred. Angry gold eyes met mine over the flames, glittering with unadulterated rage. "The Jinni snake cheated."

Used to fighting my own battles, I expected Koda to let me handle it the way Shem would. My mouth was open, ready to tell him I'd broken no rules, but Koda spoke first.

"You've always been a sore loser, Ahriman," he growled with a cold look in his eyes. "I've been spoiling for a reason to hit someone all day." Slowly he leaned forward on his knees, as he added in a soft tone that somehow seemed even more dangerous, "Feel free to say something else you'll regret."

Ahriman eyed him, swaying slightly. I worried whatever he was drinking would impede his judgment, but he managed to hold his tongue. Glaring at me, he stood and stumbled away from the fire.

Now that the sun had set, twilight was turning everything gray, including the forest, where he entered the shadows and disappeared.

I shivered once he was gone, feeling exposed and anxious with an angry Vaade wandering out there in the dark somewhere behind me. Discreetly, I scooted my log closer to Koda when he stood to put another on the fire.

A few other Vaade stood to leave as well. Their faces were unreadable, but Koda didn't relax fully until they were gone, leaving us alone.

"Would you really have fought him?" I whispered, unable to help myself, though I stopped before I added *for me?*

A muscle twitched in his jaw. He kept his eyes on the fire as he shrugged, but didn't look at me.

It was growing steadily darker, lending an almost intimate feel to the moment. I considered asking Koda why he'd been gone the entire day, opening my mouth to do so, when a twig snapped.

It was so light that at first, I thought it came from the crackling fire.

Some instinct made me tense though, sensing an attack. *Is it Shem? Is he finally coming to rescue me?*

Koda had heard it too, swiveling to face the unknown sound.

In the split second that followed, I found myself worrying for him, hoping he'd run when he found himself outnumbered instead of trying to fight.

But it wasn't Shem.

It wasn't anyone from Jinn.

16

FOUR SNEERING VAADE MATERIALIZED in the dusk of the forest at our backs, hidden from the rest of the camp by the trees.

The inebriated Ahriman had come back with friends. "Stay out of this," he said when Koda stood, widening his stance in front of me. "Even the Dragon wants it gone. I put you down earlier today, and I'll do it again."

"Only because I let you," Koda said on a roar, lunging at the same time they did. He met Ahriman mid-air, crashing to the ground, rolling in a blur of fists.

I froze as the other three stalked toward me.

How could I face three?

Panicking, I circled the large fire, keeping it between us.

My mind raced.

I didn't know the woods beyond this spot and couldn't see far enough to travel. I could either shift and face them—three to one—or I could attempt to run…

They circled the fire after me.

Having seen how far Koda could leap, I knew they were toying with me. They could cross this fire in a heartbeat.

Growls came from behind them. A fist connected with flesh. *Oof,* the sound of air knocked out of lungs. Another groan, followed by a snarl. Koda's struggle didn't sound like it was ending anytime soon.

This was up to me.

Run first, I thought, backing toward the woods, not taking my eyes off the Vaade's sneering faces. *Duck behind a tree. Shift. Disappear.*

Would it work? Or would they be able to follow my trail of magic like Koda had?

The Vaade leading the group crouched to spring. I didn't have time for a better plan.

Without a second thought, I jumped over the bushes into the dark woods and ran, dodging dark silhouettes of trees as they rose before me.

A rough hand latched onto my wrist, throwing off my balance. I fell, taking the Vaade down with me.

Grappling wildly, I shrieked, "Let go!"

I felt it the moment my Gift took effect on him, even though I hadn't looked in his eyes, growing stronger in my terror. His hands and body pulled back, just long enough for me to scramble to my feet and run.

Sheer panic flooded my body.

I'd never been so out of control before.

Trembling hands turned into full body shudders, as I heard heavy breathing behind me. They were playing with me again, deliberately letting me run though they had the clear advantage. I stumbled.

Rocks bit into my knee, but I barely felt it, picking myself up and running on.

The last bit of fading sunlight hardly reached the forest floor. I should shift my eyes, but I was too frantic to focus, feeling branches rake through my hair, scraping across my skin, and ripping at Tehya's dress as I ran even harder, heart pumping.

I didn't get far.

A body slammed into mine from behind, and another hit me from the side a second later, knocking the air out of me as we hit the ground hard.

Hands wrapped around my neck.

My lungs burned as I tried to breath, but I couldn't think to shift or fight as I choked for air.

The other Vaade ground his hand into my wounded shoulder.

I opened my mouth to scream in agony, but no sound came out.

Unable to shift through the pain, I struggled weakly as another set of hands fell on my legs, stifling movement. The third Vaade hissed, "Finish it."

Struggling to breathe as my vision darkened, I choked out an anguished sob.

Then, the heavy weight on my body was gone.

My feet were freed next.

A roar of fury came from above me as someone crashed into the Vaade with his hands around my neck. I flung myself back, gasping, gulping down air,

THE SECRET CURSE

crawling away from the sounds of scuffling in the dark.

The only light now was the moon, barely reaching us through the trees.

My eyes darted wildly around, searching for more shadows, terrified more Vaade were coming. I bumped into a tree as I backed up and covered my mouth to stifle a scream. *It's just a tree. Get a hold of yourself, you've been in worse situations*, I lied to myself.

Trembling, I tried to shift. It wouldn't come. My body shook with silent sobs.

This is not *how I'm going to die.* With shaking hands, I felt for a low-hanging branch, and forced myself to climb, despite the burning in my shoulder.

More thuds sounded below along with heavy breathing and unearthly growls.

Then, a sickly crunch that sounded like a tree meeting a body, followed by silence.

I covered my mouth with my hand, squeezing my eyes shut, trying to stifle the sound of my breathing.

It had been three to one. The odds that Koda had won that fight weren't good.

They were coming for me.

I was only a few branches up. With the dim moonlight, I'd gotten stuck, unable to find another handhold.

I tried to shift again into a mouse or bird or bear or even adjust my eyes to have night vision—anything would've been better than nothing—but the ice in my veins had blocked my senses, leaving me completely vulnerable which only intensified my fear, creating an impossible cycle.

Below, a shadow in the shape of a large man moved along the ground, straight toward me. His footsteps were silent.

He was stalking me.

My head pounded from when the Vaade had pushed it into the ground, along with throbbing wounds all along the rest of my body.

When he stopped at the base of my tree, I held my breath.

"Come down, Jinni girl," an angry male voice growled.

I tried not to throw up.

A sigh came from below.

I pressed my face into the bark, not caring if it scratched me, as my arms circled the trunk. I refused to make killing me easier for him.

"Jezebel," the voice said, softer now.

My eyes flew open.

Shivering uncontrollably, I peeked down at the hulking shadow beneath me, trying to make out a face.

I couldn't, but with that one word, I *knew* who it was.

Koda.

"It's safe now," he added in a soothing tone. When his shape moved slightly, landing in a patch of moonlight, I realized he held out a hand. "You can sleep there if you want, but they won't be feeling very rational when they wake up. I'd prefer to go back to the smokehouse before I have to give them a second beating."

That got me moving.

Hurrying from one branch to another, they seemed farther apart than when I'd climbed up. Since I still hadn't managed to shift my eyesight, I slipped.

With a yelp, I fell the last few feet.

He caught me.

I wrapped my arms around his neck without thinking, dragging in a shuddering breath. He smelled like a mixture of warm bonfire and something I could only describe as *safe*.

When he set me on my feet, my legs gave out, too weak to stand. I sagged against him, embarrassed.

He held me without complaint. Quietly, he pulled me closer, tucking my head under his chin, and gently pressed my head to his chest.

I stiffened, but the sound of his steady heartbeat beneath my ear was strangely soothing. Relaxing slightly, I let myself stay where I was until the shaking subsided.

He still didn't pull back.

I knew I should, but I didn't want to.

"Thank you," I whispered into his chest finally, voice breaking.

A little moonlight touched his arm and then his face as he leaned back. It was impossible to read his expression in the dark, but I could've sworn his eyes slid over my face, stopping briefly on my lips, before continuing on. He seemed to catalog the many different scrapes as well as the evidence of tears where they'd trailed through the dirt on my cheeks.

Embarrassed, I pulled away enough to scrub at the dirt—and tears—with rough hands.

He still didn't let go.

My hands lowered until they landed on his chest, making my heart race again in an entirely different way. I dared to lift my gaze from them to his face.

His fingers tightened along my back, drawing me closer to him again.

All thought escaped me as his head dipped lower.

I tilted my chin up, lips parting.

A groan came from one of the nearby Vaade.

We stepped back as if we'd been caught, and thoughts of Shem flooded my mind. *What just happened?*

"We should go," Koda murmured. "I'll deal with them in the morning when they're thinking more clearly. Right now isn't the best time." He took my hand, as if he could tell that my eyesight wasn't up to par, and led me back in the direction of the camp.

THE SECRET CURSE

The bonfire was like a beacon. With every step closer, it whispered, *You're safe. You're safe. You're safe.*

But how long would that last?

Once we stepped into the light, the pain from my multiple injuries grew more intense as my adrenaline faded, changing from minor complaints to screaming protests. My ribs ached from a punch I'd barely registered and my arms and legs were covered in bloody cuts. Though my shoulder burned, the blistering ache around my neck where those hands had been was the worst, like a necklace of fire.

All of it left me feeling weak, fragile. Two things I *hated*.

My shifting had failed me—*I had failed*. I didn't want to think about it, but my confidence was severely shaken. I was no longer certain I could save myself if the Vaade decided to get rid of me. And, though I did my best to ignore the whisper in my mind, I was starting to wonder if Shem was going to save me after all.

17

I WALKED IN A daze until Koda stopped us at the longhouse, reaching for the door.

"What're you doing?" I hissed, pulling my hand out of his, sharply returning to the present.

"We need to dress your wounds," he replied calmly, opening the door. He held it for me, waiting.

"Can you go get what you need and come back?" my voice came out pleading. I didn't know how many Vaade were inside, I only knew that I did *not* want them to see me like this. Jinn did not show weakness. Not under any circumstances.

"No."

I glanced at the open door. Voices floated out from inside, talking, laughing, oblivious to our quiet debate. "It's just a few scratches," I told him, waving a hand through the air, trying not to wince when it pulled at my wounded shoulder, which I suspected might be bleeding again. "I don't need anything."

He grabbed the wrist of my uninjured arm as I tried to walk past him, tugging me back. "There's also food inside. You need to eat."

My stomach tried to betray me with a gurgle, but I cleared my throat loudly over it. "I'm not hungry."

THE SECRET CURSE

"Inside." He didn't give me a chance to argue again or let go as he stepped through the door.

Dragging my feet, I kept my eyes on his back. The now-familiar fear pumped through my veins as dozens of eyes turned our way and the room fell silent.

I must've looked worse than I thought.

Koda moved through the bunks along the walls to the center of the room, where every single log was taken, and at least two dozen more Vaade stood around the fire as well, all of them eating. Or at least, they had been, before we came in. Now there was a mixture of expressions: glares, curiosity, and confusion.

I tried to stop, tugging at his hand, but he pushed through the crowd, pulling me along with him and stopping in the center next to his sister, who stopped chewing at the sight of me.

"Up," Koda said to her.

His back was to me, but whatever expression was on his face made her cut off any arguments and silently stand.

He turned to me. "Sit." Again with the one word demands. When I saw the fury in his face, my eyes widened. I could see why Tehya hadn't protested but I still cleared my throat and tried, voice rasping a little, "I don't need to—"

"Now."

I sat.

And then I stopped breathing as he walked away and started digging through a trunk along the wall, leaving me in front of dozens of Vaade eyes that pinned me in place.

I expected to hear murmurs or gossip of some sort, but no one spoke as eyes darted between Koda and I. In the loud silence, we all heard Koda murmur for someone to go "take care of" the Vaade in the woods. "Lock them up for the night," he added to the men striding toward the door. "They need to cool off."

Distracted by their exit, I didn't notice at first how the nearby Vaade at the fire were staring at the bloody scratches along my bare arms and legs, or how Tehya's borrowed dress was now dirt-streaked and shredded.

I wrapped my arms around my body, trying and failing to cover the damage.

A few of those judgmental looks were pinned to my neck, where I could only imagine a cluster of bruises was forming.

When Tehya came back into my line of sight, she held an empty wooden bowl. Using the ladle in the large pot over the fire, she scooped a large helping of stew and held it out to her brother as he stalked back through the crowd with a handful of bandages and salve.

Instead of taking it, he gestured for her to give it to me, saying, "Eat."

"I'm not hungry." It wasn't true, but I'd happily go without a meal if it meant we could leave.

"*Eat*," he said again, in a tone that said he wouldn't take no for an answer.

I accepted the bowl from Tehya with a timid thank you, suddenly aware I was starving. Digging into the stew, I ignored the way it burned my tongue, eating as fast as possible.

This wasn't like the council or the castle or anywhere in Jinn, where I could pull on a cold mask of indifference and let them think nothing touched me. Here, I couldn't seem to hide anything.

Which meant they all saw me wince and gasp when Koda unexpectedly pulled a dangling piece of the dress away from my shoulder to see the wound.

"I'm fine," I forced out, willing him to let it go. *I don't want to look weak.*

"They need to see this," he said. But he wasn't really talking to me, I realized. His voice was raised, hard eyes scanning the room, landing on every single person there. "They need to see that you're human too."

"But I'm not." I whispered it without thinking, then cringed. I could see what he was trying to do, and I wasn't helping.

Koda met my eyes now. "You are in the way that counts."

I couldn't speak.

When he broke our gaze, I blinked, trying to orient myself. Warmth spread throughout my whole body. He was like no one I'd ever met before. I didn't want to think of Shem in this moment, but I couldn't help comparing the two.

I barely noticed when some of the Vaade quietly began returning to conversations, though eyes still drifted to us frequently.

"The shoulder needs stitches." Koda wasn't speaking to me, but to Tehya, who nodded.

I paled. "I'd rather not." Back home, we'd go to a Jinni healer for something like this. I'd never had someone put a needle through my skin before and didn't want to start now.

"It won't heal right without it," he answered simply, as he started to wash the wound in preparation.

Tehya brought him a needle and thread far too soon, and I started to tremble again at the sight. Pressing my lips together, I refused to shame myself in front of so many. I held in a squeak when he started, shutting my eyes tightly and breathing through the pain as he continued. Eyes watering, I tried to blink to stop the tears from escaping, but one trickled down my cheek. I kept my gaze on the floor, pressing my lips together, hoping no one would notice.

The stitches seemed to go on forever.

I was ready to break my vow to myself and beg Koda to stop when he finally tied a knot and cut the thread with his teeth.

When he went over the cuts along my arms and legs, first washing them, then covering them with yellow ointment from a jar, I barely felt any of it through the sledgehammer slamming into my shoulder with every heartbeat.

I held the empty bowl in my lap, eyelids drooping.

Hands slipped the bowl from mine.

I stiffened, sitting upright, wincing at the way that pulled the stitches in my

THE SECRET CURSE

shoulder.

A Vaade woman with warm green eyes and golden-brown hair met my gaze without malice. "More?"

I hesitated.

Koda was kneeling by my knees, carefully pulling out little bits of rocks that'd been embedded in my skin from one of my many falls. He nodded subtle encouragement.

Clearing my throat, I nodded too and murmured, "Please."

She filled the bowl to the brim and handed it back to me.

I ate it like it was my first, finally starting to feel full. Chewing my lip, I dared to look up from the food and Koda to find the woman in the crowd.

I tried not to shrink back when I found at least a dozen eyes still on me, quickly darting from one to the next until I found the green-eyed woman and made myself speak, though it came out quieter than I'd wanted it to. "Thank you."

She gave me a solemn nod, eyes lingering on me until I looked away.

"She's tougher than she looks," a Vaade man next to her said. His voice was a normal tone, but it felt like he was shouting after everyone else had stuck to whispers.

Wide-eyed, I could only stare at him. He was the first Vaade besides Koda and his sister who hadn't referred to me as an "it." That felt significant.

"You just can't handle pain, Yona," another man teased him with a laugh, causing a round of good-natured ribbing that finally took the attention off me. I drew in a deep breath for the first time in what felt like hours.

"Told you," Koda murmured as he finished wrapping my knee, giving me a meaningful look. He didn't elaborate, but he didn't need to.

They needed to see I wasn't the embodiment of evil.

But what if I was?

I couldn't hold Koda's gaze, looking down at my hands instead. I was still planning to end this so-called covenant and escape, one way or another. I just felt a bit more guilty about it now.

The lighter mood around the fire was infectious. Someone began a story about the first man's hunt as a boy and how he'd somehow shot himself in the foot. They mimicked how he'd carried on, though even I could tell it was exaggerated, prompting a lot of laughter and more teasing at his expense. Koda even joined in a few times as he got a bowl for himself and finally ate his dinner. When a man offered to let him take the seat beside me, Koda shook his head, settling himself cross-legged on the floor between us instead.

I didn't realize I was staring at the back of his head until Tehya quietly cleared her throat behind me. Flushing, I looked away, eyes catching on one laughing Vaade after another.

"Let's get you another dress," she said, bringing me back to the same bed and giving me a chance to change yet again. The new dress fell a little past my knees, with sleeves this time, and fancier needlework. Gripping the discarded dress and lifting one of the ripped pieces from the shoulder, Tehya's face darkened dangerously. "I'm going to kick their next child out of them," she growled to herself. But she tossed the ruined dress onto the bed without another thought, leading us back to the fire.

I met Koda's eyes as we returned.

His outline grew blurry.

I blinked, hoping he hadn't noticed the tears.

Koda didn't realize—or maybe he was smarter than I gave him credit for, and he knew *exactly* what he was doing—but having me here had not only caused the Vaade to see me differently.

It'd also changed the way I saw *them*.

My throat was tight. A mother tickled her little son who giggled, and the father tucked both of them into his lap with a smile. It would sound ridiculous if I said it aloud, because of course, it was obvious, but it still felt like a fresh revelation that meant something new: *They're people too.*

18

"COME," KODA SAID AFTER we'd sat by the fire for another hour or so. It wasn't that late, but my body swayed as I sat on the log, begging for sleep. I didn't argue with him.

We wove through the Vaade as we left, and I got a lump in my throat each time one of them gave me a respectful nod. Five Vaade men joined us without Koda saying a word. Cool air hit my face as we stepped out of the longhouse, making me more alert. But there was no sign of the Vaade who'd attacked us earlier. Only thousands of cheerful stars winking down at us, lighting our way. The moon had risen high in the sky, making the smokehouse visible as we approached.

The Vaade man who'd first spoken to me, Yona, held a hand up when we reached it. "I'll go first." Stepping inside, he shuffled around briefly before he popped back out. "It's empty."

Koda nodded, waving me inside.

"We'll make sure Ahriman doesn't bother you tonight," he said, clapping a hand on Koda's back as he passed.

Koda clasped the man's shoulder, murmuring, "Thank you, Yona."

And then he closed the door behind him, leaving us alone for the first time since the attack.

My lips tingled as my traitorous body remembered our almost kiss. We were close enough now that he would only need to reach out an arm to pull me to him again. We stood there for a long moment. *What's wrong with me?* I turned to sit on the furs stretched out along the floor from the night before, hoping that putting my back to him would dissolve the intensity of the moment. I tried to sort through the multitude of feelings I hardly recognized. *Why do I still want him to kiss me?*

Clearing my throat, I faced him, planning to say a formal thank you and cut off anything further.

He'd already lain down. It felt odd to talk to him from above, so after hesitating, I stretched out too, pillowing my hands under my head with a yawn.

Exhaustion stole over me. When I blinked my eyes open again, I found his face a few feet from mine, staring openly. It felt intimate to be laying here next to him. But also, if I were willing to admit it to myself, it felt safe. My body ached but not in the sharp, unbearable way it had earlier. Every scratch and bruise now reminded me of him and the gentle way he'd taken care of me.

Koda cleared his throat. "If you ever find yourself in a situation like that again, aim for the throat." He gestured toward his chin, and his throat bobbed as he swallowed. "That's the one place our skin is vulnerable."

I nodded.

He was trusting me.

That was information I could use against *him*, but he shared it anyway.

Why did that upset me more?

I cleared my throat, which seemed loud in the silence, trying to find the nerve to speak. "You didn't have to do that," I whispered.

His voice was low as well, but he had a slight smile. "Do what?"

I frowned, not wanting him to make light of it. If I said *feed me*, I already knew him well enough to know he'd brush it off with "everyone needs to eat," and if I mentioned my wounds, he'd have an excuse for that kindness as well.

So instead, I just said one word: "Care."

His smile faded as he grew serious.

For a minute he didn't seem like he was going to respond. Flipping onto his back, he put his hands behind his head, making the powerful muscles in his arms grow even more defined. "I've never liked bullies," he said finally.

"Me either." Rolling onto my back as well, I stared at the wooden ceiling in the lantern light. I was fairly confident he was talking about his father, which made me think of my own. I should've left it alone. But part of me resonated with his words so much that I was speaking before I fully realized it. "I hate that bullies force you to either be the victim or become one of them. There's no other choice." I'd turned my father into a lizard and left him alone and defenseless for predators to find… But he would've done the same to me.

"You sound like you have experience."

Wrapped up in the memories, I'd almost forgotten Koda was there.

"Is that really the only option?" he added lightly when I didn't say anything else. "I hope you're not talking about me."

My lips twitched, wanting to smile. "If there's a third option," I said, still looking at the ceiling. "Then that person isn't really a bully at all, are they?"

We let the silence stretch comfortably.

But Koda must've been contemplating my words, because just as I was about to drift off, he murmured, "I still think there's a third option."

Yawning, I turned on my side to face him, waiting.

"I don't abuse my power the way he does." He spoke more to himself than to me, still laying on his back. "But I *did* learn to fight back."

I nodded, unsure how to answer.

He seemed to be waiting for my thoughts, twisting his head to stare at me, capturing my gaze.

"I... learned that as well," I replied softly, knowing that wasn't fully true. I hadn't chosen the third option, to become better than my father. I'd simply become him.

Not wanting to think about past mistakes I couldn't change, even if I wanted to, I thought of Koda's father instead. "What did he say to you today that made Tehya so upset?" *And you?* I added silently.

He turned back to the ceiling again. Maybe I'd pushed him too far.

Closing my eyes, I tried to settle in for another long night when he unexpectedly answered. "My father refuses to reconsider the covenant."

I snuck a glance at him from beneath my eyelashes. That was hardly a revelation. There had to be more to it.

Waiting, I was rewarded for my patience when he let out a long sigh. "I tried to fight back today, but I failed."

"How so?"

"I told him I'd take Tehya and leave. He said he'd lead a hunting party and find us before we reached the mountains."

Thinking back to when Koda had tracked me, I could only imagine they'd be extremely effective. Nodding, I held back from answering, sensing there was more.

Koda hesitated, still not meeting my gaze. "Then I told him I'd fight him for leadership of our people."

Though I tried to hold in a gasp, his sharp hearing still caught the catch in my breath. Meeting my wide eyes, he smiled, though it lacked any humor. "It was one of those times where your Jinni secrecy would've been the smarter choice."

I couldn't help myself. "What did he do?"

"His men detained me until sundown. It was his way of showing me I didn't have a chance. That they'll follow him over me, no matter what."

Suddenly his absence the entire day made a lot more sense. Still, I frowned. "I don't understand. I *saw* how everyone responded to you at dinner. They adore you. How can your father's control compare to that?"

"Is that a compliment from a Jinni?" he teased.

I flushed. "It was an obvious criticism of your father. That's all."

When he continued smirking, I tried to change the subject. "What made you decide to stand up to your father today anyway, when you haven't before?"

His expression closed. "Nothing."

The way he was hiding something from me for what might be the first time made me shiver, despite the heat of the smokehouse at my back. "There's something you're not telling me."

Koda's lips pressed together firmly. He crossed his arms and closed his eyes, drawing a clear end to our conversation.

Sitting up on one elbow, I stared down at him, growing more concerned, trying to puzzle it out. "When the Dragon first introduced the idea of the covenant, you were upset, but not enough to fight him."

Eyes closed, Koda grunted. "Go to sleep."

Undeterred, I continued thinking out loud, watching his face closely for a reaction. "The covenant is supposed to create a truce between our people, right?" I didn't need him to answer that. "I barely know your kind, but I've already seen enough of your father to know that he would never want to be mere equals with the Jinn."

Though the wrinkles in Koda's forehead were already there and he didn't move a muscle, an icy chill spread over me. I somehow *knew* I was right—the Dragon had a hidden agenda. Once again, I remembered Koda's words from when we'd met. *We don't want peace.*

In a hushed tone, I demanded, "What's he going to do?"

Koda refused to acknowledge me. His eyes remained closed.

Taking a deep breath, I did something I couldn't believe I dared to do: I poked him.

Technically, I poked his arm, and a small part of me noted how firm his muscles were underneath my touch, like poking a rock.

He sat up lightning fast, making me flinch back from a lifetime of habit.

Though he scowled at me, something flickered across his face, and he didn't move closer. "You're intentionally provoking me in your position?" he growled. "Do you think that's wise?"

It wasn't.

Not at all. And yet, I couldn't bring myself to feel worried. "You wouldn't hurt me," I murmured.

Those sunset eyes narrowed, pinning me in place. He didn't agree. But he didn't disagree either.

"Tell me," I asked again, softer.

Rubbing his forehead, he shook his head. "You're my sworn enemy."

I waved a hand at the tiny wooden shack we were in. "Who am I going to

THE SECRET CURSE

tell?" I made my tone incredulous, as if I'd completely given up hope of escaping. "I'm your prisoner until the covenant is completed, remember?" At least, I sincerely hoped they'd let me go if it came to that. "By then, it'll be too late for me to do anything."

When Koda still hesitated, I leaned forward, daring to touch his arm again, waiting until he looked up. I made sure to pull my hand away before I spoke so he'd know I wasn't trying to use my Gift this time. "We both want to stop this covenant, Koda." As I said his name for the first time, something shifted between us, at least for me. I wasn't acting anymore. I meant what I said.

In the softest whisper, in case any nearby Vaade were trying to listen in, I added, "Remember, we're on the same side."

Slowly, he faced me, imitating my posture, one hand cradling his head and the other resting on the furs between us, only a few fingers away from mine.

"What was it you'd said before about keeping secrets?" I tapped my lip as if trying to remember. "Oh yes, it was something about how you get in your own way?"

His lips curved into a wry smile. "You're very persistent, Jinni girl."

"Jezebel," I reminded him absently. "And I'm only just beginning."

He sighed, already worn down. "It's a complicated story."

"I'm listening." I propped both hands under my chin.

"My father has a secondary spell that he plans to add to the covenant," he said hesitantly. "It will come after the weakening begins."

I sat up abruptly, with a rising sense of dread. "What kind of spell?"

"It's a forbidden forgetting spell."

A rush of anxiety made my heart pump faster. Spells in Jinn were rarely forbidden unless they affected hundreds—or more often thousands—of lives. "How does it work?"

"It was described as a mixture between ignorance and withering… It erases memories from existence and somehow fills in the hole left behind until the absence is no longer noticeable."

With each word, icy fear stole over me.

"You're saying the covenant—which is binding for both the leaders and their entire people—would take away all Jinni Gifts and Vaade strengths… And then we'd just *forget* that it happened?"

Koda raised himself to a sitting position as well, crossing his legs. He dipped his head in a slow nod.

My heart sank. This was far worse than I'd imagined. Every Jinni under Shem's reign would lose their Gifts *and* their memories of them.

Including me.

Koda couldn't meet my eyes.

"That's not just any spell," I whispered, lifting a trembling hand to my mouth and shaking my head. "That's a *curse*."

19

"IT DOESN'T MAKE ANY sense," I murmured, mostly to myself. "The Dragon wouldn't do that to his own people—" Raising my eyes back to Koda, I narrowed them. "Is it temporary?" Maybe his father planned to ambush Shem and the Jinn, attacking the marriage party while they were weakened? But that didn't make sense either, because the Vaade would be weakened as well…

"In this case, the curse would be anchored to the covenant, meaning it would remain in place until the covenant is completed." He fidgeted, touching the dragon tooth around his neck with one hand and flexing the fingers of the other, his eyes darting around the room, never settling in one place.

It put a pit in my stomach.

"You're a bad liar," I said in a low voice.

"It's not a lie," he insisted, forcing his body into stillness. But his eyes still flitted around us.

Staring at him as he glanced at me then away for the third time, I shook my head. "Fine, maybe you're not lying. But you *are* keeping a secret."

When he didn't argue, I pressed my back into the wall, needing the support, eyes closing briefly as I tilted my head back. "Tell me," I whispered, afraid to hear the answer.

He pressed his lips together, still refusing, but it didn't matter. My mind had

THE SECRET CURSE

already begun to puzzle it out. "The Dragon doesn't plan to *complete* the covenant, does he?"

Somehow, he wanted to leave the Jinn cursed.

A breath whooshed out of Koda, almost as if he were relieved I'd figured it out. He nodded, confirming it.

We'd be at their mercy.

Completely vulnerable.

Shock washed over me. The Vaade weren't trying to make *peace* with the Jinn. They were trying to permanently weaken our entire race, making us easy prey for them so they could violently conquer our world. Without a completed covenant, there'd be no magical truce protecting both sides. The Vaade could attack the weak and confused Jinn with nothing to stop them.

My people would never see it coming. *Shem would be ambushed.*

Another realization hit me. "Your father added the forgetting spell so that we'd never figure out what happened," I whispered, lifting a trembling hand to my mouth as I shook my head. "Koda, you have to stop this. He'll kill everyone."

Koda's face was grim as he ground out. "Not kill them."

Though he still held back the details, he made it easy to read between the lines. They'd make us their slaves. We'd be crushed underneath their heel and too weak to stop them.

"We have to stop it," I repeated, clasping my hands in front of me, pleading. "We *have* to!"

Rubbing his face with both hands before dropping them, Koda stared at me with an unreadable expression. "We can't. My father never backs down. And he never loses."

He'd already fought with his father over this.

"There's always a first time."

"No. There isn't." I could tell he fully believed that. "The Dragon always gets his way."

I sighed. "At least help me understand how the spell works?" The wooden walls scratched my bare arms as I scooted away from it toward him. "If it can be temporary, then memories and abilities aren't lost forever, right? They're just…" I tried to remember the word he'd used. "Suppressed somehow?"

Nervous energy made me want to pace. I almost stood, but I'd barely be able to take two steps in this space before hitting the opposite wall. Instead, I fidgeted with the furs, stroking them thoughtfully. "How fast does it take effect?"

"It's a bit slower than the weakening, but not by much."

It felt like Koda was still trying to hold something back with these short answers. But I could infer what he meant. "There won't be time for Shem or anyone else to react before it's too late."

He hesitated, then nodded.

I leaned forward on my knees and asked the most important question. "How is your father going to sneak it into the covenant spell without Shem and the council noticing?"

"It doesn't matter." He waved that away as if the complete incapacitation of my people was a minor inconvenience. "The curse is just one small change to the covenant rituals. The only way to stop it would be to stop the covenant itself."

"But if we can't, how would the curse be added?" I pressed. *And how can I warn the prince before it is?*

Koda clearly didn't see this secondary spell as a priority the way I did, but if Shem somehow ended up going through with the covenant in the end, I needed to be absolutely certain this curse wouldn't be placed on *me*.

Somehow, I had to convince Koda to let his guard down and tell me. "If your father couldn't weave in the curse, he'd be less inclined to do the covenant, right?"

Rubbing the stubble along his chin, Koda tilted his head, dragging out, "Right."

"Then that's our answer," I declared. We'd finally found a solution. "We'll find a way to prevent the curse. Tell me how he's planning to include it."

"Why should I trust a Jinni to help?" he asked in a flat voice, crossing his arms. "Everyone knows the Jinn are born liars."

I scowled, but couldn't argue with the generalization. My entire life confirmed it.

Before I could come up with an answer, he leaned closer, adding in a low growl, "Don't think you've fooled me for a second. I know you're still planning to escape." With a smirk, he added, "At least, you'll *try*."

I paled but held his gaze. "It didn't work out very well for me the first time, did it?" But of course, he was right, and he knew it.

"Besides," I added more truthfully, "I'm not going anywhere until I learn how to stop this covenant."

"No," he argued. "You're not leaving unless we let you." Leaning against the closed door, he casually draped one arm over a bent knee and stretched out his other leg right beside me, as if to remind me of our positions. Of the fact that he could do whatever he wanted.

I glanced at it pointedly, raising one brow. "Is that so?" This wasn't helping my cause. I sighed. "If you're so certain you'd catch me, then you have nothing to worry about, do you?" I didn't give him time to answer, because we were focusing on the wrong thing. "The truth is, whether I'm here or not doesn't matter. *If* I tried to leave, it wouldn't be to go home."

It was hard to hold his gaze. I didn't like lying to him.

"Think about it," I added as sincerely as possible. "The prince has abandoned me, along with the royal family. Why would I go back to them after that?" A little pinch in my chest made me wince at the words because there was some unfortunate truth to them. But Shem hadn't truly abandoned me, I reminded myself. He was protecting his people while looking for a solution to our problem.

THE SECRET CURSE

He would rescue me before the day of the covenant came. Hopefully sooner.

Though I hid my hurt quickly, wishing Koda hadn't seen it, he tilted his head, as if reconsidering.

"You don't have to tell me everything," I said, hoping to tip him over the edge into finally sharing. "Just what's relevant for us to find a way to stop it. Think about it." My gestures grew wilder along with my excitement. "If the curse is taken out of play, your father won't want the covenant anymore. If he doesn't want it, he'll find a reason to back out. And if he backs out, your sister doesn't have to marry the prince of Jinn. Everyone wins."

Koda gave me an appraising look. "You're good at making your case, Jinni girl. Is this how you convinced the prince to marry you?"

I flushed angrily, pulling my shoulders back and lifting my chin. "You think whatever you want—"

"I meant no offense," he interrupted, holding up both hands, giving me a crooked smile. "I just meant you make a good argument."

"There are better ways to say it," I mumbled, crossing my arms and avoiding his eyes. The insinuation bothered me more than usual, maybe because he knew about the rumors.

"Fine." He changed the subject. "I'll tell you what I know about the curse, but it's not much."

He reached across the space between us and took my hand.

I tensed.

All of my senses fixated on my tingling fingers.

"The Vaade marriages are very similar to human marriages," he began, face solemn. "The two parties each bring a ring for the other." He made a circle in my palm almost unconsciously. "And in the covenant, as you know, these rings are imbued with magic. When placed on a finger, the enchantment begins. But"—he spread out my fingers, placing them across his palm—"the reaction is different depending on which finger they're placed on."

I swallowed, trying to focus on his words instead of his warm hand beneath mine.

Koda touched my pointer finger. "Mind." He moved to my middle finger. "Body." And finally, he stroked my ring finger. "Soul." He cleared his throat after a moment and pulled back, letting my hand fall to my knee. "When placed on a specific finger, the rings will pull those elements out. In weddings, we place rings on the soul finger because it draws out the souls and binds them together."

I tried to breathe normally.

My hand still tingled.

"The covenant is designed to make a soul connection," I whispered, recognizing bits and pieces of the spell's design.

He hesitated, then softly touched my ring finger again. "A typical human marriage would only involve this one element. But the covenant requires vulnerability as proof before the rings will accept the spell."

"Vulnerability?" I repeated stupidly.

"This finger," he said, pointing to my middle finger. "Is connected to the body. It pulls out a different connection. In this case, our physical strengths and your Gifts."

I glanced down at my fingers. "Where does the curse come into play?"

Koda's hand moved to my first finger, barely grazing it. "This finger is connected to the mind."

Mind, body, soul.

"The first finger triggers the curse?" I was afraid to hear his answer. It was so simple. Jinn didn't wear wedding rings and had little to no understanding of human—or Vaade—customs. If they placed the ring on the first finger instead of the third, Shem would never see it coming.

Koda nodded.

As he sat back, head bowed, he murmured, "It acts slower. There are thousands upon thousands more memories to erase than there are abilities. But after a day... maybe two, everything surrounding Jinni magic—including any knowledge of it—will be erased."

"Everything?" I imagined forgetting I was a Jinni... What I could do... My entire world would be turned upside down. Again.

"Like I told you," Koda said finally, sounding resigned. "We can't stop this 'curse' as you call it, because the spell is built into the rings. My father will present it as a necessary part of the covenant."

I didn't know how to argue.

He was right.

We'd lose our Gifts and never know what we were missing. The Vaade would overpower the Jinn without a fight.

Silence fell over us.

I laid down eventually, hoping fresh ideas would come to me after some rest.

Koda blew out the lantern.

His breaths evened out almost immediately.

But I couldn't sleep.

I couldn't stop thinking about what he'd said.

Stopping the curse was impossible.

Rolling over for the thousandth time, half-dreaming about the Dragon shackling Shem with this curse, my body tensed as if the curse was already happening and settling onto my own body.

A heavy arm landed across my upper body, startling me fully awake.

Koda mumbled behind me, "Go to sleep."

"I *was* asleep," I complained, trying to roll out from under his grip.

He held me tighter, which naturally dragged our bodies closer.

I froze.

THE SECRET CURSE

Warm breath blew softly on my neck.

Shivering, I felt more awake than ever.

"Go... to... sleep..." he slurred again, as if he could feel my tension.

Despite our conversation, the weight of his arm across mine and the rise and fall of his chest behind me was oddly soothing. I wanted to both push him away and scoot closer, which drew out confusing feelings. Having this new all-consuming focus helped me finally stop thinking about all my other concerns, which then lulled me slowly and unexpectedly to sleep.

The last thought I had was that when I escaped—hopefully soon now that I'd finally unraveled the secrets of the covenant curse—I had perfect evidence to stop Shem from agreeing to the false truce. On top of that, we could use my knowledge of Koda and his father being on the edge of a potential civil war to our advantage. I drifted off with a confusing sense of regret at the thought of betraying Koda.

20

TEHYA'S GROUCHY MUTTERING IN the open door of the smokehouse woke me. Beside me was an empty fur blanket. Koda must've slipped out while I slept.

My disappointment irritated me. I scowled at Tehya as I exited the smokehouse.

"Sit," she said without bothering to greet me, gesturing toward a nearby log. "Koda wants me to check your bandages."

"They're fine." I brushed off her concern. Most of my scrapes were healing well, and the wound on my shoulder only throbbed dully. Honestly, the yellowroot seemed to speed the healing. I could ignore the occasional aches.

She smacked the back of my head.

"Ow!" I yelped. "What was that for?"

"It's like you don't even know how to be a prisoner," she mocked me, rolling her eyes and giving me a push toward the log. "Go. You're not a princess here."

"I'm not a princess anywhere," I muttered, but I did what I was told. "You're going to be the new princess, remember?"

Tehya glanced around, making sure no one was nearby. "That could still change." Her tone was flat and uninterested but her eyes latched onto mine, saying more. *She's desperate enough to come to me for help.*

"I don't know how," I replied as she slowly unraveled the bandage around my shoulder. But my eyes said, *Tell me how?* Turning away, I focused on the forest, as if I couldn't care less about this conversation.

Just as casually, Tehya replied, "Our spies say the prince hasn't officially broken off his engagement with you."

"What?" I forgot about staring aimlessly at the woods, spinning to face her. Was she trying to secretly give me hope or antagonize me? Whatever her intentions, it accomplished a little of both.

She unwrapped my shoulder with a firm grip, and I hissed in pain. She wasn't as gentle as Koda. "They haven't even revealed that you're gone," she continued. "Probably to avoid humiliation."

I winced at both the description and the way she rubbed that familiar yellow paste into the wound.

"My father thinks the prince is still hoping to get out of the covenant. It looks like the Jinn are keeping it hushed until they can't anymore."

"Oh, he's definitely hoping to get out of it," I replied scornfully, the way any Vaade would expect me to. Inwardly, though, I didn't know how to process the news. Was it as straightforward as Tehya said? Or was there more to it?

While Tehya finished working on my arm and wrapped a new, clean bandage around it, I closed my eyes and tried to imagine the scene.

Shem's parents seated on the throne, looking down on their son as they demanded that he think of his people first and marry the Vaade girl for the sake of the truce. But Shem yelled back that he was already engaged to a girl he loved and wouldn't abandon her.

"Done," Tehya said, breaking me out of my trance. I sighed.

I'd never seen Shem yell at his parents. Or do something for himself over his people, come to think of it.

My plans hadn't changed. Now that I finally understood the covenant, it was time to escape. And I no longer had the option to quietly bide my time, expecting Shem to swoop in and rescue me. Though I couldn't fully shake that hope, a growing part of me wondered if he was trying to save me at all.

I brushed off my borrowed skirt as I stood, trying to brush away the painful thoughts. I'd saved myself before and I could do it again—I still had time. How many days had I been here? Three? Four? I was losing track. But Shem had negotiated for two weeks.

"How long before the wound will be healed enough to move it without pain?" I asked Tehya as she led the way toward the outdoor bonfire where we'd spent most of the previous day.

Narrowing her eyes at me, Tehya shook her head. "Not before the covenant, if that's what you're asking."

I tried not to react, which ended up being a reaction of its own. These blunt discussions with the Vaade continued to throw me off balance.

"A little more than two weeks then?" I managed to say after a slightly too long pause.

"At least."

I hoped she was exaggerating. I'd give it a few more days and then it'd have to be good enough. In the meantime, I'd prepare.

Groaning at my expression, though I could've sworn my face was blank, she veered sharply toward the longhouse closest to the fire. "Here." She waved for me to join her, putting her arm above her head as she leaned into the wall. "If you're determined to use it sooner, here are some stretches that will help."

I winced as I imitated her, but held the stretch, memorizing it and all the others she showed me after that.

At meals I could start to slip food into the deep pockets of my borrowed dress—nothing too perishable at first. Dried meat mostly, though I planned to start supplementing with bread and fruit. Though the bread might dry out and fruit could go bad, hopefully they both might still be edible if it took me a few days of searching to find the daleth on the other side of the mountains.

When we entered the longhouse for breakfast and I spotted Koda by the fire, I flushed, focusing on other Vaade to avoid thinking about how I'd accidentally ended up nestling into him while sleeping.

He could've teased me, but he didn't. After we ate, he offered to take me hunting. As we left camp for the first time in days, taking a beaten path to the stream to fill the waterskins, I caught a flash of something almost white through the trees. It was too high to be a deer, too dark to be a cloud. "What's that?"

"Nothing important." Koda didn't stop moving.

I veered off the path, heading directly toward the movement. It was definitely fur... multiple furs even? In the air?

Voices came from the clearing ahead, drawing me on.

"What're you doing?" Koda hissed in my ear, as he caught up to me.

"You're hiding something." I slowed a bit as we drew close, lowering my voice as I challenged him, "I thought you said only the foolish Jinni kept secrets?"

"It's... not a secret," he ground out, but pulled me back before I could step into the clearing. Obviously, it was. The Vaade were calling loudly to each other as they set up... tents?

A dozen or so Vaade were constructing three tents out of furs sewn together, one much larger than the others. "Are more Vaade coming?" I whispered. Thankfully the Vaade were too loud to notice us. "Why aren't you setting them up in camp?"

"It's for your people," Koda said on a long sigh, rubbing a hand over his face.

I raised a brow.

"For the covenant," he added reluctantly.

That immediately ruined my mood. "They're planning to come here?"

THE SECRET CURSE

"They don't want to, but my father is making it a requirement."

"They're still in negotiations?" I supposed that was good, but it was an uncomfortable reminder that I needed to make my escape, sooner rather than later.

"They are." Koda shrugged. "But the Dragon always gets what he wants."

I snorted.

When he tugged at my arm again, I let him pull me away, thankful for the distraction of the hunt.

We returned to the stream and continued along the path until Koda deemed us a suitable distance from the camp.

He shushed me for the tenth time not much later. "Your stomping around is scaring away the game."

Rolling my eyes, I shifted into a cat, padding along on soft, silent footpads.

He grinned and shook his head.

A soft purr of contentment rumbled through me at the sense of freedom. Back home, even if Shem and I had been alone, I'd never have used my Gifts so casually.

Each day, though I kept an eye out for the Vaade who'd attacked me, they didn't show their faces. Between Tehya and the broad daylight, I wasn't terribly worried, but I paid attention just in case. When I asked Koda about it, he told me the Dragon kept them busy from sunup to sundown working on the tents and other preparations for the wedding.

I didn't ask anything further.

After what felt like weeks working on my first basket—though, in reality, it'd only been a few days—I finally finished. The weave was loose in some places and tight in others, twisting the smooth sides into lumps, but I still admired it proudly.

"Can I try making a bag like yours?" I asked Tehya after I'd shown her my basket.

Sighing as if I'd asked for something unreasonable like being allowed to go home, she sat down to teach me nonetheless.

I'd use it to hold all the food I'd been saving.

One afternoon, someone left an empty waterskin unattended, and I pocketed it when Tehya wasn't looking.

That night, I added it to my stash of food beneath the furs once Koda blew out the candle in the smokehouse and his breathing evened out.

The small knife was my best addition, though.

Late in the afternoon, the day before I planned to leave, Koda brought me inside the longhouse to get more yellowroot for my wound, but someone followed us in, calling his name. "Message for you," the Vaade said, eyes darting between Koda and I. "Not for Jinni ears."

I didn't recognize him, but this had happened on and off all week.

Though I was curious, I rolled my eyes as if I couldn't care less, moving toward the empty circle in the center of the room where the cookfire was banked.

"I'll be right back," Koda called to me, following the other man toward the door. Over his shoulder he added, "*Don't go anywhere.*"

I heard the insinuation. If I tried to repeat my last escape, he'd be ready.

As if I'd be foolish enough to run when he was expecting it.

That didn't stop me from snooping through the Vaade's things while he was outside, however.

Some bunks only had blankets, while others held random items like clothing or furs. A knife caught my eye. Glancing around to make sure the longhouse was still empty, I snatched the small knife off the bed and stuffed it in my pocket.

"I saw that," a high-pitched voice spoke from one of the beds.

I whirled around.

A little boy sat up in a bed, one row down.

"Saw what?" I said with a smile, peeking past him at the door. Koda would be back any second. Slowly, I strolled toward the boy.

He jumped up into a crouch on the bed.

He was going to run.

"It's okay," I attempted to soothe him with the full weight of my Gift, holding his gaze.

Hesitating, he was still just long enough for me to reach him and touch his arm.

"Don't be afraid." I held my smile and imagined my Gift pouring off me in waves, hoping his young mind was malleable enough to bend to my will. "You didn't see anything, did you?"

His little forehead wrinkled. "I—" He blinked, then shook his head, blinking again.

The voices outside grew louder. Koda was about to come back.

"Tell me you saw nothing," I pushed, hoping it was the right choice.

The familiar blank look spread across his face. "I saw nothing," he repeated.

"Good," I said as the door swung open, giving him another relieved smile. Softly, I added, "Go back to sleep."

As he collected the yellowroot, Koda had me sit by the light of the cookfire to help me with my bandages. He nodded toward the little boy. "Making friends?"

I felt the weight of the knife in my pocket. "Something like that."

When he pulled my bandages back, I distracted him by pretending it hurt.

I didn't get a chance to hide the knife throughout the rest of the afternoon.

Sitting by the cozy evening cookfire inside the longhouse that night, with Vaade all around, I tried to ignore the hidden weapon in my pocket as they laughed and told stories, allowing me to be a part of it.

I joined in laughing in all the right places, but Koda gave me an odd look that told me he'd noticed my mood.

I shook my head when he raised a brow.

THE SECRET CURSE

He wouldn't understand.

It'd hit me, as I sat beside the fire soaking in the warmth and company, that *this* was the sense of home and family that I should've had growing up. What I'd always been missing, even if I'd never had a name for it before.

I thought of my chilly room back at the castle where I spent most nights alone.

Uncomfortable, I shook my head, trying to rid myself of the comparison.

I stood, silently gesturing to Tehya and Koda that I needed to stretch. Since Tehya had shown me the exercises to speed healing in my arm, I'd done them faithfully every morning, noon, and night.

They nodded, not bothering to follow.

I moved to the back wall alone. Pressing my whole arm against the wood, I gently turned the rest of my body back toward the fire, feeling the gentle pull in the muscles.

Glancing at Koda and Tehya, I bit my lip. Neither watched me. I'd spent the last week being the ideal prisoner, doing everything they asked, staying in sight, always announcing before I did anything too startling.

They'd let their guard down.

It was exactly what I'd hoped for.

Turning my back on the room, I squeezed my eyes shut, tipping my head forward, trying to force my rebellious heart into submission.

Tomorrow, I'd escape.

As I did the stretch a second time for good measure, my free hand lightly brushed along the pocket where the knife lay.

The young Vaade boy hadn't said a word about it.

My other pocket held an apple and some extra cornbread I'd slipped in a few minutes ago when no one was looking.

Lifting my arm straight above my head, I leaned into the wall, completing the final stretch.

My shoulder barely pinched anymore. The skin beneath the stitches had changed from a raw wound with inflamed redness all around it to a mellow pink line.

Yawning, I glanced over the fire at Koda. At the sight, he stood, bidding everyone goodnight, heading toward me. A few of the Vaade waved at me as well, and I shyly nodded back. I wished for the thousandth time that I didn't have to deceive them. Or Koda.

Pushing through the door, I led the way outside, breathing in the fresh, cool night air. I kept my eyes on our feet as we walked. It wasn't just the deception that bothered me. After experiencing the warmth of the Vaade for a full week now, I finally admitted it to myself.

I wanted to stay.

Koda and I didn't speak on the way to the smokehouse.

There was an odd tension between us.

Maybe I was imagining it. Or maybe it was all on my end.

But I couldn't think of anything to say that wouldn't sound like a goodbye.

As we stepped inside, he didn't say anything either.

It didn't matter if I wanted to stay here. It wasn't an option. Steeling myself against the conflicting desires, I reminded myself of the reasons I needed to leave:

I'm a Jinni among Vaade.

I don't belong here and never will.

They might be kind to me, but that doesn't mean I have a home here.

The castle is my home.

More importantly, Shem is my betrothed—I love him.

I barely know Koda.

I didn't know why I felt the need to add that last part, but it irritated me enough that I lay down without another word, putting my back to Koda.

He blew out the candle, and the room settled into darkness and quiet breaths. Crickets chirped outside.

I listened to soft scuffling as he laid down and got comfortable. I counted to a hundred, and then did so a second time before I slowly lifted the furs next to me, revealing the soft bag I'd woven with Tehya's help. It was long and skinny, with a rough flap over the top, and tomorrow I hoped to learn how to weave a thin handle which would allow me to turn it into a bag I could throw over my shoulder.

Quietly, I slipped the apple, cornbread, and my new knife into the makeshift storage space and replaced the furs over it.

With that done, I tried to slow my rapid heartbeat so Koda wouldn't hear the anxiety in my breathing.

Eyes closed, I listened for his usual soft snore.

I didn't hear it.

Tensing, I tried to keep my breathing even, but in the silence, the hitch was audible.

"Don't let me stop you," Koda's deep voice rumbled in the dark, sending my pulse racing. "We can turn the light back on if that'd make it easier."

"What?" My voice came out breathless, and I cursed inwardly.

A flicker of flame returned as he lit the candle.

I forced myself to meet Koda's gaze. If only I could get my traitorous heartbeat to slow. It thundered in my ears, and I knew he heard it too.

"Are we pretending I can't smell the food supply you're keeping here?" he murmured. "For when you plan to leave?"

I coughed. "I don't know what you mean. Sometimes I keep extra food for when I get hungry at night, but that's hardly a supply."

"Is that what it would look like if I took out the bag you've been working on?" he asked, pointing directly at the corner where I'd hidden it.

My stomach sank. If he knew what and where it was, he'd already seen it.

THE SECRET CURSE

He must've come in here while I was with Tehya and found it.

He waited, but I was out of excuses, and we both knew it.

Another long silence passed as we stared at each other.

Koda spoke first. "What if you stayed?"

"You mean... after the covenant?"

He nodded.

I didn't know what to say. When I opened my mouth, the word came out in a croak. "Why?"

Another heated moment passed. I licked my lips, wanting to hear him say... I don't know, something *more*. Something that might indicate how he felt.

His eyes tracked the gesture, but he shrugged. "You're not going back, right? You said so yourself. So you don't have anywhere else to go."

Disappointment made me hesitate, but I nodded. That's what I'd told him.

"Well, there you go," he said. "If you don't have anywhere else to go, you might as well stay here."

"You make a compelling case," I said dryly, though my mind raced, imagining it. What if...

I couldn't deny anymore that I was attracted to him. We fit well together. But *together* wasn't really what he was offering, was it?

I waited, hoping he might say more.

He only chuckled at my words.

Gritting my teeth, I remembered my goal: to escape. And now that he knew about my supplies, I needed to convince him I wasn't planning on using them anytime soon.

I tapped one finger to my chin. "I'll consider it."

The relief crossing his face was unmistakable. I tried to smile convincingly, nodding when he moved to blow out the light again.

When his quiet voice spoke up again in the dark, I found myself turning toward him.

"Whatever you decide to do, no one will hurt you. Whether you choose to leave in a week... or if you choose to stay. No one will touch you either way." My heart squeezed as he added in a rough tone, "I'll make sure of it."

My throat closed. A single tear managed to escape and trickle down my cheek, landing in my ear, followed quickly by another before I pinched my eyes shut. I couldn't speak for a long moment. "Thank you," I whispered, choking on the words. "That means more than you know."

And it did.

But his promise didn't change anything.

Except to make me wish even harder that it could.

21

DUST MOTES DANCED ABOVE my head in a thin ray of sunlight that peeked through a crack in the wooden walls. At some point in the last hour, I'd given up on sleeping, waiting for Koda to wake up and trying to figure out how to take my food stores with me today without tipping him off.

I couldn't.

I'd tossed and turned all night with this problem weighing on me, but I kept coming back to one answer: leave it behind.

He wouldn't expect that, which would give me more time before he realized I was gone.

Hopefully it won't take more than a few days to find a portal anyway. If it took longer than that, it wouldn't really matter, would it? Koda had already proven how good he was at tracking. While I'd spent hours considering this as well, I couldn't guarantee that wading through streams and avoiding use of my Gifts would prevent him from finding me. It was a chance I had to take.

A creak sounded. It was the only warning we had before the door swung open, yet Koda was already on his feet before the early morning light touched my face.

It was Tehya.

"You need to talk to him," she said to Koda, glancing at me briefly, but

THE SECRET CURSE

focused on him. "It's urgent."

I knew without asking that she meant the Dragon.

Koda didn't ask for an explanation either. Nodding to his sister, he paused halfway through the door to look at me. "I'll be back when I can." Holding my gaze, I could tell he was thinking of our conversation last night. Probably trying to figure out where I stood today.

Intentionally relaxing my shoulders, I yawned and nodded back. "Take your time. I'll be here." I smiled through the lie, refusing to let myself feel the sadness creeping over me as I looked at him for the last time.

Goodbye, Koda, I added silently once he'd turned his back, allowing myself one moment to grieve. *I'll miss you.*

Tehya chewed on her nail, watching him leave as well.

I took the opportunity to grab the handbag I'd woven and hidden in the corner, holding it up as she turned back. "Could you show me how to make a strap for this today?" I asked innocently.

"Sure," Tehya replied absently, waving for me to hurry up, distracted by whatever was going on between Koda and her father. "Let's go."

She seemed preoccupied as we sat by the fire until I reminded her to teach me how to weave the strap again. Fortunately, it turned out to be simple. While I wove the long grass together, attaching the long handle to the bag I'd made, Tehya hunched over a log and stared into the fire.

"What's going on?" I finally asked, as I slung the bag over my shoulder and tested the strap. It was perfect.

Tehya and the other Vaade at the fire exchanged meaningful glances. "Nothing. Don't worry about it."

I frowned, fiddling with the remaining long grass that I hadn't used. If it was really nothing, she'd have told me without thinking twice about it. The fact that she kept it from me was worrying. Was it about the negotiations? They couldn't be failing, or she'd be happier. Did that mean they were improving? My mood soured at the thought.

"Come," I said, standing. "You can't sit here brooding all day. Let's go for a walk and get some distance from... whatever's going on."

Though my tone was casual, my plan depended on her agreement. This was the perfect excuse to get her away from the others. I couldn't take on all the Vaade, but I could take on Tehya alone—especially if she didn't see it coming.

Tehya hesitated, glancing toward the woods.

"Unless you want to wallow." I gave an exaggerated shrug, moving back toward my log.

"No." She stood, brushing off her hands. "A walk will be good for me."

Good for me, too.

I let her lead. It didn't really matter where we went, so long as we were out of earshot.

We strode through the forest, along one side of a meandering creek toward the training grounds where Tehya had challenged me days ago.

She set a brisk pace.

Breathing hard, I didn't argue. Part of me didn't want her to stop at all.

Because once she did, I'd have to move to the next stage of my plan.

I was dreading it.

Guilt over betraying both her and Koda consumed me, and I hadn't even done it yet.

I barely noticed where we were going, until we reached the clearing where we'd had our brawl.

Swinging around to face me, she held up her hands invitingly, the way she had during that first fight. "Want to go another round?" It was obvious now that she'd been aiming for this spot for that exact reason.

I wished she hadn't asked.

It made the next stage of my plan all too easy.

To escape, I needed to incapacitate her, and while she was expecting a fair fight, I'd come prepared.

She'd never see it coming.

Koda had unknowingly solved the last piece of the puzzle for me when he'd told me where the Vaade could be hurt. *Go for the neck.*

I resisted the urge to touch the small jar of paste around my neck. The Vaade had never smelled the paralytic on me or even noticed the dark paste inside.

Regret settled onto my shoulders like a familiar mantle, as I accepted what I had to do.

Waiting would only make it worse.

Slowly, I started to pull my bag over my head to set it on the ground. Halfway through, I dropped it, shifting my fingers into claws, and lunged.

Laughing, Tehya jumped back, barely noticing the light scrapes across her shoulder. Then she paused, touching a finger to the side of her neck, brows rising.

One tiny cut.

Blood trickled down the side of her tan skin, even after she wiped it away.

"I'm impressed." She laughed again, crouching to continue the fight. "Maybe the Jinn have some strength after all."

While she'd been looking at the small drop of blood on her finger, I'd twisted off the lid of the tiny jar and scooped out a bit of the paste.

I hesitated.

Once this was done, there was no going back.

But I'd never planned to stay here, had I? It had to be done.

Another unexpected leap toward her, followed by a scuffle where we rolled in the dirt.

A little paste was smeared over the cut.

Tehya slammed me to the ground making me wince as my still healing

THE SECRET CURSE

shoulder pulsed with pain.

"Sorry," she said with a grin, not at all apologetic. Then her grin fell sideways. "That's strange," she muttered to herself.

That was all the time it'd needed.

The paralytic acted fast.

With a gentle push, I easily shoved her off me, rolling her to one side so I could sit up.

Tehya's eyes widened as her fingers twitched, barely responsive now. "What did you do? What's happening?"

She tried to wrap her fingers around my wrist.

I gently pried them off.

"I'm sorry," I whispered. "Truly, I am. I didn't have any other choice."

I wanted to say more—to tell her how she'd become my friend and how much it'd meant to me, but I knew it'd only infuriate her more.

Helping her lay down as her body grew stiff and immovable, I stared into her eyes as she fumed, turning red in the face.

"You're a fool," she snapped as she tried and failed to move. "It's too late to change anything. All you've done is make things worse for yourself when I become queen of Jinn."

Ignoring her threat, despite the way my stomach clenched, I murmured, "You might feel a bit dizzy when you wake up."

Her head twitched slightly, as if she'd tried to shake it.

I reached for her hand. "You'll have to trust me, it's for the best."

Her whole body jerked in an attempt to get away.

I let my hand drop into my lap. "You don't want to marry Shem, anymore than I want you to. You'll thank me for this once I find a way to end the covenant."

She'd lost the ability to speak, but it didn't stop her from glaring at me.

What did she mean, "too late"?

Though she tried to fight the paralytic, it slowly stole over her mind as well as her body, and her eyes fell shut as it took effect.

I couldn't stop thinking about what she'd said.

Too late.

Her frantic appearance that morning came back to me. Koda hadn't returned from meeting with his father. Tehya staring into the fire, more despondent than I'd ever seen her.

Fear took root in my stomach as my imagination conjured up the worst possibilities.

What were Koda and his father doing back at camp?

Carefully, I pulled Tehya up and propped her against a tree, turning to pick up my bag from where I'd dropped it. I slung it back over my shoulder. "You'll be safe here until you wake in a few hours." Give or take. All that mattered was it'd be long enough to give me a head start.

Out of sight, a little creek gurgled cheerfully, calling for me to follow it onward toward the mountains—to the daleth on the other side. Best case scenario it could take days for me to find it. *I have a week*, I reminded myself. But did I?

Tehya might've been livid, but that didn't mean she'd been lying.

Making my way back to the stream, I started toward the cliffs, but a tug pulled at me from the opposite direction—from the Vaade camp.

We hadn't walked far.

I could go back, just for a minute, and see what I could overhear…

My feet were moving before I'd consciously made my decision.

Returning to Tehya, I crouched in front of her still form.

It was easier to shift and imitate someone exactly if I could look at them, notice every freckle, the exact way the cheek curved, the color of dark hair when the sunlight softly stroked it.

When I stood, it was done.

I was Tehya.

22

IF I RAN INTO any Vaade between here and the camp, this disguise should keep me from being captured a third time. I shouldn't take the risk, but my instincts wouldn't let me continue without discovering what Tehya had meant. *Too late.*

Too late for what?

I'd already begun my escape when she'd said it, so she couldn't be referring to that. *Too late to warn Shem?* I couldn't think of anything else she might mean, but I hoped I was wrong. I didn't fully understand it. Had they hurt him? Or had he found a way out of the covenant without my help? But if so, why hadn't he come for me?

With each new worry, my feet moved faster, until I was sprinting back to camp. Tehya's Vaade form gave me increased speed and heightened senses. It was exhilarating. If this was even half of Koda's strength, no wonder he'd pursued me so easily. I wished I'd experimented shifting into a Vaade sooner.

As I drew closer to camp, I passed the place where the Vaade had set up those tents.

I paused.

If the Vaade were hiding something, it wouldn't be in the camp where no one could keep anything private—no, whatever Tehya meant, my gut told me it had something to do with those tents and the imminent arrival of the Jinn.

Turning on my heel, I slipped through the woods toward the clearing.

Once I'd left the path behind, I knelt briefly to tuck my bag between the roots of some trees where no one would find it. If Koda saw me with the poorly made bag stuffed with food, it'd be a dead giveaway that I wasn't his sister.

Hesitating, I chewed on my lip and decided to remove the little jar around my neck with the paste, putting it inside the bag as well. If the Vaade *could* smell it, they might associate the smell with me, which would also give me away.

Underestimating them had been my biggest mistake.

This time, I wouldn't take the risk.

Slowing as I drew close enough to see the tents, I used everything I'd learned from Koda to steal through the woods as soundlessly as possible.

Thankfully, the cloth tents were thin. Deep voices drifted along the wind toward me.

Tiptoeing closer, still hidden within the trees, I stopped a few dozen paces from the closest tent. With Tehya's sensitive ears, I could eavesdrop from here without their ridiculous hearing picking up my breathing.

"This conversation is over," a deep voice growled. The Dragon.

"It's *not*." I recognized Koda's voice. "I don't care if the prince officially agreed to the covenant taking place today," he growled. "It's *not happening*."

I gasped.

The voices stopped.

Panicking, I jumped to my feet. These Vaade and their unfair supernatural hearing—

One of them yanked the tent pole from the ground on one side while the other ripped through the cloth at the back of the tent with a hiss.

I froze.

Narrowing his eyes, the Dragon shook scraps of tent cloth from his hands and scowled at me. "Get her ready," he said to Koda who held the tent pole, turning his back on me.

He thinks I'm Tehya. I wanted to laugh in relief that my disguise had worked, but Koda was still looking at me, brows pinched together.

"The ceremony begins at sunset," the Dragon added, before he flung open the entrance and disappeared.

Koda appeared more worried than I'd ever seen him as he dropped the tent pole behind him, not caring that half the tent sagged when it landed. Taking my arm, he pulled me through the trees. He didn't stop or speak until we'd put a good distance between us and the tents.

I wanted to stop him, to ask a thousand questions, but I couldn't. I had Tehya's body, but not her voice. Shifting my voice was something I hadn't done in ages. It took practice and testing to get the vocal chords right, to sound exactly like someone else. If I spoke, he'd know it was me.

THE SECRET CURSE

So I didn't.

Part of me didn't even care if he discovered me, though, because of what I'd overheard. Shem was going through with the marriage. He was *here*. It was happening *tonight*.

Koda stopped finally after a glance over his shoulder, letting go. "What're you doing? Where's Jezebel?"

I shook my head at him. Tears rose in my eyes, unbidden, as I gestured back toward camp.

He misunderstood. Grabbing my shoulders, he gave me a little shake. "You don't have to marry him, Tehya." He yanked me in for a crushing hug.

It knocked the air out of me.

My heart was splintering in my chest a little more with every second that passed.

Shem hadn't come for me and he never would.

I lifted my arms to hug Koda back, needing it as badly as Tehya would have. Gripping his tunic and trying not to sob, I let him hold me, wishing he didn't think I was his sister.

When he stepped back, I reluctantly let go.

"Stop eavesdropping," he chided. "It's time for you to run like we talked about, do you understand?" When he paused, I nodded, though I had no idea what he was talking about. "It won't stop him forever," Koda said more softly, almost to himself. "He always gets what he wants. But maybe it'll buy us a little more time." Raising his head, he added with a note of resignation, "Take Jezebel with you. She'll be more than happy to go."

I nodded again, hoping he'd accept that as an answer.

Wrapping my arms around my body, I watched him go.

He turned, walking backward as he added, "Don't tell Jezebel about her prince yet." He paused, sighing. "She doesn't need to know he abandoned her. It would break her heart."

It already had.

Tears filled my eyes again, but he was staring at the ground and didn't notice.

"We'll find a way out of this, little sister," he said firmly. "I'm not done looking for another way." He started moving backward again. "Get supplies and leave as soon as you can. And whatever you do, stay away from the tents. The Jinn are already here." With that, he turned on his heel and jogged back toward camp.

My jaw dropped.

The Jinn were already here.

If that was true, Shem was in one of those tents.

23

I HAD TO SEE him.

At the very least, if he was truly forsaking me, I needed to hear it from him, or I'd always wonder.

Determined to hear the truth, I snuck back toward the tents, still in Tehya's form, without a plan or anything even resembling one. I only knew I couldn't leave without talking to him.

The tent where I'd listened in on the Dragon and Koda's conversation sat lopsided where they'd yanked out a stake, leaving it half-caved in. There were two others. The one in the center was large, big enough for witnesses to gather, and likely intended for the ceremony. I gave that one a wide berth, heading for the smaller tent that looked like it might hold a dozen or less.

It was oddly quiet.

Too quiet.

My hopes rose—it was spelled!

Someone in the Jinni Guard would be capable of making a sound barrier to prevent the nosy Vaade from listening in on them.

If Shem was here, this was where he would be.

I didn't hesitate.

Striding around the tent, I aimed for the front flap, still in Tehya's form. I

THE SECRET CURSE

hurried, hoping no one would enter the clearing and see me.

Since I could hardly knock on fabric, I had to risk calling out. "Excuse me. I'm here to see the prince." I was counting on the fact that none of them knew Tehya well enough to notice her voice was different.

I peeked over my shoulder. Someone was coming through the trees. When he stepped into the clearing, my pulse skipped a beat. It was the Vaade who'd chased me through the woods days ago, Ahriman. He must've come back when the Dragon did. With a respectful nod in my direction, he moved toward the broken tent pole and began working to fix it without a word.

He sees Tehya, I reminded myself, trying to calm my pounding heart.

The flaps pulled back.

Two Jinni guards I didn't recognize stepped out. "The prince will see you."

I hurried inside, letting out a soft breath of relief when they dropped the flaps behind me.

Shem had stood as I entered. He gave me a formal nod when I met his eyes. It was hard not to rush toward him, but he was clearly uncomfortable standing before someone he believed to be the daughter of his enemy.

That sparked the tiniest hope that maybe he still had some unknown plan to get out of this. I needed to speak with him as *me*. "Can we have privacy?" I tried to keep my tone neutral, non-threatening but firm.

Captain Uriel stepped into view then. I'd been too flustered to survey the tent after seeing Shem, but a quick glance showed he'd brought half a dozen Jinni Guards and just as many council members. I found myself wanting to greet the familiar faces. Even Milcah's presence in the back of the group with that condescending expression on her face was welcome right now.

"I'd strongly recommend caution," Captain Uriel was murmuring in Shem's ear, before stepping back again.

That was the Jinni way of saying, *Don't you dare risk being alone with her.*

They didn't trust the Vaade, despite coming here in a supposed truce. That was encouraging. It added to my hope that Shem wasn't going through with this. Once I told him about the second spell intended to give the Vaade the full advantage, he'd implement his plans immediately.

"Please," I said to Shem, ignoring the captain and all the guards. "Your Highness," I added with a respectful bow of my head.

He squinted at me. I hoped that meant he recognized my voice, even if he didn't know why.

Fortunately, he'd always been a bit of a risk taker—at least when he thought he had the upper hand. "I'll speak with her."

Without waiting for anyone to argue, I moved toward the slit in the curtain that divided the two sides of the tent, lifting it. Entering, I held it open from the other side in invitation.

"Your Highness," Captain Uriel murmured again, anxiety written all over his face, even if it wasn't in his voice.

"I'll be fine, Captain," Shem reassured him, stepping through the divider.

I let it fall shut.

Aware of our keen audience on the other side, I met his eyes and held a finger to my lips.

I shifted.

His eyes widened. To his credit, though, he didn't make a sound. "Jezebel?" he mouthed, shaking his head a bit. In a nearly silent whisper, he added, "How?"

"It's a long story." I tilted my head toward the divider, picturing every single Jinni with their ear to the curtain.

Nodding, he returned to it and poked his head through. "Step outside, please. All of you."

"Your Highness?" Captain Uriel repeated the title for the third time, as if he was too incredulous to think of anything else to say.

"Prince Shem," Milcah spoke up now in a haughty tone. "As your advisor on the council, I'd suggest—"

"You as well, Milcah," Shem cut her off.

He waited for everyone to shuffle out before letting the curtain fall back in place.

This time when he turned back to me, he held his arms wide. I stepped into his embrace, closing my eyes and breathing him in. He stood a bit stiff as he held me and pulled back after only a few seconds.

Sniffing, I opened my mouth to tell him all about the tricks the Dragon planned to play with the covenant, but he spoke first. "I'm so sorry it has to be this way, Jezebel." He rubbed a hand on my arm, then let go completely, running a hand through his hair. "I'm actually thankful I have a chance to speak with you before the ceremony. When I arrived and they still wouldn't let me see you, I started to fear you were dead."

Before the ceremony. Dead.

The words bounced around my head but wouldn't land. "You... thought I was dead? Is that why you didn't come for me?"

He groaned. "It was the hardest decision I've ever made."

"That isn't really an answer," I said softly. Koda's straightforward manner had rubbed off on me more than I'd realized. In the past, I never would've challenged Shem. My fingers trembled. I tucked them underneath my arms.

"My council told me the chances that you'd survive if I refused the covenant were highly unlikely..." he paused. It was another non-answer, but if I was honest with myself, it told me all I needed to know.

"You're going through with it." My voice was flat.

"I don't want to," he said fervently, reaching for my hands. "Jezebel, I will always wish we could've had a chance. If there was any other way to protect my people—to protect you—I would take it. But there isn't. I must do this."

THE SECRET CURSE

All the air rushed out of my lungs as the truth hit me with the speed and force of a Vaade attack, leaving me breathless. I couldn't deny it anymore. He was truly going through with this wedding. Our engagement was dissolved in a breath, as if it'd never been.

Shaking my head, I took an involuntary step back and then another as spots danced in my vision.

He doesn't love me. Not if he's willing to marry someone else.

That was the first thought that registered, and the second was even more painful.

Maybe he never did.

My mind ran in circles, desperate to explain this the way I had everything else Shem had done over the past week.

But the heartbreak still found me, crushing my poor heart like a fly under a fist.

Shem had let me go. As if I'd never even existed.

I couldn't be more off-balance if I'd stepped off the side of an island into thin air.

Just like that, I was no one once again.

I'd been a fool to think it could've been any different.

24

"JEZEBEL," SHEM WAS SAYING as I stumbled back.

I shook my head.

I couldn't.

If I let him say another word, I'd burst into tears. And I refused to let that happen.

Shifting into fly form, I leapt toward the ceiling as I did, aiming for a hole near the top of the tent and flying hard, thinking he'd reach for me the way Koda had in the past.

He just watched me go.

It was lucky for me that my fly form couldn't weep.

I flew above the trees, heading unconsciously back toward the Vaade camp. In this tiny form, the short distance felt like miles, but I embraced the physical effort, pushing myself until I could hardly breathe.

When I couldn't go any further, I flitted down to a tree branch to catch my breath and corral my wild thoughts. *What now?*

I couldn't go home—I didn't *have* a home anymore.

In one fell swoop, I'd lost my home, my betrothed, and my future.

I had nowhere to go.

"Dragon," a voice drifted up to me from below. The bonfire was closer than

THE SECRET CURSE

I'd realized. Below, Ahriman had returned from fixing the tent to sit by the fire. The Dragon sat on the opposite side. "Why are you allowing these Jinni scum to roam our world without consequences?"

I contemplated shifting into something large with sharp teeth to show him exactly what *this* Jinni thought of that. What did I have to lose? It's not like it mattered anymore.

"Would you rather go to Jinn?" the Dragon scoffed.

"They're too close to camp," Ahriman persisted with clenched fists. He bared his teeth. "We'll have to move on to a new one. Again."

"It doesn't matter, Ahriman," the Dragon's voice rasped. A tree blocked my view of him. "After sunset, they won't remember a thing."

"Why do we have to wait until sunset?" Ahriman whined. "The rings are ready. The Jinn brought theirs with them. Why not strike now?"

"We can't give them any reason for suspicion, you fool," the Dragon snapped, losing patience. "The prince brought his strongest guard with him. They won't lose their so-called 'Gifts' until the ceremony begins."

One of the other Vaade chimed in. "That's what I've been telling him. If we attack now, they'll fight back and use their own daleth to escape. If we wait until the curse takes effect, they'll only have their flimsy spears. We'll use their own portal to go after the rest of their kind."

My wings fluttered. That sounded less like they planned to conquer the Jinn, and more like a massacre. Did Koda know about his father's full plans? He might, if he knew about the curse...

I never had a chance to tell Shem about the curse!

"I don't need your help," the Dragon spat, stepping into view as he loomed over the man. "And those spears are an offense to our treaty," he added as a sly grin replaced his usual frown. "They'll have to give those up if they want to move forward with our covenant."

He strode away from the fire without another word.

Those spears would be their only defense when the Vaade's curse fell into place.

I had to tell Shem about the curse before it was too late.

The idea of returning to Shem's tent was utterly humiliating. But if I didn't warn him, they'd use his desire for peace to remove his Gifts and memories, along with every other Jinni's under his rule—myself included.

The Dragon would attack our world in full force. And he wasn't the merciful type.

I couldn't let that happen.

Taking off, I flew back toward the tent. Fuzzy shapes stepped out of it, walking toward the larger tent. In fly form, my vision was short-distance, but it looked like the Dragon was already at the entrance with a few other Vaade behind him. They stepped inside.

Now what?

I couldn't exactly walk in after him and demand an audience with Shem.

If I didn't think of something soon, it'd be too late.

Wings beating the air, I flitted around the camp in circles, not knowing what to do. I couldn't think in this form. Below, in the shadow of a longhouse, a lone Vaade stood with arms crossed.

Flapping my little wings, I drew closer.

It was Koda.

The muscles in his arms bunched up as he held himself in place, glaring in the direction of the tents, though he couldn't possibly see them.

With some satisfaction, I thought of Tehya, asleep in the woods. Soon they'd start looking for her. I wanted to reassure Koda that the sunset ceremony wouldn't be happening. The poison shouldn't wear off before then.

But eventually they'd find her. Even if she didn't wake in time, it was only a temporary delay.

There had to be another way to stop the covenant. Not for Shem's sake, but for mine.

It was what I should've been doing all along—looking out for myself.

Fueled by anger, I flew with a purpose now. Koda would want to stop this as much as I did.

Landing behind the longhouse, I shifted into my true form again, leaning around the corner to whisper, "We need to talk."

Startled, he straightened to face me. "What're you doing here? Where's Tehya?"

"She's... away from camp," I said vaguely in case anyone was listening, knowing he'd assume she was fleeing and that I was covering for her. I felt a twinge of guilt at lying to him, but we had more important things to worry about right now.

"Why aren't you with her?" he pressed, coming around to stand in front of me with an anxious glance over his shoulder at the path to the tents. "You shouldn't be here."

"If you mean because Shem is here, don't worry. I already know."

"Tehya told you," he said flatly.

I didn't bother to correct him. Instead, I moved away from camp, gesturing for him to follow so we could talk without worrying someone was listening in.

We climbed through the woods to a steep hill, stopping when we reached a clearing that looked down on the camp, revealing a tiny glimpse of the tents beyond as well.

"Did you know about your father's plans for what happens after the ceremony?" I demanded once we'd put enough distance between us and camp.

He looked at me blankly. "After the ceremony?"

"To murder my people. You really didn't know?" I'd meant to sound

THE SECRET CURSE

challenging, but my voice cracked on the second half.

"He wouldn't," Koda declared, shaking his head. "He only wants to subdue them so that we hold the power."

"I heard him say it myself."

Frowning, Koda repeated, "He wouldn't." This time, though, he had less conviction.

"He would," I said back softly. "But there's still time to stop it. We need to steal those rings."

Grunting, he shook his head. "Trust me, I already considered that. My father has them carefully guarded, from me in particular. But it doesn't matter. It wouldn't stop them for long."

"How long would it give us?"

"Maybe..." He paused, considering. "Two or three days at most?"

"At least it'd buy us time to think of something else." But we both knew that wasn't enough.

We stared down at the tents.

What if we didn't just steal the rings... but used them too?

I held my breath.

It was an insane idea but... what if it could work?

Could Koda and I make the covenant with each other instead? *Without* the curse? If we did—and completed it—it'd render the Dragon's schemes useless. As a magical truce, it'd force the Vaade and the Jinn to get along by making it impossible for us to attack each other. It'd also prevent us from losing our abilities, which was almost enough reason on its own.

The covenant was permanent though.

Binding.

It was a true marriage.

I'd be joined with Koda forever.

Subtly, I snuck a glance at his profile. He was certainly not hard to look at. *Fine. He's extremely attractive,* I admitted to myself, tracing the lines of his face. He noticed me looking and returned my gaze, raising his brows in silent question. Shyly, I ducked my head, looking back at camp, not quite ready to suggest it.

What would forever with Koda be like?

I thought back to the nights by the warm fire, the stories and laughter, eating and working on different projects each day that contributed to the community. Being by Koda's side as he eventually became leader of the Vaade—maybe sooner rather than later. Being by his side at night as well. I shivered. It might be wonderful.

It might be *home.*

I'd never had to hide my abilities from the Vaade. I hadn't had to hide at all.

More importantly, no one would be able to dismiss me ever again. As Koda's wife, I'd be respected. Valued. The way I *should've* been with Shem.

I'd been trying not to think about it, but the rejection was still so fresh. Seething, I imagined Shem's face when he learned the covenant was completed by me instead. It'd make me irrevocably tied to the crown, impossible to ignore ever again.

The icy rage soothed the heartache, sealing my decision.

Now I just needed to convince Koda.

"I have an idea," I told him without looking away from camp. "But you might not like it."

25

THINKING THE WORDS AND saying them out loud were two *very* different things. I forgot about Shem as I stared into Koda's dragon-eyes. He didn't rush me.

I forced myself to say it in a rush. "You and I should complete the covenant instead."

Watching his face, I held my breath.

Would he consider it?

I found myself hoping he would. Maybe I wasn't the only one who could picture a future together…

"You… and me…" he repeated, taken aback.

A blush bloomed on my cheeks. I'd just proposed marriage to a man I'd only met a week ago. Not only that, I was still technically his prisoner… his enemy. If he said no, I wouldn't be surprised. I regretted asking at all. When he dismissed the idea, it'd be almost worse than Shem's rebuff.

Koda had made me feel like I *mattered*. In one short week, he'd done more to make a place for me with his people than Shem had done in months. He'd treated me like an equal. It dawned on me that my feelings for Shem had been far more superficial than I'd realized, and if Koda were to give us a chance, I might actually grow to love him.

All of these thoughts flashed through my mind in the span of a few heartbeats.

"Nevermind," I mumbled when the silence stretched longer, and Koda's stunned expression hadn't changed. "It was a stupid idea."

"No, it's not. I just... need to think," Koda said finally, shaking his head as if to clear it.

Humiliated for the second time in a single hour, I shook my head as well. "Don't bother. I don't know what I was thinking."

I tried to hide the tears in my eyes by looking down and fiddling with a loose thread on my dress.

Koda's big hand appeared beneath my blurry vision, covering my own. "Is this what you want?" he asked softly.

"It doesn't matter what I want." I shrugged, unwilling to reveal my feelings any further. But I couldn't bring myself to pull my hand away. "This will save your sister and my people, and it's the only plan we have."

He reached out and tilted my chin up, forcing me to meet his eyes, and murmured, "It does matter."

I swallowed, trying to shove the hope back down before it could betray me.

"Is it what *you* want?" he repeated, holding my gaze.

Blinking away tears, I was terrified to answer and expose myself to him. It took all my courage to nod.

He let go of my chin with a small smile. "Good."

"Good?"

His smile grew teasing. "I think I like this plan of yours."

"You do?" Hope rose against my will.

Growing serious, he took my hand again, weaving his fingers through mine. "It would be an honor to have you as my wife."

I bit my lip, unable to stop a smile of my own. "What now?"

"We'll need to steal the rings," Koda said, but his frown returned as he faced camp again. "They're imbued with the power to make the covenant on both sides. Without them, we would only be making the agreement between the two of us." He squeezed my fingers. "But my father will expect me to try that to help Tehya."

"Then, *I'll* have to steal them." I grinned at him, feeling lighter than I could ever remember, despite the circumstances. "And you can be our distraction."

26

WE PIECED TOGETHER A rough plan.

"You're sure you can do this?" Koda asked. He wasn't questioning my confidence the way a Jinni would have, though. He was merely confirming that I had the ability.

I nodded, keeping my reservations to myself. "I have to. We don't have a choice."

"Meet at the smokehouse?" he asked.

I shook my head. "Too risky. We need to meet somewhere they can't easily find us once the ceremony begins." I couldn't seem to stop blushing whenever I thought about it. Nothing about this wedding was the way I'd imagined it for myself, but I was surprised to find I was looking forward to it.

"I know a place." Koda gave me instructions on how to find a path to a lake at the foot of the nearby cliffs. He described a peninsula to use as a landmark to find each other. "It's only a few hours on foot. Wait for me there."

"I'll probably fly." I enjoyed the ease of saying those words. There was freedom in not needing to hide any part of myself.

"Always trying to show me up," he teased.

My cheeks filled with heat. I shook my head, shooting him a smile.

With the details settled, we began the descent back to camp. "I wish Tehya was here," Koda said quietly, more to himself than to me.

I cringed. I'd have to tell him what I'd done to Tehya at some point, now that I wasn't leaving. Maybe I should tell him now. I could pretend I'd done it for her own good, to help her get out of the wedding, though I doubted she'd see it that way.

In the end, though, afraid it might change things between Koda and I, I didn't risk it. "It's good she's not here," I said instead, trying not to let my shame show. "Once they realize she's gone, they'll be so busy looking for her they won't know we've started the ceremony until it's too late."

"True," he agreed.

We circled the camp until we reached the path, stealthily making our way toward the tents. Koda rolled his eyes whenever I crunched a twig underfoot, but didn't say anything, frowning as we drew closer.

When we stepped off the path toward the clearing, while the tents were still out of sight, he grabbed my hand and drew us to a stop. "A kiss for luck?" he murmured, lifting a hand to my cheek.

My heartbeat doubled. I managed a nod, eyes fluttering closed as he leaned in.

His lips brushed mine.

It was nothing like kissing Shem. With the prince, a kiss felt about the same as a handshake: pleasant and warm, but not unexpected. Koda's kiss felt like shapeshifting—affecting every single part of me. Sparks danced behind my closed eyes and heat spread from my chest to the rest of my body. Even my bones felt soft.

He pulled back too soon.

I opened my eyes with a soft sigh.

Stroking a thumb across my cheek, he stepped back slowly, a promise of more in his eyes. "See you soon."

Lifting my fingers to my lips, I watched him go, wishing the moment had lasted longer.

With a shaky breath, I crept around behind the tents and waited for the signal.

Loud voices erupted from the other side, one of them Koda's, arguing with his father.

Shifting into lizard form, I slipped beneath the edge of the tent easily.

From this height, it looked like a forest of logs, where they'd been placed as seating inside the tent. There was a table near me where a lone Vaade stood on one side and a Jinni Guard stood on the other, both standing an equal distance from a large, intricately-carved box that sat in the center of the table, right where Koda had said it would be.

The Vaade and the Jinni eyed each other as the commotion grew louder, moving as if by silent consent toward the tent entrance. Their backs were to the table.

THE SECRET CURSE

I didn't know how long they'd be distracted. I'd have to move quickly.

Slithering up onto the table, I moved as silently as possible, though I doubted the Vaade would hear me over the chaos outside.

I tried to lift the lid.

It wouldn't budge.

In this form, I was too weak.

Glancing at the Jinni and Vaade guarding the box, I worried one of them would look back, but Koda wouldn't be able to hold their attention forever.

If I shifted, would the Vaade notice the use of magic? Just in case, I hid behind the box first...

I shifted into a badger.

A second later, the Vaade in the tent shouted, "What did you do?"

"Nothing!" the Jinni Guard yelled back, but the Vaade was already hauling him by the back of his uniform toward the tent entrance—the Jinni vanished in retaliation, taking the Vaade with him.

Well, that was a happy accident.

I scurried around the box. They could be back any second.

My newly formed claws and larger size should've made it easier to open the ceremonial ring box, but without thumbs, I still struggled.

If anyone came through the entrance right now, I'd be caught instantly.

Frantic energy made me claw harder at the box as the shouting increased.

The two guards must've reappeared outside.

Finally, one claw managed to hook the lid, and I yanked it open.

Two rings nestled inside on a soft velvet pillow, which stood out amongst the Vaade logs and patch-work fur tent. That had to be a Jinni addition.

The first ring was crafted of white gold with a perfect ruby set beside a pure diamond—it clearly belonged to the Jinn. The second ring was thicker and far less delicate. It was meant to be given to Shem by Tehya, so it represented the Vaade with a dragon head curving over a shield, mouth open wide in a roar. A magical energy came from both rings, similar to what I felt around the enchanted artifacts back in the royal Jinni vault.

I scooped them up and shut the lid, pinching them cautiously between my claws as I leapt off the table.

When I reached the tent wall, I shifted back into a lizard, though the extra shifting drained my energy, to slip out beneath the furs, dragging the now-heavy rings behind me.

With one last shift, I returned to my own form, and then I was sprinting away from the tent.

Heart racing, I cheered inwardly.

Then stopped.

My bag!

All the food and water I'd gathered was in it, not to mention the knife—we'd likely need those supplies while Koda and I hid from the Vaade for a while.

Turning back, I tried to remember which tree I'd hidden it by. They all looked the same. I walked in a few circles before I spotted those overgrown roots and dug out the bag.

Unfortunately, the shouting had drawn unwanted attention from camp.

Vaade ran down the path toward the noise.

If I hadn't stopped to find my bag, they'd have run right into me.

I ducked behind a tree.

More Vaade followed.

If I traveled right now, they'd sense it, so instead I waited for them to pass by, followed by a few more, then carefully picked my way through the trees.

Only when I crossed the path and reached the stream, leaving the tents far behind, did I finally draw a full breath.

From here, I could barely hear Koda and the other's angry voices carrying on, but he was still stalling.

Good.

The longer it took them to realize the rings were gone, the better.

Time to go to our meeting place.

Though I'd boasted that I'd fly there, I couldn't carry my bag that way. Not to mention, after changing shape so many times in a row, I didn't want to exhaust myself further by shifting again.

I considered traveling, but only briefly.

It'd be agonizingly slow in these thick woods, but more importantly, it'd leave a magical trail that any Vaade could follow.

Walking would be easiest. According to Koda, it was only a short hike. And this way, he could catch up to me.

With a racing heart, I began the trek, constantly glancing over my shoulder. After at least a quarter hour passed, and then another, I began to worry.

Where was Koda?

He should've caught up to me by now.

Had the Dragon detained him? Would he put his son in confinement a second time? That would ruin everything.

My anxiety surprised me. For a plan we'd only just created, I couldn't remember the last time I'd wanted something more. Even my engagement to Shem hadn't been this exciting.

Nervous energy made me move faster, and I reached the edge of the mountain sooner than expected.

It was exactly like Koda had described. A clear, quiet lake rested at the foot of the mountain surrounded by a field of prairie grass and flowers. In the water, the mountain peaks were reflected back, creating a beautiful duplicate.

I stood waiting on the peninsula where it stretched out into the lake, feeling exposed.

THE SECRET CURSE

If the Vaade came after me instead, they'd spot me easily. I wished Koda's meeting place could've been a bit more private.

Moving to sit on a large rock, I gazed down at the water. If the worst happened, I'd throw the rings as far into the water as I could, before turning into a fish and swimming away.

Feeling slightly better, I was still staring at my reflection in the water when another face appeared over my shoulder.

27

I SCREAMED.

"It's just me!" Koda hurried to say, catching my wrist when I swung at him.

"What took you so long?" I demanded, embarrassed, pulling away. "Did they discover the rings were taken?"

He grinned. "If they haven't yet, they will soon."

"That's not very reassuring."

"You don't seem like a woman who needs to be reassured," he countered, still radiating excitement.

I couldn't keep my frown, turning to stare at the mountains as I hid a smile. "What now?"

When he didn't answer, I turned back to find him suddenly serious. He slowly took my hand again, tracing a thumb over my skin. "Now, we begin."

A shiver swept over me.

We were really doing this.

Pulling the rings from my bag, I held them in my palm for him to see. The larger dragon one was obviously meant for a man. I picked up the delicate Jinni one that had been intended for Tehya. I put it down and picked up the dragon ring. "I don't think this one will fit me…"

"It shouldn't make a difference which one you wear," Koda said, taking the

THE SECRET CURSE

gold dragon ring from me to inspect it himself. "My father explained the covenant spell to me multiple times. We prepared our ring and instructed the Jinn on how to prepare theirs—both rings are enchanted to speak for their people, but they won't begin pulling on our power or our promises until the covenant begins."

"How will we know if it works?" I met his eyes through the circle of the gold ring.

"There will be a weakening as the spell begins to slowly pull out our strength."

A weakening. The word reminded me of how he'd described the covenant when we'd first met. I still remembered my response: *Why would anyone willingly be vulnerable? I would never trust someone enough to consider that.*

Yet here I was.

I swallowed audibly, staring at the ring now instead of Koda as he lowered it.

With a finger under my chin, he brought my gaze back to his, as if he'd remembered our conversation as well. "I have full trust in you," he murmured. "Can you say the same of me?"

Afraid to speak, I managed to nod.

He ran a thumb softly over my bottom lip.

I shivered.

This time, the kiss wasn't rushed. I drew in a ragged breath, closing my eyes. His fingers slipped through my hair. Pulling me closer, he lifted me suddenly, and I broke off laughing as my feet dangled in the air. He spun us around, and with one lingering kiss, he finally pulled back, but only enough to kiss my forehead.

I lowered my eyes to hide the sudden emotion. "I haven't been to any weddings in the human world, Vaade or otherwise," I murmured. *Or any weddings at all, for that matter.* "But I believe the kiss comes at the *end* of the ceremony?"

Wryly, Koda laughed, stepping back. "Then let's hurry up and start so we can get to the end."

I bit my lip, holding back a laugh too. "I'll follow your lead. How do we begin?"

Like before, Koda pointed to my three middle fingers one at a time. "Mind, body, soul."

Had it sounded this romantic the first time he'd explained? I stared into his eyes, memorizing the amber sunset colors, and the way they warmed as he looked down on me.

"A typical human marriage places the rings on the soul finger," he repeated the words he'd said the first time. "But the covenant requires vulnerability as proof before the rings will accept the spell."

This time a different word caught my attention. "Proof of what?"

"Trust."

The one word that had haunted me since before I could remember, causing me pain at every turn. Could I accept it now? Koda waited patiently, as my inner battle manifested itself in pulling back with tense shoulders.

He reached across the growing space, fingers softly touching my cheek, tucking a loose hair behind my ear gently. "Can you trust me, Jezebel?"

Hearing him speak my name instead of *Jinni Girl* made my lips twitch.

He didn't know what he asked of me.

But in all my time here, he'd never broken a promise. He'd been the one to rescue me from the Vaade who'd attacked me. He'd tended my wounds, told me the truth about the Dragon's plans. He'd even tried to protect me from the pain of discovering Shem's betrayal. As his prisoner, I'd been obligated to rely on him, but still, he'd never let me down.

"Okay," I whispered finally, taking the hand he held out. "Time for you to make me weak and defenseless."

He chuckled. "As long as you'll make me the same."

I still held the delicate Jinni ring, so he moved to take it, holding it in front of my middle finger, clearing his throat. "The ceremony begins when we each place the other's ring on the middle finger and speak the words of the enchantment. Once this is done, the weakening starts. Our abilities will fade gradually." He paused, gazing down at our hands intertwined in front of us. "We'll say our vows, before completing the ceremony by moving the rings to the last finger with a final oath."

Wordlessly, I nodded. I couldn't have spoken past the tightness in my chest if I'd tried.

"Say this after me," he began, intoning in a deep voice, "To prepare the soul, I surrender the body."

I cleared my throat, which was suddenly dry, and rasped, "To prepare the soul, I surrender the body."

As I finished, he slid the ring onto my middle finger.

Immediately, a tingling sensation flooded through me like a cool inner wind running through my veins. When I grasped for one of my Gifts, they seemed distant, as if they were housed in my body, but had moved to another "room" of sorts. Shifting felt just out of reach, and the distance I could normally travel felt like it was decreasing steadily, shrinking away like the water lapping at the shoreline beside us.

Koda was speaking, and I made myself focus, as he repeated the vow for himself. At his nod, I slid the dragon ring onto his middle finger.

He flinched a little, clearly not liking the weakening any more than I did.

When he blinked back at me, his sunset-colored eyes were a little less vibrant. If I hadn't spent a full minute staring into them moments ago, I might not have noticed. Subtly, they continued to change, dark pupils growing less narrow and more round by the second, visibly proving that the covenant had begun.

THE SECRET CURSE

Back in the Vaade camp—and all of Jinn—our people would be feeling the covenant start to take effect, slowly leeching away their Gifts and strengths as well.

If they hadn't noticed the missing rings before, they certainly knew now.

An image of Shem panicking caused a confusing mixture of satisfaction and guilt all at once.

"Now the vows," Koda murmured, staring at our hands shyly, cheeks growing red. "There aren't any required words for this part. It's usually just the standard wedding promises... We can make up our own."

As his words sank in, I felt a full-body flush as well. He meant we needed to say how we felt. That might be even more vulnerable than the temporary loss of our abilities. "You first," I managed to squeak.

He cleared his throat. Staring out at the water, he thought for a minute, then turned back to me. "When I came to Jinn that day, I didn't expect that I'd be kidnapping my future wife," he began with an ironic grin.

I scoffed, shaking my head, but gave him a small smile.

"I promise to protect you," he continued. "Even when you might not see it that way." I frowned at his choice of words. That was an odd way to make that vow. Perhaps it was a Vaade saying? "To provide for you," he went on, distracting me from asking. "And to prove myself worthy of being a husband. I look forward to learning to love you."

He leaned in, whispering, "Based on my experience so far, I don't think it will be hard."

His breath tickled my ear.

I shivered. Warmth stole over my body as I dared to meet his eyes. I could admit now, in this moment, if only to myself, that I *wanted* this.

It was my turn.

Gathering my courage, I drew a deep breath and let it out slowly. "I vow..."

My mind went blank.

What was I willing to promise him? Nothing felt safe. But that was the point, wasn't it?

"I vow to tell you the truth," I began in the softest whisper, growing more confident as I spoke. "To always try to love you back, and to... trust you."

Simple words.

Not nearly so simple to put into action.

His eyes softened, and he squeezed my fingers gently. When he didn't continue, I blinked away the emotions and cleared my throat. "Now what?"

He hesitated.

An odd emotion I didn't recognize flickered across his face, too fast to read.

"Now," he said in a slower voice, "We say the final words to complete the covenant as we place the rings on... the next finger."

Slowly, he drew the delicate white gold ring off my finger, staring down at the ruby and diamond for a long moment before he lifted my hand.

There was that strange expression again. It was gone before I could name it.

With his hand and the ring poised in front of mine, he dipped his head lower, until there was only a breath of space between us. "With this ring, I take you, Jezebel, to be my wife in every way, until death takes us."

As he slid the ring onto my finger, he closed the distance between us and captured my mouth with his. The kiss flooded my senses as strongly as the magic had the first time. My entire body trembled.

When he pulled away, my mind felt almost fuzzy from the kiss, as if a fog had come over me.

Eyes closed, I laughed on a shaky breath as he finally pulled back. "That wasn't technically the end," I reminded him in a teasing tone. "We still have to do your ring."

"I know." His smile was close-lipped, almost tight at the corners. One hand absently touched the dragon tooth necklace. He didn't usually fidget. Our covenant must be making him more nervous than he'd let on. "I just couldn't hold back."

Pulling his own ring off his middle finger, he held it out to me and stretched the fingers of his left hand out so I could place the ring on his ring finger.

As I reached out to take his hand, a flash of white and red on my own finger caught my eye.

It struck me as strange.

My thoughts felt uncharacteristically out of reach, like I was forgetting something important.

"What am I supposed to say again?" I asked Koda to cover my hesitation, staring down at the ring on my first finger.

"With this ring, I take you, Koda, to be my husband," he chanted the rest, but I slowly stopped listening.

The ring.

It was on my *first* finger.

What had Koda said before we'd started? It was a struggle to remember his words. Straining, I found them one at a time. *Mind... body... soul.* The ring finger was for the soul—for the marriage *and* the covenant to be completed.

But he'd put it on...

The first finger.

Mind.

Something teased my memory... Something to do with forgetting?

My heart stalled as it finally came to me.

The curse.

Drawing in a slow, careful breath, I managed through years of practice to keep a calm mask on my face as I met his eyes. They were shifting from sunset orange and yellow to a darker hazel. Was the weakening completed? If so, I was

THE SECRET CURSE

entirely defenseless… and I might've made the biggest mistake of my entire life.

"What's wrong?"

All kinds of alarm bells were ringing in my head.

He wasn't stupid. He wouldn't put the ring on the wrong finger by mistake.

I hoped I was wrong.

On instinct, I kept my suspicions to myself as I repeated the vow carefully, watching his face the entire time. There was a tightness in his eyes even as he smiled. It added to my growing tension.

"… until death takes us," I finished, staring into his eyes the way he had mine.

I slid the dragon ring onto his *first* finger.

Just like he'd done for mine.

When panic flickered in his eyes, my heart sank.

The emotion was gone so fast though, I almost thought I'd imagined it.

He cleared his throat. "Good," he said as he pulled the ring off again, though I got the distinct impression he did *not* think it was good.

He placed the thick dragon ring in my palm. Stretching out his hand toward me for the third time, palm toward the ground, he said, "Now move it to the final finger, to connect the soul, and the covenant will be completed."

I took it.

Then, I slipped my own ring off as well.

Holding both of them in shaking hands, I held mine out to him, wanting despite everything to trust him. Desperately hoping he'd prove me wrong. I whispered, "You first."

Stricken, he didn't take it. "I… can't."

28

SLOWLY MY HANDS FELL to my sides, still holding both rings as my lungs constricted.

I couldn't breathe.
I couldn't think.
Everything hurt.
"You can't," I repeated.

He might as well have taken a knife and stabbed me in the chest. It hurt the same. Maybe more.

His betrayal was worse than Shem's… because I'd chosen to trust him fully. I'd been all in.

Koda looked anguished as he finally spoke. "I'm sorry. I can't explain."

Every word slammed the knife in deeper. My heart shattered into little pieces and then each of those pieces broke again a thousand times more. I wrapped my cold fingers around the dragon ring in my palm as the same ice stole over my heart, trying to mend the fragments, piecing them together in a jagged new shape that didn't resemble what it used to be.

It never would.

"You were never going to complete the covenant for me, were you?" My

THE SECRET CURSE

tone was deceptively soft, hiding my growing fury. I didn't need his explanation. "You did exactly what your father wanted. You used me."

But he shook his head. "The covenant and the curse would've happened one way or the other. My father would've made sure of it."

I shook my head as a tear slipped out.

He reached out to wipe it, but I leaned away, and he let his hand drop. "This was the only way I could—" he broke off briefly, shaking his head as if frustrated. "The only way I could protect Tehya," he pleaded, hazel eyes tightening around the corners. "She wants to marry Akeena, not your prince."

My prince? For a split second, I felt a gap in my memory like a gaping hole, then the hole was gone. He meant the Jinni prince.

"There *had* to be a marriage to use the covenant spell," he was saying. "And I know it doesn't seem like it, but this solution saves you as well as Tehya. You would've been a target along with the rest of Jinn, but now, as my wife, I can keep you safe."

I scoffed. "Safe, while the rest of my people are enslaved or worse?"

Forehead wrinkling, Koda pressed a hand to it as if searching for something. "I… I don't think that's what my father plans. He only needs the curse in place for a short time. A few months or a year at most."

"A year?" I gasped, shaking my head. "There will be nothing left of us."

"I can't explain," Koda repeated. "It *has* to be this way. But with you as my wife, I'll have the power to end the curse as soon as we—" he cut off, almost like he'd choked on something, then growled softly. "As soon as we conquer Jinn," he said instead of whatever he'd been about to say. "Your Gifts won't be gone forever."

I couldn't hold his gaze anymore. My eyes shuttered as I squeezed the rings in my hands tight enough to hurt. "You really believe that, don't you?"

"I swear it," Koda vowed passionately, trying to touch my cheek again, but I opened my eyes in time to dodge his hand. He let it fall. "I'll keep you safe in the meantime. I promise."

Your promises mean nothing.

I didn't say it aloud, though. My mind raced, tripping through the holes that kept springing up, confusing me as I tried to think. How could I stop the curse?

"I have to do this, Jezebel." Koda's voice broke a little, as if he was somehow hurting too. "For my people."

He'd always wanted to help his people conquer mine—the truth had always been there, yet somehow, I'd forgotten it, despite the fact that *he* was the one who'd kidnapped me in the first place.

"Don't talk to me about your people," I spat, taking a step back. It was the exact reasoning Shem had given me. Did I matter so little? "*I* was supposed to be your people. Your *wife*. You lied to me."

Our wedding vows weren't even fully finished, and they'd already been broken.

"No," he swore. "I meant every word. I'll protect you from all of it. You *are* my wife now, which means my father can't touch you. No one can."

Who was his father? I somehow couldn't quite remember.

His fingers continued to twitch like he was desperate to reach for me and forcing himself to hold back. "Your people will forget. It has to be this way. But I can remind you of the truth"—he squinted, as if he either didn't know or maybe couldn't recall how it worked—"every day if need be. And when the time is right, I'll make sure we complete the covenant to bring your abilities back."

"When the time is right," I repeated dully.

"It's not like you care about your people anyway." He threw up his hands as if he was truly surprised by my reaction. "What do you care if we take power away from Jinn? The Gifts are an unfair advantage."

"That's how you see me?" I stood frozen in place, fracturing further with every new revelation. I thought he'd been the first person to respect my Gifts, that he didn't resent them. But he'd wanted them to be removed all along.

"No, of course not," he was protesting, but I barely heard him.

A numbness stole over me.

I didn't know what to do.

Maybe we could find a way to backtrack this covenant somehow before it was completed.

I could go my own way, and he'd go his. I'd never have to see his backstabbing face again.

Turning away, I moved to pace.

Koda grabbed my wrist, stopping me. "What're you doing?"

I'd meant to put a little space between us, just temporarily, to figure out how to talk this through with him.

"You can't leave."

I looked from his hand on mine to his now fully-human hazel eyes, barely recognizing him anymore. "Let go."

"I can't do that," he growled. Though his Vaade strength had faded, he was still stronger than me. When I tried to tug away, he only gripped tighter.

I reached my free hand into my bag for the knife. If he wanted to bully me, I could threaten him right back.

My hand brushed against the little jar with the paralytic that I'd used on... someone... I couldn't remember who... before my fingers curled around the knife.

I yanked it out, pointing it at Koda's face. "Let. Me. Go."

Something in my expression must've told him I was serious. He finally loosened his grip, holding his hands up in surrender. "This is going all wrong." He gripped his head, shaking it slightly as if to clear his thoughts. "We're on the same side, remember? You have to finish the covenant by putting the ring on my finger."

When I took a step back, he followed. "I will if you go first."

"I already told you, I can't." He matched me stride for stride as I backed up, speeding up when I did, ignoring the knife. "Not yet. For our plans to work, we need the Jinn to be completely cut off from magic. Nothing else will be enough."

"Why? What do the Vaade plan to do?"

"I can't say."

"Why?"

"I—I don't remember," he admitted, rubbing his brow with a frustrated hand, then shaking his head again. "You have to trust me."

I scoffed.

That was the one thing I never should've done in the first place.

On instinct, I tried to travel away. But of course, I couldn't. A spike of fear raced up my spine when I realized I couldn't even remember how.

"Listen to me, Jezebel," he continued as he stalked me along the water's edge. "I swear on the dragons themselves that I will make sure the covenant is completed for you by placing a ring on your finger eventually. It will only be a few years at most. I'll protect you the entire time."

"What an offer," I snapped. "You'll only betray me temporarily."

He had the good sense to look ashamed, but it didn't stop his progression toward me.

I'd never wished for my Gifts more than I did right then. If I could've, I'd have traveled away to the mountains and out of reach. Or maybe shifted into a Lacklore and attacked him. Could I do that? It seemed more like a dream when I thought about it.

Glaring at him, I shook my head.

How could I have ever trusted him?

As he prowled closer, I spun on my heel and ran through the meadow. Behind me, long grass crunched under our heels as Koda gave chase. The steep slope of rocks at the base of the mountain rose up on all sides, quickly blocking my path.

Koda was driving me into a corner.

His betrayal became secondary to finding a way out of this. It was either him or me. He was making all kinds of promises, but I knew better now. I was the only one I could trust.

Hands held out in a gesture of peace, Koda cornered me as I backed up against the rock wall. "I don't want to hurt you, Jezebel."

"Too late," I said bitterly, clutching the rings against my stomach. "You should've thought of that sooner."

He pounced.

Swiping at him clumsily with my knife, I aimed to skewer him, but instead I only managed to slash a shallow cut along his arm.

When he hissed in pain and fell back, staring at the wound with a surprised expression, I ducked around him, trying to run back through the meadow.

He crashed into me from behind.

His weight knocked me to the ground with a painful *thump* as the knife tore out of my hand and soared through the air, landing far out of reach.

We wrestled wildly. The rings went flying, disappearing into the tall grass along with the knife.

Grunting, Koda grew less gentle in his frustration, yanking my arms down and pinning them to my sides as he used the weight of his body to hold me down.

I squirmed, refusing to give up.

"You shouldn't have thrown the rings," he grumbled, searching for some sight of them in the long grass that rose above our heads. "You're only prolonging the inevitable."

"Are you saying you'd force me to put the ring on your finger?" I asked, breathless from the struggle but also from his heavy weight on my chest, hampering my lungs. "Because that's the only way it will happen."

Though his brows drew down unhappily and he wouldn't meet my eyes, Koda nodded. "I will if I have to."

That decided it then.

As he leaned to one side, feeling around with one hand through the grass while still pinning me to the ground, he unwittingly freed one of my arms. My bag was slightly under my hip, but I managed to wriggle it out and slip my fingers inside, gripping the wooden cork at the top and easing it off.

There was a tiny bit of paste left.

I scooped it out on one finger.

The shallow cut on his arm oozed blood, dripping down onto my dress and shoulder. It was the perfect opportunity.

Still, even after everything Koda had done, I hesitated.

This wasn't the same as what I'd done to Asher, my first crush, or to Shem when I chose to marry Koda. If I did what I was imagining, it would affect an entire race.

But that's what the Vaade had planned to do to us.

"Found it," Koda declared triumphantly.

I made my decision.

This wasn't just Koda's plan, it was... another Vaade whose name escaped me. It was what all of them had wanted. If it was backfiring on them, then that was their fault too. They had only themselves to blame.

I struggled again, straining under his weight and grabbing his arm as part of my feigned attempt to break free.

Koda held me down easily.

The paste smeared across his wound.

He was too busy grappling with my other hand to notice anything strange, trying to force me to hold his ring and place it on his finger.

I made a fist. Tightening my fingers against his attempts, I gasped as he wrenched them open one by one. Though I tried to fight back, he was overpowering me.

Just a few more seconds!

I didn't know if I could hold out much longer.

He'd pressed the ring between my stubborn fingers, and his own finger was poised to put it on, when his grip began to loosen.

Gasping, I ripped my hand free.

His body started to sag as the paralytic took effect.

Finally.

I rolled him off me.

That was the Vaade weakness: they didn't think they had any.

"What did you do?" he gasped, just like his sister had, whatever her name was.

The dragon ring fell to the ground as he lost his ability to hold it.

I left it there.

As he lay gasping in the long grass, I stood, ignoring his continued stream of complaints and demands as I searched for the other ring. Koda tried to sit up and follow, but his body continued to weaken and betray him.

The Jinni ring took forever to find.

"Please, Jezebel," Koda begged as he fell back in the grass, unable to hold himself up any longer. "Please."

I refused to respond until I found the ring, struggling to focus as different gaps in my memories continued popping up, confusing me—I couldn't think straight with this second spell clouding my mind.

There.

It'd landed near my knife, which I made sure to pick up as well. Then I lifted the thin white-gold ring with its diamond and ruby from where it'd been half buried in the dirt.

Wordlessly, I drew a deep breath and faced Koda. Since he'd tried to force me to put the Vaade ring on his finger to complete the spell, I'd do the same with my own ring.

I approached carefully, making sure he'd lost all feeling in his arms and wouldn't fight me further. "Please, Jezebel," he repeated in a whisper now, as if he couldn't find anything better to say. "I care about you more than I'd like to admit. I wasn't just marrying you for the covenant."

I lifted his limp hand in mine. My fingers pinched his together so that he held the ring, and though he groaned, he couldn't move as I used his own hand to slip the ring on my ring finger.

Where it should've been all along.

I feared it wouldn't work without the vow, but we *had* both said them. The rings should be the very last step…

The cool metal circled my finger like an embrace.

Instantly, my missing memories began flooding back, making me feel like I was waking from a deep sleep. Were my abilities returned as well? I tested them out by traveling from one side of the meadow and back in the span of two heartbeats.

Covering my face, I let out a huge breath of relief, shoulders relaxing.

"Finish the covenant," Koda's voice rasped. The paralytic was working fast, but he fought it. "Your prince doesn't want you anymore," he growled, going for the jugular. I winced, remembering exactly who he was talking about now. "This is your only option."

Was it? I stared down at him, mourning everything I'd thought we had.

The return of my memories made it hurt more.

I shook my head. "It stopped being an option the moment you betrayed me."

"Please," he used his last bit of strength to beg. His whole body strained toward the ring that lay beside him, but he couldn't even lift his arm to pick it up. "I swear I would've reversed the curse."

I knelt next to him.

Reaching down, I gently lifted the ring, staring at it. "I don't believe you." But part of me still wanted to. It brought tears to my eyes against my will. I could use my manipulation Gift to get honesty from him, but I wasn't sure I wanted to know the truth. Instead, I forced the tears back with a ripping sensation, burying them deep.

I put the ring in my pocket.

"You can't do this!" Panic mixed with anger flashed across his face. "If you don't finish the covenant, you'll condemn us to live like humans… without any memories of who we really are," he managed to say, as his eyes started to drift shut. "We'll never end…" he trailed off.

"If you could do it, then so can I."

He blinked rapidly, forcing his eyes open. "We were only going to… use the weakness temporarily. It's completely… different."

"I disagree," I murmured.

"We keep written records," Koda slurred, fighting a losing battle. "You can't make us forget forever…" As he lost consciousness, his eyes fluttered closed and didn't open again.

"Thank you for letting me know," I said quietly, though he couldn't hear me anymore. "I'll make sure to send someone to destroy them."

Leaning down, I lowered my head and let my lips brush across his one last time. "I could've loved you more than anyone," I whispered, allowing the tears to fall. They dripped onto his cheeks before trailing into the grass. "If you hadn't broken my trust, I would've been yours forever."

29

I STOOD.

The cheerful setting of the prairie grass in front of the lake and majestic mountains hadn't changed much—except for the places where we'd trampled the grass—but I felt darker.

"I imagine you'll forget what happened today," I told him softly, hoping he could hear me though he slept. "And the story of the covenant will no doubt get twisted and erased over time. But just know…" I paused, throat tightening. "I won't forget you."

Now he had nothing, and I had even less.

No home.

No one to trust.

As much as I'd grown to like the Vaade, I'd never again be allowed to sit at their fire. That dream was over.

Could I somehow go back to the castle?

The Jinni prince had rejected me, while Koda, the prince of the dragons, had betrayed me, leaving me without a place on either side.

Your prince doesn't want you anymore.

Koda's words played over and over on a loop in my mind.

Doesn't want you.

Wallowing in the loss, I looked down at Koda and thought darkly. *At least I still have my Gifts.*

I sucked in a breath. My Gifts of travel, shifting, and... manipulation.

I could *make* Shem want me.

Unlike Koda, whose strong mind had been immune to my Gifts, Shem's wasn't. Before I'd grown aware of my newest ability, I'd accidentally used it on him more than once.

That would solve everything.

If I forced him to take me back, I would have a home, a husband, and a future.

If I did this, I'd be queen.

I closed my eyes so I didn't have to look at Koda, clutching the ring as I searched for any of the old guilt over using my Gift of manipulation on others.

I couldn't find it.

Instead, my resolve only hardened. Shem had been manipulating *me* by making me think he truly loved me, that he would fight for me, when in reality, he'd thrown me aside as easily as Koda had when the opportunity came.

When I imagined using my Gift on him to manipulate him into marrying me—the way he'd promised to already—I had no reservations.

Shem had already proved he would've overrun my own desires just as easily. What did I have to lose?

The answer came to me as soon as I asked the question: *nothing.*

I stood and left Koda lying in the grass without a backward glance.

Traveling to the camp used very little energy and cut the time down from an hour to a few short minutes. The camp was oddly quiet. As if most of the Vaade were gone.

Probably looking for the rings, I thought, creeping closer.

Four large Vaade men stood near the tent arguing with each other. One of them was Ahriman, the Vaade who'd attacked me. He sported a bruised and swollen eye.

Jaw clenching, I lifted my chin.

Too easy.

Though they were no match for me now, with the curse weakening them more with each passing minute, I was spoiling for a fight.

I strode out into the clearing directly toward them. "Where is everyone?" I mocked them. "Did those 'feeble' Jinn somehow get the best of you?"

"Jinn?" Ahriman squinted at me, then his eyes widened in fear. "You're a Jinni!" To the others he added, "I told you I could smell something off!"

They'd forgotten so much already, Ahriman didn't even know who I was anymore. It was oddly disappointing. "Are you the only ones here?"

They had the good sense to raise their weapons.

"No," Ahriman scoffed. But I didn't really need an answer. If there had been

THE SECRET CURSE

other Vaade here, they'd have appeared by now. The Dragon must've sent all the Vaade to hunt us down when he first felt the covenant begin.

Nodding as I reached them, I simply said, "Good. That should give me a little time."

I clapped my hands on the shoulders of Ahriman and the Vaade closest to him.

We traveled.

I chose the farthest place I could think of, besides the lake where I'd left Koda: the place where the Dragon had first held negotiations.

When we reappeared, I let go.

And traveled again.

"Filthy Jinni sna—" another Vaade was saying as I flashed into the camp directly behind him.

Beside him, the other Vaade whirled with his fist out.

But I was prepared, and he was not.

Without his extra senses, the second Vaade didn't realize I was crouching by his feet instead of standing, and he missed, setting him off-balance.

I grabbed both guard's ankles and traveled again.

We landed on the other side of the clearing this time, across from their fellow guards who were snarling and tearing through the woods toward us as soon as we appeared.

I caught Ahriman eyes.

Giving him a dark smile, I traveled back to the tents once more, leaving them there.

It was probably only an hour or two from camp, but with the memory loss they were experiencing, they might never find their way back. I didn't care.

I hesitated at the entrance to the tent.

Throwing the flap open, I froze on the threshold.

Shem and every single member of his retinue sat tied up on the floor. Only Milcah was free.

Did they not realize their Gifts were back yet?

Wide-eyed, they all stared at me. Milcah had been bent over Shem's ropes behind his back, painstakingly sawing at them with a small pocketknife. She lifted a finger to her lips.

I scowled. "Don't shush me, Milcah," I said loudly, enjoying the way they all flinched as they waited for the Vaade to storm in and find me. "Did you not notice that I used the front entrance?" I mocked her, enjoying this more than I should've. "The guards are gone."

She straightened, looking at the other Jinn. "The king and queen must've sent—"

The audacity.

"*I* took care of them," I interrupted, striding up to her and yanking the knife from my bag. With one sharp cut, Shem's ropes dropped to the floor.

Shem brought his hands around in front of him, rubbing his wrists. He, at least, looked happy to see me. "Someone stole the rings," he told me, as I made my way around the room slashing ropes, freeing the rest of the council members and the guards. "And started the covenant on their own—"

"Again, that was me," I muttered.

Captain Uriel tensed, eyeing me more closely.

Gritting my teeth, I threw up my hands. "I had to. They added a curse to the covenant, and when I tried to warn you, you didn't give me a chance." That wasn't the full truth, but they didn't need to know that. "I'm sure you felt it? After your Gifts began to weaken, when your memories began to disappear?"

"That was part of the covenant?"

"No," I repeated. "It was a secret curse the Vaade added to the covenant."

Shem ran a hand through his hair. "How did you stop it?"

The thought of telling Shem about Koda was too painful. "I'll explain later. The Vaade could come back at any time," I said, grateful that it was true, as I cut the last rope for the remaining guard. "We need to go. Now."

"Maybe this is our opportunity to get the better of them," Shem said to Captain Uriel instead, as if already forgetting me. "If they're still weak, we could call for more members of the Guard—"

"The Vaade threat is over," I interrupted, blood boiling. "I took care of it. They won't be bothering us anymore."

"You don't know that, Jezebel," Shem said with a sigh. Had he always been this condescending?

"I *do* know," I insisted through clenched teeth. "It's time to go home."

"I completely understand your desire to go home." Shem patted me awkwardly on the shoulder. "I'll have Milcah take you to the daleth on the way to call for more guards."

"Where is the portal?" I said flatly.

"Just a mile or so to the east—"

"Good." I took his hand and traveled, knowing the others would follow.

"What're you doing?" Shem protested when we reappeared.

Looking him in the eyes, I used the full force of my Gift of manipulation. "We're going home. Right now. You're taking me to your parents."

As expected, the rest of Shem's retinue quickly followed my trail, arriving in a chaotic shouting mass.

"Join hands," I shouted back at Captain Uriel as he seized my arm.

Under the influence of my Gift, his eyes grew blank, and he obeyed.

"Now," I snapped at the others.

Though I wasn't touching the rest of them, they looked from Shem to the captain, both of whom calmly held onto me, and grudgingly followed suit.

Without my previous reservations about my Gifts, I was fueled by my fury,

THE SECRET CURSE

feeling all of them expand in ways I hadn't thought possible before.

I traveled.

Shocking them all, I easily carried the entire group of twelve. Maybe it was the adrenaline or the absolute rage driving me, or both, but I barely felt tired by it. Following Shem's directions, I traveled one final time and arrived a few dozen paces from the daleth.

"To the king and queen," I repeated for everyone else's sake, watching Shem closely for signs that my Gift was fading. He remained obedient, leading the way through the portal.

We landed directly in front of the castle gates, which was as close to the castle as we could get with the enchantments surrounding it. We'd need to physically cross them, as well as one of the castle's grand entrances, before we could travel within the castle itself.

Cold fury poured out of me as Shem stepped up to politely ask the guards to open the gates.

Not waiting for him, I made my voice heavy with the full weight of my Gift, though they were too far to touch, and stared into their eyes as I snapped, "Take us to the king and queen immediately."

I couldn't be sure if it was the size of the group already obeying me, my tone, or the Gift itself growing, but something made them jump to obey.

We strode through the castle toward the throne room.

"The king and queen are currently holding court," the guard told us nervously over his shoulder, as we reached the grand doors. "They're going to share an announcement of some sort." *Probably about to tell everyone their son is marrying a Vaade.* "You can slip into the back here and speak with them after."

"No," I said in the same flat, hard tone, slamming my Gift into him with all my strength. "We'll join them on the stage. Bring us to the side door." Before he could argue, I hooked my arm through Shem's, daring him to speak back to both of us and added sharply, "Now."

30

WE WERE LED TO a side door that opened onto the stage.

King Jubal and Queen Samaria both turned at the sound, cutting off whatever they'd been about to say. "Shem?" The queen rose, hand to her lips. "What happened?"

Her gaze seemed to sweep right over me. King Jubal didn't even spare me a glance. They focused on their son, drawing him forward.

I didn't let go of Shem's arm.

With a pointed glance at my fingers, Queen Samaria finally turned her attention to me.

I stared coldly back.

This was the family who'd left me to the Vaade without a second thought. Just like their son.

"Mother," Shem was saying, bowing his head respectfully. "Father."

I kept my chin high.

Turning to the crowd, I took in the throne room, full to the brim with Jinn, waiting to learn about a marriage to the Vaade that was no longer happening. Their judgmental eyes should've made me step back—in the past they would have. Today they didn't affect me. I hardly cared what they thought anymore.

By now, King Jubal was coming to the conclusion that the marriage

THE SECRET CURSE

covenant clearly hadn't happened. He looked between his wife and son, considering.

They'd want to hear the full story privately and discuss it before revealing anything to the public.

Too bad.

I raised my voice as I spoke to them, making sure everyone gathered would hear, all the way to the back. "Good, you've gathered everyone. That's exactly what Shem and I were hoping for."

King Jubal narrowed his eyes at me. "Thank you, Jezebel." His tone was polite, but he gripped my shoulder firmly, trying to intimidate me. "That will be all."

I ignored him, speaking louder. "The Vaade threat has been extinguished. By me."

He'd lifted a hand to call for a guard, but this made him pause. Queen Samaria gave Shem a wide-eyed look in question, and he confirmed it with a slightly dazed nod.

Now, finally, I deigned to give them a small bow along with a tight-lipped smile. "You're welcome."

King Jubal caught Captain Uriel's eye, subtly summoning him.

I stepped between them, capturing the king's eyes with my own, sensing my Gift rise at the ready the more I used it. "Shem and I knew you would want the kingdom to hear the news immediately. I'm sure you'd like me to explain."

I'd never addressed the prince so informally in a public venue before, and I knew the onlookers didn't miss it.

Neither did King Jubal.

I couldn't tell if my Gift overpowered him or if he simply didn't want to lose the image of a united front, but he grudgingly nodded for me to continue.

Turning my back on him, the queen, and Shem, I spoke directly to the people. "You may have felt your Gifts weakening in the last hour or so." Though I didn't wait for anyone to nod, I took some satisfaction in the widening eyes throughout the room. Had everyone tried to hide it from their peers? Koda was right, we concealed everything. In this case, it worked to my benefit.

"The Vaade attempted to steal our Gifts." I let my voice carry, let the pause after my words grow heavy before I continued. "I personally turned this curse back on them, stripped the Khaanevaade of their strength and other abilities with a spell that will last a thousand years."

To sound more powerful, I left out a few key details, such as the fact that I had no idea if the curse would last that long. I didn't know if it would *ever* end if Koda didn't receive a ring.

"Without their magic, all currently living Vaade should be dead within a century or two at most." I paused for emphasis, lowering my voice slightly so that they had to strain to hear, which naturally added emphasis to my words. "They'll never be a threat to Jinn again."

Shock swept across the room.

The Jinn weren't usually the cheering sort, but a murmur of excitement swept across the room, and slowly, they began to applaud.

Glancing back at the royals, I held back a satisfied grin at the astonishment on their faces.

When Queen Samaria stepped forward to take my shoulders, subtly preparing to edge me away from the stage yet again. "No." I stood up to her for the first time. "You will let me speak." I'd use my Gift on her without a second thought if she didn't listen.

Stunned into submission, she loosened her grip and let go.

Turning, I caught her hands in mine, causing another surge of murmuring in the crowd at my boldness. This time I did use my Gift, leaning heavily on it as I glanced between her and King Jubal evenly. "Thank you for sending your son to come for me when the Vaade took me hostage." *I'm giving you false credit for what you should have done,* I thought bitterly. Speaking far louder than necessary, I made sure this story would be spread far and wide today. "I know how much thought you put into my rescue and how worried you were." *In other words, not at all.*

Both their faces grew blank under the influence of my Gift, and they nodded slowly. "We were terribly concerned," Queen Samaria murmured, almost to herself, agreeing with me fully now. King Jubal looked slightly confused, as if he were fighting my Gift, but losing.

Continuing loudly, I guided them on, "That's why Shem and I both knew you'd agree to the wedding taking place today." They startled, but the reaction was dimmed by my Gift and their own desire to show confidence in front of our audience.

The buzz from the crowd was growing louder. It covered the queen's quiet question, "You're... getting married?"

"Shem and I have decided to wed as soon as possible," I told her and the king, lowering my voice so no one else would overhear. "To prevent anyone else from trying to take advantage of our people again." She nodded slowly, though King Jubal still seemed to be resisting my Gift. In a harsh whisper, I added, "Your son was already going to be married at sunset. It's very fortunate for you that it will now be to his original bride."

That finally seemed to sway him. "Yes," he murmured. "...very fortunate indeed."

I waved an arm grandly toward the crowd. "And here you are, prepared for it with witnesses already gathered. It was meant to be."

My Gift made them bob their heads in agreement.

It was what they *should* have done all along.

To Shem, I added, "You'll want to share the full story of the Vaade's breach of the agreement to pass the time. I'll be back in a quarter hour." His confused expression smoothed out as he nodded in agreement.

Before I left, I made sure to raise my voice for the audience, "We look forward to celebrating this glorious turn of events with you. The wedding will begin shortly."

Though it obviously struck the onlookers as strange that I spoke on behalf of the royal family, they didn't dare question it while the king, queen, and their son stood beside me in direct support.

I strode out in a hurry.

Without experimentation, it was impossible to know how long my Gift would hold power over the royals if someone tried to talk them out of it.

Either way, after the speech I'd just made, it was highly unlikely they would find an excuse to change their minds and still save face before I returned.

Just to be safe, though, I wouldn't dawdle.

"You and you," I pointed to two of the queen's council members lurking outside the throne room doors, waiting for her. "Go get Milcah, Jerusha, and Dorcas, and tell them the *princess* needs them immediately in her rooms. Make sure they don't delay."

I allowed myself a satisfied smile as they hurried off. I'd chosen those three to help me into my dress, knowing how much they'd hate being forced to serve me. Knowing that if I had to, I would *make* them obey.

The more I used my Gift of manipulation, the more I wondered why I hadn't let myself use it before. It was untraceable. As long as I took care not to stretch someone outside of their will too much, no one around them would question it. In some ways, this Gift could be more invisible than Shem himself.

And, if anyone *did* catch on to what I was doing, it'd only take a few words to make them forget.

Traveling directly to the residential hallway where Shem's council members lived, I opened the door to my room and entered.

It was exactly the way I'd left it.

Not a single person had left a note or other sign of their presence, because no one had cared that I'd been gone.

That was about to change.

I was done living in the shadows of what other people wanted.

From now on, I would *make* them value me.

My dress hung along the side of the wardrobe.

White and pure.

As I shucked my ripped and dirty dress to the floor, I wished there was time to bathe before the ceremony. It wasn't worth the risk. But first thing when it was over.

Once this wedding was done, there'd be time to do whatever I wanted. No one would order me around ever again, least of all Shem.

That was the benefit of marrying him instead of Koda. He would do whatever I said.

As I stepped into the wedding gown, pulling the delicate lace over my shoulders and staring into the mirror, I began a shift without thinking.

The fabric darkened.

Black lace.

It was the color of mourning.

Fitting.

When Milcah, Jerusha, and Dorcas arrived a few minutes later, I'd already run a brush through my hair and taken a few minutes to shift my features in the mirror—adding a soft blush to my cheeks, removing the bags from under my eyes, and reddening my lips.

"You called?" Milcah asked dryly when I answered the door.

I didn't invite them in. Meeting her eyes with a saccharine smile, I infused my words with my Gift. "I need jewelry fitting for a wedding ceremony. You have some jewels in your room, don't you? Bring me your favorite?"

Her eyes grew blank in response.

When she obeyed, traveling out of the hallway to another part of the castle, Dorcas gave Jerusha a startled glance and shrugged.

"Dorcas, help me with the buttons." I gestured to my back, swinging the door to my room open finally and turning. I didn't use my Gift, wanting to see if she'd cave in simply because Milcah had done so first.

Dorcas stepped forward, starting at the bottom. The little pearlescent buttons led all the way from my lower back to the base of my neck, drawing the dress in to fit my curves.

Jerusha wasn't willing to stand idle in the hall, so she reluctantly stepped inside as well, closing my door softly. Between the two of them, they were finished by the time Milcah returned.

They brushed out my dark hair so that it lay along my shoulders in waves, while Milcah placed a gold headpiece with a pale blue gem the same color as my eyes around my brow.

As she carefully fit matching gold earrings into my ear, she muttered to herself, "I don't know why I'm letting you borrow these. They're my favorites."

I turned from the mirror to grab her arm, smiling innocently for the other ladies' benefit as I let my Gift flow over her. "It's because you're secretly happy for me to marry the prince." It came so naturally now, I hardly had to think about it. Her face softened in response as my words sank in.

Facing the mirror again, I touched the pretty blue gem in the center of one of the earrings. The gold pieces dangled all the way to my shoulder, making me smile for real this time. "They make a wonderful wedding present."

When Milcah didn't argue, Dorcas and Jerusha glanced at each other again. Over my shoulder, I caught a glimpse of Jerusha studying Milcah in the mirror.

THE SECRET CURSE

"Jerusha, will you take us to the throne room?" I said to distract her, using my Gift on her this time, just because I could. Taking her arm, I moved us toward the door. "I have a wedding to get to."

Smiling sweetly, I waved for the other ladies to follow, and they did with a nervous chuckle.

"To the main entrance," I told Jerusha as we stepped into the hallway, and she nodded. I could've traveled on my own. The request was strategic. Now was the time to assert my authority. When we reappeared at the great hall, I wanted everyone to see their deference to me, not rolled eyes behind my back. And, I admitted to myself, it felt *good*.

We landed in the grand hallway outside the double doors leading to the throne room. Two Jinni Guards stood outside, giving us stern looks as Dorcas and Milcah appeared behind me. Ignoring the guards, I told all three ladies. "Follow me in and lead everyone in a bow when we reach the front." Blank obedient looks passed over their faces.

Turning to the guards, I captured their gazes and demanded, "Open the doors with a bang. Let's make a grand entrance."

Slowly, they followed orders, moving stiffly like puppets with their strings being pulled.

Lips curving in satisfaction, I stepped back as the doors swung wide.

They hit the outer walls with a loud crash, as the guards gave me the striking appearance I'd asked for.

Inside, the room grew hushed as all eyes turned toward me.

Not waiting for permission, I strode forward.

An orchestra hastily put together near the front of the room lurched into song.

I didn't bother to check if Milcah, Jerusha, and Dorcas trailed after me. They didn't matter. Nothing mattered except saying our vows before the people and completing this marriage.

Jinn parted, making an aisle for me to walk toward Shem. I didn't hurry. With long, slow steps that fit the music, I made them wait, savoring the control I held over the whole room.

When I met Shem's eyes, I forced a smile for appearance's sake.

It was only a week ago that I'd looked across a crowded room seeking his face, but it couldn't have felt more different. No longer was I hopeful or naïve. Now, when I looked at him, I saw things plainly. Shem had fallen for a simple Jinni girl who didn't mind that he prioritized his crown over her. But that girl didn't exist and never had. He couldn't possibly love me when he'd never truly known me. And maybe that was for the best.

Koda's face replaced Shem's in my mind, unbidden.

A twinge of regret struck me.

He wouldn't have let me walk all over him the way Shem was now. That was one of the many things I'd found myself liking about him. He wasn't soft, but he didn't try to make me soft either.

With a slight shake of my head, I forced myself back to the present.

A malleable husband was exactly what I needed in this relationship.

It would be *me* who ordered the Jinni Guard to subtly search for the records Koda had mentioned, removing all traces of the Vaade's history permanently, while they were still vulnerable. I'd make sure they believed they were human. Shem hadn't been capable of facing them, so I'd do what had to be done. Once we became king and queen, he'd step back, one way or the other.

In the meantime, I'd make it my personal mission to find and close as many daleths to the human world as possible. King Jubal and Queen Samaria had left far too many open. I'd also appoint someone to find the spell the Vaade had used to open portals. Not that they'd remember creating them anymore. But better to be safe and remove any chance of them rediscovering it.

Though, perhaps I'd keep one open.

Then I could still check in on Koda now and then.

I bit my lip, unsure if I wanted to when he had no memory of me.

As long as the Vaade never received a sacrificial ring with the intention of marriage, Koda would never recognize me—or my Gifts—ever again. None of the Vaade would. And I'd make sure Shem was under compulsion to never speak a word of them either. All my secrets were safe—both my Gifts *and* what'd really taken place in the human world.

And if the covenant wasn't completed, neither was the magical truce. We would put the Vaade in their place.

Reaching the stage, I solemnly took the stairs, holding Shem's gaze the entire time—not to search for a sign of love in his eyes, since I wouldn't believe it even if I saw it—but because I wouldn't deign to give his parents or the onlookers a single glance.

Reaching him, I accepted the hand he held out. Remembering how so many daughters of Jinn hated to see affection between us, I leaned closer.

Over time, I was sure the tale of what'd happened today would become twisted.

But I'd know what'd really happened.

Despite my best intentions, I pictured Koda, lying alone in that field, and my vision blurred.

I blinked away the tears, smiling like the blushing bride I was supposed to be.

I'd never forget.

It wasn't until King Jubal stepped forward to begin the ceremony that it occurred to me—the ring.

Though the large dragon ring was somewhere back in my room in the pocket of my dress, the delicate Jinni ring was still on my finger.

THE SECRET CURSE

I slipped it off, tucking it into my palm and out of sight, hoping no one had noticed.

King Jubal raised a hand to the orchestra, and they fell silent. "We gather for an unexpected reason today," he began, as he took my hand and Shem's, leading us toward the thrones where we would sit during the ceremony. Royal weddings were long and full of rituals. Queen Samaria moved to a seat on one side to settle in for the long haul.

As we approached the thrones, while my back was to the audience, I tucked the Jinni ring with its ruby and diamond inside the bodice of my dress, safely out of sight.

When I turned to Shem, he took my hands in his own. They were cold. Squeezing my fingers, he probably intended to be reassuring, but I felt nothing.

We stopped before the thrones where we would wait silently until we were allowed to sit in a later part of the ceremony. Though we stared into each other's eyes per tradition, I focused on his father striding around the stage out of the corner of my eye.

King Jubal expounded on the values of a strong marriage and the importance of a wife who would represent the people. It was a slight, meant to remind everyone listening that I was no one of importance and Shem was stooping below his station to marry me. It seemed my Gift had convinced him to let the marriage happen, but that didn't make him happy about it.

I let the insult roll off my shoulders.

It didn't matter what anyone thought of me, when I could change their opinion with a word.

As the king began the first call and response with the people, the orchestra played an undertone beneath it all, and Shem took advantage of the moment to lean closer to me. "I never wanted to go through with it, Jezebel. I always wanted to marry you."

I forced a smile that I didn't feel to keep up the ruse for those watching and whispered, "I don't feel the same. But you'll think that I do, and that's all that matters."

A flicker of disbelief crossed his face, leaving as fast as it came with my final words. It felt good to speak the truth, even if he wouldn't remember.

"I'll always care for you," I told him, using my Gift to soothe his confusion. *But I will never trust you again.*

EPILOGUE

ONE YEAR LATER

SEATED ON THE THRONES, the prince and I were mid-ceremony yet again. This time, however, I casually held his hand—a habit of mine that'd formed over the past year. It made it much easier to guide him in the directions I preferred.

My other hand rested on my belly.

As a patch of warm, colorful light from the stained-glass windows danced over us, I felt a little kick.

This was my biggest victory yet.

When it'd become clear that I couldn't manipulate the king and queen day in and day out, not to mention their subjects, I'd considered other ways I might change their loyalties.

The answer had been obvious: a baby.

Though it was incredibly rare for a Jinni to get pregnant so effortlessly, with my shapeshifting Gift and a careful study of anatomy during pregnancy, it was easily done.

Somehow, though I'd barely begun to show, I already guessed it was a little girl.

I'd name her Hanna.

The corner of my mouth tilted up at the memory of Queen Samaria's face when I'd told her I'd become pregnant in less than a year's time.

It was unheard of.

King Jubal lifted the crown from his head, drawing my attention back to the present briefly. "The ancients crafted a spell called the B'har," he intoned, projecting his voice for the entire throne room to hear. "Every fifty years, this spell allows the crown *itself* to choose who rules our land."

Though King Jubal's current speech wasn't funny or uplifting in any way, I allowed my smile to grow wider. If I liked this little one well enough, I might even consider having a second child—now *that* would really set Jinni tongues wagging! Maybe I'd wait a century or two, though. I didn't want to disrupt my new life here too much.

Shem's hand squeezed mine when I glanced over at him, still beaming, though his return smile was slightly off. There was a glazed look to his eyes most days. I'd considered easing back on my Gift, but I couldn't risk losing his support right now. He'd settled into the role of doting husband agreeing with his wife easily enough. That had to mean my demands didn't bother him too much, didn't it?

"As I step down," King Jubal proclaimed in a monotone voice. "The crown will choose our next ruler based on their worthiness and the desires of the people themselves."

He raised the crown into the air.

A crackle of energy filled the room, lifting the crown from the king's hands and bringing it up toward the stained glass of the vaulted ceiling.

The crown dangled in midair.

The audience waited with bated breath.

King Jubal stared up at it reverently, while his wife followed suit from the front row. Shem and I remained seated.

I wasn't worried.

The people loved Shem.

I had no doubt in my mind they'd accept him as the next king, despite any lingering feelings about his wife.

A spell like this just needed time. There were thousands of Jinn spread across dozens of islands, but the people would choose Shem.

Eventually our patience was rewarded.

The crown slowly sank from the high vaulted ceiling toward the thrones, toward Shem.

It landed softly on his head.

King Jubal and Queen Samaria immediately bowed, followed by the people, until everyone knelt before us—before Shem technically.

King Jubal raised his voice. "Long may he live, long may he reign."

"Long may he live," the people repeated his words, their voices blending together in a powerful chorus. "Long may he reign."

"Long may I be a good ruler," Shem replied. His words resounded across the large space as he bowed his head in respect for their choice.

After a long pause filled with weighty silence, he let his gaze sweep across the solemn Jinn around the room. "Please rise."

Shuffling filled the room as everyone returned to their feet, except us.

Shem lifted my hand to his lips to press a chaste kiss to my fingers. We sat on the thrones while the orchestra played and a slow progression began to cross the stage one at a time, bringing offerings for the new king.

Thanks to Jubal and Samaria's encouragement, the rest of the kingdom was in full support of this shift in leadership. Especially now that a babe was on the way.

Though the true Jinni taking King Jubal's place would be me.

I'd already decided Shem would begin to take on more assignments in the human world, searching for any last trace of Vaade history.

Assignments that would leave me behind to rule in his place.

If something happened to him in the future on one of these missions, I'd mourn his loss… But in many ways, I'd already done that the day of our marriage.

I didn't love him anymore.

When I looked back and compared what I'd first felt for him to what Koda had made me feel, I wasn't sure I'd *ever* loved Shem.

Absently, I squeezed his hand.

In truth, I didn't feel much of anything for him at this point.

Quiet applause from the audience followed each supplication. Perfumes, gold, resin, and even the occasional cow or goat, though the animals were of course left to the side of the stage instead of paraded before us.

My serene expression never shifted, but I sighed to myself, wishing this whole unnecessary performance was over already.

My mind was already on the meeting I'd set with Milcah after this, in the vault filled with enchanted objects above the royal family's suites.

The next few hours were full of formal rites and traditions, offering artificial smiles to each new well-wisher. Thinking about what Milcah was bringing to our meeting was all that got me through the dull repetition. Finally, after the ceremony ended, we stood beside the grand double doors of the throne room as a slow trickle of guests exited, all of whom stopped to congratulate Shem, and myself by association, on their way out.

"You seem a little ambivalent for a new queen," Shem's father jibed from one side during a quiet moment. He still didn't like me much. Though he yielded to my Gift whenever I asked something of him, his will remained otherwise strong. While I could've forced him to change his mind about me, I'd come to enjoy sparring with him. On any other day, I'd have relished coming up with a sharp retort. Putting him in his place reminded me how far I'd come.

Today, however, I'd had enough of the false niceties.

Placing a hand on his shoulder, I smiled. "Make your excuses for me, would you? You know how important it is for a pregnant woman to rest."

Not waiting for his reply, I traveled across the castle, landing in the east wing, directly outside the royal family's vault.

The room where they kept their collection of enchanted objects.

Milcah was waiting in the hall outside the vault looking the other way, arms crossed, unable to get in. *Without me.*

My lips curved upward at the irony of her needing me. "Did you find it?"

She startled.

Whirling to face me, she glanced between the Jinni Guards standing at both ends of the hallway. "Perhaps we should talk inside?" she murmured, trying to shame me for talking about enchanted objects in front of them.

As if I'd ever intentionally give away my own secrets.

"Why?" I stage-whispered. "Are you worried they'll figure out we're putting something in the vault?" I glanced meaningfully at both guards. "Give them a little credit, Milcah. I think they're intelligent enough to put the pieces together themselves."

Flushing, she stiffened.

Before she could find another barbed retort, I placed my hand on the swirling iron snakes that formed a lock across the blue vault door, still chuckling. The snake heads uncoiled and struck, wrapping around my wrist. I waited patiently. The locks clicked open as the iron snakes released me with metallic scrapes, allowing me through.

"After you." I waved Milcah inside as I opened the vault.

I rarely used my Gift of manipulation on her. It was far more entertaining when she was aware that she was being forced to obey.

Inside, soft lights flickered on in response to our presence, lighting on dozens of artifacts, from lamps to mirrors to dusty old books. Most of the items, besides the jewels of course, seemed unimportant at first glance. But everything besides the jewels—and possibly some of those as well—was enchanted in some way.

Milcah pulled a small object wrapped in soft wax paper from the travel bag slung over her shoulder.

She held it out to me.

An enchanted mirror that would allow the bearer to see anyone they loved.

My heart beat faster. "You actually found it," I whispered. "I was starting to think you never would."

She stiffened at the insult. "I've only been looking for six months." Her retort was restrained, since she was speaking to her queen now and knew better than to snap at me. As a result, she sounded like she was whining.

"You're right, I suppose," I said offhandedly, as I caressed the soft wax paper, feeling the solid shape beneath. "Anybody could've tracked it down in that amount of time."

A sharp hiss of breath let me know I'd won this round again, and I held back a grin. "You may go." The sooner she left, the sooner I could unwrap the item and discover if it truly worked the way rumors described.

Milcah moved to the door, but she wasn't ready to accept defeat quite yet. With her hand on the doorknob, she spoke. "May I ask whom exactly you hope the mirror will show you, when everyone you love is here in the castle?"

I arched a brow in her direction, finally deigning to look at her. "Oh?" I replied in a cool tone. "Is my mother in the castle? I was not aware."

She flushed for the second time in as many minutes and let herself out without another word, letting the vault door slam shut behind her.

Alone now, I allowed a small smile.

Turning back to the little parcel, I peeled away the wax paper, revealing the object inside.

It was a small hand-mirror.

Slightly larger than my fist, it had a thick frame of dark silver, etched with circular designs all around the mirror and along the handle.

Would it actually show me my mother?

I had no idea.

My mouth was dry as I held it up to my face and gazed at my reflection and spoke her name: "Sariah."

I waited.

Only my pale face with dark brows, pale blue eyes, and rosy lips stared back at me.

Nothing else.

I sighed, but truthfully, I wasn't surprised. After all, I barely knew my mother. How could I love someone that I didn't even know?

No, if I were honest, it wasn't her face I was craving a glimpse of at all. The true reason I'd begun my hunt for the mirror was an entirely different person.

Nervous energy flooded my veins, making me hesitate, shifting from one foot to the other.

Would it work? Would I finally see him again?

Though I'd kept close tabs on information regarding the Khaanevaade people as they adapted to being seemingly human, I hadn't allowed myself to visit the human world myself.

If I went to see Koda, I was afraid of what he might say—of what *I* might say.

If he remembered me, he'd call me a thief and a liar. And he'd be right.

The less exposure to Jinn, the better, if the Vaade were to remain skeptical of magic like the humans. After pressing King Jubal into action, I'd convinced him to send his guard, who'd destroyed all written records of the Vaade that they could find. Now and again, rumor reached us of a zealot urging the people to see that they were descended from dragons. But the majority of the Vaade scoffed and called them lunatics. The curse held firmly in place.

Wincing at the year-old memories that still felt like they'd happened yesterday, I decided not to torment myself any longer.

I whispered his name, "Koda."

The mirror flickered. A white mist spread across the glass, quickly replaced by a quiet scene of a man sitting at a small kitchen table.

A woman swept past along the side, and I flinched.

Though he'd never technically become my husband with our vows left unfinished, it sometimes felt like he was, even more so than Shem. I *hated* the idea of another woman taking that place in his life.

I blew out a sigh of relief when I saw the woman's face. *Tehya.*

She bumped his shoulder in their familiar version of rude affection as she left the room, while he sat staring down at the little wooden table, lost in thought. As he brought a cup to his lips, I caught a glimpse of his now ordinary-looking hazel eyes. They'd grown dull.

It broke my heart seeing him like this. I could almost forget the way he'd betrayed me and forgive him. If we'd been in the same room, I might have.

Carefully, I rewrapped the mirror in the wax paper, hiding the painful images from sight.

I slipped it into one of the pockets in my voluminous navy dress and stepped out of the vault. The guards only saw me for a split second before I traveled to the royal suite of rooms that I shared with the prince. *No,* I caught myself, *the king now.*

That would take some getting used to.

Opening the door to our collective suites, I crossed the central sitting room with unseeing eyes, passing the door that led to Shem's room and entering my own private space, locking the door behind me.

I pulled out the little mirror again, setting it on my desk beside a small, but carefully detailed map of all the known daleths in both the human world and our own.

I'd made it a priority to study their locations so I'd never be caught unaware again. And while I'd had Shem give orders to close dozens of them already, I couldn't bring myself to close all of them.

They were my last link to Koda.

After that one glimpse, I'd fully expected to satisfy my curiosity. Clenching my fists, I admitted to myself that it wasn't nearly enough.

Contemplating the much larger mirror that hung on the wall beside my wardrobe, I considered my reflection, shifting my eyes, hair, and skin until I resembled the Vaade, enough to be mistaken for Tehya's sister or cousin.

It could work.

Touching the little hand-mirror again, I thought of Koda's despondent expression and how seeing him had brought up a hundred more questions than it'd answered.

I might have to make a visit.

THE END.

TURN THE PAGE TO READ
EXCLUSIVE BONUS CONTENT FROM JEZEBEL & KODA

Koda's Curse

THE COVENANT

JEZEBEL STARED AT ME waiting, but I must've heard her wrong.

You and I should complete the covenant instead, she'd said.

But not that long ago, she'd called anyone willing to do the covenant a fool. The vivid memory was still burned into my mind.

"You... and me..." I repeated slowly. Did she understand what she was suggesting? A lifetime together. Promising to stay with me. Even when I'd asked her to stay the day before, I'd tried not to get my hopes up. Now they were somewhere in the clouds.

"Nevermind," she mumbled, dropping her gaze. "It was a stupid idea."

"No, it's not. I just... need to think," I managed. Shaking my head, I tried to focus and untangle this new knot. Yesterday she'd clearly been against the idea. What had changed? Normally I'd take the time to reason this out, but whenever she was around, logic sprouted wings as easily as she did and flew off.

Jezebel shook her head, still not meeting my eyes. "Don't bother. I don't know what I was thinking."

My hesitation had embarrassed her. *Say something.*

Carefully, I reached out to take her hand. "Is this what you want?"

Please say yes.

"It doesn't matter what I want." She shrugged, but didn't pull her hand away. "This will save your sister and my people, and it's the only plan we have."

Reaching out, I tilted her chin up until she met my eyes. "It does matter," I murmured. Her reasons suddenly mattered more than anything.

When she didn't answer, I held her gaze and asked again. "Is it what *you* want?"

Blinking away tears, she gave me a single nod.

I wanted to throw my hands in the air and whoop for joy, but settled for a quiet, "Good."

"Good?"

It took everything I had not to grin like a fool. If she only knew. I'd hoped for a future with her since the day she'd led me on a wild chase through the woods. Though I'd never have guessed it'd happen quite like this. All I said though, was, "I think I like this plan of yours."

"You do?"

Did she really not see it? Anyone would be lucky to marry her.

Swallowing hard, I gently squeezed her hand, searching for the right words. I wove my fingers through hers. "It would be an honor to have you as my wife."

I was rewarded with a smile. Shyly she asked, "What now?"

That pulled me out of the happy moment all too quickly. When I spoke, I wanted to shake my head, because it was impossible. "We'll need to steal the rings."

But we can't.

As I explained to her how they were necessary for the covenant, my hopes fell. "My father will expect me to try that to help Tehya."

I'd never been so disappointed by a dream I'd only had for the span of a minute.

But Jezebel grinned up at me with a twinkle in her eye. "Then, *I'll* have to steal them. And you can be our distraction."

Just as quickly as they'd dipped, my hopes soared back up on fresh wings.

With a grin, I touched my forehead to hers, making her gasp with the suddenness. "I love the way you think."

We quickly made a plan.

Before it had even sunk in what we were about to do, it was time to act.

"A kiss for luck?" I murmured as we reached the edge of the makeshift Jinni camp. I lifted a hand to her cheek. Her heartbeat doubled. Grinning, I kissed her, loving that I could cause that reaction. If not for the voices drifting toward us on the wind from the Jinni encampment, I'd have been happy to stay like this all day.

I forced myself to pull back, stroking her cheek with my thumb. "See you soon."

Time to go distract my father.

While Jezebel circled around the tents toward the back, I approached boldly from the front, striding toward my father where he stood in the clearing with some of his men.

Picking a fight with him would be all too easy.

***

"Don't make Tehya do this," I yelled before I'd even entered the clearing. Same argument as always. Same beginning. It would have the same ending, but changing my father's mind wasn't my goal anymore.

His eyes tightened at the corners. For one short breath, a flash of sadness lit them.

He looked like the man I'd known when my mother was still with us.

Before Cain's curse transformed her into a dragon.

A curse that might as well be mine.

One of the Jinni standing outside the tents coughed, and my father's hard mask of the Dragon returned. "You dare to approach me like this," he yelled back, waving a hand in the direction of the Jinn.

Of course, my father's men chimed in, shouting as well. "We'll put you down as easily as we did before, Koda."

My father waved them back with a harsh swipe of his hand through the air, growling softly at me, "At least Tehya cares enough to make the sacrifice."

I winced.

"I. Care." I gritted out. "But I believe there's another way to stop—to change things—that won't hurt everyone involved."

With the nearby Jinn, both outside and poking their heads out of the tent, I couldn't outright discuss the curse. I hated how it allowed Cain to pluck our people from beneath their family's noses for centuries now. He turned them into the beasts we'd come to call dragons and used them for his unknown Jinni purposes. He'd never returned anyone either. Including my mother.

And Cain had made sure the curse kept us from speaking of him, the ones we'd lost, or their transformation with anyone who wasn't a Vaade.

Still, my father tensed as if I danced right up to it. "Watch your words, boy."

A scuffle from the main tent made us pause.

Jezebel was inside.

Anxiety rippled across my skin at the fear she'd been caught.

Instead, male voices yelled at each other from within, immediately followed by a Jinni guard bursting into the clearing, arms around a Vaade, grappling him to the ground.

Chaos descended as the other Vaade and Jinn ran to pull them apart.

I grabbed my father's arm, turning his attention back to me and lowered my voice until the Jinn couldn't possibly hear. "We can bring Mother back another way."

Agony flared in his eyes. "My son, after so many years without her, how can you ask me to wait another day?"

I opened my mouth to tell him everything, about Jezebel and I, how we could complete the covenant happily instead of forcing Tehya into a future she didn't want. "I'm not asking you to wait—"

"What about Chaska?" my father cut me off. "Or Hotah? Turned into dragons, just like your mother. If you don't care about her, then maybe you at least care about them? Or Iktomi, or Sunta, or—"

Fury overtook the sting of his words. "How *dare* you? I've missed her every single day. I want her and the others back just as much as you do."

"No." My father shook his head, lips flattened into a thin line as he glared at me, both of us ignoring the sound of fists landing and the shouts of Jinn and Vaade behind us. "Every full moon Cain turns another of our own into a dragon. We've found no other way to stop his cruel plague on our people." He took my shoulders in a painful grip, leaning in to whisper in my ear. "Ten years, Koda," his deep voice growled, and as he pulled back his eyes blazed like real fire. "I won't let him have a second more. Not when it might mean you or your sister could be—" his voice broke.

I clasped his hand with my own, waiting in respect for him to finish.

The Jinni captain had just managed to subdue his men, forcing them apart from our own, when a flash of Jinni magic tickled our Vaade senses.

My father and his men all snarled at the Jinn in the clearing, warning them with glares not to try anything further.

I alone knew that the flare of magic had come from Jezebel.

Closing my eyes, I could hear her soft intake of breath and the unique cadence of her footsteps as she took off from the back of the tent.

That meant she had the rings.

I could go now.

But my father still gripped my shoulders, struggling with his words. When he raised his eyes to mine, the gates holding back his sorrow had lifted once again. A single tear trailed down his cheek as he held my gaze. "My son, the next one Cain takes could be you. Or your sister."

My heart clenched.

I'd thought the same thing myself.

Many times.

"If you think Tehya's fate is bad now," he continued. "Just remember, it could be worse."

My shoulders slumped. He was right, as always. "I understand father, and I don't disagree. The covenant has to happen today, but—" Before I could tell him about my plans to do the covenant with Jezebel instead, he stopped me once again.

"No buts, Koda," he growled, and that angry mask he wore so frequently fell back over his countenance as his grip turned painful. "The Jinn will pay for what they've done." Though he spoke too softly for the nearby Jinn to hear despite the fighting settled down, I'd never heard him speak with more conviction in my life. "Every single Jinni deserves to die for what they've done."

I waved my hand at the unfamiliar faces. "These Jinn don't even know about the—" my throat closed up against my will as I tried to say *the dragon curse.*

One of the Jinn must be close enough to overhear.

We couldn't speak of the curse to a Jinni, not even a hint. Though I'd wanted to tell Jezebel many times, to explain that most of us didn't hate the Jinn, we hated what they'd *done* to us—to my mother and so many others in our tribe—I couldn't.

None of us could.

"It doesn't matter," my father turned away, ending our discussion with one last hiss. "They'll all pay."

Torn, I let him storm away, knowing he wouldn't understand how I felt about Jezebel, that no matter what I said he would hate her along with the rest of them.

Clenching my fists, I stepped back slowly until I could slip back into the forest. I moved aimlessly through the trees, trying to think.

The only way to break the curse over my mother would be to set a new curse on the Jinn—including Jezebel.

But she would see it as a betrayal.

Honestly, she'd be right.

Could I make her understand? Could I help her see why it had to be done? The curse over my mother wouldn't be broken until the very last drop of Jinni magic faded from the world, and that could take days... Which meant I might not be able to explain my choices to her for days either.

Pressing my lips together, I stared out toward the mountains where she waited, probably wondering where I was.

I could tolerate her fury for a few days if that meant I could get my mother back. Once the curse was broken, I'd explain everything to Jezebel. She'd understand.

I turned toward the mountains, growing more and more certain.

She *would* understand.

Somehow, I felt like I'd already known her for years. She might not have told me her whole story, but something told me she was the type who could do difficult things when necessary.

Though it felt dirty and underhanded, I knew what I had to do.

***

A short hike through the woods brought me to our meeting place. Before I stepped out from the trees, I paused to memorize her like this. The mountain backdrop was nothing next to her beauty.

Tucking her dark hair behind her ear, she'd turned toward the water, unaware of my approach.

Though I didn't hide my footsteps, she must've been deep in thought. When I touched her shoulder, she sucked in a sharp breath and swung at me.

I caught her wrist. "It's just me!"

"What took you so long?" she demanded, pulling away. "Did they discover the rings were taken?"

I grinned. "If they haven't yet, they will soon."

"That's not very reassuring."

"You don't seem like a woman who needs to be reassured," I countered, growing more and more excited by the second. I was about to rescue my mother and so many others from an impossible curse, while also marrying a woman I could easily fall in love with.

If I was honest with myself, I already had.

She tried to hide a smile, but I could tell she was excited too. "What now?"

Now, we break one curse with another and change everything.

I couldn't say that though. Slowly, I took her hand, tracing a thumb over her skin. "Now, we begin."

She took the rings out of her bag and held them out in her palm.

As I explained how they worked, I felt myself drawing inward, worrying. What if she didn't forgive me for this?

I gazed at her through one of the rings, memorizing her face. I would make it up to her. I would remind her who she was every single day while the curse blocked the truth. I would protect her from my father and his misdirected hatred. We would find my mother and the rest of my people who'd been taken. Equally important, we'd track down Cain, the Jinni who'd cursed them in the first place, and make sure he could never do it again. Then, I swore to myself, I would finish the covenant with her and bring her magic back. My father would just have to understand.

With a finger under her chin, I brought her gaze up to mine. "I have full trust in you," I murmured. "Can you say the same of me?"

She managed a small nod.

My hopes lifted. That hadn't come easily to her. Her trust wasn't given lightly.

I ran a thumb softly over her bottom lip and leaned in, unable to help myself.

I kissed her slowly, taking my time just in case she didn't forgive me, hoping she could sense how sincere I was. The idea of having her forever like this hit me with full force, making me lift her up and swing her around in pure joy. Her laughter flooded my senses. With a grin, I kissed her again, before finally forcing myself to pull back.

"I haven't been to any weddings in the human world, Vaade or otherwise," she said to my chin. "But I believe the kiss comes at the *end* of the ceremony?"

A full body laugh broke from my chest as I stepped back. "Then let's hurry up and start so we can get to the end."

She bit her lip, smiling. "I'll follow your lead. How do we begin?"

Pointing to her three middle fingers one at a time, I spoke softly, reverently. "Mind, body, soul." I cleared my throat, trying not to linger on any of them by accident as I explained. "A typical human marriage places the rings on the soul finger." Another pang of guilt hit me. It was hard to ignore.

Tucking a bit of her hair behind her ear, my fingers softly grazed her cheek. "Can you trust me Jezebel?" I asked again, unable to help myself, needing to know the answer.

I knew what I was asking of her.

And how she might hate me for it.

"Okay," she whispered, taking my hand. "Time for you to make me weak and defenseless."

I chuckled. "As long as you'll make me the same."

Taking the delicate Jinni ring, I began the ceremony in a slight haze.

We spoke the words, placed the rings, and allowed the weakening to sweep over us.

It itched like a coat in sweltering heat.

My father would be furious.

But I could hardly bring myself to care as we got closer and closer to the crucial moment.

Part of me was thrilled to be marrying this beautiful woman. I meant every promise I made.

On the other hand, I dreaded the way this might end.

"Now what?"

Her words pulled me out of the dark thoughts.

I hesitated.

She might hate me forever. Was this worth the risk?

"Now," I said slowly, forcing myself to focus, "We say the final words to complete the covenant as we place the rings on... the next finger."

Slowly, I drew the delicate white gold ring off her finger, staring down at the ruby and diamond for a long moment.

I don't have a choice.

Lifting her hand, I poised the ring in front of it. "With this ring, I take you, Jezebel, to be my wife in every way, until death takes us."

As I slid the ring onto her first finger—the mind finger—sealing my betrayal, I closed the distance between us and captured her mouth with my own. It was a desperate kiss. A distraction kiss. Possibly a last kiss, though I hated the thought.

When I pulled away, I watched her closely.

Eyes closed, she laughed on a shaky breath. "That wasn't technically the end," she teased. "We still have to do your ring."

She hadn't noticed.

"I know." Though I tried to smile back, I didn't feel it anymore. Regret laced every other emotion. I touched the dragon tooth necklace, reminding myself of my mother again. It had to be done. "I just couldn't hold back."

I gave Jezebel my ring while making sure to stick out the correct *ring* finger for her to place it on.

Just a few more words followed by that ring landing in place, and this would all be over.

All our struggles over the past decade would finally end.

I couldn't even remember what my mother's voice sounded like anymore. That would finally change.

Jezebel hesitated, just slightly as she stared at the ring. "What am I supposed to say again?"

My heart squeezed. "With this ring, I take you, Koda, to be my husband," I repeated, watching her closely, trying to guess what she was thinking.

Her face was a mask of calm. It reminded me of the way she'd looked when I'd first met her.

As she met my eyes, my heart began to beat faster. Had she noticed after all? I still couldn't tell. "What's wrong?"

She smiled at me as she began to repeat the words, and I tried to relax, but peace escaped me.

"… until death takes us," she finished.

She slid the dragon ring onto my first finger.

No.

Panic flooded my whole body, along with a strange heaviness.

She'd just placed the forgetting curse on me and all of the Vaade as well.

Did she know?

Keep going.

I could still salvage this.

Clearing my throat, I said. "Good. Now, move it to the final finger, to connect the soul." I pulled the ring off, handing it back to her, and pointing at the finger she should've put it on to finish the covenant. Once she did so, it should reverse the curse's effects on me immediately. At least, I thought so… the details were growing fuzzy.

I hoped this would still work.

She slipped her own ring off instead, holding both of them in shaking hands, and whispered. "You first."

Time stopped.

She knew.

Anguish squeezed my heart so tightly I couldn't breathe.

Staring at the little ring, I didn't know what to do. I couldn't explain. Part of me struggled to remember what I would say even if I could. And I couldn't force her. All I could do was be honest. "I… can't."

Though her face remained calm, I could feel the breaking going on behind her eyes.

"I'm sorry," I said lamely, knowing it wasn't enough. "I can't explain."

Deep regret swept over me. I couldn't think of anything else to say. A strange sensation of little things slipping away continued to tickle my mind—of what exactly, I couldn't say. But I had enough presence of mind to recognize the forgetting curse beginning to take effect.

A few breaths passed as we simply stared at each other, before she spoke softly, "You were never going to complete the covenant for me, were you? You did exactly what your father wanted. You used me."

I shook my head. Thinking past my shame was a struggle. For the thousandth time, I tried to shake off whatever Jinni magic kept me from telling her the full story, but it was no use. "The covenant and the curse would've happened one way or the other," I said instead, settling for something close to the truth. "My father would've made sure of it."

A tear slipped out and rolled down her pale cheek.

I couldn't help myself. Aching for her, I reached out to wipe it.

She flinched away from me.

Hiding a wince, I let my hand fall back to my side. I needed to find an explanation she could understand, but I had *nothing*. Even if I could tell her the truth, it might not be enough. But I had to try. "This was the only way I could—" the curse strangled my vocal chords, refusing to let me finish. I shook my head, wanting to growl. Fine. Another truth then. "This was the only way I could protect Tehya. She wants to marry Akeena, not your prince."

She just stared at me.

"There *had* to be a marriage to use the covenant spell," I continued when she didn't reply. "And I know it doesn't seem like it, but this solution saves you as well as Tehya. You would've been a target along with the rest of Jinn. But now, as my wife, I can keep you safe."

She scoffed. "Safe, while the rest of my people are enslaved or worse?"

Forehead wrinkling, I pressed a hand to it, trying to wrap my mind around her words. Enslaved? "I... I don't think that's what my father plans." Who were her people again? Not important, we weren't doing this to hurt anyone. At least, not that I could remember... We only wanted to take our power back—more specifically, to get our people back. "My father only needs the curse in place for a short time. A few months or a year at most." However long it took us to end my mother's curse. And to track down whoever it was who'd hurt her in the first place— I dug deep, struggling to remember, but the name wouldn't come to me. It didn't matter right now. We'd make him pay.

"A year?" she gasped, bringing me back to the present as she shook her head. "There will be nothing left of us."

How could I help her understand?

"I can't explain," I repeated like a fool, more frustrated than I'd ever been in my entire life. Of course she didn't believe me. I wouldn't either. "It *has* to be this way. But with you as my wife, I'll have the power to end the curse as soon as we—" I choked as I drew too close to mentioning the curse in her presence and growled softly. "As soon as we conquer Jinn," I said instead. "Your Gifts won't be gone forever."

She wouldn't look at me anymore.

Squeezing the rings, she whispered, "You really believe that, don't you?"

"I swear it," I vowed passionately, trying to touch her cheek again, but she dodged my hand.

"I'll keep you safe in the meantime. I promise," I swore vehemently, wishing she could read my mind and see that I meant it. Causing her pain made me want to go back in time and do things differently. I didn't want this. I'd made a mistake. I held in a groan because there was no going back anymore, only forward. I *had* to find a way to convince her, for both our sakes.

"I have to do this, Jezebel." My voice broke a little. I only had one argument left, though it didn't come close to what was really going on. "For my people."

"Don't talk to me about your people," she spat, taking a step back. "*I* was supposed to be your people. Your *wife*. You lied to me."

"No," I swore. "I meant every word. I'll protect you from all of it. You *are* my wife now, which means my father can't touch you. No one can."

My fingers twitched. I wanted to hold her and tell her I was sorry, to make it right somehow. "Your people will forget. It has to be this way. But I can remind you of the truth"—I squinted, trying to remember how it worked when the curse was clouding my mind—"every day if need be. And when the time is right, I'll make sure we complete the covenant to bring your abilities back."

"When the time is right," she repeated dully.

"It's not like you care about your people anyway." I threw up my hands. Why couldn't she believe me? "What do you care if we take power away from Jinn? The Gifts are an unfair advantage."

I thought of the one who'd cursed my mother yet again—fury stoked my memory, briefly bringing his name back to me: Cain. He'd taken her and so many others. I clenched my fists at how powerless we'd been to stop him.

"That's how you see me?" she gasped.

"No, of course not." I'd never feared her Gifts, or her. She was nothing like Cain. I frowned. Who was Cain?

She turned away.

Without thinking, I grabbed her wrist, frantic at the thought of her abandoning our covenant before it was finished. "What're you doing? You can't leave."

She glanced pointedly at my hand. "Let go."

"I can't do that," I growled, hating myself for holding on, yet unable to let her go when she tried to pull away.

Without warning, she yanked a knife from her bag, pointing it at my face. "Let. Me. Go."

What am I doing? I forced myself to loosen my grip, holding my hands up in surrender. "This is going all wrong." That was a massive understatement. I gripped my head, shaking it slightly to clear my thoughts. "We're on the same side, remember?" I spoke softly, repeating the words she'd said to me that had made me begin to see her differently. "You have to finish the covenant by putting the ring on my finger."

"I will if you go first," she said, stepping back.

I followed.

I couldn't help myself.

"I already told you, I can't."

Ignoring the knife she held, I tried to stay close to her, terrified that if I took my eyes off her face for even a second that she might somehow disappear. If we didn't move quickly, we were both at risk of not only losing our magic forever but completely forgetting we'd ever had it in the first place.

Her eyes were growing wild.

I should try to explain, at least one more time. Carefully, I chose words that were vague enough the curse wouldn't stop me. "For our… plans… to work, we need the Jinn to be completely cut off from magic. Nothing else will be enough."

That was the only way to stop… whoever it was we were trying to stop. Fear filled the gaping hole where the memory had been.

"Why? What do the Vaade plan to do?"

Grinding my teeth, I dropped my gaze for a split second, unable to meet her eyes when I admitted, "I can't say."

"Why?"

"I—I don't remember." Rubbing my brow, I shook my head. That was odd. I still knew we needed magic to fade away, but I'd forgotten why? Frustration made my blood boil, made me want to act, to do *something* with this frantic energy. All I could manage to say was, "You have to trust me."

She scoffed, and I knew my words weren't enough.

Maybe she'd never really trusted me.

It stung, but I couldn't say it wasn't deserved.

"Listen to me, Jezebel," I tried a different tactic, trailing after her along the water's edge, unable to let too much space form between us. "I swear on the dragons themselves that I will make sure the covenant is completed for you by placing a ring on your finger eventually. It will only be a few years at most. I'll protect you the entire time."

"What an offer," she snapped. My attempt to pacify her had only made her more furious. "You'll only betray me *temporarily*."

Shame swept over me and I winced. But when she moved back, I still followed.

We were in dangerous territory now. I couldn't see a solution that didn't make things a thousand times worse.

Unexpectedly, she turned and ran.

On instinct, I gave chase.

The long grass crunched underfoot as my heart thundered wildly, beating a harsh rhythm. This wasn't the right way to solve this, but panic drove me on.

I gained on her quickly.

But I didn't pounce.

Even now, when both our people's futures depended on our choices in this moment, I couldn't bring myself to hurt her.

The steep slope of rocks at the base of the mountain rose up on all sides, quickly blocking her path.

When she whirled to face me like a trapped animal, I held my hands up cautiously in a sign of peace. "I don't want to hurt you, Jezebel."

"Too late," she snapped, clutching the rings against her stomach. "You should've thought of that sooner."

Primal fear took over.

Force it now, fix it later.

When I leapt toward her, she swiped clumsily at me with the knife.

I hissed as it sliced my arm.

Though the cut was shallow, it shook me out of my animalistic reflexes, briefly clearing my mind. I stepped back to give her space, glancing down at the wound.

But the instant she ducked past me to run again, all those instincts came roaring back.

I pounced.

It was too easy.

Knocking her to the ground, I fought against the beast inside that wanted to shake her senseless, focusing on getting rid of that ridiculous knife instead. I flung it away into the grass without a second glance.

Wrestling with Jezebel, I grunted in frustration as the rings went flying into the long grass as well.

Though I wanted to be gentle, I grunted when she landed a blow in my ribs, and yanked her arms down, pinning them to her sides with my weight.

Squirming, she continued to struggle.

I *hated* this.

Choosing between her and my mother was not only devastating, but terrifying. No matter what I chose, I risked losing one or both of them. I gritted my teeth and made myself to capture her arms. Jezebel could make her own choices once this was all over. Unless I interfered, my mother could not.

"You shouldn't have thrown the rings." My voice came out gruff. I couldn't help it. Every second that she fought, I'd have to wait that much longer to explain myself to her, to help her understand. Searching through the grass for the rings, I could hear my hatred of this situation coloring my voice. "You're only prolonging the inevitable."

"Are you saying you'd force me to put the ring on your finger?" she asked between gasps. "Because that's the only way it will happen."

Another slice of unhappiness cut through me. I couldn't meet her eyes, but forced myself to nod. If that would help us get past this faster. "I will if I have to."

Leaning further to one side, I brushed my fingers through the grass, trying to keep enough weight on her while searching for those infuriating rings that were ruining everything.

She wiggled slightly beneath me, but I ignored it.

There.

"Found it," I declared in relief.

Jezebel wrapped her small fingers around my arm, straining to get away. While I didn't want to do this, I also held firm so she wouldn't hurt herself.

Time to get this over with.

Get her hand. Make her hold the ring. Put it on. End the madness.

Get her hand.

Make her hold the ring.

Put it on...

She was making a fist.

Growling, I yanked at her small fingers, losing patience. This was hurting both of us. I'd force the ring on if I had to.

One finger pulled back.

Two fingers.

Pressing the ring between them, I gripped firmly, so she had to hold it there.

Lifting my other hand across our bodies, I leaned heavily on my elbow so I could slip my finger through.

But my body kept leaning without my consent.

I tipped too far to the other side, nearly falling over before I could correct myself.

Weakness trickled into my veins like the curse had, but this time it was all encompassing, quickly spreading, growing steadily more invasive.

I barely noticed when she yanked her hand free.

Sagging over her, panic rolled over me in waves.

What was happening?

An accidental glimpse of Jezebel's face showed a mixture of sorrow and satisfaction as she pushed me off of her.

No. "What did you do?"

The dragon ring thunked into the dirt. Without my heightened sense of hearing, it was so soft I barely heard it.

As Jezebel brought one knee up, then the other, pushing to stand, I gasped like a helpless fish in the grass, unable to move. "Jezebel, it can't end like this, this isn't how it's supposed to be. I swear to you this wasn't what I had planned. Please you have to believe me!"

Turning her back on me, she quietly poked through the long grass until she found what she was looking for.

The other ring.

The Jinni ring that would complete the covenant for *her.*

"Please, Jezebel," I begged, tears filling my eyes against my will as I tried to sit up yet again but fell back against the grass. My mother would be lost forever. All of the other Vaade, truly and permanently cursed. And now, because of me, my own people as well. And I would lose the woman I was falling in love with. "Please," I whispered again, unable to defend my decisions.

She refused to respond.

Drawing a deep breath, she faced me, cautiously picking up my arm and laying it across her lap so she could easily prop the ring between my paralyzed fingers.

"Please, Jezebel," I repeated, knowing this was my last chance. No. As I gazed into her eyes, the resolve was clear. My last chance had already come and gone. But at least I could tell her one final truth. "I care about you more than I'd like to admit. I wasn't just marrying you for the covenant."

She only lifted my limp hand higher so the ring that I held against my will was facing her, and then slipped it on.

Nothing changed for me.

My body continued to weaken as a cold, numb sensation spread across my limbs, rapidly creeping toward the center of my body, making my eyelids droop unwillingly.

But she let out a breath of relief, shoulders relaxing.

The curse had lifted for her.

And for her people.

Tears for my mother blurred my vision. Our last hope of saving her had just vanished in front of me. I'd never see her again.

If I didn't do something quickly, I'd never see Jezebel again either. "Finish the covenant," I rasped painfully, fighting my vocal chords for the ability to speak. Whatever she'd used on me was working too quickly. "Your prince doesn't want you anymore," I said to remind her we were her only home now. *Please forgive me. Please give me another chance.* But how could she, when I still couldn't explain? "This is your only option."

She shook her head. "It stopped being an option the moment you betrayed me."

"Please," I said again, because it was all I had left. My whole body strained toward the dragon ring that still lay beside me. Maybe she didn't need to place it on my finger, maybe putting it on myself would be enough.

But I couldn't even lift my arm to pick it up.

My mother. My people. My wife.

The words hadn't lost their strength the way my body had. Each time they repeated, they hurt just as much. "I swear I would've reversed the curse," I said one last time, wanting her to know, somehow, that I meant it.

She knelt beside me.

Leaning over me, she picked up the dragon ring.

For two short heartbeats, my hopes rose.

She might have mercy on me yet.

The sheen of tears in her eyes brought them to the surface of my own again, but then she delivered the devastating blow.

"I don't believe you."

Words failed me.

She slipped the dragon ring into her pocket, removing my last shred of hope that someone else might stumble along and place it on my finger instead.

We were well and truly lost.

"You can't do this!" I found my voice in the midst of my panic, growing angry now. She didn't even try to understand! Why couldn't she have given me a chance! "If you don't finish the covenant, you'll condemn us to live like humans… without any memories of who we really are…" I tried to continue, but my eyes drifted shut.

Her voice was flat when she replied, "If you could do it, then so can I."

Fighting the outrageously strong muscles in my eyes, I forced them open through sheer willpower. "We were only going to… use the weakness temporarily. It's completely… different."

"I disagree," she murmured.

"We keep written records," I slurred, fighting a losing battle. "You can't make us forget forever…" My eyes won the battle and slammed shut, refusing to open again.

I couldn't move a single muscle.

She murmured something over me that my mind didn't quite grasp, but then I sensed her leaning closer.

Her lips brushed across mine softly.

"I could've loved you more than anyone," she whispered, and something wet dripped onto my face, breaking my heart wide open. "If you hadn't broken my trust, I would've been yours forever."

Agony set my whole body on fire. And because I couldn't move, I had to just lie there and let it burn as her feet shuffled away through the grass and the world around me fell silent.

Tears formed in my eyes begging to be released.

I wished I could've found another way.

How did one of my brightest days turn so dark?

As I drifted out of consciousness, I grieved the way this had gone. I knew how the curse worked. As it stripped away all my abilities, turning me into something that would pass for an average human, the curse would also wind its way through my memories, ripping out anything related to magic one by one. Any memory involving Jinni Gifts—gone. Anytime Jezebel specifically had used her Gifts, I would forget. The hunts or practice fights with my sister, my father, even my mother all those years ago, gone as well. Everything related to magic.

Would I even remember loving Jezebel?

I hoped so.

At least then, I could hold onto one part of my old life while I lost the rest.

***

Yours forever.

The words whispered to my subconscious.

Cool wind brushed my skin, along with something else that tickled. Blinking, I turned my face slowly to one side. Grass. It was grass, dancing across my cheek.

Why was I in the grass?

Straining to remember, my heart picked up speed rapidly as I found huge gaping holes in my memory.

When I glanced around the area, I could easily place it in my mind as a short distance from camp. I could remember everyone in the camp. My father. My sister. We'd had some foreign visitors staying with us, though thinking of them turned everything fuzzy.

And I could remember her face.

Achingly beautiful.

All the memories were piecemeal, like someone had randomly cut half or more of them out, but then there were others where I'd just stared at her face as she slept.

Memorizing the details.

As I slowly sat up, careful not to stand until the horizon stopped spinning, I found myself aching over those memories though I didn't fully know why.

I stood on shaky legs as the sun slipped below the trees and twilight slowly settled over the lake and woods. The path back to camp was darker than I remembered it—so dark that I hesitated, wondering if I should sleep here in the grass and wait for morning. A faint memory of the way the trail should smell taunted me, but that didn't make sense either.

A sense of loss swallowed me up, exaggerated by the inability to name what was missing.

My mind grasped onto the one thing I *knew* I should remember more of: *her*.

Her face caused a strange ache in my chest—a mixture of hope, liking, and longing.

No matter how I racked my memories for a name, a relationship, *anything*... There was nothing.

The only thing I knew for sure, was that her face would haunt me.

It already did.

20 Years Later

JEZEBEL

"YOU DON'T EVEN CARE that he's ill!" my daughter Hanna screamed at me from across the family suite, turning to storm toward her room. Over her shoulder she added, "Someday I'm going to leave, and you won't care that I'm gone either."

Her door slammed behind her, leaving me alone in our large sitting room that connected all the other rooms in our royal suites.

I sighed. Playing with the colorful tassels of a throw pillow beside me on the sofa, I considered going after her.

In the end, though, I couldn't.

Because she was right.

Though I wanted to care that her father—my husband and the King of Jinn—was slowly fading into a shell of who he used to be, I didn't feel anything besides a spreading numbness.

She was wrong about one thing, though.

Her father wasn't ill, so much as a blank canvas waiting for me to paint, unable to create much of anything on his own anymore.

And she was also wrong about my feelings for her—if I lost her, I'd care very deeply.

My headstrong daughter reminded me of a man I'd known once who always said exactly what he was thinking. It wasn't considered a noble trait in Jinn, especially not among members of the court. But still, I didn't discourage it.

I stood with another sigh, hovering in place as I debated trying to reason with her. In the end, I went to check on Shem instead, before quietly going to bed in my own room.

Were all young Jinn this troublesome?

I still wanted a second child, but not for at *least* another century at the way things were going with Hanna. Hopefully she'd calm down by then.

Sleep came fitfully, and I woke before dawn, too eager for my upcoming trip to be still another moment.

"Good morning," I greeted Shem where he sat quietly at the breakfast table, joining him.

He gave me a blank smile and returned to chewing his food.

"Keep an eye on Hanna while I'm gone, would you?" I murmured as I flicked through a stack of papers my council had left for me to go through.

"Are you traveling, darling?"

I glanced up. Had he forgotten again? His eyes were slightly vacant, though I could've sworn I hadn't used my Gift on him recently. "Just a short trip," I replied with a tight-lipped smile. "It's nothing to concern yourself with."

"All right," he agreed easily, patting my hand before picking up a worn book he'd read many times before and settling into a comfortable chair for the morning.

When the servants came for my bags, I hesitated once more outside Hanna's door, wondering if I should bid her goodbye. In the end, I decided against it. I didn't want the servants to gossip if she refused to say goodbye to her own mother.

My retinue of servants and guards and I reached the daleth that I intentionally kept open at the edge of Resh, though most citizens in the capital city had no knowledge of it. The guards stationed there nodded respectfully to myself and my small retinue.

Despite being surrounded by a sea of faces, none of them truly saw me or knew me. The desire to be *seen,* to be truly known, grew with each step toward the daleth. It was the reason I kept making this trip, year after year, under the guise of making sure the curse was still in effect, despite everything that should've kept me away.

There was only one person in the world who'd ever truly seen me.

Like the moon was drawn toward the sun in a never-ending cycle, I once again couldn't resist the draw that pulled me to him.

"Lead the way," I told my new captain of the Guard. I couldn't remember his name, but I didn't really need to.

He bowed his head and stepped through the portal with a small group of guard members, making sure the human world side of the daleth was safe before beckoning me through.

Despite the heat, I wore a long dress and a mantle over my shoulders that trailed behind me. As soon as we reached the other side, I shrugged it off and handed it to one of the servants in my retinue. Without it, I felt briefly, wonderfully free, even if that was an illusion.

We set up a temporary camp—or rather my people had done so before my arrival. I endured the long minutes of reports and presentations, and even a few self-important humans requesting an audience with the queen of Jinn, before I finally withdrew into my own small tent.

"I will rest for a few hours before we continue," I told my captain, not bothering to look at him as I untied the strings that held my tent flap open. "Please do not disturb me until I wake."

"Of course, your majesty," his voice came to me through the thin material as it fell closed.

A luxurious poster bed was set up against the back wall, but I didn't go to it. Instead, I approached the table where a servant had set some wine and cheese, taking a long drink and, after an anxious pause, another. I closed my eyes. Slowly I released the pent-up breath I'd been holding all day—all year it felt like. It was finally time.

I traveled.

The first year I'd come here, I'd used my enchanted mirror to find the place, since I couldn't travel anywhere I hadn't seen with my own eyes. Over time, I'd scoured the area, until I could pick and choose any destination within the human market and travel there with ease.

Today, I aimed for a dark alleyway at the edge of the town market.

Thankfully, it was empty.

Jinn weren't common in this part of the world, and I'd found my magic frightened most humans—or in this case, the Vaade in this growing settlement who *thought* they were human.

That was one of the reasons that I always shifted into a Vaade before going out into the human town—turning my vivid blue eyes to a more common human brown, lightening my black hair until it lost the otherworldly blue tint, and shifting my clothes to the Vaade-style of deer-skin tunics with colorful embellishments, adding pretty blue-and-red patterned designs along the sleeves.

I touched the bright blue jewel of the necklace around my throat. I'd bought it here last time, at the stall next to his. Would he recognize this borrowed face again?

That was the other reason I shifted: because I feared that somehow Koda's memories might return if he saw my true face. Worst of all, I was terrified he'd hate me on sight.

That wasn't logical to worry over though. *All* Vaade hated Jinn on sight, not just me. For some reason, despite the way they'd forgotten their magic and their history, they'd never lost their natural hatred of the Jinn.

Winding through the stalls in the chaos of the market, I could barely hear myself think over the shouting and different animals clucking or neighing as they waited to be sold. It was a nice change from the fearful quiet that surrounded me back home. Though I could've done without the distinct smell of manure that mingled with the scent of oils for sale, flatbread, and richly spiced kabobs.

I headed for the stretch of stalls near *his*. Once there, I could barter for random objects I didn't need while studying his face and listening to his voice from afar. Picking up my steps in excitement, I nearly smacked into a broad wall of a man.

Hissing, I pulled back to yell at the brute, then froze.

It's him.

Koda's long hair was still knotted in thick spirals, but the dark brown strands near his temples had a hint of gray. After twenty years, I shouldn't be so surprised. His eyes always gave me pause as well, so familiar yet foreign, now that they were a more natural hazel color.

"Back again so soon?" He grinned and let go of the arm he'd caught to steady me. His other hand hoisted a massive platter of freshly-caught fish over his shoulder.

His words hit me. "Soon?" I questioned, brow wrinkling.

He turned toward his stall where he and his sister sold fish daily, and I followed without thinking.

"I've seen you here over the years," he replied easily, volunteering information that I'd never have given up if I'd been in his position. "You were here just last fall."

It wasn't a question.

He didn't even seem to care that much, ducking beneath the shaded awning of his stall to set down the fish without a backward glance.

But he'd noticed.

Me.

Or at least, the woman I pretended to be.

Awkwardly, I stopped at the entrance, unsure what to do.

Though I'd always wanted to talk to him, I couldn't find a single thing to say now that it was finally happening.

"Well, I should leave." I spun to go, frustrated tears forming. I hadn't cried in years. Why did this man bring these feelings out in me?

"Or you could stay." His voice stopped me before I could take a single step.

It was almost word for word what he'd said all those years ago.

Slowly, I turned back to face him, meeting his eyes. He smiled. I couldn't remember the last time I'd seen a genuine smile. It struck me with an almost physical force.

I wanted to say yes—to anything he asked.

Over the years, after my fury had faded somewhat, I'd started to review our history with fresh eyes. At first, I'd blamed his father, his sister, and even his misplaced loyalty for his tribe for why he'd betrayed me...

But I'd betrayed him too.

I'd allowed the Vaade to remain cursed.

Lately I'd begun to wonder about his reasoning again, wishing I could ask him. He'd said over and over that he couldn't explain, but he'd never said why. Something didn't add up. Whatever was left unsaid haunted me.

The urge to demand answers surged yet again. The words were almost desperate to get out after being caged inside so long. To do so, however, I'd have to reveal myself. And worse, to admit the part I'd played.

Don't do it.

He'd never understand.

Gazing down at me, he waited patiently for my response.

"You don't look like you're buying any fish," a female voice commented from the entrance.

My shoulders tensed. Had Koda found a wife? I hadn't seen anything in the mirror, but it wasn't foolproof, and I didn't let myself check on him *that* often...

With a deep breath to gather my courage, I raised my chin and turned to face her like the queen I was. When I met her eyes, though, I nearly laughed.

It was Tehya.

My reaction to her was equally confusing, as part of me wanted to smile and greet her like a long-lost friend, while the other part recoiled as I remembered I'd betrayed her as well.

Without a second glance, she sidestepped me and entered the stall, pulling out a knife to fillet a fish.

She doesn't remember, I reminded myself. *Neither of them do. Keep calm.*

"I was just about to," I lied, turning my gaze to the slimy creatures for the first time.

My nose wrinkled inadvertently.

I *hated* fish.

"I'll take that one." I pointed at the nearest fish with pure white scales and a streak of pink along his side. His glassy eyes bulged at me.

Distracted by Koda's efficient movements as he wrapped the fish in wax paper, I completely forgot about payment until he was wrapping it with a string of twine.

I reached into my small purse, hoping I'd brought enough. "How much?"

Though I was probably supposed to haggle, I paid what he asked without a word, reaching for the large fish. It took two hands, forcing me to cradle it like a baby. Why had I bought the *largest* fish in his entire stall?

Clearing my throat, I managed an awkward, "Thank you."

Reaching out, Koda took the fish back. "It's too heavy. I'll carry it for you."

Well. That was impossible. It's not like I could lead him to a house, or to the edge of the market and just disappear. "Thank you, but you don't need to do that."

"No, I don't," he agreed amiably, still holding the fish. "Which way?"

My first instinct was to use my Gift to make him forget me and leave immediately, but everything in me resisted the idea. *I can't erase his memories again.*

Wringing my fingers, I tried to calm my racing heart. "I wasn't planning to head home just yet. Would it be all right if I leave it with you and arrange to have someone pick it up later?"

Was it my imagination, or was he a bit disappointed? He lowered the fish, moving to set it in the back of his stall. "Not a problem," he said with his back to me, turning to meet my eyes. "Just leave your name, and I'll make sure whoever is here knows it."

He issued it almost like a challenge.

"Bel." I gave him the nickname. Though my rational side knew he wouldn't recognize my full name, I couldn't bring myself to risk it.

"Which way are you headed, Bel?" He picked up an empty basket.

Pointing at random, I gestured to the right.

"So am I," he said, hoisting the large basket onto his shoulder. "I'll go with you."

Tehya snorted softly. She didn't look up from her work.

"Be back soon." Koda bumped her shoulder as he passed her, but she didn't say anything else. She seemed more subdued than I remembered.

For a split second, I considered making an excuse to go the opposite direction like a coward, but I couldn't pull myself away from him.

Walking through the crowded marketplace, the stalls on both sides blurred together.

All I saw was Koda.

The way he led slightly ahead and in front of me to carve a path. How he carried the basket as if it was nothing. And also… how his clothes seemed at least a decade old and ragged, as if he hadn't been able to afford anything new in a long time.

Guilt nagged at me.

I wanted to blurt out the truth: *You're under a curse, and it's my fault.*

We ducked through a narrow space at the market entrance where the crowd thickened. It let out into a wide alley with just a handful of people passing through or working nearby.

Koda followed my lead as I walked aimlessly, not knowing where to go, neither of us saying a word.

I have to tell him.

When I snuck a sidelong glance, he winked at me.

Blushing like a young Jinni girl instead of the queen, I bit my tongue.

Don't do it.

"Are you planning to catch more fish today?" It sounded ridiculous to my ears, talking about something so irrelevant when secrets were begging to be spilled.

"Possibly." Such a Koda answer, short and unhelpful.

My lips twitched in a smile.

"Is that where you're going now?" I clarified, savoring the sweet familiarity of how I used to push him in the past.

"Are you trying to get rid of me already?" he countered with a quick grin.

"Not at all." I blushed at how quickly I said it. "I just wasn't sure which direction you were going…"

"Which direction are *you* going?"

I laughed at his boldness. "Honestly?" He always brought this side out of me. I didn't mind being truthful with him. "I don't know."

"I figured," he said, making me start to regret my honesty, until he added, "That's where I'm going too."

I rolled my eyes at his smirk, allowing a small smile when he laughed.

"A walk couldn't hurt," I said, more to myself than to him. If it were anyone else, I might not have gone very far. There were only a few people in the area, and we were taking the road that led out of town. But with Koda, I'd never worried for my safety.

The light feeling from a few seconds before faded at the thought, making the pressure return.

I need to tell him.

The compulsion wouldn't go away, as if the more time I spent in his company, the more he drew the secrets out of me.

Maybe… I thought fast as we continued ambling down the road leaving the small town behind. Maybe I could find a way.

A screech came from above us, as the cobbled road turned into packed dirt with long prairie grass on both sides. Glancing up, I found a hawk circling in the air. It dove toward the stream along one side, coming up with a flailing fish.

"Have you ever heard the tale of the hawk and the fish?" I blurted without allowing myself time to second guess my idea.

When he shook his head, I began to weave a story, coming up with pieces of it as I went. "Once there was a... dark hawk with unusually larger wings who didn't... fit with the other birds of prey."

I cleared my throat, feeling my comparisons were blatantly obvious, but he just nodded, shifting his basket to his other shoulder. As we ambled down the path, it paralleled the stream where the water gurgled cheerfully over river rocks.

Already I regretted attempting a parable. I wasn't a storyteller. But it was too late to stop now without making things even more awkward. "Far below the hawk's world, in the stream, there lived a fish—"

"Just the one?" Koda smirked.

Swallowing, I only met his eyes for a brief second before dropping them back to the stream. "It was the only one that mattered." I attempted to sound lighthearted like him, but it came out far more serious.

Curiosity sparked in Koda's eyes. He'd heard the odd note too.

When he didn't interrupt again, I cleared my throat and plowed on, hoping I knew what I was doing. "One day the hawk hurt its wing and fell to earth, landing beside the stream. The fish was passing by and called out—"

"Oh, there are talking fish in this story?" Koda interjected with a cheeky smile.

I stopped to raise a brow at him, crossing my arms. "Maybe if you stop interrupting, you'll find out?"

"Apologies." He gave me an unapologetic grin.

We turned back to the path, walking slowly now. "The fish *called out* to the hawk," I continued. "And offered help. And don't"—I reached out without thinking to put a hand over his open mouth, about to cut me off again—"ask what kind of help a fish could offer."

Both of us paused for a long moment, eyes meeting and holding before I remembered to pull my hand away from his lips.

His eyes were hooded, but he didn't speak.

It took a few breaths before I found my way back to the story, trying to sound normal as I returned to it. "The fish encouraged the hawk that it didn't need wings. It could simply come swimming and find everything it needed in the water."

I cleared my throat again, frustrated that I hadn't thought this through. If he understood the point I was attempting to make with this story, it'd be a miracle.

"Anyway, after a few days living nearby, watching how the fish not only survived, but thrived in the stream, the hawk slowly began to consider the fish's suggestion," I rushed on, as if telling the story faster could ease my embarrassment. "It dipped a talon in the water, then waded in deeper, until it was surrounded by dozens—no, hundreds—of fish."

At this point, Koda's brow was furrowed as he tried to picture it, but he pulled his lips into his mouth and mimed sealing them when he saw my glance.

I sighed. "I'm not telling the story right."

Tilting his head, he came to a stop where the stream turned a bend and set his basket on one of the large rocks along the shoreline, moving to sit on the one beside it. He shrugged. "No way to tell, unless you finish it."

Drawing a deep breath, I nodded. I could do this. "All the other fish still saw a predator. Though the first fish meant well—at least, I think he did," I murmured to myself. "The rest of the fish had other plans, using their strength to pull the hawk underwater, planning to... drown it." That wasn't completely accurate. Koda hadn't tried to *kill* me, as much as weaken me and my kind to the point we could be killed if they wanted to.

"What happened to the hawk?" Koda prompted when I was quiet for longer than I'd intended. He leaned forward on the rock, clearly invested now.

Moving to sit on another rock just a few steps away from his, I bit my lip. "The hawk fought back," I whispered, then cleared my throat, forcing myself to speak louder. "It did what it had to do to survive."

"It attacked the fish," Koda filled in when I didn't.

I nodded.

He tilted his head, hazel eyes studying me and my obviously overly-emotional reaction to a random animal story. "It didn't have a choice."

My eyes whipped up to his, widening. Was he understanding my real message after all? "The problem is, the hawk hurt the fish," I argued, wanting to make sure he really understood. "Badly. Not just one or two, but all of them—as it thrashed to get out of the water," I tacked on so it wouldn't sound too ridiculous. "The hawk healed and returned to the skies, but the fish were never the same."

"Is that the end of the story?" he asked.

Is it? I didn't honestly know. For now, it was, I supposed. I nodded. "The end."

He gave a sympathetic nod. "The hawk hurt someone without meaning to, by protecting itself," he summed the story up. "It couldn't be helped."

"It's really not that simple," I argued, swallowing back the urge to tell him the truth yet again. Staring out at the water kept me from showing him the guilt swimming in my gaze.

"You're the hawk," he replied.

My stomach dropped.

Slowly, I met his eyes and nodded. "How did you know?"

He understood my story—and accepted it calmly?

Does he know? Could he forgive me after all?

I couldn't breathe past the knot in my throat.

"Whatever you did, it sounds like you had to do it," he said finally when the silence began to stretch.

Whatever you did?

Maybe he didn't know after all.

He moved toward the edge of the stream, wading in just enough to cool his feet, turning to face me.

"Who's the fish?" he asked, and I deflated.

"It's..."

I hesitated. Should I tell him? He seemed so understanding.

Staring off into the trees, I pictured telling him. "It's you."

"Me?" His brow furrowed. Tilting his head at me, he pulled back slightly. "I don't understand. We've only just met."

Say it quickly, I told myself and drew a shaky breath. "Your kind tried to curse my kind—" I stopped, shaking my head. "That's not exactly right... *You* tried to curse *me*." I spoke to my hands, breathing shallowly, terrified to look up for his reaction. Just like the rest of my story, I could only whisper the ending. "I had to protect myself... so I turned the curse around on you."

Tensing, I stare at my clenched fists, waiting for a reaction.

He was so still he could've been a statue.

The only sound was the trickling water rushing past us.

Swallowing hard, I risked looking at him.

Understanding filled his eyes as he stared back at me.

I couldn't breathe.

"You're saying I knew you somehow."

Slowly, I nodded.

"It was more than that, though, wasn't it?" As he stared, I held my breath, but he somehow saw right through me. "You loved me."

Squeezing my eyes shut, I tried to stop the tears. One slipped out. It trailed down my cheek. Koda watched its slow descent.

"You said there was a curse," he added softly. "That one, at least, is easy enough to guess. My people have large gaps in our memories that none of us can fill in. You're the reason for this?" His tone was calm, face serene, as if asking about the weather.

My hopes rose. He was taking this better than I'd expected. "Yes. I'm so sorry," I told him, letting the tears fall. "Truly—"

In the same soft tone, he spoke over me, "For years, we searched for answers, but never found any. My father died shortly after." He took a menacing step toward me as his voice lowered to a deep growl. "You ruined our lives."

I squeaked when he lunged toward me. Trying to dodge him, I fell off the rock and bruised my hip landing on another.

He was still inhumanly fast, even with the curse.

I landed on the ground, and he was on top of me in a heartbeat.

His hands wrapped around my neck.

Why did I follow him out into the wilderness with no witnesses?

Choking, I nearly shifted in self-preservation.

But years spent protecting myself and my secret had taught me that even one single witness could lead to a chain reaction of rumors. If Koda said a Jinni shifted in his town while my retinue was here, it'd allow certain council members like Milcah to put the pieces together. She was already suspicious.

"Please," I managed to say, clawing at his hands around my neck on instinct. He could easily break my spine with one snap—but he hadn't yet. Was I foolish to hope that meant something? "I can explain."

"You've explained enough," he said in that same low, dangerous tone that I should've recognized.

He's not going to stop. I sobbed, unable to prevent my tears, staring up at his blurry face. That wasn't what caused the fissure in my heart to crack wider, though. It was the revelation that he'd *never* forgive me.

I couldn't blame him.

One word was all it would take to save myself, but as I gasped for air and my vision grew black around the edges, I struggled with self-loathing.

I don't want to do this, I told him silently as I gripped his hands tighter and tried to meet his eyes through the blur of tears.

But I have to.

"Stop!" I choked out.

The strength of my Gift swept over him immediately.

His hands loosened.

Coughing, I pulled them away fully. I dragged in a deep breath, then another. "Forget," I rasped. "Everything I said… after… the end."

His glassy eyes stared down at me. Then, slowly, as if moving through mud, he reached toward my neck with a frown. "How did this happen?"

Though my throat burned and swallowing felt like shards of glass, I managed to stand. Koda rose to his feet with me. "This is not important." I waved at my throat with a still slightly teary smile, using my Gift to reassure him and help him let it go. "This is not your fault." *It's mine.*

I watched my words sink in.

Koda's memories were wiped away once again, and I could hardly breathe beneath the crushing weight of guilt. I'd sworn I'd never do that to him again.

And I couldn't even apologize.

This was the worst possible outcome.

The one I always pictured when I thought of telling him.

"Bel?" It was Koda's voice, but his mouth wasn't moving.

I blinked. One second he was standing in front of me, and the next, he was gone.

"Bel?" he asked again, and his voice was a bit further away, sounding concerned.

It finally broke me out of my trance.

Koda was back in the stream—where he'd been all along.

He cocked his head to the side now, studying me.

"Who was the fish?" he repeated after what had been, for him, an awkwardly long silence.

I put a hand to my throat, feeling phantom pains from something that had never happened.

He hadn't attacked me.

I shivered and tried to subtly shake the vision from my head.

Nothing had happened.

I'd only imagined telling him the truth.

Relief washed over me. It wasn't real.

And I could never, ever risk it becoming reality.

"It's not important." I tried to sound casual, but it came out a bit strangled as I waved my hand in the air.

Squinting at me, he let a long pause hang between us before giving me a quiet nod. "Okay. If you say it's not important, I'll trust you."

Guilt twisted into irrational fury, and I snapped, "You shouldn't."

One brow rose. Then he smirked. "You remind me of someone."

"What?" I startled so badly that I nearly tripped while standing still. "Who?"

The corners of his lips slowly lowered as he dropped his gaze. "You'll think this sounds strange but... I don't fully know."

The sadness in his voice had my guilt sliding back around me with a vise-like grip.

Unable to give him the answers he needed, I dropped onto the rock in defeat.

A tear escaped.

As it trickled down my cheek, Koda finally stepped out of the stream and strode toward me, lifting a finger to softly catch it. "That's an odd reaction." Crouching in front of my rock, he studied me closely.

He was too perceptive.

The idea of lying to him again broke my heart. I licked my lips and switched the conversation abruptly back to the parable. "I didn't finish the story."

Leaning back on his heels, he remained crouched beside me and raised one skeptical brow.

"The hawk healed and returned to the skies, but the fish were never the same," I repeated my previous ending. "The problem is, damage is never one-sided." Blinking away tears, I barely managed to get the words out, "The hawk was never the same either."

It was the closest I could ever come to an apology.

He digested the new ending thoughtfully, never taking his eyes off my face, though he shifted back to sit on the opposite rock once more.

As he stayed silent, I shivered, wondering if he might yet remember.

Instead, when he finally spoke, I immediately realized he'd misunderstood the story. "Someone hurt you," he said in that low voice, leaning forward slowly as if I might scare easily. "You don't know me yet, but I can promise I will never do the same." He made the vow with a clear conscience, unaware of the irony. "You will always be safe with me."

My tears, which hadn't flowed in decades, flooded back with a vengeance.

"I believe you," I whispered.

And maybe someday I'll tell you the truth.

SIGN UP FOR MY AUTHOR NEWSLETTER

Want more from Jezebel's world? You can get a free short story with a sneak peek of Jezebel as queen many years later plus a new character you'll meet in The Stolen Kingdom series by signing up for my monthly newsletter—not to mention exclusive bonus content, helpful tools for fellow writers, behind the scenes updates, sales alerts, and more!

WWW.BETHANYATAZADEH.COM/CONTACT

Bethany Atazadeh · 54 songs · about 3 hours

THE QUEEN'S RISE
PLAYLIST songs that reflect Jezebel in no particular order

▶ **New Kings** — Sleeping Wolf	▶ **Heroes** — Zayde Wolf
▶ **Dreaming** (w/ blackberry) [explicit] — The Score, blackboard	▶ **Your Name Hurts** — Hailee Steinfeld
▶ **Older** — Sasha Alex Sloan	▶ **Bad Dreams** (Stripped) — Faouzia
▶ **Lose You To Love Me** — Selena Gomez	▶ **Sorry** — Halsey
▶ **when the party's over** — Billie Eilish	▶ **Exhale** — Sabrina Carpenter
▶ **Consequences** — Camila Cabello	▶ **Can You Hold Me** — NF, Britt Nicole
▶ **Lonely** — Noah Cyrus	▶ **i can't breathe** — Bea Miller
▶ **Bulletproof** (with XYLO) — The Score, XYLO	▶ **Glass Heart** — Tommee Profitt, Sam Tinnesz
▶ **Wrong Direction** — Hailee Steinfeld	▶ **Bitter** (ft. Noak Hellsing) — Dylan Conrique, Noak Hellsing
▶ **Deep Water** — American Authors	▶ **birthday cake** — Dylan Conrique
▶ **This Is It** — Oh The Larceny	▶ **1 last bye** — Kiran + Nivi
▶ **Glory Days** — The Federal Empire	▶ **Let You Down** — NF
▶ **Blindfold** — Sleeping Wolf	▶ **War of Hearts** — Ruelle

page 1

Bethany Atazadeh · 54 songs · about 3 hours

THE QUEEN'S RISE
PLAYLIST

songs that reflect Jezebel in no particular order

- **The Other Side** — Ruelle
- **Lost My Mind** — Alice Kristiansen
- **Hurricane** — Tommee Profitt, Fleurie
- **Hands** — ORKID
- **War of Hearts** — Ruelle (acoustic version)
- **Walk Through the Fire** — Zayde Wolf, Ruelle
- **Armor** — Landon Austin
- **like that** — Bea Miller
- **Heart of the Darkness** — Tommee Profitt, Sam Tinnesz
- **Champagne** — Lia Marie Johnson
- **Vigilante Sh*t** (explicit) — Taylor Swift
- **Paint It, Black** — Ciara
- **Don't Blame Me** — Taylor Swift
- **Villains Aren't Born (They're Made)** — PEGGY

- **Big Bad Wolf** — Roses & Revolutions
- **How Villains Are Made** — Madalen Duke
- **Monsters** — Ruelle
- **Game of Survival** — Ruelle
- **Vendetta** — UNSECRET, Krigare
- **Midnight Oil** — Tommee Profitt, Fleurie
- **Sound of War** — Tommee Profitt, Fleurie
- **I Scare Myself** — Beth Crowley
- **Madness** — Ruelle
- **Love into a Weapon** — Madalen Duke
- **I Didn't Ask For This** — Beth Crowley
- **Moment** — Roses & Revolutions
- **Hard to Kill** — Beth Crowley
- **Slip Away** — UNSECRET, Ruelle

read more in this magical world of jinn

THE STOLEN KINGDOM

How can she protect her kingdom, if she can't protect herself?

Arie never expects to manifest a Jinni's Gift. When she begins to hear the thoughts of those around her, she hides it to the best of her ability. But to her dismay, the forbidden Gift is growing out of control.

When a neighboring king tries to force her hand in marriage and steal her kingdom, discovery becomes imminent. Just one slip could cost her throne. And her life.

A lamp, a heist, and a Jinni hunter's crew of thieves are her only hope for removing this Gift - and she must remove it before she's exposed. Or die trying.

THE STOLEN KINGDOM is a loose Aladdin retelling and the first book in a complete, four book series of fairytale retellings. Set in a world that humans share with Mermaids, Dragons, and the elusive Jinni, this isn't the fairytale you remember...

If you enjoy fantasy worlds, magical races, and surprising spins on classic fairy tales, then you'll love this spellbinding retelling of Aladdin.

READ THE STOLEN KINGDOM NEXT...
books2read.com/thestolenkingdom

KICKSTARTER SHOUT OUTS

A.C. BABBITT, CHRISTIAN AUTHOR
ABBY WHITE
ABIGAIL
ALBERRY
ALEX GREGG
ALEXANDRA CORRSIN
ALEXIA
ALEXIS P
ALEY
ALLI
ALYSSA HECK
AMANDA BALTER
AMANDA HARPER
AMBER D
AMY MURDOCK
ANASTA SIDHU
ANGELA BUBLITZ
ANGELA MORSE
ANGELA POWERS
ANGELA RIESBERG
ARWYN CUNNINGHAM
ASHLEY BETTENCOURT
ASHLY NICOLE
ATHENA
AVIONNE
BIANCA-TATJANA
BIG BAD JOHN
BILLYE HERNDON
BRITTANY SACREY JENKINS
BRITTANY WANG
BROOKE CLONTS
BROOKLYN CANNON
C COLEMAN
CAITLYN PRICE
CAITY LYUBOV
CARISSA
CAROLINE O.
CARRIE CROSS
CASSANDRA STUBBS
CHARITY MARIE
CHARLIE
CHEYENNE THOMPSON
CHLOE RUGGIERI
CHRISTINA WHITE
CORINA
COURTNEY DENELSBECK
COURTNEY FRASER
COURTNEY PYGOTT
CRAIG SISSON
D.C. CONTOR
DANAE
DAVID
DAVID HOLZBORN
DAVID OKEEFE
DAVID PINSON
DAVID STEWART
DAWN MONTOYA
DEL MCCOOL
DM GEARHART
ELIZABETH
ELIZABETH DUIVENVOORDE
ELIZABETH KIEFER
ELIZABETH KING
ELIZABETH MURRAY
ELIZABETH RUTH
EMILY MERRITT
EMILY ROUSELL
ERICA ROWAN
ERIN SLEGAITIS-SMITH
EWELINA SPARKS
G.E. ADERHOLDT
HEATHER CAMACHO
HECTOR T TORRES
HOLLY DAVIS
HOLLY FYFE
INDIA
IVEY TUCKER
J.J. OTIS
JA'NEAR
JACKIE REUTER
JACLYN MASDEN
JANINE B
JEAN KNIGHT PACE
JENNA MARSHALL
JES DREW
JESSICA
JESSICA KIDD
JESSICA PORTILLO
JESSIE JONES WILBANKS
JOANNA WHITE
JOHANNA RODRIGUEZ
JORDANNA BLUESTONE
JOSEE SMITH
JUDY PRESCOTT
MARSHALL AUTHOR
JULIA E LINTHICUM
JULIANNA JURVELIN
JULIE E. MCATEE
KARA BLACKWOOD
KATHERINE SCHOBER
KATHY WEREB
KATIE KNIGHTLEY
KATIE S.
KATRINA GILLES
KAYLA ANN
KAYLA WRIGHT
KELLI SCOTT
KJERSTEN LILLIS
KIERYN PARKIN
KIM HARRINGTON
KIRBY MOUNTIFIELD
KOUNT VON KULMBACHER
KRISKA
KRISTJAN VISNER
KYLE JOHNSON
KYLIE MACDOUGALL
KYNSIE RENE'
LEAH KANTHACK
LENA
LESLEY BARKLAY
LIA ANDERSON
LIANA MILLER
LILLIAN SJERVEN
LISA L
LIZA BAILEY
LORELEI ANGELINO
LUCIA SALDANA
LUNA1206!
LYDIA WOODWARD
MADDIE S.
MAKENNA ZORNES
MANDI GRACE
MARIA MEJIA
MARIA OTT TATHAM
MARIANNA PALMER
MARIE KNEELAND
MARILÉNE F
MARK
MARVIN TURNER
MARY MENSAH
MEGAN ASTELL
MEGAN KELL
MEGMALLOW
MELODY FAE
MICHELLE FOX
MICHELLE WINKLER
MICKI HESS
MIKE MCCUE
MIKE PORTER
MOLLY KLUNZINGER
MORGAN G.
NATALIE COLBURN
NENA
NEW DOOR MEDIA
NICHOLE
NICOLE PORTER
NOEL LAUGHLIN
RACHAEL LANDERS
RACHEL HETRICK
RACHEL SIKORSKI
REBECCA HILL
REBECCA K SAMPSON
RHIANNON BIRD
RICK PETTY
RODNEY D. LOPEZ
S. SHARBER
S.J. PALMER
SAGE KIESSLING
SARA
SARAH RODECKER
SARRA CANNON
SELENA GARCIA
SERENA RUBY FOSTER
SHANNEN INGRAM
SHANNON MCKEEVER
SHIRSTEN SHIRTS
STACY WARD
TABITHA CASWELL
TAMMIE GIPSON
TANIA NYGMA
TERESA BEASLEY
THE CREATIVE FUND BY BACKERKIT
TIFFANY A. SMITH
TIFFANY MILLARD
TIFFANY SIERRA
VANNESSA GOODWIN
VICTOR JULIUS 3RD
VIRGINIA MEZZATESTA
Z

ALSO BY BETHANY ATAZADEH

THE STOLEN KINGDOM SERIES :

THE STOLEN KINGDOM

THE JINNI KEY

THE CURSED HUNTER

THE ENCHANTED CROWN

THE COLLECTOR'S EDITION

THE QUEEN'S RISE SERIES :

THE SECRET GIFT

THE SECRET SHADOW

THE SECRET CURSE

THE NUMBER SERIES :

EVALENE'S NUMBER

PEARL'S NUMBER

MARKETING FOR AUTHORS SERIES :

HOW YOUR BOOK SELLS ITSELF

GROW YOUR AUTHOR PLATFORM

BOOK SALES THAT MULTIPLY

SECRETS TO SELLING BOOKS ON SOCIAL MEDIA

PLAN A PROFITABLE BOOK LAUNCH

Bethany Atazadeh is best known for her young adult fantasy novels, The Stolen Kingdom series, which won the Best YA Author 2020 Minnesota Author Project award. She is a mama to a cute little boy and a corgi pup, and is obsessed with stories and chocolate.

Using her degree in English with a creative writing emphasis, Bethany enjoys helping other writers through her YouTube aka "AuthorTube" writing channel and Patreon page.

If you want to know more about when Bethany's next book will come out, visit her website below where you can sign up to receive monthly emails with exciting news, updates, and book releases.

CONNECT WITH BETHANY:
Website: www.bethanyatazadeh.com
Instagram: @authorbethanyatazadeh
YouTube: www.youtube.com/bethanyatazadeh
Patreon: www.patreon.com/bethanyatazadeh